Douglas Terman was born in Pittsburgh, Pennsylvania, and attended Cornell and Columbia Universities before joining the US Air Force. Between 1955 and 1963 he worked in Intelligence, flew night jet interceptors and jet bombers, and was launch crew commander for the first Atlas ICBMs. After leaving the Air Force he spent several years cruising in the Caribbean, made a number of transatlantic voyages, and developed a small island resort. He now lives in Vermont.

Douglas Terman's first novel, *First Strike*, was published to great success in 1979, and was followed by *Free Flight*, *Shell Game* and *Star Shot*. *Cormorant* is his fifth novel.

FIRST STRIKE

'A top quality thriller! Exciting, gripping, agonizingly intense'   *Wall Street Journal*

FREE FLIGHT

'As distinctive and carefully crafted a suspense novel as we are likely to see ... lean, taut, beautifully articulated'   *Washington Post*

SHELL GAME

'A terrific narration of espionage, love and a starkly brutal war'   CLIVE CUSSLER

STAR SHOT

'Spies, Star Wars technology, revenge, hate and heart-stopping suspense ... a taut zinger of a tale'

STEPHEN COONTS

DOUGLAS TERMAN

CORMORANT

HarperCollins*Publishers*

HarperCollins*Publishers*
77–85 Fulham Palace Road,
Hammersmith, London W6 8JB

A Paperback Original 1994
1 3 5 7 9 8 6 4 2

A catalogue record for this book
is available from the British Library

ISBN 0 00 647309 1

Cormorant is a work of fiction. All characters and incidents in this
novel are fictional. Any similarities between the characters (or any
fictional corporate body) to any person living or dead (or to a real
corporate body) are purely coincidental.

Set in Meridien

Printed in Great Britain by
HarperCollinsManufacturing Glasgow

This novel is dedicated to my wife, lover, first mate, best friend, sounding board, editor, research assistant and reasonably restrained cheerleader, Seddon Johnson.

ACKNOWLEDGEMENTS

I wish to thank the following for the encouragement and assistance they so freely gave in the research and writing phases of *Cormorant*. The linguistic and technical accuracies are of their doing. The errors, of which there are undoubtedly many, are mine. So thanks to:

David Barber, Larry Bond, Major Terry Breithaupt USMC, Kenneth N. 'Punky' Coates, Laurie and Jonathan Eddy of the Waterfront Diving Center, Jake Eddy (no relation to Laurie and Jonathan but a good man all the same), Red Goodman, Robert Gottlieb, Captain David Howe, Jan Iserbyt, Big Al Kildow of Insuppressible Imag-engineering and Ukulele Strumming Ltd, Captain William L. Kullman NWA, Greg Lambert of the Congressional Merchant Marine and Fisheries Committee, James Plumpton, Nick Sayers, Ward Smyth, Michael J. Steer MD, Lydia Thomson, Dr Chuck Wagner, Johnny Walker (the Man, not the Whiskey), and with special thanks (and my solemn promise to replace the leather buttons on his sports coat that my dog ate) to:

Michael M. Barker AICP, DOM, DGH

In Xanadu did Kubla Khan
A stately pleasure-dome decree:
Where Alph, the sacred river, ran
Through caverns measureless to man
Down to a sunless sea.

Coleridge: Kubla Khan

Just getting over a little cold (war)

PROLOGUE

October 1988

The Black Guy was on the nozzle, Finn just behind him wrestling with the writhing hose, trying to wrestle it under control. And behind Finn was Stone, sweating bullets.

The arc light which illuminated the work sputtered, electric-blue and flickering, dancing its long snaking shadows over the wet muck and fallen rock.

The Black Guy was an artist, a sculptor, a Michelangelo; sensuously carving out sections of muck, then undercutting the embedded rock, keeping the nozzle moving like a finger caressing the tunnel's face, never pausing too long, just softly *stroking* it until the skin fell away, exposing another layer, the process forever.

Forty-three meters deep in this part of the shaft, the ceiling low enough that you had to bend over to walk and the air stinking of sweat, methane gas, and hydraulic fluid. Three hundred and twelve meters into East Germany, another 288 to go before canting the shaft up toward the surface. Then another sixty-three meters and Kagg, the Man from Langley, said they would run into a brick wall in an unused cellar of an East German bakery.

The hose bucked once, spit air, surged again, Finn literally lifted off his feet, then slammed against the tunnel wall.

The Black Guy almost lost his hold on the nozzle but held on long enough to yank the cutoff valve. The hose went tumescent, a limp dick, its wad shot. Finn had said that weeks ago and they had laughed. Finn had said it several times since and no one laughed any more.

1

Only the sound of heavy breathing and water dripping from the tunnel's ceiling, seeping from the walls in little rivulets, plopping into puddles on the tunnel's floor.

'Bitch,' said the Black Guy, no particular anger in his voice.

'Corrigan. New kid on the pump,' said Finn, picking himself up and examining a cut knuckle, then sucking on it. 'Doesn't know shit from Shinola.'

'Takes getting used to,' said Stone, master of the obvious. He measured the distance between the peg and the face of the cut. 'Eight point seven meters. Decent shift. We'll knock off a little early, let the next shift muck it out. Want some shoring in anyway before they start tunneling again.'

He dug a sample of the earth from the tunnel's face with his knife and didn't like the look of it. Getting into broken ground, conglomerate, faulted schist. Like the ground on the far side of the Seikan rail tunnel, the same unpredictable crap that he had run into, just before the blowout. Happy memories, Stone thought. *I'll drink to that*, said the voice within him.

A red light hung from a bracket further back up the tunnel, normally steady, now belatedly blinked. Intermission time. The Stasi were up there on the surface, listening with their portable probes for the sound of jackhammers. Guys in dishwater-gray uniforms with earphones, sticking rods in the ground, sniffing for spook holes. *Lotsa luck, fellas, 'cause there ain't no jackhammers down here*. Instead, Stone was cutting the tunnel using high-pressure hydraulics, his technological contribution to keeping the Cold War cool.

Stone always made a point of being the last one out. Captain of the ship stuff. Black Guy squeezed by him, then Finn; both hand-picked by Stone, the best of the best. *My turn to buy drinks tonight*. Cheers from the voice within.

Twelve meters back up the tunnel, they crawled into the mucking trolley. Stone rang the buzzer and they accel-

2

erated down the tracks, the rubber wheels making squiggling sounds on the wet rails.

Just another crummy day at the office, he thought. And what the hell was he doing this for? *You know what for*, piped up the voice from within. *'Cause you owe your soul to the Company store.*

Up the long incline, the car decelerating, past Station 23. Bad ground here as well. Had to put in rock bolts spaced on half-meter centers. Not enough; should have been coated with shotcrete. Kagg said they were already running over the max budget, yet weren't three-quarters finished. Had told Stone that the equipment he ordered wouldn't get to Berlin for another three weeks, and to just tough it out until the stuff arrived. Toughing it out could well mean having fifty tons of rock bounce off your head, but then again, Kagg didn't visit the face of the shaft so *he* could well afford to tough it out.

Kagg. Had told Stone that he was an engineer as well. Stone wondered what kind. Erector set? Lego blocks? The man didn't know from nothing but loved the blueprints, the hard hats, the bloated technical reports. Kagg had bragged to Stone about how he ran a tunnel four kilometers under the Korean DMZ for the good gooks. Private contract, no foreign aid involved, strictly paid for by one of Langley's off-the-books slush funds. Proud of it. Of what? Stone had heard that they lost twenty-two men on the drive before the North Koreans detected it. Clever devils. They bored their own hole straight down, intersecting the tunnel, then packed it with liberated C-4 they bought on the black market – your American tax dollars at work.

Most of the guys got out, according to Kagg. But Kagg wouldn't say how many didn't.

Kagg. He wore a spotless white boiler suit with a *Merikan* flag sewn on the shoulder. *Merikan* was how Kagg pronounced it. From Oklahoma. Had a shoulder holster with a .38 Special stuffed in it, a permanent part of his wardrobe. Stone supposed Kagg was aching for the day when the tunneling crew broke through and a battalion of Stasi were waiting there, ready to storm the tunnel: the first wave in the Inevitable Assault on the West. Horatio at the Bridge, Kagg at the tunnel, real Death before Dishonor stuff.

Kagg had another Oklahoma buddy in the Agency. The man who brought the funds in and took the reports back. Called himself a *Merikan* as well. Stone idly wondered whether there was a form of air pollution wafting around the air of Oklahoma that caused this particular speech defect.

Past the last thirty meters, lined with doubled corrugated steel arches, all they had to work with in the way of shoring. Stone and his crew had run into a pile of bones there. The surface, four meters above, was an interior courtyard paved with brick. The two-story complex that surrounded the courtyard had been a nunnery for over 140 years. Finn, a Roman Catholic, had been spooked by the bones, worried like hell that it was consecrated ground, until Kagg *swore* he found out through Archives that the place had been a slaughterhouse a century before that. Stone had never told Finn about the human skull the third shift had mucked out.

The trolley rolled out into the cellar and squeegeed to a stop. Kagg was waiting.

'Office, Stone,' he said, gesturing with his head toward a glassed-in cubicle. Stone would swear the man had just said *orifice*. Actually the air? Or, maybe, just possibly, hormones they fed beef cattle in the feed lots to fatten them up which then migrated up (down?) through the food chain.

'How long a drive on your shift?' Kagg had a nifty graph plastered on the glass divider wall, progress stripped in with colored tape.

'Do they eat a lot of meat in Oklahoma, Kagg?'

'Does a bear shit in the woods? That's a dumb-fuck question.'

'Just wondering. Call it 8.7 meters. Getting into bad

ground. I think we should knock off the drive until we can shore up some more.' Okay – probably hormones. After all, the air over Oklahoma drifted in from Kansas and those folks didn't have this particular speech impediment.

'Balls to that, Stone. We're behind. We've got operations backed up, waiting for the tunnel to get finished. The *Direc*tor is all over my ass on this one.'

Which was a pleasant thought to grab on to during sleepless nights, Stone reflected. 'I'm running into mica schist and amphibolite, some traces of decomposed shale. We need serious shoring.'

'You got it.'

'Corrugated sheeting doesn't qualify in my book as serious shoring, Kagg. What's the delivery on the plascrete equipment?'

Kagg fiddled with the roll of red tape, thinking hard, tossed it on top of a filing cabinet, then burrowed in his top drawer. He pulled out a thick report, licked his thumb and fluttered through the pages. 'Test phase. Slight delay. "Difficult to regulate the set-up time", it sez here.'

'Mind if I take a look?'

Kagg's mouth puckered with displeasure. 'Shit *yes*, I mind. I mind like hell. The report's addressed to me, Stone. Classified *Eyes Only*. You're not on the distribution list.'

'It was my idea,' Stone said, working hard at keeping his voice even. 'I could have put the equipment together in five days, worked out the bugs in another week.'

'We've already beaten that dead horse.' Kagg squirreled the report away in his top drawer and made a big deal of locking it. 'We would have tipped off the Stasi with local procurement. Half of Germany's on their payroll. No way, Stone. We keep this a purely *Merikan* operation.'

'Listen up, Kagg. I'll drive the tunnel for another shift, but if the ground gets any worse, I'm closing the operation down until I get proper shoring. I mean *shoring*, Kagg – not galvanized tin sheeting. We've got forty-three meters of overburden just aching to fall in on our skulls.'

'You quit on me now and you're off the contract, Stone. We've been through this shit before. You've got a performance clause in the contract. Screw that up and you're outta here.'

'Just might do that, Kagg.' Which both of them knew was bullshit because Stone, with no other options and with the IRS hard on his heels, had signed the contract because he needed the money, despite the performance clause which no tunnel engineer in his right mind would have ever signed. Beggar-chooser syndrome.

Kagg skated his castored Bauhaus chair over to the progress chart and studied it, as if it were the missing link to the Dead Sea Scrolls. 'Real plain, Stone. You're way behind on the drive. If I wanted to, I could cut you off right now and you'd automatically forfeit the performance bond money. One hundred thirty grand plus cleanup costs.'

'You want to explain to the Director of Operations a cave-in, maybe the loss of a shift crew? Forty-three meters' overburden of mud and rock comes crashing down. How much time do you think that would take to clean up, and where would you find another tunneling contractor that would take this fucking job? No shoring, no boring, no blasting, no jackhammers, not even a shield to contain a breakout. Shit, Kagg – this is eighteenth-century tunneling technology. I have no geological data to work with, no technical support, crapped-out equipment. What the hell do you people expect?'

'You signed . . .'

'Yeah, I know, ". . . the goddamned contract".' What the Agency wanted was blood from a Stone. Even Kagg had laughed at that one, probably sent it back to the Director by diplomatic pouch, classified *For Your Amusement Only*. 'Well, Kagg, you can shove the contract up your ass.'

Kagg rose from behind his desk, looming a head higher than Stone, leaned forward, supporting his weight against the desktop with his knuckles like an ape in heat, ready to charge. Blond clumps of hair poked out from his nostrils and ears. He had no color to his eyes, the irises almost transparent, a beef-eater's complexion, crooked teeth and burger breath from his steady diet of Big Macs.

'You fuck with me, Stone, and I'll give you so much heat you'll be swinging a daisy-cutter on a road gang for the rest of your natural-born. You drive the tunnel and let me worry about shoring. I've got a degree in mining. I've been down to the tunnel face and I don't see any problem.'

Stone opened the door, paused and looked back. 'Then you better take another look, Kagg, but don't cough too loud.' Stone slammed the door.

The Black Guy and Finn were waiting for him, Finn smoking and the Black Guy on his second can of Pepsi.

'How'd it go?' said the Black Guy. His real name was John Buckkins, had cut his teeth on Anaconda #3, helped reopen the Glory Hole in Central City when the price of gold spiked in 1980, then shifted to tunneling for the steady money. Stone had first met him in Colorado when he was working on the Overlook Tunnel. The Black Guy had pulverized a gang boss for taking chances and consequently gotten canned. Stone figured then that, sometime in the future, if he ever was in charge of a drive, he'd have the Black Guy on the payroll. This was the second drive they had worked on together, no regrets on the part of either man as far as Stone could tell.

'It didn't. I told him we'd do one more shift. If the ground gets worse, we're closing down until we have proper shoring.'

'. . . Or until they take us off the contract.'

'That's about it.'

'How about the progress payment?'

Stone shrugged.

Finn coughed and dropped the cigarette on the concrete and ground it out with his clodhopper, working at it more than necessary, but then again, Finn was given to making moot points. 'I'm behind in my alimony payments, Stone.'

So what else was new? Stone was already six months

7

behind in payments to the IRS. His old man had written that they had seized his Camaro and were making enquiries about the lakeside lot Stone owned in Latrobe. Like they said, the future belonged to those who owned the databases.

'I'll write you a check on my Maine account, Finn. By the time the check is submitted, I'll have money in the account.'

'I'm not bitching, Stone. She is.'

Stone was watching Kagg over Finn's shoulder through the glass of the cubicle. Kagg was on the phone, his face red, not getting a word in edgewise. The report on the plascrete was in front of him, and Kagg was thumbing through it, obviously looking for some specific reference. Kagg started to talk, paused, puzzled, rapped the hangup bar a couple of times, then slammed the phone into its cradle.

Blue funk time, which was in charming color contrast to Kagg's bursting nose capillaries. Kagg pulled on a coat, swiped the report and a notepad into his top drawer, then barged out the door and up the stairwell that led to the courtyard, pointedly ignoring Stone and company.

The second-shift mucking crew was just coming on. Stone talked to them for a few minutes, then watched them head down the tunnel in the trolley.

'You ready to go?' the Black Guy asked. Some gang boss had called him that and it had stuck, but was inevitably shortened to Bee Gee, assuming you wanted to keep your teeth.

'See you in the courtyard. I'll be up in a few minutes,' said Stone, itching to stick it to Kagg.

'I wouldn't,' said Finn. Stone gave him a look and Finn shrugged. 'Hey, just a suggestion, buddy.'

Stone gave it a few minutes, then checked. Garvey was hanging out in his cubicle, playing with work schedules, drinking cold coffee from a paper cup. Stone watched him for a few minutes, sipping a Pepsi. Their eyes met twice,

Garvey looking up out of mutually shared mistrust. Garvey was head of security for the operation, a new boy. Stone had no bones to pick with Garvey, but neither did he have any to share with him. Garvey looked up a third time, a trace of suspicion flickering in his eyes. Stone smiled thinly and headed for the stairwell.

Kagg's and Garvey's cubicles were side by side, separated by a concrete block wall, topped with a glass partition from the waist up. Kagg had his famous progress chart taped to the glass, obscuring most of the view between the offices.

Stone gave it three minutes, then peeked.

Garvey was hunched over, reading time cards, pausing occasionally to jot down numbers on a pad to his left, his head turned away from the glass partition.

Stone ducked back behind the stairwell and shucked off his boots, then checked again. Garvey was spending the government's money wisely, giving good value, caught up in the process of recording numbers for dead eyes that would never read them. It was pure bureaucratic make-work, although Garvey hadn't glommed on to that yet.

Doing it doggy-style, Stone crawled down the stairs, keeping to all fours below Garvey's line of sight. Kagg's door was unlocked. Stone reached up and released the catch, eased it open a few degrees, waiting for a reaction. Two minutes and nothing. He edged it open to fit the width of his hips. If Garvey caught him, Kagg would charge Stone with a security violation, probably high treason. As Kagg often said, 'There are rules. Break them and expect to take serious heat.' Anticipating heat, Stone sweated profusely.

Into the office, keeping his buns down, around the desk. The top drawer was ajar. Stone mentally tried to calculate the visual geometry. Same level as Garvey's desk, probably line of sight, not entirely blanked by the progress chart. Stone eased out the drawer from the bottom with the tips of his fingers, held his breath, then blindly swept his hand into the drawer, fingers probing.

The first pass yielded a notebook and two sheets stapled together which heralded the fifteenth reunion of Kagg's senior high school basketball team in Chickasha, Oklahoma. *The Chickasha Cluckers' Triple Nickel Bash, Y'all Come! R.S.V. Pee.*

Don't I wish y'all would come, thought Stone.

A creak and a groan came from the adjacent office, Garvey shifting his atrophied buns. A file cabinet door opening, then closing, the scratch of a match, the chair creaking back as Garvey settled in for the next breathtaking report.

Stone gave it another minute, now beginning to worry that Finn and Bee Gee were getting thirsty, might come down to find out what had happened and blow the deal. Stone's turn to buy rounds tonight, and when he did, he always dragged them to a bar that had a piano the customers could bang on. With two beers in him, Bee Gee could generally be talked into playing the thing. And with four beers in him, Bee Gee did his Debussy thing.

Once, when Stone had hired Bee Gee to run second shift on the Lebo Tunnel drive, they had both rented apartments over a store on Saw Mill Run Boulevard. The store's owner hustled amplified twang boxes, bongos and boom boxes, but also carried a line of Yamaha pianos. Stone had come back one night, shit-faced. He lay in his bed, hanging on to the rails, afraid that he was going to slide off, when he heard the Debussy stuff. Cascades of bright notes falling like leaves in September, all in myriad colors, crisp and dry, each a miracle in its own precise way. Next morning, he mentioned it to Guerber, the shop-owner. Guerber smiled and shook his head. 'You mean you didn't know?' He pointed a parchment-like finger toward the ceiling, toward Bee Gee's apartment, and smiled.

Stone took a deep breath and moved his hand up, more cunning this time, and probed deeper into the drawer. The tips of his fingers closed over the report, positive about that, because it was sandwiched between acetate covers, held together by brass pins. Victorious, he stuffed it under his belt and retreated, doggy-style.

Three minutes later, he was in the courtyard. Fine, light snow falling, the stuff swirling in small vortexes that scoured the bricks, then whirled upwards in miniature cyclones. Bee Gee and Finn were in the VW microbus, the windows fogged with condensation. Stone slid the back door open and piled in.

'You didn't . . . ?' Finn started to ask.

'You don't want to know,' Stone answered. 'Let's try the Ku'dorf.'

I'll drink to that, croaked the inner voice, obviously parched, nerves jangling, in the early stages of withdrawal as usual.

Stone fingered through the report that night. *Plascrete Tunnel Lining: An Appraisal*. The exact title that Stone had used, except that this was printed in slick, Helvetica type, fourteen-point.

The idea had not been all that unique, just the lucky cross-fertilization of one technology with another, Stone the catalyst.

Tunnels started out with boring, drilling or blasting a hole. But the walls and ceilings of tunnels often had to be lined to keep out water infiltration and to support the overburden. There were all kinds of liners. Segmented concrete liners, precast tubes, lattice girders and liner plates.

Shotcrete was another method — dry-mix concrete pumped to the work site, then mixed with water and sprayed on. The concrete could be reinforced by the addition of steel fibers with kinked ends. Reasonable in some applications but not suitable for rapid-setting applications or early high-stress loads like the tunnel he was presently chewing on.

Stone had dreamed up the idea one night, inspired by a liter of Johnny Walker's second-best. He had read about a quick and dirty boat-building technique which used a mixing gun that combined polyester resin, accelerator and glass fibers, the glop sprayed under pressure against the side of a mold. The results weren't as strong as normal fiberglass cloth lay-up, but it was quick, and, in sufficient depth of build-up, strong enough.

Stone had pondered the concept through the brown fog of whiskey and came to the conclusion that the same process could be used in certain tunneling applications. Same principle, right? Except the 'mold' would be the wall of the tunnel, and instead of using glass fiber, he'd used steel fibers for greater rigidity and yield-strength, and instead of polyester resin, epoxy with a chemical accelerator geared to set up almost instantaneously. Admittedly, the applications were limited, but in close quarters with bad ground that steadily weakened under seeping conditions, it should work.

He ran some calculations the next day and was encouraged; good energy absorption, highly ductile, impermeable and suitable for overburden support given sufficient build-up.

Stone knocked off early for the weekend and took a train up to Denmark. Aalborg Danske was the name of the firm in the article. They were using the method for glass lay-up on mid-sized work boats. Stone cut a deal to use the equipment after hours, then worked with a machine shop for three days to fabricate a hopper and dispersal system for the steel fibers, finally merging the two systems on a blue-steel-cold November afternoon. The test panels exceeded his expectations by a factor of 1.3.

Necessity is said to be the mother of invention, but the dream of fat future royalties stoked Stone's enthusiasm. He boxed the test pieces and shipped them back to Berlin, personally carrying the fan-fold reams of computer print-outs with him. Like a cat, proudly dragging in a dead mouse and looking for approval, he had shown the stuff to Kagg, who, if not innovative in his own right, realized Stone was on to a good thing.

Stone cobbled together a list of equipment and an estimate.

'It'll take at least 30,000, Stone,' Kagg had said. 'Can't authorize it myself – have to go back to Langley for approval.'

At that stage, the tunnel was only eighty-three meters into the underbelly of the GDR. Three weeks was what Stone figured it should take from the git-go to shipping. Double that to allow for the Agency's blinding bureaucratic inefficiency. 'Tell them we'll do it ourselves.'

'Can't,' answered Kagg. 'Procurement procedures, see? Form eighty-nine twenty-one.' He waved the paper form like a flag, as if he expected Stone to salute. Stone ultimately caved in to Kagg's pure logic, dreams of sugar-plum royalties dancing in his head. And why the hell not? Let the Agency fork out the funds for research and development, the funds necessary to accomplish that not within Stone's resources.

Stone and Kagg were still wary friends then, working together in the common cause of freeing the planet from the scourge of Borscht-eaters, but with their eyes still discreetly locked on the capitalistic ball. Stone allowed as how he might cut Kagg in for a piece of the pie if Kagg pushed Langley to fund the project. Kagg surprisingly agreed to five per cent of Stone's royalties, although Stone was prepared to go higher. Gentleman's agreement. Which assumed that Stone was dealing with a gentleman.

That was four months ago. By now, they were no longer friends.

Stone thumbed through the last pages of the report, the tide line on the bottle of Red Label steadily falling.

Not part of the main document, this section. Legal parchment, pink double lines framing the margins, all legal mumbo-jumbo: *party of the first part, whereas*es, *hereinafter referred to as the LICENSEE, such expression to include its successors, agents and assigns, et cetera*. Stone flipped back to the first page of the section and dumbly read the title:

Licensing Agreement for Plascrete Tunnel Lining
System (patent applied for), by and between
Orcus Resources Ltd, A Panamanian Corporation
(Licensee)
and
Normetz-Kondor GmbH, An Austrian Corporation
(Licenser)

All there, spelled out in precise and well-worn boiler-
plate: percentage of royalties (3.25), terms of license
(seven years, renewable for another five years with the
approval of both parties but subject to good-faith re-
negotiation of royalty percentage), scope of license
(universal), co-ownership of patent (Orcus Resources
Ltd and Milton G. Kagg, also listed as Managing Director
and Chief Executive Officer with his sprawling signature
on the dotted line).

It wasn't a bad apartment. A nice but slightly sawed-off
view of the Bergmannstraße in the Kreuzberg, decent
enough furnishings if you liked Early Ersatz Teutonic.
Stone topped up his scotch and parted the draperies. Four
or five centimeters of snow on the pavement, still falling,
probably enough accumulation by morning so that a few
of Siegfried's hearty heirs could skinny-ski to work. Have
to get snow tires for the VW pretty soon, he reminded
himself.

He knocked back the remains of scotch, then heaved the
tumbler at the ersatz fireplace, the gas flame innocently
flickering yellow above ersatz logs. The tumbler shattered,
shards and slivers arcing in the gaslight, littering the tiles
and ersatz oak parquet flooring. Stone got another bottle
of JWRL out of the cupboard and expertly slit the seal with
his fingernail. *I'll drink to that*, moaned the inner voice in
sympathy, still thirsty, never *quite* satisfied, the fatal worm
burrowing in Stone's guts.

*

14

Kagg was apoplectic. Garvey backed him up, cheerleading from the sidelines, quoting chapter and verse from the security regs.

'You're never going to work on a tunnel again, Stone – my fuckin' word on that,' said Kagg, his face flushed with bursting capillaries.

'How about your fuckin' word on whose idea the plascrete was?'

Kagg turned to Garvey. 'You heard about it from me first, right? Told you that I sent Stone up to Denmark to work out the bugs.'

Garvey looked doubtful, uncertain of his ground. He was still fresh enough out of the Agency's training to question dubious ethics, regardless of whether there was a payoff that kept the World Free for Democracy.

Which Kagg explained in tiresome detail. 'Nothing worth diddly-squat in this for me, Stone. The Agency is the beneficial holder of the patent. Understand that Congress doesn't fund us for certain kinds of operations. Bunch of pussy-whipped liberals. So the Agency has an assortment of its own profitable companies to fund off-the-books operations. *Salus populi suprema lex est* – for the good of the people – whether the dumb shits know it or not.'

'It was my idea, you bastard!'

'Maybe, maybe not. I'll admit that you got my brain all hot and bothered, but that don't make a shit. Your contract reads that all proprietary . . . uh . . . read it to him, Garvey.'

'. . . All proprietary instrumentalities, intellectual planning, devices, creations, methodologies, drawings, calculations, et cetera, et cetera, however derived and by whom, if used in the design, construction or maintenance of said underground structure, immediately revert to and remain in perpetuity the sole property of the Proprietor.'

Garvey looked up at Stone, flushed with victory. 'You signed it, Stone.'

'*Gotcha!*' Stone shot back. 'Nobody ever anticipated the use of plascrete in the design, construction or maintenance

15

of the tunnel. It's something outside the scope of the contract. Read the specifications, Kagg.'

Kagg curled his forefinger at Stone and bid him come hence. 'Got a little old surprise for you in the courtyard.'

It was sitting in the back of a Mercedes truck, shrouded in canvas and mounted on skids, painted a bright, bilious yellow. Diesel-engine-driven pumps, mixing hoppers, hose connections, regulating valves. The metal placard on the radiator proclaimed that this was a *Plascrete Application System, Model III*, built by the venerable firm of Normetz-Kondor GmbH, Wiener Neustadt, Austria, all rights reserved, patent pending.

'So what happened to Models I and II?'

Kagg brushed an offending flake of chimney soot from the sleeve of his boiler suit. 'Doesn't sound good if the prospective customer thinks he's the number-one or two guinea pig, does it?' Kagg exuded marketing know-how, patting the machine.

The unit was pretty much the way Stone had envisioned it. Off-the-shelf parts except for the bent-wire hopper. Someone had done a nice job on the design of the nozzle. He fingered a fitting, slightly puzzled. 'What's this gizmo?'

'Flush out the nozzle with acetone once you've used it. Keeps things from getting gummed up.'

'How long does the plascrete take to set up?'

'Depends on the temperature and the percentage of accelerator fluid you use. The tables are in the manual. But anywhere from five minutes to practically instantaneous.' He emphasized *instantaneous* by snapping his fingers. Kagg was now smiling, open, old buddy. 'Just the ticket, Stone. Now you can drive the tunnel and shore up as you go.'

'I'll want breathing apparatus for the crews.'

Kagg nodded to a wooden crate in the back of the truck. 'Self-contained, same stuff that Navy SEALS use. And by tomorrow morning, we'll have forty drums of epoxy specially trucked in from Italy. Take your time getting used

16

to it. That is, supposing you still want to finish the job.'

Kagg had left a thin wedge open for negotiation, a bone tossed. Stone caught it. 'Okay – no penalty clause and Langley ups the completion price by twenty per cent. And I want to be paid up to date in cash. Otherwise, anything they shove in my Stateside account will be grabbed by the IRS.'

Big grin. 'Seems like all of us gotta operate off the books some of the time, right, buddy?' Kagg puffed out his cheeks like he was considering real hard. 'Okay. You're one hel-luva horse-trader, Stone, but I'll run it by Langley with my endorsement for approval.' He stuck out his hand. 'Deal?'

'Deal,' Stone said, mentally crossing his fingers. 'One thing, Kagg – where'd you come up with the name Orcus Resources?'

'Roman god of the underworld. Like in tunnels. Got it outta crossword puzzle dictionary. Real cute, huh?'

'Not bad,' Stone agreed. Actually, given the players, appropriate.

February into March, the snow turning black, then melting to mush and refreezing into concrete. But the drive went a lot faster now. Drill, muck and plascrete, one smooth, seamless operation. Except for the stench of epoxy, the tunnel was a lot more habitable and infinitely safer.

Fifty meters, then thirty from the *target*, Kagg's exact words. Another fourteen meters, then eight, three and, in the second hour of their shift on 21 May, Bee Gee's hose revealed bricks. He throttled the nozzle and leaned back against the tunnel wall.

'How 'bout that? Didn't even need a visa to get here. Think we should knock or just barge right in?'

Stone was smiling, the idea he had been working on now clear in his mind. 'You guys clear out. Take the plas-crete unit back up to the courtyard and refill it.'

Bee Gee's forehead wrinkled. 'Come again? This sucker oughta be stripped down and cleaned.'

17

'I'll take care of it personally. Meet you in the courtyard in an hour.' He headed for Kagg's orifice, a spring in his step.

Kagg beamed, a twenty-one toother. Stone slid down into a chair opposite his desk. 'Bee Gee and Finn are cleaning up. The second shift can tie the ribbons on it.'

'You hear anything on the other side of the wall?'

'No, but you can smell pine.'

'Pine? You're shitting me.'

'Sawdust. They use it as filler in their bread. Makes the flour go further and also cleans the plaque off your teeth as you chew. The GDR's contribution to sturdy German fangs, the better to eat you with, my dear.'

'You're kidding.'

'You're right.' Stone shifted gears. 'Forty-three thousand, eight hundred. That's the balance of the contract money owing.'

'No sweat. I'll cut you a check.'

'Cash. That was the deal. I've got to pay off Bee Gee and Finn. They've got tickets out of Tempelhof tomorrow afternoon, PanAm.'

Kagg shrugged. 'Still have to issue an IRS 1099, miscellaneous income report. Best you declare your income to the revenue boys whether you pay it or not. Your butt's in enough trouble already, Stone.'

It wasn't the deal but Stone wasn't going to argue. 'Whatever turns you on, Kagg,' he answered.

Bee Gee and Finn were lounging against the VW, waiting.

Stone paused by Kagg's new 500 series BMW. Black, with a luster so deep that it looked like liquefied coal. Tan leather upholstery. Just smelling the interior gave you a hard-on. Kagg *loved* the machine, undoubtedly bought with royalties that were rightfully Stone's.

Finn came over to where Stone stood. 'One helluva pussymobile, Stone. Had to cost him over thirty grand.'

'What's Kagg make?'

Finn scratched his crotch in happy contemplation, sighing deeply. 'Maybe forty-two, forty-three thousand max including the hazardous duty pay.'

'My thoughts exactly,' said Stone.

Stone, hung-over, picked up the packages of fifties from Kagg at nine in the morning. Terrific day, the sun hot, the lindens budding. Bee Gee and Finn were packed, waiting for him in the van. Stone slid into the front seat. He counted out two piles worth 13,000, then threw in another 4000 each. What the hell, they earned it.

Bee Gee gripped his hand. 'You staying on here?'

'Not for long. You know how to reach me?'

'Mail it to your daddy's place in West Virginia?'

'The same.' He reached across the seat and took Finn's meaty paw. 'Later,' he said.

'You sure you don't want some help? It'd be pure pleasure.'

'I don't think either of you guys need the hassle. But I'll take photos for the archives.'

The microbus snorted gray smoke and trundled away, Finn looking back, grinning.

Stone had already set up his exit from Berlin with a British platoon sergeant, a fellow alcoholic and admirer of Scottish adult beverages. Stone's exit was to be in the back of a British Army lorry headed for Norway. From there, he was booked on a freighter that would, in its own good time, call at the Port of Boston.

He got the compressor going and patted the machine, now an old friend and co-conspirator. From a bag, Stone withdrew ten meters of water hose and snaked it into the vent system of the BMW, providing a crude snorkel. Then he headed for the operations area.

Kagg was in his office. He looked up, surprised.

'Thought you were already outta here.'

'PanAm, 6.30 tonight. Overbooked on the early flight. Gave my seat to Finn. He's got a lady waiting in Boston.'

'What's your pleasure?'

Stone held up the Cannon 35-mm. 'Wanted to get a picture of you and Garvey.'

'No way down here. Secure area, remember?'

'I was thinking in the courtyard, in your BMW.'

Kagg's face beamed like a harvest moon. *'GARVEY!'* Hardly necessary, as Garvey was in his accustomed place in the next cubicle, pecking out his accustomed reports.

They meandered up to the courtyard, Kagg stretching in the early heat of the May sun. He slid into the BMW with casual grace, like he practiced doing it a lot.

'Smile,' Stone called out across the courtyard, backing away, fiddling with the focus.

They both grinned on full hot, Kagg with his shoulders squared, hands in the ten and two position, black leather driving gloves on, Ray Bans glinting.

Stone kept backing away until he bumped into the throbbing compressor. He shot the first frame, the *before* shot.

Then dropped the camera in its sling and whipped the nozzle toward Kagg's BMW, adjusting the flow valve to *rapid mix/full aeration* as he swung it.

Kagg's smile was frozen, words probably starting in his throat, never quite making it to his lips. The electric window zipped into the closed position, Kagg's expression transitioning from concerned to frenetic.

The stuff built up rapidly, foaming, then hardening in seconds. Stone snaked the hose around to the passenger side, cutting off the escape route.

He could take his time now. He made it as artistic as he could, building the initial shapeless mound into a gigantic tit, complete with nipple, then, dissatisfied, swirled the pale foam into a Dairy Cream Vanilla Jumbo Frosty. It took concentration, dedication, and skill, but Stone was up to the task and he whistled as he worked.

And if chilling out in Maine was the price he had to pay, it was worth every goddamned minute and then some.

The Mid-Nineties

ONE

The wind buffeted the glass of his penthouse office, smearing it with streaks of sooty rain. The sky was domed by a bleak layered overcast, the lowest clouds torn into ragged fragments by the west wind, the dull horizon within his quadrant of vision merging the City's skyline into the gritty suburbs to the south.

Although it was only mid-afternoon, motor cars, delivery vans and lorries had turned on their headlamps. Like a procession of primitive insects, they crept forward in obedient order, their minds numb to the tattered vestiges of a burned-out empire crumbling around them. Nelson's heirs, England's stout-hearted men, this happy breed, this realm of kings? Sir David Michael Coosworth thought otherwise.

He stood at the window for long minutes, the Brunschwig & Fils curtain drawn back by his purple-veined hand. And, as always, his eyes were drawn down to the River. Immediately below him flowed the Thames. It was the reason he had selected this building site four decades ago. Then, three of his senior accountants and two of the directors had screamed at the cost of the land in varying degrees of falsetto. He fired the accountants and quietly terminated the directors. Sod the buggers. His was a firm connected to the sea and the Thames was England's symbolic artery to the heart of world commerce, hence to the fortunes of Blue Riband Lines. The bean-counters and clubmen had never comprehended that reality – not then, not even now.

He had to squint, damned annoying. Hated wearing spectacles and couldn't abide those damned contact things – gave him headaches. Eyes good, just tired from the strain, he lied to himself. At age seventy-three, self-deception was a means of explaining away the inevitable rule of corporal decay.

Below him, the Thames had been beaten into a dull sheet of hammered lead by the winter's rain. Isolated wisps of mist lay on the River and swirled in eddied gusts. A small tug breasted the current, working its way upstream toward the Pool of London. From the height of his seventeenth-story office, he could see no evidence of current, but it was there, remorselessly flowing toward the sea, like black blood seeping from a mortal wound in the commercial heart of England. He unconsciously warped his lips in distaste. The metaphor was overly dramatic, yet, he thought, appropriate.

Sir David lit a gold-tipped Benson and Hedges, sighed and dropped the hem of the curtain. He moved to the bar hidden in the paneling above the stock quotation monitor and poured a small whiskey, then eased back into his leather chair. The spreadsheet printout lapped over the rosewood surface of his desk, light green and white striped rows, organized into dense columns of numbered print. It was the bottom line, of course, which drew the uninformed eye. Profits reasonably good, although off six per cent from the previous quarter. He would keep the dividends artificially high, of course, to appease the shareholders, because he had to float a new management compensation plan and needed a *quid pro quo*. Let the financial analysts in the City howl. The share price of Blue Riband stock would remain reasonably firm – for now.

The bad news was buried in the line items; not each entry stunning in itself, but altogether a disaster. He examined them separately. Blue Riband Lines was hemorrhaging at the rate of £400,000 a month, no end of it in sight. Long-term contracts being renegotiated, suppliers hedging on their commitments, credit terms becoming tighter, and the short-term loans being called in by the banks without justifiable reason.

He leaned back and studied the framed oil portraits on the paneled wall opposite him – his father and his father before him, and a succession of five other men immortalized in seven cracked oil paintings, back through two and a half centuries to Mad Michael Coosworth who had founded Blue Riband Lines with one ship, purchased with a loan from a moneylender at ten per cent per month and an override of thirty per cent on the landed profits. The ship had been rotten by all accounts; an old transport of 220 tons, a relic of the East Indian trade, four hours on the pumps for every hour off. Mad Michael had run muskets to Africa, slaves to the West Indies and Jamaican rum back to the docks of London, each leg of the triangle earning a bloody fortune. Without knowing it, Mad Michael had laid the foundations of a commercial empire.

In those halcyon days, one successful passage paid three times over for the ship and her crew's wages. Now, the bean-counters amortized the cost of ships over sixteen years and prayed to the Gods of Statistical Analysis that the company's profits, after taxes, would out-earn the yield on Treasury gilts. It seemed stupid, he thought, now to risk so much for so little. Yet there was an inertia generated by prior decisions in any corporation's life, and Sir David accepted that it would never be any other way. It was just that he chafed at the dictatorial democracy of the shareholders' insatiable thirst for profits, even though one man at the top was better positioned to make the hard decisions, despite temporarily depressed profits. If nothing else, Sir David took the long view, provided it was his own.

Blue Riband now had forty-three ships with an accumulative displacement of a quarter of a million tons, all in the cross-Channel trade. His ships carried passengers, motor cars, lorries and railway wagons between Great Britain and the Continent. And they were profitable, according to the sacrosanct bottom line. Cross-Channel trade had been growing at an annualized rate of twelve per cent per annum through the late eighties and early nineties, but now, with the speed, safety and convenience of Eurotunnel, the seaborne freight tonnage and passenger loads were beginning to slip. Soon, Sir David knew, they would begin to fall – precipitously.

The progress reports arrived by courier twice weekly, courtesy of Matsuo Ashida. Ashida, a senior man with Komoto Securities and Investments Ltd, had been retained by an investment underwriting firm working for Eurotunnel in the hope that he would be able to attract Japanese and Pacific Rim investors to the next round of Eurotunnel financing. The initial cost overruns on the Chunnel had been staggering, but already some in Eurotunnel were quietly prodding management to drive two more tunnels, doubling the Chunnel's capacity by the year 2002. Only in Japan and on the Pacific Rim was that kind of new money available, the European banks – exhausted from the original round of financing – now wary of new commitments before a profit from Eurotunnel share dividends graced their portfolios.

A clever and multi-faceted man was Ashida, Coosworth reflected. And a dangerous bastard to boot, now that Coosworth understood the game Ashida was playing. Met him at Wimbledon – had actually bumped into the bloody chap. Coosworth now realized that their meeting had been far from 'accidental'.

In the early days, when they were still friends, they had frequently met at Ashida's discreet Regency Park *pied-à-terre*, always liberally supplied with good whiskey and charming (but vacuous) popsies. Friendship being what it is, Sir David had casually asked Ashida as to his access to Eurotunnel's financial prospects, their traffic load factor and knowledge of any problems that they were experiencing. After all, it *was* necessary to learn what one's competitors were up to, Sir David had said with a wink and a nod.

Surprisingly, Ashida willingly supplied him with reams of highly confidential information, thus laying the groundwork for the 'Arrangement'.

The 'Arrangement' had now been in place for three years. For an insignificant annual 'honorarium' of £20,000, Ashida supplied Sir David with an ongoing summary of Eurotunnel operations. This week's report was no less comprehensive than the previous ones: current and projected revenues, traffic load factors, maintenance costs, anticipated value of contracts currently in negotiation, an analysis of British Rail's privatization and its impact on Chunnel traffic, problems with security, safety probe monitoring readouts – the lot.

Eurotunnel was Blue Riband's most dangerous competitor and Ashida's reports allowed Sir David to gaze clandestinely into its corporate crystal ball. Increasingly, that crystal ball forecast the success of the Eurotunnel endeavor, and by simple extrapolation the demise of Blue Riband.

Sir David leaned back and closed his eyes. Nearly three centuries of work for nothing, and he was at the helm of the sinking ship but damned if he would let it go down without fighting back.

His intercom buzzed twice and he fingered the switch.

'Sir David . . . they're here except for the Brigadier, and his driver has just called by cellular. Caught in traffic, perhaps ten minutes' delay.'

'Show them the boardroom and make them comfortable. I'll be there shortly.' He flicked the switch off.

Not once in his life had he committed a clear-cut crime. Oh, perhaps danced on the edges, but nothing like *this*. He flicked his gold Dunhill lighter absently, glancing at the clock. Let them cool their heels for twenty minutes, give them time to read through their confidential copies of the quarterly report, worry about the rapidly diminishing worth of their stock options, the curtailed directors' fishing rights in Scotland, the downscaling of their fees, all the other perks that would melt under the blast of reduced profits. He would give them time to reflect, set their nerves on edge, make them more receptive. The few directors who counted would ultimately give their consent to his proposal, either directly or through a generalized agreement that would leave the sordid details to his own discretion. Ashida had insisted on the board's participation in the endeavor, but why? If anything, it made the whole thing that much riskier. Still, Ashida was calling the tune and there was no denying him.

Sir David did not exactly look forward to this, yet, in a way, he did. For this was a scoundrel's business and Mad Michael would have been proud of him.

'Seconded,' said Bradley-Gresham. His hand was raised. Seven other hands joined his; white cuffs shot from suits crafted by the best tailors in London, Patek Philippe watches glinting, manicured fingernails gleaming softly in the subdued light of the boardroom.

'Agreed, then,' said Sir David. 'The declaration of quarterly dividends stands as proposed by a majority of the board. Any new business?'

Gerald Farington leaned forward and raised a finger. Bald, brittle, aged, Farington *was* Farington Electrics Ltd. For close to a century, his firm had made electric light switches and wiring receptacles. It was said that Farington's design philosophy had frozen sometime around 1934. The Farington Standard Home Model Two wall switches were still molded from Bakelite plastic with sturdy copper contacts and robust springs. They never failed, backed by an unstated but binding lifetime warranty. But they were also half a century behind the times in design. Ungainly things, meant to be screwed into a wall with exposed wiring, rather than being flushed into modern-day dry-wall construction.

Corporate lore explained it anecdotally. Back in 1961, a Farington engineer, tainted by a trip to America, had suggested to the old man that Farington Electrics enter the space age with flush receptacles and some damned innovation called 'touch-press' light switches. Seemed that people were actually building new homes and running the wiring *inside* the walls. The engineer blathered on, suggesting that different *tints* could be selected for the switch face-plates – a concept he called 'color coordination'. Appalled, Farington discharged the man on the spot.

Now, with the advent of the EC, the trade barriers had dropped overnight. German, Finnish and French light switches were going head to head with Farington products, no longer protected by punitive import duties. Farington, with no stockholders to answer to, had always firmly believed that the British public would see straight through these flimsy, *foreign* frauds and still buy Farington. Matter of common good sense and – well, damn it all – patriotism, when you got right down to it. *Buy Better – Buy British*. Of course, Farington was wrong and he was now reluctantly coming to that realization.

'Sir David, I assume that you have an update.'

Sir David smiled and looked around the table at the eight directors, all malleable men. Twelve thousand pounds each for their annual directors' fees, yet they didn't earn a damned farthing of it. Rubber stamps, the lot, which is exactly what Sir David expected of them.

'Don't want to take up your time unnecessarily with trivial reports which are not a matter for the official minutes. I know some of you have important schedules to meet. Any of you who wish to stay, please do so. Otherwise, this meeting is officially adjourned. Thank you, gentlemen.'

Four of the eight filed out leaving Gerald Farington, Brigadier-General Malcolm Campbell, Ret. (DSO with bars), Freddie Barnsworth and Ian Page.

Sir David dismissed the recording secretary and nodded to the remaining directors. 'Sherry, gentlemen? Tio Pepe; excellent stuff, half a century old from my man in Spain.'

Nods. Sir David poured, then sat down on the edge of the table, in his informal mode.

The Brigadier and Farington would go along with the scheme, he was sure. Barnsworth probably would as well, assuming that his alcohol-addled brain comprehended the necessity of it. Only Page was a question mark.

Sir David offered cigars around. All but Page accepted one. Page was a hard-charger. Positively glowing with health, in his forties, said to ride a push bike in Hyde Park during his lunch-hour, for God's sake. He was one of the young Turks, software development, making a packet internationally. Page had been a mistake, Sir David acknowledged to himself. *Should never have offered him a directorship. Not really our kind of man.*

The four men settled back in their chairs, waiting.

'The report from Folkestone is not particularly noteworthy except for some bumph about British Rail's privatization. Once their new high-speed lines from Liverpool and Cardiff are tied into the Chunnel route, we can count on a further twenty-one per cent reduction in Blue Riband's railcar transport revenues.'

'Damned thing!' snorted the Brigadier. 'John Major was dead wrong when he agreed to open the thing to foreigners. Sold out England, I say.'

'I disagree,' said Page. 'Without the Chunnel, we'd still be cut off from the Continent, both in terms of rapid movement of goods and full integration into the EC, psychologically speaking.' He nodded to Coosworth. 'No offense, Sir David. I realize that Blue Riband will suffer to some extent, but it's impossible to buck an idea whose time has come. I think it would be prudent for Blue Riband to examine alternatives to the cross-Channel shipping trade.'

Page was in a position to speak that kind of codswallop, Sir David thought, his expression blank. Page didn't own any shares in Blue Riband. Had some stock options, of course, but the man wouldn't be concerned with the cost of a hideaway in the Caribbean or the upkeep for a tart in Mayfair; not with the dividend stream from his firm's business. His shares in Page Software Solutions Ltd were said to be worth eight million, with a share price growth projection of twenty-eight per cent per annum.

As a consequence, Sir David didn't rise to the bait, but continued, 'I also have a copy of an internal White Paper prepared for the Board of Trade concerning the impact thus far on Great Britain's entry into the European Community. Somewhat expensive to procure, I'm sure you can appreciate. Not even to be published, I understand. Might cause a stir.' He pulled a slim document out of his briefcase and laid it on the table.

'There is supporting statistical analysis although not in my possession, but this document summarizes the situation neatly.'

He leafed through the pages as if to refresh his memory, although he had read through the damned thing at least five times. 'There are, predictably, winners and losers in Great Britain. Winners – the financial markets are prospering, as are such business sectors as insurance, banking, specialized consulting firms, computer software firms on the leading edge of technology . . .' He glanced up at Page and smiled thinly, Page passing this revelation off with a modest shrug. Sir David continued. '. . . Import agencies, transport firms, particularly Eurotunnel and British Rail, hospitality industry firms catering to upscale business visitors from the Continent, providers of international communications, et cetera, et cetera.'

He turned the page. 'Losers are cross-Channel shipping interests, textile mills, finished-garment firms, automotive manufacturers, food production and processing firms, except for unique British carriage-trade goods, breweries . . .'

Sir David glanced briefly at Barnsworth. Freddie Barnsworth owned one of the largest breweries in Great Britain – that and 418 pubs to distribute his product. The problem was twofold: Freddie loved to sample his own

31

wares, was said to consume a raw egg folded into a glass of Barnsworth Noble Stout upon rising and never looked back for the rest of his waking hours. Freddie's other problem was what he broadly categorized as 'YTTs' – young trendy types, university-educated, moving up rapidly in the corporate world and tainted by distinctly non-British tastes. It was fashionable now in that crowd to drink imported lager, *chilled* to indecently frigid temperatures so as to hide the inferior taste; stuff with brand names like Heineken, Saint Pauli Girl, Beck's and San Miguel – all of it *foreign* trash. That and wine. Waves of it from France, Italy and Spain, lapping at the shores of England, diluting Freddie's bottom line because of the faddish tastes of these young people. With the import duties now dropped and with rapid, pilfer-free, low-cost delivery via Eurotunnel assured, Freddie's brewery profits were being devastated. Of course, the older generation of solid English working men would never in their life lift a bottle of German beer or Italian wine to their lips, but they were, literally, a dying breed.

Sir David needn't have bothered to have looked. Freddie's eyes were already glazed over, his expression frozen, ears deaf. Actually dreamy.

Sir David continued. '. . . Machine tools, fabricated steel products, computer-associated hardware . . .' He sighed and closed the report. 'The list goes on for another two pages, gentlemen. Most depressing. In a few short years, England will be a beggar on the Continent's doorstep.'

'Scandalous,' said the Brigadier. 'I said that to Maggie eight years ago and damned if the blasted *woman* would listen.'

Ian Page sighed, closed his briefcase and zipped it. 'I think all of you are swimming against the stream. The European Community is a fact. We have to adapt to the reality. It may be painful in the short term, but . . .' He left the sentence unfinished and stood up. 'Sir David, gentlemen, I must be off.'

No one looked up as he departed.

Sir David waited for long seconds until he was sure that Page wouldn't pop in again. *Hope the bugger bashes his push bike into a tree.*

The room was silent, except for the sound of breathing, the hush of the air conditioning and muffled sounds drifting up from the streets.

'I want to discuss the problem of the Chunnel and how to permanently rectify that problem,' said Sir David, his voice barely audible. Three pairs of eyebrows raised, heads slowly turning toward him.

'The English common man doesn't want the EC. Repeated polling incontestably reveals that fact. Nor, certainly, do the union lads, despite what the Labour Party tells them. Nor does the solid core of the middle class. Nor do we, as representatives of unfairly threatened industries. Agreed?'

Of course the poll was balderdash, out of date by three years, but Sir David had dredged it up for this particular occasion.

One head nodded, then two, then three. *They'll go along,* he thought, because they *have* to go along.

Confident, his spirits lifted, Sir David began to hit his stride, just as he had when he was a marathon man at Oxford; that moment when the runner knows the race is his, when the oxygen comes sweetly to the lungs, when the muscles know no pain, when the trophy is for the taking.

'We can do nothing to reverse England's entry into the European Community. At least not directly. But indirectly, we can.'

That roused their attention, even Barnsworth looking up, trying to focus.

Not that it was necessary, more for effect, Sir David moved to the door and locked it. He then poured a second round of sherry. 'I must ask each of you to pledge that what I am about to say will forever remain secret. If you disagree with my proposal, you will be free to leave this room, but what is about to be discussed remains in the strictest of confidence. Agreed?'

Like small boys banding together in conspiracy, perhaps to flatten the tires of the headmaster's Austin, each solemnly pledged undying fidelity. Barnsworth actually made a motion of zipping his lips.

'What I am proposing will preserve the cultural identity and commercial position of England and the rest of Great Britain. No less than that, gentlemen. What is required is an event of such dimension that it will stir the sluggish blood of Englishmen into rebellion against union with the Continent. I would suggest that our involvement, regardless of its difficulty and cost, will be an act of unparalleled patriotism.'

The Brigadier loved that, actually smiling. ''Bout bloody time,' he rumbled.

'This will require a financial sacrifice on our part . . .' – scowls – 'but in the end, it will come right – more than right.' He laid out copies for each of the three men; copies of his own handwritten calculations.

'At present, Blue Riband is quoted at 1360 pence a share. Down, I would note, from over 2100 last year. As things stand, within two years, Blue Riband will likely be bankrupt and your shares worthless.'

Blank stares.

He pressed on smoothly, ignoring words forming on bloodless lips. 'I know what the annual shareholders' report says. ''Conversion of Blue Riband ships to specialized carriers of goods otherwise prohibited to Euro-tunnel traffic, mini-holiday cruises, luxury surface ferries with gaming salons, and catering to those averse to transiting Eurotunnel because of claustrophobia.'' So much rubbish. We'll try all of that, of course, until the firm's reserves run dry, but realistic projections of these schemes, thus far, are quite depressing.'

Farington started to interrupt but Sir David pressed on.

'But suppose that the Chunnel was, ah, rendered incapable of service on a permanent basis with no residual financial or political will to rebuild it. If that were to happen, the market value of our Blue Riband shares would soar. Anticipating this, er, fortuitous turn of events, we might even individually purchase options on Blue Riband stock with an expiration date of, let's say, July of this year, thereby leveraging our positions. I have done some discreet research on this and for fifteen million or less we could buy option contracts on nearly all publicly owned Blue Riband shares.'

The Brigadier, perhaps the canniest if not the brightest of the lot, had the beginnings of a smile on his lips.

'All very well and good for Blue Riband, *if* the Chunnel was put out of action,' said Farington.

'All very well and good for each of us,' Sir David corrected. 'Blue Riband's share values would double, triple, quadruple, quintuple. My calculations only assume a modest tripling of share values within two years. The second and third columns of my calculation reflect the present and projected future value of both your shares and options. I believe you'll find the differences substantial.' They were. A minimum of an eight-million increase for the Brigadier, substantially more for the other board members. What Sir David hadn't shown was a forty-three-million increase in his own account. Of course, very little of it would be his. Specifically, only five per cent, with the balance going to his silent partner, Komoto Securities and Investments Ltd.

Slightly more than two years ago over a cozy dinner, Ashida had described the potential of investing in Nikkei Dow futures contracts (which he claimed he had insider knowledge of) and Coosworth began investing – just moderate sums at first, but as the Nikkei soared, so did the value of Coosworth's portfolio and his investment commitment. The real money in the family had always been Alice, his wife's – with Coosworth's wealth tied up in Blue

Riband share holdings. Coosworth had been drugged with the prospect of acquiring a fortune on his own account. And, after all, the investment was a sure thing. Ashida was a man in the know, at the vortex of things as it were; a man who spoke of his powerful connections and insider knowledge of Japan's rigged stock market.

And then the Nikkei Index headed south with a vengeance. Between 1990 and 1992, Sir David Coosworth lost over sixteen million pounds. Ashida apologized and assured him that this was just 'a temporary and regrettable reversal', with an upward resumption in the index a virtual reality within a few short months. He had actually suggested that Coosworth *increase* his investment in futures contracts to 'eventually double your profits'. To cover Coosworth's massive debt, Ashida assured him that '. . . we at Komoto will discreetly cover your shortage of funds with an unlimited line of credit, your shares in Blue Riband serving as collateral.'

As it now stood, Coosworth was bankrupt on paper with an overhanging debt that exceeded twenty million pounds, and the only way out was Ashida's Chunnel plan. To defy Ashida would mean public exposure and prison at a minimum, but Ashida had obliquely referred to other distasteful consequences, not the least among them physical harm.

Ashida had suggested the Chunnel plan with a dismissive shrug, '. . . As a means of enhancing the value of your Blue Riband shares which, in turn, underlies the security of our loan to you.'

As to the 'project', Ashida, of course, would in no way be involved other than to supply Coosworth's share of the seed money and to select the 'contractors'.

The Brigadier seemed genuinely disturbed, his patriotic bubble pricked. 'Dammit, man. You're blathering about Blue Riband share values. Assuming that something can be done, we'd all make a bloody fortune, but that doesn't do anything to restore England's supremacy.'

What supremacy? Sir David wondered. *We lost that fifty years ago and the old bastard hasn't wakened to the fact even now.*

'I was going to address that situation, Brigadier,' Sir David went on smoothly. 'The Chunnel is the most visible symbol of Great Britain's entry into the EC. Soon, we will no longer be a proud, independent island nation but rather a tatty suburb of the Continent. English quality products will be crushed in the marketplace by inferior goods from the Continent, simply because Continental trash is cheaper. It is a sad comment that the average Englishman's loyalty is first and foremost to his purse. I also fear that *foreign* firms will continue to build factories in Great Britain, exploiting our labor force in the production of goods to sell to our own markets, with the profits flowing back to the Continent. I hesitate to even mention the corruption that will be visited on our people due to the *influence* of Continental moral standards, or the uncontrolled spread of rabies.'

There was an audible sucking-in of breath.

'But let us assume that the Chunnel were to structurally fail – that it were to become permanently closed to traffic due to, ah, an accident. Billions of pounds would be lost by imprudent banks and investors who have foolishly underwritten the scheme. Lloyd's could, probably would, fail.' He relit his Romeo y Juliet Number Four and continued.

'My conservative estimate is that the government would fall from a vote of no confidence, and regardless of which party replaces it, there will surely be proposals put forward in Parliament to remove Great Britain from the EC, once and for all. The idea of union with the Continent is uncommonly despised by the public, by the union rank and file, and by all thinking men of English blood. The failure of the Chunnel would be the final straw.'

Overdoing it a bit, he thought, yet two of the three directors nodded their approval. The Brigadier was actually smiling, displaying yellowed teeth that once flashed white in the sun of colonial India.

Farington was the reluctant bridesmaid. 'Then what would Great Britain do? We'd be cut off from the EC, from a lucrative Continental market.' Somehow, the old boy still clung to the fragile belief that Frogs and Huns would buy his Bakelite abortions in preference to their mod-con *tinted* switches.

Sir David thrust home at their collective jugulars. 'There is a very quiet movement within the House of Commons to form an English-speaking trade bloc as a counterweight, perhaps even an alternative, to the EC. Composed of Great Britain, of course, coupled with Canada, the United States, Australia, New Zealand, and some of the former colonies. We might even let in the Irish. Mind you, such an economic union would be built on our *own* standards, our *own* traditional quality – with all of the trading partners united by a common language and shared values.'

'Who in the House of Commons?'

There wasn't a movement such as Sir David had alluded to, but it fit his scenario neatly. And perhaps, in time, there would be, but his goal was the salvation of his own skin and Blue Riband's, not Great Britain's. 'Backbenchers, of course. But backbenchers of both parties backed by men of substantial means, men whom each of you know well, but men who for the moment must remain anonymous.' He winked.

'Would the Yanks *actually* go along with it?'

'My reading of that is an emphatic *yes*. They're gradually being cut out of the EC by protectionism. Nothing overt, of course. Just delays in customs clearance, quotas, high duties, impossible standards, mandated majority ownership by European shareholders, that sort of tripe. You would have thought they would have learned from their experience with the Nips. Oh yes – they'll come in. But Great Britain will, of course, supply the leadership.'

The Brigadier gradually spawned a smile, then swelled

his chest, satisfied, as if his doctor had just pronounced him fit for another eighty-one years of service. 'Just how will these blasted tubes under the Channel be permanently closed?'

'There is a terrorist group on the Continent which needs only a bit of funding and some encouragement to make a political statement. What their political motivation is shouldn't concern us in the least. I am in contact with a very able man who has links to this group. What I am suggesting is that we engage him as a conduit to fund the destruction of the Chunnel.'

Alarmed eyebrows shot up in unison.

Sir David raised his hand as if in benediction, calming the troubled masses. 'Mind you, there would be no direct connections. My man is discreet. Our involvement would be that of an anonymous contributor to their just cause, whatever that cause might be. My man would not ask for any details of how it would be done. Just the assurance that it would be done properly, with no loss of life, of course.'

'What would be the budget for such an endeavor?'

'Eight million, perhaps a bit more.'

'And when would they go over the top?' The Brigadier still related to trench warfare.

'By the spring of this year, say April or May.'

'Possible?' Freddie Barnsworth asked.

'Anything is possible, Freddie. I have detailed drawings of the Chunnel's construction provided by our anonymous Japanese friend. Bags of geological data, details of Euro-tunnel's security arrangements. A third-form engineering student with a couple of O-levels should be able to both find and exploit the fatal flaw.'

'And who pays . . . ?'

'We pay,' Sir David answered. 'I will personally under-write fifty-five per cent of the expense, and if you are all in agreement, each of you fifteen. I *will* require *all* the funds in advance.' He firmly emphasized that although he kept his voice even. It was a simple business deal, cash on the barrel head. Which translated to £1,275,000 for each of the three men seated opposite him.

The Brigadier was no longer smiling. 'Rather pricey, Sir David.'

'I did not plan on a rag-tag effort. Quality work is expensive. But I would suggest that the effort will reward us well. I would add that Eurotunnel shares might be vulnerable were the Chunnel to be put out of service. I should think the share price would fall through the cellar. I caution you not to short those shares. The profits would be enormous, of course, but damned embarrassing if any of you were linked with massive short-selling and the roof of the Chunnel caved in.' He paused for effect. 'Of course, one could always short Eurotunnel stock through offshore accounts held in nominee names. No direct connection, of course, and complete confidentiality. I believe that offshore banks provide such services with absolute discretion. At least, so I've heard.'

The Brigadier was smiling again, already counting profits. As were the others.

'More sherry?' Sir David asked.

The directors lifted their glasses and the Brigadier spoke for them with one voice.

'Damned good show, Sir David.'

TWO

Ito Wantanabe hunched before a low teakwood table, his withered legs painfully folded beneath him. Occasionally, he sipped from a bowl of green tea as he turned the pages of the document, committing its contents to memory.

The room was minimalist, reflecting the esthetic purity of the *Kamakura* shogunate; soft rush *tatatimi* mats, three sliding *shoji* panels, lighting so subtle that it seemed to have no source, and a single white iris in a roughly fired ceramic vase which was positioned within a small alcove. A charcoal brazier glowed softly in a corner, its heat delicately balancing the dry coolness of conditioned air which whispered from artfully concealed registers.

The *shoji* panel behind him led to an antiseptic Western-style bathroom, for Wantanabe, of necessity, had been forced to draw a line between traditionalism and hygienic practicality. At age seventy-nine, Wantanabe's organs were gradually shutting down, leaving only his mind, like a glowing coal at the core of cindered ashes, still bright and vibrant.

The *shoji* panel to his right opened to a sleeping-room, its structural components, paneling and sparse furnishings taken intact from a *ryokan* in southern Hokkaido, then meticulously reassembled in this windowless black marble building which edged the Forest of Soignes on the outskirts of Brussels.

On the far wall of the sleeping-room, accessed through sliding sandalwood doors, was a traditional Japanese garden which had been assembled on the top of this

41

four-story building, the European headquarters of Komoto Securities and Investments Ltd. It was a precise replication of a fifteenth-century garden located at the Ryoanji in Kyoto. On summer days, the translucent liquid-crystal fiber roof could be folded back to admit a pale Belgian sun, but for most of the year a sophisticated system of lighting and climate conditioning supplied the garden with its requisite moisture, heat, nutrients and artificial sunlight.

The third *shoji* panel, directly across from Wantanabe, led to an anteroom which accessed a single elevator. Original manuscripts and essays on the *Thirteen Classics* and *The Four Books of Ta Hsùh*, prepared by scholars in Japan, as well as the more mundane reports concerning Komoto's progress in ensuring Japan's trading dominance in Europe, were delivered, the messenger unseen, to the anteroom.

The anteroom itself was a smallish chamber whose sole furnishing was a stand where materials were placed for Wantanabe's eventual attention. Set behind a framed rice-paper panel – graced with an ink drawing of a single wheat straw – was a hydraulically actuated Kevlar door which accessed the elevator. Only three people had keys to the elevator.

The three rooms, the anteroom and the garden were Wantanabe's universe, and he rarely left them except for a visit to Japan, now increasingly rare. His meals were prepared and delivered by an old woman from a Japanese mountain village, for Wantanabe's tastes were traditional and entirely vegetarian.

It had been a sacrifice of enormous magnitude for Wantanabe to head up the European effort with its attendant obligation of residence in Belgium. He would have preferred to have spent his remaining years in a simple house, built by his great-grandfather a century ago on the shores of the Inland Sea. But the underlying concept of Komoto Securities' hidden agenda had been his intellectual creation and he had regretfully acknowledged from its inception that he was personally responsible for its success or failure.

As far back as 1986, Wantanabe had identified those economic postulates which, if combined, would be the ruination of Japan's economy.

With no significant natural resources or cheap power sources of her own, Japan's only means of creating wealth was to import raw materials, add value to them through superior technology and a quality workforce, then export the finished products to foreign countries which could pay for them with hard currency. Market share was established through predatory pricing, a fanatical obsession with quality, but, most of all, by production of innovative products based on intensive market research that focused on what foreign consumers craved and not the superficially updated junk which foreign competitors *thought* consumers wanted.

Otherwise intelligent Japanese economists had termed it 'Our Japanese Miracle'. With just a superficial analysis of the phenomena, those learned men had extrapolated trends, then pontificated that Japan would be the world's leading economic power by the turn of the century. But the fatal flaw was that they made those predications on a 'full belly'.

Wantanabe's father had told him once that a man with a full belly was incapable of remembering hunger. For that reason, Wantanabe had disciplined himself to remain lean, both physically and intellectually.

For what those full-bellied economists hadn't foreseen was the eventual collapse of the dollar and the subsequent breakdown of the US economy, which had in turn quenched America's consumption of quality Japanese products. No American with surplus money still in his pockets was going to buy a Toyota or a Sony when a Ford or a Zenith was just as good and half as cheap. Not that many Americans had money in their pocket, let alone adequate food on their table. Since the collapse of the

American banking system in '95, over fifteen per cent of her workforce were unemployed.

Likewise, Japanese exports to the Third World had fallen dramatically, both because of the faltering world economy and because goods produced by the other Pacific Rim nations, the *Little Dragons*, had stripped Japan of its competitiveness owing to the lower labor rates of Taiwan, Hong Kong, Singapore, Korea and Malaysia.

Which left only the European Economic Community and its leech-like economic satellites as a viable market, but that market too was withering. Importation of Japanese goods had been severely restricted in the mid-nineties through protectionism, and even Japanese subsidiaries operating on European soil were experiencing difficulties in producing profits for their Japanese parent companies as the EC inexorably raised the mandatory percentage of European share ownership and parts content. Through a complex net of regulations, Japanese firms in Europe were slowly being taken over by European shareholders at bargain prices and, therefore, the dividends flowing back to Japan had dwindled to a trickle.

There were only two possible solutions to the problem as Wantanabe saw it. One, that the EC would voluntarily throw open its doors to Japanese goods, dropping its protectionist practices which sheltered Europe's producers — a highly unlikely scenario; or, two, that the European Economic Community would miraculously dissolve, leaving Japan to deal with individual nations on her own terms rather than having to go head to head with a powerful and integrated community of nations, speaking with one voice for over three and a half million consumers. It was this latter condition that Wantanabe sought to 'facilitate'.

Wantanabe sighed, his eyes weary. He applied his long bony fingers to the bridge of his nose and pressed upwards and inwards, the pain gradually easing. Ashida was waiting.

Matsuo Ashida was one of those with access to the elevator and a discreet light over the *shoji* panel indicated that he had arrived, had now been patiently waiting in the anteroom for over three-quarters of an hour. Wantanabe had no use for the power game that kept subordinates interminably waiting, but he wanted to be sure as to the details of the plan and the suitability of its principal player. He read on, his lips moving ever so slightly, his fingers unconsciously stroking the fire-scarred tissue that covered his hairless skull.

The report was from an old friend and head of Komoto Securities' 'Research Bureau', Taro Tagawa. Tagawa was Wantanabe's principal source of intelligence, which he drew freely from classified Japanese Defense Force files and from paid informants in intelligence agencies worldwide. Tagawa, with essentially unlimited funding supplied by Komoto Securities' clandestine owners – the *keiretsus* which comprised the seven largest Japanese industrial manufacturing giants – and with the shadowy acquiescence of Japan's Ministry of Industry and Trade, had resources at his disposal which probably exceeded those of the CIA, MI5, and the German BND combined.

Wantanabe trusted Tagawa's judgement implicitly, for they had been friends for more than sixty years – both Meiji-men in their old age as well as lifelong adherents to the nationalistic dreams of the National School of Learning, and, during the war years, fellow officers in the Imperial Navy's intelligence service.

If anything, Tagawa's report had artfully understated the capabilities of the candidate. The report profiled what little was known about the German whom Wantanabe had ultimately selected for the 'endeavor' from an initial roster of eight men, all of them obviously respected masters of their trade.

Wantanabe had initially been disturbed by the lack of detail on this German, but as Tagawa had dug deeper and submitted additional information, Wantanabe had grown to admire the German for the thorough manner in which he had brushed over his tracks. Wantanabe smiled as he read. Tagawa, Zen-like in his approach to intelligence, had revealed far more for what he *didn't* say.

The German's real name was unknown; all that was known was that he was vaguely rumored to have grown up in a suburb of Dresden. Consequently, the church and civil records of his birth and upbringing had undoubtedly been incinerated by the English night-bombing raid of February 1943. Not that it mattered. Wantanabe – in an attempt to personalize the man – had come to think of him by the name a *Der Spiegel* journalist had conferred on the former Red Army Faction organizer following the discovery of his penetration of a NATO Q-clearance vault in 1967, and the subsequent transfer of those papers to the Stasi for a reputed two million deutschmarks. The journalist had labeled his renegade countryman *der Maulwurf*, which aptly translated as 'The Mole'.

Sometime in the late sixties, *der Maulwurf* had crossed the line from his allegiance to the Red Army Faction to become a full-time agent for the Stasi. Wantanabe mentally shrugged. It was like an Irishman crossing over from Sinn Fein to the IRA Provisionals – both cut from the same kind of cloth, only the texture of the weave differing.

What little that Tagawa had been able to piece together concerning *der Maulwurf* indicated a solid grounding in engineering, superb organizational skills, a firm belief in superior communication techniques, a ruthless pursuit of security, and a curious sense of honor which seemed to compel him to carry through on whatever task he had committed to. For this project, these qualifications alone would have been enough to convince Wantanabe that the German was the one to handle the destruction of the Chunnel, but there was something even more interesting about the man that confirmed *der Maulwurf* as Wantanabe's choice. *Der Maulwurf*, it seemed, had good reason to hate the British, and that particular motivation was likely to be the most compelling rationale when it came to fulfilling this particular task, for Wantanabe understood the power of hate and how it could be shaped into an unyielding discipline to accomplish the impossible.

Satisfied, his thoughts finally in order, Wantanabe sat upright, straightening his back, then rang the bell.

The *shoji* panel to the anteroom slid back. A slight, middle-aged man in a Western business suit stood there, hands pressed to his sides, bowing deeply. Wantanabe nodded and motioned him in.

Matsuo Ashida, nominally an employee of Komoto Securities and now consultant to the Eurotunnel consortium on Far Eastern financial sourcing, withdrew two papers from the breast pocket of his jacket and laid them before Wantanabe. Wantanabe scanned through them briefly and nodded.

'Then Sir David's presentation to Blue Riband's board of directors was accepted without dissent?'

'Yes, Wantanabe-san. I have a taped recording of the event. The three men named here have given their assent to the Chunnel project and have already transferred their share of the project's anticipated costs into Sir David's Channel Island offshore account. Sir David is awaiting further instructions from me as to its disposition.' Ashida hesitated fractionally, as if he desired to comment.

The relationship between the two men was not quite that of the traditional roles played by superior and subordinate. Wantanabe's brilliance as an Imperial naval intelligence officer, innovator of a business management technique now aped by the West, and for the last nine years the clandestine head of Japan's efforts to dissolve the bonds of the European Community, was grounded in the belief that ideas, like water, could flow freely in many directions. But his relationship with Ashida went much further, for Ashida would eventually replace Wantanabe after his death, and that required the affiliation between the two men sometimes to be that of *sensi* and student. Even beyond that, as Wantanabe's strength and mobility waned, Ashida had grown to be a physical extension of his master's will, and from this, unexpectedly, evolved the unstated but binding relationship of the stern father and his obedient son.

Wantanabe nodded and Ashida continued. 'I have reservations about the wisdom of involving these men, Wantanabe-san.'

Nodding, Wantanabe looked down at the desk, silent for a moment. 'Perhaps, Ashida-san, you overlook the subtlety of the obvious. I *want* them involved, both as co-conspirators and as witnesses to Sir David's treachery. The people of Great Britain will demand vengeance when all this is over. If things go as we plan, we will ultimately allow the transfer of Blue Riband funds to *der Maulwurf* to be traced back to Sir David and his board members. Great Britain will demand scapegoats and we, indirectly, will supply them.'

Wantanabe's bladder was burning but he tried to ignore the irritation. It would be an embarrassment to have to rise and leave the room. Worse still, it would be an indication that he had not prepared for this meeting. Wantanabe suppressed his body and collected his thoughts.

'But the point of our meeting,' he said, 'is your appraisal of *der Maulwurf*, whether you have been able to establish contact with him and the results obtained?'

Ashida marginally nodded his head. 'When the Stasi was broken up in 1990, *der Maulwurf* was able to have his files destroyed, leaving no traces. He took his talents, some of his best agents and a great deal of money from Stasi-funded bank accounts and started operating freelance for profit. Tagawa's intelligence summary indicates that *der Maulwurf*'s people have conducted at least six assassinations of Middle Eastern leaders, popularly ascribed by the press to Mossad but actually paid for by the Syrian and Libyan governments. He has also apparently been involved in the transfer of eighteen kilos of fissionable material from the Ukraine to Pakistan, the looting of two branches of the

Bank for International Credit and Commerce on the Asian subcontinent, and, of special interest to our requirements, four major "terrorist" bombings. The Trade Center explosion in New York was, Tagawa believes, *der Maulwurf*'s work.'

Wantanabe frowned. 'It seemed obvious to me that it was the work of Islamic fundamentalists.'

Ashida shook his head. '*Der Maulwurf* may have used them as subcontractors, in concert with their own political aims, but the real reason for the bombing, according to Tagawa's intelligence, was purely commercial gain. A small investment firm, Netherlands Antilles Associated Ventures Ltd, had offices located two floors directly above the blast epicenter. The firm claimed that over three hundred million guilders' worth of Dutch bearer bonds were destroyed by the blast and ensuing fire. Fortunately for the Netherlands Antilles firm, these bonds were fully insured. The insurance investigators found the charred remains of a few of the bonds but not enough to confirm a total loss. However, they were obligated to pay off the face amount of the claim and have already done so. Tagawa estimates that *der Maulwurf*'s fee would have been ten per cent of the covered loss. In brief, the German is a man without politics or national allegiances, dedicated only to personal gain.'

'But he surely left some ties behind when he left Eastern Germany?'

'He did. Tagawa's people were able to find a man in Argentina, now retired, who had been a Stasi associate of *der Maulwurf*. Tagawa's people were able to persuade the man that it would be in *der Maulwurf*'s best business interests if there were a way he could be discreetly contacted. Consequently, the man gave them a facsimile number. I traced the number. It is assigned to an earth satellite station, similar to those used by CNN reporters during the Gulf War. The attraction of such a device is that it can be contained in a suitcase and set up anywhere in the world where there is electrical power. However, much like a cellular telephone, although the number is known, the location of the telephone is impossible to determine. Thus, *der Maulwurf* can be anywhere on the surface of the globe and still have secure communications without his location being known.'

Wantanabe was unfamiliar with the technology but was able to understand its capability. He nodded his approval and said, 'I take it then that you've contacted him?'

'Yes, but first I rented a flat in Antwerp for the sole purpose of installing a fax machine so that we can communicate with him without revealing our identity. One of my people is manning that machine twenty-four hours a day. Next, I set up a numbered bank account in the Cayman Islands and deposited 200,000 deutschmarks to it, then sent a fax to *der Maulwurf*'s number, indicating that we – as an anonymous client – wished to make contact with him through a trusted third party in order to negotiate the cost of a project. I included the number of the Cayman account in the fax and told him that it was his to retain, regardless of his decision – essentially a gesture of good faith on our part.'

'And what purpose would this meeting serve us if we can communicate directly by facsimile machine?'

'*Der Maulwurf* will need technical information concerning the structure's fabrication in order to destroy it. This data would obviously be too great in volume to be sent by fax. Consequently, I have copied that information onto a floppy disk which will give him sufficient basis to make a decision as to the project's feasibility and cost. There will also be the matter of negotiating the contract price and setting up a mechanism with which he can communicate with us.'

'And who will represent us at this meeting?'

'An American lawyer with ties to organized crime. He features himself as a facilitator of business between parties who do not wish their identity to be known to each other. A "middle man" is the American expression.'

'And *der Maulwurf* agreed to such a meeting?'

'Yes. The meeting will take place on a small Greek island, Aegina, accessible only by a local ferry. I gave our assurance that the American lawyer would not be shadowed by any of our people except from the time of my meeting with him in Athens until he actually disembarks from the ferry at Aegina, and that coverage only to ensure that the lawyer performs his services in a proper manner. At that point, our shadow will make no further attempts to trace the lawyer's movements. *Der Maulwurf* has agreed to this arrangement.'

Wantanabe pinched his nose again, the nerve throbbing. 'If *der Maulwurf* consents to go ahead with the project, how will we be able to make future contact with him without exposing ourselves? Surely, given time, he will be able to track down the apartment where your facsimile machine is located, thus exposing us.'

Ashida motioned to the other paper lying on the desk. 'I have contracted with Global Data Systems through a Delaware shell corporation for an earth satellite station similar to *der Maulwurf*'s. The unit will be delivered to a Delaware warehouse, then shipped to Belgium and installed on the roof of this building. I have assumed that *der Maulwurf* will require ongoing intelligence as to Euro-tunnel security procedures, as well as answers to specific technical questions. We will communicate with him by a digital data link, using a modem. For security reasons, the data will be encrypted. I have supplied a copy of the encryption software on the floppy data that the lawyer will carry to the meeting, as well as a set of passwords.'

Wantanabe considered the location of the meeting. Was it significant that a particular Greek island had been chosen? Perhaps the German had a villa there but, on consideration, he decided that *der Maulwurf* had chosen the place because he could easily monitor access to the island simply by observing who got on or off the ferry. 'When do you meet with this American lawyer?'

'Tonight, in Athens, at his hotel. He will board the ferry tomorrow morning at first light.' Ashida hesitated. 'And the disposition of the lawyer? He will know nothing of Komoto's involvement but, of course, he would be able to identify me at some later date.'

'That will be up to *der Maulwurf*, of course,' Wantanabe responded, 'but I have a feeling, based on *der Maulwurf*'s background, that the lawyer will not present any problems.'

The interview was at an end. Ashida rose to his feet and bowed, then backed away. Wantanabe lifted his hand. 'One thing that must be emphasized, Ashida-san. There are to be no Japanese fingerprints on this operation, no link that can tie us, Komoto Securities, or our superiors in Japan, to the endeavor. Only the lawyer and Coosworth would be able to link us.'

'Coosworth . . . ?'

Wantanabe pressed his hands together, fingers arched. 'You are to make suitable arrangements. Sir David has scheduled a salmon-fishing trip to New Zealand two weeks hence. The streams there, Ashida-san, are said to be both swift and dangerous.'

3 February

Victor Roselli fidgeted with his cigarette, pissed-off that his contact hadn't showed up yet, half an hour late already. Roselli wasn't used to being hung out to dry, even by his principal client back in Newark. When you came down to it, respect cut two ways.

He sat in a small *taverna* that fronted the edge of the harbor of Aegina, drinking something that tasted like warmed-over turpentine. No bourbon, not even rye. These dickheads didn't know from squat about keeping the *turistas* happy.

He squashed the cigarette out beneath the sole of his loafer and leaned back in the chair, casually studying his image in the crazed mirror that backed the bar. Roselli was a heavy man, but it wasn't fat. He did an hour every day on the machines at Lorenzo's Gym, along with Bean Bag Benny and some of the other guys from the boss's construction company. Roselli could normally bench-press 308 pounds, something even Benny couldn't handle on an off-day.

Not that pumping iron was part of his job description, but he knew hulks were intimidating – handy as hell when you were trying to get a reluctant client of Gino's to see it your way.

For the last fifteen years, Roselli had worked for the Gino Peduzzi Construction Company. That kept him nailed down at his office, working through piles of litigation, depositions and motions to appeal. Roselli knew he wasn't one of those hot-shot Gucci lawyers – more like NYU night school, bottom third of his class – but he was thorough, knew the essentials of criminal law, and so far those skills had enabled him to keep Gino out of the joint.

Roselli pushed his sunglasses back on his head a bit farther, the ringlets of his hair capturing the frames. *Not a bad profile for a bastard wop from the South Side,* he figured. A few creases around the eyes, but that just heightened the maturity thing. Jurors, the majority of them liberal wimps, loved maturity in a trial lawyer, just like they were getting the word straight from daddy. Broken nose, too, and that had been a plus when he was a kid, working as a union enforcer on the docks.

A woman came into the tavern, distracted, thumbing through a stack of mail, the bell over the door doing a tinny clink as she entered. She slumped down at a table, stretching out long legs clad in blue jeans that matched her denim jacket. Long black hair, dark eyes and lashes, and a body ripe enough to turn a guy's brain to mush. The waiter dropped by her table as if she were a regular, his tray bearing a tiny cup of coffee.

Roselli inhaled deeply and turned his head away from her. Another time, sweetheart. Business first.

He had done this kind of thing three or four times before – not on a regular basis yet, but who knew? He liked traveling, liked the negotiating end of it, and the money was good to fuckin' excellent – in this case, the promise of thirty big ones plus expenses for the deal.

He had done the first job of this sort about a year ago. The client had been a friend of Gino's who wanted some Cleveland guy and his bimbo whacked for shorting product on a drug shipment. Ordinarily, Gino would have had Bean Bag Benny take care of it, but there was some kind of truce between Gino and the Russo Family in Cleveland, so the job had to look like it had originated from out of town and the guy who did the job shouldn't know from nothing about who was paying the tab. So Gino had laid the problem on Roselli.

It had been a no-brainer. Roselli had gone to Miami and hired a Haitian who had a street rep for doing untraceable hits. The guy and his lady in Cleveland expired on schedule and the spook got paid in cash by Roselli a day later, when the papers came out with the glad tidings. The spook didn't know or care who had hired him and the client didn't know who had done the hit. Perfect insulation both ways. Roselli liked to think that, rather than setting up an assassination, he had simply been the facilitator in a delicate business deal.

Gino's buddy – pleased with the handling of the job by Roselli – had let the word get around that Roselli could get things done without raising feathers, and within two months Roselli had his second shot as a 'facilitator'.

It turned out to be a relatively clean job. A West Coast aircraft company had developed a ground-attack bomber, perfect for blowing the shit out of the advancing Soviet hordes, investing over a billion of their own bucks in the development of the aircraft. Problem was, the Soviet hordes, if they ever had existed, were now running the

Moscow rackets or pedaling time-share condos on the Black Sea. An appropriations bill to fund the bomber was coming up for a vote and it was going to be close. Three Congressmen on the committee held the swing vote and the smart money was that they'd vote for approval if they were paid off.

Roselli, after receiving one brief telephone call, met with a man in a LAX airport hotel room. The guy, otherwise suited out in a three-piece Armani, had actually worn a ski mask to hide his identity. After handing Roselli three brick-sized packages, the guy said, 'It's your job, Roselli, to get these into the hands of the men on this list. They don't want to know where the money came from and that's why you're the go-between.'

'Right – so you want them to vote for funding the bomber?'

The man shook his head. '. . . Against it, Roselli, *against* it.'

The authorization to fund the project was voted down by a very slim margin and the aircraft manufacturer subsequently went tits-up, then was sold off to a Korean company which promptly shipped all the plans, tooling, prototype aircraft and 7000 jobs to the land of *kimch'i* and kung fu.

This job was his fifth. Roselli had received an envelope which contained a round-trip ticket to Athens, a room reservation confirmation at the Grande Bretagne hotel, and a photocopied bank deposit slip for thirty big ones stashed in a numbered account in the British Virgins. That same night, some bozo called him, asking whether he wanted the job. Roselli allowed as how he could handle it.

Six days later, he had met the bozo in Athens. The guy was a Chink but talked like he came straight out of Harvard. The briefing had been just that – brief. Roselli was to carry specific details of the job on a floppy disk to the 'contractor' and negotiate the fee, assuming the guy was willing to dance. Which was why he was presently cooling his heels in this fly-blown boozer, drinking crap wine that was probably reject paint-thinner.

Roselli checked his watch. Fifty minutes late. He signaled the bartender. 'You got any of this stuff but without pine tar in it?'

'Ask him for *aretsinto*,' the girl at the table said, glancing up. 'Try Elissar. Or if you're the brandy type, Camba.'

Roselli trotted out an award-winning smile from his inventory. 'How 'bout you join me for one?'

She shrugged like it wasn't a big deal one way or the other, came over and sat down opposite him. She had a terrific set of hooters and he made a point of staring at them. It didn't faze her.

'You from around here?' he asked.

She shook her head.

'Vacation?'

'No.'

Not getting anywhere. He tried again. 'Name's Roselli. Vic Roselli.'

'Francine,' she answered. 'You're here to meet someone, I take it?'

'Yeah.' He had been sniffing the Camba, about to get into it when it occurred to him that she had been waiting for him, using the time to scope him out, see whether he had a tail or a back-up.

'What's your business?' she asked.

'I'm supposed to meet a German guy. You with him?'

'I represent him, you might say. What's your business, Mr Roselli?' she repeated.

He shook his head. 'I only talk to the German. But before that, my client told me to make sure he looked at a floppy disk I got for him before we talked. He got a computer?'

She smiled as if he had said something faintly amusing. 'I should imagine he does,' she said, and put out her hand.

*

She came back just before sundown with a heavily muscled dude, with a ponytail and pock-marked, sallow skin like it had never seen the light of day. The guy looked Malaysian or maybe Filipino, and it was obvious he was packing heat under his windbreaker. Roselli wasn't intimidated because where he came from carrying a concealed weapon was about as bizarre as wearing socks.

The three of them walked down the quay to a landing where a launch was waiting, the driver decked out in a sailor suit with a pompon hat, knuckling his forehead. *Class act*, thought Roselli, impressed. *Lifestyles of the rich and famous, me included.*

The four of them tooled out to a big powerboat that was swinging to an anchor at the mouth of the harbor. The chick escorted Roselli to a big living-room near the back of the boat and left him there after fixing him a double shot of Wild Turkey on the rocks. Roselli was beginning to enjoy this but had begun to wonder whether agreeing to a lousy thirty grand had been real bright. Fifty big ones seemed more appropriate, given the circumstances.

'Good evening.' No accent, but he clipped the words off like a European who had learned his English from watching *Masterpiece Theater*. The man was early sixties, hair the shade of slightly tarnished silver, good build, tan that didn't come out of a bottle, and a smile that would have made his dentist proud. He wore linen slacks, a polo shirt and one of those European sports jackets that was tailored tight at the waist and probably sold for a little less than a Honda Civic.

Roselli stood up, slopping Wild Turkey on his pants, his hand out. 'Vic Roselli's the name. Didn't get yours.'

' "Karl" will do.' He didn't offer his hand.

'You got the computer floppy okay, Karl?'

The man nodded. 'Very interesting project. Who is your client and how did he get my satellite fax number?'

'Can't tell you who the client is because he didn't tell me, I didn't ask and, even if I knew, I wouldn't tell you.

That's the way these things work, Karl. Party A wants somethin' done by Party B but doesn't want any ties that bind. So he uses a trusted third party with a reputation for keeping his mouth shut and his nose clean. That's where I come in, right?'

The man lifted his shoulders fractionally, not so much in agreement but rather as if he really didn't give a damn how Roselli fitted in or didn't. 'My privacy, Mr Roselli, is very dear to me. Only three people have that number.'

'Figured from the start you might be uptight about that, Karl . . .' Roselli decided to embellish a little, show he was looking out for everyone's interest – even-handed, like. '. . . So I told my client that you probably wouldn't be interested in the deal unless you knew who was passing out your number.' He pulled a slip of paper out of his pocket and passed it across the table. 'Does the name Gunther Hess mean anything to you?'

The man studied the slip, the corners of his mouth turning up in a smile. He turned and left the room but was back forty minutes later.

Roselli was into his third refill, a nice buzz working. 'Everything check out okay, Karl?'

The man seemed more relaxed. He paused at the wet bar and poured himself a glass of wine, then sat down on the white leather couch, carefully crossing his legs so he didn't screw up the crease in his slacks. 'Yes, entirely, Mr Roselli. Gunther and I both worked for the same employer at one time. He's retired now but apparently felt I would be interested in the job.'

'Great. That's settled. About the project – you up for it now?'

'I'm interested but still undecided. Just how much do you know about the project, Mr Roselli?'

'Nothin'. My client told me to give you a floppy disk which had technical specs on something he wanted blown up. I'm supposed to emphasize that whatever it is he wants popped, it has to be completely gonzo, not just busted up a little. Based on that, he figured you'd be able to quote me a price and, if it's in the ballpark, I'm authorized to okay it on the spot.'

Which really wasn't the whole truth and nothing but. The part about negotiating was accurate enough, but not the part about being in the dark about the project. Roselli had learned from Day One that closely held information was a commodity which could either be translated into hard cash or held as insurance against an uncertain future.

Probably to make sure that Roselli didn't have the opportunity to copy the floppy disk, the Chink had delivered it to Roselli's hotel room this morning just before it was time to leave for the ferry. And Roselli had to assume that he'd be tailed, so the idea of trying to make a copy of the disk hadn't seemed possible. That is, until he had spotted the Nerd.

Halfway through the hour-long trip to Aegina, Roselli was pretty sure that he had scoped out his tail – a Slavic-looking guy in his late forties, decked out in working-slob clothes and carrying a cheap overnight bag. The Slav fit in just fine with the locals except for his haircut. Roselli could recognize a twenty-five-buck razor-cut when he saw one, and he was damn sure no working stiff was going to shell out that kind of bread for his weekly trim. Still and all, being tailed didn't bother Roselli worth a shit. He had expected it, would have had big-time doubts about his client if he hadn't set up a tail. Roselli, who featured himself a professional, knew the way professionals worked.

The fact he had a tail was confirmed when Roselli headed for the ferry's bar and bought a beer. The tail kept it discreet, keeping his distance, but twice Roselli caught the Slav eyeballing him. So no big deal, Roselli thought.

He took his beer back to the passenger lounge, lit up a Camel and relaxed, just taking it easy, passing the time watching a bunch of college kids dorking around.

One of them caught Roselli's attention – a nerd with

Hubbell-sized granny glasses. He seemed like he was with the crowd but kept on its fringes, reading a tourist guide-book and occasionally making notes. Roselli's eyeballs had started to shift to a chick whose T-shirt was bulging with goodies when the Nerd pulled a little Toshiba laptop out of his rucksack and started pecking the keyboard. What had been a wistful idea in Roselli's mind now sprung full-blown. Still, he didn't give it more than a one-in-eight shot.

The Nerd had been drinking from a bottle of fizzy fruit juice and, sure as shit, finally began to fidget. He crossed and recrossed his legs a couple of dozen times, then tapped the arm of one of his buddies and whispered a question. His buddy stuck his fist in his pocket, jerked it around, then nodded toward the far side of the lounge, all the while panting with his tongue hung out a yard. That got a couple of snorts from the rest of the crowd, the Nerd, fer chrissakes, blushing.

That did it. Roselli got up, flipped the butt and headed for the can, casual-like, still beating the Nerd to the door by a good thirty seconds.

Nobody in the can unless you counted the flies. Roselli took a stall, sat down, swung the door closed and waited.

He heard the Nerd come in, unzip his fly and start to water the plants. Roselli hung tight, doubtful that the Slav would barge in, but stringing it out as long as he could to make sure. Like he figured, the Slav was smart enough not to risk it.

The Nerd was washing his hands when Roselli opened the door. He shot the Nerd a big grin.

'You want to make twenty bucks, kid?'

The Nerd looked like he was going to piss his pants, probably figuring that he had just been nominated Queen for a Day.

'Ya . . . yes — I m-m-mean, no.' Cracked voice, up a couple of octaves from normal.

'Relax, sonny. I saw you got a computer. I need a disk copied real quick. You got some blank spares?'

The Nerd's expression looked like he had just been told his Wassermann had come out negative. 'N-n-no problem. I'll . . . I'll do it outside.'

Roselli put a hand on the Nerd's shoulder and squeezed, real hard, feeling the bones shift. 'Tell you what you do. Let me leave first, give it a minute or so, then go back to your seat.' He produced the 3.5-inch floppy from his jacket pocket and handed it over. 'Once you get back, make a copy of this for me and leave it with the original disk under the seat cushion of the bench you were sittin' on. Five minutes before we dock at Aegina, you gather up your stuff and head for the gate. I'll shift over and take your seat so I can retrieve the floppies. You got that straight?'

The Nerd nodded rapidly, like one of those spring-necked plastic chickens that redneck assholes suction-cup to the rear window of their pickup trucks.

Satisfied, Roselli beamed at his accomplice and peeled a twenty off his roll, then added another twenty because he liked to encourage the American entrepreneurial spirit.

Roselli paused by the door and looked back, cocked his finger and aimed it at the Nerd. 'Don't say nuttin' to no one and don't fuck up, right? I got a long memory.'

Like he figured, the Nerd came through.

The German brushed his hand through his hair, laying down a few errant strands which had managed to dodge his hair spray. 'Of course, it would be unwise if you did have any knowledge of the project, Mr Roselli – an obvious violation of your "trusted third party" status.'

Roselli hunched his shoulders, perfectly at ease. 'You could give me a polygraph for all I give a shit. I don't have a fuckin' clue what it's about.' True, because he didn't. As yet.

The German nodded like he believed. 'Then let's settle on the price. My overhead is going to be extraordinary, at least two million and possibly more. Payroll, say another three, and as for the profit margin – ah . . . say five million. Round the total up to eleven million just to be on the safe side.'

Roselli swallowed. He was authorized to go to nine and his commission was contingent upon acceptance. 'I can go seven and a half, Karl. That's the top. My client told me he's got a load of other guys lined up, all of them panting for a job like this.'

Shrugging, the German twirled the wine glass's stem in his fingers. 'My problem is that I'm emotionally involved. I want the project. Ten million, Mr Roselli. Pounds sterling, that is – seven immediately, wired to the Cayman account and the balance on completion.'

Still too high. The Chink had given him an Athens number to call in the event he ran into problems. 'I'll have to go ashore and get to a phone. I can have an answer by tomorrow morning.'

'Perhaps it would be best if I just faxed back to your client's number.'

Roselli didn't like the sound of that one bit – like the Kraut was planning to bypass him and deal direct.

'Can't do that, Karl. The client wants me to handle it directly.'

Karl nodded, looking a little disappointed. 'You're probably unaware, Mr Roselli, that the floppy disk you gave me had a form of copy protection – and if any attempt were made to copy it, the original disk would automatically record the number of duplicates made?'

Roselli closed his eyes. He realized that the Nerd had screwed him, probably making a duplicate copy for his own purposes. What the hell – he would have if he had been in the Nerd's Reboks. But he had been around Gino enough years to know how these things worked. He opened his eyes, wishing that he could get a refill on the Wild Turkey before the fun and games started. Ponytail was standing at the far end of the living-room, looking like he was going to enjoy this.

'I don't suppose, Karl,' Roselli said wistfully, 'that you'd settle for my commission?'

The German shook his head, actually smiling. 'No, Mr Roselli, I wouldn't.'

Alone, Karl Brunner sat on the cushioned helmsman's seat of the *Valkyr*'s bridge. His view encompassed the harbor and the faint lights of villas that speckled the hillside beyond.

It was nearly midnight. He sipped at a snifter of cognac, relaxed and well pleased with the turn of events.

The project was more than possible but the engineering analysis necessary to do it was beyond his own capabilities. He would have to involve Hans Maas. It would be good to work with the Dutchman again after all these many years. And there would be other specialist skills required as well, but he had the means of contacting the right men – particularly for this job.

The money was reasonable, he thought. He would be able to bargain for more but that part of it was unimportant. His real interest lay in the destruction of the Chunnel. That was the unexpected prize.

He heard her naked feet on the carpet behind him. She sat down in the lounge chair next to the navigational table.

'Did Roselli talk?' he asked.

'Of course,' she answered. 'Roselli admitted that eleven million was probably acceptable.'

'But did he know who his client was?'

She stood up and walked to the place beside him, resting her arm on the back of the helmsman's seat, working her fingers along the muscles of his neck. 'No, except that the client was an educated Oriental.'

'Japanese?'

She shrugged. 'He wasn't sure but thought so.'

Brunner nodded and laid his head back so that her hand cradled it, and he looked up at her. 'Who copied the disk?'

'Roselli described him very accurately. An American in

his late twenties who was on the ferry with Roselli – possibly a graduate student by his description. Joss and Dieter have already gone ashore. I should think that they'll locate him before morning.'

'But why did this American make *two* copies? That's what concerns me.'

'Roselli certainly didn't know,' she said. 'It could be that the student was in a hurry, under pressure, and made an attempt to copy but accidentally interrupted the process. Consequently, he would have to start the copy process over again.'

'More likely,' Brunner responded, 'that he made one copy for Roselli and one for himself. Wouldn't you if you thought the disk held valuable information?'

'I suppose that's possible.' She wandered over to the wing bridge door and opened it, allowing the night wind to blow in the scent of mimosa. 'What now, Karl? I'm bored with this place, its tiresome expatriates and its greasy-haired locals. There's no fun here.'

Brunner couldn't blame her. She was young, a good thirty years his junior. They slept together sometimes but she was free to make her own arrangements. Her real value resided in her extraordinary ability to seduce fools and pump them for information. 'I'll have to call the Dutchman before I go much further. Assuming he's available, we'll have Klaus fly us in the Hughes to Athens and take an onward flight to Amsterdam. But the matter of the copied disk must be resolved first.'

'What if you can't find the American student or he has transferred the copied disk to someone else?'

He considered her question carefully. The floppy contained proprietary engineering data on the Chunnel but made no reference to the client's real objective. And the security afforded by the encryption software could be preserved simply by changing the passwords – something that he could do once he was in contact with the client on the satellite link.

He leaned back and stretched, slightly weary and yet strangely elated. 'I have no doubt that Joss and Dieter will find the student and retrieve the copied data. But regardless, I'm going ahead with this project.'

'Why the change in plans, Karl? We've already committed to the treasury-raiding operation in Brazil and the payoff from that will be more than twice the money that Roselli was authorized to offer.'

Brunner turned to her in the darkness, took her hand and gently squeezed it. 'Indulge me, Francine. You should understand by now that revenge is an old German tradition.' He squeezed harder, pulling her to him, and she didn't resist.

THREE

Hans Maas was swaddled in an ancient fleece-lined leather coat of uncertain vintage, the collar a monk's cowl which wrapped around the back of his head and protruding pink ears. The surface of the leather had long ago crazed into a spider's web of cracks and it was unevenly stained, as if he had applied oil to waterproof it. His feet were clad in rubber boots that had patches vulcanized over the toes. His whole ensemble creaked as the two of them scuffed through the snow and stubbled fields toward a distant hedgerow.

Two crows cawed from a leafless elm, contesting the invasion of their territory, then took flight. Momentarily distracted, Brunner watched them climb, then circle over a neighboring field before spiraling down to an unseen roost.

It was dry and bitterly cold, the product of an unusual spring storm. Brunner's nose was running and he felt like a child, constantly sniffling. *God – at his age, how can the old bastard stand to live in a climate like this?* Yet Maas's great veined beak seemed immune to the cold, perhaps petrified with age or alcohol. The Dutchman, to reinforce this impression, nipped from a silver flask which he pointedly declined to share with Brunner. But knowing the Dutchman as he did, Brunner guessed that the unwillingness to share was more of a hygienic consideration than one of mean-spiritedness.

The Dutchman had not been here when Brunner and Francine had arrived last night. A silent woman with blem-

66

ished skin and bird-like eyes – apparently Maas's Indonesian housekeeper – had shown them to a room on the second floor, brought them bowls of fish broth, black bread and wedges of cheese, then pulled the door closed behind her as she left. They had eaten in silence, then Francine, unconcerned, quickly stripped naked and crawled under the down comforter, asleep within seconds. Brunner had joined her minutes later, molding his body to hers for warmth rather than passion. Exhausted, they had slept through until dawn.

'We will turn back in seventeen minutes for breakfast,' said the Dutchman, checking his gold pocket watch. His breath made fat balloons of white in the pale morning sun. Brunner half-expected to see Maas's words drawn in block characters within the envelopes of the balloons, the way it was done in cartoon strips. Certainly the Dutchman's face was a caricature: beaked nose, hollow cheeks, eyes recessed under overhanging brows whitened with age, fleshy folds of skin drooping beneath his chin like those of an old rooster.

The Dutchman had maintained silence, except for grumbling about the weather throughout their walk, and Brunner was uneasy. He needed answers, wanted to get on with the process, even though Maas had told him to save his breath until later. Maas did everything at his own speed, the agenda dictated by his own preconceptions of priority. Maas was the finest explosives expert and bomb-maker in Europe, and Brunner had used the Dutchman's services for nearly a quarter of a century. Thus, a certain homage had to be paid to genius before bargaining began, but enough was enough. He needed answers.

'So what's your opinion, Hans? Do you think the project is viable or not?' Brunner asked. He damned well wished he had brought some lip balm, his lips were cracking with the cold.

'I would prefer to save all of that for after the meal.'

'I want an answer now, Hans. I didn't come 2500 kilometers for a walk in the snow.'

Maas brushed the back of his gloved hand across his face, his voice flat with just a tinge of superiority to it. 'You are older, Karl, and going to fat with easy living. Your network is undoubtedly flimsy. You no longer have the Stasi to back you. Are you really up to this? It will be more difficult than you imagine.'

'I don't see it that way, Hans. Perhaps a few hundred kilos of plastique explosive. Concealment will be a problem but not insurmountable. The project should take no more than a month to put together.'

'You were an engineer, were you not?' Brunner nodded. Maas looked at him for a few seconds and continued. 'I brought you to this field for a demonstration which has some relevance to the project at hand. The technical end of things is complex and not as elementary as you seem to believe. This way.' Maas picked up his pace, angling off toward a low stone wall.

Brunner followed. He had no boots and snow was infiltrating his shoes, wetting the leather. His feet felt as if they were encased in ice, his toes numbed beyond agony.

Pausing, Maas squatted down next to a snow-covered mound of sand, perhaps five meters long, piled up to a height of a meter. From either end protruded a concrete drainage pipe approximately the diameter of a small grapefruit. A pair of black and red wires, their ends stripped to bright copper, led from one end of the pipe.

From his pocket, the Dutchman withdrew a small device and attached the wires to the device's terminal posts. He looked up at Brunner, his lips slightly parted in a smile. Crystals of ice glittered on his eyebrows.

'We have here a miniaturized and vastly simplified version of the Chunnel. At the mid-point of my little Chunnel tube is a block of Semtex plastique explosive; 200 grams to be exact.' He twisted a knob on the device. 'It will detonate in thirty seconds. You may care to stand back.'

Good God! This old aufgeblasenes Arschloch *was out of his mind!* Brunner wheeled and ran. Twenty seconds later, he slowed, then turned his head, glancing back over his shoulder. The Dutchman was now sitting on the sand pile, unconcerned, lighting his pipe.

Brunner estimated that he was more than a hundred meters away. He crouched down, waiting. Brunner felt the fool for his reaction, now realizing that Hans had done it not as a joke but to establish control.

Seconds later, a double-ended lance of flame flashed from the ends of the tube with a hollow *whump*, throwing shockwaves which billowed the snow into roiling white plumes. The Dutchman hardly moved. The sound of the blast wave echoed back from the stand of trees on the far side of the field, followed by the frenetic screams of crows.

Brunner trudged back, irritated. The Dutchman, amused at his prank, was chuckling in an uneven rhythm that sounded like a diesel tractor engine missing on half its cylinders. He looked up at Brunner, still chuckling and wagging his head, then retrieved a shovel which had been covered by the snowfall and scooped a trench through the middle of the sand pile.

He brushed away the remainder with his gloved hands like a dog burrowing, exposing the concrete pipe. Brunner bent over his shoulder.

There were hairline cracks in the pipe but it was still in one piece. 'This is the problem as I see it, Karl,' Maas said. 'There is nothing to contain the blast because the tube is open-ended. Furthermore, the pressure of the sand surrounding the tube exerts an inward pressure – a form of natural reinforcement to the tube itself.' He stood up, shoving his hands into the deep pockets of his jacket. 'It is time we started back.' Without an acknowledgement, he turned and headed for the farmhouse. Brunner caught up with him, feeling manipulated.

'I'd hardly call that a scientific analysis.'

The Dutchman shrugged. 'Agreed. I was merely illustrating a concept. The magnitude of the explosion remains to be calculated. But my preliminary conclusion is that either the amount of Semtex will have to be much greater than presently seems necessary, or we will need to find a way to tamp the explosive so its effects are localized and directed against the liner. And I would not discount other avenues that have yet to be fully examined.' He pulled his hands from his pockets and chafed them together. 'But it makes the project all the more appealing, doesn't it, Karl? The most devastating act of terrorism in the history of the world. That, and a stunning technical challenge to those of us in the autumn of our careers.'

Speak for yourself, you old bastard, Brunner thought.

Maas was a born anarchist and, during the 1930s, a member of a radical splinter group of the Dutch Communist Party. He firmly believed that the old order had to be destroyed before the new order could be built. His talents lent themselves to the destructive side of the equation, and over the fifty years of his career he had become technically superior and far more innovative than any ordnance specialist Brunner had ever worked with, including the best that the Soviets had to offer.

Now, in his old age, the more difficult the task, the greater Maas's enthusiasm.

From the inception, Brunner had recognized that the structural analysis of the Chunnel would be difficult and had already made a phone call to a small town in the eastern part of Germany. Germany, if nothing else, was not known for a shortage of good engineers, and Kitzner was one of the best of them.

Brunner paraded a chain of thoughts through his mind, trying to get them to march in lockstep for the Dutchman's edification. 'I have a man in Germany, Hans, who once taught structural engineering at Nürnberg. He is old and disinclined to adapt to the new ways of modern Germany since *deutsche Einheit*. And like us, Kitzner has no love for

70

the English. We've already had preliminary discussions and, assuming that you're willing to provide the detonation circuits and explosives, I'll fly there to meet with him. His analysis will determine exactly the methods required for the demolition and the quantities of Semtex required.'

'That was hardly necessary. I have already made a start in gathering the necessary information,' the Dutchman responded. 'But we will eat first.'

A mangy dog had come romping across the field, his fur matted with ice. He ignored the Dutchman and wheeled in beside Brunner, tail thrashing through the brittle air.

Somehow, the Dutchman's initiative surprised Brunner. 'Just where did you obtain the information from?' he prompted.

'The technical institute in Utrecht. Simplified stuff churned out by English writers for the edification of the masses who are being conditioned to believe that it's perfectly safe to travel through a thirty-eight-kilometer-long death-trap. But the work had a bibliography which gave a number of other textbook references which I have now explored in detail.'

Brunner frowned. He didn't like unsolicited help, and it now appeared to him that the Dutchman would want a bigger cut for these trivial efforts.

'Hans, you will make the detonating mechanisms, of course. I was thinking about two per cent of the contract price. More, of course, if you can get the appropriate amount and type of explosives together. Beyond that, I will handle the details.'

The Dutchman responded with a disdainful snort.

They had come to the back of the farmhouse. There was a shed which connected the outdoors to the kitchen – a place used for the storage of boots and jackets and baskets that held moldering apples. The Dutchman opened the door and passed inside, not holding it open for Brunner. The dog made an attempt to sneak inside but Maas kicked

71

at the animal's ribs. The dog seemed to have expected it and deftly sidestepped, wheeling back, briefly colliding with Brunner, then trotting off toward one of the barns, unconcerned, pride intact. Brunner suspected it was an oft-repeated ritual between the two of them – the form, not the substance, that mattered.

The kitchen was a hot box, the ceramic stove radiating waves of heat. Only two places were set at the table.

Brunner checked his watch. It was exactly nine. The housekeeper placed plates of food on the table, followed by mugs of tea. Maas spoke to her in slurred syllables; some kind of Dutch Indonesian patois. She answered, her voice hesitant. Maas shook his head in disgust, then motioned for her to leave.

'She says your bitch has taken a bath and used up the hot water. I take my bath each morning at ten. Instruct your bitch that she is not to take a bath before eleven.'

The eggs were runny, the sausage dripping with fat and the tea bitter. Yet Brunner was hungry. The two of them ate in silence.

Finished, Maas pushed back from the table and relit his pipe, resuming a conversation that was fifteen minutes old. 'Of course I will make the detonating mechanisms, Karl. Three per cent of the contract price. As for the explosives, there is a problem and it will cost much more than in the past. Times, as you know, are changing.'

Getting up, Brunner moved to the coke-fired oven, removed his shoes and socks and placed them on the warming rack. Using a towel he had taken from the mud room, he carefully wiped the moisture from his feet. They pulsed with pain as the blood began to circulate again. 'What's the difficulty?' He suspected the Dutchman was creating problems that he had already solved, probably angling for a higher price.

'Plastique is in very short supply. My Rotterdam contact has less than a hundred kilos on hand and most of it's very old. One other problem is that although the Czechs are

72

still making Semtex, they've added a tracer scent that is easily detected by electronic sniffers. Very risky to attempt transporting a load across Europe by truck. I suspect that we'll have to find alternative supplies in the East, perhaps on the Polish black market, then ship it in by sea from one of the Baltic ports.'

As far as Brunner was concerned, explosives were explosives. As long as they did the job, he wasn't concerned with specifics, but the Dutchman was leading up to something and he decided to play along.

'You're hinting that there's an alternative to the plastique?'

'A fuel-air bomb.'

Brunner had heard of the things, used in the Gulf War to pulverize the Iraqi trenches, but the Dutchman had the bit between his teeth. 'Enlighten me, Hans.'

The Dutchman failed to detect the hint of sarcasm in Brunner's voice. Either that, or he ignored it. 'The essential component in a fuel-air bomb is ethylene oxide, a highly volatile liquid. Prior to being detonated, it is atomized, forming a cloud of vapor through a dispersing mechanism – something along the lines of a diesel injector nozzle. Once the cloud is formed, an ignition charge sets it off.'

'It sounds overly complicated.'

The Dutchman scratched at his unshaved chin, the hair so white as to be invisible, then shrugged. 'Perhaps. But the attraction is that the explosive yield of a fuel-air bomb is eight to nine times that of conventional plastique explosive, and in many ways, liquid is easier to conceal than blocks of plastique.'

'Where would you buy this chemical?'

'Buy?' The Dutchman made a coarse noise in his throat. 'One doesn't *buy* ethylene oxide, Karl – not in the quantity we need. We'd steal it.'

'From whom?'

'That, of course, is your problem. But the best source would be from our NATO allies, the Americans. They stockpile the stuff in England – at an air base in Surrey according to my contacts.' He grinned like the Cheshire cat, his teeth unnaturally white and glossy, as if they had been molded and fired from the same porcelain as the kitchen tiles.

Brunner didn't like it. Each segment of the operation would have its own risks. Piling up too many segments multiplied those risks to an extraordinary degree. But it was an interesting concept.

'Have you ever worked with ethylene oxide, Hans?'

The old man nodded. 'Yes – or near enough to it. You read about the Düsseldorf café bombing that occurred in August?'

Brunner had. Five British servicemen and eight German nationals incinerated in a fireball, but the medical examiners had concluded that they had actually died from concussive shock, their bodies crushed by the blast wave. The IRA had, predictably, taken credit.

'I used something similar – decane – fired with a piezo-electric igniter of the type used in table lighters, all of it packed into a fire extinguisher the size of a large flashlight. My calculations indicated that the power of the explosion was roughly equivalent to twelve kilos of Semtex.'

Impressive, Brunner thought. 'How difficult would it be for me to assemble such a bomb?'

The Dutchman curled his lip over his lower teeth, thinking. 'I would fabricate the nozzles and igniters for you, of course. The container that would hold the ethylene oxide would have to be a tanker truck of some sort, supposedly containing a fluid that would be acceptable to Eurotunnel security – perhaps bulk milk, for example. You would have to weld a false bottom in the tank a meter or so below the filling port. The ethylene oxide would be stored in the lower part of the tank and ordinary milk used to fill the space from the false bottom up to the filler port so that a physical examination by a security inspector would yield no unpleasant surprises.'

It would be possible, Brunner thought. But hijacking the ethylene oxide would be very tricky, at least a six-man effort.

'Earlier, you alluded to an alternative method of destroying the Chunnel, Hans.'

'By drilling down from the seabed. If you could somehow place explosives on or near the roof of the Chunnel's liner, a much smaller quantity of explosives would be needed. You are familiar with the Pacher-Fenner curve?'

'Vaguely.'

'It's used in the structural analysis of domes or vaulted ceilings. From the loading tables contained on the floppy disk, I've calculated that if the roof of the Chunnel were deflected inward in excess of 150 millimeters, the entire Crossover Cavern would collapse. How much explosive I can't predict, but my guess is that 600 kilos of Semtex would do it.'

Brunner considered it, then decided not to tell the Dutchman that Kitzner, the East German engineer, had already outlined this possibility and had requested that Brunner obtain substrata data on the English Channel's seabed along the Chunnel's route. With a portable satellite communications link similar to the one on the *Valkyr*, Brunner had queried his Oriental 'client'. Two days later, the information had come back on the satellite link, and buried within the data was a footnote that the Le Havre-based firm of *Société Techniques Maritimes* had contracted to drill boreholes in 1973 but had possibly failed to grout them. Brunner had immediately ordered Joss and Dieter up to Le Havre to see whether they could obtain the old drilling logs so Kitzner could look at them. And if the boreholes hadn't been grouted, Brunner had a ready-made solution to the destruction of the Chunnel. But if they had, then the Dutchman's fuel-air bomb would be the alternative solution.

'Hans — I like the idea of the fuel-air bomb. I want you to concentrate on that, develop the nozzles and ignition

75

system. To back up your effort, I'll have one of my people survey the Polish market for plastique explosives. I've heard the Russians are selling it and my guess is that the stuff will leak out to the West through the Poles, just like everything else.'

The Dutchman nodded. 'I'll make a start on it, Karl. I should have something to show you in three weeks. What are your plans?'

Brunner stood up, retrieved his socks and pulled them on. His shoes were still soggy and he left them by the hearth to dry overnight. 'To Germany,' he said. 'Then back to Greece. We'll start to move the *Valkyr* east to Gibraltar, then north to a commercial port on the Dutch coast. I'll use it as my base until the planning firms up.' He paused by the stairwell that led to the upstairs bedrooms and looked back. The Dutchman already had a notepad out and was scratching down calculations.

Brunner climbed the stairs and entered the bedroom. Francine had taken the rental car and driven to Amsterdam, leaving a note that she wouldn't be back until tomorrow night. Brunner wondered what sort of creature she would find to service her sexual appetites, not that he cared any more. She had her uses and, above all, he trusted her judgement to keep pleasure isolated from business.

He lay down, pulled the comforter over him and shut his eyes, but he couldn't sleep, both his mind and body exhausted.

The planning was coming together now, at first just scraps, then stitched together into larger pieces, with finally the whole pattern emerging. It was firm in his mind now that the separate means of attacking the Chunnel, each with its own unique attractions and difficulties, should be pursued in parallel paths. If one method failed, he would have the other to fall back on with no time lost.

Reaching across to the nightstand, he shook two capsules from the vial, then swallowed them. As he waited for the sleeping medication to take hold, his eyes settled on the wire-framed photograph of his parents, now gone sepia with age. It was the only thing he owned that remained of them and he carried it with him wherever he traveled.

He lay back on the pillow, his eyes closed, trying to let his mind go. But it kept reeling backwards through time, the images blurred.

He had been born in March 1931 in the small town of Heidenau which edged the banks of the River Elbe. His father was a *schienenleger*, a maintenance worker in the rail yards; a thin, cheerless toad of a man from what little Brunner remembered of him.

But his mother was bright in his memory — uncomplicated, loving, solid, warm — and he had adored her. His first memory was of her holding him in her arms as they watched a marching band pass by, the brass bells of horns flashing in the sunlight, the drums booming, their martial percussions making buzzing vibrations in his chest which had caused him to laugh. He clearly remembered laughing.

Delighted, because he was normally such a serious child, she had held him up high so he could see better. A truck following the band had a movie camera mounted on the flatbed and young Karl Brunner's laughing face charmed newsreel viewers across all of the Third Reich.

Such a perfect, Aryan child, women had whispered to their husbands in the dark theaters, and the men had nodded, secure in the knowledge that the future of the Fatherland would be in good hands.

He had been a good student, an obedient son; strong, sure, and intelligent. His parents never had cause to criticize him. By eight, he was husky enough to go to the coal yard with his wagon and bring back the sacks of anthracite for their stove. He built model airplanes from sticks and paper, and he followed the news every night with his father, placing thumb tacks on a map as they followed the sequence of endless victories.

There were two framed photographs above the Grundig radio; one of the Führer and one of his father who had fought with Turkey in the Great War. As a boy, Karl could visualize the third photograph that would someday hang there – one of himself with the Knights Cross on a ribbon dangling from his neck, the flashes of an officer on his collar tabs.

An artillery unit *feldwebel*, back from the Eastern Front on medical leave, told Karl that he must apply himself because he would be a fine officer, although, for some reason, the *feldwebel* suggested he prepare himself for the supply corps. Karl was sure that the supply corps would be far too dull for him. He featured himself in a crack Panzer unit or piloting a Stuka.

And there was a girl with silver-blonde hair he remembered; the daughter of a grocer. She smelled of oat bran and laundry soap, but sometimes she shared chocolate with him which she had stolen from her father's hidden hoard. In a darkened schoolroom where the teacher was showing a film on hygiene, she had taken his hand in hers and touched his fingertips to her secret place. He remembered that vividly, even now.

Then there was the night in February 1943. His parents had taken the tram to Dresden which was less than a fifteen-minute ride, leaving Brunner in the care of a neighbor woman. A massive political rally was planned and his father, a Party member and block leader, had been required to attend. Not that his father minded. His proudest possessions were his Party pin and arm band, and there would be refreshments afterwards for the block leaders and their wives.

Brunner, unable to sleep, had sat by his bedroom window, looking out at the night, dreaming of summer youth camp. He was good at boxing and had won a medal the summer before, beating even boys who were heavier than him.

A single British aircraft had flown over just before midnight, and dropped a stick of red flares. Brunner later learned that such planes were called 'Pathfinders'. He thought the flares were probably meant to mark the rail yards which were east of Dresden, about two kilometers away. The sirens had sounded before the plane droned over, but for some reason the all-clear wailed even as the flares ignited. Fifteen minutes later, the world exploded.

Karl Brunner woke two days later, his hair and eyebrows singed, his right arm seeping pus beneath the bandages, both his legs encased in plaster. They didn't tell him how his parents had died but he overheard a nurse tell an orderly that thousands of *Engländer* firebombs had incinerated Dresden and its suburbs. *Vernichten* was the word she had used. More than 12,000 bodies had been buried in a mass grave in a meadow south of Dresden, almost all of the corpses charred beyond recognition. Four stone shafts were placed to mark the corners of the meadow, but there was no plaque to list the names of the dead.

Brunner was placed in an orphans' camp. The State provided the food, the bed, the education, the political inspiration, the chants and the Mauser 98 rifle that he trained with. Brunner had been very proud of his uniform and kept it immaculate. He was boxing champion of his barracks and popular with his classmates. The State even taught him how to use condoms, the procedure illustrated with precise, anatomically correct drawings.

In 1945, the leadership of the State changed. The flag changed. Oaths changed. Old enemies became new friends. Brunner was sent to a special camp. There he was taught languages and unique skills. His instructors were men in gray uniforms, not all of them German. In his sixteenth year, he was sent to a school near Leipzig where he learned yet more skills. He graduated near the top of his class and was sent to a technical school to learn the skills of a draftsman. Then on to yet another camp where only a select few were sent.

In 1951, at the age of twenty, Karl Brunner (with some intensive tutoring provided by a man from the Stasi) climbed an electrified fence and ran a very complicated (but predetermined) zig-zag course through a minefield. Four shots were fired at him and the Austrian spotters said he had been damned lucky to make it because five out of six didn't. Fresh-faced, blond-haired, strong of limb, obviously intelligent, Brunner carried a knapsack which contained a pair of wire-cutters, a bottle of water, two tins of canned meat, his school transcripts (or what certainly *looked* like his school transcripts) and the framed photograph of his parents. He told the Austrian border guards that, above all, he wanted freedom. The Austrians gave it to him, along with a hot meal and a bath.

The rest had been easy.

His eyes closed and he slowly drifted into sleep. He dreamed he saw his mother coming down the street toward their home, carrying a string bag filled with impossibly huge oranges which she had somehow found for him – his favorite food. He ran to the gate, ecstatic, and called to her: *'Mutti.'*

FOUR

Melissa van der Groot signed the last check, stuffed it into
an envelope along with the printer's billing invoice, then
sealed it. Gratefully, she eased back into her chair, and
reached for the glass of Chablis which perched precariously
on the telephone stand. She sipped, reflective, the beginnings of a headache nibbling at her temples.

It had been a barely break-even month for the travel-
guide sales, February always a slow month. But there had
been a nice order from an American chain of discount
booksellers for the newly revised *Caribbean on the Cheap*,
and the profits from that order alone would keep her
creditors at bay for yet another month.

The ship's clock on the wall above her desk chimed four
bells: 22.00 hours. The clock was made by Chelsea, solid
brass with spokes like a ship's wheel. It gleamed, the metal
polished faithfully each week, and wound each day exactly
at eight in the morning, just as Pieter had always done.
Dear God – I miss him, she thought, the pain still hard and
intense after four lonely years.

She poured herself one last glass of wine from the bottle
in the mini-fridge which supported the copy machine.
Blanking off her guilt receptors, she sneaked two chocolate
chip cookies from a package on the bottom shelf and secretively munched them, as if her mother's ghost were hovering in the shadows, ready to chastise her for caving in to
her perennial vice.

Bugger it! she thought. So I'm thirty-four and a little
heavy – call it *lush*. A couple of cookies won't blow what

waistline I have left, assuming that I skip tomorrow morning's *café au lait* and a croissant, which of course I jolly well won't.

Not that another half-kilo of weight would drive off her non-existent suitors. The local frogmen were only interested in jumping her bones. The bastards expected her to shuck her knickers and spread her legs at the snap of Gallic fingers. Abstinence did not make the heart grow fonder if there was nothing there to be fond of in the first place.

For good measure, she slipped another cookie out of the package and ate it — let the fat fall where it may. Eighty calories each, so proclaimed the package. Not to worry — she'd burn off that and more just fuming over her tax bill which was due next Wednesday.

The dog snoozed in front of the coal stove, pink tongue barely showing between white teeth. He moaned in his dreams, feet twitching, chasing rabbits. Pieter had bought him in Wales from a farmer five years ago — a handful of wiggling parts connected to a fat, furry body. *Sailor*, of course, was to be his name.

She eased back into her chair again, tired, reluctant to go. Half a kilometer to the boat through a knifing February wind. She clicked off her desk lamp, sorry that she had rented the upstairs apartment — so close, just a stairwell away, warmed from the heat of her offices below, a good bedroom and a cozy kitchen. Still, by allowing Anna to live there for free as an offset on her wages, it kept the payroll to a minimum.

She could faintly hear the strains of a record playing, probably a *Moody Blues* cut, usually an indicator that Anna had been dumped on by one of her boyfriends. Undoubtedly, Anna would be hung-over from either booze or drugs tomorrow morning, assuming the unlikely eventuality that she even showed up for work.

Still, I'd be a damned fool to fire her, Melissa thought. Anna was on the dumpy side and frizzy-haired — a sixties-type reject — but she took the raw manuscripts sent in by Melissa's freelance travel writers and converted them, via the black magic of desktop publishing, into camera-ready copy ready for the printers.

Melissa had planned to take tomorrow off. The varnish on *Night Watch*'s rail was going spotty and the weather promised to be fair — unusual for February in France. And she could use some time away from the shop. *Good luck, lady*, she thought regretfully.

She rose and pulled on her jacket. The dog raised his head, ears flopping forward in slow motion, thumped the floor with his tail for a couple of strokes, then shambled to his feet, stretching. There was a rabbit in the field that bordered the road to the marina and Sailor was always keen to terrorize the poor thing, even though Mel doubted he would ever catch it. The dog, now fully awake, nuzzled her leg, ready for the hunt.

She dampened the stove, washed out the wine glass and turned off the desk lamp. She was about to leave when she heard glass breaking in the apartment above her. *Dammit! Anna's trashing the place again. Best to see if she's all right.* Mel dialed the apartment's number, hearing its muffled ring echo over the phone lines, slightly out of sync with the sound of the real thing.

'Yeah?'

'It's Melissa. I heard something break. You okay?'

'Bottle of gin, my last one. You got any?'

Melissa sighed. Anna was predictably half-blotto. 'No, just wine. Anyway, I was getting ready to leave.' She hesitated. 'Sure you're okay?'

'I got somepin' you gotta see. Like right now!'

She glanced down at her watch. 'Look, I'd like to but it's late. Can't it hold for tomorrow? Let's both come in a bit early and chat before we get down to the final edit of *Norway on the Cheap*.' Subtle, but she doubted that Anna would catch the hint.

'Bring up the grappa. You'll need it.'

'Only for five minutes, Anna. It's really late,' but she was talking to the dial tone.

Mel took the bottle from the fridge – also grabbing another cookie to soothe her nerves – pulled the front door closed behind her and walked around the corner of the building to the alley. A stairwell led up to the second floor. Anna already had the door open, her baggy hippie-sixties tie-dyed dress billowing in the wind, frantically puffing away on a Gauloise like the Little Engine That Could.

The flat was a shambles. Dead spider-plants drooped runners over the rims of parched pots that hung from the ceiling in soiled macrame slings. A Dylan poster, splotched with red wine, was thumbtacked to the wall. The rug hadn't been vacuumed in God knows how long and the sink overflowed with grimy dishes. The bed – *black satin sheets!* – looked like two sumo wrestlers had just finished a match on it. Sailor, exploring old territory with a nose for new treasures, sniffed at the putrefying garbage piled up under the sink. He snorted, turned away and curled up in the corner.

Anna expropriated the bottle of Chablis and poured most of it into her glass, then plunked down on the chair in front of her IBM clone. 'Take a look at this stuff!' she said.

Melissa leaned over her shoulder and studied the screen as Anna scrolled through the pages. It was technical litera-ture, engineering drawings, stress tables, yield curves. None of it registered but it surely didn't have anything to do with *Norway on the Cheap*. 'What is this stuff, Anna?'

Fingering the keyboard, Anna resumed scrolling the screen, blurring through images, then paused. 'Catch a load of this.' The screen read:

Confidential and Proprietary Information
Not for circulation or public release under penalty of prosecution. Access strictly limited to Transmanche Link Engineering Group, Grade 0–8 and above. Refer to current access list for authorized users.

'What's Transmanche Link?' Melissa asked.

Anna, her eyes red-rimmed from booze and staring into the computer for twelve hours non-stop, rubbed her fist in her face, smearing her Arizona Sunrise eye shadow. 'The Anglo-Frog group that built the Chunnel. All this crap is on how the thing was built, security procedures, where the structural weak points are – stuff they wouldn't dare leak to the public.'

'Where did you get it?'

'Jimmy Teller, the Fulbright Scholar guy who covers the Greek Islands and Albania for us between semesters, mailed it in two weeks ago along with his regular travel notes on a separate floppy. Asked me to hold it for him until he stopped by Rouen on his way back to Limey Land.'

'So . . . ?'

'Jimmy ain't coming back no how, no way. I got a call today from his significant other in England. The bitch asked whether Jimmy had any royalties coming to him and wouldn't it be *terribly reasonable* if we sent them to her to help soothe her anguish – that Jimmy would want it that way. Seems that yesterday, Jimmy and some other guy – an American lawyer by the name of Roselli – were found washed up on a beach off Crete, the two of them chained together. Bullet holes in their heads, execution-style. The Greek cops figured it was a Corsican drug deal gone screwy, except I personally know Jimmy hated drugs, had a friend that got hooked on the big H and picked up AIDS through a dirty needle.'

'I'm not making the connection, Anna.'

Anna poked her finger at the monitor. 'This is what he got killed for. Somehow he stumbled into possession of this floppy and mailed it off to me for safe-keeping. Except whoever owned the floppy got to him.'

'Maybe Jimmy didn't say anything – I mean, he might not have told whoever it was that killed him where he sent the floppy.' It sounded flimsy, even to her own ears. Quite suddenly, she was afraid.

Anna leaned back and finished off the wine, then wiped her mouth with the back of her hand. She shook her head. 'I figure Jimmy talked. The police report said his fingernails had been trimmed down to the cuticles, probably with a pair of pliers. I've seen Jimmy damn near faint at the sight of uncooked hamburger. He'd talk, for sure spill everything he knew, including this address.'

'You . . . we could ask the local gendarmes for protection. They'd probably keep an eye out. And after all, it's been a few days since Jimmy was killed. If they were coming for you, they'd probably have done it immediately.'

Anna lit another Gauloise and exhaled. She was agitated, constantly flicking the cigarette with her finger to knock off non-existent ash. 'No cops, no way. The only thing those Frog fuckers are really good at is violating your civil rights.'

This was an old, tired refrain that Anna was playing — paranoid about any contact with the police. Mel had always suspected that some of Anna's previous life in Alaska had not been spent just marveling at the Northern Lights. 'What are you going to do?'

'Move. I got a friend up in Denmark who makes wind chimes shaped like doggy bones for sale to the kennel-club set. Plus the guy's got more hash than he can handle. If things cool out, I'll be back late summer.'

Melissa slumped down in a bean-bag chair, the headache now pounding. 'Anna — what about the publishing schedule? We've got three revisions in the works plus the new travel guide on Bermuda.'

'I'll take a laptop and mail the stuff back to you, but I'm not hanging around here.'

'Can't you finish off the Norway revision before you leave? Please!'

Anna had taken on that look when she was working her brain cells overtime. 'How long we talkin' about?'

'Two weeks. That should do it.'

'How 'bout you pay for my train ticket and give me a thousand francs bonus if I do?'

It was blatant extortion but Melissa, with no alternative, nodded. She glanced back at the computer monitor. 'What about *that*?'

'I don't want nothin' to do with it. I never seen it.'

'But we should do something. Send it to the police.'

'No cops, I told you.' Anna pushed her bulk upright, reached over and popped the disk-eject button. She tossed it to Melissa. 'All yours. Once you told me your old man's a lawyer or something. A guy with connections.'

'A barrister, in England. He handles a certain amount of litigation but it's mainly on behalf of "names" in Lloyd's. I don't talk to him enough to really know the extent of his contacts. We're not exactly close.' Which was an understatement.

'So send it to him.' Anna had slouched down on the chesterfield, her wine glass propped up on her bosom. 'But keep my name out of it,' she added.

Melissa desperately wanted the whole thing to evaporate. Her father would laugh at her in his restrained upperclass way, and she feared his scorn as much as she needed his love. Better to settle for neither.

She took the diskette and nodded. 'I'll send it to him. It's probably nothing anyway.'

Portree, Isle of Skye, Scotland, 7 March

Ian Macleod slowly climbed Brick Kiln Road toward the cluster of cottages which overlooked Portree and the Sound of Raasay beyond. Pausing, he used his walking-stick to knock clods of mud from his boots and looked back.

It was a fair enough day, the sun dazzling the Sound as if the light were reflecting off shattered glass. A light easterly wind was blowing, but Macleod calculated that the wind would back around to the north-west by evening and with that would come rain, sleet by midnight and a few centimeters of snow by morning. Tomorrow it would clear, but with a north wind blowing like the devil himself. Best to bring in a bit more wood this afternoon, because other than the hearth and the electric fire the cottage was unheated and without insulation.

He sniffed hard, wrinkling his massive nose, then swiped at the dribble from his nostrils. The cold he'd picked up was going down to his chest, but a dram of whiskey would cure that, he reckoned. He smiled at the thought and began to climb again.

Macleod was a big man, even for a Highland Scot. His father had topped two meters and weighed sixteen stone. Macleod was within a hair of that, but on his last physical he discovered that he was losing height.

'Old age, Macleod,' the doctor had told him. 'Happens to us all.'

Sod him, Macleod thought. Age seventy-one wasn't old. Not when he could still swim the Sound without getting his wind up and heave the clabber with the best of the lads. Well, nearly so.

He breasted the small rise. John Fetters' cottage was the first on the left, the shutters closed and boarded over. Fetters, divorced less than a year ago, was working the North Sea rigs on a two-month rotating schedule and wouldn't be back until late March. Macleod missed him. Besides the occasional natter over a game of cribbage, they generally shot grouse together in the fall and poached salmon in the spring. 'The poaching of the beast makes it all the tastier,' Fetters had always remarked. 'And the conspiracy of a friend makes it all the more so,' was Macleod's response.

Beyond Fetters' cottage was his own, close to three centuries old. It had been his uncle's, left to him as a worthless stone hut but now worth a small fortune, what with the inflow of fancy money from the city people. Quite in vogue to have 'a place in Skye' these days.

As he cleared Fetters' cottage he hesitated. A Land-Rover with English plates was parked off to the side of his own cottage and a small curl of smoke rose from the chimney, although he had not lit a fire before his morning trek to the village.

He hefted the knapsack from his back, gripped his walking-stick tighter and gently pushed open the door.

A man was stretched out on the rug in front of the fire, a pillow under his head, shoes off and mouth open, the occasional clot of a snore breaking the silence. Macleod eased his knapsack onto the kitchen's counter and sat down in the easy chair. He poked the man in the ribs with his stick.

'What brings you to the wilds of Scotland, Manning?' Macleod knew the man vaguely, had even had lunch with him and a couple of other chaps just after the report was published. In those days, he was a lamb for the killing, although he hadn't known it then. Manning was with Lloyd's of London, some obscure branch involved with 'risk assessment'. He remembered Manning as 'drauchty' – just a bit too clever for his own good.

Manning opened his eyes mechanically, squinted slightly, then focused. He yawned, forced a grin and said, 'Sorry for the intrusion, old boy, but knew you wouldn't mind. Your bloody phone was out of order so I just thought I'd drive up and see you. Get out of the City, smell the peonies, clear the cobwebs, et cetera, et cetera.'

Macleod believed that like he believed in the fairy folk. 'I don't think you'll want to tarry long, Manning. Temperature's dropping with a storm brewing up. The roads will be slippery come nightfall. You might end up in a bog with your head through the windscreen, more's the pity.'

Manning stood up and tucked in his shirt. He turned to the fire, chafing his hands together. 'Thought you'd be happy to see me, Macleod. What's happened to the famous Highland hospitality I've heard so much about?'

The bastard hadn't even offered his hand, which had set

Macleod's teeth on edge. More to the point, it had to have been either Manning or the other poofter from Lloyd's Bureau of Internal Development who had been ultimately responsible for Macleod being canned by Transmanche Link. He had realized that only months after the incident.

'State your business, Manning, and forget about staying the night. I don't run a bloody bed and breakfast.'

Manning turned slowly, a fallacious smile on his lips, his eyes hard. His face was gaunt, eyes deep-set, the Adam's apple prominent. A stubble of beard rimmed his jaw. He shrugged, then lifted his hands in supplication.

'You see before you a humbled man, Macleod. Your discredited report on the Chunnel's vulnerability would now seem to have some validity, given recent events. Internal Development selected me to hie my arse up to Scotland, hat in hand if you please, to beg forgiveness and negotiate a reconciliation.'

'Eighteen months went into the analysis of that report, Manning – and close to seventy thousand pounds sterling out of my own pocket. Then you and that other toad from Lloyd's trashed it with a three-page memo. That cost me the contract and my reputation as well. I'm not well disposed to reconcile anything.'

Manning hunched his shoulders. 'Your report was speculative, Macleod – wildly speculative. If it had ever surfaced, the banks who put up money to build the Chunnel, Transmanche Link, *and* the bloody shareholders of Eurotunnel would have howled to the heavens and the ensuing stink would have driven the Chunnel project under. What would happen if an airline like Lufthansa or British Airways released a report to the public saying that their planes were prime candidates for terrorist attacks? You bloody fool! You were given a brief to construct a series of worst-case scenarios and how they might be countered, but to keep circulation of the damned report limited and for internal use only. But no – you had to threaten to release it to the press. Too clever by half, Macleod.'

'I *did* circulate the damned thing as confidential, Manning! It passed across the desks of nine men, all of whom marked it *no action required*. It might have cost a few more million to put the required security measures in place, but that's a trifling amount compared to the potential risks involved.'

Manning shook his head slowly, as if he were an impatient schoolmaster, forced to listen to a new boy's ill-prepared recitation.

'You never worked it out, did you, Macleod? After eighteen years in the security consulting business, I'd think you'd have learned the drill. The Eurotunnel consortium would have surely been willing to drop almost unlimited additional money into security, *provided that the procedures that go along with that additional funding don't unduly slow down productivity*. But to turn a profit – in the words of the efficiency wallahs – Eurotunnel has got to have reasonable product through-put. In simple language, Macleod, that means they've got to keep the Chunnel stuffed with high-speed trains, not sitting on sidings in France or England with bloody bomb squads ransacking every last cargo container and BMW boot for lumps of explosive as you suggested.'

'So they'd just turn a blind eye, then?' Macleod was seething.

'Of course not. They'll be thorough enough, Macleod, more thorough than even the airlines, because instead of just a few hundred passengers that you'd have on a jetliner, there will ultimately be thousands of passengers transiting the Chunnel at any given moment. They're laying on top-of-the-line metal and nitrate detectors, X-ray machines, squinty-eyed inspectors, psychologists who are trained in recognizing potential terrorists, bomb-sniffing bloodhounds, the lot. But just as great an effort will go into identifying and stopping terrorists before they've even got started. To blow the tunnel, your own report states that over two thousand kilos of explosive would be required.

Absolutely nobody comes by that much of the stuff without raising eyebrows. The word would leak out. And who the hell's got the motive any more? Red Army faction, Baader Meinhof gang, the Justice Committee, Action Direct? Christ, man! They're all too busy keeping up with their Mercedes hire-purchase payments or walking their pedigree dogs, now that the Russians are out of the game. IRA? The Yard's Special Branch doesn't think the boyos would touch it. Yes, they might kill a few Brits but at the same time they'd also kill a bunch of American tourists and business types, and that's not the IRA's style. Bad for public relations in Boston, where their money comes from.'

'So if the Chunnel's safe as a church, why are you here?'

'Ah – we're down to the nub of things, aren't we?' Manning turned toward the fireplace and threw in a log, then stirred the coals, trying to get the wood to catch fire. He turned back, stuffing his hands in his pockets, rocking back on his heels.

'Less than a fortnight ago, a London barrister by the name of Simmons contacted me. He has occasionally handled litigation for us and got on to my department without having to stumble through the normal channels. His daughter who lives in France spun him a yarn about receiving a floppy disk which contained highly sensitive engineering and security data on the Chunnel, all of it pulled from different classified documents, internal use only. The person she got it from was killed, execution-style, although the details are sketchy. But the obvious conclusion is that someone in the Eurotunnel organization or Transmanche Link has sold sensitive data to parties unknown and intends to communicate further information as it becomes available. We think it smells of a bomb plot – your speciality, Macleod.'

'Has anyone interviewed the daughter?'

'The barrister won't give us her married name. Wants to keep her out of it, adamant on that point.'

'Special Branch involved?'

'Out of their bailiwick.'

'What about MI5?'

'We informed them but who knows if they'll act. They've never been the ones to share bugger-all with us, even when we've put them on to something. Of course, they made the usual round, dulcet sounds about "probing their contacts on the Continent", but I don't think they'll shift their arses given the current state of the budget.'

'Which leaves it up to Lloyd's?'

Manning smiled sweetly. 'Laying off on our bets, let's call it. Lloyd's is on the hook for close to thirty billion pounds in insurance and reinsurance. Still, no one's taking this very seriously, but I suggested that it would be worth a few quid to have a closer look. Told them that old Macleod up in Skye might still have contacts on the Continent, could sniff around to see whether anyone's buying plastique, update his threat analysis, the usual drill.'

Turning away to the window, Macleod studied the western sky. Already hazing over with cirrus, the wind getting up. He could hear Manning stirring the fire with a poker, killing time, waiting for a response. *I told them it was possible, and what is possible eventually comes to pass*, he thought. And if he took on the job, perhaps in the end, he'd be vindicated.

The common wisdom now was that with the Russians and their puppets out of the game, terrorism would dry up and wither away. But Macleod hadn't subscribed to the common wisdom. There were still two types of terrorist threats in play that he had outlined in the discredited report.

The first was as simple as one man with a burning grudge. That man could be a deranged former employee of an airline, an Arab fundamentalist on a one-way trip to paradise, or, at the extreme end of the scale, the power-crazed leader of some tin-pot, fly-blown country. Motive, the willingness to take seemingly insane risks and a supply of explosives were all that was needed, and no amount of Interpol threat profiles could ever deflect such a madman.

But Macleod's primary concern had been molded into a theory based on a bank job in Northern Ireland. The Brits claimed it was the work of the Provos, but they were only half-right, as usual. Three men had tunneled their way into a bank using sophisticated boring equipment, rerouted the security circuits by hacking into the central computer, then blown the safe with shaped charges. Four million was the haul and they never would have been caught had not one of the men blathered to his Sheila. The men *were* Provos. Or, more specifically, *had been* Provos. They had been thrown out of their unit for unspecified political transgressions and had turned 'commercial'. Thus, in the complex evolution of a craft's progression, serious terrorism would now be based on a for-profit motive.

All over Europe, there were thousands of men and women who had spent a lifetime in Soviet-sponsored clandestine operations and knew the value of the ultimate weapon — terrorization of the masses. They knew no alternative legitimate trade, had forged interlocking and sometimes cooperative links with other terrorist cells, and could move transparently through national borders. They knew where to obtain the tools of their trade and had no moral inhibitions in using them. Many of them had acquired a very un-Bolshevik-like taste for money and consumed it at a prodigious rate, not only for their personal enjoyment but also to pay for the necessities of their secret existence — false papers, bribes, security apparatus, bodyguards and the cost of constantly being on the move, for in most cases, they were wanted by the police in their own land — even in the former Eastern Bloc countries — foreclosing the option of a gentle and unremarkable retirement in their homeland.

All of Europe had been blind to this new reality, so Macleod had settled back in the Isle of Skye seven months ago after accepting the golden handshake. Lloyd's had threatened to sue him if the report were leaked to the press and his own solicitor had convinced Macleod that Lloyd's would prevail because of the air-tight confidentiality clause in the contract. The settlement, arrived at after acrimonious negotiations, had been dear enough – ample to retire on with a goodly surplus building up in his account – but still a bitter pill to swallow.

The Chunnel was bound to be a magnet for an attack, and Macleod knew that a truly determined and enormously well-funded group could pull it off. His report had outlined six distinct, if somewhat outlandish, avenues of attack and the security measures necessary to counteract them. The authorities felt they had done all that was humanly possible to meet his recommendations, but still Macleod had doubts.

Of course, Manning was right and Macleod had recognized the problem from the onset of his employment with Transmanche Link, the prime contractor to Eurotunnel. When you came down to it, for Eurotunnel to ensure a high level of security, every container transiting the Chunnel, right down to little old ladies' handbags, would have to be minutely scrutinized, and yet there was no longer time for that sort of thing in a high-speed, commercial transport venture. It was a classic case of 'damned if you do and damned if you don't'.

Macleod had no doubt that the contract Manning was going to offer amounted to little more than a means of covering Lloyd's' collective arses in the unlikely event a terrorist event did occur. By using Macleod's own updated report, they would point bony fingers at the supposed inefficiency and laxness of Eurotunnel, Interpol, Special Branch and MI5, beseeching exoneration from an outraged Parliament with the argument that it was *only* Lloyd's who acted to uncover the threat.

It all came down to whether it was worth the effort. Macleod concluded that, if he worked by different rules than he had initially agreed to, it damn well would be worth the effort.

He turned back to Manning, then opened a cupboard over the sink and withdrew a bottle of Talisker Scotch whiskey. He poured two measures and handed one to Manning.

'I will take the assignment only on two conditions. One – I run my own operation without interference from you or anyone else. If I need assistance of any type, you will be responsible for securing it.'

Manning hesitated, the whiskey halfway to his lips. 'What else?'

'Two – there will be no cap on my expenses. I'm going to draw on the best people there are and those sorts don't work on the cheap. You'll be provided with a complete accounting when my work is finished, not before. I'll require one hundred thousand pounds expense money just to get started.'

'And your own fee . . . ?'

'A pound sterling, Mr Manning. A *Scottish* pound sterling. That and a published apology from you and your cohorts for the smear campaign that was orchestrated following my termination.'

Manning swallowed twice in rapid succession, even before he downed the whiskey.

FIVE

Green Island, Maine, 19 March

Stone heard the rock crack, saw the fissure spread like forks of lightning across the crown and down the walls of the tunnel, the face of the dig beyond the boring machine bulge ominously, then rupture. He turned to scream a warning, his voice somehow frozen in his throat, then started to run as tons of water and rock cascaded into the shaft from the sea above, men screaming behind him as they were crushed, the first wave of sludge and water sucking at his boots, dragging him down, snapping his legs like matchsticks, flooding his lungs, engulfing him in blackness.

He shot upright in bed, his heart banging against his ribcage, his body bathed in cold sweat.

A lance of sunlight, nearly horizontal, shot beneath the window blind, spearing across the bedroom, igniting motes of dust with its incandescence, then impaling the overstuffed chair on the far side of the room in a blossom of fire.

His heart gradually slowed. Wind hummed in the eaves, water dripped from the kitchen tap. Normal.

Some Windham Hill stuff on the CD was playing softly, George Winston rippling through an arpeggio, scratching around for the resolution to an augmented seventh. Stone reckoned that his heart could have seized solid, his body stiffened and turned black, but Winston would have played on to eternity or until Maine Electric cut the juice off for non-payment.

His mouth was foul, his head pounding, his nose freezing. He squinted at the heat gauge on the woodstove. It was off the lower end of the scale, the shack's temperature below freezing. Stone blew a tentative balloon of fog from his lips, groaned and burrowed deeper into the down sleeping bag. Ten more minutes, he promised himself.

He had eaten at Cappy's the previous evening with Sid and Cyril, both lobstermen who worked the reaches of Blue Hill Bay. Stone had been on the wagon this time for more than a month, and had started off with a mug of hot cider which Sid thought was fuckin' hilarious.

'Jesus, Luke. That stuff will eat your guts out.'

'Just taking it easy for a while, Sid,' Stone answered, willing to kill for the double shot of Seagrams Sid was pouring down his gullet. Not to think about it, he told himself.

He pried open a clam shell and stripped off the muscle, dipped it in butter and let it slide down without chewing.

The alcove was warm and smells of overheated fat wafted in from the kitchen. Cappy's was a bar and grill, popular with the locals in Camden, particularly in the off season when the tourists weren't stumbling all over themselves or asking dumb questions like where the cheapest factory outlet store was – *ya know, where* real *Mainers go*. During high season, a man couldn't sit at the bar and get drunk in peace.

'What's this I heah 'boutcha visit downta Sou'wes' Habah?' Sid asked, prying a bit of clam from his teeth with a fingernail. The waitress was happening by and Cyril splayed out three fingers, indicating another round.

'Just down there to collect a debt,' Stone said, smiling secretively, laying it on a little thick. Sid must have heard the whole story because he grinned back like a whale taking on a load of krill.

Last August, the US Coast Guard cutter *Griswald* had put into Southwest Harbor with a bent rudder. Seems that the third officer had the con, and while the vessel was backing down on an anchor the rudder racked over a shoal of rocks in the process. 'The dumb shit doesn't know cornbread from batshit,' the engineering officer had told Stone, who had been called in to check on the damage and see whether he could effect temporary repairs.

For the last five years, Stone had operated under the name of Luke S. Walker with stationery, calling-cards and invoices printed up with the name of a phony corporation, *Walker Marine Services Ltd.* He normally worked on long-term contracts for underwater construction firms, placing piles, blowing up obstructions and laying electrical cables, but on occasion he took on the odd below-the-waterline work if the money was right.

Still, he had been leery about doing any work for the government because of the paper trail, but the engineering officer winked and assured him that payment would be 'cash and carry'.

The job had turned out to be more difficult than Stone first estimated. The plating on the rudder was peeled back like a banana skin, which meant cutting away the warped plates with an acetylene torch, some grinding, then welding on new plates. All in all, twelve hours of underwater work at $90 an hour, plus $290 in materials, for a total of $1370 and forget the tax.

When the job was finished, the engineering officer, now in civvies, took the bill to the bridge while Stone cooled his heels in the wardroom over a cup of coffee. Eventually, a gangling ensign with fair hair, freckles and the reek of the barnyard still upon him showed up with a stack of forms.

'The skipper left word that you've got to fill out these in triplicate. Ballpoint pen only and press hard. BUSHIPS will review it, mail you a retro-something procurement order which you then submit along with the billing, your tax ID number. Should only take about four months.' He grinned, displaying a full mouth of milk-fed teeth set in pink, healthy gums.

'I was supposed to be paid cash,' Stone shot back, not at all amused.

'The exec got it all screwed up, Mr Walker. Sorry about that, but I gotta go by the book.'

'Get the engineering officer down here, like *now*!'

The kid shrugged. 'He just took off on a forty-eight-hour leave. The skipper's ashore and so's the exec. I'm the officer in charge so, like Truman said, "the buck stops here".' The kid grinned again. Stone could swear that there were still traces of Iowa straw stuck between the kid's teeth.

'Look,' Stone said patiently, 'I'm in business – what you guys call the "private sector". I've got bills to pay and I pay them on time. I also expect to get paid on time, all without having to do a shitload of paperwork. That's the way it works around here.'

The kid's eyes hardened. ' "How it works around here" doesn't cut the mustard, mister. I'm going by the regs. By the way, you got a license?'

'What kind of a license?'

'Approved defense contractor's. If you don't have one, we can't contract with you. 'Course, you can sue.' The kid was positively enjoying this, a little farm brat bossing the hired help while daddy was in town picking up a load of chicken feed.

'Look, admiral, I don't have the time or the money to sue. I've seen that sort of thing take years and I don't have years. I've got close to 500 bucks into the job just in materials. You pay me that and we'll forget the rest.'

The kid shook his head slowly, like a dim-witted spectator at a tennis match that had finished an hour ago. 'No way, Walker. That's a discretionary procedure, up to the officer in charge, and I just happen to be in charge. What if the plating doesn't hold? The Coast Guard would be out for 500 and who knows what unkind words the skipper would put on my effectiveness report.'

'Based on what I've seen, he'd probably suggest that you be reassigned as second in command of a tractor, which is probably what the hell you were doing before you started parading around in that uniform.'

The kid went ballistic, said some words unbefitting an officer and a gentleman, then ordered Stone off the ship, never more to darken its gangway.

Stone had patiently waited a month until the *Griswald* had put into Southwest Harbor again on her run south. Stone timed his arrival for just after dusk. It was a Friday night and, although the ship was well lighted, Stone guessed that most of the crew were ashore. He prayed that the dingbat ensign was officer of the deck, totally in charge, and that the buck truly stopped there.

He tied up his work boat to a mooring off Hinkley's yard, pulled on his scuba gear, armed himself with a gas cutting torch, and went diving.

The propeller shafts on the *Griswald* were about eight inches in diameter. Stone selected the starboard-hand side shaft and cut about three-quarters through it with the torch. It took all of nine minutes.

He was back at Green Island in two hours, cleaned up, then took his dinghy over to the mainland where he kept his 1956 Dodge pickup. An hour later, he was at Denny's house in Bar Harbor for the weekly booze, poker and bitch session.

The *Griswald* had put to sea the following morning, or tried to. In the middle of the channel abeam the Cranberry Islands, she lost the starboard prop when it sheared off as revolutions were increased to breast the incoming tide. Unable to maneuver in a restricted channel and with no major dry dock in Southwest Harbor, the *Griswald* had to proceed down the channel, then limp to the Bath Shipyard for a proper haul-out.

When the cops made enquiries the following day, everyone who had been at the poker session was willing to swear on a Bible that *Walker rolled in early Friday afternoon, played poker until midnight, then crashed on the couch for overnight 'cause he was too damn drunk to drive back.*

It was odd, the *Camden Herald* noted in the following

day's op-ed page, that only one diving contractor had been willing to undertake a salvage contract for the propeller (valued at $4000 in scrap). But along the Maine coast, from Boothbay to the Canadian border, no one else thought it was the least bit odd. The word had gotten around. Mainers took care of their own, even the drunks.

'So how much you git for the prop, Luke?' Sid asked. The waitress arrived at the table with three double shots of Seagrams.

Stone, responding to the siren call of the booze, pushed the mug of cider aside and raised his shot glass. 'Sold it to a scrapyard in Portsmouth for 1370 bucks. Seemed like a fair price.'

Sid and Cyril clicked their glasses with his, both of them grinning like they had just won one for the Gipper. 'Fuckin' A, buddy,' said Cyril, which was the longest sentence Stone had ever heard him utter.

He must have dozed off because when he woke up it was half-past eleven. The shack was still freezing and wasn't going to get a damned degree warmer without a fire in the stove. Naked, his flesh puckering, Stone pulled on a one-piece snowmobile suit, pushed his feet into a pair of L. L. Bean gummies and attended to fueling the stove. He dropped in three split halves of birch, a bunch of twigs, threw in a half-cupful of kerosene and torched it with a match, once again burning the hair off the back of his hand. He'd done that with gasoline once when he was drunk and nearly blew the place up.

He shuffled into the galley, dumped a spoonful of instant coffee into a mug, filled it with tap water and chucked it in the microwave. While he was waiting, he fingered through the mail that he had picked up in Camden yesterday afternoon before heading for Cappy's. Three bills, a couple of catalogs and a large, recycled mailer from a clothing company with the return address scratched out and his dad's penned in. The envelope was postmarked Charleston, West Virginia, which meant that his dad had felt it was important enough not to mail from Weer Hollow where enquiring eyes might take note.

Stone wondered how the old man was getting along. He did some mental addition and figured out his dad would be seventy-three come August. Retired from the mines, the old man spent a good deal of his time fishing and the rest of it writing letters to the editor or calling *Larry King Live*. They had never been close, but Stone figured they shared common cause in their mutual loathing of government, be it foreign or domestic.

The Internal Revenue Service was still on Stone's case, so his old man served as a mail drop and forwarded the occasional letter from a discreetly remote mail box. Stone wrote back about once a month and, when he could, slipped in a couple of twenties. The old man never thanked him and Stone would have been shocked if he had. Like his dad said, the stuff was just paper with printing on it and if a fool worked for it and another fool accepted it in payment for services or goods, they were both high up in the cosmic order of self-duplicity.

The microwave pinged. Stone took the steaming cup of coffee and his dad's package back into the communal bedroom/living-room, checking the stove on the way. It was starting to roar. Stone quickly threw in two more splits of hardwood, slammed the door and adjusted the damper, then crawled back into the sack.

The coffee tasted like warmed-over Milk of Magnesia but Stone forced it down, desperate for the caffeine kick. No more booze for a month, he promised himself. *Tell me another one*, the inner voice taunted.

Inside the package was a note from his old man and a separate bulky envelope. The note was sparse, just a few lines about local politics and mention that he was seeing a woman who ran a Seven-Eleven over in Beckley who believed in both the gold standard and free love. Stone grinned at that one.

He examined the sealed envelope. The ink on the

postmark was smeared, making it unreadable, but it had stamps with the Queen's profile on it. He pried the staples from the flap of the envelope and pulled out the contents. There was a handwritten letter and a printed report bound with plastic rings.

Dear Mr Stone,

I've been in contact with Brian Woolsey, with whom I think you're quite familiar. I contacted Brian relative to employing him as a consulting engineer on the structural integrity of the undersea tunnel which links England with France, commonly referred to as the 'Chunnel'.

Brian was unable to undertake this work because of a prior commitment to Balzari & Schudel AG as heating and ventilation consultant on the Grauholz Hill Tunnel, but he strongly suggested that I contact you as he believed that, although your methods are somewhat unorthodox, you would be the ideal man for this particular job.

I have enclosed a report which I authored concerning the Chunnel's vulnerability to terrorist attack. The report was rejected by Transmanche Link, the Chunnel's prime contractor, as too speculative, but there is now some spotty evidence that terrorist elements on the Continent are intent on confirming my findings. I need you to reexamine my calculations concerning the structural integrity and resultant vulnerability of the Chunnel, and to detail those countermeasures you feel would be most appropriate.

I also understand from Brian that you're somewhat at odds with the American tax authorities. I can assure you that, should you undertake the project, payment for your services will be forwarded to the bank account of your choice without notification being sent to either your tax authorities or to our

Inland Revenue. Contact me at the letterhead telephone or fax number if interested.

   Yours faithfully,
   Ian G. Macleod
   President
   Dundeedum Security Services Ltd

Interesting, he thought. Stone thumbed through the
report. Not bad. Macleod had the basics right but had made
a couple of flawed assumptions based on textbook engineering wisdom, not hard tunneling experience. They were
seemingly marginal, yet might be the sort of thing that
could be exploited. He finished off the coffee and ambled
out to the kitchen again, grabbed a Bud from the refrigerator and sat down in the chair opposite the stove, rereading
Macleod's analysis.

   Out of professional interest, Stone had followed the
progression of the Chunnel's construction and service
trials through his subscription to *Tunnels and Tunneling* –
otherwise known in the trade as *Bores and Boring*. Brian
Woolsey had been peripherally involved in the ventilation end of things and had once written Stone
that 'the damned thing's a bloody great death trap.'
At the time, Stone had put that down to Brian losing
the bid.

   Undersea tunnels were bastards to drive and dangerous
as hell until they were stabilized and lined, but once completed, safe as houses. The Chunnel was all of that, in
spades. Whether by nature's accident or divine inter-
vention, a thick stratum of chalk ran under the seabed
between Folkestone, England and Sangrette, France – the
shortest possible distance between England and the Continent.

   As a tunneling medium, the chalk was ideal: homogene-
ous, largely without fractures and nearly impermeable. The
lining segments – generally interlocking collars of reinforced concrete – were almost superfluous to the

structural strength of the Chunnel, largely cosmetic in purpose. Or so said the glowing progress reports in *T & T*.

To Stone's knowledge, no commercial tunnel within the last century had ever been blown up, either accidentally or otherwise. And the reason was simple: a tunnel, by definition, is a tube open at both ends. The pressure of the earth which encases a tunnel exerts an inward force. Any explosive detonated within a tunnel did little more than to offset the inward force and was otherwise dissipated down the open bore of the tunnel. That premise, of course, presumed that a *reasonable* amount of explosive was detonated. Stone's job, as he saw it, would be to find out how much explosive was *unreasonable*.

By seven the following morning, Stone had his work boat cranked up. He cast off the dock lines and headed south for Murry's place at Burnt Coat Harbor. A cold blue norther was blowing, foam spitting off the curling wave tops, cormorants working the ridges of Blue Hill Bay, their eyes cocked for smelt. Seals occasionally poked their snouts through the surface as he passed, warily eyeballing him.

There hadn't been much to closing the shack on Green Island. He had turned off the power, emptied the fridge and left the key to the lock on the window ledge where Sid knew it normally resided. Sid *jus' fuckin' loved* dropping into Green Island with a ladyfriend when Stone was out of town. Sid would show up with a case of Seagrams, some jacked deer steaks and the makings for a big pot of chili. Stone had pointedly left a stack of clean sheets on the chair next to the bed and a gallon jug of laundry detergent on the drain board. Sid was somewhat prone to forgetting the finer points of housekeeping when he was courting.

By 10.30, Stone throttled back the diesel and eased past the number-two buoy into Burnt Coat channel. Not much activity – a couple of lobstermen stacking bait boxes on the town wharf and some laundry flapping on a clothesline behind Belsin's place.

Stone turned to port after he came abeam of the number-six can and idled down the privately maintained channel.

Murry's place was a multi-decked structure built into the side of the hill with floating docks angling out from the shoreline near the workshop. An old schooner was tied up at one of the docks, a guy aloft wooding down the spar, getting ready for spring charter work. Off to the left on a separate pontoon was a Cessna 180 on floats.

Easing his work boat in behind the Cessna, Stone killed the engine and looped a spring line over the float's docking cleat, then, clambering over the gunwale, led a bow and stern line.

Murry was already shambling down the dock with the gait of a bull seal. Stone took one last turn on the cleat, stood up and stuck out his hand. 'Howzit going, John?'

Murry took Stone's hand and flailed it for half a minute. He wore grease-stained canvas trousers, a faded denim shirt and had chest hair sprouting out between the bulging buttons. Murry beamed a ruddy Irish smile.

'Going good, Stone. How's by you?'

Stone had told Murry his story some years ago – the only person in Maine who knew his background. Stone had often wondered why, and the only reason he could come up with was that Murry inspired conspiratorial trust. Murry had his own stories to tell, and if half of them were true it was a wonder he hadn't been lynched by any one of a dozen cuckolded husbands, or thrown into jail by any number of Maine magistrates.

'Got a job, a good one, I think, John. Headed out for Scotland to do some engineering stuff. Might be away for some time.'

Murry looked at him sideways. 'Gopher work?' They headed up the dock toward the Cessna.

Stone shrugged. 'Yep, the Chunnel.'

'How you feel about going down in an undersea tunnel again?'

'Scares me shitless.' The odd thing about his phobia was that it didn't apply to tunneling under solid ground, even though a rock cave-in could kill you just as dead as a seabed hydraulic blowout. It all came down to the echoes of men drowning in his dreams, and it had been his own damned fault. The Japanese consortium was behind schedule and they wanted the drive pushed harder. To make faster progress meant not waiting for the linings to be erected. Stone, his job on the line and trying to make a name for himself, pushed the tunnel without adequately supporting it and the result was the death of twenty-one men and nearly the loss of his own life.

Murry switched subjects. 'How's your love life?'

Shrugging, Stone stuffed his hands in his pockets. 'Great.' But there wasn't any. And he didn't bother to ask Murry how his was because that was like asking Nero how the fiddling was going. 'Feel like flying today?'

Looking up at the sky, Murry was obviously pleased with an excuse to get away. 'Where to?'

'Peggy's Cove in Nova Scotia. Got a friend there who would put you up overnight. I already checked with him. He knows a couple of ladies . . .'

Murry lifted his eyebrows and fingered his *Got Mit Us* belt buckle. 'Now would we be clearing immigration, old son?'

'Thought that it would save some time if we didn't. My buddy has a seaplane ramp so you can haul out overnight and he'll run me up to Halifax by car so I can catch tonight's flight for Ireland. You could come back down tomorrow morning or whenever.'

'You still having problems with the tax people? Is that why you're ducking immigration?'

'John! Fer chrissake, you know me better than that.'

Murry smiled. He had heard it all before.

Macleod pushed the bottle of Talisker toward Stone and nodded. 'Keeps the chill off your bones, lad.'

Stone poured for both of them. The stuff slid down like liquefied gold. No wonder the canny Scots didn't export much of the stuff.

There was a roast of venison in the oven and yams baking in the hearth's embers, the smell permeating the small cabin. Macleod was stretched out on a lounge chair in front of the fire, mulling over figures that Stone had concocted. He absently fiddled with his eyebrows, occasionally wrinkling his nose.

Stone had been in Scotland for ten days, working twelve hours a day, seven days a week non-stop. Taking all the engineering drawings and calculations that Macleod had collected, Stone had driven down to Glasgow Technical Institute and locked himself in a room with a work station tied to a mainframe computer to run 'what if' assumptions. He had returned to Portree only this afternoon. The summary that Macleod was now rummaging through detailed Stone's calculations.

'You're saying here that even in the most vulnerable part of the Chunnel, the Crossover Chamber, it would require 1500 kilos of explosive to breach the damned thing?' Macleod pushed his glasses down on his nose, squinting over them at the numbers.

'Sixteen hundred, plus or minus ten per cent,' replied Stone. 'Even less, if it were focused properly, but with that large an amount, focusing is damn near impossible unless it was divided into a number of shaped charges, each machined out of a solid block of explosive.'

Macleod exhaled slowly. 'No group could get that much stuff together without inviting attention. Still, if they did, it could possibly be contained in the back of a lorry or a cargo container.'

Stone shook his head. 'Chemical sniffers would pick up

the characteristic trace scent of nitrates, even if the truck or the container were sealed. But even if you got past the sniffers, it wouldn't do the trick. As far as it goes, my calculations indicate that the explosive would be sufficient to blow out the top of the tunnel lining. The shockwave would gouge out a lot of chalk beyond the liner and possibly fracture enough of the chalk marl above it to cause some minor seepage, but I seriously doubt it would lead to a massive failure.'

'But surely to God, Stone, we're talking about a pile of explosives the size of a small motor car. It's got to do more damage than make a few pockmarks.'

Shaking his head, Stone took a pencil and sketched a cross-section of the Chunnel and the seabed above. 'Twenty-five meters of chalk and compacted conglomerate between the roof of the structure and the floor of the English Channel. The pressure of the shockwave would be more than counteracted by the weight of material pressing down.'

'But with the liner no longer there to support the roof, I'd expect that the whole seabed would cave in.'

Stone drummed his pencil on the pad. 'Ever hear of the nuclear waste storage site the Department of Energy built out in Nevada? Twenty-five hundred feet below the surface, all of the tunneling and chambers scooped out of raw salt. There's no liner on the walls or ceiling and yet salt is a lot softer than chalk. Once in a while, some flakes fall off the ceiling, but that's about it. Simply put, the liner in the Chunnel is cosmetic.'

Macleod shook his head. 'All of this technical jargon is so much blather to me. I understand security systems, Stone – how to stop crazy men from getting into buildings or onto airplanes. People like you are hired to show what happens if I don't do my job properly.' He took off his glasses and rubbed the bridge of his nose. 'Forget all the technical bumph for a minute. Knowing what you know, given unlimited resources, how would *you* destroy the Chunnel?'

'I've got two workable scenarios laid out on the last page. You might go over them, but it comes down to the following: either by an explosion of massive proportions inside the Chunnel or by boring down from the seabed right over the Chunnel and blowing it inward with shaped charges.'

'How large an explosive charge to blow it from within?'

'That's a tricky number to calculate, but let's say you take a tanker truck of gasoline, about 8000 gallons in size, then disperse it in a fine mist. Gasoline is more explosive than C-4 or Semtex, say by a factor of two or three. What you'd have would be an equivalent of 47,000 kilos of explosive. Of course, there'd be a problem with getting perfect dispersal but it *could* be done. Probably mean that you'd have to shut down the air conditioning and stop all the trains so there wouldn't be dissipation of the gasoline mixture prior to ignition.'

'Eurotunnel regulations prohibit any combustible liquids from transiting the Chunnel.'

'Where there's a will, there's a way, Mac. The gasoline container doesn't necessarily have to look like a tank truck. Maybe an ordinary moving van specially fitted out with a rubber bladder inside, a number of concealed nozzles and a high-speed pump.'

Getting up, Macleod stretched, kicked the yams closer to the embers and lit his pipe. 'What about boring down from the seabed?'

'A much more elegant solution,' Stone answered. 'There's no security to breach, no inspections, but the flaw in my thinking is that it would take something the size of a North Sea drilling rig and a couple of days in position to bore out the holes, and those holes would have to be accurately placed to within a few meters of the Chunnel's structure. I assume that the presence of a North Sea drilling rig right in the middle of the most heavily trafficked waters in the world would capture somebody's attention. But *assuming* that holes could be bored, then the full length of the boreholes – from the seabed down to the Chunnel's liner – could be packed with Semtex or C-4, and with that kind of load, you'd be able to blow the bejesus out of the Chunnel.'

'How so?'

'The initial explosion in the bottom of the bore would breach the liner of the Chunnel. The balance of the explosive would enlarge the borehole from, say, eighty-five millimeters, which is a more or less standard coring-sized bit, up to several meters in diameter. The sea would start to hose down the enlarged bore and into the tunnel. The pressure would be enormous and the sides of the bore would erode under the pressure and volume of water flowing past it like a cutting torch going through butterscotch pudding – the breach becoming progressively larger and larger. And as the breach became larger, whole new sections of the liner would tear away or collapse. At a minimum, you'd flood the tunnel for sure and the damage *might* be irreparable.'

'How long to flood it?'

'The answer to that would take a supercomputer quite a few days to work out and even then it would still be a ballpark guesstimate. I'd say maybe an hour, but again, it depends on how large the borehole would initially be, which, in turn, would determine how much explosive could be packed into it.'

'Cheerful bugger, aren't you?' Macleod moved to the stove, opened the door and probed the roast with a fork. 'Not done enough. We'll give it another half an hour.' He closed the oven door, then leaned against the stove, frowning. 'None of it makes real sense, Stone. I can see some odd bloke sneaking in a couple of pounds of explosive or maybe derailing a train, but that isn't going to do any real long-term damage. Of course, the possibility of terrorists using a bloody load of gasoline might do it, and that's something that no one, including me, has really studied. You were talking about dispersion of the gasoline. What would that take?'

'As I said, a very large container for the gasoline, but you'd also have to have high-speed pumps and one helluva lot of nozzles to atomize the liquid. Very tricky to get the right effect, particularly with a train running at over 150 kilometers an hour. Like I said before, any dissipation or non-uniformity of the gasoline mist would yield unpredictable results.' Stone's mouth was watering. The venison had already been in for five hours and the Scots had a reputation for overcooking everything. He settled for another glass of Talisker to take the edge off his hunger.

Like a terrier that wouldn't let the rat go, Macleod kept worrying with the problem. 'Could boreholes be drilled with anything less than an offshore rig?'

'Nope. The weakest part of the Chunnel and therefore the most vulnerable section is the Crossover Chamber on the English side, and the seabed above it is twenty-three meters deep at low water. You'd need a rig big enough to have legs that reached all the way down to the seabed. We're talking "massive".'

Pointing his pipe stem like he was taking aim, Macleod asked, 'What about boreholes drilled before the damned Chunnel was built?'

'Forget it.' Stone flipped through a stack of engineering reports and pulled out a computer printout. He ran his finger down a column. 'Total of 221 boreholes drilled along the Chunnel's intended route between 1953 and 1990 to sample the substrata. But they were all plugged with concrete grout after coring. That's just standard practice.'

Macleod shook his head. 'GEM – name of a North Sea offshore rig that drilled seventy-three boreholes back in the late autumn of '74 for some aborted tunnel scheme. French-backed – never got off the ground financially. They drilled in November, bad weather according to the reports. As you say, the drilling crew was supposed to pack the bores with grout but the inside story I've heard is that they didn't because the rig dragged in a gale. Big brouhaha about it, threatened litigation but no one was willing to fund the necessary money to locate the holes and prove the point. But when Transmanche was driving the south-running tunnel in the autumn of 1989, they hit what they later assumed to be one of GEM's open boreholes. They had the shield in place but it was a near thing. Hell of a row but it was hushed up because the banks already had their wind up due to cost overruns.'

'Seventy-three boreholes. Jesus! Even if a third of them weren't plugged . . . Where were these boreholes located?'

'Not sure. Never considered the boreholes as a security threat because the liner's in place. Besides, I was told that the bores have probably silted up and would present no further threat. However, I've got a contact at Lloyd's. I'll fax him if you think it's worth looking into and see whether any records still exist.' Macleod shook the bottle of Talisker. It was empty. 'You drink too much, Stone. Particularly when it's my whiskey. Bad for both your liver and my wallet.' He took his mackintosh from a peg and pulled on his boots. 'Hustle up, lad. We'll be going down to the village. I'll scratch out a letter for the fax machine and we can wait in the Rosedale's public room for a response. The roast can wait.'

'I thought you had your own fax machine.'

'It's an economically beneficial arrangement that most Americans wouldn't countenance, Stone. I occasionally drink the Rosedale's whiskey and they occasionally tend to my communications needs. Do ya suppose that I'd buy a cow just because I needed a pitcher of cream?'

Mac sent the fax from the Rosedale's front office, then retired with Stone to the public room.

The return fax came back two hours, six whiskeys and half a dozen pickled eggs later.

For the attention of Ian Macleod, re GEM boreholes:

Firm which contracted with GEM was Société Techniques Maritimes based Le Havre, France. We have no data available concerning present disposition of this firm, borehole numbers or locations of same. Await your further enquiries with both interest and amusement. Road conditions on the drive back were as awful as predicted. However, didn't connect with a bog as you had hoped and thus both windscreen and cranium are still whole.

Manning

Lloyd's Bureau of Internal Development

'That's it, then,' Macleod said. He finished his whiskey carefully, then stood up.

'What's *it*, then?'

'You'll be taking a self-drive to catch the evening ferry from Armadale over to Mallaig. Drop the vehicle off at the coach garage next to the station and take the West Highlander to Glasgow. Should arrive sometime around 23.00. From there, catch the next express down to London, then the cross-Channel ferry to Boulogne and hire a motor car, their cheapest, mind you. With a bit of luck, you'll be in Le Havre for breakfast.'

'Christ, Mac! I haven't had a day off since I got here! And how about my social life? There's a sheep in your paddock that seemed like she was available.'

'Bugger that, mate,' Macleod snorted. 'I'm paying you a fair wage for an honest day's work. Get over to France and find out what you can about the boreholes from this Frog outfit, then up to Rouen to interview the barrister's daughter.'

He scribbled two numbers on the back of his business card, then wadded up the fax and threw it in a trash bin. 'The first is the number of a woman by the name of van der Groot who lives in Rouen. Simmons, the barrister who is her father, was reluctant to part with that information but I convinced him that it was in her best interest to cooperate. It was her tenant who received the floppy disk. Might be worth the while to interview the both of them. Mind – neither one of them wants to be involved, so tread softly.' He pulled on his mac and put the exact amount of the bill on the bar.

'The other number is for an operations center I'm setting up in Ramsgate. Old machine shop which fronts the harbor. By the day after tomorrow, I'll have someone manning the phone twenty-four hours a day. We'll be using the name "Highgate Engineering".'

'Where's Ramsgate?'

'About thirty kilometers up the coast from Dover. Good location, not far from Folkestone and the Chunnel. Now, let's get up the hill. While you pack, I'll make you up a bit of a meal to travel with.'

Together, they left the Rosedale and started climbing. A thick fog had rolled in, blurring the shapes of the cottages that lined the road. Blue television screens flickered behind lace curtains, the moving images surrealistic.

'One other thing, Stone . . .'

'What's that?'

'That wee darling sheep you referred to is already spoken for.' Macleod's laughter boomed in the fog, unnaturally loud.

SIX

Stone rolled into the outskirts of Le Havre in a rented Peugeot just a few minutes after nine. The Peugeot had a defective heater and a driver's seat that was jammed in a position previously selected by a midget. To compound his unhappiness, he had only been able to snatch two hours' sleep in the last day and a half and had the beginnings of a cold – by all indications a humdinger.

He pulled off the motorway into an ELF service station, swapped pounds for francs at a rip-off rate and called the offices of *Société Techniques Maritimes*. The connection was good, the linguistic barrier impenetrable. The guy who answered either didn't speak English or preferred not to. Stone hung up, bought a map and tracked the place down.

It was a three-story brick building in the dock area, a marine electrical supply store on the first floor, the offices of STM on the second. He climbed the stairs and opened the door into a shabby office walled with filing cabinets and framed photos of offshore drilling rigs.

The receptionist – an emaciated crone with a sharp nose and flinty eyes – first examined Stone with distaste as though he had an uncontrollable drool, then scowled at his business card.

'And exactly what is it that you wish, Monsieur Walker?'

'I want to see whoever's in charge of offshore drilling contracts.'

'That would be the specialty of Monsieur Le Fonde, our director of technical operations.' She consulted a schedule. 'He is unavailable.'

'Look,' Stone said, exasperated, 'it will only take a second. Check with him to find out whether your outfit has a record of the boreholes that the GEM rig drilled along the Eurotunnel route in the fall of '74.'

She gave him a odd look and, without explanation, got up and disappeared down a hallway. Ten minutes later she came back, followed by a man – late fifties, yellow-tinted glasses, a suit ten years out of date, and hair parted down the middle of his scalp. He smelled of blueprints and dusty files.

'I am René Le Fonde, Monsieur Walker.' Le Fonde offered a limp hand but pointedly didn't invite Stone to his office.

Stone made his pitch.

Le Fonde seemed vaguely familiar with the GEM drilling project, almost *too* vaguely familiar with it. Yes, regrettably, although he currently held the position of technical director, he was not with the firm in 1974. No, to his knowledge, no records remained of the GEM drilling activity – quite possibly destroyed when the GEM was sold to a Venezuelan firm in 1978. *But of course*, all the boreholes would have been grouted – a contractual condition of work such as that. No, he doubted whether others in the firm would remember the GEM project since most of them were younger men, only with the firm for a few years, but he would make a *most thorough enquiry* and give M. Walker whatever information might come to light. He paused, then drew a small notepad from the breast pocket of his jacket.

'Unfortunately, I will be traveling to St Malo tomorrow morning, but it would be possible for me to meet with you for breakfast at your hotel so I can present my findings, if any – say about eight, if that would be convenient?'

Stone, with no hope of speeding up the process, agreed. But he had caught the brief shadow on the secretary's face as Le Fonde spoke, almost as if she was about to contradict him but then had thought better of it.

Le Fonde seemed slightly nervous. He lit a cigarette and said, 'For the time being, that is the extent of my knowledge, Monsieur Walker. Ah . . . exactly what is your interest in this matter?'

'Just doing some background research on the history of the Chunnel. It might lead to a book.'

The Frenchman's mouth twitched momentarily. 'How interesting.' A long drag on the cigarette, then a longer exhalation. 'Ah . . . your hotel?'

'Thought I'd stay at the Hôtel de Ville.'

'A good choice. In the meanwhile, I will do what I can, but you should not have high expectations.' He shrugged elegantly, then offered his hand.

Within half an hour, Stone had checked into the Hôtel de Ville, taken three antihistamine pills, two whiskeys, and zonked out.

Once the man who called himself Walker had left the office, Le Fonde made several transatlantic calls from his private line. Next he placed a call from his private line to a cellular telephone number – which meant its location might be anywhere in Europe. How convenient, he mused, but as his father had once told him, when you danced with the Devil, you didn't call the tune.

'Yes . . . ?' It was a man's voice, cultured but unfamiliar.

Le Fonde cleared his throat. 'This is René Le Fonde with the firm of SMT. Three days ago, two, ah, gentlemen visited my office. The one who gave his name as "Joss" instructed me to call this number if there was ever an enquiry concerning the GEM borehole contract or the whereabouts of Monsieur Le Borveaux. I would like to confirm that I will be paid a fee for this information.'

A pause, then, 'An envelope will arrive within forty-eight hours with 12,000 francs enclosed, assuming that your information is useful.'

'I believe it is. A man came to the office this morning enquiring about the GEM borehole contract.'

'His name?'

'A Mr Luke S. Walker, the chief executive officer of Walker Marine Services Limited based in Camden, Maine. I made enquiries. His firm's telephone number is not in service and no such firm is incorporated in the State of Maine. Neither Mr Walker nor his firm is registered with any Canadian or American engineering society. It is my opinion that Mr Walker is not who he claims to be.'

'Where is he staying?'

'At the Hôtel de Ville near the train station. I made an appointment to meet him for breakfast tomorrow morning.'

'That was wise. Call me immediately after you've met with him. I am particularly interested as to his travel plans. I would add that it is obviously not in your interests to tell him anything about the GEM contract or Le Borveaux. Do you understand?'

'Completely,' Le Fonde answered. The line went dead and he eased the handset into its cradle.

The back of Le Fonde's shirt was soaked and he wondered whether 12,000 francs was adequate compensation. Le Fonde had not known Le Borveaux well – the old man was no longer a member of the firm, only being employed for occasional consulting work. But he had thought to call Le Borveaux's number and warn him after the meeting with the two men who had unexpectedly barged into his office eight days ago. On reflection, he realized that some things were best left undone.

Stone came to sometime around seven in the morning, his stomach hollow, the cold still hanging in there but containable. He called down to room service for coffee, then showered, shaved and dressed.

At 7.30, he tried the van der Groot woman's number in Rouen. He got an answering machine which rattled French at him. He left a message that he'd call back later.

Le Fonde was waiting in the lobby, obviously agitated,

120

nervously checking his watch. He had a briefcase, umbrella and overnight bag stacked on the seat next to him.

Le Fonde apologized that he was running late and had only a few minutes before his train left – an unexpected business trip. 'Unfortunately, Monsieur Walker,' he said, 'I have no new information, although I found reference in the files concerning a firm in Marseilles which may have done some of the hydrocarbon analysis on the cores that the GEM extracted. You must understand that these things take time. I will contact them at the earliest opportunity and telephone you if there is anything of significance to report. You will be, perhaps, staying in Le Havre for some time?'

'No,' Stone answered. 'I'm going up to Rouen this afternoon and I'll probably head back for England tomorrow.' He scribbled out the two numbers Macleod had given him and added, 'The Rouen number might not work but the number in England will take a message for me. If I'm not there, ask for Ian Macleod. He's head of a firm called Highgate Engineering which we do work for.'

Le Fonde took the slip and wanly smiled at him. 'I must say *au revoir*, Mr Walker.' They shook hands and Le Fonde left hurriedly. Stone watched him dodge through the traffic as he crossed the street, then disappear into the stream of people entering the railway station.

Stone was about to return to his room and pack when he noticed Le Fonde had left his umbrella behind in his haste. No way he would be able to track him down before his train pulled out. He considered it for a minute, then thought, *What the heck. It's ten minutes out of my way*.

He returned to the room, packed and checked out. Traffic was heavy, and it was just after nine when he pulled up in front of the brick building.

The secretary had probably arrived just a few minutes earlier and was removing her coat. She turned as he entered, puzzled.

'You did not meet with Monsieur Le Fonde?'

'Yeah, I did, about an hour ago. He was in a hurry and left his umbrella behind at the hotel so I thought I'd drop it off.'

Her face eased into an unexpected smile. 'That is very thoughtful of you, Monsieur Walker. I hope that Monsieur Le Fonde was able to assist you.'

'He wasn't able to come up with anything.'

She hesitated before she spoke, as if she were balancing one thing against another. 'Perhaps he forgot about Monsieur Le Borveaux but, of course, Monsieur Le Fonde was not a member of the firm when Monsieur Le Borveaux was still active. That was some years ago, of course, when I first started work with the *Société*.'

'Le Borveaux? Le Fonde didn't mention him. Was he involved in the GEM contract?'

'It is my belief that he was. Monsieur Le Borveaux is retired now but he does occasional consulting work. It is very difficult for him, you understand? His wife is ill and her treatment is expensive. He might welcome the work.'

'Would you have his telephone number?'

She looked down at her desktop, considering, then looked up at Stone. 'I'm not sure that Monsieur Le Fonde would approve. He is very . . . formal . . . in these matters.' She raised her eyebrows. 'Would you be able to pay Monsieur Le Borveaux for his services? He was a very kind man and I would feel assured if I knew that by giving you such information, he would benefit.'

Mac hadn't given him a budget and would probably scream to bloody hell, but the drilling logs were the key to the whole thing.

'Probably a couple of thousand if he has the technical information I need.'

She looked relieved. She wrote down an address and handed it to Stone. 'Neither Monsieur Le Borveaux nor his wife speak English. You will need an interpreter. The hotel may be able to help. And Monsieur Walker . . .'

'Yes . . .' Stone paused in the doorway.

'I would appreciate it if you would not mention my involvement to Monsieur Le Fonde. He is not what you would call a sympathetic man, you understand?'

Stone nodded.

As he pulled out from the curb and pivoted through a U-turn, he caught a glimpse of a gray van edging out into the traffic. It stayed half a block behind him, following.

Vaguely paranoid, Stone took a left without flicking on the turn signal and circled the block. The van showed up in his rear-view mirror after each turn. For sure a tail, he thought, but who and why? Someone connected with Le Fonde? That was the only possibility.

At a traffic light, the van slowly closed the distance, and when the light turned green it shot past Stone's Peugeot and turned right. A Toyota with two men in it, German plates. Coincidence? Stone didn't think so any more but he had to be sure.

He parked on rue Emile Zola outside of Henri's, a warm and fuzzy looking brasserie.

After buying a copy of the English-language *Herald Tribune* at a kiosk, he entered the place and took a seat next to the window. The sausage was good, the croissants — roughly the size of a 38D-cup — better, the coffee excellent. Stone fortified it with a shot of Calvados to keep the cold at bay. He settled in, thumbing through the classifieds but casting an occasional glance toward the street.

It didn't take long. The van showed up, half a block down, double-parked. Minutes later, a slot opened up and the van jammed into it, nosing out a Fiat by half the thickness of a paint job. The French driver catapulted out of her car and pounded on the van's hood in frustration, probably doing nothing to enhance Franco-German relations. The van apparently prevailed by ignoring her. The driver remained behind the wheel for several minutes, working a cellular phone, then got out, the other man remaining in the passenger seat. The driver slowly sauntered up the street, casually looking at goods displayed in windows but always glancing toward Henri's, his lodestone.

Professional, Stone thought. Stone watched, the Calvados glowing warm in his gut.

The van driver was slightly younger than Stone's first impression. He had short blond hair, hollow cheeks, the mouth thin, the eyes caged in shadows behind sunglasses. The effect was skinhead chic-mod, rounded out by a black leather jacket, jeans and denim shirt, Wellington boots and a white rayon scarf. Oddly, Black Jacket was carrying a shopping bag. He casually scuffed past Henri's front window, briefly glancing at Stone, then entered, paid for a coffee and took a stool at the fast-service breakfast bar.

Somehow, Stone knew he had to shake this guy, find an interpreter and hunt down Le Borveaux. Nice if he could combine all three functions.

The street was busy — the usual crowd of shoppers, a few enlisted men in naval uniform, an old bag strolling a twinset of beagles, the occasional cop. Then two women, arms linked, ambled past the window. Both in their twenties, one a blonde, the other a dubious redhead. It dawned on Stone that this was just what he had been looking for. He smiled broadly at them, then pointedly winked.

The women hesitated. The blonde pointed to herself, smiling, and Stone nodded, mouthing the words 'Speak English?' The blonde cocked her head, not quite comprehending, then nodded in acknowledgement.

If there was one trade where fluency in English paid off, it was hooking in a seaport town. Stone got up, dropped a ten-franc note on the table, and headed for the street.

The girls were waiting for him, primping their hair. The redhead was actually the better looking of the two, with delicate features and a fresh, country-bred face. She wore a jumpsuit, high heels and a faux fox-fur jacket. Gold bangles dangled from her ears; her eye shadow was a deep purple. Her front teeth were slightly crooked, which only enhanced her innocence.

The blonde was older, perhaps a little more worldly, built for comfort, not speed, with full hips and swelling breasts barely contained by a sheer black blouse. Sensible flat shoes, considering her trade, and a leather skirt, a scarf wrapped casually around her throat, and a trenchcoat open but loosely belted, completed the package. She had a nice full face, touched up with very little make-up. Her eyes were arresting, pale blue, a sure trace of her Norman ancestry. Not exactly what you'd call innocent but somehow honest, with a hint of mischievousness thrown in. Stone liked her immediately.

'You are looking for a friendly engagement, monsieur?' the blonde asked.

'Not exactly what we call it where I come from, but that's close enough.'

'I am Nicole and this is Babette. You wish us both?'

'Never tried it that way but sounds real interesting. Let's say that it's just you for now, Nicole, and I'll catch Babette some other time.'

'For 'ow long would you like to be with me?'

'Say about three hours.'

'You pay in pounds or dollars?'

'Pounds.'

'Two 'undred.'

'Say seventy-five now and another seventy-five if you do like I tell you to.'

A shadow passed across her face. 'I do not like it rough, monsieur.'

'Stone. Call me Stone. Just like you say, Nicole. Nothing rough. Just smooth and easy. A little walk, a little talk, maybe a drink afterwards.'

Black Jacket was leaning against the building, about two meters away, studying a street guide, obviously well within hearing range. He looked up briefly, his expression blank, his eyes black marbles behind the dark lenses.

Stone turned to Babette and bowed slightly. 'Sorry. Another time, okay?'

She said something in French, her voice soft and conciliatory, pursed her lips, brushed Nicole lightly on the cheek with her lips, then headed up the street in pursuit of employment, hips swinging slightly in synchronized magic beneath her jumpsuit.

Stone cocked his elbow and Nicole took it, falling into step with him.

'You are from New York, no?'

'Nope. West Virginia. *Country road, take me home, to the place that I be-long . . .*' he sang softly, off key.

She squeezed his arm. 'Jacques Denver. 'E is my favorite. We can play 'im while we make love. I have a place near the *Union Chrétienne de Jeunes Gens*. We go there now, no?'

'No. Something else we have to do first. You know a supermarket somewhere within a couple of blocks?'

'Ah − *supermarché*. You know Prisunic? Like your K-Mart, no?'

'No, but close enough. Lead on.' Reflected in the glass window of a shop, Stone saw that Black Jacket was following them. He started to hum.

'You are here on business?' she asked.

He squeezed her arm. 'Monkey business.'

She picked up the pace. 'What are we going to Prisunic in search of? I have all things necessary.' She fluttered her eyelashes in a slow semaphore.

'I'm looking to get something for a friend of mine. Well − not exactly a friend you'd take home to mother.' He glanced in a butcher's window. Black Jacket had fallen back, pausing to examine the latest in orthopedic braces and wheelchairs. Stone turned to her, smiling. 'Don't look back but the guy I'm talking about is behind us − in the black leather jacket. He's following me and I want to get rid of him.'

'I know of a man whose business it is to do such things.' She cocked a finger and stuck it in his ribs. 'Very discreet, not expensive. He enjoys it, you understand?'

He shook his head. 'Nothing permanent. Just to get him

out of the way for a while. Thought maybe you could help me.'

'In what manner?'

He told her.

She cocked her head, considering, then nodded.

Prisunic was part grocery store, part mini-mart and part bistro. Tables were scattered along the central aisle, dogs under the tables scarfing up discarded tidbits, kids yowling in shopping carts, a zillion tennis shoes in neon colors spilling from the shelves, spider plants dangling from hanging pots, minnows gulping in bubbling tanks, everything you never needed.

'What do you think, Nicole?'

'There is a department *photographique* on the next floor that will suit our purpose. You will wait here for a few minutes, then proceed up the lift. When everything is right, you will see me touching my hair with my left hand.'

'You're a doll.' He leaned over and kissed her lightly on the cheek.

'And if I am successful, you will pay me another thirty pounds, yes?'

'If it works out okay. I presume that you've had some experience in this sort of thing?'

'You like my trenchcoat, yes? And my shoes? And my watch?' She flashed a smile, pivoted, heading for the escalator.

Black Jacket was hanging over the take-out bar, fingering what was probably a discarded coffee cup, turning the pages of a newspaper.

Stone sat down at one of the tables and took off a shoe, shook it out and put it on again, taking his time to fuss with getting the laces tied just right. His father had always told him to tie his laces properly, about the only parental advice he had ever taken to heart.

The department *photographique* was surprisingly large, complete with projectors, film-splicing machines, bottles of chemicals and the like. The expensive cameras were behind locked glass cases, but five of them were spread out on the counter, Nicole leaning over them, poking at their controls with her fingertips, a salesman joking with her and obviously positioning himself to get a look down her blouse.

Stone moved to the far end of the counter and studied a Nikon under glass. He looked up after a few minutes, annoyance on his face, and snapped his fingers.

The salesman glared at him. *'Un moment, monsieur!'*

'Hey, I don't have all day. You here to help the customers or not?'

The salesman obviously didn't speak English, but Nicole touched his arm and whispered something. The salesman hesitated, ground the muscles in his jaw, then moved down the counter and unlocked the display case. He reached in but Stone was shaking his head.

'No, no, no – I'm not looking for some crummy camera. I want film, *F-I-L-M*.' He stabbed his finger at a cutout of Bill Cosby flashing a mouthful of teeth and waving the Kodak banner.

The salesman, a short man with an incipient pot and smudged eyeglasses, was obviously exasperated.

Stone pointed to the right-hand end of the rack. 'The twenty-four exposure rolls. Four of them. You know, *quattro, por favor.'*

The salesman fished out four and dropped them on the counter as if they were contaminated fecal specimens. Stone pulled out his wallet and slid a hundred-franc note across the counter. In the process his hand knocked one of the film cartons off the counter and onto the floor.

The salesman took a very deep breath and bent down. He retrieved the roll and put it back on the counter, then picked up the banknote with his fingertips, muttering under his breath.

Nicole was brushing her hair with her fingertips. She smiled briefly at Stone and wandered away toward a stack

128

of photo albums. Where there had been three cameras, now there were two.

Black Jacket was just one aisle over, checking out a complicated tripod. Stone could only see the top of Nicole's head as she turned the corner and came down Black Jacket's aisle. There was a minor collision, some sharp words, then they parted.

The clerk had returned with change. He slapped the coins down on the counter along with a sales slip and headed back toward where Nicole and the cameras were.

The clerk did a slow take of his camera inventory, then looked up at Nicole. He hesitated, then started to say something, but she put her finger to her lips, leaned over, then whispered in the clerk's ear. His eyes narrowed.

He whispered to her. She whispered back. He craned his neck, looking toward the aisles. Black Jacket was now playing with the knob on an enlarger.

The clerk swept the cameras from the counter and locked them in the display case, then picked up a telephone and stabbed in two digits. His face was set in a hard mask, the eyes boresighted on Black Jacket. Justice would be done.

Nicole nodded to Stone. They were on the down escalator before she spoke. 'Their procedure will be to let 'im go through the checkout counter before they stop 'im. The camera was priced at over a thousand francs. It is a major offense.'

'Best thirty pounds I ever spent,' Stone said, and squeezed her arm. She squeezed back.

They were out the door and onto the sidewalk when the alarm bell clanged. Behind them in the doorway, there was a serious scuffle in progress between Black Jacket and an older man in a stockkeeper's apron. Black Jacket was definitely winning until another man stepped into the scrimmage and belted him with a liter bottle of olive oil. The glass shattered. Black Jacket sunk to his knees, then folded forward like a stuffed doll.

An older woman arrived on the scene in a dressed-for-success business suit, obviously *la boss*. She issued a flurry of instructions to hovering employees, then turned to examine Black Jacket's shopping bag, dramatically removing each item, holding it up for the patrons to see, playing to the gallery.

First was a Minolta camera, the price tag still attached. A low rumble went through the crowd. The next was a pair of leather gloves. Murmurs of disappointment. Then a cellular telephone which generated a few *ah*s.

There was a pause, *la boss* maximizing the dramatic effect. She withdrew a revolver with thumb and forefinger, as if she were extracting a dead rat from her lingerie drawer. Gasps, then dark mutterings from some of the older patrons. In the distance was the two-tone warble of a police siren.

Nicole tightly gripped Stone's arm, her eyes wide. ''E 'ad a gun.'

'So 'e did,' Stone answered.

The van was gone. He drove, Nicole beside him keeping a watch behind them. He found an underground garage and drove in, spent half an hour explaining what he wanted her to ask, then rolled back onto the street. She guided him through the back streets toward the northern parts of the city.

Le Borveaux's apartment was on a tree-lined street in an older suburb of Le Havre, the area undamaged by wartime bombing and still untainted by gentrification. But it had a run-down air to it.

Nicole told Stone that there was a very nice park not far from here where a brass band played on summer evenings and children flew kites on windy days. It was a place she loved to go to read poetry beneath a certain chestnut tree. 'With your lover?' Stone had asked. She had shaken her head. 'I 'ave no lover.' She said it as if it were either a testament to failure or indifference to allegiances.

A woman in a robe hesitantly opened Le Borveaux's

130

apartment door. Stone could understand why Le Borveaux's wife consumed what pension Le Borveaux brought in. The woman was emaciated, her flesh parchment, eyes hollow. A badly fitting wig covered her scalp. The stench of slow, undignified death seeped from the room.

The woman's face clouded, first in puzzlement, then in fright. She hesitated for a second, shaking her head with agonizing slowness, then started to close the door. Nicole spoke rapidly, her voice low and insistent. Reluctantly, the woman backed away from the door and motioned them in, too weak to resist, too tired to argue.

After a short, intense conversation, Nicole made tea for Madame Le Borveaux while Stone sat stiffly in a chair, trying to keep a smile plastered on his face. Yet he felt as if he were an intruder in this room, the acrid taint of rubbing alcohol and medicine fogging the air, the drapes drawn, what little light that filtered in hazed with motes of decades-old dust. The woman, her eyes dull and unfocused, breathed with a dry rasp.

When Nicole reentered the room with a tray holding a steaming cup of tea and two biscuits on a plate, Madame Le Borveaux spoke to her in a low, cracked voice.

Nicole nodded and whispered in Stone's ear, 'She says that she wishes you to go. She is uncomfortable in your presence.'

Stone started to protest.

Shaking her head, Nicole touched his shoulder. 'She 'as difficult problems with her organs. She does not want to be embarrassed. I know what information it is that you seek. Stay outside in the corridor and wait for me, please. This will take only a little time.'

It was more than a hour before Nicole emerged from the apartment. 'She is sleeping. So tired. She has sores all over her body. A woman that I know will arrive shortly to take care of her. Come with me.'

They walked to her park, Nicole holding his hand.

'Two men came for him very late last night,' Nicole told him. 'Monsieur Le Borveaux told 'is wife not to worry: that 'is services were needed and that 'e would be paid well. 'E wasn't sure 'ow long 'e would be away but that arrangements would be made to employ a nurse to care for 'er until his sister could come from Boulogne. 'E left 'er ten thousand francs – part of 'is advance payment. 'E didn't say so, but she thought 'e was very frightened.'

'Did she have any idea who the men were?'

'She saw them only briefly when 'er 'usband came into the bedroom to pack 'is luggage. From 'er description, the man in the black jacket was one of them. 'E spoke French but with a German accent. The other was older, 'is face pitted and with long hair. She 'ad the impression that 'e was Euro-Asian – perhaps a Malay.'

'Did she have any idea where they were headed?'

Nicole shook her head. 'Madame managed to get to the window after they left the apartment. They went in a van but she could not see the license plates. She 'as not 'eard from 'er 'usband since then.'

They had reached a small cul-de-sac in the pathway. There were a few benches, and a small pond, now empty. She pointed toward a slope where a tree stood apart from the shrubbery. 'That is my special place. You will come 'ere some day and read me poetry, then we make love in the bushes, yes? When it's warmer, of course.'

Stone smiled, a little sad. 'I think I'd like that, Nicole.'

They sat down on one of the benches. She fussed with a cigarette, trying to light it in the rising wind. Her hands were pale with the cold.

'Did you ask her about her husband's work in the Pas de Calais?'

'Madame Le Borveaux taught science classes in the *lycée*. She took an interest in 'is work.'

'The boreholes . . . did she know whether any of them were left ungrouted?'

Nicole nodded. 'More than you suspected, in fact, all

seventy-three. The GEM rig for drilling was not properly equipped to supply grouting. That was to be done by a separate service ship but it never arrived, first due to an engine breakdown and then because of the bad weather. When the autumn storms came, the GEM abandoned the project. Madame said that no one except an English geologist by the name of Monsieur Harriman, who was on board the GEM to sample the cores for traces of petroleum, and 'er 'usband were concerned with the grouting. The drilling contractor told Monsieur Le Borveaux that the bore 'oles would silt in with no one the wiser and that 'e was to keep 'is mouth closed if 'e wanted to be paid.'

'Did Madame Le Borveaux know where her husband kept the GEM's drilling logs?'

She nodded. 'Monsieur Le Borveaux was concerned that if the truth came out, 'e would be unjustly blamed. Therefore, 'e reduced the drilling logs to film negatives, yes? 'E kept them in 'is library desk. We looked. The films were gone, along with many of 'is papers and 'is passport.'

'I could use a drink,' Stone said.

They sat together, Nicole sipping Pernod, Stone into what the French passed off as whiskey. He had picked a small, poorly lit café opposite the hotel so that he could monitor the entrance for signs of the opposition. The watery late-afternoon sunlight backlit Nicole's hair and she chain-smoked Gitanes but kept silent as Stone juggled his thoughts.

It had to be Le Fonde who had fingered him unless he had been followed from England. Go back and confront Le Fonde? That seemed like a lousy idea because Le Fonde had the home-court advantage and at least one of the heavies was still in action.

What *was* apparent was that the drilling logs existed and that the boreholes probably hadn't been grouted. The only information missing was whether they had been bored close enough to the Chunnel's structure to be dangerous.

And to determine that, he had to find the drilling logs.

He got up for the third time and tried Mac's Ramsgate number. No answer. He tried the woman's number in Rouen and got the same rapid-fire phone-answering device, the French incomprehensible. He slammed down the telephone handset and checked his watch. Nine minutes past four. Time to get on the road.

She looked up at him and smiled as he returned to the table.

'You will stay with me tonight,' she said. It was a statement, not a question.

He shook his head. 'I'd love to, Nicole, but I've got to get moving.'

'I would not charge you, Stone. You are my friend. We will make a nice dinner and drink a bottle of wine. What 'appens then will 'appen.'

He counted out the sterling notes, folded them and placed the wad in her jacket pocket. She tried to give them back but he shook his head. 'Nope. Deal's a deal.'

She looked down at her glass of Pernod and spoke in a soft voice. 'I want you to stay because I like you, not because of your money.'

'Same here, Nicole, but I'm worried about another person who's involved in this thing. But I'll make a stopover in Le Havre on my way back, say in a day or so.'

She looked up at him, the rim of her eyes moist. 'I don't think you will, *cher*, but thank you for saying that. You are a good man.'

He leaned down and kissed her on the forehead. Whoever came up with the story about whores having hearts of gold must have done his homework in Le Havre.

SEVEN

Rouen, France, 3 April

Two hours after sundown, Stone reached the outskirts of Rouen. The Peugeot's heater still didn't work worth a damn and his cold had worsened. Dumb, he thought. Should have stayed in Le Havre with Nicole. A hot bath, a couple of whiskeys, a square meal and a warm body intertwined with mine. *C'est la stupido.*

Finding a cooperative local who could help him locate Ms van der Groot's part of town had been a bust, and it took him another hour and a half to sniff it out on his own.

It was a dumpy little neighborhood, mainly mom-and-pop stores, with a scattering of apartment buildings and vacant lots. Only one streetlight, and that was halfway down the block. Otherwise, black as pitch, as if most of the locals rolled up the carpet by nine.

The address turned out to be a store of some sort, paper-back travel guides from a dozen countries displayed in the windows.

There was a light on behind drawn shades in the second story of the building, probably her apartment. He got out of the Peugeot, taking his briefcase because he had his notebook, passport and traveler's checks in it. He knocked on the shop's door. No response, but behind the glass of the door was an emergency number. In the alleyway beside the shop, he found a call box, fed in some coins and tapped in the number.

She answered in indecipherable French.

'Sorry,' he said. 'I don't parley voo. You speak English?'

'Who is this and what do you want?'

'My name's Stone. I've come over from England and I'm calling from the pay phone next to your shop. I wanted to meet with you concerning a letter you wrote your father. Mind coming down and letting me in?'

First, silence, then, 'What is your involvement in this?'

'I'm here on Lloyd's instructions to interview you about the floppy disk you sent your dad,' he lied.

He heard her softly sigh. 'You've talked to my . . . to Mr Simmons?'

'He gave me your number, said to tell you it was okay.' Again, the big lie, but Stone didn't want to waste any more time and he was beat, wanted to get it over with, get to a hotel, swallow a bottle of aspirin and sack out.

Her voice relaxed slightly. 'Meet me in my office tomorrow. Say mid-morning.'

'Not possible. I'm due back in London by late afternoon.' Another lie.

A touch of agitation in her voice, although it was softened by her accent, not quite American, not quite English but, for sure, not French. 'I really can't give you any more information than I've already set down in the letter to my father. But if you've come this far, then I'll make time to talk to you for a few minutes. I don't live in the shop but my residence is only a couple of blocks away.' She gave him directions and said that she'd meet him in fifteen minutes at the entrance gate of the road she lived on.

Stone decided to leave the Peugeot parked across the street from the shop and leg it. Mom had always preached that walking cleared the lungs, countered by his father's acerbic comment that if walking cleared the lungs, how come all the damned quacks drove BMWs? Stone decided to go with mom's advice. Cozy mist, crisp air, real healthy stuff, and it would give him a chance to work the kinks out of his muscles.

Following directions, he headed down the alley that bordered her shop, then turned left along a metaled roadway. Less than five minutes later, the gentle mist turned to rain.

Further down the block, a gray Toyota van with German plates rocked slightly in the rising wind, rain starting to pelt off its roof. Two men sat in the front compartment, intent, watching. The older man passed a cigarette to the other, who deeply inhaled then slowly released the smoke from his lungs.

'You get a good enough look at him?' the older man asked.

Dieter shook his head. 'The light's bad. How do you expect me to see in this *verdammt* shit? But who else could it be? And it's the same Peugeot.'

Dieter was on edge. Being arrested for shoplifting had been bad enough and Brunner, if he found out, would be furious. Of course, Dieter had a license for the .38 and had settled the shoplifting charge by taking aside the manager and paying her off to drop the charges. But by the time he had been able to get back to Joss, the American and his whore had disappeared.

Panicked, he and Joss had checked Walker's hotel. Joss had taken aside one of the desk clerks and exchanged a few francs for information. No 'Walker' was registered at the hotel. The only American who had been in the house over the last three days had paid his bill this morning with a credit card issued in the name of Christopher Stone, the address a post-office box in West Virginia. The clerk, sensing that there was more money to be made, mentioned that M. Stone had made three calls which had been billed to his room, all to the same number in Rouen.

Dieter had called Brunner for instructions on the cellular. Brunner, furious, had told Dieter to get up to Rouen fast while he, Brunner, correlated the Rouen telephone number with an address. How Brunner was able to get the information in under forty minutes was a mystery, but he did, and called back on the cellular just as the van passed through Barentin, three kilometers west of Rouen. As it turned out, they had beaten Stone to Rouen by an hour, had checked the building out and were waiting when he arrived.

Joss eased back in the driver's seat, finished off the joint and snuffed it out in the ashtray. He suddenly sat upright and stared into the darkness. 'Here we go. He's headed for the alleyway. The stairs that lead up to the apartment are around on that side of the building.' He lit another joint but didn't offer to share it.

'So what do we do?'

'We just hang on for a while until they're settled in.'

Less than a minute had elapsed when another light in the apartment snapped on. There was the brief silhouette of a backlit woman approaching the window, then the blind was drawn.

'Probably the hallway. She's let him in and now they're going to have a cozy little fuck. That's it, Dieter. Get the Dutchman's canister out of the cargo compartment and set it up.'

'. . . under the Peugeot?'

'No. We'll get them both. The store's built out of wood. It'll go fast and we'll hang around just long enough to make sure they don't get out.'

'Brunner is not going to like this. His instructions were just to eliminate Stone.'

'Yeah, but Brunner's not here to make that decision, is he, Kraut-head?' Joss shot back. 'Stone is probably planning to stay for the night and that would leave us exposed to any cops cruising around. On top of that, Brunner wants us to meet him up in some town south of the Hook of Holland by tomorrow night with the stuff we got from Le Borveaux, so get with it. I'll monitor the cellular.'

Dieter flexed his shoulders, pulled on a jacket and opened the door. It was raining even harder and the droplets pelted off his scalp, trickling down his collar. Joss, the bastard, would of course stay dry in the van.

He kneeled on the puddled street and groped under the Toyota for the release handle. The van that Brunner had supplied had come equipped with a compartment built into the underside of the chassis – an optional extra not offered by Toyota dealers. On occasions like this, it came in useful.

The rain suddenly hardened, sleet mixing in, stinging his face. But Dieter didn't mind. He loved the warmth of a good fire.

In less than three minutes, Stone had turned down a rutted dirt road, overgrown on either side with dead weeds. A figure hooded in a foul-weather jacket stood next to a chain-link gate, a large dog quartering the weeds behind her, growling.

'Mr Stone?'

'The same. I decided to walk.'

'My name's Melissa van der Groot. I presume that you have identification?'

'My passport do?'

She swept the beam of a flashlight into his face. 'Toss it to me, then step back.' In the peripheral glow of the flashlight, Stone saw the shape of a 12-gauge Winchester pump-gun under her arm, casually held, in the manner of an experienced duck-hunter.

Satisfied after examining his identification, she motioned him to precede her. Down the road, then along a dirt path to a concrete quay. It fronted a small yacht basin. To the south-east, the basin joined what he supposed was the Seine, marked by the firefly blinks of navigational lights edging the main channel.

Tied up along the quay were the black silhouettes of moored vessels. She paused at a finger pier and motioned him past her, the dog between them, a rumble in his throat, overly protective.

'You first,' she said. 'Knock the dirt off your shoes and go below. Neither the dog nor I like sudden movements.'

He couldn't accurately estimate the vessel's length, but it was large, probably over fifty feet. Two spars thrust upwards into the blackness, a spider's web of rigging supporting them.

Once below, Stone was enveloped in the warmth of a coal stove and the smell of brewing chocolate. It was not a sterile production-plastic thing but built of wood, polished mahogany paneling reflecting back the soft glow of oil lamps. Stone, having only sailed on Maine work boats that reeked of gutted fish and dry rot, immediately recognized the craftsmanship that had gone into this vessel and the labor of love that was required to maintain it.

'Down,' she said, and Stone obediently sank onto a soft settee, not immediately realizing that she had commanded the dog.

She handed him a large mug of chocolate and placed a bottle of rum on the table in front of him. 'What I wrote in the letter is all I know. You've wasted your time, Mr Stone. I'd appreciate it if you'd be brief.'

Stone poured a slug of rum into the cocoa and leaned back against the cushions. Initially, he kept silent, carefully offering his hand to the dog who seemed suspicious but not particularly predisposed to take a hunk out of him. He glanced around. Bookshelves, a navigational desk, a compact galley, a large mahogany dining-table, Oriental throw-rugs on the cabin sole, gleaming brass portholes. 'I like your boat,' he said.

'My husband would not appreciate your calling his yacht a "boat", but that's beside the point. What do you need to know that you think I haven't already stated in my letter?' She stood in the galley, leaning against the counter, her face shrouded in shadows, sipping at her mug.

Very touchy, he thought. But obviously a dog lover. What was the salesman's creed? Something like 'Break the ice before you talk business'. 'What kind of mutt is he?'

'Airedale. His name is Sailor. He is not a mutt, Mr Stone.'

Touchy-touchy, he thought. The dog was dozing but his

eyes, under drooping lids, watched every one of Stone's movements.

He pulled a notebook from his briefcase and began to ask questions. Had she seen anyone suspicious around the neighborhood since the grad student's murder in Greece? A shake of the head. Had the grad student ever mentioned a man by the name of Roselli? She thought for a few seconds and said no, not to her knowledge. Did the grad student have any criminal record or was he a drug user?

She hesitated. 'I don't know. It was mainly Anna who dealt with him. You'll have to ask her.'

She shucked off the foul-weather jacket. She was dressed in jeans and a black polo-necked sweater. Her hair, a dark russet, was tied up in a bun but she loosened it, the strands cascading down beyond her shoulders.

Her face was not beautiful but, rather, strong, the nose prominent, her cheekbones high, her eyes widely spaced. Green, he thought. Either green or hazel. He wished the light were better. She caught him staring at her, then ignored his rudeness, completely self-contained, unflappable. Stone felt slightly off balance, intimidated by her cool beauty, his own ineptness.

He finally glanced back at her. She was adding more cocoa to her cup. Handsome, he thought. Not exactly what you'd call pretty. But with the unmistakable mark of good breeding, the English genes undoubtedly. In all, an intriguing lady. Her husband was a lucky man, and Stone momentarily wondered where he was on a bum night when he had *this* to come home to.

'Your husband?' he asked. 'Did he know the student?'

'Possibly. Jimmy occasionally stopped by on his research trips to drop off material or pick up his royalties. My husband, Pieter, might have met him but I doubt it. Pieter spent most of his time at sea.'

Odd, he thought. Past tense. 'Your husband be back soon?'

She shook her head but didn't elaborate.

Stone folded his notebook closed. Useless. She didn't know anything. 'This woman, Anna, your renter . . . do you think I could call her from here?' Stone had noticed a telephone on the galley counter. I ought to call Mac as well, he thought, but better to do it from a hotel where he'd have some privacy.

The woman shrugged again. 'Her telephone is disconnected. She's moving out tomorrow, so she's undoubtedly in her apartment packing. You could try knocking on her door. Whether she'll see you is up to her.' She pulled the jacket around her and zipped it up. 'I'll see you to the gate with Sailor. I apologize about the shotgun. It's just that one never knows these days . . .'

'I have to tell you something. I was in Le Havre earlier today. A man was following me. It's my guess he's connected with this floppy disk thing.'

'And where is he now?' Her voice was even, almost formal. Good control, he thought.

'He was arrested for shoplifting and he was carrying a gun. You could possibly be in danger.' Listening to his own words, he realized it took a leap of faith to connect the two. Actually, it sounded ridiculous, like dialogue out of a thirties detective flick.

She shrugged her shoulders slightly. 'I would sincerely doubt that, Mr Stone. I know nothing about any of this, other than what I wrote in the letter. Therefore, I represent no threat to anyone. If you think Anna is in danger, you should personally warn her.'

He considered it. 'She's probably okay for a couple of days, or at least until the guy gets out of the slammer.'

'By tomorrow, Anna will be gone. To Scandinavia, I think. She has friends there.'

Curious. 'Why she leaving?'

'She's the one who received the floppy in the mail and she's frightened of the possible consequences.'

Stone checked his watch. Just a little after 21.00. He'd be able to wrap this thing up in an hour. He'd seen a reasonable place to bunk down, the Hôtel Normandy, advertised at 130 francs, *douche* included. Even Mac would approve of that rate, *douche* or not.

They retraced their way up the path, the dog just behind Stone, occasionally nudging him in the leg with a stick, begging to play. At least I scored points with the pooch, he thought wearily.

Just short of the gate, he turned to thank her.

'Really appreciate . . .'

There was a tremendous flash which lit the skyline, then a second later the massive rumble of an explosion.

Initially, they hesitated, then both began to run toward the source of the explosion. By the time they hit the alley, her store was engulfed in flames, all the glass on both stories blown out, flames roaring, glass littering the street, burning books strewn helter-skelter.

'*Anna!*' she screamed, but he knew it was too late. The wooden structure was burning like a tinderbox, the outside stairwell to the second floor blown away, the raw stink of gasoline in the air. Stone grabbed her arm to pull her back but she twisted away and broke loose. She shouted back over her shoulder. '*Front of the store. There's a stairway inside! We've got to help her!*'

He started after her, yelling at her to stop. As he rounded the corner, he knew it was useless. The whole store front was engulfed in roiling, yellow-black clouds of smoke and flame, the heat searing.

Headlights flashed on from down the street, then tires squealed, a vehicle pulled out and accelerated hard. It flashed past, a light-colored van of some sort, then suddenly slammed on its brakes, nose-diving with the deceleration, then grinding into reverse and backing up. The side door on the passenger side slid open, the man in the passenger seat swinging a black shape toward them. Instinctively, Stone knew what was going to happen. He sprinted the few remaining yards and tackled her, both of them coming down hard on the glass-littered pavement as bullets ripped a swath of tracers above them. Gasping for breath, Stone rolled sideways, grabbing her shotgun, chambered a round, propped himself up on his elbows and pumped a round into the vehicle. Another burst of automatic weapon fire from the van, this time scarring the pavement, cement chips showering him, stinging his face.

Get it right this time, dummy! He adjusted his aim and fired three closely spaced shots. The vehicle lurched to a stop, gears grinding again, then leaped forward, careening off the curb, wiping out a bicycle stand, ricocheting off a parked Fiat, then stabilizing. It tore down the street, swaying drunkenly as it skidded into a side street, disappearing.

In the background, Stone could hear the two-tone warble of an emergency vehicle. Nothing he could do here and damned little point in getting involved with the gendarmerie, particularly being a foreign national in possession of a shotgun.

The store and the apartment above were a holocaust, timbers falling inward, walls collapsing. The heat was so intense that the paint on the rental Peugeot had started to burn and one tire was flat, probably punctured by a flying shard of glass. Shit, he thought. Didn't take out comprehensive insurance when I rented the damned thing. Mac will love that when the bill comes in.

He bent down, shielding his face from the heat, shaking her. 'We've got to get outta here!' She was still sprawled on the sidewalk apparently unconscious, her coat smoldering, the dog pawing at her, whining, its fur starting to singe. Stone hefted her in a fireman's carry and sprinted for the alleyway, the dog loping along beside him, its eyes wild.

He stopped at the other end of the alley and stripped off her smoldering jacket, then hoisted her again into a fireman's carry and headed for the river. She was moaning a little now, fighting him. Another block away, he veered off the road into a clump of trees and lowered her to the ground. She was groggy, a cut on her forehead, bleeding badly.

She touched her teeth with her tongue. 'Dammit – I chipped a tooth.'

He didn't think it was appropriate at this time to tell her that she might have been dead meat by now. 'Think you can walk? I'll give you a hand. We'll make better time that way.'

She nodded. '. . . Try.'

He checked the street. No sight of the van. 'How many people know that you live on a boat?'

'It's a yacht. A lot. Almost everyone in the neighborhood.'

'Can we move it somewhere – like for now?'

Nine minutes later, the fifty-one-foot ketch, *Night Watch*, was under way, first easing out of the Bassin St Gervais, then altering to starboard into the main channel, headed for the sea.

Once in the channel, she turned the helm over to him. 'I've got to get a compress on my forehead and stop the bleeding. You steer. Keep the red lights in the channel on your right side and don't bump into anything. I haven't turned on the running lights so be extra careful.' She disappeared down the hatch.

It was still raining, mixed with the occasional splatter of sleet. Mist hung on the river, cutting visibility to a couple of boat lengths, and the wind quartered over the bow, chilling his body. He felt like hell, but by his guesstimate they'd be in the English Channel and headed for England by mid-morning, and that suited him just fine. He leaned down and edged the throttle forward a notch, the engine picking up the beat by a couple of hundred revs.

She was up on deck in seconds, jumped into the cockpit and yanked back on the throttle. 'I didn't tell you to increase revs, you idiot! The oil-pan gasket leaks and I don't have any more oil on board. It'll seize up if you run it hard.'

'Okay, okay! So what do we do for oil?'

'I know of a place about three hours downriver. It's a shallow canal that T's off from the Seine. The canal used to service a bulk cement plant but someone recently told me that the place is now abandoned. From there, it's a half-hour walk into Duclair. There are a couple of garages there.' She glanced over the side at a passing lighted buoy. 'We've got the tide with us. Should be there by early morning.'

She started for the hatch, then turned. 'I'm sorry, Mr Stone. I didn't mean to shrill at you like an old bitch. You saved my life. Just hang on for ten more minutes. I'll toss you up a set of oilskins, get some coffee going and then take over the helm.'

He took it as an apology.

It was 02.41 when she put the helm over, moving out of the main shipping channel and into a narrow backwater canal. In the glow of the spotlight, he could see that the banks were overgrown with brush and a few scrawny trees. The air stank of industrial waste. She threw the gear shift into neutral and edged into the bank. The ketch lost way and grounded in soft mud.

Stone threw mooring lines ashore and took a flying leap, but his bum leg betrayed him. He almost made the bank but instead landed in shin-deep muck, swearing. He tied up the lines to stunted trees and waded back out, climbing up the dolphin striker. She gave him a hand up.

They stood side by side for a few minutes, letting their nerves wind down. She handed him a cup of cocoa.

'Anna's dead, isn't she?' she said, her voice flat.

He nodded. 'Probably.' Not probably – for sure. No one could have lived through that inferno.

'Was it me they were after?' she asked softly.

'No,' Stone replied. 'More likely me. At any rate, we're safe for now.'

'I think not. Whoever it was will check and find out that the yacht's missing, then start searching. Not upriver because Rouen has a low bridge which we couldn't possibly get under because of the masts. No, they'll start at Rouen and work their way downriver either by car or by boat – that's the way I'd do it if I were them. We've got to get out of here no later than tomorrow night and make a run for the sea.'

'The police . . .'

'I wouldn't count on the police, Mr Stone. I seem to remember you using the shotgun – an idiotic pastime common enough in your country but very much frowned upon in France. You're a foreign national, as I am. And even if they believed us, which is doubtful, how long could they protect us? The sea is seventy-three kilometers from here, about an eight-hour run. You're welcome to stay, but I'm leaving France.'

It seemed like a good idea to Stone.

'We better set a watch tonight just in case . . .' he said.

She nodded, then turned to him. 'Tell me – how good are you with a needle, Mr Stone?'

'I've been known to sew on a button or two.'

She led the way below, then took off the compress. It was a deep gash just at the hairline but it had clean edges. She had already blotted most of the blood away but the wound was oozing, not something that would heal without sutures. A sail needle lay on the galley counter, already threaded.

'You're going to have to do it,' she said. 'Just please try to make the stitches neat.'

The remains of a bottle of rum stood on the counter. He slid it toward her. 'Bottoms up.'

She pushed it away. 'This is going to hurt bad enough in the morning. I don't need a hangover on top of it.'

Stone sutured her wound. She gritted her teeth, tears flowing down her cheeks, but she didn't flinch or make a sound. *Tough*, he thought, tough as nails, tough enough to break your heart.

He finished off the last stitch, knotted it and cut the thread with her nail scissors. 'I'll take the first watch.'

'Not necessary.' She snapped her fingers. 'Sailor,' she softly commanded. *'Anchor watch!'* The dog grunted his displeasure but climbed the companionway.

'He'll freeze out there,' Stone said.

'He was born in Wales, Mr Stone,' she said, as if that explained it. She went to her cabin and closed the door.

Stone took a shot from the rum, then stretched out on the salon's settee, pulling a blanket over him. Above him on deck, he could hear the dog pacing, then pausing occasionally to shake his coat. 'Better you than me, buddy,' he thought, fading out.

07.00, 4 April

Stone woke to weak sunlight shining through the porthole and the nudge of the Airedale's nose sniffing at his stockinged feet. There was the smell of coffee brewing, the hiss of eggs frying in fat. He was still groggy but edged into a sitting position.

Her forehead was swollen slightly, her eye blackened. She smiled at him, displaying a chipped tooth, and handed him a mug of coffee. Turning, she reached up to an overhead locker on tiptoe to retrieve another mug, placing her body in profile. Stone swallowed hard. Unbelievable knockers, a gently swelling butt and legs that went on forever. She was dressed in paint-splattered jeans and a white polo-necked shirt – obviously no bra needed. He felt suddenly a bit dirty, as if he were one of those wine-swilling man-goats who had peeked through the branches primeval to catch a naked young nymph sunning.

Then he remembered her husband. Which made her unavailable unless he chose to be a cad and work his dubious magic on her – naughty but not absolutely unthinkable.

The coffee was terrific and he sipped at it, trying to put the situation in perspective, yet involuntarily he kept returning his thoughts to the woman.

Obviously independent as hell and with a will of iron, he thought. And undoubtedly, with my luck, not the sort of woman to cheat on her husband. Superimposing her personality over all the women he had known, he couldn't make a match. He decided he'd like her, even if she was a man. It was just that the hormones were different and that complicated things.

'You're rather quiet this morning,' she said. She was standing over him.

He looked up. She put a plate of fried eggs cushioned by buttered toast in front of him. The dog came smartly to attention, drooling.

'Lot to absorb.' He speared an egg, letting the yoke hemorrhage into the toast, the way he liked it. 'How about your husband? He'll be frantic.'

'I don't think so.'

She had said it casually, as if she was sure. Divorced? he wondered.

She sat down on the edge of the table and stirred her coffee. 'I listened to the local morning newscast on my Walkman. They said that my shop was probably destroyed by an explosion and arson was suspected. It seems traces of gasoline were detected. The remains of one person have been found and they're trying to identify the body although the police think I'm the victim.'

'The problem is, somebody else knows different.'

She nodded. 'But why did they do it?'

'I'm pretty sure that it was me they were after. They thought I was in the building. Nothing else makes sense, Ms van der Groot.'

'Melissa will do. What's your Christian name, Mr Stone?'

'Christopher. My father named me after his favorite saint. Good karma, I suppose, but I can't stand the name. I keep thinking of all those millions of medals on chains hanging from rear-view mirrors. Everyone calls me Stone.'

'Sounds cold.'

'Never thought about it like that. How 'bout *solid*, as in the rock of Gibraltar.' He pumped a flaccid biceps.

She favored him with a subdued smile. 'Or "He built better than he knew, the conscious stone to beauty grew." Ralph Waldo Emerson. Are you growing beautiful, Stone?'

He grinned. 'Not last time I looked.'

She studied his face. 'Plain but definitely not beautiful. Certainly not ugly. 'Twixt and between.'

'But you are. Beautiful, I mean,' he said solemnly.

Her smile evaporated and she turned away from him, studying the fields beyond, then said, 'I'm off for town. To get some engine oil and food. Are you good with tools?'

'Fair to middling. What needs to be done?'

'The oil pan. The gasket's leaking. If we run the engine at more than 1200 revs, the oil leaks out in bucketloads. As you've seen, 1200 revs doesn't push *Night Watch* at much more than four knots, and we'll need all the speed we can to stem the incoming tide tonight. I don't have a new gasket but I bought some goo that's supposed to turn into a gasket. The tools and the goo are stored under the quarter-berth.'

'I'll give it a go.'

'Anything you need from town?'

'How's the rum supply doing?'

'You drink a lot, don't you?'

'Not so you'd notice.' It didn't sound convincing.

She studied him for a few seconds, then nodded.

The dog went with her. Stone watched as the two of them, gazelle-like, effortlessly made the leap from deck to dry ground.

She's trying to humble me, he thought. And doing a damned fine job of it.

The builders of *Night Watch* had contrived to place the diesel engine in the most inaccessible part of the bilge. Stone had to lie on his back, his head lower than his feet, head wedged under the oil pan, a flashlight in his mouth.

It took him an hour to remove the pan and clean off the old gasket and another hour to replace the pan and torque in the bolts. He assumed that the gasket goo would work because the surplus stuff that squeezed out between the mated parts had set up like gum rubber in his hair, impenetrable to a comb. He cut off the matted hair with her scissors and checked the results. The mirror reflected back the image of a jaded, oil-smeared, shaggy-haired Oliver Twist with bags under his eyes.

Swaddling his feet in paper towels to prevent oiling the rugs, he tip-toed forward. There was a shower compartment adjacent to her stateroom. Shivering, he stripped down, lathered up with a jug of laundry detergent and turned on the hot water tap. A couple of drops of frigid water dribbled on his scalp. Stone swore, working through most of his vocabulary.

The door to the shower suddenly swung open, Melissa standing there, studying him, her face expressionless. The dog looked on from between her legs, a neutral but interested observer.

'I forgot to tell you,' she said. 'The electric pump doesn't work.'

Stone had crouched down, hands crossed over his vital parts.

'Really, Stone, I can't believe you're blushing. Stay right there and I'll heat up some water. The galley's supplied by a hand pump. It'll take some time so just be patient.' She closed the door gently.

From behind the door she asked, 'Does the cold temperature make it shrink or is that your regular size?'

Stone swore again, with feeling.

They had taken turns monitoring the river through the rest of the afternoon, the one off watch sleeping. River traffic seemed light – the usual coal barges, an occasional freighter, a few fishing trawlers, but nothing suspicious. Just before getting under way, Melissa had called on the ship's VHF marine radio to a friend, a retired English businessman, whose houseboat was tied up in the marina where *Night Watch* had been moored.

'He's an old reprobate,' she told Stone. 'Calls himself "the Viscount", but all he ever did was broker London bus tours for tourists. That and collect stray cats. Has nineteen of them, and you wouldn't want to stand downwind of his houseboat. Still, he's an old dear and one of the few people I trust.'

The Viscount had responded almost immediately, as if he had been expecting her call. They switched to another frequency in order to avoid being overheard by the casual listener.

Dear me, no, he told her. The police hadn't checked the marina yet, but two other men had, asking the marina manager, Albert, about her whereabouts. No, m'dear, of course he hadn't spoken to those *horrid* men. *Thugs*, he said, and repeated himself twice, savoring the word. 'Oh yes, one other thing,' the Viscount said, his voice wavering. 'They bought a copy of *Navicarte One* by Editions Cartographiques Maritimes from the marina office. You understand my drift?'

Stone had raised his eyebrows.

She signed off with the Viscount, then switched the unit to the deck speaker. 'He's referring to the chart of the Seine River, from Paris to Le Havre. Which means they'll be looking for us in a vessel of some sort. Let's get under way.'

Just after sundown, she backed the *Night Watch* off the mud, swung the wheel over and reversed course, then bumped the gear-shift selector into forward and nudged out into the main channel. Turning downriver, she kept the revs low, *Night Watch* just noodling along at a crawl.

He leaned down to look at the instrument panel. 'Oil pressure's good.' He had already checked the oil pan for leakage and had seen none. 'You can push up the speed a bit.'

'Look behind us.'

He did. A large tugboat with three garbage barges in tow was plowing a deep furrow in the muddy waters, overtaking them.

'We'll let him pass us, then fall in behind and stick close with our running lights off. Be difficult for anyone to spot us at night, coupled with the fact that our friend is running interference for us.'

Brains as well as beauty, he thought.

Sometime after 21.00, she went below and returned with some food and a bottle of mineral water.

She had heated up a pot of chili from the freezer. In the cockpit, they shared it, mopping up the remains with hunks of bread torn off a baguette.

Stone had a powerful thirst. 'You get any rum in town to go with this Frog water?'

She shook her head. 'I want you sober, Stone. You can get as drunk as you want when we reach England.'

Bitch, he swore to himself. The inner man groaned in sympathy.

They had been motoring for more than two hours and were keeping up with the tug *Orion* but just barely, the *Night Watch*'s engine pounding out maximum revs. Stone had been monitoring the engine instruments, concerned because the engine-cooling water temperature had started to creep up. He looked down once again and saw the gauge's needle now solidly in the red caution zone.

'I've already noticed it,' she said. 'We've got to ease off on the power.'

'We'll never catch up.'

'I hate it when people state the obvious, Stone, don't you? Of course we won't catch up. We'll cool off the engine and wait for the next vessel that's headed for the sea. There's no other option, is there?'

She retarded the throttle and edged over toward the bank of the river. The *Night Watch* slowed to a crawl. Based on the strength of the incoming tide, Stone estimated that they were actually losing ground, slowly being pushed back upriver.

A few minutes later, she bent down and checked the water temperature gauge again. 'It's not cooling down!'

The engine was running rough and Stone could smell the scent of burned oil from the engine's exhaust. 'I'll check it. Maybe the water-pump belt's slipping.'

He cursed himself for not checking before. Mooning around with this woman, playing Fletcher Christian to her Bligh. He grabbed a flashlight from the rack in the companionway and lurched aft.

The engine was in a compartment aft of the galley. He removed the panel, exposing the rusting beast.

Christ, it was hot! He ran the beam of the flashlight over the block, then aimed it down toward the sump. The beam of the light was clouded by a fine black mist. He realized he had just struck oil, the stuff blowing out between the pan and the block, the bilge sloshing with Texaco Premium 10W-40, nearly all ten quarts of it, the stuff that he had added just a few hours ago.

He back-pedaled into the galley and found the container that held the measly three quarts of oil that he had scavenged from the morning's operation. Back in the engine room, he grabbed the oil filler-cap, burned his hand, found a rag, then twisted it off. He slowly added the old oil on the theory that a transfusion, even a small one, would prolong the patient's life.

But it was too late. The diesel engine, a machine which Stone calculated had first seen light thirty years ago, grunted, loped a few more reluctant revs, then died. It was very quiet now. Almost peaceful.

He sighed, sucked on the burn and climbed back up the companionway. 'The gasket material didn't hold. Most of the oil blew out. We're screwed.'

'Plan B,' she said, her voice steady.

'Which is . . . ?'

'We sail. We can't make the sea, not with the direction

of the wind and against an incoming tide. We've got to head back upriver. My hus . . .' She hesitated, then started again. 'My husband was good friends with a retired Seine River pilot, a Monsieur Perocette. He has a small home on the River Rancon, just past the high bridge we went under thirty minutes ago. The Rancon is shallow but I think we can make it. Monsieur Perocette has a wharf we can tie up to and it's out of direct view of anyone on the Seine. Perhaps you'll be able to repair the engine properly this time.'

Smarting from the insult but keeping silent, he helped her get the mainsail up, then the jib. The ketch heeled slightly as she spun the wheel over, the sails luffing, then filling with a *whump*. Steadying on, the *Night Watch*'s wake gurgled contentedly, now in her element.

He sat down on the coachroof, disgruntled. It was an all-American boy's wet dream: on board a go-anywhere classic yacht and alone with a thoroughly desirable woman. Except she was a fucking power-mad tyrant and they were headed the wrong damned way.

'Stone,' she said softly from behind him. 'I apologize. You did your best — it's just my nerves. You'll find the bottle of rum under my bunk. Make one for me as well.'

He smiled.

EIGHT

Shortly after midnight, they picked up the leading lights
to the River Rancon. Stone went below and dipsticked the
engine – halfway between the *add oil* and *empty* marks –
then returned to the cockpit and twisted the ignition key.
The engine balked at first, rumbled through a few turns
and started.

The oil-pressure gauge jittered, then stabilized on the
low end of the scale. 'Should be enough oil in the sump
for about ten minutes' running at minimum revs,' he cau-
tioned her.

She nodded without comment, her face lit from the glow
of the binnacle light, her features intent as she maneuvered
through the narrow entrance.

They edged up the river, but in reality it was not much
more than a sluggish stream hemmed in with stone walls
on either side, less than thirty meters wide. Stone swept
the spotlight in arcs. Set back from the banks were gingerbread cottages, most likely the summer retreats of the
French *bourgeoisie*, most of them undoubtedly boarded up
during the winter months. Still, the little clutch of cottages
had a nice feel to it; a place of summer dreams and lazy
days.

The fifth cottage on the starboard side was slightly larger
than the rest with a rickety but usable dock fronting the
river. The yard was bordered with bushes, carefully tended.
A massive ship's anchor was firmly planted in the center
of the yard, its chain leading to the columns that supported

the porch. Obviously, the home of a retired seaman who, as the saying went, had swallowed the anchor.

As confirmation that it was Perocette's place, two whip antennas sprouted from the roof, undoubtedly connected to a VHF so that Perocette could keep in contact with his still-active river buddies.

She nudged *Night Watch* alongside the dock and Stone secured the lines. The cottage remained dark.

'It doesn't seem as if we woke him up. I'll go in and talk with him in the morning,' she said.

'Think it's safe here?'

She exhaled tiredly. ' "Safe" is a relative word. We can't be seen from the river, but at this time of year there aren't too many yachts moving about. Eventually, word's likely to get out.'

Stone checked his watch and sighed. 'I'd better start pulling the sump pan off.'

She shook her head. 'It's not exactly brain surgery, is it? I think the gasket material blew out because we couldn't give it enough time to allow it to set up properly. I'll remove the sump pan and clean off the muck tonight. You can bolt it back together in the morning. That will give it twelve hours to set up before we leave tomorrow evening.'

Nice of her to offer, sort of a back-door apology for her previous comments about his mechanical prowess. But it was a man's job. 'I'll do it, Melissa. It's a filthy job.'

Her voice was more relaxed now, unwinding. 'And if I do, then you'll just have to help me scrub up.' She bent down and kissed him lightly on the forehead. 'Get some sleep, Stone, and give your manhood a rest. I'll be just fine.'

There was mist on the river, but overhead the stars were hard points of light, dazzling in their seeming proximity, yet remote as eternity.

He had to take a shot at it, to understand what the rules were and how the game was to be played. 'Melissa, there's something I have to know. It's not my business, but where's your husband?'

She didn't look at him, just absently stared off into the night. 'He was the first officer on a liquid propane tanker. The ship blew up in the South China Sea four years ago. It's not something I can talk about – not to you, not to anyone.'

'I'm sorry,' he said softly, but deep down inside where his lonely heart lurked, there was a spark.

He woke at first light to a muzzy-gray dawn. The mist had become fog and condensation ran in rivulets down the portholes.

Her stateroom door was closed and an oil-stained boiler suit lay discarded on the cabin sole.

The dog was sound asleep on the quarter berth, obviously no longer on anchor watch. Stone ruffled his head. The dog opened one eyelid, thumped his tail twice, stretched, then slid back into dreamland where the squirrels were clumsy, the cats were slow, and sirloin was the common currency. His paws began to twitch.

Stone stoked the stove and added coal, then dressed. Sliding back the hatch, he checked first for signs of life in the cottage. A single light burned in what looked to be the kitchen and he could hear the faint strains of someone singing *Don Giovanni*. He walked through the wet grass and rapped on the door.

Through the windowpane, Stone could see a heavy-set man in a bathrobe and slippers, a river pilot's cap cocked to one side on his head, a cigarette that was mostly ash dangling from his lips, presumably Monsieur Perocette.

Startled at the sound, the man wheeled, pushed the cap back on his head and shuffled to the door. He threw off a chain and opened it, his face initially puzzled, then looked beyond Stone to where the *Night Watch* was tied up. His eyebrows knitted together, face flushing, mouth twisting, eyes bulging.

'*Qu'est-ce que vous foutez ici? Je ne vous ai pas permis d'utiliser ce quai. Foutez-moi le camp. Tout de suite. Je ne veux pas voir votre bateaux ici!*'

Stone had to step back, Perocette's spittle spraying his face. 'Hey — take it easy.' Stone made calming gestures with his hands. 'We got in late last night. Didn't want to wake you up.'

Perocette's head cocked to the side, the eyebrows knitting together even more tightly, the chin jutting out, lower lip protruding beyond the upper, teeth actually gnashing.

'Ameri-*can*?'

Stone smiled weakly.

Perocette lifted his arm, hand extended, finger pointing rigidly toward the far horizon, the whole apparatus quivering with rage. 'OUT. OUT, OUT, OUT!'

'But I . . .'

'OUT. NOW!' The door slammed in Stone's face, the glass rattling.

He slunk back to the yacht.

She was up, her body wrapped in a blanket, standing at the foot of the companionway. Her nose had a smudge of oil on it which she had missed. 'I could hear the shouting from here. What's the problem?'

'I don't think he likes Ameri-*cans*. He wants us to move.'

She shook her head slowly, then pushed back the strand of hair that had fallen over her forehead. 'You should have waited for me to handle it. Pieter told me that Perocette was an officer in the French Navy back in World War II. The American fleet shelled the French Navy at Oran. Perocette's ship was sunk, some of his friends killed. He doesn't like Americans.'

'Obviously.' That seemed to go for most Frenchmen he had met, so Stone wasn't particularly offended. It was just the general principle, now that the New World Order had arrived and all men were supposed to be New Age sensitive asshole buddies.

'I'll go up and talk to him,' she said. 'Help yourself to

159

some coffee first and, after that, the oil pan's ready to bolt back on. Goo's on the workbench. Fair enough?'

'Okay. But see whether Perocette will let me use his phone for a long-distance call to England. I've got to get in contact with the man I work for and let him know what's going on.'

'I'll try.' She refilled her coffee mug and drank it down quickly. 'Time to climb into my armor and go do battle with the dragon.' She swirled her blanket like a bolero and swished back into her stateroom, closing the door behind her.

Stone was on his fourth cup of coffee when she opened her stateroom door.

She had done her hair in a French twist and applied make-up.

She wore a cream-colored silk shirt and form-fitting slacks that looked as if they had been sprayed on. Not exactly suitable for early April but the effect was ravishing.

'You don't think you're overdoing it?'

She favored him with a devastating smile. 'Would you turn a perfect body like this away from your door?'

'You got a point there,' he said, trying to keep his eyes above her neck level.

She must have noticed it. 'There's hope for you yet, Stone,' she teased, then threw on a raincoat and was gone.

The sump pan wasn't any easier to install than the first time, but he finished up shortly after eleven. As an afterthought, he tracked down the fresh-water pump and tore it apart. The neoprene pump diaphragm had a tear in it. In the parts locker, he found a replacement and installed it, then switched on the pump's circuit breaker. This time, the shower worked and, although not up to Stone's American standards of near-scalding, the water was warm enough to shower with.

Through the afternoon, he puttered around, cleaning up the yacht. Occasionally, he glanced through the porthole. There were lights on in Perocette's cottage and the faint strains of opera from a hi-fi. So she had worked her magic, he thought, not a little jealous. He resumed puttering, fortified by cups of cocoa, supplemented with blasts from the rum bottle.

Night Watch was elegant but she was old, probably built shortly after World War II, he figured. Conventional layout for that era. The companionway was a simple teak ladder, leading down from the cockpit into the main cabin. Galley to port, navigational desk to starboard with the pilot berth aft of that. A U-shaped settee wrapped around a mahogany dining-table took up the rest of the space.

Melissa's cabin was just forward of the main cabin and connected to a head compartment where the shower, wash basin and head were located.

Stone hadn't been any further forward and now he explored — a guest cabin on the starboard side, two bunks, one over the other, the place musty and unused. And forward of that was the fo'c'sle. He pushed open the door, expecting the usual sail bins and anchor-chain locker.

Instead it was a workroom of sorts; a bench with a vice bolted to it on the starboard side, fitted out with a few simple machine tools and a small diesel generator. On the port side, another bench with scuba-diving bottles beneath it, secured in brackets, and an assortment of diving gear neatly stowed in bins above the bench.

Tacked on the bulkhead was a color photograph. Stone looked closer. A couple; Melissa in a stark white swimsuit, ridiculously large sunglasses and floppy straw hat, her face thrown back to the sun, mouth open, laughing, as if she had been surprised by the photographer.

Her arm was stretched out, her fingers trailing gently along a man's shoulder, the intimacy almost unbearable to Stone.

The man was fair-haired, the color bleached out by the sun. He wore a quizzical grin, his lips forming a question. His face was unremarkable but the blue eyes were somehow arresting, a certain patience in their depths, the kind of man Stone instinctively knew he would like.

He tentatively touched the photograph as if it somehow held the answer, yet he knew it didn't. The unanswerable question was: how could he compete with a dead man whose goodness was frozen in time but whose faults had long vanished in the South China Sea?

She came traipsing back late afternoon, a little tipsy, a pink wine stain on her blouse, her lipstick smudged.

'Honestly, Stone. He's a *mar-vel-ous* man. Pieter said he was a gem, but you just can't believe . . .' She hiccuped twice, held her breath and made a stern face, trying to suppress her breath, then hiccuped again and burst into laughter.

'The engine's fixed. Did you get the oil?' Stone was petulant; the keeper of the flame, the loyal vassal, the worker-drone guarding the hive while the queen bee had gone cavorting.

'Oh, *Stone*, lighten up. Of *course* I've got the oil. We drove into St Wandrille after lunch. A whole case. It's in the boot of his motor car.'

'I better get it if we're going to get going by dark.'

'Can't,' she said. 'I'm having din-dins with him. By the way, he said you could make your call as long as it doesn't exceed three minutes. He's got this egg-timer thing shaped like Mae West.' She giggled, then bent down and ruffled the dog's fur.

He lost it. '*Dammit!* Do you even vaguely recall that someone tried to blow us to hell and they're undoubtedly looking for us this very minute?'

She gave him a look that royalty generally reserves for the peasants. 'Really, Stone. You're so *impenetrable*. Perocette has it all worked out. He contacted a friend of his on the radio, a Seine River pilot who's piloting some dumpy little freighter that's headed for Denmark. Once it reaches the entrance of the Seine tonight, Perocette's friend transfers to a pilot boat, heads back to Le Havre and then takes the train up to Rouen. Tomorrow afternoon, he'll be piloting an ocean-going tug towing this *gigantic* dredge owned by the Dutch government. We just have to wait until the thing's abeam the River Rancon and nose out. There's a notched-out place at the stern of the dredge where they normally tie up some sort of a work boat and we'll be able to wedge in there, completely out of sight except for the mast. The dredge has a crew of twenty-two Dutch seamen so we'll be safe.'

'Perocette contacted the pilot on the radio? Why in hell didn't he just take out a full-page ad in the *Terrorist Gazette*? These guys aren't stupid. They'll be monitoring the radio.' Stone was shouting, totally out of control.

She set her lips tightly, trying to control her anger. Then, in a steady, measured voice, 'The river pilots have a special radio channel reserved for them only. It's not even authorized for installation in commercial VHF radios. He told me that the frequency is absolutely secure.'

She picked up the bottle of rum and sloshed the remaining dregs from side to side. There wasn't enough left to float a flea.

'If you want something to eat for dinner, you've got a choice between tinned steak and kidney pie or beef stew. If you want something to *drink* other than coffee, which I highly recommend, there's instant lemonade in the dry locker.' She set the rum bottle down on the counter a little too firmly and went to her cabin.

The dog looked up at Stone, his head cocked, undecided as to where his loyalties lay, then followed Melissa.

Blew it again, thought Stone.

He took a walk in the late afternoon along the River Rancon, the fields beyond Perocette's cottage unkempt. Not much more than 500 meters inland, the river petered out into cat-tailed shallows and mudbanks. The mighty River Rancon, he thought. Somehow, he had hoped it would offer an escape route from the Seine, but like most other things in his life it was a dead end.

The afternoon's sky was clear but high cirrus feathered toward the north-west, a sign of heavy weather coming. The thought of having to beat across the Channel into a gale made him wince.

What the hell am I doing here? he wondered. Alone, he could have worked his way north into Brussels and slipped over to England on a ferry. But trying to get the *Night Watch* out of France meant having to get through a bottle-neck passage at the entrance to the Seine – the *Chenal de Rouen* – less than a thousand meters wide. Even with the protection of the dredge, anyone monitoring the river would be able to spot the mast, conclude that it was stepped on the deck of a yacht, and take appropriate and somewhat messy measures.

Okay – it comes down to the fact that I've involved her and, therefore, I'm damned well responsible for her. He tried that one on for size but it didn't fit because it was just partially the truth. The real reason was that she was unique – the kind of woman he had searched for all his life, yet never found.

Stone checked his watch. Just after 19.00, the appointed hour. The dog had finished doing his thing in the fields. Stone whistled him back and headed for Perocette's cottage.

The door was unlocked. He entered the kitchen, embraced by the smells of a succulent pork loin roasting in the oven. A wine sauce simmered on the stove's back burner. A plate of partially eaten pâté and cheese rested on the work counter, a salad with endives and anchovies next to it, ready for presentation. His mouth watered.

Noises from the next room. He checked the dining-room, inching open the partially closed door.

Perocette was wearing a French naval officer's mess dress uniform, elegantly tailored to contain his gut, and at this moment was lifting a fluted champagne glass to a stunning Melissa, outfitted in a simple but elegant green silk sheath. She was laughing at something he had just said. They had just finished off a pastel-tinted sherbet. Although they must have heard him, they didn't bother to turn their heads. Stone felt like a scullery maid caught snooping and edged the door closed.

The egg timer was pointedly positioned next to the telephone. He scooped up the remaining wedges of cheese and gnawed on them while dialing Mac's number. As an afterthought, he flipped the egg timer.

Mac's Ramsgate number rang four times in the distinctive double buzz, then was picked up by an answering machine. A fruity voice identified the number as belonging to Highgate Engineering.

Irritated, Stone started to leave a message, but Mac came on the line before he had finished the first sentence.

'Sorry for the delay, lad. Had trouble getting the lines installed, some kind of a strike by the British Telecom workers. Where are you?'

'Still in France but planning to come across the Channel tomorrow night. Should be in Ramsgate by sun-up Thursday. I'm with the van der Groot woman on her boat . . . ah, yacht.'

There was a long silence at Macleod's end. Then, 'I believe I heard correctly that you're with Simmons' daughter on her yacht. I presume that you're having a nice time of it.'

'It's not exactly the way you think, Mac.' He looked down at the egg timer – a third of the sand already gone.

There were a couple of faint clicks on the line. 'Mac, you still there?'

'I'm here. Those clicks have happened twice before but my people assure me that the line's not tapped. Is someone listening to the extension on your end?'

'Not that I know of but it's possible. I'd better keep this brief. I checked out the firm in Le Havre. They stonewalled me but I found out about a guy who had worked for them back in the seventies. I tracked down where he lived but he was gone – most likely kidnapped. All the records that he had on the GEM were also missing but his wife said that he had microfilmed the drilling logs because of potential litigation and she was quite sure that the boreholes had been left ungrouted.'

'Did she have any idea of the borehole locations?'

'No – just that they were roughly aligned with the Chunnel's present path.'

'What was this man's name?'

'Le Borveaux. See whether your people can get together with the French police on his whereabouts. Other than that, nothing else.'

The last grains of sand had run out. Like magic, Perocette pushed open the dining-room door and glared at Stone, tapping his wrist.

'Mac – I've got to hang up. Monitor VHF Channel 16 starting tomorrow evening. When I'm in range, I'll give you a call. It's possible that I might need your help.'

'I'll do that. Take care, Stone.' The line went dead.

Perocette glowered at him, then slammed the dining-room door closed. Stone grabbed the remains of the pâté and slunk back to the *Night Watch*.

He was too tired to mess around with waiting for the oven to heat up so he opened a can of baked beans and ate them cold. The tin of instant lemonade had pointedly been left on the counter. He ignored it but found a half-empty bottle of red cooking wine wedged behind a sack of potatoes in the vegetable locker. Any port in a storm, although the stuff tasted more like Burgundy. He finished it off, the wine yielding a nice little buzz, making him sleepy.

After adding coal to the stove, he damped it down and pulled a blanket from the overhead rack. The dog was stretched out on the settee Stone had been sleeping on. Stone tested the quarter berth and found it saturated with dampness from a deck leak in the overhead, explaining the dog's migration from his favored pad.

'Sailor,' he softly commanded. The dog lifted his head, ears flopping forward, alert. *'Anchor watch!'*

The dog considered it for a second, grunted and dropped his head back onto the berth, eyes closing.

Stone, now thoroughly cheesed off, started to pull at the dog's leg, trying to pry him off the settee. The dog growled, a low rumble originating deep down in his gut.

'Nice boy.' Stone gritted his teeth and patted the animal. The dog relaxed, thumped his tail twice and closed his eyes again.

The lower bunk in the guest cabin was lumpy and smelled of mold but he finally drifted off.

Sometime in the night, he sensed someone standing over him. The shotgun was on the cabin floor next to his trailing fingertips and he tensed, then smelled her perfume. She bent down and tucked the blanket under his feet. He reached up to take her hand but she gently pulled it away, then headed aft toward her own cabin, softly pulling the latch closed. Stone heard her turn the key in the lock, the sound of it hollow in the stillness.

Joss turned up the gain control of the Sony ICF Pro 80 scanner, trying to hear over the muffled roar of the sport fishing boat's engines. The scanner was a state-of-the-art handheld receiver, capable of sweeping all frequencies from the AM broadcast bands up to 216 megahertz, including the police, marine, aircraft, weather and business bands. Joss had it locked on to the marine VHF band with the priority scan set on Channel 11, the Seine River pilot service's secure frequency.

He both loved and hated the thing. Loved it, because it gave him the ability to monitor damn near anything that went out over the air, a useful thing in his profession. Hated it, because it took a genius with a PhD in astrophysics to operate it, which he damned well wasn't.

Brunner had actually made him study the manual, then demonstrate that he knew how to operate it. German efficiency, undoubtedly. Apparently came with the genes.

A self-propelled barge loaded with containers passed in the opposite direction, probably heading upriver for Paris. Joss countered the barge's wake with a twist of the wheel, then steadied back on course.

Grudgingly, he had to admire Brunner's thoroughness. Brunner believed with a passion in the power of communications, claimed that the edge went not to the quick but to the informed. He had equipped each member of the land-based team with both the same model of Sony scanner and a handheld cellular telephone, specially fitted with a scrambler. Joss figured that all they needed now were Captain Midnight Secret Decoder rings. Brunner hadn't laughed at that one.

At first, Joss had sneered at the idea of space-age electronic terrorism. His operating concept was that you went out and *did* the job, unburdened by communication schedules, replacement batteries, rude operators or indecipherable operating manuals. But now, he saw it differently.

He glanced at the Sony which was propped up on the instrument console. The scanner's digital readout repeatedly flashed through a sequence of channels, pausing only when a frequency was in use. It slurred through an exchange between two offshore trawlers working the Banc de Seine, a lock-keeper harassing a Dutch motor barge, then back to a river pilot calling Honfleur radar control for a reading on upstream-bound traffic. But there was nothing more from the pilot on *Le Champe*, the little freighter headed for Denmark which Joss had been shadowing for over nine hours.

Actually, it had been Turner who picked up the exchange this morning between a land-based station run by a man who identified himself as 'Maurice' and the river pilot of *Le Champe*. Turner had been listening for any transmission from the van der Groot woman's yacht, the *Night*

Watch, but had made the connection once the word 'sailboat' had been mentioned. From then on, it began to fall into place. 'Maurice' was careful not to identify himself or give away his land-based location, but it was obvious that Maurice's buddy, the pilot of *Le Champe*, knew where Maurice was transmitting from and, therefore, it was the pilot of *Le Champe* that Joss had to get hold of, the missing piece of the puzzle.

His back was aching from concentrating on holding course, and it would be a long night. He decided that he'd get some coffee from the galley. He clapped Dieter on the shoulder. 'I'm going below for a minute. You got it.'

Dieter slid down from the upholstered stool next to Joss and took over the helm. He wasn't skilled at steering the Bertram but he was good enough, as long as he didn't have to manipulate the throttles. Dieter seemed to believe that a throttle had only two positions – idle and flat-out.

'We're too far back,' Dieter said, predictably, his hand reaching for the throttle quadrant.

Joss rapped Dieter's hand. 'We're equally matched in speed with *Le Champe*, just the way I want it. Move that throttle and I'll break your back.'

Dieter stiffened slightly, then relaxed. 'I was making a joke, Joss. You know my ways.'

'I know your ways,' Joss agreed. 'Too damn well.' He paused and checked *Le Champe*'s return on the radar. 'Keep an eye out and give me a call if the fog rolls in. The forecast says it'll get thick by midnight and if it does we'll have to close up tight behind her.'

Dieter nodded and lit a cigarette.

Joss paused for another few seconds, watching the hazy stern light of the vessel ahead. Probably less than 1000 tons deadweight, *Le Champe* was making slightly over nine knots. Both vessels were now abeam Tancarville, Le Havre less than twenty minutes away. Once *Le Champe* cleared the sea buoy marking the entrance to the Seine, she would slow and a motor launch would come alongside her to retrieve the pilot. In less than two hours, Joss would know exactly where Stone and the van der Groot woman were. He was willing to bet the pilot's life on it.

Joss ambled down the companionway, past the galley with its adjacent bar, and into the salon. He wanted a brandy, but the first thing he had locked up after they hijacked this plastic piece of shit was the booze. Joss considered himself a professional and, like all professionals, he set rigid priorities.

Turner was sprawled on a leather couch in the salon, watching a skin flick on the VCR. After the fuck-up in Rouen which he had attributed to lack of manpower, Joss wanted another body, particularly someone who knew powerboats. He had called Turner on his cellular. Turner had been scouting out suitable shipyards along the Dutch coast for the next phase in Brunner's project.

Joss had told Turner to catch a commuter flight down to Le Havre. By the time Joss and Dieter had reached Le Havre in the van, Turner had already picked out the eighteen-meter-long Bertram power yacht. The rest had been a piece of cake.

Joss had known Turner for a long time — both his strengths and weaknesses — and had recommended that Brunner hire him for the project based on Turner's expertise in welding and boat systems. Because most of Brunner's people on the project were ex-Stasi types, Joss wanted one of his own next to him if things got tight. Turner and Joss had first met in Colombia back in '83, both of them out of work and trying to break into the Trade. They found they moved well together in a tight situation, could anticipate what the other was thinking. Neither would ever have described the relationship as a friendship. Rather, like wild dogs running in a pack, the extent of their loyalty was limited to not biting the other when bringing down the game.

'How's our host taking it?' Joss asked.

Turner looked up. 'He was whining about us ripping off

his boat and like how it was gonna blow his insurance bill outta sight. So I kicked him in the nuts to give him something halfway decent to whine about.'

'The woman?' Joss nodded toward the opposite cabin.

'No problem.'

Joss opened the cabin door. She was in the sack, the sheets pulled up so that he could just see the cleavage of her boobs – a teaser. She was munching chocolate turtles.

'You doing all right?' Joss asked, throwing her a smile that had warmed the hearts of countless cruise-ship passengers. In those days, a smile wasn't worth much more than a buck tip, but times had changed.

'Is Marc well? I thought I heard him call out.' She was French but her English was good, like she worked in some kind of international job.

'Last I heard, he was playing with himself. You go for that kind?'

She brushed the sheet with her arm so that the edge exposed more of her body, like it was a casual thing. 'He's a lawyer for foreign companies doing business in France. He works sometimes for the firm that employs me. I know him just a little.' She held up thumb and forefinger spaced a couple of millimeters apart, indicating the depth of their relationship.

'What's your name again?' he asked. They hadn't been formally introduced. He, Dieter and Turner had strolled past the marina's security guard, boarded the yacht like they owned it, then quietly kicked the shit out of Marc. Ten minutes later, they were cruising up the Seine.

'Michelle. Or you can call me Didi.' She giggled.

'Say I come back with a couple of drinks later on? You go for that?'

'It would be very nice, I think. I'm lonely, all by myself.' Her face clouded momentarily. 'You won't hurt us?'

'Not if you're good, Didi babes.' He winked.

Turner tapped him on the shoulder. 'Fog's rolling in and the freighter's starting to slow down.'

'Keep it warmed up for me, Didi. I'll be back by and by.'

She smiled, then patted the bed beside her. 'Champagne,' she said. 'And there is another box of chocolate-covered turtles in the refrigerator.' She pursed her lips and licked them.

He had guessed right – a teaser. He reminded himself to bring some nylon rope as well.

Captain Pierre Fornier – licenced Seine River pilot and ship's master, all tonnage, oil and steam, master as well of the art of boules, a faithful husband to his wife of forty-three years and, in the considered estimation of those who were qualified to judge such things, an extraordinarily gifted chef – paused near *Le Champe*'s boarding ladder and shook the hand of the first officer.

'I wish you a fine passage, Eric, but I suspect the Pas de Calais will have dirty weather in store for you tonight.'

'One takes what comes,' the Dane said pragmatically. 'But after two more runs, I'll be qualified to sit for my master's ticket. And once I have that, you won't see my backside north of the tropics. The cold gets to your bones once you reach fifty.'

'That it does,' agreed Fornier, who was sixty-three.

Fornier climbed over the rusty bulwarks and carefully descended the boarding ladder to the pilot launch which was keeping station alongside *Le Champe*'s hull.

Fornier hesitated for just a second before transferring to the launch, and looked up. The Dane was peering down. *Decent man*, Fornier thought. He gave the Dane a last wave and leaped to the deck of the pilot launch. Even at his age, Fornier was light on his feet.

The pilot launch's engine gunned and it veered off smartly to starboard as Fornier watched the wall of steel that formed *Le Champe*'s hull slide by into the fog. For a few minutes, he listened to her screws biting water, growing fainter, then lit his pipe. It had been a good trip and the Danes, as usual, were generous with their aquavit. Yet there was something odd gnawing at him – a pervasive sense that he would never see *Le Champe* again. It was a premonition of loss that he knew was improbable. She was old but the Danes maintained her well. He pushed the thought from his mind.

The sea was starting to kick up a bit and he had to steady himself as he swung down into the wheelhouse.

'*Bonsoir*, Claude,' he said. 'Didn't expect to see you working tonight. Heard you were off for the rest of the week.'

'Was,' Claude grunted. 'But Vincent called in sick. They stuck me with the duty, the filthy shits.'

Fornier frowned and relit his briar. He didn't care for Claude, but as the Dane had said, one took what one got. And in less than an hour, he'd be on the train for Rouen and, with luck, he'd see Perocette tomorrow. Besides ships, the river and the sea, they both shared a passion for food, and Perocette had reported in this morning's transmission his success with a new formulation of *tripes au beurre noir*. In exchange, Fornier would divulge his most closely guarded recipe to Perocette: *maquereau aux pommes à l'huile*. Indeed, it would be good to see Maurice again, and he looked forward to the exchange. And, of course, the matter of the yacht would be amusing. Perocette had been most mysterious about the sailing vessel tied up on his doorstep, but that was entirely consistent with Maurice's love of intrigue.

Fornier ambled over to the radar screen. It was on five-kilometer range, blank except for sea clutter and a small return up to the east of them. He tapped the screen. 'Have you been watching this one?'

Claude grunted again. 'It was behind the Dane all the way out into the bay. A trawler, probably.'

Fornier studied it. 'He's altered heading for us, although he looks to be slowing down.'

'I'll give him a wide berth,' Claude said, turning the wheel to pass astern of the return which was now a half-kilometer away.

In response, the return altered heading again, re-establishing a collision course.

'He must have radar as well,' Fornier said. 'It looks intentional on his part, as if he's trying to close with us. Try to raise him on Channel 16.'

Claude tried but there was no response. The range separating the two vessels had now closed to less than 200 meters, both vessels slowing to a few knots.

'Keep on this course, Claude. He may be in trouble. I'll go topside and see whether I can spot him.'

It was wet and windy topside, the fog thick, the chop starting to get nasty. Fornier sighed. Fools and their boats. Nights like these were best spent in port with a good woman.

He edged forward on the slippery deck, keeping one hand on the lifelines, the other shielding his face from the spray.

At first it was just a suggestion of light, more of a glow. Fornier listened intently and could now hear the growl of two idling engines drifting down on the wind.

The glow became a misty pink and, as the distance closed, blossomed into an aching red glare. He had been right. Whoever it was had ignited a distress flare.

Claude had flicked on the launch's spotlight. Its beam picked up a white fiberglass sport fisherman, a man on the yacht's deck waving madly.

'Ha-looo,' Fornier shouted.

'Fuel filter's clogged up. We need a tow!' the man shouted back.

The two vessels were closer now, a few meters separating them. Fornier's eyes were smarting from the salt spray and he was annoyed. Stupid yachtsman, out in a toy boat on a night like this, and to make it worse, positioned squarely in the middle of a shipping channel. He didn't stop to reason why the sport fisherman's engines were still running if the fuel filters were blocked.

A coiled line from the sport fisherman arced over Fornier's head and he caught it, then bent down to secure it to a bit on the pilot launch's deck. Best to tow them out of the shipping lane, he thought, and into shallow water so they could anchor, then call Le Havre for a salvage vessel. Fornier had a train to catch, a ship waiting for him to pilot and an old friend to meet, and he didn't suffer fools gladly – particularly English-speaking ones.

When the line was secured properly, Fornier stood up, bracing himself against the roll of the vessel. The man on the sport fisherman was holding a stubby machine pistol.

'You the pilot that was on *Le Champe*?'

'Yes. What . . . ?'

'We're closing in. You jump on board my boat when the timing's right.'

'I won't . . .'

'If you don't get over here pronto, you're going to get a bullet up your Frog ass, understand?' The man motioned to someone in the sport fisherman's wheelhouse. 'Bring her in, Joss,' the man shouted.

The sport fisherman nudged closer. With the seas heaving, the two hulls collided, and Fornier felt a hand grab his, yanking him forward. He landed heavily on the yacht's fiberglass deck, its anti-skid tread grating his face.

Another man had come out of the sport fisherman's wheelhouse and the two of them half-dragged, half-pushed Fornier through the door opening. He tumbled down a short set of steps, onto a carpeted floor.

'Finish the job, Turner,' the man behind the wheel said to the one holding the SMG.

'Pleasure.' Turner plucked a flare pistol and three cartridges from a rack and turned to the third man. 'You toss the jug when I tell you to, Dieter.'

Fornier was dazed, stupidly sprawled on the carpeted

175

deck, his bridgework loose in his mouth, composure fragmented.

'What is this thing you are doing?' he mumbled, looking up. The man behind the wheel had an automatic tucked under his belt. He was relaxed, smiling. He looked out through the windshield and nodded. 'You might enjoy watching this, Pilot.'

The man called Turner had cast off the line, the two vessels starting to drift apart. Very methodically, Turner raised his weapon and sprayed two short bursts into the pilot launch's wheelhouse, shattering the glass. Fornier couldn't see Claude, knew he was probably already on the deck, trying to crawl to the radio to call on the distress frequency. *Mother of God, help him.*

'*Now!*' Turner yelled.

The man called Dieter heaved a plastic jerry jug across the black waters. It landed in the cockpit of the launch, ricocheting sideways off a thwart, its contents spilling.

Turner slung the SMG from his shoulder and fitted a cartridge to the flare pistol, aimed and fired. He must have been thrown off by the heaving deck because the flare traced a shallow parabola just over the top of the launch's wheelhouse. Turner didn't seem perturbed. He methodically fitted another cartridge and fired again.

The red flare rocketed through the launch's wheelhouse window. Staring in dumb fascination, Fornier saw its propellant still burning white-hot, the cartridge banging around within the launch like a pinball gone insane. The jug must have contained diesel fuel because it ignited with a soft *whump*, the flames a dirty yellow. Suddenly, Claude was standing, his arms outstretched, his mouth open in a silent scream, his face and body a torch.

Turner unslung his SMG and fired three closely spaced shots. Claude bucked under the impact, spinning backwards into the flaming wheelhouse.

Fornier collapsed, bile filling his throat, the cross-like image of Claude burned into his retinas.

'We'll have a little chat now, Pilot,' the man standing over him said, and he felt a foot slide under his chin, forcing him to look up. The man was smiling down at him.

NINE

He came awake with a jerk, a wet tongue licking dirt from between his toes. Startled, Stone sprang upright, smashing his head against the overhead bookshelf.

'Beat it, mutt!'

The Airedale hesitated, grinned at him, then jumped up on his chest, working over his face, tail flailing. Stone wrestled the dog off the bunk and probed his scalp for obvious damage.

She entered the cabin, ruffled the dog's head and handed Stone a mug of coffee. She had a large bath towel wrapped around her body, her face freshly scrubbed, her hair wet and smelling of conditioner. Stone felt a pang of domesticity denied.

'Thank you for fixing the water pump. It works beautifully now. Incidentally, you owe me half a bottle of wine.'

'So what's the big deal? You were swilling the stuff down with Perocette last time I noticed.'

'Some of us can handle it, Stone, and some of us can't. Let's just leave it at that.'

What the hell was it with this damned woman?

She leaned over his shoulder, wiping moisture away from the cabin's porthole. 'The fog's starting to clear. We have to get *Night Watch* ready to go.'

'In daylight?' He checked his watch: 09.23. 'I thought the master plan was to wait until nightfall.'

'Was, but not now. I checked the VHF a few minutes ago to see what kind of weather we'd have in the English Channel, but it was clogged with chatter. There's a search and rescue effort going on for a pilot boat that went missing in the bay off Le Havre last night. No report of a collision but a fishing trawler found debris and both men who were on board are presumed missing.'

'So what's the big deal about that?'

'One of the missing men was Perocette's friend – Pierre Fornier – the Seine pilot Perocette talked to on the radio yesterday morning. During that conversation, Perocette never identified himself by his name or location because a private VHF shore station is illegal, but Fornier obviously knew.'

'That's paranoid.' But on closer examination, maybe it wasn't. He finished off his coffee and held the mug out for a refill, the caffeine starting to kick in.

'Paranoid or not, I want to get *Night Watch* ready to move. If they got their hands on Fornier, they'll know where to find us.' She took his empty cup and turned to leave the cabin, then looked back at him. 'I'm going up to the cottage for a few minutes. Maurice has to be warned. In the meanwhile, get things ready and we'll leave when I get back.'

'Give him my love,' Stone called after her.

He cranked up the engine and checked for oil leaks. None. Then he singled up the docking lines.

Fifteen, then twenty minutes elapsed. Stone checked Perocette's cottage from the companionway. Lights were on in the kitchen, faint strains of *Don Giovanni* wafting from the library. *Come on, lady, move your butt.*

Irritated, he went below and puttered around in the galley, frying up a twinset of eggs and supplementing them with a box of cookies he found stashed in the back of the dry-goods locker.

The bottle of Burgundy he had finished off last night was still on the counter, his silent betrayer. Until they got to England, it looked like he was going to have to dry out, a truly nauseating prospect.

The dog was back on station in the quarter berth, dozing.

Stone was about to go forward to make up his berth when he heard a low rumble and the sound of a woman's voice.

He glanced through a porthole. A fiberglass sport fisherman was trundling through the water, angling in toward the *Night Watch*, fenders over the side as if it was getting ready to come alongside. On the yacht's deck was a knock-out babe holding a boat hook, togged out in a white jumpsuit with the zipper pulled down from *here* to *there*. Behind the helm was an older guy — fleshy cheeks, thick, puffy lips, gold chains around his neck, wearing a dumb yachting hat with scrambled eggs on the bill. Definitely not the opposition, but he didn't want a boat tied up alongside when he and Mel would be getting under way in just a few minutes.

Stone scrambled up the companionway, waving them off.

'Hey! We're leaving. This here's a private dock. *No es permiso!*'

The Bertram was within a couple of meters and drifting closer.

'Ah. You are *Englaise*, no?'

'Yes. Well, no. Not exactly. American.' She had a lovely cleavage, inviting even at ten in the A.M. Stone now desperately wished he had shaved, brushed his fangs and combed his hair.

Behind him at the bottom of the companionway, the dog was growling softly. Stone told him to shut up, then turned back to the babe.

A man casually rose from behind the fish-well deck bulkhead of the Bertram, an Ingram MAC-10 leveled on Stone. 'Where's Perocette?' He was handsome in a hard way, his face slightly pitted, ponytailed, vaguely Spanish-looking with some Indian genes thrown in — but undoubtedly the bird who had been in the van with Black Jacket back in Rouen.

'What's a parrot-seat?' Stone asked, his recent sexual ardor now rapidly waning. Unconsciously, he betrayed himself, his eyes swiveling across the lawn toward the cottage.

The man nodded toward the cottage. 'Dieter, Turner. Check it out. Get the woman, then yank the telephone cord, smash the VHF radio and clean things up. Don't screw up and no noise.'

Two men, one of them Black Jacket, the other a crew-cut type, jumped from behind their hiding place in the Bertram's well deck and onto the deck of *Night Watch*, both gripping silenced handguns. They crossed over to the lawn without giving Stone a glance and headed in a crouched, zagging run toward the cottage.

'You . . . !' Pit-face snapped. '. . . Hands clasped behind your head.' He boarded *Night Watch* and shoved Stone down the companionway, following closely.

He motioned Stone to sit down on the settee. 'You're Stone, aren't you? I didn't get a good look at you in Le Havre.'

'. . . Or Rouen. Fucked up there, didn't you,' Stone slid in sideways. He saw the look on the man's face. Major mistake.

Pit-face smashed the barrel of the MAC-10 across Stone's shins. The pain was incredible and Stone shrieked.

Sailor had been quietly hanging out in the shadows of the quarter berth, mildly interested in the current events. Over his five years on the boat, strange people were always coming on board and that didn't normally concern him. But an outsider striking an occupant already given the Good Housekeeping Seal of Approval by his mistress did, because he had been trained by Pieter to guard his territory and all the approved occupants thereof. The new Alpha Pack leader, the man his mistress called 'Stone', seemed marginally to qualify. His duty clear, the Airedale lifted off on all fours, jaw set for maximum bite, and tore into the stranger's leg.

Pit-face's reaction was instantaneous. He slashed the Airedale's head with the MAC-10. But the distraction was just long enough for Stone to snatch the empty wine bottle still resting on the counter and clobber Pit-face just slightly north of the frontal lobe. The bottle exploded into shards.

Both the Airedale and Pit-face were temporarily incognito; blood, glass and the remaining dregs of wine splattered across the cabin. Stone found himself panting, heart-rate stratospheric.

He grabbed the Ingram which had fallen from Pit-face's hand and checked the safety. Off, with the Selector on Full Automatic, forty-round clip. God, his knees were screaming. He tested them and they still functioned, marginally.

He examined Pit-face first. Leg bleeding, irises dilated, scalp dark with blood, possible concussion. The dog was in slightly better shape, semi-conscious. Stone ruffled Sailor's neck and, in response, the dog twitched. Reasonably normal there.

Decision time: either take on the two guys at the cottage or wait until they returned, hopefully with Mel still intact. The latter made more sense.

He checked Pit-face again. His eyes were fluttering. Stone got a roll of duct tape from the parts drawer and bound Pit-face's hands, then took several wraps around his head to cover his mouth.

Time running out and he had to get ready for them. It was an idea, a little thin around the edges, but the only one he could come up with.

He checked the cottage first through the porthole. The back door was closed, no noise except Pavarotti wailing away on *Don Giovanni*. Next, he boosted the Airedale up the companionway and slung him over the lifelines and onto the deck of the powerboat. Both the owner and his babe were wide-eyed, frozen in place.

Stone waved the submachine-gun at them. 'Just do like I say and you won't get hurt.' He cast off the single docking line that secured the Bertram to *Night Watch*, then motioned with the Ingram. 'I'm moving the sailboat off the dock. Once it's clear, pull your boat in alongside.'

Stone jumped back into the cockpit of the *Night Watch*, locked the helm amidships, flipped the eyes of the dock lines off the dock's bollards, snicked the engine into forward and leaped to the deck of the Bertram. His knees were screaming, but he was running on pure adrenalin, immortal as long as it lasted.

The canal was straight, both sides lined with flat rock walls. Without a helmsman to guide her, *Night Watch* slowly nudged out into the stream, gradually wandering toward the far side, then, scraping against it, rebounded slowly back to mid-stream. At a speed of less than a knot, she headed inland toward the mud flats.

He motioned to the Frog at the helm. 'When they come back, you tell them that I overpowered Pit-face and took off with him in the sailboat. If you want to live, don't let on that I'm on board your boat. I'll take it from there.'

The man, his eyes still bugging out, nodded.

Stone hefted the Airedale in his arms and took him below. The dog, still groggy, wasn't going anywhere for a while, he figured. Stone stuffed the animal into the engine room between the two turbo-supercharged engines, then checked for activity on the lawn through the bronzed Lexan windows of the powerboat. Black Jacket was just coming through the kitchen door, Melissa in tow, the other guy, Turner, right behind him.

The cabin of the powerboat was laid out with couches, a TV console built into the bulkhead, a wet bar, connecting galley, the usual airliner plush that powerboat owners seemed to go for. Stone chose the galley, hunkering down behind the counter. From there, he could see most of the bridge deck.

It was less than a minute before the two men piled onto the deck. The one called Dieter had Melissa by the arm, her arms bound behind her with a length of electrical cord.

There ensued an animated conversation on deck, part in German, the balance of it in French. Suddenly, the engines gunned and the Bertram started to move, following the *Night Watch*.

Stone was gambling that they'd try to overtake *Night Watch* and save their boss, all the time assuming that he, Stone, was still on board the sailboat.

Which was exactly the way they reacted. The one with the crew-cut, Turner, herded Melissa below and shoved her into the forward cabin, locked it and headed back out on deck. He passed so close that Stone could smell the stink of the man's body odor.

Thumps on the deck, the two men clomping forward to the bow in their hard-soled shoes, shouting at the *Night Watch*.

Stone chanced it, cautiously moving up to the bridge deck. The Frog was driving, the babe next to him, hanging on to an overhead grab rail. The Frog started to say something but Stone, in a crouch, shook his head. 'Keep your eyes on the road, Kermit, and your mouth shut.' He moved up behind the Frog's shoulder, within reach of the controls.

Stone had always hated the flimsy chromed life-rails that adorned most power yachts. They were devilish devices, slightly higher than the average person's knee. If one intersected a life-rail at a rate faster than a casual stroll, the body from the thighs up (as Sir Isaac Newton had sagely predicted) tended to keep going in a straight line while the legs and feet were restrained. This imbalance in forces induced a rotational movement with the rail as the pivotal point. Generations of seamen had cursed these things and the men who designed them. Stone himself had experienced the evils of one first-hand, falling overboard from a yacht during a cocktail party in Newport Harbor.

The sport fisherman, now making fifteen knots, was rapidly overtaking *Night Watch*. Both Turner and Dieter were standing, their thighs braced against the bow railing, their weapons aimed at the *Night Watch*.

It seemed as good a time as any. Stone reached past

the Frog's elbow and slammed the gear-shift levers from forward into reverse. The transmissions howled, trying to blow out of the engine room. The Bertram shuddered to a stop and reversed direction at a smart clip. Stone eased the shift levers into neutral. The Frog still had his hands on the helm but he was paralyzed, in shock.

Turner surfaced first, swimming for the shore. Dieter was nowhere to be seen, hopefully embedded in the bottom mud. Stone smiled; Newton's theory once again proven correct.

Night Watch was slowing, dragging a yellow stain behind her as she grounded in the shallows of the mud flats.

He had the bastards now. Stone scrambled out on the foredeck of the Bertram, the Ingram ready. *'Freeze, Turner!'* Turner was just crawling ashore, covered with mud, an amphibian surfacing from the primordial ooze. He hesitated for a second, unsure, then started to run. Stone squeezed, the Ingram bucking in his hands, empty shell casing spewing from the blow-back slot. Turner slammed on the brakes, turned and raised his hands.

Stone didn't hear the report of the shot, but a bullet whined past his head and impacted with the Bertram's windshield, scarring the Lexan. Stone swiveled to the right, suddenly feeling very naked on the wide-open deck. Another shot, then two more, closely spaced. Sounds of distressed fiberglass shattering behind him. Stone jerked the trigger reflexively, spraying a swath of 9-mm slugs into brown shrubbery on the opposite bank. He caught the flash of clothing diving to the ground behind a grassy knoll. Stone fired again and saw clods of dirt jumping, grass wilting.

Turner was running again, this time back down the embankment. Stone tried to keep his bursts short, stitching the shallows as Turner high-stepped. Too late. Turner had made it to the *Night Watch*, was now hidden by the curve of the hull.

Another shot from the grassy knoll where Dieter was

hiding. Stone felt the rush of wind, the crack of the bullet as it whined past him.

The engines suddenly barked, the Bertram heeling hard over in a turn, accelerating, the Frog frantically spinning the helm. Stone, off balance, fell to the deck, skidding toward the low side. The Ingram slipped from his hands, slithered across the deck and went overboard. *Ah shit!*

His fingers caught the shaft of a stanchion but his legs were halfway over the gunwale, flailing at thin air. Starting to lose it, nails breaking.

Just as suddenly, the Bertram was upright, on an even keel, picking up knots as it thundered out of the River Rancon, spray from the bow thrown back by the wind, soaking him.

He caught one last glimpse of *Night Watch*, heeled over in the mud, Turner scrambling on deck.

The Bertram was past the entrance buoy, arcing through a curve toward Le Havre and the sea. The Frog's forehead was covered in sweat, his fingers flicking at a toggle switch marked 'trim tab', talking out of the side of his mouth in French to the babe. The Bertram lifted slightly, her stern coming up. The knotmeter flickered past forty, rising.

Stone let out a long breath. The babe was staring at him, her mouth open. He nodded toward the Frog. 'Tell him to keep this thing flat-out for now. You okay?'

She nodded, trance-like, hair askew, face pale, jumpsuit stained with sweat. She was now about as attractive as a hand-me-down Barbie doll.

He found the VHF radio telephone and pulled the mike jack from its receptacle and stuffed the microphone in his jacket pocket. Best not to leave temptation in the way.

He found her in the locked forward cabin, hands tied with telephone cord to the leg of the bed.

'Where's Sailor?' she asked.

'He's okay. Sleeping. Lump on his noggin but he'll live.' He fumbled, untying the knot. He had expected praise for his gallantry and intelligence. Fat chance.

She suddenly collapsed on the floor, her body racking. He crouched down next to her. 'It's okay, okay. Melissa – it's fine now.' He was awkward, touching her face, her cheeks wet with tears. She was holding back, trying to suppress it.

'They killed Perocette. The man . . . the man in the leather jacket did it – as if it were the most normal thing in the world – just raised his gun and shot Maurice in the head – twice. His skull exploded. It was terrible.'

He held her, rocking her a little. Then lifted her and lowered her to the bed. 'Just rest a little. I've got to go on deck for a minute. I'll be back.'

'. . . *Night Watch*?'

'She's on the mud flats. A couple of scratches, nothing serious.'

'But . . .' Her voice was thin, broken.

'We'll get her back, Melissa. Promise.' He closed the door. Then wondered how he could make good on that one.

Stone found some beer in the cooler and returned to the cockpit. The babe was steering now. She had throttled back but the Bertram was still making thirty-five knots. A bean-bag ashtray rested on the throttle quadrant, two separate cigarettes burning, both with lipstick marks on them. Stressed out, he thought.

He sat down beside her. 'How you doing?'

She just nodded, staring ahead, mechanical.

'My name's Stone.'

'Mine is Didi.' He noticed that she had gray eyes and the lashes were real. Her sleeves were rolled up and he saw that there were bruises on them. Also, one on her neck, actually a hickey. Stone was surprised. The Frog didn't look like he was the passionate type.

'Were you, ah, mistreated?'

She didn't respond, her eyes hidden behind dark glasses.

'Where's your friend?' he asked.

187

'In our cabin. He did not feel well – his nerves. It will pass.'

'The man with the pitted face and the long hair. You know his name?'

She made a non-committal shrug. ' "Joss" was what he called himself, I think.'

'How did Joss and the other two guys get on board?'

Her expression hardened. 'You understand that I cannot talk about it now. It is a matter for the gendarmerie.' She pointed a finger to a scattering of houses. 'Vieux Port. In thirty more kilometers, we will be to Honfleur. There are authorities there.'

She had a strip chart clipped to a bracket on the dash. Stone studied it. Honfleur was opposite Le Havre on the south side of the River Seine. Beyond Honfleur was the sea. And beyond that, England. He spanned off the distance to Ramsgate with his fingers – roughly 140 nautical miles, say five hours' running time at this speed.

'How much fuel do you have left?' he asked.

She glanced down at the gauge and delicately tapped it with a red fingernail. 'Marc keeps the tanks always filled. There is more than enough to arrive at Honfleur.' She turned to him a little and tried to smile but there was no real warmth in it, just going through the motions. Stone could understand her frame of mind. The adrenalin had burned out, leaving him brain-dead and jittery, and he noticed that his hands shook a little.

'Does Marc ever go over to England in this thing?'

She lifted her shoulders, then dropped them. The cleavage shifted nicely. 'In the summer when the sea is very calm. To Southampton for shopping. He has enough fuel for the trip over and back with some remaining.'

Which opened a second option. Stone eased back in the seat, sucking on the beer, trying to put it together. It seemed rational to pull into Honfleur and let the cops sort it out. God, he was tired, wanted to dump the problem in somebody else's lap. But somehow, he didn't think Joss, or whatever he called himself, and his buddies would hang around, and that meant, as long as he and Melissa remained in France, they'd be at risk. And without doubt, the cops would put some awkward questions to him which Stone didn't want to answer without a damned good lawyer on his side; one he couldn't afford unless Mac was willing to foot the bill.

The alternative prospect was more appealing. Five hours maximum, he calculated.

'You want something to drink, Didi? Calm your nerves down. A little cognac maybe?'

She nodded, just the smallest movement of her head, then lit another cigarette.

'Be back in a second.'

Stone went below. Aft was the owner's cabin. He eased the door open a crack. Marc was in bed, the sheets pulled over his head, his bare feet sticking out. A bottle of pills lay scattered on the nightstand.

'Hey, you okay?' Stone nudged the body with his shoe.

The sheets held by little pink fingers tentatively dipped down to reveal Marc's terrified face, then were drawn back up tight. Still functioning after a fashion, Stone thought. He eased the door closed.

There was a second cabin opposite Marc's. Empty, but the sheets were rumpled and an empty bottle of champagne rolled back and forth on the cabin sole. A tube of lubricating jelly had been left on the floor, mashed flat by somebody's shoe, the goo staining the carpet. Stone wondered how Didi would explain that one to Marc.

Stone was about to leave, then hesitated. Lying in the corner were two zippered flight bags and a canvas attaché case. The flight bags were el cheapos, not the sort of thing that Marc or Didi would be caught dead carrying. He opened them.

One held six forty-round clips and a screw-on silencer for the Ingram. The other contained blocks of a yellow clay-like substance wrapped in oiled paper.

189

Stone had handled the stuff before – C-4 plastique explosive. The detonators were in a plastic box, each cushioned in its own foam-padded receptacle. In another box were two small printed circuit boards, each fitted with an LED readout screen, a battery case and two terminal posts. Firing timers, he guessed. Home-brewed, but nevertheless fabricated by a talented craftsman.

He turned to the canvas attaché case. There was a thick notebook, its cover strapped down by a rubber band, the writing on the cover in French, somewhat faded with time or salt air. The pages were covered with calculations and a tight, copperplate script. *Le Borveaux's drilling reports!* he guessed. Had to be!

No time to look through it now. He rummaged around in the bottom of the attaché case and came up with a holstered semi-automatic handgun. Well used, the bluing worn to bright metal. It was a Beretta 9-mm, Italian Army issue, the serial numbers filed off, the clip of fifteen shells missing three rounds. He smelled the muzzle. It had been fired recently. He grabbed the attaché case, jammed the gun in his waistband and headed for Melissa's cabin.

The door was open, swinging gently in the seaway.

He found her in the cockpit, talking to Didi in French.

Stone curled his finger at Melissa and she came aft to where he was standing.

'We're not going into Honfleur,' he said, his lips close to her ear. 'I'm dropping Didi and her buddy off at the first dock I can find. We can make England in five hours.'

Her eyes went wide. 'We can't! Perocette, the boat . . .'

He gripped her arm. 'Keep your voice down, for Christ's sake.' He glanced over her shoulder at Didi who was studying the chart. If she heard anything, it hadn't penetrated. 'Look, the Mafia types we left back there will be vamanosed by the time the cops get to Perocette's place. And as long as they're on the loose, we've got big problems.'

She backed away from him, shaking her head. 'I'm not

going with you, Stone. You're out of your mind. The police will protect us. If you run, they'll think you're implicated.'

That did it. She had made her point as usual, but his mind was made up and he was damn well going to run the show from here on in, with her or without her. He picked up the binoculars and studied the river ahead. There were a number of commercial wharfs lining the river but they were cliffs of concrete, well above the deck level of the Bertram. He needed a dock where he could pull up alongside, dump the passengers and blast off.

On the south side of the river, he picked up the shape of a concrete pillar with a mushroom dome capping it. The land between it and the river was low-lying and he could make out the shape of a small dock fronting it.

He pointed, then handed Didi the glasses. 'What's that?'

'Honfleur radar tower. From there, they watch boats on the river who are proceeding in fog. That is where we turn, a small canal. It is marked by a buoy with the number nineteen.' She pointed to the chart.

'Okay. Got it.' He slid in behind the helm, displacing her. 'You get Marc up here quick.' He pulled the VHF microphone from his jacket pocket and plugged it in. 'I'll give them a call and set things up.'

She ducked her head in acknowledgement and scrambled below.

Melissa leaned against the control console, staring ahead. 'Stone, you're not going to do this.'

'Like hell I'm not. The Frog cops will hold us for God knows how long, probably charge us with Christ knows what. Try arson, homicide and hijacking for starters.'

She actually stamped her foot. 'Damn you, Stone. You may not like the French but they've got laws and a legal system. *Night Watch* is lying in the mud, perhaps holed – and you were the one who put her there. I've got to file a claim with the insurance company, and what of Anna's remains? Someone's got to make sure she's properly taken care of and her relatives notified. You *bloody twit*! As usual, you're just thinking of yourself and your own precious agenda.'

Stone was seething but he kept it under control, just barely. 'Fine by me, lady. You do your thing, I'll do mine. Just keep in mind that you'd be dead twice over if it hadn't been for me. How your hubby ever put up with you is beyond me.'

'Just what do you mean by that?'

'Exactly the way it sounds. You think you're some kind of princess, holier than thou. You're damn right that I've got an agenda, and that's currently getting my butt back to England in one piece.'

'You . . . you . . . you . . . !'

He was throttling back, coming off the plane, angling in toward the dock. *Screw her,* he thought.

Marc and Didi were standing in the cockpit now, holding on to the overhead grab rail, Marc pasty-faced, Didi obviously bewildered. 'What are you doing?' she demanded. 'The canal is *there.*' She pointed to a marked channel beyond the tower.

'You're getting off here. Tell Marc that I'll make sure someone gets his boat back to him.'

'You can't . . .'

Stone pulled the Beretta from his waistband. The Bertram was nearly alongside the dock. He chomped the gear shift into reverse, stopping the boat on a dime, swinging the stern in.

'Off. NOW!' He thumbed back the hammer.

The three of them clambered over the side and onto the dock, Melissa last. 'Stone, you're insane!' she yelled at him, her fist clenched. She had lost one shoe overboard and was hopping around on one foot.

Someone was running across the lawn toward them, waving his hands. Someone in uniform.

'Hey,' he shouted at Melissa.

She turned.

'What do I do with your damned dog?'

She was stunned, her mouth gaping open.

'I don't have all day. Make up your mind.'

She reached out and grabbed at the life-rail, trying to pull the Bertram back.

Marc and Didi were running across the grass toward the guy in uniform. Stone could see a leather holster attached to his belt, a little képi cap on the guy's head. Cop.

'Let *go* of the damned rail, Melissa. I'm leaving.'

She tugged at the Bertram, not willing to let go, not willing to come aboard, her face red from the effort.

He snicked the gear shift into forward, applying a little throttle, not wanting to jerk her off the dock, figuring she'd let go when she realized that it was useless.

She kicked off her other shoe and dug her heels in, grunting to hold the vessel back but gradually losing ground.

The cop was fifty or so meters away, feet flailing, his arm stuck out, hand splayed, as if he were trying to stop traffic.

Stone sighed and slid off the helmsman's seat. He moved aft to the rail, wrapped his hand around her wrist and yanked. Already off balance, she catapulted over the rail, landing heavily in the cockpit.

In two strides, he was back at the helmsman's seat. He crammed the throttles to the firewall. The Bertram lunged forward, dragging its stern at first, then bodily lifting onto the plane, the knots piling up.

Stone glanced back. The cop tried to stop but his hard-soled shoes skidded on the dock. He toppled into the drink, all four limbs windmilling.

Add yet one more crime to the rap sheet. They'd charge him with assault by default, he figured.

It was raining heavily now, the seas shredded into white spume, driven by a wind gusting at over thirty knots. Ahead of him, a black frontal-roll cloud was sweeping in from the Channel, blotting out the western horizon.

He looked aft. With difficulty, he could just make out the office towers of Le Havre and a container ship exiting the River Seine, cranking around in a slow turn to port, headed for the Mediterranean, he guessed.

Reaching up, he turned down the gain and increased the anti-clutter on the radar. Nice little thing, Japanese, made by Sitex. Maximum range about thirty-two miles, although in this sea he doubted it would pick up anything much over half that. Except for the ship behind him, the screen was blank. So far, so good.

But there had been a moment of doubt in the bay off Le Havre. The search and rescue effort was still on, maybe a dozen vessels bird-dogging the area, a lot of chatter on the VHF.

Stone had throttled the Bertram back to twenty-five knots, an innocent stroll in the park. But a police launch about half a mile away suddenly altered course toward him, strobe lights flashing, undoubtedly alerted by Honfleur Radar. Stone hadn't waited to find out whether the Frog cops had anything heavy-duty in their engine room. He powered up to max speed, the knotmeter occasionally clipping forty-five, and within ten minutes put the Frog hull down behind him. For the next twenty minutes, he had been on edge, always glancing back, amazed that they hadn't sent something faster after him. But they didn't.

For the time being, he had the Bertram throttled back to twenty knots, the seas on his beam, rolling the vessel through forty degrees, sloppy going and not in harmony with his queasy stomach. He checked the chart. In another twenty minutes, once he was abeam Cap d'Antifer, he would be able to alter to starboard, bringing both wind and sea on the stern. Then he could flat-out fly.

He flopped the switch on the autopilot, letting the thing take over, and lit a cigarette, the first in a very long time. He had kicked the habit once, twice, third time a charm, so he had thought. Nerves, he guessed. Lung cancer wasn't going to be the death of him, given his present situation.

She was down below, had been since recovering from the high dive. Probably in the owner's cabin, since it was aft and not subject to as much motion as the forward one. She had rescued Sailor from the engine room, then told Stone that he was despicable to have forced a poor dumb animal to cower on a greasy floor in a room filled with howling machinery. The dog didn't have the good grace to corroborate her story, happily thrashing his tail when he spotted Stone.

Stone sighed and flicked the cigarette butt into the sea. His original estimate of five hours was already half gone. It was going to take more like six. Which would put him into Ramsgate by sundown. Once he was within English coastal waters, he'd try to call Mac and have him make docking arrangements. Perhaps up some cozy backwater creek where the natives weren't too curious.

'You hungry?'

He turned. She was behind him in the companionway, dressed in a man's foul-weather jacket, a size far too large for her. She looked like a canary whose body had shrunk inside a skin that hadn't. She was braced against the door frame, swaying with the roll, holding a couple of sandwiches wrapped in waxed paper.

He nodded and she tossed him one. It was some kind of mystery meat with cheese and mayo. He ignored his stomach and bit into it.

'Where are we?' she asked. She used the overhead handrail and pulled herself hand over hand to the passenger seat next to his.

He pointed to the chart, then to a lighthouse on a promontory, not more than a few miles distant. 'Cap d'Antifer. Once we're around the point, the seas will smooth out. How's the pup?'

'He's probably deaf as a stone, but otherwise fine. I've got him bunked down in Marc's lavatory compartment to keep him from sliding around. Seems reasonably happy there.'

'How are you?'

She folded the paper away from her sandwich and nibbled. 'What am I supposed to say? Confused, frightened, pissed-off?' She picked something out of the sandwich that she didn't like and threw it overboard, then turned her face to him. 'Let's settle for pissed-off.'

'Sorry for the stuff I said.' Actually, he wasn't. Well, almost wasn't.

She nodded absently. 'Probably most of it was true. But it doesn't matter anyway, Stone. We're just strangers on the same train. I get off in England.'

'I meant it about helping you get your boat out of France.'

'It's a yacht, Stone. *This* is a boat. And I doubt they'll let you take the time off.'

'You mean my firm?'

She shook her head, the hood flopping sideways a little. 'No, the constabulary. I'm turning you in.'

'Oh yeah?'

'Why is it that Americans find themselves incapable of speaking English, let alone understanding it? But in terms of one syllable, *yeah*. Unless the authorities interview you and learn what happened, I'll be your accomplice in crime. Which also means I won't be able to recover the *Night Watch*, collect insurance on the shop or use my passport. But don't concern yourself. I'll testify on your behalf.'

'Terrific.' But she sounded as if she meant it, had to force-feed him just one last slice of humble pie. Mac and, by extension, Lloyd's would be thrilled. As would Her Majesty and her assorted bureaucratic servants. And it was highly likely that the IRS read the foreign editions and would be waiting for him when he walked out of Newgate Prison. Stone had never visited Fort Leavenworth, Kansas, and didn't intend to.

They had been running in rain showers but the visibility was starting to improve. Off to the north-west, two ships plodded one after the other, like elephants nose to tail, headed for the Straits of Dover. Both freighters, by the looks of their superstructure, making good time. As he got out into the shipping lanes, the traffic would get a lot thicker, but the Bertram was agile — a no-sweat proposition.

He stayed a couple of hundred yards out from the promontory, carving an arc to the north around Cap d'Antifer, opening up a new coastline, chalk cliffs as far as he could see. With the seas now abaft the beam, the motion eased. He set a course for Ramsgate, 032 magnetic, and inched up the throttles to 2400 revs, twenty-eight knots showing on the speedo. Piece of cake.

He relaxed a little, now free of France. He glanced over at her. She was staring at the radar, intent. Stone took a look. It was a big return, heading down the coast toward them, coming fast.

He got the binoculars out and searched the horizon. There were some low clouds with rain showers hanging around to the north, the remnants left over from the frontal passage. As he watched, a large gray ship emerged from a curtain of rain. Magnified seven times in the binoculars, the ship looked like a massive knife on edge. It was throwing a bow wave, probably doing close to thirty knots.

A minute elapsed as they closed the distance to six miles. Then a finger of flame spat from a box-like structure just under its bridge. Three seconds later, a large geyser erupted a good quarter-mile in front of the Bertram, staining the water a dirty yellow; the proverbial shot across the bow.

Stone slapped the switch of the autopilot to off and wheeled the Bertram to the north-west, increasing power to maximum revs. The knotmeter crept up to forty-two knots, the hull pounding like hell.

He looked again through the binoculars. The ship was flying the French flag, the sea-going pride of fifty-four million Frogs. A frigate, Stone guessed.

As he watched, the frigate smoothly altered heading

toward an invisible point in the sea beyond where, by the canny calculation of her navigator and the immutable laws of physics, the twain of Bertram and frigate would meet.

TEN

The Bertram was flying, airborne off the tops of waves, props screaming as they bit air. Then, faltering, she'd crash into the next sea in an explosion of white water, staggering, then picking up speed as she rebounded, launching back into low earth-orbit again. Stone prayed that the factory hadn't skimped on the construction of this one.

He had made a rough calculation of his own; picking a point to intersect the freighter nearest him, duck behind her, then hide in the freighter's radar shadow to mask his course. That was Plan A. There was no Plan B.

He glanced back. The frigate was throwing a mustache of white water, massive and curling. As he watched, he saw a light blinking in code from the bridge, aimed in his direction.

Trying to signal me, he reckoned. He started to turn on the VHF, then dismissed the idea. Nothing he could say would change anything. And if he guessed right, he would outrun the frigate with the Bertram's ten-, maybe twelve-knot advantage. In an hour, that speed differential would put the frigate hull-down on the horizon and, in less time than that, Stone would be in the Frog-free territorial waters of England.

He turned back to the helm, trying to ease the Bertram's passage through the sea, then thought briefly about the fuel supply. He was burning it at a prodigious rate, wasn't sure whether the tanks would last to Ramsgate. Both oil and water temperatures were starting to creep up a little, the oil pressure . . .

The shockwave of an explosion reverberated through the hull. A dirty yellow geyser of water erupted ten boat-lengths away. It took a second to register. No more warning shots across the bow. The bastards were actually shooting at him!

He flicked the wheel to starboard, skirting the yellow-stained pothole, then jogged back on course again, a shower of water from the shell-burst cascading over the Bertram, streaming off the windshield and partially filling the aft fishing well. The air momentarily stank of cordite, then was whipped away by the wind.

She was yelling at him over the scream of the engines. 'Stone — you're going to get us killed! Stop this damned thing!'

She was hanging on to an overhead grab-rail with both hands, her body bouncing like a rag doll on a bungee cord.

He shouted back at her. 'What — and give them a sitting target? You crazy?'

For emphasis, he tried to ram the throttles forward, but they were already hard up against the stops. Frustrated, he unconsciously shoved against the wheel, trying to make the damned thing go faster.

Ahead, the freighter was growing larger in the windshield, a tattered South Korean flag snapping at her stern, brown rust stains trickling down her hull. A couple of crew in sweatsuits stood on the afterdeck, peering at him with binoculars.

The jarring of the hull was starting to get to him. He had been standing on his toes, trying to cushion the shock, but his arches were screaming in agony. He wondered how much longer both the Bertram and he could take it before starting to come unglued.

No more shells as yet. Probably close enough to the freighter so that the Frogs didn't want to risk hitting her. He altered course slightly to pass just astern of the ROK freighter. There was a guy on the bridge now, wind whipping his nylon jacket. He actually waved at Stone, smiling, his face all teeth. Friendly folk, Stone thought, and made a note to buy himself a Hyundai the next time around.

In seconds, he had passed behind the stern and swung to starboard in the lee of the ROK freighter, cutting the visual and radar link between the Bertram and the frigate.

He could see it in his mind — positioning the ROK between himself and the frigate, angling out for another ship in the line of shipping traffic plodding up the Channel, then repeating the whole exercise over again. The Frog didn't dare fire if there was any possibility of hitting a ship and, during that time, Stone would be increasing the distance between the twain.

He played cat and mouse with the frigate for the next hour, positioning the Bertram behind a ship, then dashing in its radar shadow for the next one. By now, he was in the actual shipping lanes, the traffic heavy, ships separated by less than a mile. The afternoon light was slipping away, a few rain showers still lingering to the west but the sea beginning to calm down. The Bertram was hitting a consistent forty knots, the gauges high in the caution zones, but steady. It was only the fuel consumption that worried him.

Over twenty minutes had elapsed without sight of the Frog, and he was beginning to feel pleased with himself. He looked aft to see how Melissa was making out and to ask her to fetch him a beer. It was thirsty work but exhilarating.

She was scrunched down on the deck with the microphone in one hand and a set of earphones held to her head with the other.

'DAMN YOU!' He kicked hard, knocking the mike from her fingers.

She screamed, a gash on her wrist welling scarlet. Her hands flew up to her face, protecting it, her body cowering. He reached over the dash and snapped off the VHF's circuit breaker. 'You were talking to the frigate, weren't you?'

She nodded hesitantly.

'Just what in hell did you tell them?'

Her body slowly relaxed. She dropped her hands, then sucked on the wound, two twin tears trickling down her cheeks. 'You're rotten through and through, Stone,' she finally said. 'There was a time I had some respect for you . . .'

Which was news to Stone. He nodded at the VHF radio. 'What was the conversation about?'

'I told them that I was a hostage and not to shoot. They said that they couldn't catch you anyway and were breaking off the chase. That was thirty minutes ago. Last thing the captain of the corvette told me was to stay on the frequency if I could.'

He suddenly felt a warm and fuzzy feeling creep over him. Just like that, they had caved in. He grinned, then, remembering the fuel, backed the throttles off to what he guessed was best cruise speed. The Bertram slowed slightly, the pounding less pronounced.

'I guess I ought to thank you,' he said, trying to make it sound reasonable.

'You have a damned odd way of expressing your gratitude, Stone.' She stood up and staggered to the starboard side, looking north-east toward the Straits of Dover, absently licking at her wound. She studied the horizon for a while, then came back and slid into the passenger seat opposite him.

'How far?' she asked.

'About sixty miles to Ramsgate, say two hours maximum.' He had altered course again, not quite sure of his position, not that it mattered. The stream of vessels heading out of the Channel stayed within the tight confines of the shipping lanes marked on his chart and, inshore of that, there would be identifiable sea buoys to pinpoint his position. Relaxing now, he stabilized his course on 043 degrees magnetic and switched on the autopilot.

He glanced off to port. Somewhere out there in the patchy scud, rain showers and cloud shadows was the coast of Kent, probably no more than twenty-five miles at its nearest point. But Ramsgate lay a considerable distance up the coast, and he was trying to lop some mileage off by going the direct route, rather than the scenic one.

He nodded to her wrist. 'How's the scratch?'

'It's all right.' She favored him with a sardonic smile, as if she were mentally pawing the ground – scheming how to get past his cape and gore him on the next *pase de capa*. He'd made a mental note to keep an eye on her, but he doubted that she'd defy him now.

He breathed in deeply, then let it out. Tired. And the thirsty inner man was banging on his stomach lining.

'What about getting me, ah, us a couple of beers?'

'Help yourself, Stone. I'm not your handmaiden.'

'Don't think I can trust you with the controls, *Mizzz* van der Groot.' He said it easily, trying to lighten her up.

She wasn't buying it. 'You're damned right you can't, *Mis*ter Stone.' She stuck out her tongue at him. He felt like doing likewise but didn't. The victor could afford to be magnanimous.

So he laughed. 'Come on – get us a beer. The good news, *Mizzz* van der Groot, is that I'll be out of your hair by tonight. I'd think that would be cause for celebration.'

'That is indeed good news, *Mis*ter Stone.' She hesitated for a split second, then turned to him, her eyes hard, glittering. 'The bad news, *Mis*ter Stone, is that the Navy is sending a ship, the HMS *Alacrity*, to escort us in.'

She had let it slip out – too quick with her tongue.

'How do you figure that?'

'The captain of the corvette told me. Said he had called on the NATO high seas distress frequency as soon as he saw you had the speed advantage. Said not to worry and to try to convince you to give up peacefully, which to me sounded like a damned fine idea.'

'And just what kind of a boat is the *Alacrity*?'

'The captain of the corvette said it was a Royal Navy

frigate. "A very fast frigate", he emphasized.' She said it with a smirk.

'And just where is this frigate, *Mizzz* van der Groot?'

'That, *Mis*ter Stone, is entirely unknown to me.'

But she had already told him. Somewhere up to the north, where she had been staring just a few minutes ago.

He hadn't been paying much attention to the radar. He reached over and flipped the range up to the maximum and studied the scope. On this side of the western approaches to the Channel, all the traffic was bound southwest, probably obeying some mandated speed limit, staying inside of the imaginary yellow lines. Nothing else on the scope that seemed out of place, but if the *Alacrity* was closing on him from the north-east at thirty knots, combined with his speed of thirty knots in that direction, the rate of closure would be more than a mile a minute. By the time he picked up her radar return, it would be too late to run for it.

He considered the alternatives. Back to France was definitely out. Another was to head for Kent, but he knew in his gut the whole coast would be on the alert for him and the Bertram wasn't exactly inconspicuous, what with French registration plastered on the hull. But there was a third alternative — it was just that it was slightly messy.

He glanced at his watch. Two hours, maybe less to sundown, three hours to total darkness. He switched off the autopilot and altered course for Kent, studying the inshore weather. Ahead of him was a gaggle of clouds with curtains of light rain beneath them, obscuring the horizon. He twitched the wheel a hair, aiming for the closest one, then reengaged the autopilot.

'You won't get away. They'll find you on their radar.'

He grabbed her roughly by the arm and yanked her off the seat, dragging her below into the main cabin. 'Get your mutt. There's a string shopping bag in the galley. Fill it with beer and bottled water. Anything else that looks edible, as long as it's packaged in plastic. And I want you back on deck in three minutes flat.'

'What do you think you're doing?'

'Jumping ship.'

'I'm not going with you.'

'Like hell you aren't. If I left you here alone, you'd be on the radio in nothing flat.'

'So break the radio.'

'Same result. Once they picked you up, you'd spill the beans.'

'I'm *not* going with you, Stone.' Her voice was adamant, the tone dangerous.

He pulled the Beretta from his waistband. 'Yes, you are.'

'You wouldn't shoot me.' She kept her voice calm, the original Ice Queen.

'You're right. But I'll shoot your dog.'

Her eyes widened.

He emphasized the point by thumbing back the hammer. 'Do we do it my way or not?'

Her jaw muscles were jumping. For a second, he thought she was going to swing at him, then all the fight drained out of her as she realized he was serious. She nodded slowly.

Stone wasn't satisfied. 'I want your word on it – nothing funny, you do as I say, and no arguments, no playing around.'

She nodded again and said it very softly. 'You have my word, but you're the most loathsome man I've ever met. You make Attila the Hun seem like a saint.'

'Just what my mother always told me. Now go do it.' He dropped his hold on her arm and ducked into the guest cabin, snatched the canvas attaché case and headed back to the cockpit.

He found a chart book of the English coast in the cockpit drawer and tore out the section that covered Kent, stuffing it in the bag. Two flashlights and some batteries cocooned in a blister pack followed. Compass. He'd need a compass.

He checked the one fixed to the panel in front of the helm. No time to unscrew the fasteners that held it in place. He pried the compass housing loose with a screwdriver, ripping the wood, then wrapped the thing in a towel.

The Bertram had almost reached the curtain of rain. Not heavy, but dense enough to mask him once he was in it. He took a quick glance back toward the shipping lane. There was an oil tanker about three miles away, plodding south-west, a rising sun on its hull. He couldn't take the chance that the coastal stations hadn't alerted all shipping to keep an eye out for him, so he cranked up the revs, impatient. In less than a minute, the Bertram had been swallowed by the rain, the stuff heavier than he had guessed.

He eased the throttles back to idle and shifted them into neutral. The Bertram slowed to a crawl, wallowing in the seaway.

The dinghy was a twelve-foot inflatable Zodiac, hung from davits over the stern. The motor was a Johnson Twenty, reasonably new and a close cousin to the fifteen-horse that Stone used on his crab boat in Maine. Scrounging around, he found both the fuel tank and a spare jerry jug of gasoline in a vented locker. Grunting, he hefted the motor into the dinghy, following it with the tanks, then lowered away after securing the dinghy's painter to a stern cleat.

In the live-bait well, he found a rusty knife in a sheath. Stone stashed it in his pocket. *Ready.*

She was back on deck with the dog, the string bag stuffed with food and bottles. The dog wasn't wagging his tail and his ears were flattened back. That's loyalty for you, thought Stone.

'Get into the Zodiac,' he snapped at her.

Lips set tightly together, she clambered into the dinghy, the dog jumping in after her.

Get set. Stone went back to the console and twisted the autopilot's dial to 250 degrees magnetic, switched on the autopilot and eased the gearshift levers into forward. Magically, the wheel turned, the Bertram slowly circling to port, then steadying down on a south-westerly heading. The speedo crept up to a knot and stabilized.

Secured in an overhead rack were an assortment of expensive deep-sea fishing rods and reels. Stone pulled down two of them, tossed one into the Zodiac and reeled out some line from the other. He formed a noose with a slipped bow line at the end of the monofilament and dropped it over the throttles, led the line forward over the windshield-wiper knob, then trailed it aft, reeling out slack as he went. He clambered down into the dinghy.

'Cast off the painter,' he commanded.

She untied the dinghy's bow line and they slowly drifted aft of the Bertram, the monofilament line tightening as it slowly pulled the throttles forward. The engines increased revs and the Bertram began to gather speed.

Go! He fished the knife out with one hand and yanked on the monofilament with the other. The Bertram's engines snarled, props churning the wake into white froth. The stern squatted down and the Bertram lunged forward, the monofilament line twanging tight. Stone hacked through it with one stroke. The Bertram roared off into the rain, screaming at full throttle toward the south-west. How long the fuel would last was anyone's guess, but it would give them something to chase.

They sat in the dinghy, listening until the roar faded to a whisper, then to silence. It was now dead quiet except for the sounds of waves slapping against the rubber tubes of the dinghy and the soft hiss of rain on her foul-weather jacket.

She tiredly handed him a beer and he popped the top. It was French stuff, bitter with a fuzzy aftertaste, but it tasted better than anything Stone had ever put to his lips.

'Oh, you're a bastard all right,' she said softly, 'but a clever one.'

*

He kept the speed down to about fifteen knots, conserving fuel and trying to keep the Zodiac from pounding too much. He sat on the starboard tube, one hand on the throttle of the Johnson, the other wrapped around a can of beer. It was warmer now and the seas shorter, the off-shore wind diminished by the coastal land mass.

Twice in the last hour, he had seen choppers in the distance, both headed south-west, their camouflage paint dull in the sun. Stone wondered whether the Bertram was still running full-tilt down the western approaches, HMS *Alacrity* in hot pursuit. The course he had set would probably fetch her up somewhere near Cherbourg or the Channel Islands, provided she wasn't run down by a ship or blown to fiberglass bits by the *Alacrity*.

He could no longer see any Channel shipping, the distance too great. It was likely, however, that there would be some local traffic as they got further inshore. He estimated they'd make the coast in half an hour, just at sundown, with enough twilight left over to sort things out. Still, the final approach to the coast would be critical. He didn't want to land on an open beach, chancing surf, hidden rocks and curious locals. Stone was looking for a harbor — a safe harbor, where dumb pleasure-boaters dropping in would be nothing out of the ordinary to the local gentry.

The dog was snoozing under the spray-dodger, his head cushioned in her lap. She had dropped the hood of her foul-weather jacket, letting her hair stream in the wind, her cheeks burnished red by the wind and sun. As he studied her, she absently stroked the animal's flank, detached, her eyes forward, watching the coastline grow from a low-lying smudge to a scattering of chalky cliffs and green fields. She hadn't spoken to him since they abandoned the Bertram.

Stone was into his fifth beer, his nerve endings pleasantly dull. He casually studied the coast, eyes straining against the glare of the setting sun.

Far up to the north was a hazy promontory with a number of structures jutting up into the evening light. As he watched, the most seaward structure winked – a lighthouse. But which one?

Dead ahead was low-lying – the countryside seemingly unpopulated except for the occasional farmhouse and paddock. A few church spires spiked the skyline further inland.

Off to the west were chalk cliffs, their bases battered by booming surf. *Better not land there*, old son, he thought. Where there were cliffs, there were bound to be rocky shoals and slashing undertows as well. He had no desire to swim ashore.

He tapped her on the back. 'Hand me the chart.'

'No need to. Up ahead, you're looking at the approaches to Rye Harbor. The lighthouse to the north is Dungeness.'

'You been into Rye before?'

She nodded, still not looking back at him, her words blown back by the wind. 'Just once. We had to bring *Night Watch* in at high water. The River Rother's quite shallow but probably deep enough for this thing at any state of the tide.'

'Rye. What kind of a place is it?'

'Little English town. God-fearing, law-abiding, peaceable. You should feel right at home.'

'Any cops, military?'

'Forgot to mention that, didn't I? The town is swarming with SAS. They're all charming lads but a bit on the stroppy side, particularly when it comes to terrorists of your ilk.'

'I'm serious.'

'Since when and about what?' She turned around to face him. 'It's a small town, Stone. That's all there is to it. On the east side of the river there's a harbormaster's office and a customs house. Next to that is a launching ramp for small boats and a car park with a public loo. My bladder would appreciate it if you stopped there.'

He looked forward again, trying to make out the approaches. He caught the blink of a red light slightly to the left of where he was looking and waited. It blinked again about five seconds later. He altered heading slightly, putting the lighted entrance buoy on his bow.

As he watched, he saw a mast moving across a green field. Then the boat that the mast was attached to popped out from behind a stone breakwater. Local fishing boat, headed out to sea. Stone was closing on it fast and he throttled back to a fast idle.

'Take one of the fishing rods and start trolling.'

'You can't be serious! In case you hadn't noticed, it's quite shoal in here. For us to be trolling would look quite odd.'

'Do like I say. I want to look dumb. That's what locals expect from out-of-town pleasure-boaters. I'm from the coast of Maine, remember?'

They passed the fishing boat within a stone's throw, both rods out. Stone waved like an idiot and the guy who was steering the fishing boat barely nodded back in acknowledgement, pipe clenched between his teeth, cap stuffed on the back of his head, a study in restrained English exuberance. First test passed, Stone guessed.

They were up to the buoy and passed it, the river opening up, the channel markers previously hidden by the sea wall marking the way inland.

He headed for the first blinking red light, intending to leave it to starboard. Basic rule when inbound from the sea: red, right, returning. But somehow, it didn't look quite right.

She shook her head. 'In England, it's the other way around when you're coming in from the sea. Green on your right, red on your left.'

'That makes perfect sense, doesn't it? Like the way you guys drive your cars on the wrong side of the road.'

He adjusted his course and throttled back, barely making five knots, posing as the happy weekend sailor home from the sea. He tried to whistle a tune but couldn't, his lips parched, his mouth suddenly dry.

Rye wasn't much to write home about, and that was exactly what he wanted. On the west bank of the river were a few homes, a small commercial district and a church. Somewhere, he could hear a piano playing and people singing. It smelled good, he thought. Early spring, the trees just starting to bud, the grass coming up. Maine would be the same by the time he got there, and he felt an unexpected pang of homesickness.

On the east bank were mooring stages and a jetty, backed by official-looking offices. Stone cruised past them as if he owned the place. Nobody hailed him.

Just as she had described, there was a concrete small-boat launching ramp which led to a parking lot in the field above it.

Stone puttered alongside the ramp, tied up and killed the engine.

She started to get out of the dinghy. He took her by the arm and squeezed. 'Where do you think you're going?'

'To spend a penny. To the loo, the potty, you know, Stone. Pee-pee.'

'Do I have your word?'

'Of course you do,' she said mechanically, out of sorts.

He didn't trust her worth a damn. 'I'll go with you.'

They went up the ramp, Sailor tied to a light nylon line which served as a makeshift leash. Stone's gait rolled, unused to the land, his senses still at sea. His leg hurt like hell; always did in damp weather. Too bad she hadn't bought some rum.

He let her enter the women's side, keeping Sailor as a hostage.

Stone waited outside, impatient. A couple walked by chatting and wished Stone a good evening. Afraid that his accent would betray him, Stone just smiled and nodded.

He checked his watch. She was taking too damn long. Stone entered the Ladies, Sailor in tow. She had started to write on the mirror with her lipstick. He whacked it out

211

of her hand and wiped the letters 'HELP CALL POL . . .' off the mirror with a paper hand-towel.

'So much for your word, lady.'

She yanked her arm from his grip. 'My father told me that the courts wouldn't uphold a contract made under duress. I was within my rights . . .'

'So you're a fucking lawyer now?'

The door suddenly opened and an older woman entered, then stopped stock still, her hand rising to her mouth.

Stone jiggled the zipper of his pants. 'It's all right, love. We were just leaving. The gentlemen's loo is knackered.' Stone smiled weakly and pushed Melissa out ahead of him, dragging the dog in tow.

She sniffed. 'You sounded exactly like what you are, Stone – a dumb American trying to imitate a Brit with an accent out of date by fifty years.'

He was tired of playing games, tired of her smart mouth. 'Okay, *Mizzz* van der Groot, where's the telephone?'

She showed him, a call box near the trash bin.

He had to reverse the charges and used the name 'John Talisker' as the calling party.

Mac came on, still talking to someone in the background. 'Who is this?'

'Mac – it's Talisker, your old friend. Thought I'd ring you up to find out whether your sheep misses me.'

'Where are you?' His voice was guarded. More voices in the background, the sound of a door slamming, another telephone ringing, a printer chattering.

'In a parking lot on the east bank of Rye Harbor. I need a ride.'

'You're all right?'

'Tired. I could use a stiff drink and a long sleep. Might have to lay up with you for a few days till things cool off.'

'You're quite the celebrity, you know. All over the telly.' He paused, a paper rustling. 'I just did a quick check on the road map. Should take me less than an hour.'

'Mac . . . ?'

212

'Yes.'

'See whether you can come in a van. I've got some evidence to dispose of.'

The line went very quiet.

'Mac . . . ?'

'I'm still here. What have you done with the woman, Stone?'

'Don't sweat it, Mac. It's just an inflatable boat and outboard motor I'm talking about.'

There was something that passed for a laugh from the other end of the line.

They picked up a bucket of sweet and sour pork – hold the MSG – a side order of fried rice and two Guinness stouts from a Chinese drive-through joint in Hythe, Mac taking care of the transaction while Stone, Melissa and the dog huddled in the back, out of sight. Three minutes later, Mac pulled out, heading north on the A259 toward Ramsgate, skirting the coast.

'How bad?' Stone asked between spoonfuls.

'Awful,' Mac answered, lighting a cigarette and exhaling. '*Bloody* awful. Peugeot and everything in it was destroyed by the fire. But they traced it back to the rental firm in Le Havre and got your name and a description. The French police lifted a set of your fingerprints from the rental agreement and put them on the Interpol wire. Turns out you're wanted in the US for various unspecified but serious felonies. I knew that you were in trouble with your own people, Stone, but they've made it sound as if you were some kind of one-man crime wave.'

'Anna . . . ?' she asked.

'The charred remains of a body were found in the ashes, but it was unidentifiable. Initially, arson for the insurance money was suspected. But the SDS are now hinting that the deceased was a drug pusher and a confederate of yours. Something murky about a cocaine deal in Corsica gone sour, and that the two of you burned the building to get

213

rid of her after hijacking a load of cocaine. They published a photo in the papers of you, Mrs van der Groot, taken from your French work-permit application. I must say it doesn't do you justice.'

'Anything new about Le Borveaux?' Stone asked.

'Nothing yet. I've made enquiries through some associates over there. But given the pattern of events, I would suspect he won't be heard from again.' He paused and knocked the ash on the edge of the rolled-down window, sparks streaming away into the night like a miniature Roman candle. 'What actually happened at this chap Perocette's place?'

Stone told him. That and the rest of it.

'Not quite the story the French are putting out. People working for you stole the Bertram power yacht at Le Havre and rendezvoused with you in the River Rancon to transfer the cocaine from the *Night Watch* to the Bertram for onward transport to England. There was an argument over ownership of the drugs. Perocette, a man of considerable reputation and a decorated war veteran, got in the way and was, I quote, "ruthlessly gunned down".'

'What about the Bertram?'

'Royal Navy has egg on its face. Chased the thing for close on an hour before it ran out of fuel some twenty miles south of the Isle of Wight. Boarded it and found no one was home. Still, they didn't come up empty-handed. Discovered two machine-pistol clips of 9-mm ammunition and a hundred grams of cocaine. The owner of the Bertram and his companion claim the small quantity left on board was part of the main shipment you were carrying. Claimed you were snorting the stuff, high as a bloody kite.'

'The lying bastard. There wasn't any cocaine on board, not that I saw. It had to be the owner's stash and he lied to cover his ass. What about Joss and company? The press say anything about them?'

'Nothing yet. But, as you might imagine, there's a massive search under way, centered around Southampton and the Isle of Wight.'

Stone forked down another load of fried rice. 'Something bothers me. Why would the Frog and Didi lie? What did they have to gain?'

Mac's face was gaunt, older-looking than Stone had remembered. He sucked on the cigarette, then blew smoke at the windscreen. 'The Frog you refer to, Monsieur Marc Borges, is a respected member of the French bar and a married man with wife and three young bairns. I suspect that he's telling the police what they want to hear and thus diverting attention from his own foibles. Infidelity and a drug habit would be damaging to a man of his standing. It wouldn't be the first time a gentleman has lied to protect his reputation.'

Practically the history of mankind, Stone thought.

They had already passed through Folkestone and Capelle-Ferne. On the outskirts, Mac slowed and turned left onto a secondary road, then right again between a set of brick entrance posts marked 'Channel View'.

'What's this?' Melissa asked. She scrubbed at the moisture on the side window, peering into the darkness.

'Caravan campground,' Mac answered. 'Not what you'd call proper accommodations, but the best place I could think of at short notice, given the situation. Bit early in the season for most people, but the management rents out units to the occasional young couple seeking privacy. You'll be safe here.'

Her voice rose in anger. 'I'm not going to hide out in some tatty caravan with *this* thug. You're taking me into Ramsgate, Mr Macleod. I'll make my own arrangements, thank you very much.'

'I wouldn't do that just yet, Mrs van der Groot.' Macleod's voice was weary. 'I think you'd better wait until morning, read the papers and absorb the gravity of the situation. Then we'll talk.'

'My father's a barrister. He can help me.'

'And he's the last man in the world you should call. There's a leak somewhere. I can't explain it, but someone on this side of the Channel knew, from the very beginning, what my brief was and what Stone's mission was in France. It could well be that my telephone in Skye was tapped, but I wouldn't discount that the leak originated when your father first received your letter and contacted Lloyd's. Given that situation, his line might be tapped, either by the police or by the terrorists. Please − to protect yourself, be patient. I'll be back in the morning with food. Then we'll go over the whole situation and attempt to establish a pattern. You have my word that I'll sort this out.'

'What about the *Night Watch*? Stone, your valued employee, left it stuck in the mud.'

'The French police have confiscated the vessel. They towed her to a marina in Le Havre and left a guard on it, pending an auction.'

'What auction?'

'I'm afraid that's their policy in terms of assets seized in drug-related cases. Normally, she'd be auctioned off in less than a month after seizure. But I'll see what I can do. If necessary, I'll send someone over to bid for her, then arrange to bring her back to England.'

She sat back in the seat, obviously relieved. 'I presume that you'll cover all costs.'

Clearly embarrassed, Mac shook his head. 'I don't have sufficient funds in hand and if I were to ask my principals for an advance of that magnitude, I'd expose you and Stone. Could you raise any money? Generally, an item seized goes for less than half its true value.'

'She is, or at least was, in absolutely beautiful condition, worth close on £100,000, Mr Macleod. That's what she was appraised for less than five months ago. And just where do you think I'd be able to find even half that much money, even assuming that it would be sufficient to win the bidding?' Her voice was brittle.

Mac downshifted, slowing the van. 'Don't worry your

head, lass. We'll have this thing sorted out soon enough.'

She made an exasperated noise and leaned back in the seat. Stone could almost hear her fuse burning.

Mac pulled the van up in front of a scruffy house-trailer. 'This is it, I'm afraid. I'll go about making better arrangements tomorrow.'

'By tomorrow, I'll be gone,' she said.

'Perhaps,' Mac answered non-committally.

Stone had kept out of it up until now, defeated by guilt and weariness. But he had one shining prize.

'Mac – this Joss creep had Le Borveaux's papers in his attaché case. I've got it.'

There was a long silence. 'Are you sure it's Le Borveaux's?'

'Haven't had time to go through it yet, but I will, first thing tomorrow. Melissa speaks Frog. She can help me with the translation.'

'Right. But for now, I've got to get back to Ramsgate and attend to a few things. Incidentally, no one in my group knows where I am or that the two of you are with me. Thought it best for now.' He slid open the door of the van and stepped out, Stone, Melissa and the dog following.

The caravan was cramped. One large bed and a sofa, a small dining-table and a kitchen. It smelled of fried cabbage and stale beer.

'Charming,' she said, flopping down on the bed, exhausted.

As usual, he got the sofa.

Angus K. Paine, a.k.a. 'AK' – a subject of Northern Ireland, white male, one meter seventy in height, twelve stone in weight, pale-complexioned, brown hair, hazel eyes, the only mark on his body a sixteen-centimeter scar running from his right shoulder-blade to his lower back – walked past the converted machine shop which now had a sign in the window identifying it as Highgate Engineering. Paine swatted a newspaper against his leg, thoroughly agitated because, quite simply, he had screwed up. His current boss, should he learn of this monumental fuck-up, would likely have Paine's balls for breakfast.

Paine's last legitimate employer had been the Royal Air Force, his trade an aircraft ordnance specialist with a secondary rating as electrician. That was three years ago. Paine – whose chums called him 'AK' not because of his initials but rather because of his enduring love affair with fully automatic weapons – had been quietly mustered out after certain items of ordnance had gone missing from an RAF warehouse that Paine had access to. During the enquiry, Paine knew they had nothing they could prove and had told the investigating officer to get stuffed. Up to *here*, mate.

After being demobbed, AK had drifted back to Northern Ireland. Hanging out in the right pubs, he met men who thought as he did: Prods who had a passion to kill the Irish Papists. AK, seeing a few bob to be made by cannily matching politics with the laws of supply and demand, used his old connections in the RAF to liberate 'surplus' explosives and weapons which AK then moved north in a pig delivery van. It wasn't all beer and skittles and the smell of pig shit seemed to permeate everything he owned, but the arms racket, with some casual cocaine-peddling on the side, kept him in pocket change. AK also believed that, eventually, someone within the Movement would steer him into work even more lucrative.

Predictably, his name had eventually been passed along by one of the bosses in the Movement to a German bloke who needed a job done. The Kraut had kept it simple.

First, AK was to tap into a telephone cable that serviced an outfit called Highgate Engineering. Once AK had a tap on the cable, he was to connect the tap to a box the size of a small milk carton and screw that into the utility pole. AK had marveled at the device: it was a miniature transmitter of some sort, complete with an antenna not much bigger than a cockroach's prick. On top was a solar cell which probably fed a battery inside the box. *Too cute by half,* he thought.

The second part of the assignment was keeping track of some old Scots bastard by the name of Macleod. It was this that AK had screwed up on this particular evening. Around dinner-time, he had knocked off for a pint of bitter and a plate of scampi at the local. The Scot always worked late, never left the office before midnight, lived upstairs in the loft. Except tonight.

AK had missed him. The Scot's van was missing. Not to worry, he thought. He'd be back, and from now on AK would stick to the old bastard like a leech.

ELEVEN

South Coast of England, 7 April

The three of them sat around the small dining-table of the caravan having breakfast, Melissa translating Le Borveaux's notebook between bites of Marmite on toast and sips of Bovril. Stone thought it was a revolting way to start the day and said so. Macleod had then looked up at Melissa and they both shrugged, as if silently agreeing that there was no accounting for American tastes or lack thereof. Disgusted, Stone fed the toast to the dog and pined for a cup of decent coffee.

'That's all there is,' she said finally. 'Just a personal diary he wrote while he was on the GEM. No specifics concerning the location of the boreholes, just that they were never grouted and his nagging concern about being involved in litigation. He comes across as a bit of an academic twit, but still, he's obviously a man with deep moral convictions.'

Mac had been making notes. 'Le Borveaux refers to the drilling log five times in the last fourteen pages of his diary.'

She nodded. 'But they were the property of the English geologist who was on board the GEM with Le Borveaux . . . ah, a Mr Ronald Harriman.'

'Yet Le Borveaux's wife said her husband had made duplicate copies of the logs,' Stone interjected.

'*Had* is the operative word,' Macleod replied. 'He probably borrowed the originals from Harriman for duplication but they're gone now.' He nodded to a pile of papers that were stuffed in a blank envelope. 'What about that trash?'

Stone hadn't looked yet, the diary being first priority. He pulled them out and leafed through them. They were a jumble of receipts, maybe twenty in all, from motels, restaurants, and service stations. 'All made out to cash . . .' He turned over a pink slip. '. . . except this one. The receipt for an overnight delivery by DHL from Le Havre to their office in Utrecht. The sender's name is Antonio Bontoc, no address given, paid for with a credit card.'

Melissa frowned. 'But if this Bontoc is a criminal, why would he pay with a credit card when everything else he purchased was paid for in cash?'

'If he was trying to keep his identity secret, he obviously wouldn't use a credit card, but who knows . . . Possibly, the DHL desk clerk didn't have enough cash on hand if Bontoc had a large bill and Bontoc was therefore forced to use a credit card.'

Mac put his cup down and examined the receipt. 'You mentioned that this fellow Joss spoke with an American accent but had the features of a South-Eastern Asian. Bontoc sounds like a Filipino name, even if it's an alias. I'll run the card number and name past a friend of mine in Special Branch to see whether he can match it with any records on the Continent or the UK, but I doubt that it will lead to anything. Generally speaking, people like this Joss person use three or four passports when they're traveling, both depending on the circumstance and as a means to cut the continuity of their movements. And the card could well be stolen.' He scratched down the name. 'What address was the package sent to in Utrecht? That sounds more promising.'

'General delivery to the DHL office in Utrecht. Addressed to a H. Maas.'

Mac made an unpromising grunt. 'What were the contents and the value of the materials sent?'

'No value declared. Contents are listed as commercial papers.'

'How recently was it shipped?' Mac leaned forward, his pencil tapping on the paper.

'3 April, 08.40, sent from Le Havre.' Stone counted time

backwards in his mind. 'That was the day after I arrived in Le Havre – and the morning following the night that Le Borveaux was kidnapped. It fits.'

Macleod leaned back in his chair, his mouth twisted in disappointment. 'I expect that we now know what the contents of the package were. They were after the drilling logs and Joss shipped them to whomever's running the operation as soon as he got his hands on them.'

'How about Maas. You can trace him, can't you?' she asked.

'Unlikely,' Mac said. 'Maas or whoever it was that picked up the package had to know it was coming. Went into the DHL shop and flashed some identification, probably not his own.' He sighed. 'I'll make enquiries but I wouldn't get my hopes up.'

Stone stood up and stretched. 'That leaves Harriman, the English geologist, Le Borveaux's buddy on the GEM. He'd have the original logs.'

'You're talking about an event that happened more than two decades ago.' Mac swiped at his nose. 'He could be dead as a dormouse by now.'

'But someone was paying his wage to examine the core samples for traces of petroleum-bearing sands – probably a British oil company. The records would have survived him.'

Mac nodded, then started writing. 'Yes . . . quite possibly, quite possibly. And there would undoubtedly be a professional organization of some sort that Harriman belonged to. From there, it would be a straightforward job to find whom he worked for. Good thinking, Stone. I should be able to have an answer on this by next week.' He stood up, folding his notebook. He opened a worn leather briefcase and placed the notebook in a compartment, then extracted a camera. 'I'll need some shots of both of you. Best we drape a white sheet for the background.'

'What for?' Melissa asked.

'Passports. Yours will be that of an Englishwoman, of

course, Mrs van der Groot. I think that Stone could pass for a Canadian. Do you have any preference as to names?'

She slumped down on the couch. 'Mr Macleod. You haven't listened to me very well. I'm not involved in this stupid game that the two of you are so keen on playing. Someone tried to kill me. I've lost my business and my yacht. But, thank God, my father's a barrister at law. Given his connections and knowledge of the law, he can clear this up for me.'

'I shouldn't doubt it,' Macleod answered. 'But I can't allow you to expose either yourself or Stone. Not yet. Stone's the only one who's likely to recognize Joss. But if you go to the police, you'll necessarily expose him in order to validate your story. Additionally, there's damn little to substantiate your claims of innocence. The French would put pressure on the Foreign Office to extradite the lot of you. It might take months to sort out and I don't have the luxury of time on my side.'

Stone shook his head slowly. 'That goes for me as well, Mac. I didn't sign on to get killed. I've found out what I can and that's it. Get me a passport and I'm out of here.'

Macleod made an exasperated noise in his throat. 'I don't give a damn what you *want*, Stone. You actually *saw* these people, know what they look like, have an idea of how they operate. Right now, we don't know whether they're going to attempt to blow the boreholes or whether they're planning to blow the Chunnel from the inside. Either way, we have to cover both possibilities and you're my best bet at identifying them.'

'Sure, I can help put together a composite like the stuff the cop artists draw. But you've got plenty of manpower to do your leg work, Mac. Don't give me a bunch of baloney about me being indispensable!'

Macleod sighed. 'As to manpower, yes, I have twelve people, most of them specialists or former coppers. But I can't tell them about you, understand? All it would take would be for one of them to get an attack of righteous indignation and turn you in. There's a reward for information leading to your apprehension. And Lloyd's has already put me on notice. I filed a progress report with them based on the information you gave me on the telephone from the French pilot's home. So they know I hired you and now they're most unhappy with the muck you've stirred up, blaming me, you see? If Lloyd's knew that I was harboring you, I'd be sent packing on the spot.'

'Lloyd's doesn't know?'

'No, and I can't afford to tell them until we have something substantial to go on — something, I might add, that would probably clear both of you of charges at the same time.'

She was sitting there, her head bent down, slowly shaking it from side to side. 'I want out of this thing, Mr Macleod. I can't take it.'

Macleod bent down and lifted her chin. Her eyes were wet.

'I understand, girl. Just try to be patient with me. I'll personally go up to London tomorrow afternoon and explain the situation to your father. Give me four days. At any rate, it'll take that long for my people to forge your passport and I'm afraid that you might have use for it until this thing's over with.'

She hesitated, dropped her head, then slowly nodded.

Standing up, Macleod laid the camera on the table. 'Take several shots full front profile, full frame, Stone. I'll pick up the film tomorrow morning on my way up to London.' He moved to the door, curling his finger at Stone. Stone shrugged and followed him outside.

It was actually warm, rare for early April. Beyond the caravan grounds, Stone could see a scattering of houses, the roadway and the sea beyond.

'You have a firearm of some sort?' Mac asked.

'A Beretta. Joss's.'

'Keep it handy but try not to shoot anyone, lad. The police take a dim view of that in this country.'

224

'What about a rental car? We're stuck here.'

'Don't want to chance you wandering about. With your luck, you'd run down a constable and the fat would be in the fire. I've brought food enough to last a week and I'll bring some clothes and toilet articles tomorrow morning when I drop by to pick up the film. What I want you to do is to keep to the caravan until I come back on Tuesday. No exposing yourself unnecessarily. And I'm holding you responsible for making sure that the girl doesn't wander off either.'

Mac checked his watch. 'Tomorrow's Friday. I'll try to see her father then, but I can't chance calling him. Just have to go up to London direct from here and take my chances that he'll be in. The passports are promised for Monday, latest Tuesday. Cost a bloody packet but one of the best commercial forgers in England. I'll have new accommodations set up for you by then and, hopefully, Melissa's father can take over custody of her.' He stuck out his hand. 'Take care until then, Stone.'

'Mac . . . ?'

Macleod paused by his van, buttoning his jacket. He had aged a decade in a week – an old man trying one last time to make the world safe for fools.

'Yes?'

'Thanks for your help but the answer's *no*. This wasn't the kind of job I signed on for.'

Macleod slid into the driver's seat, his expression unchanged, as if he hadn't heard.

'AK' Paine crouched behind the low stone wall more than eighty meters away, one thousand quid's worth of Nikon telephoto gear screwed to a tripod, the lens just nosing over the rocks.

He had followed the old bastard this morning when he left Highgate Engineering just after seven, surprised when the Scot's first stop was a greengrocer's in Deal and the second a Paki mini-mart in Dover. Four big boxes of food

225

– enough to keep Macleod in tucker for a month. Now, AK understood the buying binge. Macleod was harboring someone on the run.

The two men in the viewfinder were talking, Macleod doing most of it. AK tripped the shutter, then zoomed in for individual portraits. The younger one's face was wind-burned, tanned, a working bloke's puss. *Click*. The film automatically advanced with an expensive purr. AK took four more, then three of Macleod.

The bloke was the American chap, Stone, AK guessed. Had to be, in all the rags and on the telly. Five thousand quid on his nose, the coppers were offering. 'Armed and extremely dangerous' was the word ITN was putting out. The £5000 AK was being paid for this job was good, but AK intended to push up the price to twice that. AK was just dying to get to a phone and call Horst. *Proper job, mate, worth £10,000 for starters.*

They passed Friday and much of Saturday in silence. She brooded while Stone either stared out at the sea or slept. She thought it was as if an unstated truce had been arrived at, the opponents too exhausted to press the fight.

She had put up a blanket to privatize her sleeping-accommodations, not that it did much good. It was like living in a shoe box. Stone, perhaps more sensitive than she might have expected, seemed to take pains not to look when she wrestled into her new clothes, dowdy things that Macleod had picked up at Marks and Sparks, spring sale, twenty-five per cent off.

Sailor, poor thing, probably bored with inactivity and bedeviled by split loyalties, alternately padded between her and Stone, as if seeking benediction. Because Macleod had not brought dog food, Sailor had dined on tinned bangers and instant mash, no worse for the experience, she thought, except for the predictable gas attacks whose tox-icity, she reckoned, would have laid low the lads in the trenches.

She folded the *Daily Mail* closed and checked her watch: 17.50. She was leaning against the wall of the caravan, her cheek touching the window. It was twilight, the soft April night folding over the coast. The running lights of ships tracked silently down the Channel, outbound for tropic islands in distant seas. She desperately wished she were on one.

'Stone – let's go for a walk. It's nearly dark.'

He grunted, turning over on the sofa. 'Can't. Macleod said we shouldn't expose ourselves.' He got up, stretched, scratched his elbow and opened the door of the minifridge. 'Where's the beer?'

She sighed, weary to death of this man. 'I only drank one of them. And *that's* the only one I've had, Stone.' She expected him to go into low earth-orbit but he didn't.

He sniffed and shuffled to the window, looking past her to the sea, his body just touching hers. She wanted to draw away, yet didn't, not wanting to offend him, to start the whole agony of confrontation over again. She had to last it out until Tuesday.

'There were three six-packs of Watney's,' he said. It wasn't exactly an accusation and yet it was.

'You're right. There were three cartons, eighteen tins of beer. You've had seventeen of them in the last forty-eight hours. I expect that Mr Watney will be pleased with his bottom line this month.' She had said it to be amusing, to cut the tension, but it had come out as a bitchy chastisement. How odd, she thought. I never did that to Pieter, even when he was being insufferable about achieving *his* goals, ignoring mine. Then why was she acting this way now? Was it that she actually loathed Stone, or was it something else, perhaps a defense mechanism on her part? If so, a defense against what? She buried the thought, not wanting to examine it or where it would lead her.

He cleared his throat, probably wanting to defend his drinking habits but unwilling to violate the terms of the truce. Instead he asked, 'What's for chow?'

She had planned carefully, knowing the moment would come. 'Roast beef, rare. Yorkshire pudding, snow peas topped with sliced almonds, bib lettuce with Roquefort dressing and probably a trifle for dessert. Coffee, of course – Jamaican Blue Hill. Alternatively, you might try the breaded scampi, caught fresh today.'

He moaned piteously. 'I'm serious.'

'So am I.' She picked up the brochure from the bedside table and handed it to him. She had found it, along with car-rental literature and a tour guide, in the dresser, probably left there by the last occupants.

The brochure was a blurb for a local pub called the Crown and Bridge, '. . . on charming Suttle Lane in the historic village of Capel-le-Ferne, overlooking the White Cliffs of Dover and convenient to the Folkestone Ferry.' A simplified map was on the back cover page. She had calculated that it was less than a kilometer walk over open fields, only one public roadway to cross.

'We can't . . .'

'Stone. Two days have passed. We're old news, buried in the back pages. National attention has turned elsewhere. There's a front-page flap on about an animal right's group who are bashing some chap who sexually abused his daughter's pony. All captured in exquisite detail on a neighbor's home minicam. As for us, the police have probably concluded that if they didn't catch us in the first day, we've gone to ground. International drug runners of our stature just don't hang around the scene of the crime. Just isn't done, Stone.'

She poked him in the ribs, trying to get him in the mood. 'Come on, Yank. Shave your face, get dressed and take your girl out to dinner. It's a little pub in a little town, well off the trodden path.' She laid down her ace card. 'It says here . . .' She leaned lightly against him and pointed a finger at the text beneath a photo of a ruddy-faced publican beaming over a polished bar. '. . . that "the Crown and

Bridge stocks the widest possible selection of single distilled malt whiskeys in the South of England".'

Stone didn't say anything, just pursed his lips, then got out the razor and soaped his face, humming.

The Crown and Bridge was as advertised and she loved it – had missed the gentle familiarity of the British local for these many years. Oaken posts and beams turned umber from tobacco smoke and smoldering wood fires, the sweet-thick scent of stout in the air, brick floors polished smooth by generations of leather boots, the tables grainy from two centuries of scrubbing. She chose a candlelit table by the fire.

The food was solid pub fare: generous portions, soul-satisfying with no pretensions. She had Dover sole, Stone, predictably, the roast. Between them, they shared a bottle of hock.

He raised his glass to her. 'Pretty good idea you had.'

That he approved pleased her. They touched rims.

He sipped at the wine, then set the glass down, twisting the stem, obviously working up to something. He was a bit awkward, hesitating as he said it, like a small boy admitting an inconsequential sin. 'I've given you a good deal of trouble. Beating up on you and all. I apologize, Melissa. Truly do. Never meant to hurt you.'

She lowered her head slightly, examining her hands, a little embarrassed because she hadn't been much help to him, had wanted to do it her own way, not considering the consequences. She looked up, capturing his eyes. 'I was thinking about it too, just this afternoon. I'm bitchy sometimes, Stone. I don't mean to be, it's just that I've lived alone for so long that I've forgotten there are other people with other agendas. I understand why you did what you did . . . and you didn't hurt me, really.' She hesitated. 'Just one thing I have to know. Would you really have shot Sailor?'

He leaned back and laughed. 'That clown? I could never bring myself to kill an innocent like that. But it was the only thing I could think of to get your undivided attention short of clobbering you. Speaking of Sailor, thought that if you needed someone to take care of him while you're getting things sorted out, I could fly him back to Maine with me. He'd love it there. Small island, raccoons and squirrels to chase, three squares a day and I'll teach him how to shuck clams.'

He was smiling, even white teeth, sun wrinkles around his eyes, his hair flopping over his eyebrows, tan, boyish despite his age. Her heart hesitated for a second, a feeling that startled her, not felt in so long. Not since Pieter. She tried to push it away.

'You're really serious about going back?' she asked.

He nodded. 'Yeah, but only after we get the *Night Watch* out of France. Obviously, Mac wants to use me as bird dog, but if I went along with him, eventually, I'd come in contact with your cops. Bound to be questions, delays, and in the meanwhile, the US Department of Injustice would get wind of it. Either that or the French. Both of them will ask for extradition and probably get it. I'm just the kind of example that they love to make.'

'What did you do in the States that was so awful?'

He told her about the mix-up in tax reporting, the tunnel under the Berlin Wall and Kagg's plastic entombment, then the grim details of the *Griswald* propeller story. At first, she listened to him seriously, then, realizing how outrageous it all was, tried to keep a straight face and, unable to contain herself, burst into laughter.

He looked up at her, first probably thinking she was laughing at him, then realizing that she was enjoying his company, laughing with him, visualizing David smiting Goliath with the sword of divine justice, guarded by a shield of black humor.

She had to wipe the tears away, still laughing, then got the hiccups. He made a big thing about her having to drink water from a glass while bending over, her head between her legs. He demonstrated. She tried. It didn't work. By this time, their serving girl and the publican were looking on, half-amused, half-concerned, full of old family remedies.

Nothing they suggested worked, but she drew the line at stuffing beans up her nose. She finally got it under marginal control.

'We're not exactly . . . *hut* . . . inconspicuous . . . *hut* . . . Stone. Mr Macleod would . . . *hut* . . . have a stroke if he knew we were here.' She broke out laughing again, then held her breath, forcing her breathing to calm. A giggle leaked out. It's the wine, she thought, but realized that she was actually enjoying the pleasure of his company.

She caught his eyes studying her, grinning back, Stone slowly twirling the stem of his empty wine glass. He must have been thinking the same thing. 'It wasn't all that bad, was it – our time together?' he asked softly.

Initially, the idea struck her as absurd, then she realized that for the first time in her life she had lived on the edge, had been part of something bigger than the endless repetition of dull days, had actually relished the danger in a perverse sort of way. Frightening, but also something that had brought her senses alive. Now, she felt whole, vital, somehow transformed. And, in a sweeping realization, she recognized that he had saved her from death twice, possibly three times, at risk to his own life. He had done that, she thought guiltily, and I never even thanked him.

She nodded. 'Yes, and I shan't ever forget the time we had together.' She reached across the table, placing her hand on his. His hand was roughened by weather and hard work, the skin dry. But warm. His other hand folded over hers, pressing it firmly, yet gently.

He dropped his voice to almost a whisper. 'You're very tough and very beautiful and very, very desirable. I had to say that, Melissa, just had to so that you'd know . . .' He frowned as if he had surprised himself. 'I mean . . .' He couldn't finish it but he didn't have to.

The warmth of his hands transferred to hers, rushing through her arteries and veins, through her heart, warming her whole body in a flush of heat. There was suddenly an odd, hollow aching between her thighs.

Oh my God, I want him, she realized with a shock. Had subconsciously known it almost from the beginning, that first night they arrived at Perocette's, yet had pushed it away, not sure of what it would mean to her, the unknown to remain safely forever the unknown.

Their legs, perhaps accidentally, touched beneath the table and some kind of electrical current arced between them, a jolt which triggered hammering in her heart. And she could see the same reaction reflected in his eyes, feel the increased pressure of his hands, see the acceleration of the pulse in his throat.

Their candle flickered and bent in a cold draft, the door of the pub opening and closing, voices behind them.

Melissa looked up. The serving girl led a young woman past them toward a table in the corner and, as she did, the woman looked at their hands joined together, a condescending half-smile on her face.

Self-consciously, Melissa withdrew her hand and Stone froze, not understanding.

The woman in the corner was shaking her head, saying something in a low voice. Melissa saw her pass a five-pound note to the serving girl who quickly stuffed it into the pocket of her apron. The serving girl smiled solicitously and indicated a table next to theirs which shared the warmth of the fireplace.

'This do? Nice fire in the grate, bit of a chill out tonight, isn't there, now?' She drew back a chair for the woman and took out her order pad. 'Starters tonight are jellied eel or Spanish prawns. Soup's leek *au gratin*. Everything on the menu's available except for the chops. Do you fancy something to drink?'

The woman smiled mechanically, handing back the menu. 'I'll have a bottle of wine — a *Pouilly Fuissé* if it's a decent year. And bring two glasses, please. A gentleman will be joining me shortly.'

The woman was behind Stone and he couldn't see her, hadn't really noticed her. He slowly pulled back his empty hands as if he didn't know what to do with them, a vague hint of hurt or irritation in his eyes.

Melissa smiled at him, trying to bring him back to her. 'Stone – don't misinterpret what I'm about to say but I've had a wonderful time tonight. What would you think of leaving now . . . a nice walk back across the meadow. And we could take a bottle of bubbly with us. Muted howls at the moon from our doorstep. Just a final drink between parting friends.'

His face softened, the beginnings of a smile in the corners of his mouth.

'I'm so sorry to disturb you but do you have a light?' The woman had gently tapped Stone on the shoulder, completely ignoring Melissa, a cigarette held in the V of her fingers.

She's at least eight years younger than I am, Melissa thought, irritated. Not just beautiful but an absolute knockout in an exotic, primitive way. Perhaps Greek or Lebanese. They always looked fabulous when they were young but bulged out like sows when they grew older – she could just imagine what she would look like in ten years. Melissa bit down hard as she watched Stone fumble for matches.

The woman had widely spaced dark eyes, high cheekbones, flawless olive-tan complexion and long black hair which trailed over her shoulders, catching highlights from the candles.

It was the dress that did it. She was clothed in a black thing that was deceptively simple, enormously expensive and perfectly tailored to fit her extravagant body, accentuating her high breasts. The woman exuded raw sex. Melissa caught a whiff of the woman's scent – *Safari* by Ralph Lauren, a killer fragrance if there ever was.

233

Frustrated, she watched the act begin – the storyline so bloody obvious. The woman was out hunting, a predatory bitch, and she had set her sights on Stone.

'There *is* a lighted candle on your table,' Melissa said, refrigerating her voice.

Stone threw her a quick frown, probably embarrassed by her lack of civility, then pivoted in his chair, a matchbook held in his fingers, the guardian of the flame, the last purveyor of chivalry.

Instead of reaching for it, the woman bent forward with the cigarette held in her mouth, waiting for Stone to light it. The movement of her body flopped the top of her dress away from her body, exposing and accentuating the mounds of her breasts. *The slut wasn't wearing a brassiere!* Stone nearly burned his fingers lighting her cigarette.

'Thank you ever so much,' the woman said, her eyes locking on to Stone's. She blew a thin plume of blue smoke toward the ceiling.

He fumbled out a reply and turned back to Melissa, but she had already gotten up, had to get him out of here before the woman ruined it. 'You might ask for the bill. I'll be back in a sec.' She headed for the women's loo, trying hard to keep her carriage erect, her movements graceful.

Once inside the loo, she stood before the mirror, examining the damage. *God, I look like an old hag*, she swore to the figure in the glass. The dress made her look like the aging matron of a delinquent youth's correctional institution. *I'm plain as oatmeal, pushing forty.* She bared her teeth. Damned chip. Stone had hit her with a tackle; she could remember the concrete rushing up to her face. Have to cap that eventually.

She took her comb from her handbag and started to pull it through her hair, yanking at the knots, still studying her reflection.

Why on God's green earth would he be attracted to me? She combed harder, trying to tame the strands into submission. *Come on, old girl. He's not your sort anyway.* She splashed cold water on her face, scrubbing the skin with both hands, trying to infuse a little color, then blotted up the moisture with a paper towel. She touched up her lipstick, then raked her comb furiously through her hair once more and called it quits. Some things you could change, some you couldn't.

She wondered whether he'd make the first move. Probably not. For all his masculinity, she sensed he was shy. But could she? She wanted it to happen and yet she didn't – her logic conflicting with her heart. And where would it lead? To bed, of course. To sheets thrown back and bodies intertwined, to lips on lips, his heart to hers, beating wildly. The mental image became more graphic than she thought her mind was capable of, and she wanted him now, the pressure intense in her thighs, her hormones singing. And realized that where it led didn't matter.

Before going back to the table, she intercepted the serving girl. Melissa passed her a twenty-pound note, her last. 'A very nice bottle of champagne, chilled please. To go. And please bring our bill immediately.'

The girl actually curtsied. 'A special evening, is it?' She winked.

Melissa didn't answer, just pursed her lips and winked back.

The bitch had moved her chair closer to their table, talking intently to Stone, her eyes smiling, her body language begging for him to reach out and take a handful. And the stupid bugger was lapping it up, probably had an erection pinned down between his crossed legs.

She tapped Stone on the shoulder. 'Sto . . . ah, darling,' she said. 'We'll be late for our appointment.' She had caught herself just in time from using his name. *Idiot!*

He turned to her, looking up, a little surprised. His face was flushed.

Dammit! She wasn't going to let this bitch ruin it. She sat down tentatively on the edge of her chair, ignoring the woman, ready to leave. 'I already ordered the bubbly. The girl's bringing the bill. Are you finished?'

He looked at her, then back to the bitch. 'Ah . . . I'm sorry. Your name again?'

'Francine. Francine Margeaux.' She extended her hand to Melissa as if she were royalty, expecting it to be kissed.

'Mel . . . ah, Melanie. Melanie Simms. I'm very pleased to meet you. Terribly sorry, but we were just leaving.'

Their eyes met, the bitch's hard as glass, black as ancient ice.

'I was just asking Christopher whether he had any idea of how long it would take to drive down from Dover,' the bitch said. 'My friend's late and I'm concerned.'

Melissa was enormously relieved. So the bitch actually had other plans, just practicing on Stone, just keeping her talons sharpened. 'It can't be more than a ten-minute drive,' she answered evenly.

The woman glanced down at her delicate and extraordinarily expensive watch. 'He's late and that's so unlike Karl.'

'Who's late?'

Melissa turned her head. He was older, mature, silver-haired, his face deeply tanned, his teeth even and white. He was dressed in casual but elegant clothes: a ribbed polo shirt, rust-red slacks and a Harris tweed sports jacket draped over his shoulders. He was unquestionably one of the most attractive men she had ever seen.

His eyes captured hers and he bent forward in the slightest suggestion of a bow. 'I'm so pleased to meet you. My name is Karl Brunner,' he said.

TWELVE

Stone stood up awkwardly, bumping the underside of the table with his knee, his chair penned between Melissa's and Francine's. The man stood there, a relaxed smile on his face, his hand extended. Stone grasped it and pressed well-manicured flesh. 'Good evening. My name's Sto . . .'

Melissa's shoe connected with his shin. He glanced down at her momentarily distracted, then understood.

'Ah, Christopher . . . Walker. Pleased to meet you, Mr Brunner. This is my, ah, friend, ah . . . Mizz . . .' *Damn – what was the blasted name she had just given Francine? Tip of the tongue . . .* 'Ah, . . . Mizz Simms . . . Melanie Simms.'

Brunner nodded, flashing a mouthful of exquisite teeth. They were either the product of unbelievably expensive dental work or, alternatively, Brunner had maintained them to perfection with some formidable assistance from the Tooth Fairy. Stone subscribed to the former.

'Just "Karl", please.' Brunner reached down and brushed a fingertip off Francine's nose. 'How's it going, Francine?' He didn't wait for an answer, but positioned a chair next to Melissa's. 'Francine looks after my interests while I'm away from England,' he explained. He turned his head, searching for the serving girl. She was already under way, making flank speed toward the table with an ice bucket under one arm and a tray balanced on the other. Stone reflected that there was a unique set of people in the world to whom serving people were drawn as if they were lodestones. Stone had long ago recognized that he wasn't one of them, but Brunner evidently was.

'. . . Which is most of the time,' Francine laughed, picking up on Brunner's remark. 'Karl seems to find his Mediterranean interests in constant need of close, personal supervision. Your tan looks fabulous, Karl. When did you get in?'

'About two hours ago. Sorry for being late. There was a delay in the ship's clearance at Dover.' He turned to Melissa, beaming full on. 'I really don't do Francine justice. She runs the business and makes all the decisions. I just spend the profits.'

The serving girl had arrived, burdened by her load and probably flustered with the mixed-up seating arrangements. She clamped a bucket containing a bottle of Dom Perignon to the table next to Brunner, then distributed four glasses.

She held up a tab. 'Whose bill's this on?' Brunner plucked it from her fingers as if he were a magician pulling a coin from behind a child's ear. 'Mine.' He glanced at the label and nodded in apparent approval. 'Bring another one of these immediately, please.' He removed the foil and wire basket in a succession of deft movements, then expertly applied his thumbs to the cork. It slid out with a polite cough.

'Please . . .' Melissa had her hand on his arm. 'I ordered that.'

'And an excellent choice you made,' Brunner replied. He filled a glass and handed it to Melissa. 'You're elected the official taster. How long have you and Christopher known Fran?'

Melissa had the glass to her lips and nearly choked.

Francine did the honors. 'We've just met, Karl.'

Brunner looked confused, then dramatically banged his fist against his forehead. 'Good God in heaven! You two must think me a fool, barging in. I had no idea . . .'

Stone struggled to get up again. 'It's okay. We were just leaving.' Things were getting complicated and he wanted to get out of here with Melissa before it went any further,

Mac's warning against undue public exposure now ringing in his ear.

Brunner turned to him. 'I'm *terribly* sorry, Christopher. I just assumed . . .' He turned to Melissa. 'How idiotic of me. The champagne was yours then, wasn't it? And here I've opened it.' His hands made a dismissive movement in Stone's direction. 'Please sit down. The girl will be back with another bottle in a minute. I give my solemn word not to deflower it. Here – let's all have a glass while we're waiting.' He poured three more glasses and passed them around. 'Cheers, then.'

Reflexively, they clinked rims.

A small dance band was tuning up in the next room; a lonely rush of notes from a clarinet, the soft whish of brushes on a drum head, a few subdued chords from a piano.

Without explaining, Brunner stood up and headed for the annex.

'You have to excuse Karl,' Fran said, delicately sipping at her glass. Stone could feel her leg touching his, her hand lightly on his thigh. 'He's like a puppy. Bounds in, licks everyone in the face, and expects that you'll play with him.' She shifted slightly in her chair, the movement causing her hand casually to brush the inside of Stone's thigh. 'But he's terribly nice. Most wonderful employer that one could ask for and, in his way, an absolute genius when it comes to making things happen. I wasn't going to do anything tonight, but about six he called and said that he was arriving in Dover and to meet him here. Karl collects English pub experiences like some people collect stamps. Tells me he's been in thousands of them, actually keeps a score card on authenticity and ambiance.'

Brunner was already back. 'Asked whether I could sit in on the piano between sets. Black fellow from the West Indies told me that they were union lads, amateurs not allowed.' Wide-eyed, he made a comic gesture with his hands, fingers splayed out, hands held up like a minstrel's, moving them in circles as if he were cleaning an imaginary window. 'No way, boss. Yawl can't play heah nohow.'

The accent was all wrong and the parody racist as hell, but Brunner still pulled it off pretty good. At least Melissa and Fran were laughing. Brunner pounced on their glasses and refilled them, then held up his own and gestured to Stone to do likewise. 'To new friends, old friends and those we left behind.'

They all clinked.

The piano began with a few solitary notes, picking out the theme, then augmenting it with chords. The clarinet eased in and began to elaborate, the brushes softly establishing the rhythm. It was an old Vera Lynn thing, 'We'll Meet Again', reminiscent of the war years and the Battle of Britain.

Cocking his head, Brunner listened to the music for a moment, then turned to Melissa. 'One of my favorites. Suppose that dates me. Dance?'

'I don't think . . .'

Brunner was smiling at her, that vast white expanse of enamel gleaming in the candlelight. 'Just this one, please.'

She looked helplessly toward Stone, an unstated question in her eyes. Stone felt trapped, unable to refuse. Outmaneuvered, he nodded.

Brunner pulled back her chair and took her hand as she stood up, then guided her toward the dance floor.

As with all men who had never learned to dance, Stone felt inadequate, the underpinnings of his ego once again undermined by a man who did. Just ten minutes before, Melissa had given herself to him, the promise in her eyes, the compact then sealed with the touch of her hand. It had not been just the promise of sex that had stirred Stone, but the hope of something much more complex than that. And now it was slip-sliding away.

'You have been friends for a long time?' Fran asked. Her hand moved slightly higher on his thigh, her touch light as a moth's. Stone's senses were clouded by her perfume, the stuff as potent as meat tenderizer, permeating his brain and turning it to mush.

'Not for long,' he answered automatically, trying to catch a glimpse of the dancers, but they were skirting the floor in the shadows and he could only see movement, not form.

'Are the two of you – *together*?' He could feel her breath on his cheek, smell its tangy sweetness.

'I don't understand . . .' He was temporizing, distracted, trying desperately not to understand.

She studied him closely, as if the answer was there for the discovering. Her eyes were black, deep and liquid as the ocean was at great depth. He felt slightly dizzy, as if he was experiencing an onset of vertigo.

'I was asking whether you are having an affair with her?' She didn't wait for his reply, looking beyond him toward the dance floor. 'She has a very nice body,' Fran said. 'I envy her. I'm too skinny.'

'I wouldn't say that.' It had been an automatic response, not thought through, and he mentally kicked himself.

'Then you've noticed me after all?' She was gently mocking him. 'Come on – drink up and fortify yourself. You're going to dance with me.'

'I really can't . . .'

She was already standing up, both of her hands on his arm, gently tugging at him. 'You must know by now that you can't refuse to dance when a lady asks you.' She made a little face, something between pouting and teasing. She was bent over as she spoke and the top of her dress fell free from her bosom. He caught a flash of erect nipples, the aureoles dark pools of pink. Stone tried but he couldn't take his eyes away.

'Honestly, Francine, I'll mash your feet.'

'Then we will not move our feet, will we? Just our bodies.'

It was just as she had described it.

The band had slid into 'The White Cliffs of Dover', the clarinet laid aside, replaced by a tenor sax which moaned the melody. It was aching sweet music, stirrings from a time they had never known yet somehow knew.

In the darkness, she molded her body against his, no gaps remaining. They swayed to the slow rhythm, her lips on his neck, her arms around his shoulders, her hands gently cupping his head, her nipples whispering against his chest, her groin firm against his, everything sweetly swelling. She smoldered, her heat infusing him. Stone's tumescence had transformed itself into an erection the size of a brick. Impossibly, she moved tighter and closer, enveloping it with her groin, her arms pressing hard into the small of his back, drawing him deeper into the fold. Her breath made little catching sounds in her throat and he found it impossible to breathe. Minutes, hours, days, a millennium passed by unnoticed.

His body was still moving against hers when he realized that the music had stopped. He opened his eyes.

Fran's head was still buried against his neck, her lips wet on his flesh, eyes closed. And beyond her shoulder, he watched Brunner and Melissa, arms around each other's waists, walking back toward the dining area. Brunner's head was bent down, saying something in her ear and she was laughing.

In the darkness, the mirrored globe on the ceiling showered sparks of light which swept across Francine's shoulders and face. He gently released his hold on her, trying to kickstart his heart.

She looked up at him, her lips parted, glistening. 'You see now? Dancing is not just about moving your feet.' She reached between them and gently brushed her hand over his groin. 'I think we would be very good together, don't you?'

Stone swallowed. He was drenched with sweat, shaky. 'We better get back.'

Another bottle of champagne was on the table, unopened. The bill was on a plastic tray, Brunner in the process of smothering it with Swiss franc notes. 'Melanie has already agreed on your behalf, Christopher, and I won't take no for an answer. Grab the bubbly. We're off.'

'Where to?'

But Brunner was already bouncing toward the door, Melissa's arm linked in his. He was doing an 'Off to See the Wizard' routine, skip-dancing, arms flailing the air, conducting the music in his head, three steps forward, one step back. Stone thought he looked ridiculous but vaguely envied him for his unselfconscious flamboyance.

Fran tucked in alongside Stone, her jacket already on. 'He gets this way when he's had a few drinks. Still, he's fun, don't you think? Let's go.'

'Where we going?'

She picked up the champagne bottle and poked him in the back with it, prodding him on. 'To his play-pen, I suspect.'

Brunner had already flagged down two taxis, he and Melissa clambering into the one in front. Stone wondered how in blazes Brunner had arranged that so easily.

By default, he and Fran took the second one. Their hack wheeled through a U-turn, following the first one, heading north-east along the coast. The driver was straight out of *Andy Capp*, fag stuck in the corner of his mouth and scarf around his neck. He had called Stone 'Guv' and told him to relax and enjoy the ride – that it was all paid for by the gent up front.

Fran cuddled against him, playing 'Itsy Bitsy Spider' up and down his buttons, paying particular attention to the bottom ones. Stone felt things slipping out of control; he was no longer in charge of his own destiny, had to get the reins back. But that old, dynamic duo of alcohol and testosterone were in charge now, blurring his resolve.

He settled back in the seat, his eyes closed, giving in to the pleasure her fingertips inspired. What the hell. Go with the flow and see where it leads, he decided.

The cab eventually peeled off the main motorway into

the outskirts of Dover, twisted through narrow streets into the town and past a floodlit castle, then turned right at a sign marked 'Eastern Terminal' into a maze of parking lots.

She sat up, straightening her dress, realigning her pantyhose, then leaned over and rubbed at a lipstick smudge on his collar. 'None the worse for wear. We're almost there.'

'Where?'

'Here.' She pointed ahead to rows of white Christmas-tree lights outlining the superstructure of a vessel. 'Karl's play-pen, the *Valkyr*.'

Their cab drew onto a quay, opposite the vessel. A man in a white uniform, the epaulets banded with gold braid, opened the door of Stone's cab.

'G'evening, sir.' Aussie accent, sandy-haired, a little on the thick side, ruddy-faced. 'I'm Capt'n Allen.'

Brunner was already out of his cab, standing back, looking up at the yacht with a proprietary air, pointing at something. Melissa was standing just behind him, her mouth slightly open, staring up at the beast, probably as impressed as Stone was.

It was more a ship than a yacht. About fifty meters overall, perhaps more. Acres of varnished teak, fancy awnings, smoked Lexan ports, a zillion antennas sticking out from the top of the bridge like hair on a punk rocker, a satellite communications dome on the after sun-deck, and aft of that, on a deck over the stern lounge area, a small chopper strapped down, its rotors folded.

What impressed Stone were the lines of the vessel. Not a fat cow-like mega-toy so favored by the Palm Beach crowd, but rather lean and efficient – obviously laid down on military lines. That became obvious as Stone examined her hull plating more closely. Not the fine finish of a yacht but rougher, more utilitarian, the welds showing, the hull plating horse-staved and uneven in the bow area as if she had known heavy offshore weather.

'She's a conversion, sir,' Allen remarked. '*Patra* class patrol boat hull fitted out as a proper yacht.' Allen was standing beside him, tapping a cigarette out of a pack, then lighting it with a complicated brass thing. 'Added a section fifteen feet amidships when they built her to accommodate the bigger engines. Does thirty-five knots when you put the go-fast pedal to the wall.'

Stone raised his eyebrows. 'This *belongs* to Brunner?'

Allen took off his captain's hat and wiped his hand through thinning hair. 'Sure does. And, thank the good Christ, he moves her around. Always on the go. Just got in from the Mediterranean this afternoon. Me, I can't stand sitting around dockside. You know the saying, "When in port, ships rot and men go to the devil." Whoever said that got it dead straight.'

Stone nodded toward the helicopter. 'You fly that?'

Allen thumped Stone's arm, laughing. 'Me? No way, mate. Those things scare the livin' piss outta me. Mr Brunner's got hisself a proper yabo to do that. Ex-Kraut air force bloke. Does all the maintenance as well.'

'*Christo-pherrr?*' Fran was already on deck. She was leaning over the rail, calling him, waving her scarf to catch his eye.

'Catch you later,' Stone said, breaking off and heading for the gangway.

The two women and Brunner were already in the salon, Brunner giving orders to a compact man in ship's mess uniform – something about making up canapés. The crewman nodded, bent forward slightly and clicked his heels together. More like it, Stone thought. Good help was hard to find these days.

The salon was simple but elegant: a vast, white expanse of carpeting with stuffed black leather loungers facing each other, separated by a long teakwood coffee table. Aft on the starboard side was a wet bar with recessed lighting and, opposite that, a spiral staircase which descended, presumably to sleeping-quarters and the galley. Further forward and dominating the room was a massive dining table inlaid with the compass rose and fitted with ten chrome and leather chairs. From a hidden compartment, a stereo system oozed New Wave music. The whole place smelled as if it had just been sprayed with money.

'We're having French seventy-fives, Christopher. You're surely up for one?' Brunner was bobbing around behind the wet bar, rocking a cocktail shaker. Melissa and Fran were just traipsing down the staircase, probably headed for the lavatory. Fran gave Stone a little wave as she descended. Melissa ignored him.

Why not? He nodded. 'Nice vessel you got here.'

'Not perfect as I'd like her, but quite serviceable,' Brunner answered. 'Being a Swiss, I used to keep my offices in Geneva, but as you probably know, it's such a dreary town. So I bought the *Valkyr*. Completely self-sustaining for months on end, full range of navigation and communications gear, able to go anywhere. Makes a marvelous base of operations. I'll give you the grand tour later on if you'd like.'

'You said that Fran works for you?'

Brunner nodded. 'Been with me for years. She's presently managing a project that I'm doing in England. Converting warehouses into upscale flats for – what do you call them? – yuppies.' He gave the shaker one last rattle, eased the glass out and poured two drinks. He held his up to the light, then sipped. 'Ah – splendid. Amazing how the French do occasionally get it right.'

Stone tried Brunner's concoction. It went down smoothly, leaving a citrus tingle on his tongue. Undoubtedly lethal.

'And you?' Brunner asked. 'What kind of business are you in, Christopher?'

It really didn't matter if he told Brunner. The papers had never identified him by name or profession. 'Marine engineering and consulting. Piers, bulkheads, that sort of thing. A little diving on the side.'

Brunner's eyebrows raised. 'I presume you're here on the Chunnel scheme.'

That had hit close to home. 'Not really. Vacation. Just visiting friends.'

Brunner smiled graciously. 'Must say I envy you. Melanie is a lovely woman.' He hesitated for a second, concern clouding his face. 'I hope that you didn't take offense with me asking her to dance. There's so little time to play, but when I do, I tend to go a bit overboard.'

'No offense taken. She and I are friends. Just that.'

Brunner seemed relieved. 'Excellent. So now we are all friends.' He moved closer, his voice low and conspiratorial. 'Speaking of friends, I think Francine has taken a fancy to you. My suggestion is that you hang on tight and enjoy the ride.' He actually winked.

'What do you mean by that?'

'Oh – just that she has the healthy appetite of an uninhibited young woman. I've seen it happen before. She wants you but, in a month, it will be someone else.' He moved closer yet. 'What I'm saying is that she loves both the giving and taking of physical pleasures, but she impresses me as a person who has always avoided complicated or lasting relationships.'

'You and she . . . ?' Stone didn't finish it.

Brunner's face broke into a broad smile. 'Good heavens, no! I'm too ancient for her tastes and I probably wouldn't last the night. And from a practical standpoint, such a relationship would be disastrous because of her being my employee.' He shook his head with emphasis. 'No, Christopher, I'm an old man, book-by-the-fire sort of thing. Go back to Geneva occasionally to see my married daughters and, on the rare occasion like tonight, kick up my heels a bit, but . . .'

Somehow, Stone didn't quite swallow it. Brunner was probably early sixties but he looked ten years younger. A bit of flab around the middle but otherwise probably as tough as case-hardened steel. Most men in his position didn't get there by being wimps.

In ten minutes, the two women returned and the waiter whom Brunner had called 'Manfred' took over mixing drinks and dispensing finger goodies. The four of them eventually drifted out onto the broad afterdeck, the only light a dim wash of yellow reflected off the harbor waters from buildings along the quay.

Brunner had stacked up some compact disks in the player and the four of them danced to the music of the Big Bands. This time it was not as sexually intense but, somehow, even more sensuous. Fran intentionally kept her body separated from his, just touching when they turned or dipped. It was that occasional contact that electrified him, the movement of her breasts slowly brushing across his chest, her groin suddenly hard against his, then gone. Pressure, then emptiness. Denial then satisfaction. His body ached for hers and her fingers promised him that it would be so, constantly moving along his back, alternately stroking him softly, then her sharp nails biting into his skin when their bodies merged.

Twice in the dim light, he had seen Melissa watching, her face neutral of expression. Brunner was a skilled dancer and the two of them moved effortlessly. And when she turned her face up to him, she was smiling, the animation real.

'You see – you have a natural talent for the dance,' Fran said softly. 'And I am a good teacher, am I not?'

'You're a very good teacher.'

'I can teach you other things as well,' she whispered. 'When Karl asks you, agree. For me, please.'

'Asks me what?' They dipped as the song ended, and Stone felt the throb of her body hard against his, the pressure intense.

She sighed and gave him a secret smile as they parted.

'We should be going,' Melissa said, her voice distant and a little dreamy. She and Brunner were standing apart but

Brunner was holding her hand as if reluctant to let her go. He finally did and her fingers trailed from his hand slowly. Stone felt a small pang of jealousy, then realized that he could hardly play dog-in-the-manger when he already had a bone for the taking.

Rotating his wrist and shooting his cuff, Brunner checked his wafer-thin gold watch. 'Nearly midnight. And I, unfortunately, have business tomorrow. Well, there will be other nights.' He motioned to Manfred, who had been standing silently in the door frame which led to the salon. Brunner spoke in a low voice and Manfred nodded stiffly, then disappeared.

Brunner turned back to them. 'I've asked Manfred to call a taxi for you. There's a rank at the terminal. Shouldn't take more than a few minutes. One more drink?'

Stone was awash, didn't want another, shook his head.

'Champagne, perhaps,' Melissa said. She did a solo twirl, her skirt flaring, obviously a little tipsy. 'Really, Karl. It's been a lovely evening. I enjoyed it so much.'

'I did too, Melanie. Enormously.' He checked the bar cooler. 'There's just your bottle of Moët left,' Brunner said, making a face. 'Perhaps we should save it for another time. I promised not to open it, remember.'

Melissa nodded. 'You're right . . . for a special occasion.'

Stone said his goodbyes to Fran, just the brush of lips and the touch of hands between them. Brunner saw them down to the dock and into the taxi. He bent down, his face framed in the opened window.

'Tomorrow afternoon . . . I'll be back from the City with nothing on my schedule for a few days. Weather forecast's to fair with a full moon tomorrow night. Pity to waste it. Would the two of you enjoy a brief excursion across the Channel? We'd be back in Dover by Tuesday afternoon, my word on it.'

'I don't think . . .' Melissa started to say.

Brunner put his finger to her lips. 'Don't refuse me. Not now. Sleep on it. If you can find the time, then come to the dock by five tomorrow afternoon. We'll leave port at sundown, have a fine dinner, then dance the night away.' He laid his hand on hers and grasped it tightly. 'Please.'

She sighed. 'Really – on short notice, it will be hard to arrange.' She turned to Stone. 'What do you think?'

He heard just the hint of regret in her voice and knew then that she wanted to go. Small wonder. But he would play this hand out by turning over just one card at a time.

He reached over and offered his hand to Brunner. 'Thanks so much for the evening, Karl. As Melanie says, it might be difficult to change our existing plans. But who knows, it could work out.'

Brunner beamed. 'Please try. Really. We've all had fun tonight and it would be a shame to stop the party so soon.' He waved as they drove off.

Stone told the cabby to drop them off in the parking lot next to the Crown and Bridge. They waited until he wheeled away, then headed home through the moonlit fields.

She kept her distance from him, softly humming something under her breath. He finally recognized it: 'We'll Meet Again'. It hurt him more than he would have imagined, the idea that she was mooning over Brunner. And his mind seemed clearer now, away from Fran. He had made a fool of himself and he didn't know how he could salvage it. Amazing how a tantalized dick could shout louder than the brain.

Sailor went berserk, bouncing around, tail flailing. Stone slipped a leash on the animal and the two of them skirted the borders of the caravan park, both marking their territory against intruding males. Stone casually wondered whether the idea was commercially marketable. Could call it 'She's Mine', package it in a little spray dispenser so you could squirt it on the hem of your favorite lady's dresses. Nah. It would never get past the Pure Food and Drug Administration dorks, he decided.

When he returned, she was already in bed, the curtain lowered into place.

He pulled off his jacket, tie and shirt, then dropped one shoe and waited.

'Very funny,' she finally said, her voice muffled.

'Was just thinking. Still want to sit on the doorstep and howl at the moon?'

'I think that time's past, don't you?'

'I had sort of hoped it wasn't.' Truly.

There was a rustling of bed sheets. She pushed aside the curtain. 'Stop trying to manipulate me, Stone. You were just dying to tell Karl that we'd come but decided you could trick me into believing it was my decision. You think I couldn't hear those rusty little gears in your brain going round and round?'

'I haven't tried to talk you into anything other than howling at the moon.' He wanted her to drop it. Letting Brunner and Fran crash the party had been a major mistake but it was over, finished.

But she misinterpreted. 'So you want to go by yourself, right? Do you *really* think Karl is going to be happy playing mein host to an oversexed Yank, mixing love potions and turning down the bed sheets for you and that bitch?'

That got to him. 'What sharp teeth you have, *Mizzz* van der Groot.'

'They pale in comparison to that creature's fangs. She was sucking on your neck like Count Dracula in an advanced stage of dehydration.'

Getting nowhere fast. 'Look, Melissa, letting Brunner horn in was my mistake. And I don't give a damn about Francine.'

'Save your explanations for your memoirs, Stone. I'm going with him.'

A long silence. 'I don't get it.' Then he did. She wasn't jealous of him. It was something quite different. 'Brunner, right? You've got a thing for him. Absolutely *amaz*ing.'

'That's part of the equation. You probably didn't notice

but he's a gentleman — well-traveled, intelligent and a lot of fun.'

'And loaded with dough.'

'That doesn't factor in.'

'Then what else does?'

She heaved out a long, irritated sigh. 'Did it occur to you that the *Valkyr* is a private yacht? No immigration procedures in the normal sense. The captain just goes ashore with the crew list and clears the ship, no other immigration procedures required. I'm sure if I ask nicely, Karl would list me as crew. And there are no border-crossing checks any more between the EC countries. Brunner's yacht is the best way for me to get out of England and onto the Continent. From Belgium, I'll cross into France, find *Night Watch* and bring her back.'

'They'd nail you when you reentered England. Out of the frying pan, et cetera.'

'There are other places. Ireland, perhaps. As a sovereign republic, they're not particularly keen on enforcing British laws.'

'You really think you can get her out yourself and sail singlehanded to the Old Sod without help?'

'I could if I had to. She's got an autopilot.'

So maybe it really wasn't Brunner she was interested in. He tried it on for size. 'You might recall that I volunteered to help.'

The sheets rustled again, her voice now muffled. 'I could use the help but I won't hold you to your promise. It's strictly up to you and your conscience.'

He smiled in the darkness. Second chance. The question was, who had manipulated whom? Not that it *really* mattered.

Brunner sat back in the leather lounger, his stockinged feet propped up on the coffee table. He swirled the ice cubes around in his glass of Vichy water, then drank from it, trying to bank the fires after the fact. He was getting too damned old for this sort of game. The liquor caught up to him more quickly these days, and the role of the charming, exuberant host was exhausting. Twenty years ago, he could have gone all night. Not now.

Francine had been mixing a nightcap, a brandy and soda. She curled up next to him, the cold glass held up against her cheek. The scent of perfume mixed with sweat aroused him.

'Do you think they'll come?' she asked.

'I'm sure of it if Stone has any voice in the matter. Incidentally, your handling of Stone vastly exceeded my normally jaded expectations. Perhaps even better than your manipulation of the Italian in '89.' It had been a Stasi job, Francine used as the bait. She had casually asked to share a table with an Italian bureaucrat while he lunched at his favorite Milano restaurant. In an hour and forty minutes, she had taken him to a transient hotel, seduced the fool and, while he was showering, made a wax copy of the key to his safe where a list of names of unsavory campaign contributors was kept. Two weeks later, the government had fallen on a vote of no-confidence.

She returned his compliment. 'The woman likes you, Karl. I could see it in her eyes.' She toyed with her drink.

'I thought so as well,' he answered. Actually, Brunner thought that the van der Groot woman was no more than mildly interested in him. The degree of her determination to get the *Night Watch* out of France would be the deciding factor.

Still, it had gone well. It had only been necessary to create the proper inducements for Stone and the woman. After all, if you scattered enough crumbs, the sparrows would come.

'I presume that you'll dispose of them at sea,' she said, touching the rim of her glass with her lips, not really drinking. 'Just give me enough time before you do so I can test-drive Stone. His equipment appears to be formidable.'

Brunner snorted, amused at the idea – her concept of a

condemned man's last wish. 'You can play all you want, Francine, as long as you're discreet. But I don't want you to create an open fracture between Stone and the woman, not while they're still on board. Just enough divisiveness to keep them off balance.' He ran his hand through his hair, tired. 'My intentions are to help him in any way I can, to be both his mentor and guide, so to speak.'

She wrinkled her nose. 'I don't understand. Why risk exposure when you could just as easily have Horst kill them?'

He didn't normally brief her on the details of an operation, preferring to keep her knowledge limited to only the role that she would play. But this was quite different, because instead of laying down an artillery barrage, you sometimes obtained better results by launching one single but extremely precise missile.

He absently touched his finger to her throat and trailed it down to the cleavage of her dress. He felt her shiver involuntarily beneath his touch.

'To ensure destruction of the Chunnel, Francine, I am preparing two very separate and distinct operations – one by land, the other by sea. During the final weeks of preparation, if one operation begins to appear less likely to succeed, I will throw all of my resources into the other. And as applied to the present situation, should either operation appear to be in danger of being uncovered by our worthy opposition, I will sacrifice it as a decoy to mask the other. To do that, I need to keep Stone and the woman alive long enough to find out exactly what they know and whether it's feasible to use them to create such a diversion.'

She nodded. 'Very clever, Karl. Just like Paul Revere – "One if by land and two if by sea." But just what exactly do the operations entail?'

'That, Francine my dear, will be revealed in the fullness of time.'

She knew the rules and didn't try to press him further. Setting her glass down on the table, she stood up, smoothing the material of her dress with her hands, unselfconsciously emphasizing her body – an obvious invitation. 'You will be coming down soon?'

The thought pleased him but he was realistic enough to understand that she was still sexually aroused by her contact with Stone and merely needed to be serviced. Not that it mattered. He would enjoy it for what it was – a second-hand gift, but nonetheless pleasurable for its unintended recipient.

'Yes,' he finally answered. 'Horst should be here shortly. It won't take more than a few minutes.'

When she was gone, Brunner stood up and climbed the companionway to the bridge of the *Valkyr*. He treasured sitting there alone, looking out over her bow at the harbor beyond. The ship's very presence infused him with a vitality. After this was over, he would take the *Valkyr* to Brazil. He yearned for the heat of the tropics and would be well advised to avoid the less benign heat that would be generated by the British constabulary.

The final wire transfer from Komoto Securities – he had traced the ownership of their satellite link through a complex chain of shell corporations – had been made three days ago and Brunner's Credit Suisse account specifically set up for this operation had swelled to a current balance of over £10 million. There would be the expenses to cover, salaries to pay. But of the twenty-one bodies presently on the payroll, he anticipated that only five of them would live to collect their fees. As he recalled, the American corporate jargon for that kind of managerial decision was appropriately termed 'downsizing'.

It was largely his handling of Stone that would determine which operation Brunner chose to run. He turned over the current phase of the sea operation in his mind. The Dutchman had received the GEM drilling logs from Joss and pronounced them authentic. There had been some problems correlating the Decca-generated co-ordinates of the boreholes with actual latitude and longitude, but that was now solved. The one unknown was what important details, if any, had been given in Le Borveaux's diary. Joss claimed that there had been no borehole coordinates given in his quick scan of the diary, but Brunner wasn't willing to bet the success of the whole operation on Joss's lack of thoroughness. He had either to see the diary for himself or find out from Stone what it contained.

Then, there was the other thing he needed Stone for; a willing assistant to help him with the grand illusion.

Actually, he thought of it as a magician's act. While he diverted the audience's attention with one hand, he would execute the trick with the other. Thus, Horst's upcoming land operation in England would be the diversion and *Cormorant* the trick.

From the top drawer of the navigational table, he withdrew a panatella and lit it. The ship's chronometer on the bulkhead read after one. It had been a long day and he was anxious to finish it. Brunner smoked in silence, waiting.

Ten minutes passed. Then he spotted a figure passing through the security gate, heading for the ship. The figure passed under lamplight, the fair hair and carriage unmistakable.

Brunner eased out through the sliding door and onto the wing bridge. 'Horst – up here.' The figure glanced up and nodded.

Two minutes later, Horst appeared on the bridge, wiping the neck of a bottle of beer which he must have taken from the wet bar. He was slightly above average height with the lean body of a long-distance runner. His face was unremarkable, except for the pale blue eyes. His passport identified him as an Austrian immigrant who now held UK citizenship. Horst, working as an independent lorry driver, paid his modest taxes on time, never spoke in his native tongue, and kept his name off the police blotters.

Horst had originally been Stasi-trained and controlled. Brunner – recognizing Horst's potential – had broken him off as an 'independent contractor' after arranging to have Horst's Stasi records shredded so that no connection could ever be made. Brunner admired the man's intelligence and ability to work on his own; was confident that Horst could run this end of the operation and be relied upon to clean it up when it was finished.

'How has it gone?' Brunner asked.

'Paine, the man that's doing our surveillance, will be leading the charge. He's an ex-RAF troop man with a deep grudge against his former employers. Heard about him through my Irish contacts. Bright but not too bright and he follows orders.'

'Any record?'

'He was drummed out of the military for arms pilfering. Since then, he's been running guns into Northern Ireland for the Prods. Some small-time drug dealing. Three arrests, no convictions.'

'Your fax indicated that you've identified the target,' Brunner prompted.

'Paine, through some of his old service buddies, pin-pointed two air bases in England with supplies of ethylene oxide which the Americans brought in during the Gulf War. I've been to both aerodromes, checked out the conditions, done my homework. The best one for the operation is located at Lakenheath Air Force Base in East Anglia. I've leased a small farm in the countryside about thirty kilometers north of the base. No neighbors to speak of and the nearest town, Swaffham, has just one constable. Told the estate agent I was going to fix it up for my mum and me when I had the time. It's nothing more than a cottage, a couple of paddocks, and a cow shed. I've also bought a used milk tanker and parked it inside the shed. Doesn't look like much but I had new tires put on and checked out the motor. Top notch. Have all the papers for the truck, proper decals, the lot.'

'What about the transfer equipment?'

'Two pumps. One's electric, the other gasoline-driven.

I've timed how long the transfer takes. Eighteen minutes.'

Brunner nodded. 'When?'

'We've been ready for a week. Now that Joss is coming over here to help, the timing's up to you.'

'The sooner the better,' Brunner answered. 'Say the day after tomorrow if the weather's good. How many men besides you and Joss?'

'Paine and three others that he's worked with before, most of them from his smuggling days. They're in it for the money, no politicos, and they haven't met me so there won't be any connection. Paine takes care of the payroll.'

'You have all the equipment you'll need?'

'Everything. Thought I might need an estate wagon with military markings but the gate guards always have one parked just inside the fence. Keys in the ignition, piece of cake.'

'Another beer, Horst?'

Horst shook his head. 'Can't. I'm on my bike. Wouldn't do for me to get nicked by the coppers just now, would it?'

Brunner nodded. Horst always had good judgement. 'What's the physical layout of the storage area?'

'Basically, your average fuel dump. Stashed away in an isolated area, about two kilometers from the base. Danger of fire, see? It's a tank farm. Jet fuel, gasoline, lubricants, that sort of thing, as well as the ethylene oxide, of course. The ethylene oxide is stored in 30,000-liter tankers, five of them, already filled and prepositioned so that the stuff can be driven directly to the flight line for loading into bomb casings. It's liquid, of course, but no trickier to handle than butane camping gas according to Paine's contacts.'

'Security?'

'Low level. Two roving perimeter guards working the outside of the fence, both equipped with automatic weapons and hand-held wireless radios. In addition, there are two gate guards at the compound's entrance, same equipment. Both lots call into central base security every half-hour like clockwork. Checked for a solid week with the Sony scanner you gave me.'

'Any other men on duty inside the compound?'

'Ten or so during the day but only two during the night shift,' Horst said. 'Sergeant and an enlisted man have a shack where they keep the keys to the transfer pumps and make up the paperwork. No radios, just a telephone.'

'How long will it take?'

'In and out, less than six minutes. Should be tucked away at the farm before the balloon goes up.'

Brunner stubbed out the cigar. 'When you've done the job, fly to Gibraltar and wait for me. In the meanwhile, I'll be in touch. Just don't fail me, Horst.'

Horst grunted in amusement, then said, 'Have I ever, boss?'

THIRTEEN

South Coast of England, 10 April

When he woke, both mistress and mutt were gone. Probably out, he guessed, for what she euphemistically referred to as 'the pong patrol'. He squinted, slightly hung-over, checking his watch: 10.20. Still muzzy-headed, he pulled the blanket over his head and drifted off.

Twenty minutes later, he edged awake again. *Not back yet*, he realized. Swinging his feet over the side of the day-sitter, he padded from one window of the caravan to another, expecting to see the pooch fertilizing the grass with Melissa supervising its placement. Nothing. The camp grounds were deserted except for a scattering of sparrows pecking in the grass.

He tried to suppress the panic growing in his gut, wondering whether she had cut a private deal with Brunner to leave early, then found her note scribbled on the face of an envelope and tucked in the door handle of the fridge.

> Back early afternoon. Gone shopping and stuff. Didn't wake you because I knew you wouldn't let me out. Not to worry. I'll be careful. Incidentally, DON'T drink my champagne if you value your testicles (regardless of how sore from unrequited lust they must be).

It was signed with a swirling 'M'.

Stone grunted, not amused. Actually, they *were* tender,

what his buddies in Maine callously referred to as 'blue balls'.

Well, she would either be picked up by the cops or she wouldn't be – beyond his control. If she was, he trusted her not to lead them back here and, if she wasn't, she owed him a big one for breaking the rules.

Stomach rumbling, he strip-searched the food lockers and found a half-empty tin of baking chocolate. *Caffeine, right?* He boiled up a pan of water, added non-dairy creamer, half a box of sugar cubes, dumped in the cocoa powder, mushed the muck into submission with a rusty gravy ladle, and found it drinkable.

He sat down at the table, pondering his agenda for the day. Not much he could do other than clean up, pack and write Mac an explanatory note. He wondered whether Mac would be sore enough not to pay him for the time he had already put in but decided that, in the event Mac wouldn't or couldn't loosen up his expenses, he'd handle his complaint by transatlantic mail. Much better than posting it from Wormwood Scrubs Prison.

He poured a second cup after refining the mixture with more sugar. Not exactly up to Cadbury's standards but the caffeine was now singing in his veins. He pulled on his slacks and a sweatshirt, then poked his head out the door. Amazing for England in early April – still fair weather. It looked as if Brunner's forecast had been accurate.

Retreating to the table with a third cup of cocoa, he reread the *Daily Mail*'s sports section, puzzling over how the Brits scored cricket, then cleaned up the kitchen, in general killing time.

Not much to pack, he thought. Joss's canvas attaché would be large enough to hold everything he currently owned. He laid all his articles on the bed: socks, change of underwear, a new shirt from Marks and Sparks, shaving gear, Le Borveaux's diary, his Swiss Army knife, and the Beretta encased in its leather holster.

He casually picked up the holster, examining it. It was a

fancy thing with a shoulder loop and strap that presumably attached to the wearer's belt. Well worn, the leather holster showed traces of polish that indicated it had been cared for over the years. He strapped it on, feeling vaguely like 007, then tried a quick draw, succeeding only in scratching the web of skin between his thumb and index finger on the Beretta's hammer.

He sat down and field-stripped the Beretta, pushed wadded toilet paper soaked in sewing-machine oil through the barrel with a pencil, then wiped down the exterior surfaces and reassembled the thing. He shoved in the clip and chambered a round, then carefully lowered the hammer and flicked on the safety. It felt heavy and reassuring in his hand.

About to shove the Beretta back in the holster, he noticed that the stitching between two layers of the holster's leather casing had intentionally been removed, leaving a slight gap. *Interesting*. He compressed the leather, feeling for something that might be hidden, but the leather betrayed no lumps.

Not satisfied, he took the holster to the doorway and held it up to the sunlight, spreading the gap between the leather with the blade of his knife. In the gap, he could just make out the edge of a thin piece of cardboard. He tapped the holster against the kitchen table and a business card fell out; slightly oil-stained and frayed around the edges but still legible.

It was a business card for a firm in Hamburg, Germany – Weshiem-Munden GmbH, exporter of medical equipment. A telephone, telex and fax number were printed in the lower left-hand corner. Stone turned the card over. On the back, the writing had been done with a fine ballpoint pen; presumably a list of telephone and fax numbers, but the last entry didn't seem like a telephone number. It was written with a different pen, probably more recently since it was last on the list. Squinting, he read: 'DMV *Cormorant*, NE 78781.'

Somebody's name, a place, a *thing*? Didn't matter. The list had to be eyes-only stuff that Joss hadn't trusted to his wallet in case it was lost or he was picked up by the cops and searched.

Mac would know how to handle the stuff but Mac, as far as Stone knew, was still up in London, not due back until Monday, possibly even Tuesday.

What now? He could call Highgate Engineering and take a chance on giving the information to one of Mac's minions, but he couldn't be sure that the information would reach Mac intact. Nobody in their right mind was going to take information over the telephone without asking who was dispensing it, and Stone didn't know how long one of Mac's ex-cops, if so inclined and equipped, would take to trace the call. Another problem: Stone didn't think his phony British accent would hold up for more than a few mumbled sentences before his American twang began to crack through. His only acquaintance with the nuances of the British accent had been gleaned from listening to lip-lacerating announcers on the BBC. He decided against calling in.

Which left only one way to handle it – stuff the card along with a note in an envelope, mark it 'personal', and address it to Mac at the Highgate Engineering address, then drop it in a mail box. Not exactly high-tech and he felt queasy about entrusting it to Her Majesty's Postal Service, but it was the only way left to him.

He first transcribed both sides of the business card on to a slip of paper to keep with him in the event the original was lost, then penned a short note about his decision to help Melissa snatch the *Night Watch* out from underneath the Frogs' noses. He also explained that the enclosed card had come from Joss's holster but he had no idea of what its significance was, other than the phone numbers and the word *Cormorant* should be checked out. He didn't mention the *Valkyr* trip, knowing that Mac would assume he had either used the Sealink ferry or the Chunnel train.

263

Regardless of their friendship, Stone thought it was wise not to leave a trail.

In the final paragraph, he held out a vague promise that he'd help Mac out when he got back to England, then signed it 'Stone'.

For the next hour, he sat on the doorstep of the caravan, soaking up rays, yearning for a cold beer and growing more edgy with each minute of her prolonged absence.

She came back slightly after 15.00, *sans* Sailor, two shopping bags full of stuff in her arms.

'Figured you'd be chained up in the Tower of London by now.' Then it dawned on him. 'Where's the mutt?'

She gave him a withering look. 'He's not a mutt. And he's staying with a friend.'

'You contacted someone?'

'Matilda, my father's secretary. She's single, lives alone, the soul of discretion. She'll take care of Sailor until I get to Ireland, then bring him up there.'

'Undoubtedly, you told her the whole story.' He put his finger to his head and pulled the imaginary trigger.

'Didn't, as a matter of fact. Just that I was innocent, which she naturally accepted. The only crime Matilda thought I was guilty of was bringing Sailor into Great Britain without a proper rabies clearance. Went on and on about rabid rats from the Continent streaking through the Chunnel and infesting the English countryside.'

'Ought to put up signs on the French side, warning the poor bastards that they'll probably end up on English dinner plates, based on the texture of the stuff you've been feeding me.' He gestured to the bags. 'What's in those?'

She spilled the contents on her bed: a couple of shimmering dresses, a high-quality sweater, slacks, pumps, black lacy underwear and an astonishing brief bikini. He lifted the material with a finger and held it up to the light. The sun shone through, practically unhindered.

'Definitely X-rated. Your mother would not approve.'

'Don't act like a prude, Stone, because I know you're anything but. See-through is the fashion now.'

For Brunner's eyes, he thought. 'Looks like you spent close to a couple of hundred pounds.'

'Nine hundred and twelve and sixty pence. Matilda loaned me three thousand.'

He found that hard to believe. 'Your father in on this?'

She shook her head, holding up a dress against her body, preening before the tiny mirror. 'No. And Matilda won't say a word.'

He took her by the shoulder, turning her toward him. 'Melissa, I want you to think hard for a few seconds. You know that trying to get *Night Watch* out of France could be very dangerous? Or the fact that we might fail. In two days, we'll have fake passports. In three days, we could be in Maine.'

She studied his face, undoubtedly believing that he was trying to back out. '*You* could be in Maine, Stone, and if you're so inclined, get on with it. Mr Macleod said that there was just one man guarding the yacht. That shouldn't be too difficult for me to handle.'

He sighed. 'For us to handle,' he corrected. 'But that's based on information someone gave him. Whether there's one cop or a whole division of them remains to be seen.'

She shaded her forehead with her flattened hand, mimicking Cochise at the pass, checking for dust clouds kicked up by the approaching cavalry. 'We'll scout it out, Stone. Isn't that the expression?'

He nodded. 'Like you said . . .'

In the late afternoon, they crossed through the fields again, headed for the Crown and Bridge. The sun was setting, the late afternoon air smelling of spring grass and summer's promise. She had paused on the edge of a puddle to pick a bunch of delicate purple flowers – 'late Spider Orchids', she called them – happy as he had ever known her, more

265

child than woman. He didn't want to ask himself why, but he could guess. Brunner.

Her hair was piled up in a French twist and she was wearing slacks and the wool pullover which accented her body in an understated way – the sort of thing that Hepburn would wear for a jaunt over English moors. Stone, vaguely disgruntled and silent, walked behind her, toting the bags.

Slightly after 17.00, they turned off Swinge Hill Road and into the lane where the Crown and Bridge was located.

There were a dozen automobiles in the parking lot, all of them empty except for a tan VW Polo parked near the side entrance to the pub. A youngish man with a thick mat of hair sat slouched behind the wheel, the *Sporting News* draped over it. He was smoking a cigarette which he occasionally tapped on the sill of the open window, the ashes spilling down the door. He looked up at Stone momentarily, then back to his paper. Off-duty fuzz? Stone wondered. Nah, he thought. Too coincidental. Still, it was hard to keep the paranoia under control.

Inside, there was a pay telephone next to the coat room. Some voices were coming from the taproom down the hallway, arguing in a good-humored way, a TV sports announcer mumbling through a list of rugby scores. The place smelled of stale beer and dusty carpets, far less exotic than the musky essence of the previous night.

Stone squinted, his eyes adjusting to the darkness, and spotted the cards of several taxi services thumbtacked to the wall. He picked up the handset, fumbling for change. There was no dial tone, the line dead. Then he noticed an 'out of service' note taped to the coin slot. *Damn!* Looking more closely at the armored cable between the handset and the phone box, he noticed that it had been partially severed with what must have been wire-cutters.

The VW driver had just entered, still holding the paper, digging in his pocket. 'You on that thing for long, mate?'

Disgusted, Stone tapped his fingernail against the 'out of service' note.

The man took a step forward, scowling, then rocked back on his heels. 'Soddin' things. Don't work worth a wanker when ya need 'em. Never shoulda gone along with privatizin' British Telecom, I sez. Maggie and her fat-cat friends screwed the workin' class again.' He said it flatly like he had said it before and often.

'Know where there's a taxi rank or another public phone around here?'

The man smiled a little and cocked his head. 'Yank?'

'Canadian,' Stone lied. 'Nova Scotia.'

'Lovely. All them lakes and such.' He expertly folded his newspaper with one hand, jiggling change in his pocket with the other. He rolled his eyes up, as if he were studying the cracks in the ceiling. 'Let's see now – taxi rank.' He scuffed at his day-old beard. 'You know Merchant's Row? About three blocks down, turn right, two blocks . . .'

'How about a pay phone?'

'Don't fink I know of one close by. Where are you headed?'

'Dover. The docks.' He tried to remember. 'Eastern Terminal.'

'I was headin' home after I had a pint. It's before hours but the landlord here's a chum of mine. Say – wouldn't mind taking you up to Dover if you could break loose a couple of quid for petrol.'

Relieved, Stone pulled out a ten-pound note. 'All yours if you don't mind skipping the beer. We're in a hurry. It's me and the lady outside.'

'Nice,' the man said. 'Very nice indeed.' He took the note with one hand and stuck out the other. 'Name's Angus. Angus Paine. Friends call me "AK".'

'Walker,' Stone said, taking the man's hand briefly. 'Christopher.'

'Right you are, Walker Christopher. We're on our way.'

He and Melissa squeezed into the back seat of the VW,

her bags on the front seat, passenger side. Angus stuffed the Polo in gear and ground through the remaining gears, whining east on the A259. As if to justify the money, he played tour conductor, keeping up a running commentary, pointing out the sights, replaying local history.

'Took a proper pasting during the war, all through here. My old dad was a sergeant in the RAF posted not too far from here, up at Biggins Wood. Spits, Hurricanes, the lot. Took a chunk of German steel in the leg for his troubles, he did.'

He pointed to the right. 'Over there's Shakespeare Cliff. Can't see it, underground an' such, but the Chunnel tubes head out to sea there.' He turned his head briefly, looking back at Stone. 'Couldn't get me in that effin' thing if you paid me a packet, mate. Cave in on their noggins one of these days, ya ask me.'

You got that right, Stone thought.

Then remembered the letter. 'Any post boxes along here?'

'Not likely, mate. But there's probably one in the terminal area for people sending postcards back home and such.'

'Keep an eye out for one when you turn in, all right?'

Angus nodded, slightly distracted, as he did the Lambada through heavy Sunday traffic.

They passed a little town marked 'Maxton', then hung a hard right. Past the castle up on the hillside, through the town, the same route as last night.

Angus turned in where it was marked 'Eastern Terminal', threading through slowing traffic. 'Where to now, Guv?'

Stone pointed off to the left. He could see part of the *Valkyr* beyond a small freighter tied up inshore of her. 'The eastern arm of the breakwater. You can drop us off next to those forklifts just short of the gate.'

'Say – we forgot all about the post box.'

Stone had been preoccupied, keeping his directions

straight. Not much time left, running late, and he didn't want to wander around a terminal building that probably would be thick with cops.

Angus must have read his mind. 'Want me to drop it off, Guv? Letter box right across the street from my flat.' He wheeled through a U-turn and braked to a stop, then turned his body, one arm over the seat, looking back at Stone, fingers fishing a cigarette out of his shirt pocket. 'Nuffin' in it that's valuable, is there, like you don't want it registered or such?'

'No. It's just a note to a friend.'

Angus hunched his shoulders. 'No problem, mate. She'll be in the post tonight – just put it here in the windscreen demister vent where I can't forget it.'

It seemed all right to Stone. Even if Angus held it up to the light, he'd be able to see that there wasn't anything worth pilfering inside, and it saved exposing himself to curious cops in the terminal building. 'That'd be fine, Angus.'

Paine got out and opened the door for them. He smiled, displaying a collection of tobacco-stained teeth. 'Good trip, Squire.'

Karl Brunner sat at his desk in the communications compartment of the *Valkyr*, reading the Dutchman's weekly fax update.

The costs were mounting and the report, as usual, reflected the Dutchman's obsession with detail. Brunner lifted a cup of coffee and sipped, then set it down, still scrolling through the document, as pleased as an astute investor reading the stock-market quotes and noting that all his shares were on the rise.

The prefabricated pieces of the Tank were scheduled to arrive from Finland on time and most of the other equipment had either arrived or was en route from suppliers in the Netherlands, Belgium and Germany.

Brunner unconsciously frowned when he read that the

nickel-cadmium batteries for the Tank's power supply were back-ordered, but in the next line entry, the Dutchman said that he had gone ahead and purchased an equally capable set of heavy-duty marine lead-acid batteries in the event the ni-cads didn't arrive on time.

The best news – something that had been worrying Brunner – was that the Dutchman had finally received the shipment of 1356 kilo blocks of Semtex, the bulk of it purchased in hundred-kilo lots from fourteen different black-market dealers in Poland. Kruger, a German with Polish blood who had worked for Brunner before, had been the buyer, posing as a 'purchaser' for the IRA. Kruger had carefully assembled the Semtex, packaged it, then arranged for its delivery by freighter from Gdansk to Rotterdam, the shipping manifest listing the stuff as 'No. 2 Beef Tallow, Unrefined'. Kruger had taken five weeks to assemble the load, but it had arrived and was now safely stored at the shipyard.

The Dutchman had added a personal note at the end of the document, cautiously hinting that he was pleased with the progress. Brunner smiled, imagining how difficult it must have been for the Dutchman to have acknowledged that he was pleased with anything.

The intercom buzzed and Brunner punched the bar without taking his eyes from the computer screen.

'Yes?'

'Cap'n Allen here, Mr Brunner. They're on quay dock and they got their bags with 'em.'

'Very well. Show them aboard and break out some champagne. Inform Francine of their arrival. I'll be down before we sail.'

'Right, sir. We finished loading diesel fuel twenty minutes ago. Docking lines singled up and the engine room's on line and ready to go. Permission to disconnect shore cables.'

'Go ahead and disconnect shore power but leave the telephone lines plugged in. I'm expecting a call before we leave.' Brunner hung up the handset, leaned back in the chair, pleased. He had never been in doubt that they would come. He was looking forward to this little excursion.

He spent the next five minutes composing a reply to the Dutchman on his word-processing software, downloaded it, then transmitted it through the satellite fax channel.

The shoreline phone buzzed twice. Brunner picked it up.

'Yes?'

'It's me, Horst. Tate, Paine's number-two man, kept surveillance on the caravan for most of the day. No visitors. However, the woman went out shopping. Took the dog. Paine tried to follow but lost her in the crowds. She came back to the caravan at 15.21 without the dog. He figured she left it in a kennel.'

'How did it go at the pub?'

'Paine was there waiting for them, no problems. He cut the telephone line just before they arrived.'

'How did Paine think Stone and the woman were getting along?'

'Said that they didn't seem to be too cozy. Fact is, the lady didn't even talk to Stone on the drive up to Dover.'

About what Brunner had expected. 'You still on for Tuesday night?'

'Right. It's all laid on. I'm meeting Joss at an inn in Newmarket this evening. Show him the farm tomorrow morning. Paine and his people will be coming up early Tuesday morning.'

'Good luck, then, Horst. I'll see you in . . .'

'There's one other thing. Maybe it's not important, but Stone had a letter he wanted to mail. Paine volunteered to take care of it. I have it with me now.'

'Where are you?'

'I'm calling from a *schnellgaststätte* in the terminal area.'

He thought for a minute. 'All right. Bring the letter to the ship. Allen and the electrician should be on the wharf taking in the power cables. Tell Allen to bring it to me

271

immediately. After that, go back to the snack bar and call me in exactly thirty minutes.'

'Right. Incidentally, I just picked up the most recent photos that Paine took. Do you want them?'

He didn't need them with the two dozen that he had already received, but he didn't want Horst carrying them in the event he was picked up. 'Yes – bring them as well,' he said, then broke the connection.

Nine minutes later, the envelope was in Brunner's hands. It was addressed to Highgate Engineering, marked personal to Macleod, no return address. He didn't want to take the time to steam it open and the envelope's address would be easy enough to forge if he had to. He ripped the flap open.

Stone's note to Macleod was short. Nice that Stone felt his job was over. Perhaps Macleod felt the same way. And the fact that Stone intended to help Melissa get the yacht out of France confirmed Brunner's forecast. There was a ridiculous offer by Stone to help Macleod when and if he returned. 'If' was the operative word, Brunner thought.

But it was the enclosed business card that shocked Brunner. He had set up the Weshiem-Munden firm years ago. In theory, Weshiem-Munden GmbH exported medical equipment, mainly to clients in the Middle East. But in fact, Weshiem-Munden exported a great deal more than that and its client list included Syria, Iraq, Iran, Libya, India, Pakistan, Burma and mainland China.

That Joss had been careless enough to carry the card shocked Brunner's sense of security. It was the same one that he had given Joss a month ago, Brunner's own handwriting on the back listing the *Valkyr*'s satellite fax and phone numbers, as well as Turner's and Horst's cellular numbers. The *Cormorant* registration number had been added, presumably in Joss's handwriting.

Brunner was enraged. He had specifically warned Joss to memorize the numbers and destroy the card when he had first given it to him. The stupid, incompetent bastard!

Yet, in a bizarre way, Brunner suddenly recognized that Joss's stupidity could actually enhance the illusion that he was creating.

He reread the note, slipped it into the desk drawer, then leaned back and lit a panatella.

The problem now, as he saw it, was that Stone could identify Joss and, based on Stone's enquiries at *Société Techniques Maritimes*, he probably suspected that the threat to the Chunnel was real and focused on an attack from the seabed. That had to be changed.

Joss made too many mistakes, despite the fact that Brunner regarded him as one of the most effective contract agents that he had ever worked with. But Joss was like a bearing that was going bad in an otherwise smoothly running machine. Still, bearings could be replaced.

He rang for Allen.

The Australian knocked on the door in under three minutes.

Brunner let him in. 'How are my guests doing, Captain Allen?'

'Happy as pigs in shit. They're all swilling champers on the lounge deck. Francine's with Stone. The women aren't talking.'

'Have their baggage sent up here and if either of them asks where it's gone, tell them that it's already been sent down to their cabins.'

Allen nodded. 'Anything else?'

'We'll depart in half an hour unless you hear from me to the contrary.'

Allen threw a sloppy salute and left.

Horst called seven minutes later. There was the sound of a bawling child and the clanking of metal trays in the background.

'Can you hear me, Horst?'

'Some rug rat's screaming bloody hell in my ear but I hear you good enough.'

'There's a change. When the tanker arrives at the farm

and after the liquid's been transferred, you'll take care of Paine and the driver just as we discussed before. The alteration is that I want Joss handled in the same way as you did with the Rumanian Securitate defector back in '87. Make sure that you sanitize anything Joss is carrying that relates to the project but leave his passports where they'll eventually be found.'

'Joss might not . . .'

'I don't give a damn what the *verfluchte* says. You're acting on my direct orders. His choice is that he cooperates or it's a bullet in the head.'

'But . . .'

'Listen carefully, Horst! I hold you responsible. Do you understand my instructions?'

There was a long pause, then a snort. 'Just took me by surprise, boss. Not that it bothers me worth a shit. It's your operation.'

Brunner hung up. He sensed that Horst had been smiling.

The *Valkyr* eased out of Dover, slowly picking up speed as she cleared the breakwater, shaping a course to the north-east for Belgium. Through the soles of his shoes, Stone felt the vibration of the engines smoothly building up revs.

The four of them stood in a loose gaggle on the open afterdeck, foam boiling out behind them, the sea air clean, no longer tainted by the stink of the harbor. Gulls – startled from their rest – took flight, wheeling and squawking as they swooped over the crests of seahorses turning rusty rose in the setting sun.

Stone slouched against the teak railing, sipping at the champagne, his mind at ease. England was behind him. So were whatever obligations that he might have encumbered himself with. Despite his guilt about ducking out on Mac, he had done his best and it was finished now.

Melissa had not spoken to him except for the necessities,

yet he felt that she must be sharing the mood that had come upon him.

Something magical, almost spiritual, about a departure by sea, he thought. The end of one thing, the beginning of another, the transition between them seamless.

Brunner was on his left, pointing out something to Fran, his laugh generous and easy. He turned to Stone, still smiling, the contrast of his startling white teeth against his deep tan bordering on the theatrical. A few of his silver-gray hairs not nailed down with hair spray tentatively lifted in the wind.

'More champagne, Christopher?'

'. . . a touch.'

Brunner was decked out in cream elkhide deck shoes, russet slacks, white turtleneck and a double-breasted navy blazer with gold buttons. Probably *real* gold, Stone reckoned. Brunner wore one of those ridiculous Greek fisherman's caps on his head, slightly askew and at an angle he probably considered rakish.

Brunner splashed a large dollop into Stone's glass, then added to his own. He eased in alongside Stone, bent over slightly, elbows planted on the rail, glass held like a chalice between his hands. 'Spring, moonlit night, the company of beautiful women. Not exactly hardship duty is it?'

Yes indeed, Stone thought, a little bemused with Brunner's naked attempt to pander Francine's wares while simultaneously cutting Melissa out of the herd for himself. It was going to be dicey – keeping Francine at arm's length without ruffling either her or Brunner's feathers. That, while firmly inserting himself between Melissa and this latter-day Ezio Pinza look-alike. Not that he was ungrateful. A ride was a ride and *this* particular ride was ticketed in the first-class compartment.

He tried to shift the subject. 'Terrific yacht you've got, Karl.' Stone glanced over the side, figuring that the *Valkyr* was making over twenty-five knots. 'We must be doing close to twenty,' he said, trying to sound polite but not too impressed.

'Thirty-two knots,' Brunner said, a slight edge to his voice.

Stone had learned from long experience that power-yacht-owners seemed to equate the speed of their boat with the size of their dick. 'Really? That fast? Wouldn't have thought it.'

'It's the height above the water that deceives,' Brunner explained. He slapped Stone on the back with a little more oomph than was required. 'Come with me. I want to show you my playroom. It's just aft of the bridge.'

Brunner led off, his arm draped around Stone's shoulder. He nodded at Manfred, who had just delivered a plate of smoked salmon to the women, and Manfred nodded back, then fell in step behind them.

Gave Stone the creeps, Manfred did. Middle-aged and balding, blank face but light on his feet, as if he practiced kick-boxing in his time off. Every time he saw him, Stone mentally dressed Manfred in a black leather coat and fedora – the type the Gestapo had worn. That and glinty wire-rimmed glasses. A real *You vill cum mit me* kind of guy.

Allen was parked in the helmsman's seat, Ray Bans on despite the deepening dusk, monitoring a vast array of gauges. He turned slightly to check who was invading his territory, flicked a salute at his boss, then resumed his vigil. Above him, a radar scope strobed, a satellite receiver beeped and a depth-sounder whined – all duplicated with identical units at the navigational desk on the port side of the bridge.

'How fast, Captain Allen?' Brunner asked.

'Thirty-two knots and a bit, skipper,' Allen said, tapping the knotmeter. 'Burn off some fuel weight and she'll be flying.'

'How long to Antwerp?' Stone asked Brunner.

'Five hours to Flushing which is at the entrance of the

Honte Everingen Channel.' He moved to the chart table and traced his finger along a penciled track. 'From there on in, we'll have to slow down. Tricky piloting because of the sand bars, so Captain Allen tells me. I plan to anchor off the town of Terneuzen for the night. Pleasant place.' He turned to Stone and smiled agreeably. 'Good to get out of England, isn't it?'

Brunner didn't have any idea how good. Stone nodded. He was suddenly a little edgy, as if this dog and pony show had been contrived. 'Very nice up here but we better rejoin the ladies.'

'Not quite yet,' Brunner said, guiding Stone by the arm to a closed bulkhead door. 'My play-pen. More appropriately, my workroom. Everything here that I need to keep in touch with my various enterprises.'

He opened the door and stood back. 'You first, Stone.'

Stone automatically took a step forward, then hesitated, turning to Brunner, knowing by the very fact that he did that he had unconsciously betrayed himself.

Manfred moved in behind him now, the Beretta held easily in his hand, nudging Stone's ribs.

'We really *must* talk, Mr Stone,' Brunner said.

FOURTEEN

'I'm deeply disturbed, Mr Stone, assuming that's actually your name,' Brunner said wearily. 'You've abused my hospitality and now I don't quite know what to do with you.' Brunner had eased into a padded leather chair behind a desk with a computer flushed into the walnut surface. Behind him was a technologically stunning array of sophisticated communications gear – two high-frequency SSB radios, a laser printer, a fax machine, a flat-screen video monitor the size of a billboard, and a bank of telephones. It looked to Stone as if Brunner was going into competition with Radio Shack.

Manfred stepped off to the side, the Beretta held casually in his hand. Stone guessed that Manfred was trying to dredge up memories of Gestapo interrogation techniques from tales his father told him.

'I think you've gotten some bum information, Karl,' Stone replied, a bit incredulous, trying to see if he could bluff it out.

Brunner wasn't really listening. His fingers flicked through a stack of photographs, playing with the edges of each one as if he were about to deal. He looked up suddenly, his face blank of expression, giving nothing away. 'The driver that brought you here today – who is he?'

Stone marginally relaxed. It was a dumb question, nothing to do with him. 'Ordinary guy. Angus something or other. Don't remember. Mel and I were at the Crown and Bridge, trying to get a cab. The telephone was screwed up and this guy offered to drop us off in Dover on his way home. That's it.'

'Interesting,' Brunner said. 'Your Angus something or other was on the docks most of the morning taking photographs of the *Valkyr* with a telephoto lens of formidable dimensions. One of my people noticed him. Not initially suspicious, but one never knows. He left about 14.00 . . .' Brunner glanced at a typewritten report. '. . . 14.04 to be exact. The fact that he turned up again, oddly enough with you in tow, prompted my people to follow him when he left the terminal area. They briefly exchanged pleasantries with Angus after forcing him off the A259 at a secondary turn-off.' Brunner held up the photographs. 'He had these in his possession, presumably taken over the last few days.'

'What do you mean, "your people . . ."? Like who?'

'Most are ex-policemen or retired military, now in the security business, Mr Stone. My interests are wide-ranging – wood products in Norway, industrial ceramics in Spain, jet engine components in Italy, office complexes in England, resort properties in the Mediterranean, and a software development firm in Germany, to name just a few. I try to keep what you would call "a low profile", but there is always the possibility of kidnapping, industrial espionage, extortion for profit and, of late, environmental terrorism. For those reasons, I employ security firms in five different countries to help keep my profile low and my business secrets confidential.'

He held up a newspaper clipping, now four days old. It featured a composite drawing of a Neanderthal-like Stone gaping out at the reader. 'Manfred told me last night that you bore a striking resemblance. I laughed at the idea then.' Brunner looked at the page, then studied Stone again. 'But now, on second glance, there are some similarities. This *is* you, I presume,' Brunner said.

'If it is, they didn't get the brow quite right, did they?' Stone answered, temporizing.

'That doesn't answer my question. Nor does it answer

why your travel bag held an Italian Army-issue Beretta with the serial numbers obliterated. Nor does it explain why your Swiss Army knife has the initials "C.L.S." scratched on its handle. As I recall, you gave your last name as Walker.'

Sighing, Stone shifted his weight in the chair, uncomfortable, a trickle of sweat dribbling down his back. Brunner was undoubtedly going to give the order to turn the *Valkyr* around and put back into Dover unless he could convince him to do otherwise. Mom had always told him that honesty was the best policy, but this situation went deeper. More like sheer necessity. He heaved his shoulders. 'Okay. My name's Christopher L-as-in-Luke Stone. I'm an American engineer and I'm not fond of drugs unless you're talking about alcohol. I was indirectly working for Lloyd's of London – threat assessment – involving a structure that they've written a policy on. I got in the way of some people who want to trash that property and they manipulated the events to make it look as if I were responsible.'

Brunner perked up his eyebrows, a smile curling on his lips, exposing his pearly whites. 'You don't say! "Manipulated events." What modesty! The article claims you and Ms van der Groot were involved in the brutal death of at least two people, the kidnapping of two others, the hijacking of a Bertram power yacht, the fire-bombing of a business in Rouen, and various bungled attempts at drug smuggling. And I always thought Lloyd's was a stodgy old-boy firm peddling insurance. I presume that they'll confirm your story.'

'The truth is, they probably wouldn't. I was subcontracting as an engineering specialist to a firm hired by Lloyd's – an outfit called Dundeedum Security Services based in Scotland but now operating out of Ramsgate under the cover name of Highgate Engineering. You can have your people check with a man by the name of Macleod who runs the operation. He'll verify who I am and that what I was doing in France was legal.'

280

From the stack of photographs, Brunner picked out one and slid it across the desk. 'This is the man you're speaking of?'

It was a good photo of Macleod, obviously shot with a telephoto lens. The hood of Mac's van showed up on the left of the photo with the caravan looming in the background.

Stone nodded to the print. 'Angus took that?'

'I presume so. As well as these thirty-four other photographs. They were in the boot of his car, along with a Nikon camera.'

'So ask Angus. He wasn't working for me.' Which left open the question as to who in hell Angus was working for, but Stone had an uneasy feeling that he already knew.

'Angus's driver's license was real enough. No other identification, no photos. Several hundred pounds sterling in new bills but nothing else of interest in his wallet. And he didn't have anything in the vehicle that would indicate any criminal activity. My people had to let him go but they're checking on his background through their connections in Scotland Yard. I should have a report on him by morning.' Brunner plucked a panatella from his desk drawer and lit it with a lighter shaped like a naval cannon. He blew out a rich blue-gray stream of smoke. 'So tell me, Mr Stone. Just what did your "threat analysis" for Lloyd's deal with?'

'I'm not at liberty to discuss that, Karl. Confidentiality agreement and such. Ask Macleod if you want to know, but I doubt he'd tell you. At any rate, my end of the job is finished. Melissa and I had to get over to the Continent to retrieve some property she left there. The *Valkyr* seemed like a good way of getting there without having to use public transportation.'

'. . . Or exposing yourself to the port authorities. Very understandable. I'm disappointed, of course. Interesting friends are so difficult to find these days.' He tapped a few millimeters of cigar ash into a ceramic basket held by a smiling peasant girl. 'Just a few more questions.' Brunner removed a paper and a business card from his drawer and laid them on his desk, turning them so that Stone could view them.

'About these, Mr Stone. There was an envelope on the dash of Angus's vehicle. My people thought it might have some bearing on the matter and I took the liberty of opening it. Just who is "Joss" and what is the *Cormorant*?'

'As far as the *Cormorant* goes, I don't have the foggiest except that it sounds like it's a *thing* – a pub, maybe, or a club. "Joss" is a professional killer working for some kind of a terrorist organization that's trying to trash the property that Lloyd's has insured.'

' "Joss?" Unusual name. As I recall, it refers to a Chinese deity. A nickname, perhaps Asian?'

'Filipino, I think, but I'm not sure. I met him under rather strained circumstances but I did note that his English was good — he'd possibly spent time in America.'

'And the terrorist organization he's working for?'

Stone shrugged. 'No idea. Lloyd's hasn't received any demands for money in return for the terrorists backing off. Therefore, I assume somebody's trying to make a political statement.'

'There was a diary of some sort in your travel bag. What bearing does it have on your activities?' Brunner was leaning back in his chair, slowly rotating the cigar, relaxed.

'It's the property of an engineer I know who was working on a project that I was interested in. Doesn't really have anything to do with the present situation.'

'That remains to be seen, doesn't it? Francine's French is better than mine. We'll discuss it later.' Brunner motioned to Manfred. 'Show Mr Stone down to the galley store-room and call up one of the engine-room people to guard him.'

'What are you going to do?' Stone could smell the stink of his own perspiration, the stuff that oozed out when the fight or flight glands were pumping.

'Turn you over to the Belgian authorities, I should think,' Brunner said. 'I'd rather keep it quiet. In England, the press would play it up, but on the Continent, I have friends who can ensure that my peripheral involvement is not disclosed.'

Manfred motioned Stone with the Beretta when Brunner spoke again. 'Francine will be *so* disappointed, Stone. She was looking forward to this evening.' He turned to Manfred. 'When Mr Stone has been made comfortable, please ask Ms van der Groot to come to my office.'

'She doesn't have anything to do with . . .'

'I should hope not,' Brunner replied. 'But then again, one never knows until one asks, Mr Stone.'

The store-room was black as a lawyer's heart, stuffy as a church parsonage, and reeked of over-ripe fruit. In the blackness, Stone stumbled over packing crates of produce before clearing a resting-place on the floor.

About an hour later, one of the galley staff brought him a plate of corned-beef hash and a bottle of beer. Standing behind the galley slave was a guy in a white boiler suit, armed with a crowbar. The guy actually held the bar cocked and ready in a two-fisted grip, as if he were Casey and Stone the ball. Stone laughed out loud, told the guy he couldn't make it in the bush leagues, but regretted it later when he rapped on the door and asked for seconds.

Brunner showed up thirty minutes later, an apologetic smile wired on his lips. 'She's very persuasive, Stone. Melissa told me the whole story. It does have its amusing aspects, you must admit.'

'Never noticed any, Karl. What now?' Stone stood blinking in the hard glare of the light, brushing flakes of onion skin off his clothing.

'We pick up where we left off. We're just about mid-Channel. We might talk a bit more in the morning. I have a few ideas that I'd like to share with you then, pending the receipt of information that I've requested from friends on the Continent.'

That struck Stone as curious. 'Just like that? You believed me?'

'Just her,' Brunner corrected him. 'And if you don't mind, Stone, I'll put your Beretta in the ship's safe. I'm averse to violence and all things connected with it.'

The four of them went through the motions of partying but there was no spontaneity to it – more as if they were actors, playing out a scene that they had already done a thousand times before. The champagne went nearly untouched.

The four of them danced on the afterdeck but the night air was cold, the moon obscured by a bank of clouds, and they failed to recapture the essence of the previous night. Initially, Francine clung to him as if she were a second skin, but Stone was sober and no chemistry catalyzed between them. After their third dance, she pecked him on the cheek, excused herself and said she was going down to her cabin. It was an invitation of sorts but offered with only mild enthusiasm and received in the same manner.

Brunner finally yawned, told them to enjoy and disappeared in the direction of the bridge for a last-minute check on their position before retiring. Manfred was still on call but had withdrawn to the salon, clearing away the remains of the buffet.

'Smoke Gets in Your Eyes' was playing. He bowed to her formally. 'This is the last one before they play "Good Night Sweetheart" and we all tear down to the drive-in for Cokes. Will you dance?'

Almost reluctantly, she moved into his arms, keeping the distance between their bodies to church-social standards. But by degrees, she relaxed, finally seeming to enjoy it, allowing herself to be held closer, her head lightly on his shoulder.

'What did he ask you?' Stone said. Her ear was just

millimeters from his lips and he had the overpowering desire to munch on it.

'How we met and everything that happened after that. I told him the unvarnished truth except for the part about you quivering stark naked with cold in the shower compartment.'

He cringed, remembering the incident, the embarrassment all the more acute because she had dismissed it as amusing.

'So he knows about the Chunnel, Le Borveaux, the *Night Watch*?'

'Everything.'

So be it, he thought. 'I have to say he handled it pretty well, considering what he must have thought he had on his hands. Not every day you have suspected drug runners for yachting guests.'

She nodded. 'He's a very decent man,' she said, her breath warm and sweet on his neck, smelling vaguely of cinnamon.

'You're talking about Brunner?' He had closed his eyes for a second, half dreaming of things that he hoped could be.

'Of course Brunner. The last of the Old World gentlemen. You could take a few lessons from him.'

'Dancing or otherwise?'

'Both. He's quite a marvel.'

'I hadn't noticed but I'll take your word for it.'

She hummed a snatch of the melody. 'I haven't danced this much in years. You're not bad, Stone. Just that you're not supposed to count out loud.'

'I had a good teacher.'

She snorted a little. 'I suspect Francine's instructional talents go far beyond dancing, Stone. I'd suggest that you start on a course of antibiotics tomorrow morning if you poke your thing into hers tonight.'

He pulled his head back from hers, looking into her eyes. 'Not fair, Melissa. Don't you know the difference between infatuation and love?' The words came out semi-slick, contrived, not the way he had wanted them to sound.

She batted her eyelashes. 'Was that heart-wrenching declaration of unrequited adoration aimed in my direction?' But she had a nice smile on her face.

'Just trying to say that I wasn't planning to sleep with her.'

More batting of eyelashes. 'I didn't know people slept when they were doing the dirty deed.'

'You know what I mean, dammit.' The music was ending and he tried a dip but forgot to lead. The effect had all the grace of two shoppers trying to shove past each other in the checkout line.

The CD player eased into 'Moonlight Serenade', Tommy Dorsey. The clouds parted a little, letting a stream of moonlight through, its reflection glazing the sea with mellow yellow.

She had paused, about to move away from him, but he held her hands, gently drawing her back to him. 'One more, for old times' sake,' he said, surprised to find that his voice had lowered an octave.

She hesitated, then slid into his arms again, her eyes closing slowly as she did.

His feet were now magic things: artfully gliding, hesitating, turning, smoothly crossing over, her body his, the scent of her filling him, her touch unbearably gentle on his back. It was the first time that he had really held her, could feel her breasts gentle against his chest, her heart beating, her curves molding to his as if they were both two pieces of a cosmic puzzle, at last and forever fitted together. He was surprised that he was not sexually aroused, but it was not there, not exactly – instead something wholly different and infinitely more.

'Things change, don't they,' she said, her voice languid. 'I couldn't tolerate you at first.'

'And now?'

'Definite improvement. Now I can barely stand you.'

She glanced up at him, wrinkled her nose, smiling, then laid her head back on his shoulder.

They drifted with the music across the varnished deck, the primitive scent of the sea a counterpoint to her perfume, a fullness within him. *Complete* was the only word that came to his mind.

He vaguely wished he knew the words to the music, believed that they could say for him what he felt. On impulse, he pressed her more tightly and she came to him completely, not resisting. Her hands moved from his back to his neck, stroking it softly, touching him as if she were gentling an animal, her lips saying something so softly he couldn't understand the words.

If this would go on forever, he thought, I would need nothing more to sustain me. Just her with me, like this, floating forever in mid-air.

The music was trailing off into the last bars, the sound blending with the wash of the sea, the end of it. They slowed, barely moving, still embracing.

She turned her face up to him. Stone gently framed her face in his hands, bending down. Her lips parted very slowly, just the smallest bit, eyes closed, and he kissed her.

It was like falling and not caring that you were falling, knowing that it would go on forever and you would never be hurt.

He held her, even after their lips no longer touched, swaying lightly, brushing his face against her hair, her fingers moving in a slow adagio along his spine.

She finally stood back from him, her hands still holding his, a funny smile on her lips, waiting.

If there was a time, it was now. He cocked his head, nodding toward the staircase. For a few seconds, she hesitated, then squeezed his hand in response.

They went down the spiral staircase together, bodies touching in gentle agony, hands linked. The carpeting was green and deep as mountain moss, the hum of the air conditioning a distant secret sound, like slow surf breaking on sand. Hidden lights recessed into the bulkheads lighted their feet, leaving their faces in shadows.

He had not been below before and she guided him past doors, putting her finger to her lips to indicate silence.

She paused. There were two doors, opposite each other. 'Yours. And mine,' she said softly.

He knew of no other way to put it. 'Will you?' he asked.

She kicked off her shoes and on tiptoes arched her body toward him, then kissed him very hard.

'Will you?' he asked again more insistently.

She hesitated, then backed away a step, her head slightly bowed. She put her arms straight down against her body as if she were unconsciously restraining herself. 'I don't know what to say, Stone, or how to answer. Will you hate me if I don't?'

He wanted to see her eyes, knew that she'd come with him if she looked up. 'No,' he said. 'Of course not, Melissa. But that doesn't stop me from wanting you.'

She still didn't look up, her voice barely audible. 'I'm not sure yet, Stone. This wasn't supposed to happen, I didn't want it to, it just did. I need time . . .'

He leaned over and kissed her forehead a little awkwardly. 'I can wait,' he said. 'It's not just tonight that I'm talking about. If I have to, I can wait until the Second Coming and then some.' He turned away reluctantly, his hand on the door knob of his stateroom.

Behind him, he heard her voice and turned to face her. 'Stone . . . I wasn't saying that I didn't want you, because I do, oh God I do. If you truly want me as well, I'm . . .'

It was if she were afraid to finish the sentence. She slipped into her stateroom, her door closing softly. But in that split second, he had seen her eyes and he was sure what those missing words would have been. He hesitated, unsure, listening for the sound of her latch locking . . . but it didn't.

Inside his stateroom, he leaned against the door, his heart bounding. She had left the latch unlocked, perhaps, because she forgot to secure it. Or, more likely, didn't want to. He looked down at his hands. They were shaking. Someone had once said, *He who dares, wins.* In ten minutes, he would find out.

The recessed lighting of his stateroom glowed from hidden fixtures. He fiddled with the knob on the wall and the lights dimmed. Another switch illuminated the bed with soft light. Gray silk sheets, almost liquid to the touch, the pillows stuffed with down. He punched one pillow experimentally, his fist disappearing into it.

He found the bathroom and stripped with one hand as he twisted the shower controls with his other. It was as hot as he could stand it, hard needles of spray raking his skin. He finished off with ice-cold, his whole body puckering.

A terry-cloth robe was draped over a heated towel rack. He pulled it on, feeling like a horny monk, then furiously brushed his teeth.

After hanging up his clothes, he padded around the room, exploring its possibilities. A hidden panel revealed hi-fi controls. He found a late-night FM station, a flute and guitar duet – a Brazilian composition by Jobin he half remembered. Her stateroom would probably have a unit just like his and he memorized where the station was on the dial.

Beneath the dressing-table, he discovered a metal latch and tugged. It opened to reveal a mini-fridge, stocked with splits of wine, champagne and a dozen miniatures of scotch. The lower shelves held little crocks of pâté and tinsel-wrapped wedges of Camembert. He chose a split of the Cordon Bleu, decided that Brunner could afford it, and on second thought recruited its mate as a reinforcement.

Still, like a schoolboy, he was a little frightened that she might reject him. It suddenly came to him that it wasn't just that he wanted her. Something more, something unfamiliar within the scope of all his previous experience, possibly that alien emotion they called love. Unravels the soul and unnerves the spirit, so it was said. The symptoms seemed to fit. He decided that he didn't care if there was the risk of rejection – that not to try was unthinkable.

Ten minutes had gone by, he estimated. Enough for her to undress and bathe, then to lie down in an empty bed and, hopefully, to listen for his coming. He felt lightheaded, breathless and insanely happy.

He was in the process of twisting the wire basket off when fingernails brushed the outer panel of the door. The sound sent a shiver raking down his spine.

He pushed his hair out of his face and slicked it back with the flat of his hand, fumbling the door open.

She stood there in white lace, little rows of seed pearls rimming the bodice, a gleaming waterfall of hair cascading over her shoulders. The effect was both child-like and devastating.

'It is my favorite nightdress,' she said. 'Do you approve?'

He swallowed. 'Francine, I . . .'

She moved slowly against him, her hand on his cheek, her eyes closing, her lips parting.

Beyond Francine's shoulder, he saw the handle of Melissa's door rotate, the door opening the barest fraction. Just part of her face showed. He saw her lips compress, her eyes slowly close. The door shut softly, the effect more deadly than if she had slammed it.

'Oh God,' he groaned.

Her voice was deep in her throat, husky. 'Yes – I feel it too. Now. I want you now.' The pressure of her body against his was pushing him backwards. Her breathing was labored, her scent overpowering.

'No!' he rasped, pressing her face away. *'NO!'*

Her eyes flashed open. ' *''No'' what?'*

He shook his head. 'I can't.' He backed away.

Her jaw took a dangerous set. 'What are you telling me?'

'Just that I can't.' His mind tumbled through a list of seemingly implausible excuses that he had heard before, desperately looking for one that fit. 'Because . . .'

290

Her eyes were hard. 'Because why?' Her voice was barely audible.

'Because ... because ... because it's my time of the month.'

She looked like she had been transformed into stone, stock-still, her eyes impossibly wide.

He placed his hands on her shoulders, guiding her backwards through the door. He smiled weakly and closed it, then twisted the latch.

There was the sound of a bare foot smashing against his door, then, *'PIG!'* The solitary word seeped through the insulation, muffled but distinct.

He stood against the interior of his stateroom door, perspiration dripping from his body. Just the sound of machinery deep in the guts of the ship, the rush of the sea against the hull, the pounding of blood in his brain. Other than that, silence.

He gave it another five minutes, then eased his door open. The corridor was empty. He tried Melissa's door. Locked.

11 April

He woke late and came up on deck mid-morning. It was cooler than the day before with low humidity and a west wind snapping. The *Valkyr* swung leisurely at anchor about two hundred meters from the seawall that fronted a small village. The surrounding land was marshy and unrelieved.

He found Brunner on the afterdeck where a table and chairs for four had been set up.

Brunner was reading a report of some sort with one hand as he spooned grapefruit wedges into his mouth with the other. He looked up.

'Ah – the tardy riser. I take it you slept well?'

Whether it was a smile or a smirk, Stone couldn't fathom.

'Pretty good. Where's Melissa?'

'Neither of the ladies have graced me with their presence. Coffee?'

Stone sat down opposite Brunner. Manfred appeared from nowhere with a silver coffee pot and poured.

'Vot vood you vant for breakfast, Mister Stone?'

Stone couldn't resist. 'Pig's knuckles over easy with a side order of kraut.'

'Vee haf no . . .'

Brunner gave a restrained laugh. 'He's teasing you about your accent, Manfred. Bring Mr Stone some orange juice, eggs Benedict and a scone.' He waited until Manfred had left then said, 'Manfred's a bit sensitive, Stone. He misunderstands American humor. His parents were killed in a B-17 raid and consequently he's not overly fond of Americans. You understand, of course?'

Sensitivity was a trait that Stone hadn't associated with Manfred but he nodded. 'Sorry about that. No offense intended.'

'Good. I knew you'd understand.' Brunner forked in the last of the grapefruit wedges, then sat back in his chair, stretching. 'What are your plans, Stone?'

'It's up to Melissa, of course. As she probably told you, *Night Watch* is in Le Havre, impounded by the French authorities. Basically, we'll make our way down there and see what the situation is. Macleod told me that the French have just one man guarding her, a retired *flic*. Might be able to bribe him. Alternatively, might have to overpower him. One way or the other, we'll sneak her out of France and sail her to Ireland.'

Brunner scratched his chin. 'I've given the situation some thought. I think I could help you.'

'Nice, Karl, but why? I wouldn't want you to get in trouble.'

'I don't intend to, but that doesn't prevent me from using my considerable resources to advantage. As you've probably noticed, the *Valkyr* is equipped with a Hughes 500 helicopter. Rather than you and Melissa trying to get to Le Havre by public transportation which would entail the risk of being detected by the police, my pilot could fly you there direct. It's about 350 kilometers — say a little under a two-hour trip. No flight plan, no passenger list. He'll fly at treetop level, under the air traffic control radar, and drop you off in the countryside a few kilometers from the port.'

It was a stunning offer, too good to be questioned. 'When?' Stone asked.

'Tomorrow morning, crack of dawn. In the meanwhile, I'm having some of my people check on the *Night Watch* to see whether it's well guarded. I'll have a report in by evening.'

'One other problem — she's low on diesel fuel and oil.'

Brunner made a note. 'I can't make any promises, of course, but my people might be able to assist in that as well.'

Stone was overwhelmed. 'Karl . . . I can't begin to tell you how much your help is appreciated.'

Brunner made a gesture of dismissal as if he had done nothing of value, then said, 'There's another aspect of this that I want to talk to you about, Stone. The attempt to sabotage Eurotunnel. Melissa said that you were convinced there would be an attempt to destroy it.'

'That's pretty well out of my ballpark now, Karl. I'm off the job.'

'It isn't out of mine,' Brunner replied, his facial muscles hardening. 'Terrorism is the plague of Europe. It has to be stamped out because it affects all of us.'

'Not that easy,' Stone replied.

'Perhaps not, but it's the same old thing, isn't it? A few discontents spoiling it for everyone else. If we're to have a civilized world, then each of us has the moral obligation to act.' He ruffled the paper in his hand. 'I've got two separate reports in already, the first on your friend, Angus K. Paine. Too bad my people didn't have sufficient cause to turn Angus over to the authorities. He's been associated with an Irish Protestant terrorist group for several years, runs explosives for them.' He glanced down at the paper. 'Before that, RAF ordnance specialist, drummed out of the service for suspected theft of explosives. Some drug-related crimes as well.'

Which left Stone with the unanswerable question of what Angus had been up to. Surveillance only, or something more deadly?

Easing his sunglasses back on his head, Brunner studied a second sheet of paper. 'I've also received a preliminary report on the numbers that were written on the business card from a retired friend of mine in Austria who was with Interpol but still has friends in the organization. As I thought, the list was composed of telephone and fax numbers.'

He passed Stone the printout, obviously from a fax machine. No letterhead but signed by someone named Frans Shiffe.

'You can get faxes at sea?'

'Sat-com. The dome you see aft of the bridge. It continuously tracks a communications satellite. I can be in contact worldwide, regardless of the location. Somewhat expensive, but actually a small price to pay for the freedom of movement it affords me.'

Suitably impressed, Stone resumed reading. Opposite each number was a comment. The first number was from the face of the business card, Weshiem-Munden GmbH. 'Legitimate firm in Hamburg, import-export business specializing in medical imaging equipment such as CAT and MRI machines. Established 1911, listed on the DAK exchange. Will interview principals tomorrow.'

The next three numbers had an 'X' next to them with the comment, 'Cellular telephone numbers, disconnected, but originally registered in the name of New World Realty Ventures Ltd with a corporate address in Manchester, England. A company-records check with a law firm in Manchester reveals that no such firm exists.'

Stone lifted the page. 'English firm?'

Brunner shrugged. 'It is a bit odd, isn't it, when all the activity you've described would indicate a European orientation?'

Stone nodded and resumed reading. The last entry was 'DMV *Cormorant*, NE 78781'. Next to it was the comment, 'DMV = Dutch motor vessel? Will check with authorities for correlation of registration number with ship's name.'

How bloody stupid I've been, Stone realized. Of course – a ship of some sort. It made even more sense since a vessel would have to be used to transport divers and equipment to the Chunnel.

'I think the guy who wrote this is right on.'

Brunner lifted his eyebrows. 'Why is that?'

'Fits in.' Stone laid out the borehole theory.

'You can't be serious! I can accept a couple of mad IRA bombers trying to blow up the Eurotunnel with a carload of explosives, but what you're describing entails a massive operation with costs in the millions. And I hardly need remind you that a vessel anchored over the Chunnel would immediately attract the attention of the authorities.'

'I agree, but from an engineering standpoint, it's the only thing that works for me – particularly the crossover chamber. My calculations indicate that's the most vulnerable part of the Chunnel.'

Brunner scratched at his jaw, reflective. 'Perhaps. We'll see what my people turn up if this *Cormorant* actually turns out to be a vessel. But it still all seems to revolve around this Joss person. You don't seem to know much about him, do you?'

'Only the list of the numbers, the reference to *Cormorant* and some receipts that he had in his attaché case. One was from a DHL office in Le Havre made out to an Antonio Bontoc for a package sent to Utrecht. Could actually be his real name although Macleod thinks it's probably an alias.' Stone paused, thinking. 'One other thing, although it's pure guesswork. Joss could have been a merchant seaman.

It seemed to me that he was familiar with boats and that's not something that happens overnight. That would fit in with the *Cormorant*, assuming it's a vessel.'

'Then if he was, he would undoubtedly have belonged to a seaman's union of some sort, quite possibly a Filipino seaman's union. I can contact my Austrian friend, Frans Shiffe, and have him cross-check Interpol's database. It's very long odds, but if there's a match-up in names, he might be able to have a photo of the man transmitted to us for identification.'

'But like you said — it's a long shot.'

'Now that I've considered it, perhaps not as long as it sounds. This Joss person might have a false passport and driver's license, but it's doubtful that he would bother to falsify his seaman's records — not the normal thing one would use as identification. It's my guess that, if this *Cormorant* is a vessel, Joss might be trying to get aboard as crew, and if he is, then he'd need seaman's papers. In other words, Joss might be planning to hijack the *Cormorant*.'

Brunner's theory sounded tenuous to Stone but Brunner seemed to have the bit well and truly in his mouth. 'What can I say except "good luck". But I'll be damned surprised if you turn up anything.'

Brunner stood up, passed his napkin across his lips and threw it on the table. 'Don't underestimate me, Stone. I generally get what I want because I'm willing to pay the price.'

Stone spent the balance of the morning in the salon reading a book from the *Valkyr*'s library. The author had a five-point program on becoming the happy landlord of one's libido by evicting the injured child within. Somehow, Stone was unable to contact the injured child within, although he had to admit his libido needed a good tune-up. He gave up by the third chapter which promoted the healing powers of primal-scream therapy.

Drinking lunch, courtesy of Brunner's well-stocked bar,

he spent an uncomplicated afternoon browsing through magazines.

Just after noon, Francine passed through on her way to the sun deck, suitably fitted out in a bikini of micro proportions. She ignored Stone, her chin held high. Ten minutes later, Melissa passed through, presumably also headed for the sun deck.

He scrambled to his feet and called to her. She looked back briefly, her face neutral of expression.

'I have nothing to say to you, Stone, and I'd prefer that you don't bother me. Furthermore, I hope that you've started in on the antibiotics because if you haven't, they'll eventually have to amputate.'

'*Dammit*, Melissa, I didn't . . .'

The salon door banged shut behind her. *Ice queen*, he thought, passing summary judgement, but he knew that what evil lurked in the hearts of women was generally of man's making, his own in this instance.

Brunner, as animated as an eager puppy, bounded in just after 16.00 with a fax fluttering from his fingers.

'Let's go. Frans Shiffe has come through with a match-up.'

FIFTEEN

'My God! You mean this guy Shiffe got results that fast!'

'Frans is not a genius,' Brunner answered. 'But he is a very competent man who goes several steps beyond what's expected of him. That's why he was head of my corporate security for those years.' Brunner checked his watch. 'No time now to talk how. We're due there in twenty minutes.'

'Where?'

'Shiffe has set up a meeting for us with a ship's agent in the port area of Antwerp – a man who may possibly actually know Joss. We'll take the helicopter – less than fifteen minutes' flight time.'

They were airborne by 16.08, the Hughes whacking low over the estuary, then inland, paralleling a canal. Below them, the land was low-lying and marshy; sunlight glittering back from saturated soil, an occasional farm building, cows heading home for milking, a solitary figure on a bicycle who looked up and waved.

The Hughes intersected the River Scheldt and altered course eastward, the roadstead and Port of Antwerp growing on the horizon.

Brunner sat next to Stone in the back seat, Manfred and the chopper's pilot in the front. Brunner handed Stone a set of headphones with a boom mike attached, then fiddled with the intercom controls.

Brunner puffed in the microphone, testing it. 'Do you hear me all right?'

'Fine. Exactly what did Shiffe find out?'

'Just as he guessed, the *Cormorant* is a motor vessel and,

until a month ago, registered in the Netherlands. The number given was not her official ship's registration but rather her radio call-sign – something you'd need to make a ship-to-shore call to her through a marine operator, most likely the reason Joss was carrying the number.'

'What kind of vessel is she?' Stone asked.

'Shiffe said that Dutch maritime registry records show she's a 500-ton coastal freighter built back in the late forties; been through seven owners and was just recently purchased by a German corporation. According to Shiffe, she failed a survey after the sale had already gone through and was declared unfit for service.'

'What about Joss?'

'Shiffe checked with the authorities in Manila and learned that there *was* a seaman by the name of Antonio Bontoc listed in their records. It's not conclusive because Bontoc seems to be a fairly common last name over there, but at least it's a start.'

'Not exactly pay dirt, is it?'

Brunner ignored him and continued. 'On a hunch, Shiffe contacted both the US and British merchant marine seaman's registration offices. Both of them implemented digitalized registration about five years ago. Admittedly, it was a long shot. The British came up with a blank but the Americans had a file on a man by the name of Antonio Bontoc, age forty-two, licensed able seaman. The Americans were able to modem a photo of Bontoc and his fingerprints to Shiffe and he'll be transmitting them to me within the hour. If it's the same Bontoc, he originally worked for an American bulk carrier shipping firm, Holsen Caribbean Lines, then jumped ship in Jamaica and signed on one of those Bahamian-flagged cruise ships that do the Caribbean run. Worked on the *Caribbean Star* for two years as a steward, then was fired for suspected theft and drug use. There's no further record of his movements after that, although there was a note in his file that the Colombian police have a warrant out on him – something about his potential involvement in the disappearance of an American-registered yacht, along with an accomplice by the name of Turner.'

'*Turner?* An American?'

'Shiffe didn't mention Turner's nationality. Only that Turner was a marine engineer who was employed on the yacht in question. He dropped out of sight about the same time that Joss did.'

'During the dust-up I had with Joss in Rouen, he called one of his men "Turner". I'm positive of it.'

Brunner drove his fist into the palm of his other hand. 'Excellent. Then we're on the right track.' He glanced at the fax again. 'Shiffe could have stopped there but instead he took the problem to its logical conclusion, trying to tie Antonio Bontoc to the *Cormorant*. Given that the *Cormorant* has been in the North Sea trade for nearly fifty years and has probably traded in every port on the Continent, Frans commandeered the entire staff of my home office in Switzerland. He had them contact all the ship's agents listed for every European country bordering the North Sea and the Mediterranean – 289 different agents in all. My staff reached all but eight of them. Of the ones they reached, four of them had files on a crewman identified as Antonio Bontoc: one in Italy, one in Spain, one in the Netherlands, and one here in Antwerp.' He pointed to the port area below. 'We'll find out soon enough.'

The chopper banked steeply, burning off altitude. Stretched out below was a chain of freighters tied up alongside the commercial docks, cranes and gantries cluttering the foreshore. Containers were stacked six deep like Lego blocks, trucks wheeling onto the docks, forklift trucks hustling in and out of warehouses – an orchestrated medley of maritime commerce.

Leaning forward, Brunner tapped the shoulder of the pilot and pointed at a green patch next to a parking lot.

Minutes later, Brunner and Stone were standing on the grass, the blades of the chopper still scything the afternoon air as the turbine spooled down, both of them watching as an obese man climbed out of a small delivery van that was double-parked in the lot. The man fluttered his hand, then half shuffled, half ran toward them. His face was bright red and beaded with sweat, glasses glinting in the sunlight, an old-fashioned schoolboy's briefcase lurching in his grip.

'De Ruiter,' the man said as he reached them, sticking out a pudgy hand. 'Hans de Ruiter of IBUH, ship's agents. Mr Shiffe contacted me. You are Herr Brunner?'

Brunner nodded. 'Grateful that you could take time to meet with me. My chief of security, Frans Shiffe, told me that you have information on Antonio Bontoc.'

Still panting, de Ruiter motioned to a bench edging the grass. 'If you don't mind, we will sit down. My heart is not young.'

As they walked, de Ruiter rummaged in his briefcase and came up with a photograph. 'This is the man?'

Brunner handed it to Stone. It was a cheap passport shot, the man's eyes squinting, mouth slack, the skin pitted.

'That's him,' Stone said.

De Ruiter took the photo back and studied it. 'Antonio Bontoc.' He scowled, his nose wrinkling. 'Insisted that everyone call him "Joss" – told me that the name brought him luck. Came to me three years ago with seaman's papers and a couple of average recommendations. Put him on board a Dutch coastal freighter as an able seaman. He stayed with her over two years before he was stopped when he reboarded the ship after shore leave in Alicante, a half-kilo of cocaine concealed in a shoe box. The officer on watch locked him in the ship's pantry and called the *Guardia Civil*. But before they arrived, someone let him out and he dove overboard, as they say, "never to be seen again".'

'What was the name of the ship?' Brunner asked.

De Ruiter eased down onto the bench, wiping his neck with a handkerchief, still breathing heavily. 'Not a real ship, mind you. Little coaster, one of the Van Heil Line vessels, all of them named after seabirds. The *Osprey?* He shook his head. 'No, I forgot. She was lost in the Biscay with a load of cement in '86.' His face brightened. 'It was her sister ship, the *Cormorant*. Ya, the *Cormorant*.'

Stone started to ask a question but Brunner held up his hand and asked de Ruiter, 'Do you think Bontoc had an accomplice who remained on board the *Cormorant*; perhaps someone who was in the drug trade with him – someone he'd want to stay in contact with?'

After thinking for a short while, de Ruiter shook his head. 'Not in the sense of an accomplice. But there was a Dutch girl who was working as ship's cook. It turned out he was having an affair with her.' He thumbed through a smudged notebook. 'Lousja van den Broek. Not pretty, mind you. A bit wide in the beam, but a good girl, understand? After Joss went swimming in Alicante, she was called in by the *Guardia* for questioning because she was the only person on board the *Cormorant* who had keys to the pantry. After two minutes of questioning, the poor girl broke down. She admitted being pregnant by Joss. He had told her he was going to marry her once he had a little money stashed away. His parting shot was that he promised to contact her once he got clear of Spain. She must have believed him because she telephoned me every time the *Cormorant* made port to find out whether Joss had shown up. She finally signed off the ship when she got too big, then went to live with her parents up in Hoogeveen. That was about, ah, last November. Had a baby boy and called him "Hans" after me. Photo of the lad somewhere in here.'

De Ruiter rummaged around in his briefcase and pulled out a greeting-card with a pop-in photo of a baby. 'Sent this last Christmas. A good girl, like I said. I'm a ship's agent, Herr Brunner, and I make most of my fees through ship's provisioning and brokering cargoes, but I've always followed the kids that I've signed aboard ships, lent them

302

money when they were short, remembered their birthdays.' He beamed. 'Ask anyone. They call me "Uncle Hans".'

'So Joss just skipped?' Stone asked.

De Ruiter nodded. 'But six weeks ago, I received a letter addressed to Lousja at my firm's address with a request to forward it. It was postmarked somewhere in England — Newmarket, as I recall. No return address but it was Joss's printing — compared it to his old résumé — and it had a "J" with a stroke through in the upper left-hand corner, just in the way that Joss initialed paragraphs on the ship's articles he had to sign. Naturally, I forwarded it to her. Then another envelope just like it arrived two weeks ago, postmarked Rouen, France. Forwarded that as well.'

'You read them?' Brunner asked softly.

De Ruiter looked shocked. 'What do you think I am, Herr Brunner? I respect the privacy of my clients. It's a sacred trust.'

Brunner homed in. 'Why do you think Joss is trying to reach the van den Broek woman?'

De Ruiter smiled. 'It's just my opinion, Herr Brunner, for what it's worth. Man is immortalized by his children, even if they happen to be bastards. Joss wants to establish that link with immortality. He wants to know about his son. And who knows, he may miss the woman. It's that simple.'

'I want you to notify Mr Shiffe if you receive any further letters from Joss . . .' Brunner said '. . . and if you do, hold on to them until I can arrange for one of my employees to pick them up.' It was a command rather than a request.

Studying his veined hands, de Ruiter was obviously struggling with his ethics. He shrugged, then looked up. 'I'm getting old, Herr Brunner. There is no pension for a man like me so a few guilders here and there help. What you ask is possible, as long as you don't involve the girl.'

'What about the *Cormorant*?' Stone asked.

Tugging at his earlobe, de Ruiter scowled. 'Let's see. Last I heard of her, she was anchored somewhere up in the Hook of Holland. The knacker's yard for her. She's scheduled to be broken up for scrap in Norway come next month, soon as they can find a patch of calm weather to tow her up there. She was built of good Dutch steel back in '48, but her plating has rusted away to the thickness of a beer can. One good storm and she'd go down.'

'Do you have any idea who owns her now?'

'Of course. It was an enormous joke, everyone in the marine trade talking about it. Some German environmental group that calls itself Sea Greens bought her on the cheap back in February. Bonehead scheme about installing a tank in her cargo hold to contain garbage from the ports of Europe. Thought they'd compost it and use the methane gas given off by the pig swill to drive the engines – their idea of an environmentally safe perpetual-motion machine. "Save the World from the Greenhouse Effect by Recycling Garbage" kind of nonsense. Any damned fool on the coast knew she couldn't pass a survey, would never qualify for a certificate of seaworthiness. And the amount of methane gas generated wouldn't amount to a mouse fart – let alone enough to even drive an outboard motor if you ask me.'

He interlaced his fingers and cracked his knuckles, obviously enjoying center stage. 'After she failed the survey, the bank that had loaned the money foreclosed on her. The German kids dry-docked *Cormorant* and had anything that was worth salvaging stripped out of her and sold. She's just a hulk now, so I hear – only fit for scrap. Sad that old ships have to go that way. Rather see them towed out to sea and sunk, flags flying.'

Brunner retrieved an envelope from his jacket and handed it to de Ruiter. 'There's a bit extra in there over the sum that Mr Shiffe said I'd pay you. I want you to follow up on the *Cormorant* – let Mr Shiffe know if there's any change in her status. And as I said before, if you receive

304

another letter for the girl from Joss, you're to call Mr Shiffe immediately. Joss is wanted by the police.'

De Ruiter raised his eyebrows as he took the envelope. 'Sad when these boys go wrong. Drugs, is it?'

'Perhaps,' Brunner answered, signaling the pilot to get the chopper cranked up. He hesitated, turning back to de Ruiter. 'You mentioned that the first letter had an English postmark?'

'Ah – it was from Newmarket. Small town up in East Anglia if I recall my lessons.'

Brunner nodded, briefly shook hands, then turned and guided Stone by the elbow toward the Hughes. They walked across the grass, the evening shadows stretching out, the glass windows of buildings reflecting the setting sun.

'Newmarket,' Brunner said, almost to himself. 'Strange place for a man like Joss to be hanging out, don't you think?'

Stone nodded, but he didn't have the slightest idea where Newmarket was, let alone East Anglia. But now that Brunner had mentioned it, it did seem odd.

Dinner on board the *Valkyr* had all the ambiance of the Last Supper. The two women ate in surly silence and individually excused themselves, both pleading headaches, even before the dessert was served. Stone had not once been able to make eye contact with Melissa and his probing toe had been rebuffed with a kick.

After finishing up, Stone and Brunner retired to the salon for a cognac, Stone in the dumps.

'I don't suppose that I should ask what transpired between you and the women last night?' Brunner asked, obviously amused.

'It's a little complicated,' Stone answered. 'Two plus one equals zero is about as close as I can come to explaining.'

Brunner gave a refined laugh. 'I suspect a little celibacy never hurt anything except the ego. But take heart, my

305

friend. Things generally come out right in the end.' With this gratuitous homily delivered, he topped up their snifters. He held his up to the light to check for whatever it was that connoisseurs checked for, then sipped. He set it down, apparently pleased.

'Incidentally, I checked with Captain Allen before dinner. The weather in the Channel will be calm tomorrow morning but you'll probably run into some fog. Light south-westerly winds in the afternoon and clearing. Kiss the Blarney Stone for me when you get to Ireland.'

'What's with the retired French cop guarding the *Night Watch*?'

'Amazing what 10,000 francs can do. My people had a talk with the *flic*. He's on a pension, has an ailing sister who lives in Tours. Conveniently, her condition has suddenly taken a turn for the worse. He should have left Le Havre by now and will remain in Tours until the day after tomorrow. That will give you and Melissa a thirty-six-hour head start. I have a rough map so you'll know where the yacht is tied up.'

Brunner pulled a hand-drawn map out of his jacket pocket. 'The *Night Watch* is tied up in a marina at the Digue Nord.' He pointed his finger to an inlet just to the west of the commercial docks. 'Slip C-3. Once you're out of the marina, turn to starboard at the breakwater and you'll be in international waters within twenty minutes.'

'Diesel fuel?'

'All arranged. My people paid the *flic* to refuel her prior to his departure. They'll check over everything, make sure nothing's amiss. I also told them to lay on food sufficient for a five-day passage. You'll find the keys to the engine in the port cockpit locker.'

'What's the schedule for the flight down to Le Havre?'

'You and Melissa will leave the *Valkyr* at 03.30 in the Hughes. The timing is such that you should be ready to cast off just before dawn.'

Impressed, Stone tried to make a rough calculation but

couldn't. 'This had to cost you a bundle, Karl. I can't repay you now but when things get sorted out . . .'

Brunner shrugged, vaguely magnanimous. 'Forget it, my friend. The whole exercise has been most instructive and I think that things are now much clearer.'

'How so?'

Brunner ticked the points off on his hand. 'One – Joss's connection to the *Cormorant* is long past, or so it would seem. If it isn't, then de Ruiter will let me know and I'll forward that information on to you or Macleod. Two – the telephone and fax numbers on that business card were probably written down some time ago. But now, they're either disconnected or seemingly unrelated to anything Joss's currently involved in. And three – from the limited evidence that I've seen, I seriously doubt that Joss is a terrorist. Drug running seems much more likely, given his background.'

'I can't buy that, Karl. There's the floppy disk with confidential data on the Chunnel's construction as well as Le Borveaux's abduction. And why in blazes were Joss and his two buddies trying to kill Melissa and me?'

Fiddling with his snifter, Brunner slowly shook his head. 'Does it occur to you, Stone, that you're looking at this from the perspective of already having convinced yourself that Joss is working for people who are out to destroy the Chunnel? You've fitted all of his actions into your tightly molded theory, yet ignored the obvious. Cocaine was found aboard the Bertram powerboat, possibly the owner's, but more likely Joss's. And don't ignore the fact that Joss has a lengthy history of drug dealing, and for that matter, so has Angus. It seems likely to me that Joss has gotten it into his head that you're connected with a drug enforcement agency of some kind. I think his actions as concerned you were designed to eliminate a perceived threat.'

Possible, Stone thought. Brunner's drug theory *could* explain the chain of events but, still, Stone couldn't shake the idea that it was all tied in with the destruction of the Chunnel.

He stood up and walked to the salon windows, looking out over the water. The moon was a pale disk, the fabric of low clouds drifting across it. As he watched, he noticed the *Valkyr*'s launch heading for shore, the running-lights not showing. Probably Manfred headed for the nearest plumber's shop for a new supply of lead pipes, he reckoned.

He turned back to Brunner, who was now fiddling with the hi-fi.

'What you say makes sense, Karl, but there are too many things that are left unexplained. I just can't shake the idea that Joss is bent on destroying the Chunnel. Yet I can't come up with a motive.'

'Political?' Brunner was still fiddling. A couple of lights on the hi-fi blinked and a string quartet filled the salon with soothing sounds.

'Doubt it. He doesn't act like a political animal and there's nothing in his background to suggest that.'

'Revenge seems unlikely,' Brunner suggested, 'but who knows?' His tone was dismissive.

'That doesn't fit either as far as I can see.'

Brunner yawned. 'All right, Stone. Have it your way. Let's say Joss actually is intent on destroying the Chunnel for whatever reason. You've described it as a highly technical task requiring a massive amount of equipment and specialized skills. What makes you think a common drug runner with little or no education could muster that kind of capability?'

'Okay, Karl. You're probably half-right. I've pretty well given up on the idea of Joss blowing it from the seabed. But he might try blowing it from inside.'

Brunner shook his head wearily. 'Eurotunnel has extremely rigid security screening. I seem to recall that even minute quantities of plastique explosive can be detected by chemical sniffers and I'm quite sure Eurotunnel's security personnel are equipped with such machines.'

Stone poured himself another brandy. 'I was thinking about liquid explosives – something that could be dispensed inside the Chunnel, then ignited. There was a similar situation a couple of years ago. Back in '92, you probably remember that there was an explosion in the sewers of Guadalajara, Mexico.'

'Intentional?' Brunner asked.

'Don't think so. A methane gas leak maybe, or some kind of cleaning fluid. Whatever it was, it blew out a mile of sewer, the street above it and all the buildings on either side. Same principle as a fuel-air bomb. The thing about a liquid explosive is that if you get the mixture just right, the explosive effect is a large multiple of what you'd get from the same weight of plastique.'

'Interesting,' Brunner commented, but it didn't sound as if he really thought it was. He yawned. 'You're going to have to forgive me. I'm tired and I'd suggest you turn in soon as well. I'll see you off in the morning, but before we wind this up, I have a suggestion. I think you should send a fax to your friend, Macleod, and let him know what we've found out here in Belgium. It might be useful to him.'

'Thought about that, Karl, but I can just as easily call him from Ireland.'

Brunner frowned, obviously not in agreement. 'That will be at least four or five days from now, Stone. I would think that the results from our efforts and the considerable expense we've gone to warrant an immediate report. Keep it short. Just give him the facts with no mention of my help. You might also consider that Lloyd's should be more inclined to pay Macleod for his and your services if he can show some early results on his investigation.'

Damned true, Stone thought. He had nearly spent all of Macleod's advance and was now digging into his own pocket. And the possibility that Joss might presently be in England would give Mac something to chew on.

'You're right, Karl. If we can use your fax, let's do it.'

In Brunner's office, Stone pecked out a report on the word processor, Brunner making the occasional suggestion. Stone had the body of the text finished in half an hour. To the text, he attached Joss's photo and fingerprint scan which Shiffe had transmitted to Brunner.

'Do you have some kind of a fax cover-sheet, Karl? If Mac gets this tonight, he might want to call or fax back assuming he has questions.'

'Frankly, I'd just as soon have my name left out of it for now, Stone. I'm violating the laws of several countries helping you out, and knowledge of that at any level wouldn't enhance either my corporate or personal reputations. Once you've met with Macleod face to face, you have my permission to tell him about me, but for now, I'd appreciate it if you made no mention of either me or the *Valkyr* in the document you're transmitting.'

As usual, Brunner made perfect sense. 'Okay. No return fax number, no mention of you or the *Valkyr*. He'll think I sent it from a hotel or something like that. Probably just as well.'

'Just one final question,' Brunner interjected. 'How will he be able to verify the fax was actually transmitted by you?'

'I'll sign it "Talisker". It's a brand of scotch that he likes. I've used it before to identify myself.'

Brunner shrugged. He reached down and saved the document to memory, then tapped a couple of keys. The screen reformatted, the cursor blinking on a line marked 'Transmit fax to what number?'

'You have Macleod's fax number?' Brunner asked.

Stone gave it to him.

Brunner typed it in, then touched the return key. The screen dissolved, replaced with a blinking 'Transmission in progress. Please wait.' Thirty-eight seconds later, the screen cleared with the message, 'Fax transmission complete. Three pages received OK.'

'That wraps it up,' Stone said.

Brunner nodded, turning the computer off. He favored Stone with a mechanical smile. 'I think it does,' he said.

He saw Stone and the woman off at 03.33, the three minutes' delay due to Stone's insistence that his Second Amendment rights not be infringed on.

'In other words,' Stone said, 'I want the Beretta back.'

Brunner tried to keep a straight face. 'Violence begets violence, Stone. You surely don't need a firearm' – but after further hounding by Stone, he signaled Allen to get it from the safe. There was a timetable and Brunner didn't want to throw it off. And, regardless – a firearm wasn't going to help Stone where he was going.

They shook hands one more time under the dazzle of the decklights, Brunner overlaying Stone's hand with both of his.

'You've done a lot for me, Karl. God knows I can't repay you for all the help you've given me.'

'Your thanks are more than enough,' Brunner answered warmly. 'Have a safe passage, my friend.'

He watched as Stone joined Melissa in the back seat of the Hughes. There was a short delay until Manfred scrambled down from the bridge and crawled into the chopper next to the pilot, a briefcase under his arm. Manfred had insisted on checking the batteries but Brunner knew that the Dutchman didn't make mistakes like that. Still, he appreciated Manfred's thoroughness. Old-world devotion to duty was now rare in a workman.

Gunther, his face shrouded by his headset and baseball cap, gave Brunner the thumbs-up and Brunner nodded. Gunther was as good as they came. Over 3000 hours in rotary-wing aircraft, including the time he had been on loan from the Stasi to the PLO during the pullout from Lebanon.

The rotor blades began to scythe through the damp night air as the turbine spooled up, the exhaust stack of the

311

Hughes belching blue feathers of flame. In seconds, the chopper lifted off, dipped forward and disappeared to the south, its navigational lights extinguished.

Allen had climbed back to the bridge, and almost immediately the decklights were extinguished, leaving Brunner standing in darkness.

He didn't notice her until she was standing next to him in a bathrobe, a cup of coffee in her hand.

'Did it go well?' she asked.

'I think so,' Brunner replied, sliding his arm around her waist. 'De Ruiter or whatever his name was gave a superb performance.'

'How did you arrange it?' Francine asked, but he sensed she wasn't really interested. He felt her body shivering in the early-morning cold.

'I called Turner before we left England. He drove down from the shipyard to Antwerp and contracted with de Ruiter – a man whom the Dutchman had recommended as both reliable and talented. Seems that de Ruiter actually spent some time on the stage in his younger years but has made his living for the last thirty years as a con-man. Turner rehearsed him, of course, but still, de Ruiter did a magnificent job. I sensed he actually enjoyed it.'

'Stone believed him?'

'Completely, I should think.'

'What now?' she asked.

'Back to bed for a few hours. We'll get under way for the shipyard after breakfast.'

'What about Gunther and Manfred?'

'They'll probably need most of the day for a job I've given them, so I don't expect them back at the shipyard until late tonight or tomorrow. Nine hours in the cockpit is a long time, even for a man of Gunther's stamina.'

She undoubtedly wanted to know what the job was, but he sensed that she knew enough not to ask.

He turned to her, lifting her chin, and kissed her lightly. 'So tell me, Francine. Did you bed Stone?'

He felt her body shift slightly beneath his hand. 'I thought better of it at the last moment. He didn't suit me.'

Which Brunner knew was a lie, because he had listened to the conversation transmitted by the hidden microphone in Stone's cabin. Knowing Francine as he did, she would be craving sex by now, desperate to reassure herself. It would be both violent and satisfying.

'Then perhaps you have room in your bed for an old man with young ideas,' he said.

She didn't answer, but she reached over and squeezed his hand very hard.

04.30, 12 April

She wouldn't talk to him on the way south to Le Havre, had rejected the headset he offered her, kept her face turned away, nose pressed to the oval window of the Hughes.

The ride was rough as a cob, most of the time down in the weeds, weaving through valleys and cresting ridges by the slimmest of margins. Stone had to admit that the pilot was damned good, but the flight, nevertheless, scared the hell out of him.

They had been airborne for little more than an hour when the pilot eased out over the sea, paralleling the French coast. There was just the hint of first light in the east, and with it the realization that the sea below was blanketed in fog. *Not good*, he thought, given that the heaviest seagoing traffic in the world would be trooping directly across their intended course. Still, it would help in getting out of Le Havre undetected, and Brunner had mentioned that the fog would clear in the late afternoon.

At 04.53, the pilot swung back in toward the coast. He skimmed over a prominent bluff, up a sloping rise, then down into a shallow valley. In the first light, it was postcard perfect, the sort of thing travel agents tacked to their wall. There were neat fields laid out between tall rows of trees, crops already starting to green, a hedgerow, a string of telephone poles, a tumbled-down shack that looked more quaint than dilapidated. Little patches of fog lay in the hollows, enhancing the fairyland quality. Stone half expected Fred Astaire to come prancing down the hill with Ginger Rogers on his arm.

The pilot eased back on the stick, choked the collective and reduced the throttle setting. The Hughes nosed up slightly, lost airspeed, began to sink, finally settling into the corner of a field.

'We are there,' the pilot said, and jerked his thumb toward the door. 'Quickly.'

Manfred had already hopped out. Without looking back, he strode briskly toward a thick wooded patch. Stone followed him, Melissa still in the chopper, fumbling with her meager luggage.

The light was still weak and Stone almost bumped into Manfred once he was under the canopy of trees, Manfred's dark coat blending in nicely with the dense foliage.

'There iss a map under the driver's seat. Herr Brunner asks that you leave the car in the marina parking lot. It must be locked, the keys left inside the grill. Someone will pick it up later.'

'What car?' Stone asked.

Manfred motioned to a shape set further back in the brush. He reached down and tugged. A camouflage drop-cloth whisked over the metal and glass, revealing a black Audi 5000.

'Do not get stopped,' Manfred instructed. 'The car iss stolen.' He smiled for the first time that Stone could remember and put his hand out. 'Haf a nice day.'

SIXTEEN

Stone drove. Down a misty cow path, through a dry stream-bed, onto a rutted country lane. Melissa suddenly tapped his shoulder and pointed. He backed off on the accelerator and craned his neck. It was just a shape in the half-light, blurred by tendrils of fog. The Hughes had lifted off from the field and was climbing. It circled once as if uncertain of its direction, then headed north toward Belgium.

'On our own,' he said, but she didn't comment – the ice-queen-cometh routine again. Trying to convince her that he hadn't screwed Francine bordered on the impossible. Should have gotten an affidavit to the effect. Might have to call for binding arbitration, a stay of execution, whatever.

The Audi hummed beneath him. Nifty set of wheels. Absolutely pristine, as if the thing had just rolled out of a dealer's showroom, although there were over 10,000 kilometers on the odometer. He noticed that there were no cigarette butts in the ashtray, no smudges on the glass, and the upholstery still showed marks from a recent vacuuming. The glove compartment was empty, except for an owner's manual. The Audi was undoubtedly stolen and had been expertly sanitized. No wonder Brunner didn't want his name connected with the operation.

The farm road intersected a two-lane highway. Stone kept within the speed limit, just his foglights on. There were a few cars on the highway, the occasional delivery truck, but no cops. He checked his watch – just after five.

It was overcast, light mist, with the occasional patch of heavy fog.

She was studying the map. 'Bear right at the fork up ahead.'

They rumbled over railroad tracks and onto a divided tree-lined avenue populated with tatty apartment houses and restaurants, most of them Algerian. A few signs of life: a garbage pickup truck, a patisserie with a couple of bicycles outside, a little kid with a book bag trudging half in, half out of the gutter, pausing occasionally to solemnly stomp puddles.

Stone's stomach rumbled for food and his nerves whined for coffee. Later.

As they drove through the suburbs, the fog thickened, bleary streetlights muzzled by the mist, traffic almost non-existent. He made a wrong turn but realized his mistake within two blocks, retraced his route and got it right the second time.

Whoever had laid out the route had taken care to avoid the populated areas of the city. The routing led them through the outskirts, then through an industrial area. At the end of a potholed street, he found a shipyard and parking lot marked 'Port de Plaisance, Digue Nord'.

The marina was sparsely populated, mostly small plastic runabouts. Visibility wasn't much more than twenty meters. For a few minutes, they sat in the parking lot, watching for movement, the engine still humming.

She pointed. 'Over there.' He could make out a set of spars, varnished wood, not aluminum things, poking up through the fog. 'That's her.'

'Do we go for it?' he asked.

She answered him by getting out of the car.

He did as Manfred had instructed: locked the thing and left the keys inside the grillwork.

She was ahead of him, running, already to the outermost pier. Stone strolled after her, trying to look like he owned the place, waiting for the shrill of a police whistle or a heavy hand on his shoulder. Nothing; as if whoever had sanitized the car had also done a job on the marina.

She had already disappeared below. Stone took one last look around the marina, then dropped down the companionway. Almost like home, felt good. She had the navigational desklid open, pulling out charts. She apparently found what she was looking for and laid it out, mumbling to herself. She wrote some numbers on the back of her hand with a ballpoint, evidently magnetic courses and distances to get them out of the channel and into the bay.

Stone cleared his throat.

She looked up, agitated. 'Can't you think for yourself, Stone? Check the engine. Oil, water, fuel filters, hydraulic fluid. Make sure the fuel supply valve is on, then check the diesel tank's sight gauge to make sure they filled it up.'

She was back into her power-trip mode, in *command*. Like, who the hell needed it? He was about to bite back, then subconsciously examined the pressure she was under. If the cops stopped them now, it would mean the loss of *Night Watch* and twenty years of stamping out license plates in a French jail. He decided to let it pass.

The engine room didn't yield up any surprises. All fluids normal, valves on. He grabbed a flashlight from the overhead rack and checked the bilge under the engine for oil, hoping that the goo he had put on the oil pan had held. He was rewarded by a thin layer of clear salt water that had drained down from the packing gland with no slick or oil scum. One problem he wouldn't have to deal with, thank God.

Melissa had gone back on deck and he could hear her footsteps moving forward. Undoubtedly getting the lines singled up but waiting until he had finished before starting the engine. Once the engine was running, it was going to have to be sayonara in double-quick time lest someone woke up and blew the whistle.

The diesel fuel tank was under the starboard cabin sole, an identical-sized tank on the port side holding water. A small teak plate with a pull ring was flushed into the cabin sole amidships, making it reasonably easy to check the sight gauge on the fuel tank. He lifted the plate and played the beam of the light on the vertical glass tube. Full, the liquid in the glass a murky yellow, right up to the top. Not only to the top, actually overfilled, because he could smell the raw, sweet-acid stench of diesel. He dropped the plate back into place. Once they were out to sea, he could dump some fresh water and detergent into the bilge, slosh it around with a broom handle, then pump it out. Diesel wasn't nearly as flammable as gasoline, but the stench of it was enough to give you the heaves if you had to button up the boat in rough weather, and Stone had heard stories about the Irish Sea and the weather that lurked therein. Later, he promised himself.

He grabbed a foul-weather jacket from the locker and headed up the companionway. She was in the cockpit, ready to go, impatient.

'Cast off,' she said, her voice low but with an edge of tension in it. He ran along the deck, retrieving the docking lines. When the last one was off, she kicked the engine over. It fired on the first crank and settled into a steady rumble. To Stone, it sounded like a 747 blasting off, the noise ungodly loud in the otherwise silent marina.

She snicked the transmission in gear and nudged out of the marina, then put the wheel hard over, turning into the channel that led from the marina to the breakwater.

The *Night Watch* ghosted past a few fishing boats and a rotting cabin cruiser, then nosed through the gap in the marina's breakwater. A pelican, perched on the rocks, tried to stare Stone down, then flapped off to join his buddies.

She angled starboard into the outbound shipping channel, steering precisely. One buoy after another slipped past them, each bent down in the outgoing tide like frost-blackened weeds swept before a hard autumn wind. In the distance, Stone could hear the moan of fog horns. Didn't want to think about the hulks of floating iron attached to those horns. It was like walking blindfolded in a shooting gallery.

In five minutes, they were clear of the last channel marker, ghosting seaward into heavy fog and an uneasy swell.

He went aft and sat down in the cockpit. Her hair was matted, rivulets of moisture from the fog running down her face and slicker. She looked vulnerable and he wanted to say something to reassure her, but couldn't find any words that worked.

'Looks like Brunner's people set it up perfectly.' He gestured to the helm. 'I'll take it if you want to work on the navigation. What's our heading?' he asked.

'Two eighty-eight. That will keep us inshore of the shipping lanes but clear of Cap de la Hague. Once we're abeam Cherbourg, we'll alter for Land's End on the south-western tip of England, then head north-west for Ireland.'

'Where in Ireland?'

'Not sure, but I'll probably put into Cork. My father has an old classmate who lives there, teaches law at the university, I think. He can probably help me out.' She pushed a damp wisp of hair from her forehead. 'You can fly out of Shannon, you know.'

'No passport, remember?'

'I'm sure you'll be able to talk Macleod into forwarding it.'

He tried for an opening. 'You could probably use an extra hand for the transatlantic. I'm available, cheap, and I don't eat much.'

She got up, making room for him at the helm. *'You?'*

'Me,' he answered.

She brushed past him on her way below, her face expressionless. 'I'll make coffee. Call me if the wind begins to pick up. I'd like to get sail on as soon as possible.'

They took turns on the helm, one hour on, one hour off. She didn't trust the autopilot to do the steering because if the steel hull of a trawler suddenly loomed out of the fog there would be no more than a second to act – too long in a collision situation to disengage the autopilot and take over manual steering. Stone didn't mind. It kept his mind occupied and his hands busy.

The shipping in the Baie de la Seine had slowly thinned out. No longer the deep throaty blasts of ships' horns and the hollow thump of their propellers – just the occasional squawk of a trawler's air horn or the muted clank of a drift fisherman's bell. But the fog, if anything, was thicker – a real pea-souper that put the Maine stuff to shame.

By 11.00, they got the sails on in a light northerly but kept the engine going. The speed picked up to 8.6 knots.

She brought up a thermos of soup and a package of saltines around noon. She had changed into denims and her white polo-neck sweater, Wellington sea boots and a Navy watchcoat which was much too large for her.

'How's it going, skip?'

She sipped from an enamel mug, then wiped her lips on the cuff of the watchcoat. 'Not bad. The loran swears we're halfway across the bay and the BBC forecast is for the fog to clear mid-afternoon.' She favored him with a tentative smile.

Good, he thought. She was starting to ease up. 'Nice watchcoat you got or is that a tent in disguise?'

'It was Pieter's,' she said without inflection.

Stone cursed himself, should have guessed. It was probably her version of a security blanket. Step one in any conversation with her: engage brain prior to moving tongue.

She slid onto the helmsman's seat. 'I'll take it, Stone. My watch.'

'Anything you want done? Otherwise, I thought I'd catch a few zees.'

'Did you spill any diesel this morning when you were checking the tanks? The salon smells like a lorry stopover.'

He shook his head. 'Nope. Think Brunner's people must

have overfilled it.' It was easy enough to do if you didn't know the eccentricities of a yacht's fuel system, and all of them were uniquely different.

She nodded. 'There's a ten-liter jug of industrial-strength detergent in the fo'c'sle. You might slosh out the bilge if you can spare the time.'

What he had planned on doing voluntarily had become a command performance, but it was his fault: could have, should have done it in a previous off-watch. Instead, he had spent the time monitoring the VHF emergency frequency for sounds of possible pursuit, but all he had heard were fishermen bullshitting to each other in three languages. He flipped her a ragged salute but she didn't respond, just stared ahead into the fog.

He retrieved the Mag Lite from the rack over the nav station, then pulled up the floor plate. He flashed the beam into the bilge. There was an iridescent sheen to the water which surged sluggishly between the frames. It didn't look like a lot had been spilled, probably less than a liter or so. The program would be to dump in plenty of detergent and fresh water, then suds it up. The bilge pump would take care of the disposal problems provided the Greenpeace types weren't looking.

He got out a large cooking-pot and filled it with water from the galley pump. The detergent was in the fo'c'sle as she had said. He paused a second to check the photograph over the workbench. It begged for a family photo album caption like 'Melissa and Pieter – the happy lovers on vacation'. He felt like a stranger who had intruded, the idea vaguely depressing him.

Dumping the water into the bilge, he followed it up with a couple of gurgles of detergent, then sloshed the mixture into a frothy brew with a mop handle. The bilge pump sucked it dry but the stench was still strong.

He kneeled down on the cabin sole and stuffed his arm into the narrow gap between the floorboards and the top of the fuel tank, reaching back as far as he could. His hand touched wet metal. He withdrew it, rubbed his fingers and sniffed. Slick and slippery. Diesel fuel. Puddles of it, probably trapped by the raised edges of the tank.

It would be a simple matter if his hand could reach the entire top of the tank. Some paper towels, a slosh of soapy water and that would do it. The only problem was that most of the fuel tank was recessed under the floorboards, inaccessible except for the corner of the tank where the sight gauge was located.

He popped up the companionway. 'Any way that I can get the floorboards up? There's diesel fuel puddled on the top of the tank.'

'Remove all three drawers under the starboard settee. That will expose the floorboards. They're held down by flathead screws. Once you've got the screws out and the boards up, you can reach ninety per cent of the tank top if you've got long arms. I'm sorry, Stone – didn't think it would be such an involved project.'

'No problem.' Not much, that is, if you were a masochistic type who enjoyed groveling on the floorboards and breathing diesel fumes in a rolling seaway.

He pulled out the three drawers and stacked them on the pilot berth, then got a screwdriver from the tool box.

Scrunching down on the cabin sole and using one hand for the flashlight and the other for the screwdriver, he torqued out the screws.

Odd, he thought, examining them. The bronze screws, otherwise grungy with corrosion, showed fresh scratches in their slots as if someone had recently removed them. He mentally shrugged and put the screws in one of the drawers to guard against losing them, then attacked the floorboards. Surprisingly, they came up easily.

After pulling the floorboards up and laying them in the galley, he studied the tank with his flashlight. It was a conventional construction: built out of iron, strapped down to the frame with galvanized bands. There was a clean-out plate about the size of a saucer bolted on the outboard side, something that you'd normally remove once every five years so that you could get your hand inside and clean out any muck that had accumulated in the bottom. Not a pleasant job, he knew, but occasionally necessary.

On the top of the tank in a slight depression, a small puddle of fuel had accumulated. He mopped it up with paper towels, then sponged it with a paper towel dipped in soapy water. He was about to replace the floorboards when he noticed an insulated wire running from a hole in the center of the access plate to somewhere up under the settee. Sloppy, he thought. Wires carried electricity, and unless you strapped the critters down the motion of the boat at sea could cause the insulation to chafe through – a potential fire hazard.

He brought the flashlight closer, squinting at the wire. Single-strand stuff, the plastic insulation absolutely clean as if it was fresh out of the package. He checked where the wire passed through the access plate. A hole had been drilled to accommodate the wire, then sealed with a glob of mastic putty to keep fuel from leaking out. But the mastic – partially dissolved by the diesel fuel sloshing against it – hadn't stuck, and that had been the reason for the fuel seepage.

The dumb bastard, he swore under his breath. You'd think that a yard worker would know better.

The guy should have used epoxy putty. Stone cleaned the mastic off the wire and the access plate with a paper towel, then rummaged around in the parts locker. No epoxy putty.

He popped up the companionway. 'You have any epoxy putty?'

She frowned. 'No. What do you need epoxy putty for?'

'The wire that runs through a hole in the access plate on the fuel tank. Some idiot sealed it with plumber's mastic, but the fuel dissolved the bond. That's where the diesel fuel's leaking out.'

323

'*What* wire that runs through the access plate?'

'You know. It's single-strand with black plastic insulation. Thought it was for a fuel transducer or something like that.'

'There *isn't* any wire through the access plate to a transducer, Stone. That's what the glass sight gauge is for.'

'There sure as hell is a wire. Maybe something that Pieter installed but forgot to tell you about.' He started back down the companionway but she called to him.

'Stone – are you absolutely sure about the wire?'

He popped back up. 'Not to worry. I'll sort it out.' And he would. Instead of using epoxy, he had just remembered the oil-pan goo – undoubtedly capable of resisting both oil and fuel. *Should have thought of it in the first place, dummy.*

He found the goo in the engine room. Next he examined the wire – best to secure it first before sealing the tank. He traced the wire from the access plate. It led to the underside of the settee, but it was too far back for his fingers to trace. He stood up and removed the cushions from the settee. The wire poked up through a freshly drilled hole and led outboard where it turned upward again through the bottom of the bookshelf, then up to the overhead. There, it disappeared through a drilled hole which undoubtedly led to the deck. The wire had been led with cunning, virtually unnoticeable.

Weird, he thought. He had expected the wire to go to a power source or an electrical gauge – had convinced himself that Pieter had installed the wire as part of a fuel-quantity measuring system.

He climbed the companionway and went forward on the starboard side, trying to spot where the wire exited the deck. He found it: a glossy black electrical wire poking up from the covering board, the hole in the deck through which the wire led plugged with the same mastic putty. From the covering board, the wire snaked through a drilled hole in the cap-rail and on up into the rigging, strapped to a shroud with neat layers of electrical tape. About two meters above deck, the wire was cut off, obviously not connected to anything. A wire to nowhere? Didn't make sense.

'What are you doing?' she yelled at him.

'What's this wire all about?'

She punched on the autopilot and came forward. She frowned as she examined the wire. 'Not something I put there. Is this the wire from the fuel tank you were talking about?'

Stone nodded. 'I can't figure it out. It goes to the fuel tank but it's not connected to anything on this end.' A wire to nowhere? No electrical wire was open-ended except . . . then he bloody damn well knew what it was. An antenna. *Couldn't be!* He tried to visualize a use for a hidden antenna, and a cold chill rippled up his neck and back, his armpits suddenly wet.

'You have a life raft?' he asked, trying to sound reasonably normal.

'On deck, behind the mizzen mast. That fiberglass suitcase thing that's strapped down in chocks. There's a cord on the side that you pull to inflate it. Should have mentioned it. But why?'

'Tell you in a minute.'

He tore down the companionway, back to the tank. To cut the wire? Not sure what that would do. It would be a very sensitive receiver, he guessed. An incoming radio signal would be measured in microvolts and just the static electricity of his body might be enough – more than enough – to trip it. Even the radar energy from a nearby ship could . . .

He checked his watch, sweating. They'd been under way for nearly seven hours now – say forty-two miles out to sea. Nice and lonely, far enough off shore, deep water. There was no doubt in his mind that somewhere behind them – probably no more than a couple of miles back – was a powerboat equipped with radar which was shadowing them, waiting. Another ten minutes? Another couple of miles? Because they sure as hell weren't going to follow the *Night Watch* all the way to Ireland.

He found a wrench in the tool kit and backed out the bolts that held the access plate to the tank, then gently lifted the plate. He passed his hand through the access-plate hole into the fuel, his fingers following the wire. The wire terminated in a metal cylinder, about the diameter of a can of soup but perhaps twice as long. He ever so gently pulled it out and cradled it in his hands – a dripping, new-born bomb.

The thing was fabricated from aluminum alloy, beautifully machined, then anodized to a dull black. Whoever had made it *cared* about the niceties. The wire led from one end through a protective grommet. On the other end was an anodized cap, held in place by six machine screws, the joint between the cap and the body waterproofed with an O-ring seal. *Very* nice.

He gently hefted it. Say three kilos. Take away half a kilo for the housing, 200 grams for the circuit board and another 300 grams for the batteries. That would leave about two kilos for the explosives.

The placement of the radio-controlled bomb in the fuel tank was such that it would blow through the bottom of the *Night Watch*, but as it blew it would flash off 600 liters of diesel fuel. What didn't sink or was blown to bits would be incinerated. All that remained would be a burning oil slick. *Not nice, not nice at all.*

He made a nest with his foul-weather jacket and cushioned the bomb in it, then headed back to the cockpit.

'Seen any ships?'

She wiped a trickle of condensation from her nose. 'The fog's so thick, I can't even see the bowsprit. Heard a ship's horn, though, about five minutes ago.'

'They'd be using radar in this weather, right?'

'I hope for our sake they are, Stone, unless you want an 8000-ton freighter goosing us.'

The wind had calmed in the last hour, the sails furled,

a gentle swell running, *Night Watch* under power. Stone reached over and pulled the throttle back to idle.

'*Hey!*' She reached for it but he pushed her hand away.

'Don't touch it and no questions now. I'll explain later. Just trust me.' Slick Willie had said that, hadn't he? And faked out 150 million voters. All Stone was asking was for one to believe in him, and even that was turning out to be a hard sell.

He stepped past her to the afterdeck. He had noticed it before, yet hadn't really examined how it worked. A lanyard was taped to the seam of the fiberglass case. He yanked hard on it, not quite prepared for what would happen.

The fiberglass case split open with a roar of rushing gas, the raft unfolding as it inflated, the thing bigger than Dumbo.

'*STONE! Are you out of your mind?*' She had scrambled out of the cockpit, trying to drag him back.

He dumped the raft overboard, still hanging on to the lanyard to keep it from floating away. '*Just shut the hell up and get in. NOW!*'

She stared at him, immobilized, her eyes crazy. 'Dammit, Stone! That life raft cost me over 800 pounds sterling! Get it back up on board right now, you damned idiot!'

No time for niceties. Grabbing her arm, he yanked, then slammed his body against hers as she tumbled past him. She went overboard and surfaced seconds later, spluttering. Stone cast off the lanyard. 'Be back in thirty minutes. If I don't, you'll eventually be picked up. Tell Mac everything, got that? Brunner's the one who's going to blow the Chunnel.'

'*STONE! I CAN'T HEAR YOU. PLEASE!*' She had stroked her way to the raft and was pulling herself aboard it, coughing up water. The raft, with Melissa in it, floated further and further astern.

Pulling the man-overboard pole from its bracket, Stone heaved it after her. The strobe on top of it began to flash.

He watched as the raft, the woman he loved and the strobe were swallowed by the fog. Now to put distance between her and the *Night Watch*. At least one of them would survive.

Jumping back into the cockpit, he pushed the throttle up to cruise rpms and checked the compass: 087 degrees. He checked the autopilot switch. On. She must have engaged it just before she jumped him. He leaned down and tapped the reset button on the electronic mileage log, zeroing it.

Below, the stench of diesel fuel was stronger. He flipped on the overhead lights, then dumped the tool box on the salon table, looking for wire-cutters. The purpose of all this, he told himself, was to cut the antenna so a firing signal couldn't reach it. The problem, he reminded himself, was that his body's capacitance might be enough to trigger the receiver, which in turn would fire the detonator, which in turn would make a terminal mess of his various bodily organs. He had heard that computer chips could be ruined just by touching them. I've got something very sensitive here, he thought, and maybe the bastard that put this thing together wired it so that it would blow up if the wire was cut – a kind of backup booby-trap.

His throat was dry and he wished he had something to drink. Prerogative of the dying man, right? Screw it. He'd go to his Maker sober, assuming that his Maker was willing to extend the invitation.

He studied the bomb for half a minute, his nerves screaming at him to do something, anything, but do it *NOW*. Okay – there had to be batteries inside, some way to service them. Ergo – remove the cap and disconnect the batteries.

He pulled his Swiss Army knife from his pocket, then flipped open the miniature Phillips-head screwdriver blade.

Keeping pressure on the cap with his thumb, he backed out the screws. Six of them. When the last one was out, he eased the pressure that his thumb exerted on the cap by just a tad. It felt as if there were a compressed spring inside, forcing the cap away from the body of the bomb. Trusting his otherwise untrustworthy instincts, he brought the thing up to eye level and continued slowly to ease the pressure, examining the gap for any irregularity. When the gap was about four millimeters wide, he saw the switch. Itsy-bitsy thing, neatly flushed into the body of the bomb. It had two positions, one marked by a white dot and the other by a red dot. The switch was positioned at the red dot. Arming switch? He pulled the little plastic toothpick from his knife, swallowed hard and repositioned the switch, trying not to think too much. There was a faint *click*.

He continued to ease the cap off until it was clear of the body of the bomb, then peered inside. There was a micro switch on the inside of the cap, wired to the switch flushed into the side of the bomb. He wasn't sure but he could guess. If you took the cap off without repositioning the switch, the damn thing would blow. *And they said that talented craftsmen were hard to find these days.*

Gently, he up-ended the bomb. Two mercury batteries slid out, their terminals connected to red and black wires. He snapped off the connector and shoved the batteries in his pocket.

There was that great line from the *Marathon Man* flick when the mad dentist Mengele starts probing Dustin Hoffman's mouth with a shrieking drill, repeatedly asking, 'Is it *safe*?'

Yes, Stone thought. It's safe.

Back on deck, he checked the mileage meter: 2.3 miles. He reset the mileage log to zero, then disengaged the auto-pilot and reversed course by 180 degrees. In theory, she was 2.3 miles in front of his bow. In practice, things didn't normally work out that neatly.

At exactly 2.3 miles, he threw the gear shift in neutral and ghosted, the fog opaque as tofu, the sounds of the sea's wash muffled. He shouted a couple of times and heard nothing but the muffled echo of his own voice. Swallowing hard, he reengaged the gear shift and started a slow turn to starboard, spiraling outward. No wind to speak of, he told himself, so she couldn't have drifted far. But then again, the current did strange things. *Hang in there*, he whispered to her. She'd be cold as hell and he worried about hypothermia. Then he smiled. The best way to cure that, so they said, was to lie naked next to the victim and rub gently.

One complete circle and nothing. He shouted again and again.

On the second circle, there was a muffled sound but he couldn't make out where it had come from, its direction masked by the fog. He started on his third circle, spiraling outward a bit more. He heard her better this time, then saw a red glow in the fog off to port and behind him.

She was hanging on to the canopy of the raft, the red flare in her hand spluttering its finale. He eased up alongside the raft and she tossed him the lanyard first, then scrambled up over the railing.

He pulled her to him and she came, unresisting. She was shaking, her hair plastered down, the watchcoat matted to her body like the coat of a wet dog.

'You okay?' he asked.

She nodded, her face buried against his throat. 'Cold. Terribly cold.'

'Go down and change but don't touch anything. I'll tend the store up here.'

'What wa . . . was it?' Her teeth were chattering.

'A bomb, radio-controlled. Brunner's people. Toss me up the Beretta. They're somewhere behind us, probably close.' He slapped her lightly on the thigh. 'Get going.'

He turned back to the 087 heading and pushed up the revs as high as he dared. The knotmeter rose to a solid 8.2 knots, the prop cavitating and the shaft vibrating. She passed him the Beretta through the hatch and he chambered a round, but he knew that it was a toy compared to the stuff they were probably packing.

Reality-check time: if they were back there, they would have seen the *Night Watch* circling on their radar. That could be explained by any number of screw-ups – something lost overboard, maybe a line from a fish trap wrapped around the prop which had taken time to clear. They wouldn't think it was so unusual, but they would want to finish it now, would first close in for a look, then back off to a safe distance and transmit the firing signal. *Kaboom*, then home for chow, a few beers and a couple of frames of bowling.

In less than five minutes, she was back up on deck, decked out in après ski boots, Bogner stretch pants, a turtleneck and parka. Very fetching, he thought. She was carrying the shotgun. She slid in next to him behind the helm.

'You could have been killed,' she said softly.

'I didn't think it was likely. They say that only the good die young.'

'I *hate* your jokes when I'm trying to be serious.'

'Sorry. If you want to know, I was scared shitless.'

She reached up and held his face in her hands. 'Stone – I actually might have been wrong about you after all.' She kissed him as if she meant it and his heart soared.

Till death do us part, he thought, suddenly calm.

A quarter of an hour passed. They heard the distant sound of a jet passing high above them, the methodical grunt of a distant fog horn and the squawks of fog-bound gulls, but beyond that, nothing.

'They're not coming,' she said.

'I wouldn't bet on it.'

'Could the firing signal be transmitted from very far away?'

'Nope. The circuit board in the bomb looked like it was commercially made. Probably something out of a kid's

331

radio-controlled model airplane. They'd have to be within two or three miles' range, maximum.'

'Maybe they . . .'

He held up his hand. 'Just a second. Listen!'

It was very faint. He pulled the throttle back to idle. Still too noisy. He killed the engine. The *Night Watch* slowed, gliding silently, only a whisper of wind in the rigging and the liquid wash of the sea.

Turning, cupping his ears, he could hear it better now. A faint *whump, whump, whump*. A chopper – the goddamned bloody Hughes. They had set back down somewhere and refueled, then waited. Probably had someone watching the marina to give them the *Night Watch*'s departure time. Brunner would have been able to calculate the best course to Ireland and guess at her speed. Which meant that all the chopper had to do was to fly that course above the fog and start punching the transmit switch until there was the glow of fireworks in the fog below them.

And if nothing happened, what then? Brunner would be waiting for them in Ireland – or, more likely, Joss and company.

He restarted the engine but didn't put it in gear. 'Pull the life raft up alongside.'

'We can't . . .'

He didn't bother to listen to the rest of her sentence. He scrambled below and stripped the insulation from the last few inches of the bomb's antenna wire, then taped it to the body of the bomb. He wasn't sure, but it seemed like a good bet that the antenna would be ineffective as long as it was grounded, but he had no way of knowing whether the thing was wired that way or not. Then again, life was full of unknowns, death being the greatest one.

He grabbed the can of detergent and tossed it up on deck, then threw the cushions from the port settee after it. Next, he lifted the lid on the spare-parts locker. He had seen the thing before when he had searched for water-pump parts. It was a portable plastic bilge pump, its sole virtue being that it would fit through the access hole of the fuel tank and had a long enough hose to reach from the salon, up the companionway and overboard.

He positioned the pump in the fuel tank, then checked back on deck. She had tied the life raft alongside. It was a big raft, two meters in diameter with an inflated side that was roughly knee-high.

'Throw some life vests in the raft – oars, junk, anything that will float or burn.'

'What . . .'

He dropped the end of the hose into the raft, dumped in all of the detergent, then went below and pumped like his life depended on it. He guessed that the pump threw about a liter per double stroke, so he gave it 400 licks, the muscles in his arm howling in agony. When the fuel tank was half empty, he figured he had pumped enough to do the job.

She was standing on the coach roof, her hands cupped to her ears. 'It's closer. Back and forth, but closer.'

The raft was half full of fuel, cloudy yellow, the detergent mixing nicely as the raft rose and fell in the swells. He sat down on the deck and fished out his knife. First he connected the batteries, then reinserted the screws. He gently pushed down on the cap, leaving the recessed switch just visible. She was crouched beside him, watching intently.

'Get the engine started,' he said. 'When I say so, get this thing moving as fast as it will go.'

'Is it safe?'

He had to laugh but it came out like a croak. 'Funny you should ask. If it isn't, we'll never know.'

He waited until the engine caught, then flicked the switch to the red dot, crammed the cap down and tightened the screws.

Sliding off the rail, he positioned the bomb cylinder on the floor of the raft on a life preserver, pulled the antenna wire free of the tape and twisted its end around the metal center pole that supported the canopy.

Grabbing the rail of the *Night Watch*, he heaved himself up onto the deck and cut the towing lanyard.

'GO!'

He held his breath as the raft slid along the side of the hull, bobbled in the turbulent wake, then drifted aft into the fog. He figured a quarter of a mile would be the minimum safe distance and unconsciously counted time.

Thirty seconds, then sixty. Two minutes, three, five. He breathed deeply. Had to have covered half a mile by now, he calculated.

'Put it in neutral and coast,' he told her softly.

The engine noise diminished, the ketch slowing, bow lifting to the swell from the south-west, the motion easier. Then he could hear it.

Whump, whump, whump. Off to starboard, getting fainter. Stone silently cursed himself; hadn't left enough antenna wire to be effective, maybe screwed up the switch, got the batteries in wrong, something.

Whump, whump, whump. About the same – no – getting louder. He could guess who it was up there – probably his good old bosom buddy, *Cum mit me* – frantically pressing the tit of the transmitter, frustrated as hell.

Whump, whump, whump, whump. Getting much louder. Loud enough that the fog bounced the sound around, hard on the ears, like living in a bass drum with Ringo beating on it. The chopper had to be damn near overhead, close enough to . . .

Bright flash, blinding white, like a stroke of summer heat-lightning on a black night which burned its jagged image into your retinas. He slammed her to the deck and dropped down beside her. Four seconds later, the hot blastwave hit and with it came the roar. The whole ship bucked, shrouds vibrating.

The sound echoed around for a long time, slowly dying.

He found that he had been holding his breath.

They stood up, both of them silent, listening. She was gripping his arm tightly. The chopper sound lingered for a few minutes, see-sawing in volume, then tapering off. He guessed it was heading north.

'Why the detergent?' she asked.

'Intensifies the explosion, next best thing to napalm. Lots of black, greasy smoke.'

'Do you think they believed it was us?'

'Wouldn't you?' he asked, and sneaked a kiss. It was, as the song went, sweeter than wine.

SEVENTEEN

With Stone sweating up on the halyards and Melissa grinding the sheet winch, they hoisted sail, including the big drifter. The wind was light from the south-west but slowly increasing, the swell starting to stretch out under the force of the fresh breeze.

He stood back for a few seconds, watching as *Night Watch* slowly accelerated, then turned to her. 'I'll clean up below,' he said.

'How much fuel is left in the tank?' She had the chart laid out on the cockpit cushions, spanning off distances with her fingers.

'About a third. That enough?'

'Depends.' She frowned but didn't elaborate. 'Why don't you get a couple of hours' sleep?'

He could use it. She had flaked out early last night while they were on the *Valkyr*, but he had been up with Brunner until nearly midnight and these last few hours playing at bomb disposal had emotionally drained him. He checked his watch. 'It's 16.20 now. How about waking me at 18.00.'

'Will do.' She pushed back the hood of her parka. Freed, her hair cascaded over her shoulders. She twisted a strand of it around her finger, her forehead wrinkled. 'I have a question but you don't have to answer it.' She had said it hesitantly, as if she had thought about it a lot, perhaps too much.

Whatever it was, he knew it was going to be loaded. 'Shoot.'

'Did you really sleep with Francine the other night?'

'Of course not. I had plans for another lady.'

'Honestly? Don't you dare lie to me, Stone.'

That pissed him off. 'Dammit, I said I didn't!'

She was now wrinkling her nose, not a good sign. 'Okay. So you didn't *sleep* with her. Perhaps I should have phrased it another way. Did you – you know – *do* it with her?' Holier than thou.

'A-hah! You've cleverly nailed me on semantics. You're dying to know all about sweaty bodies locked in passion, tongues searching, seeking, sucking, teeth gnashing flesh, whips and chains whistling through the musk-scented air, right?' He put his hand up, taking the oath. 'Okay, I'll come *relatively* clean. We did it but only half a dozen times, hardly worth mentioning. And no need for you to worry about me catching the dreaded hickey virus. "Safe sex all the way" is my motto. Wouldn't be caught dead in a ladies' boudoir without a six-pack of condoms – fabricated especially for a sensitive New Age guy like me in all the hues of the rainbow coalition. We started with pussy pink and finished off with pulsing purple, but the stealth-black was truly awesome – a high-tech Japanese ninja jobbie. Had ticklers, a built-in vibrator and . . .'

She flung a plastic coffee mug at him. He had just enough time to duck down the companionway before the thing whistled over his head and clattered against the mainmast. Sand-bagging it for a few seconds, he then poked his head up above the hatch, just at eye level.

Her head was tilted up, checking the luff of the mainsail, and she didn't notice him. But he could see that she was smiling. Actually . . . laughing.

Black as pitch and the sound of the sea swishing past the hull. *Night Watch* was gently heeled, a lonely and discordant hum in the rigging, the bow lightly plunging and lifting to the swells as if she had a heartbeat of her own.

Totally relaxed, he lay still for a few minutes, slowly coming awake, luxuriating in the miracle of being alive and in love. It was self-evident now, only now, how close they had come to death.

This was literally the first day in the rest of his life and he felt reborn, wanted to capture this feeling of fulfilled contentment forever, to lock it away so that he could pull it out in years to come, knowing the precise moment when it had begun. His father had said it. 'Our minds are mainly made up of memories, so be damned sure to hang on to the good ones.'

Yawning, he lifted his arm and squinted at the luminescent numbers of his watch. *Christ!* It was past nine. He sat up, banging his head on the bookshelf, and swore. She'd been on the helm for nearly five hours. He squirmed into his jacket, grabbed a bottle of beer out of the fridge, changed his mind and switched it to mineral water in honor of the new abstinent Stone he was trying to be, and shambled up on deck.

He paused at the top of the companionway, trying to orient himself. The fog had lifted, the air was dry. Off to starboard, he saw the range-lights of a ship moving up Channel and away from them, slowly burying her hull beneath the horizon. Constellations of stars wheeled overhead, their lesser sisters rimming the horizon. Bloody glorious!

The weather was cooperating, the wind soft, probably not more than eight knots, the mainsail eased, the drifter full and drawing well. Perfect.

He felt his way aft to the cockpit, not yet able to see her. The binnacle light was off but in the dim starlight he could see the varnished spokes of the helm turning in small increments, probably on autopilot.

'Thanks for letting me sleep in.'

No answer.

'Melissa . . . ?' he said softly.

No answer. His heart leaped, suddenly afraid, visions of her having fallen overboard.

'MELISSA!'

A small, muffled voice. 'Stop shouting. I'm here – aft. Watch your step.'

He now noticed the reflection of a light in the wake. Its beam moved, catching a flash of her hair as she shifted her position. She was flat on her stomach, half her body hanging over the transom, her head bent down.

'You scared the hell out of me,' he said, kneeling down beside her.

'Working girl. Take a look.'

He hung his head over the transom. The varnished teak gleamed and into it were carved the words 'SNOW GOOSE, Southampton'.

The inlaid letters had been freshly touched up with gold paint.

'She was launched with the name *Snow Goose*.' She wiped off a fine-tipped brush with a paper towel. 'I loved the name, from the title of the novel by Paul Gallico. But Pieter couldn't stand it – typical stubborn Dutchman – had to do it his way. So he renamed her and had a new nameboard made, then screwed it over the original carving.'

'I don't understand.'

'We're not going to Ireland. I figured out the fuel consumption. If we got into headwinds, which is more than likely, we'd run the tank dry. I've altered heading for Southampton waters. By morning, we'll be up the Hamble River on a mooring, along with 10,000 other yachts.'

'She'll be recognized.'

'I hope so. The former owner of *Snow Goose*, a retired RAF officer, still lives up there. I was with Pieter when we bought her. Squad-rooon Leadah Nigel Scott-Hughes insisted that Pieter use his private mooring whenever we were in the Hamble, and she's still listed in Lloyd's Register of Yachts as *Snow Goose*, a proper Clyde-built and currently registered English yacht. Pieter never switched registration because he wanted to avoid paying French import duties. As long as no one asks for our passports, we'll be all right.

In a day, we'll be able to rest up, get some provisions and refuel – all without attracting the slightest bit of attention.'

'What's our story if someone bothers to ask?'

'We've been up in Scotland for the past year, living on the *Snow Goose*. You're working on a book, I'm working on a baby. Nationality-wise, I'm English, you're Canadian. The English love Canadians. They're such an innocuous and peaceful lot, but you have to remember to end every sentence with an "Ey?" and use the word "shed-u-all" a lot. You'll pass as either a Canadian or, at the very worst, a decaffeinated American who ran over the border during the Vietnam thing. Just be a little vague if you get caught out.'

'Still, she's a big boat. She'd attract attention.'

She squirmed back from the transom and sat up, capping the paint can and washing out the brush with turpentine, talking as she worked.

'She's not a big boat by south-coast-of-England standards. The whole area is chock-a-block with yachts – big, expensive gold-platers. We'd be a pan-sized fish in a large pond.'

'And then we head for Ireland . . . ?'

'We can't chance going to Ireland because Brunner might see through your little fireworks display and send his goons up there. But this time of year, there'll be plenty of experienced sailors available along the south coast of England; any one of them dying to make a one-way passage to the West Indies.' She looked up at him, something different in her eyes. 'That's where I'm going, Stone. I want you to come with me.'

'Would this be an arrangement of the permanent variety?' His mind was galloping ahead. A couple of years drifting through the islands with the love of his life. Let things die down in the States, maybe send his dad an obituary notice concerning Christopher L. Stone's untimely demise in the English Channel, then let the old man leak

340

it to the IRS. Like they said, you can't get blood out of a stone.

'We'd find out whether it was permanent, wouldn't we?' she answered.

'You *were* actually jealous, weren't you?'

'Angry, hurt. And, yes, if it pleases your stupid ego, jealous as well.'

'Why the rejection routine before that?'

'Pride, frumpishness, lack of self-esteem. Or maybe that I couldn't rid myself of Pieter's memory that easily. Or because you do dangerous things and I don't want to lose someone again that I care too much for.'

They stood up and moved back into the cockpit. A falling star streaked yellow-green and gold toward the northern horizon. Wish upon it, he reminded himself. 'Then there's hope for me?'

She cocked her head, inscrutable as usual. 'Some. Perhaps a lot. But don't plan on me sharing my bed with you – not yet. The other night would have been a mistake.'

'Just exactly *when* do you think we will share the same mattress? Mind you, not that it's all *that* important. As far as I'm concerned, stuff like breathing always had priority over sex.'

'You unfortunately picked an old-fashioned girl, Stone. I've never slept with anyone other than Pieter, so you're going to have to do some old-fashioned romancing.'

'Give me a clue.'

'Sweet words with champagne and a bouquet of roses under a full moon for starters.'

He picked up a strand of seaweed from the cockpit floor and draped it across her nose, shone the flashlight down on them and offered her his bottle of mineral water. 'For now, dear heart, this will have to do, except to tell you that from almost the very beginning I've loved you, your chipped tooth, your flatulent dog, your broken-down boat, and everything else that goes along with the package.'

She ducked her head against his chest, holding on tight.

Her voice was soft but it vibrated within his chest. 'Stone. You're a rotter and a silver-tongued devil to boot, but all that said, I believe you. Just that you have to give us both time to work it out.'

Time was what they both had a lot of, he reckoned.

He took the helm while she slept, as content as he had ever been. The westerly wind was soft as a lover's lips, whispering promises in his ear. A waning moon rose over France and followed in the ketch's wake, climbing higher, casting dream-images along the deck.

Stone had spent a lot of time in small boats but little of it under sail. He wondered now why he had never made the transition, had never really even considered it. But he comprehended the magic of it now. Sailing was about the unification of the mind, the body and the soul, all in synchronization and at peace with the ship and the sea – the easy lift and fall of the hull as it mated with the swells, the sails asleep under a blanket of wind, the soft rush of the water hissing along the hull, the creak of the spars and rigging.

Happy, he sang softly to himself, songs almost forgotten, songs from a kinder and gentler time before that expression became despised. Songs like 'Kingston Market', 'Jamaica Farewell' and 'Brown-Skinned Gal'. Grow a beard and learn to play the guitar, he thought. That and swim naked under tropical skies with his lady of choice.

He was thirsty and went below, leaving the autopilot to find their way. He thought once again about getting a beer but nixed that. The new Stone, he promised himself, polished to a dazzling gem-quality by the grit of abstinence. Instead, he found some cocoa mix, added milk and, while it was brewing, checked in on her. She was asleep, her arms around the pillow, hair fanned out across the sheets. He bent down and kissed her gently. She made a little noise, sort of a low hum, and rolled over. God, he thought, I love her.

Her Walkman was stashed in the navigational desk and he took it with him, returning to the cockpit with the cocoa.

With the autopilot handling the steering chores, Stone propped the cockpit cushions behind him and leaned back, sipping cocoa and diddling with the FM tuner. He found a late-night station that was peddling an obscure string quartet by Mendelssohn.

As she had predicted, he was starting to pick up the loom of the Isle of Wight and the occasional blink of Selsey Bill lighthouse. Another four hours to the Nab Tower, he guessed. With luck and a fair tide, they'd make the Hamble by dawn. He decided he'd let her sleep in return for the watch she had stood for him.

The world news came on just after the hour.

An animal rights activist group had chucked cow pies at 10 Downing Street. Heated debate in the House of Commons over a proposed immigration exclusion act. Riots in India, a Sikh temple trashed, six dead. Squabbling between the Republic of Quebec and the rest of Canada over cultural diversity inequities. Yawn.

Then, 'This evening, French authorities reported the presumed sinking of a pleasure yacht thirty kilometers to the north-east of Cherbourg. Search and rescue vessels of the French Navy responded to reports by a fishing vessel which observed a massive explosion in the fog to the south of their position in the mid-afternoon, local time. A search of the area has yielded no clues as to the cause of the explosion or the name of the vessel involved, but several scorched items of debris have been recovered, including a life preserver marked with the name *Night Watch*. The search is ongoing but all on board are presumed dead. French authorities will release further information as it becomes available. In other news . . .'

Stone smiled, the undisputed master of deceit.

He got her up at first light, dawn still an hour away. He had sailed the ketch by himself past the Nab Tower, Horse Sand Fort and into the Solent. The entrance to the Hamble was less than three miles away.

She came on deck with two cups of coffee, passed one to him, and admired the misty shoreline. There was the strong smell of land and growing things carried on the wind. 'Love this place, the best part of England,' she said, stretching. 'Everything normal on your watch?'

'Little item on the radio at 04.00. Some Frog fisherman saw the explosion. They found the life-ring with *Night Watch* painted on it.'

'What was the explanation of the yacht blowing up?'

'. . . Didn't say.'

She tipped her face up and kissed him lightly. 'Isn't it marvelous to have our very own fifteen minutes of fame?'

'Fame like that we don't need.'

The ketch was sliding past South Bramble Buoy and there was a course change coming up. Sailing this close to land made him nervous. 'We better start getting the sails off.'

'Stone. One thing I have to know. What are you going to do about Brunner once we're in England?'

He had thought about it a lot. 'On the face of it, it looks like he set us up, but when you go over it carefully, we don't have any tangible proof of his involvement except that his people were the ones who put fuel on board the boat.'

'But it was his helicopter!'

'*A* helicopter. Remember, we never saw it, just heard it. What I'm saying is that if Brunner's behind the plot to blow the Chunnel, there's no hard evidence of it.'

'But surely you're going to tell Macleod?'

'I'd just as soon not, but I think I have to. I owe him

344

that much. Just as long as he doesn't drag me back into it again.'

'But do you really trust him? Macleod could conceivably turn you in to the authorities if he thinks you're not going to play by his rules.'

'I don't really believe Mac works that way.' He leaned over and started to coil the mainsheet. 'Anyway, the thing's Mac's problem, not mine.'

The density of yacht population in the Hamble was as she had predicted. Stone estimated that there were thousands of yachts tied up in marinas edging the shore and moored up in trots along the sides of the river. *Snow Goose* fitted in like an old shoe at a rummage sale.

With the sun just breaking the horizon, she found Scott-Hughes' mooring, marked with an RAF roundel and 'Scott-Hughes' painted on its side in a neat, flowery script. Inshore, a broad green lawn rose from the beach to a rambling collection of buildings, seemingly assembled over centuries from different architectural periods – the bulk of it Tudor, a touch of Georgian, with some Victorian gingerbread troweled on. The whole was less than the parts, yet somehow pleasing, as if generations of Scott-Hugheses who had tacked it together didn't give a fig for what generations of table-thumping neighborhood architectural watch committees had demanded.

They had breakfast in the salon – dehydrated eggs, canned sausages and biscuits. Finishing off his cocoa, he yawned.

Reaching across the table, she took his hand. 'Just stay awake for a bit longer. After I've cleaned up and changed, drop me off at the dock across the river and then you can go back to bed. The bags under your eyes look like they're rejects from the lost-luggage department.'

'Yeah, I could use a couple of hours. What's your shed-u-all?'

'Going up to London. Remember the mutt? I'll have to

345

ring up my father's secretary and make arrangements for me to pick him up. And I've got to stop at O. M. Watts for charts of the West Indies.'

'What about your father? Are you going to contact him?' He realized that he was possibly talking about his future father-in-law. A lawyer in the family he didn't need, but if that was the price he had to pay . . .

She frowned a little but nodded. 'I'll have to but I'll do it through his secretary in case his phone is tapped. We're short of money. We'll need quite a bit of cash to carry us over until we reach the West Indies, which I'll have to borrow. Besides, my father will be worried sick once he hears the morning news.'

'What do you want me to do once I've had my beauty sleep?'

'Make a list of stuff that you think we'll need for a year's operations in the tropics. I'll take it down to Mercury Marine first thing tomorrow morning.'

He took an imaginary pencil and wrote in an imaginary tablet. 'Fifty cases of rum, one hundred cases of tonic, three gunny sacks of limes . . .'

'Mechanical stuff, Stone. Gaskets, V-belts, engine parts.' She wrinkled her forehead. 'Now that I think of it, you didn't drink any booze on the trip over, did you?'

'Figured I'd knock off drinking for a while. If we're going to be together till death do us part, I thought I'd do my best to prolong your agony.'

She looked at him intently. 'You're quitting because of me?'

He shrugged, a little embarrassed. No big deal except for the occasional rat gnawing at his gut. 'Total abstinence I'm not promising. I draw the line at champagne taken in moderate quantities under a full moon.'

She didn't say anything, just stood up and cleared the dishes off the table. She turned and went into her cabin, closing the door behind her, and soon he heard the shower running. But he had seen the beginnings of tears rimming her eyes.

346

He must have fallen asleep at the table. He woke with a start to the sound of an outboard motor puttering, then the sound of a dinghy thudding into the hull of the *Snow Goose*. He checked his watch. Just after eight. Voices drifted down the companionway: Mel's and that of a man. Immigration or the fuzz? Either spelled disaster. Stone eavesdropped at the bottom of the companionway.

'*Absolutely* first class!' the man said. 'Pieter has done a *marvelous* job on the old girl.'

'I'm pleased that you approve.' There was a hint of petulance in her voice, Stone thought. Melissa had done at least half of the restoration work while Pieter was still alive and, since his loss at sea, all of the maintenance.

'Still, you should share the credit, my dear girl.'

'Oh, how so?'

Warm, chummy, conspiratorial with slightly naughty overtones in the man's response. 'Well, beneath every good man lies an equally good woman. Ha-ha. Keep the home fires burning, the old boy's belly full, the socks darned and all that sort of thing, eh? Makes for a good union.'

'I'm not with Pieter any more,' she said, her voice flat.

Best that he got up on deck before things got out of hand, he reckoned. He poked his head out of the companionway. The visitor was early-seventies, slightly overweight, cheeks mapped with burst veins, face and arms speckled with liver spots, balding with a fluff of dandelion hair. He was standing in a dinghy but dressed in immaculate white linen slacks and a gaudy floral shirt. He noticed Stone and impulsively stuck his hand through the lifelines.

'Name's Nigel Scott-Hughes. Used to own the old girl. Damned sorry I sold her but she's obviously in good hands. Saw you come in early this morning and just had to come out and make my number.'

'Pleased to meet you, sir. My name's Christopher, ah, Walker.'

'*Delighted* to meet you, Mr Walker. Sorry for the

347

intrusion. Retired now, just spend my time pottering around. Any excuse to poke my nose in other people's business.' He handed up a bag containing a folded newspaper and half a dozen sticky buns. 'Always nice to get the morning paper and some fresh pastry for breakfast when you've been out cruising. My housekeeper just popped them out of the oven and thought you'd enjoy them. Yank, are you?'

'Well, I . . .'

Melissa gave him a sharp look.

'Canadian,' Stone answered. 'Saskatchewan. Little town called Moose Lips. Smoked-meat sandwiches, caribou wrestling Wednesday nights, Quebecquois-bashing on weekends, ey?'

Melissa glared at Stone and Scott-Hughes frowned slightly, not sure whether he was being put on or not. 'Right, then. Good to see our Colonials returning to the Mother Country. Actually, had a lot of your chaps over here in the last dust-up. Keen lads, they were. Awful accent, though.'

'Can I make you some tea to go with a pastry?' she asked.

Scott-Hughes thought that would be *smashing*.

While she was below brewing tea, Stone helped Scott-Hughes climb over the cap-rail onto the deck. The old boy wiped his brow with a red bandana and plunked himself down on the coach roof. 'Awful thing in the Channel,' Scott-Hughes said. 'I flew Lancasters in the Coastal Command during the last bash. Hard to forget the ships that blew up because of Jerry U-boats. Don't suppose you saw anything.' His blue eyes glittered.

'Heard about it on the BBC but we've just come down the west coast from Scotland. Spent a year up there. No smoked meat to speak of, and damned few caribou. Glad to be back.'

Scott-Hughes cocked his head, then leaned close to Stone, his voice a whisper. 'What exactly *is* the arrangement between you and the lady? I'd think that her husband might be rather put out by his wife and another man cruising about on his yacht.'

'Pieter died at sea a few years ago. Melissa and I are, ah, sort of engaged. Nothing formalized yet, but . . .'

Scott-Hughes leaned back, his sense of propriety evidently appeased. 'Well, not to worry. Things are more relaxed these days. Give and take, I say.' He paused. 'And what is it that you *do*, Mr Walker?'

'Writer.'

'Spies, high-tech gadgets and such?'

'Nothing that exciting. Non-fiction. I'm working on a book about the history of, ah, the Eurotunnel.'

'You don't say! My God, it's a small world. Dicky, my nephew, is an editor for a quarterly put out by the Institute of Mining and Metallurgy. Gets submissions about the Chunnel all the time. You've heard of that mob?'

Stone had and nodded. 'Dicky must have quite a research library on the subject if he's an editor.'

'Don't rightly know. Anything that you're specifically lacking in your research? I could call Dicky, you know.'

'Actually, come to think of it, Dicky might be able to help. I'm stuck on some of the early efforts by the French to sample the underlying geophysical composition of the seabed. Seems they did some test drilling back in '74 but the drilling logs were lost. Where's Dicky located?'

'One never knows. Dicky flits around from site to site. Last I heard, he was up in Denmark. Some tunnel project up there that's got his liver up, but I'll try to remember to ring up his wife and get his telephone number. Incidentally, come up to the house anytime. I've got bags of hot water. The two of you might want a proper shower and I have some old photographs of the *Snow Goose* you'd probably enjoy browsing through.'

Stone mechanically thanked him for the offer. A few minutes later, Melissa brought up a mug of tea. They talked a little about the weather and, eventually, Scott-Hughes made his excuses and departed.

'He's straight out of a Noel Coward play,' Stone remarked to her as they watched him puttering toward the shore, standing bolt upright in his dinghy, steering by means of a golf club lashed to the handle of the outboard.

'But he's solid, Stone, once you get past all the old-boy routine. Wish there were more like him, even if he thinks the definition of a liberated woman is one that wears blue eye-liner.'

The sun was up, the air warming. She did a pirouette, luxuriating in its warmth. 'It's the nice thing about England,' she said. 'It's a century behind everyone else except the Irish, but the people are lovely. I hate to see it change.'

She ducked below for a few minutes and came back on deck rigged out in town clothes. 'Off to see the wizard,' she said. Tight cotton slacks, a sassy blouse and thong sandals. With the suntan and freshly washed hair, she was stunning.

They pumped up the dinghy, attached the Seagull outboard and motored across the river. Stone dropped her off at the landing in front of a little inn.

'With any luck, should be back by tea-time,' she said. 'If you go up to his house, don't let him ply you with liquor. I'm possibly open to your devious ways, should you plan to employ them this evening.'

Before he could absorb this news, she had planted a badly aimed kiss on his forehead and headed off down the rickety dock. Stone stood there for a few minutes, admiring the view of her backside twitching beneath her tight cotton slacks – undoubtedly intentional on her part. He hummed a snatch of a melody from *West Side Story* on the way back to the boat.

He slept for a few hours and got up at noon, made himself a peanut butter and jelly sandwich and washed it down with mineral water. The siren call of Heineken beckoned but he successfully blanked off his receptors.

Through the afternoon, he surveyed the parts locker, taking inventory, then started in on his wish list, thumbing through manuals to pick off parts numbers. At 15.00, he brewed up some coffee and took it to the cockpit, along with the copy of *The Times* that Scott-Hughes had left.

Nothing about a yacht blown up in the Channel, the edition probably printed before the news was in. He leafed through the sports section, hoping that there would be coverage of spring training in the American League, but baseball didn't seem to stir the sluggish blood of English sportsmen.

On page nine, something caught his eye. 'Investigation of Newmarket Truck Deaths Yields No Fresh Clues.' The article was sketchy, no more than a couple of column inches. Two tank trucks filled with 'explosive toxic chemicals' valued at £63,800 had been stolen from an unidentified 'government facility'. One truck was still missing but the other one had been found by a local boy searching for his missing dog. The truck had been discovered parked inside a shed located on an abandoned farm. Two men, whose identities had not been divulged by the police, had been found dead 'nearby', both burned beyond recognition. The Special Branch of Scotland Yard had been called in and an enquiry was under way. The article implied a news blackout or cover-up of some sort.

Newmarket! From where Joss had mailed the letter to de Ruiter! And what kind of 'explosive toxic chemicals' were they talking about? Stone knew it was time to contact the Scot.

Scott-Hughes was in his garden, wielding an impressive pair of clippers. He looked up as Stone approached.

'Quite warm, wouldn't you say? Unusual for this time of year.' He stood up, brushing dirt off his knees. 'Sun's almost over the yardarm. Time for gin and tonic. You'll join me?'

Stone felt awkward asking but he did. 'Sir — I'd like to use your telephone. Long distance. I'll get the time and charges.'

'Wouldn't hear of it.' He pointed to a screened structure. 'There's a telephone on the far side of the porch. Help yourself.'

Stone punched in the Highgate telephone number. An unfamiliar voice answered.

'Is Ian Macleod there?' He had mumbled with a Limey accent and it came off pretty good.

'No such name at this number,' the man abruptly answered. 'Who's calling?'

There was a double click on the line — possibly someone implementing a phone trace. Or was the asshole just recording the conversation? Paranoid, Stone hung up.

It was a long shot but he called Mac's number on the Isle of Skye. Mac answered on the eighth ring.

'It's me,' Stone said.

Long interval. 'Rather surprised to hear from you, that is, if it really *is* you. What have I just poured into my tea?'

'Talisker.'

Longer interval. 'There's been some queer chaps working on my telephone line. How many digits in the number you're calling from?'

Stone counted them. 'Nine.'

Mac breathed into his mouthpiece. 'All right. Add the five digits of your father's post-office box number to your local number and give me the result.'

Stone fumbled for a pencil and pad out of Joss's attaché case and did the arithmetic, then gave Mac the sum.

'Got that,' Mac said. 'I'll ring you back in thirty minutes from a public call box.'

Actually, it took him less than fifteen. 'Surprised to hear from you, Stone. Thought that you and your lady would be feeding the fish by now, old son. Prime-time coverage on the morning tube. You've caused quite a stir, you have.'

'What are they saying?'

'Nothing particularly complimentary. Involvement in drug trafficking, a stolen Audi dumped in Le Havre with your fingerprints all over it, the murder of a retired policeman who was guarding confiscated property which apparently you then purloined, unlawful flight to escape prosecution . . . the usual thing.'

'What did they say about the *Night Watch*?'

'It seems that besides the French fishing vessel, two other vessels saw the flash of the explosion. Both the Royal Navy and the Froggies sent out divers but the current runs at over four knots in the area and it's nearly sixty meters deep. Given those conditions, what remained of the vessel could have been carried on the tide to the far corners of the globe. The TV wallahs don't expect that anything will be found.'

'So they think we're dead.'

'It would seem so. The consensus seems to be "good riddance".' A pause, the sound of Mac lighting his pipe. 'I also presume, based on the number you gave me, that you're in the south of England.'

Stone didn't want to answer that one and shifted the conversation. 'I called Highgate and they never heard of you. What's the deal?'

'They sacked me. Seems Charlie, one of the lads I hired, was on Lloyd's payroll as well as mine, except Lloyd's was paying him a good deal more. Wanted to keep tabs on what I was doing, so it seems. Charlie was on duty when your fax came in the night before last. He retransmitted it to Lloyd's Bureau of Internal Development before giving me the original. Yesterday morning, some snotty-nosed MI5 bastard came down from London and told me that I had "exceeded my charter – consorted with criminal elements, broken every law in the book – all very distasteful, et cetera". First swore me to the Official Secrets Act, then sent me packing.'

'What was their reaction to my faxed report?'

'Oh, they went for that in a grand way, particularly after

the hijacking up in Newmarket. They're definitely concentrating on the theory that the Chunnel will be attacked from within the tubes with liquid explosive. Contrary to your calculations, they've now got some American explosives expert who says it's possible.'

'That's exactly why I called you. The Newmarket thing in the last edition of *The Times*. Any idea of what happened?'

'There's a news blackout, but I still have contacts in the Yard. Parties unknown, but thought to number at least six, garroted two perimeter guards and shot two gate guards at the fuel depot that services Lakenheath Air Force Base – the aerodrome where your F-111s are based. The upshot was that the intruders stole two tanker trucks loaded with ethylene oxide, the fuel-air bomb stuff the Americans used in the Gulf War. One of the trucks is still missing. The second one was discovered accidentally. Found in a farm shed about thirty kilometers north of the base by a local lad on the lookout for his dog. The ethylene oxide had already been transferred to another vehicle, probably a civilian petrol tanker. Found heavy tire tracks leading out to the main road.'

'The article mentioned two dead men.'

'They were in a shallow pit behind the shed. Each shot with a small-caliber pistol through the temple, execution-style, then burned with gasoline. Their fingertips had been cut off prior to incineration and their faces made, ah, unrecognizable.'

'So there was no way to identify them?'

'The forensic types were able to do a DNA match on the younger one. Ex-RAF ordnance type with a criminal record, forgotten his name. There was no DNA match on the other man, but about a kilometer north of the farm one of the local constables noticed the tire tracks of a heavily laden lorry in the dirt where it had pulled off the road. No footprints, so the constable assumed that whoever was in the truck had pulled over just momentarily so as to toss something from the window. He then nosed around and eventually found several items scattered at random as if they had been thrown, including three fingertips, an empty man's purse and three passports. Obviously, there are now experts on the scene who are on their hands and knees, combing the ground within a two-hundred-meter radius for other clues.'

'Passports!'

'Right. One Belgian, one Uruguayan, and one American. The first two were forgeries, but the American one was authentic, issued in Puerto Rico to a Mr Antonio F. Bontoc.'

'BONTOC? Sonofabitch. You're sure?'

'Quite positive. The Yard checked with the American State Department. The passport was authentic. And they had a green card on file in his name with a complete set of prints. One of the fingertips found by the constable matched up with Bontoc's green card fingerprint file – a positive match.'

Stone wanted to believe but couldn't. Why would Joss be assassinated by, presumably, his own people? Unless it was an attempt to throw them off the track. 'I'm not buying it, Mac. And who'd be fool enough to carry a valid passport on a job like that?'

'It does smell a bit gamy, doesn't it, but not to worry – the Yard has the bit well and truly between their teeth and they're headed for the barn. One hundred and eighty coppers on the loose, stumbling over each other, looking all over Great Britain for two tankloads of ethylene oxide – close to 60,000 liters' worth. That lot would make the Guy Fawkes effort look like a schoolboy prank, assuming that the people Joss was working for could get the stuff into the Chunnel and touch it off. Which is damned unlikely. Eurotunnel has increased security and they're triple-checking everything that shows up for loading at the Folkestone terminal.'

'It's a cover-up, Mac. I'm positive that they're going for the borehole plan and this is just a diversion.' He told

Macleod about Brunner, the *Valkyr*, de Ruiter and the *Cormorant*. What he didn't say was that he had been played for a sucker, but Mac, no fool he, would eventually work that one out as well.

Mac had apparently been making notes. He asked a few more questions then said, 'I'll pass this on to the Yard, but I doubt that anyone will listen. It's been repeatedly pointed out by the so-called experts that the borehole plan would involve a ship equipped with hydraulic dredges anchored over the Chunnel for at least twenty-four hours. Eurotunnel management has already alerted shipping interests to report anything along that line. And now, with the ethylene oxide hijack, they've got something definite to sink their teeth into.'

Stone thought for a minute. 'Mac – the telephone and fax numbers that I found in Joss's holster. Brunner said he checked them out and claimed that they were duds – old stuff or disconnected. Any way you could independently check them out?'

'Not likely. I'm off the payroll and *persona non grata*, remember?'

'Let's say that one of the numbers somehow links Brunner with Joss. Then we'd know almost for certain that the fuel-air bomb theory is a blind and Brunner's going for the boreholes. I know it's a long shot, but if there is a link, then it would be worth looking into both de Ruiter's background and the *Cormorant*, not to mention tracking down the *Valkyr* and questioning Brunner. For starters, he could probably be nailed on conspiracy charges.'

Mac grunted. 'I could try, Stone, but remember that I'm bound by the Official Secrets Act. If they catch me paddling around in their official bath water, they can put me in the nick for twenty years, which is about twenty years more than this old body can endure. And based on the number of rude chaps cruising around here in delivery vans and telephone trucks, I suspect they're keeping an eye on me. Neither MI5 nor the Yard wants to be embarrassed over their previous lack of zeal, understood? We blotted their copybook and now they've gone daft that the word will leak out.'

'You're sure they've tapped your telephone?'

'I think it's likely.' He sniffed a little. 'Just out of curiosity, I'll make a few enquiries into those numbers. If you want to get in touch with me again, call Jimmy, the chap that runs the Rosedale Inn. He'll get word to me and I'll call you back at this number. Incidentally, just *where* are you?'

'Don't think I should say over the phone, Mac. And I won't be at this number for more than a day at most. After that, I'm gone.'

'What are your plans?'

Stone didn't want to answer that one either. Helping Mac was one thing, but he couldn't get directly involved again. That, and the fact that he had a date with a lady.

There was silence on the line, Mac waiting for an answer. 'Look, Mac, I'm sorry I can't give you any additional help on this but I've done my best. If I hang around England for more than a few days, I'll either get killed by Brunner's people or arrested by yours. Neither appeals.'

Again, a long pause. Finally, Mac spoke. 'You did more than I expected, Stone, but less than I had hoped for. I'll make out a check from my own funds and send it to your father's address for forwarding. It should cover your expenses at a minimum. Now it's time that I rang off. One of those chaps that I told you about is up a telephone pole outside the shop I'm calling from, and I don't think he's looking for robins' eggs.'

'I'll drop you a card from Maine and, Mac . . . watch out for yourself.'

When Macleod answered, he sounded tired, almost depressed. 'Aye, lad. Because I surely don't know of anyone else who will.'

EIGHTEEN

The Hamble River, 13 April

Groveling around on his hands and knees, Stone puttered about, caulking deck seams between the teak planks. He was particularly intent on plugging a leak over the quarter berth that inflicted an insidious kind of Chinese water torture on the occupant beneath.

He had stripped down to cut-off jeans, the spring sun hot on his back, the Walkman cranking out early Beatles stuff from *Rubber Soul*. He croaked along, off key, as he laid down a fresh bead of black seam compound.

Unexpectedly, a tap on his back banged his nerves into overdrive. He swiveled around, startled, smearing the goo. Scott-Hughes was standing up in his dinghy, clutching the lifeline, his face beaded with perspiration, his lips moving. Stone ripped off the headphones.

'Terribly sorry to bother you, old boy, but I've been screeching from the blasted beach for the last half-hour. Telephone message for you.'

'Wasn't expecting one.' Stone wiped the gunk from his fingers, smearing the stuff farther up his palm.

'Two, actually,' Scott-Hughes said. He glanced at scribbles on a notepad. 'Your dear lady rang up. She's in London, didn't say where. Just that a sailor she seems to know had to get a round of vaccinations.' His face clouded momentarily. 'Hope it's not another new epidemic popping up.'

Stone grinned. 'Sailor is the name of her dog. I guess she had to bring his shot record up to date.'

Scott-Hughes seemed relieved. 'Good. One can barely

breathe in a public place these days without contracting some damned sort of alphabet-soup virus. At any rate, she said she won't be back until tomorrow evening. Very apologetic and all that but hoped you'd understand. Emphasized that you should pick up a dozen roses. That make sense?'

'Perfect sense.' Absolutely perfect, erotic, carnal, erogenous, procreative sense. Sailor, undoubtedly the jealous type, would have to be blindfolded. 'You mentioned another message?' Odd, because he hadn't expected Mac to get back to him this quickly.

'*Splendid* news. Rang Dicky's office and he's back in England. Arrived two nights ago. His office is in Burnham-on-Crouch and he thinks it's possible that he has the gen on your Channel drilling job. His former boss was a member of the Petroleum Institute and told Dicky he had all the bumph on test drilling in UK waters for the past fifty years. Dicky's never been through the stuff but said you'd be more than welcome to browse.'

Stone's heartbeat picked up the pace. 'When can I meet him?'

'He's off again on Friday next with his wife. Nepal. Some hydro project *thing* on the Kali Gandaki River. Expects to be there for two weeks, then take a climbing holiday in the Hindu Kush. Tax write-off sort of thing. Be back in six weeks, give or take.'

'Burnham-on-Crouch is somewhere on the east coast, right? I could be there by noon tomorrow if I caught the morning train, and still be back here by the late afternoon.'

Scott-Hughes shook his head. 'That's not on, old boy. Dicky's off to a wedding tomorrow, best man to an old school chum, then up to his place in London to pack. Today's the only time he has available to let you rummage through his files.'

Stone inwardly cursed. Mac needed his provenance — the proof that the borehole theory held water. He briefly thought about renting a car but immediately chucked the

359

idea because his credit cards were probably flagged by Interpol. He shook his head. 'It doesn't look like I can make it.'

''Course you can, my dear chap. I'll run you over there. Give me something to do besides gassing grubworms in my garden. Already told Dicky we'd be coming up together and to lay on hotel accommodations. We'll spend the night and be back by noon tomorrow. Won't take no for an answer.'

There was no point in arguing, and whatever he could find to help Mac would be in partial atonement for bugging out on the job. Stone grabbed a quick shower, dressed, and stuffed a clean change of clothes into the attaché case. He was about to close the drawer of the bureau when he noticed the butt-end of the Beretta poking out from beneath a pile of underwear. Melissa had been worried sick about having *the thing* on board because British courts came down very heavy on possession of an unregistered firearm. If, for any reason, the *Snow Goose* was searched in his absence, the discovery of the weapon would put her in even deeper trouble with the law. He made a decision to take it with him, then wrote her a quick note explaining where he was in the event she came back before he did. As an afterthought, he scooped up a stack of road maps that were bound together with a rubber band on the off-chance that Scott-Hughes might get lost wandering around the countryside.

He found Scott-Hughes in the driveway, behind the wheel of a vintage Morgan roadster. Astonishingly, he was dressed in a sweaty flight suit, his overnight bag in the boot. 'Strap in, Mr Walker, and hold on.'

After five sphincter-puckering minutes of blasting down country lanes, Scott-Hughes slewed the Morgan through a drifting turn into the graveled driveway of a small boatyard. On a concrete ramp which sloped down to the river was a twin-engined Grumman Mallard amphibian, engines ticking over.

360

Scott-Hughes motioned Stone to climb in while he did a quick walk-around inspection. A mechanic in an incredibly filthy boiler suit chatted briefly with him, then, astonishingly, saluted him.

Scott-Hughes clambered into the pilot's side. 'Tommy's appearance tends to put one off but he's a first-class fitter – been with me for the last forty-odd years, first in the RAF, then followed me into retirement; takes care of my toys. Actually dragged the Morgan off a rubbish heap and rebuilt her from the chassis up. And what he doesn't know about aircraft isn't worth a bent farthing.'

Stone was sweating slightly. RAF or not, Scott-Hughes was an old man. But he ran the checklist with practiced precision, his movements economical. Satisfied, he gave a 'thumbs up' to the mechanic who then pulled out the chocks and, once more, saluted.

The amphibian trundled down the ramp into the Hamble River. As Scott-Hughes taxied, he flicked on the de-ice and carburettor heat, then the boost pumps. From a map pocket, he pulled out a pair of Ray Bans and carefully fitted them on.

At the mouth of the Hamble, they turned into the broad expanse of the Solent Estuary. With the big radial engines grumbling, the Mallard eased past a starboard hand-marker labeled 'Bald Head'. Scott-Hughes advanced the throttles, mushing the Mallard through a turn, aligning the aircraft into the wind. 'Designated seaplane operating area,' he said. 'One hundred and ten miles to the River Crouch, Mr Walker. Here we go.'

Minutes later, they were climbing through 3000, the cockpit now cooler. Like a caterpillar turning butterfly, Scott-Hughes had metamorphosed from a rummy good old boy into a precise pilot. Years seemingly dropped from his age. He kept a tight instrument scan going, and when he fingered switches he had no need to look where they were located.

'You fly, Mr Walker?'

Stone felt as if he were meeting the real Scott-Hughes for the first time. 'Most everyone calls me by my nickname. It's "Stone".'

Scott-Hughes turned and grinned. 'Nigel. Forget the Scott-Hughes bollocks. I play the part that people expect of me. Comes with the money and the honors, most of which were totally unwarranted.' He gestured to the instrument panel. 'You watched every movement I made on take-off. Do you? Fly, I mean.'

Stone nodded. 'A little, but not anything like this. I've taken a few lessons, and someday I thought I'd get a small floatplane. Back home, I live on an island. It'd come in handy.'

Scott-Hughes smiled thinly, scanning the sky to the east. 'Everyone lives on an island, Stone. Most just don't realize it. Take the controls. I'll play nanny.'

It took less than an hour. With Stone at the controls and Scott-Hughes coaching, he set up a descent over the Thames Estuary, leveled off over Foulness Point on the coast, then turned on finals for the River Crouch. Scott-Hughes didn't touch the controls, just kept a soft monologue going, prompting rather than commanding.

'Full, rich mixture . . . good. Fine pitch. More flap now and stabilize your airspeed. Ease off on your throttles, Stone. Not that much – up a bit . . . good, *good*. Level her off a little, controls coming aft . . . there . . . there . . .'

The hull kissed the water, was briefly airborne again, then settled on the plane. Stone slowly eased the throttles back, awash with the giddy feeling that he had done it right the first time.

'Proper job, Stone,' Scott-Hughes said, a smile on his face. He directed Stone to taxi into a protected cove on the northern shore. An inflatable dinghy drifted alongside a ringed buoy, a man standing up in the dinghy holding a mooring pendant and a portable radio to his ear. Using a marine VHF handi-talkie, Scott-Hughes coordinated the hook-up.

Dicky Barker was a gangling man in his late thirties — charming, exuberant, 'terribly keen' on everything. His thinning blond hair fluttered in the slightest breeze, and he wore white flannel slacks and a white V-necked sweater which gave the impression that he had just ducked out of a cricket match.

Dicky's 'office' was the partitioned half of a World War II Nissen hut, tacked on to a crumbling brick building which housed the administrative staff.

Dicky's working space looked as if a paper blizzard had just blown through: piles of reports and memos, charts and engineering drawings scattered over Chesterfields, chairs, work tables and the floor.

He explained that his secretary had just cleaned things up. 'Can't find a damned thing now, but still, she's a good sort. Means well.' He paused and lit a cigarette, then stabbed it in the direction of a door. 'Right — over here. Let's take a look.'

He waded through piles of paper to a broom closet and opened it, revealing eight nose-high stacks of manila files, each bound with a pink ribbon. 'Somewhere in here.'

'Is there any particular order that this stuff is filed in?'

Dicky frowned. 'Not sure, really. Probably whatever came in the door was put on the top of the heap. My former boss was originally head of the British Petroleum Research Institute. Had a gentleman's agreement with all the geologists working in the UK to get a copy of their reports. Government was going to fund some sort of a database to organize it, but the Labour Party came into power and never requisitioned the money. Frankly, I haven't been through the lot myself. Rather suspect that you'll be the first to read the damned things.' He checked his watch. 'Back to my word-mangler. Got to finish off some editing. Have fun.'

It took Stone half an hour to find the report. Like all the rest, it was a stack of photocopies which had been bound in a ledger book, the edges of the pages already turning brown.

He leafed through the report. Literally, dry as dust. Analysis of the cores for undrained modulus of elasticity determined over unload, reload cycle prior to failure, typical mass permeability, typical intact UCS, geological description of the core, column after column. But on the last two pages was a list of the boreholes with their exact latitude and longitude, down to the tenths of seconds, cross-checked by both optical survey and Decca electronic readouts.

Stone asked Barker whether he had a large-scale chart of the English Channel with a detailed overlay of the Chunnel. Barker pulled down a roll of charts from a ceiling rack, kicked aside some papers and laid them out on the floor, finally finding the right one.

Stone plotted carefully. Most of the boreholes were between twenty and forty meters north of the Chunnel, but two, CP0021 and CP0023, were positioned just a few scant meters from the Chunnel structure at station CH.27,088.23.

Curious, Dicky bent down and examined the plot. '*Good God!* Nearly on top of the UK Crossover Chamber.' He stabbed the chart with his finger. 'This indicates that two of the boreholes were drilled *there.*'

Stone rechecked the coordinates and replotted. The point of the divider fell in the same pinholes. 'Looks that way. And from what I've heard, they weren't grouted.'

'Damned good thing the drilling teams didn't bore into them. Could get very nasty, poking into a hole that runs right up to the seabed.' Barker checked the soundings. 'Thirty-five meters lower than the seabed, with another thirty-five meters of water on top of that.' He whipped a calculator out of his jacket pocket and pecked at it. 'Sixty-nine thousand, three hundred and four kilograms per square meter. Could have been a bad blow-out had they tunneled into it.'

Indeed, Stone thought. But if even one of those same boreholes were cleaned out, then packed with C-4 plastique explosive, *absolutely* catastrophic. 'Just how large is this crossover cavern?'

Barker thumbed through the spring 1991 issue of *Tunnels and Tunneling*. 'Ah . . . 160 meters long, 15.4 meters high, 21.2 meters in span. Massive thing. Largest underground cavern ever attempted. But they had good geological information to work with. As you can see from the cross-sectional drawings, the cavern liner is relatively thin – just steel mesh, shotcrete and rock bolts – because the natural rock arch over the cavern is extraordinarily stable. Actually, takes all of the load, you understand? The cavern walls are primarily shotcreted to keep out the occasional trickle of moisture and also for cosmetics. Wouldn't do to have train passengers see the raw chalk walls weeping water, would it?'

'Don't ungrouted boreholes that close to the structure concern you?'

Dicky shrugged elegantly. 'Shouldn't think so. Might crack the shotcrete due to the sea pressure behind it, but the lads would just throw in a couple of rock bolts and plaster it over. Not a problem, and after all, that cavern's been in existence for years with no structural troubles yet apparent. Besides, the engineers have all kinds of probes sticking out into the surrounding caulk and mudstone; rock-pressure cells, extensometers, creep gauges and such. No large water infiltration has shown up to my knowledge, and the settling has stabilized within the expected limits.'

'Suppose that one of those boreholes was packed with high explosives?'

'How did a bizarre idea like that pop into your head?'

'Terrorism is always a threat that should be considered, right? I've reserved the book's last chapter to cover it.'

'But you're not talking about a couple of bolsheviks in baggy pants slinking around with bombs. The boreholes, even if they weren't grouted with concrete, have filled up over the years with silt and gravel. They'd have to be excavated, either with a drilling rig or with hydraulic hoses.'

'My thoughts exactly.'

'And you've overlooked two vital facts, Mr Walker. An offshore drilling rig would have to be used. Look a bit odd to see something like that plodding around in the English Channel. And also consider that the rock surrounding the cavern is monitored for stresses from potential shifting of the rock strata, as well as water infiltration and swelling. The sensors would immediately pick up any noise or vibrations from an attempt to clean out the boreholes.' He rolled up the chart and stuffed it in a tube. 'I would tread very softly if I were you, Mr Walker. Sounds almost as if you're writing a pulp thriller instead of a detailed engineering history, and the Eurotunnel people would eat you whole for such speculative penny-thriller stuff in the guise of a factual history. Messy lawsuits against you and your publisher for loss of business, diminishment of public confidence, et cetera.'

Stone grinned weakly. 'Worst-case scenario. I agree that an attempt like the one I've described is almost impossible. Just covering all the bases.'

Barker relaxed marginally. 'Still . . .'

'Let me ask a favor of you, Dicky. Would it be possible for me to see the Crossover Cavern, talk to the people that do the sensor monitoring?'

Barker scratched his scalp, then examined his fingernails for dandruff. 'Difficult, probably impossible. The Eurotunnel people are very restrictive on whom they allow to poke around. Can't blame them, of course. If they didn't keep a short leash on whom they take down there, they'd be inundated with swarms of Girl Guides and garden clubs looking for a way to pass the afternoon.' He scratched again and apparently hit the mother lode by the look of his nails. 'Still, I could make a phone call. What are you after?'

'I'd like to take a look at their monitoring setup. Also,

I'd like to know how many and what type of sensors are monitoring the chalk stratum near CH.26,088.23.'

Barker wandered off, rummaged through piles of paper, until he found his telephone. He dialed, was put on hold, then got through. The conversation dragged on for fifteen minutes. Barker finally dropped the headset in its cradle.

'Nothing,' Barker said flatly.

'What do you mean, "nothing"?'

'Just that – nothing. Talked to Bobby Knowles – in charge of subsurface electronic maintenance for Eurotunnel, old school chum of mine. First off, they're not taking visitors unless you've got the proper introductions and all. As to the sensors, Bobby said that a week ago, a subcontractor's quality control engineer by the name of Clifford Rumsley showed up with a work order to have his electrician check out some sort of intermittent sensor reading in the Crossover Chamber. Bobby's people didn't have anything on their fault list but they gave this Rumsley chap the go-ahead because, after all, he had the proper credentials. 'Bout half an hour later, there was a cock-up of the first magnitude. Rumsley's electrician accidentally jumpered 480 volts AC onto a low-voltage terminal strip that carries signals from the sensors and snuffed out no less than thirty-two of them. They'll be replaced, of course. Tedious job. Six days to change the lot.' He shook his head. 'But a complete fiasco.'

Alarm bells were clanging in Stone's mind. 'What explanation did Rumsley give?'

'Said that the schematic was wrong, not his electrician's fault. Obviously, it was. The electrician was German, barely spoke English. Chap probably made a mistake in translation. At any rate, Bobby's people tried to get hold of Rumsley three days ago but both Rumsley and the electrician had resigned, no forwarding address. Bobby is *most* unhappy with the situation.'

'Sabotage?' Stone suggested softly.

Barker gave him a puzzled look. 'You on that again?

These things happen all the time. Just your common garden variety of stupidity. And mind you, I'd play this borehole thing down. Not to ruffle the feathers of the powers that be.' He checked his watch. 'God, still have that article on the Danish tunnel drive to finish off. Anything else I can help you with?'

Stone shook his head and Scott-Hughes eased into the conversation. 'Thanks ever so much, Dicky. We'll take our leave now, let you plod on with your word-mangling. Have a super time on your holiday but don't drink the bloody tap water. Was in Nepal once, mind you. Nearly rotted my guts out.'

The evening sunlight was hard in their eyes as they walked toward the Burnham Inn, less than half a kilometer away.

Both of them were silent, preoccupied, when Scott-Hughes finally asked, 'What are you really up to, Stone?'

They were taking a shortcut through a lane, its edges lined with low stone walls, the cobbled roadway overhung with budding oaks. It looked as if nothing had changed since William the Conqueror had passed through, assuming that Burnham-on-Crouch had been on his agenda.

Stone had heard but didn't answer immediately, turning Scott-Hughes' question over in his mind. What *was* he doing? It wasn't his fight, not even his playing-field. This was the end of it, as far as he could go. He decided he'd phone Mac tonight and give him the information. It would be up to Mac to convince the various government knuckleheads that they had a serious threat on their hands.

Scott-Hughes was still waiting for an answer. Stone kicked a rock with his shoe. 'What am I doing? Just gathering information for the book.'

'You're not Canadian, are you?'

There didn't seem to be any point in lying. 'No. American.'

'Thought that might be the case. The accent doesn't ring

true. Also noticed that some screwholes in the transom of the *Snow Goose* weren't plugged and had been painted over where another nameboard had been previously attached.'

'You've been very decent, Nigel. I'm not going to lie to you, but I want you to give me your word that you won't repeat anything I tell you. If you did, it would put both Melissa and me in an awkward situation.'

They had come to the inn, a three-story Tudor affair. Stone indicated a bench on a knoll of grass overlooking a rose arbor. 'Let's sit down here. This might take a little time.' He started his story from the beginning, telling Scott-Hughes everything, from muddled start to inconclusive finish.

'Then it *was* the two of you in the Channel, the *Night Watch* thing?'

Stone nodded.

Scott-Hughes drew his hand along his jaw, making a face. 'Something odd has been going on in the markets with Eurotunnel shares. A lot of short selling by anonymous nominee shareholders, as if *someone* knew that the price of the stock was headed for a tumble. Ever consider this Brunner person is trying to make a killing in the market?'

'Doesn't fit. Destroying the Chunnel would be one hell of an expensive operation, and not at all a sure thing. There's got to be easier ways to make money.'

'Still, someone out there knows, is somehow involved, and is trying to capitalize on the possibility regardless of how slim.'

'Who?'

'It wouldn't be a short list by any stretch of the imagination, Stone. British nationalists, criminal elements, seaman's unions, Channel shipping interests, manufacturers of British goods who know they can't compete with Continental interests, the IRA. That's just for starters. Chuck in your own government as well. The Americans don't want to see Great Britain sucking up to the EC's tit —

undoubtedly lead to a diminishment of American influence on the Continent. Then there are the Japanese.'

Stone lifted an eyebrow.

'Oh, yes, indeed,' Scott-Hughes responded. 'The Japanese are beginning to feel the bite of European countries which, individually, were vulnerable to Japanese commercial pressures but now, collectively, can stand up and fight. Our Nipponese compatriots don't want the European Community to succeed and the failure of the Chunnel might trigger Great Britain's withdrawal which, in turn, could lead to the weakening and possible dissolution of the EC. It's not all that popular an idea, even on the Continent, you know. More of a marriage of convenience arranged by self-appointed Eurocrats than a love match entered into by eager lovers. Your country seems to muddle through with its melting-pot of cultures, but do you really believe that chucking Germans, Italians, Dutch, Belgians, Greeks, Danes, Spanish, French, English and Irish into the same pot will produce anything but a witches' brew of discontent?'

'I take it you're not all that enthused over the common-market philosophy?'

A look of distaste passed over Scott-Hughes' face. 'Like most Britons, I'm of two minds. Europe's great strength and its great weakness, I must admit, has been the *diversity* of cultures, not the homogenization of them. All this claptrap about having a common currency, common political goals, common labor laws and common health benefits is so much common codswallop. Perhaps the EC thing will yield some gains in terms of international bargaining power, but it destroys initiative, innovation, smothers the national spirit and reduces every man jack of us to the least common denominator. Still, I suppose that if we're in bed with the Germans, we won't be fighting them. Pity. We'll both probably miss a good bash-up every generation or so.' He gave Stone a wry grin. 'Remind me to tell you how I forced a Jerry U-boat to the surface in the Denmark Straits. December of '43, as I recall. Johnny Hawkes —

370

although all the ladies called him Johnny Come Early —
was my bombardier and we had this . . .'

'Have to be later, Nigel.' Stone stood up. 'I've got to call
Macleod. What say we meet in the dining-room about
seven thirty?'

He left Scott-Hughes sitting on the bench, his head
tipped up to catch the last of the sun. Stone checked in
and had a large glass of orange juice sent up to his room.
He retrieved the Rosedale Hotel's number from his wallet
and dialed it.

A woman answered, nice Highlands lilt to her accent.
Stone asked for Jimmy. There was a long wait, the sound of
singing in the background, the occasional clink of glasses.

'Hullo. Who's this?'

'I'm a friend of Mac's — was with him drinking in your
lounge about ten days ago. He told me to call you if I
needed to get hold of him.'

'Right. Macleod made mention of you. You're the Yank
engineer?'

'The same. How long will it take for you to get Mac to
the phone? It's important.'

'Call 'im yourself. Got his number right here.'

Stone gritted his teeth. It looked as if Mac hadn't
adequately explained the situation to his friend. 'Look,
Jimmy, I don't want to argue with you, but Mac told me
to do it this way.'

'Look yourself, Yank. Mac left Scotland last night. Flew
up to Ireland to shake off the watchers, then on to Antwerp. Told me to tell you that one of the phone numbers
he was supposed to check up on was for a German yacht,
Val-something or other — got it written down right here —
Valkyr. Said he checked with the overseas operator and
she told him that the prefix was only assigned to ships
equipped with satellite gear. She looked it up on her computer and that's how Macleod found out the registration.'

'Yeah, but why did he go to Antwerp?'

'Something about a ship's agent you told him about —

chap named de Ruiter. Wanted to track him down, then go from there. I've got his hotel number in Antwerp. He's staying down near the docks, a place called the Verdhoffin.'

Stone clenched the phone in his hand. Bloody stupid of Mac to stick his head in the noose. Brunner was the type to keep an eye over his shoulder for anyone following. He had proved that in spades, hadn't he?

Stone got the hotel number from Jimmy, rang off, then dialed the Verdhoffin in Antwerp.

The desk put him through and Mac answered on the twelfth ring.

'Got me out of my bloody bath, Stone,' Mac grumbled.

'I'm in Burnham-on-Crouch,' Stone said. 'Tracked down a copy of the GEM drilling logs today. Two of the boreholes are within three meters of the Crossover Chamber.' He waited for Mac's breathless praise.

The line was silent for a while, just the sound of Mac's breathing. 'Doesn't leave much to the imagination, does it?' Mac finally said.

'Not as far as I'm concerned.' Stone hesitated. 'Jimmy said you went to Antwerp to check out de Ruiter.'

'Seemed the logical thing to do since you've turned in your resignation. I called the shipping agent's firm first. They're in business all right, but nobody in the firm ever heard of a Hans de Ruiter. And I suppose Jimmy told you about the *Valkyr*? You swallowed that one too, didn't you?'

Mac's voice had just an edge of sarcasm in it, but Stone wasn't going to get into an argument. Brunner had been so damned *positive*, so damned *efficient*, and, consequently, so goddamned *believable*. Stone now realized how easily he had swallowed Brunner's concoction, but he knew that if Mac had been in the same position, he would have as well.

'Point well taken, Mac. Did you find out anything else?'

'Checked on the *Cormorant*. What de Ruiter or whoever he is told you is true as far as that goes. She's on Lloyd's Registry of Ships as "decommissioned and out of class".

Which means she's uninsurable. Most of the ships surveyors in Antwerp have known her for donkey's years, said her hull plating is as thin as bog paper and that she's overdue to be broken up for scrap. Couple of the chaps reckoned that she was up north, somewhere around the Hook of Holland, possibly Europort. I checked with an assurance society and they had a list of surveyors who normally work on that part of the coast. Spent seventy-eight pounds on phone calls but I finally tracked down the bloke that surveyed the *Cormorant*. He was in Greece on another job, devil of a time getting hold of him.'

'So what'd he say?'

'The *Cormorant* was fetched up for about a week in Oostvoorne, Holland – a little shipyard just south of Europort owned by the van Velsen brothers. Van Velsen actually commissioned the surveyor to do the work. When he finished the survey on the *Cormorant*, an older Dutch chap who was representing the new owners asked the surveyor where he could find a good man who specialized in inert gas welding – had an aluminum tank to install.'

There was the sound of Mac blowing his nose – a healthy honk, then he resumed. 'The surveyor told him to forget it, that the *Cormorant* had failed survey and that it would cost a fortune to make her seaworthy, let alone to install some fancy tank. But the Dutchman said that she was fine for their purposes and to hell with the insurance companies – that they'd self-insure.'

'What happened?'

'The surveyor recommended a welder friend of his, thought he'd get a cut of the fee. The welder, local chap by the name of Holwerda, met him four days later to give him his ten per cent and fill him in on the details, although he mentioned that the old Dutchman had told him to keep his trap shut. Holwerda said that the *Cormorant*'s owners had brought in a load of specially fabricated alloy plates from a shipyard in Finland, then had him assemble the whole lot in the forward cargo hold. Literally built a bloody great tank within the hull, took up the entire space. The Dutchman gave Holwerda a cockle-brained story about it being a bio-conversion plant that runs on pig swill and produces methane gas to power the engine.'

'That's the same story de Ruiter gave me,' Stone said.

'Aye, but the interesting thing is that the owners didn't spend a quid on replating the rest of the ship. Didn't even spray fresh anti-fouling paint on the hull. Moreover, once the *Cormorant* was back in the water, she took on three containers of stuff that had come in from a German firm, Weshiem-Munden GmbH. That name sounds familiar, doesn't it?'

Stone felt a chill ripple up his back. The business card that Joss had written on had listed the same name. 'Probably Brunner's outfit. What was in the containers? Any invoice or packing list?'

'Holwerda said the containers were sealed. No need to open them due to EC customs procedures. Just the general description of "marine equipment for vessel in transit" plastered on the outside. And in addition to the containers, they took eight or nine drums of number-two beef tallow on board. Does that make sense to you?'

'I don't know what in the hell beef tallow is used for other than greasing skids on construction projects.'

'Doesn't make sense to me either,' Mac responded, 'so I'm running up to Oostvoorne first thing tomorrow morning. Want to see whether I can talk to this van Velsen chap who owns the shipyard and get some details firsthand. Might even be able to find out where the *Cormorant* went.'

'Hang on, Mac. Between the two of us, we've got enough background on Brunner to get the British authorities interested in following through, and if you want my advice, don't start messing around with Brunner's operation without some substantial assistance on your side.'

Long silence. Mac sniffed. 'Catch my death of cold, Stone. I'm standing here with a bath towel the thickness

374

of a snot-rag wrapped around me. And the cheap buggers don't heat these rooms properly.'

Stone realized that Mac was going to do it his way, now that he had something substantial to go on. 'I have an idea, Mac. I'll meet you day after tomorrow, somewhere on the south coast of England – say at the caravan park. We'll hammer out an updated report that will surely convince Lloyd's and the cops that we're right about Brunner.'

Longer pause, as if Mac was balancing his curiosity against his projected longevity. 'Maybe you've got a point, Stone. I'm getting close to the grave but I wouldn't want to expire just yet. I'll think about it. Ring me back shortly after eight thirty. The cost of the lodging includes an evening meal and I'm not going to let these cheeky buggers get off with not feeding me.'

Stone had to smile. 'Okay, Mac. Eat 'em out of house and home. I'll call back at 20.30 hours.'

Stone found Scott-Hughes in the lounge. He looked up. 'You got through to your friend?' He was nursing a glass of sherry and was decked out in a white shirt, ascot, blazer and gray slacks.

Stone filled him in.

'Not exactly proof positive, is it?' Scott-Hughes said. 'I mean, all that Macleod has established is that this de Ruiter chap probably doesn't exist. Other than that . . .'

'I know. But Mac's sticking his neck out. The police may not buy into it, given what we've got to go on, and we need someone who will at least listen. Do you have any contacts in government that might be willing to get involved and follow up on what we've learned?'

Scott-Hughes paused, then slowly shook his head. 'Always avoided politicians and Civil Service types – a bunch of ponces, if you ask me. Mainly, just friends from the military – chaps you know will stick it out. Still, I'm fairly pally with Air Marshal Lindsey. His brother, Sir Bloody Alfred Lindsey, is connected with some cloak and dagger branch of the Foreign Office and he might be able to kick down a few doors. I'll ring Lindsey up when we get back to the Hamble.'

'One thing, Nigel – I'd appreciate it if you'd keep mention of Melissa and me to a minimum.'

Scott-Hughes considered it and nodded. 'I'll quote my information coming from "informed sources". That should do.'

They had roast lamb and potatoes, the first decent meal Stone had eaten in days. They retired to the reading-room for coffee. Just before the appointed hour, Stone excused himself and phoned Mac from his room.

The desk clerk in Antwerp answered, other voices in the background.

'Room 303, please,' Stone said.

A brief pause. 'I am sorry, but Monsieur Macleod is not in his room.'

Oh Christ! 'What do ya mean – he checked out?'

'No. He was apparently displeased with his waiter over the quality of service and went elsewhere to eat – to a McDonald's, no doubt.' There was a conversation in the background, the sound muffled as if the clerk had put his hand over the mouthpiece. Then, 'You are the same gentleman who was enquiring for him?'

It was an involuntary reaction that Stone sometimes experienced when he looked down over a cliff – a momentary contraction of his sphincter muscle. '*What* gentleman?'

Hesitation, then a certain degree of bored arrogance in the man's voice. 'I would doubt that you are the same gentleman. Do you wish to leave a message, monsieur?'

'*What gentleman were you referring to?*'

'That is *not* your business, monsieur. I can only disclose that there was another person enquiring for Monsieur Macleod half an hour ago, but he did not leave any message. It is not all that unusual, no?'

'Listen! Give Macleod this message as soon as he comes in. Tell him "somebody's checking on you". You got that?'

The voice was decidedly chilly. 'Yes – I have *got* that. Is there a name you wish to leave?'

'Tell him the message is from Talisker and that I'll call back in exactly half an hour. Just make damned sure Macleod gets the message.'

Stone heard the man snort. He hung up on Stone without answering.

Scott-Hughes was draining the last of his coffee. He looked up, concerned. 'You look a bit out of sorts, Stone.'

'Someone's been asking after Mac. It could be one of the people he was talking to today updating information, but on the other hand, it could also be one of Brunner's people. I'm worried as hell. Are there any cross-Channel ferries out of here tonight for Antwerp?'

'Shouldn't think so,' Scott-Hughes replied. He flagged the publican who checked the ferry timetable.

The man rubbed his nose vigorously. 'There's a Sealink ferry out of Felixstowe for Rotterdam 'bout mid-morning tomorrow, guv.' He squinted at the fine print. 'Sorry, got that cocked up. Don't run except Fridays and Sundays now with the Chunnel in operation.'

Scott-Hughes thanked the man, patted his lips with the linen napkin and eased back into his chair. 'Give it an hour, Stone. Probably nothing to be concerned about.'

He's probably right, Stone thought. I'm blowing this thing out of proportion. Still, he was edgy. A drink would go down very nicely just now, but he resisted the temptation and settled for a glass of milk which seemed to curdle in his stomach.

He called at 21.00 exactly.

The man who answered in Antwerp was someone different, his accent decidedly more French.

'My name's Talisker. Did Mr Macleod pick up my message?'

'There is no message in the box for Monsieur Macleod so I presume that 'e 'as already picked it up.'

'Ring his room for me, please.'

377

'As you wish.'

Mac's phone rang fifteen times before Stone jiggled the hang-up bar in exasperation to get the desk clerk back on the line.

'Yes?'

'Macleod's room doesn't answer. Are you sure he's in?'

An exasperated note in the desk clerk's voice. 'I am not sure if 'e is in or not, monsieur. It is not the business of management to spy on our guests.'

'Can you check the bar?'

A deep sigh, then a minute's delay. ''E is not there. Maurice said that Monsieur Macleod has not been in the bar since noontime. 'E remembers Monsieur Macleod well because, like most of the English, he did not leave a gratuity.' The man sounded as if he had been personally offended.

Stone left the same message that he'd call back in an hour and hung up.

Scott-Hughes was standing just a few meters away, frowning. 'I take it that you didn't get through to Macleod?'

'Something's up and I don't like the smell of it. The desk clerk thinks Mac picked up my message but he wasn't in his room.'

Scott-Hughes checked his watch, then asked, 'How important is it that you get over to Antwerp?'

'If I possibly could, I would. I'm worried as hell. My fault in a way.'

Scott-Hughes moved to the window and glanced up at the evening sky. It was twilight, the sky a pearl gray. He nodded to himself and turned back to Stone. 'Get your kit and let's go.'

NINETEEN

The Crouch River, 21.10, 13 April

Scott-Hughes ran the engines up, checked the tachometers
for mag drop, then, satisfied, pulled the throttles back to
idle. He reached up to the overhead panel and selected the
main fuel tank, then flicked on the boost pumps and nav
lights. Adjusting his headset, he turned to Stone.

'Keep a lookout for small craft and give a shout if you
spot anything. My old eyes aren't all that good and visibility's bloody awful this time of evening. You ready?'

Squinting, Stone peered ahead, trying to judge whether
the river was clear of traffic, but he couldn't pick up any
hard shapes in the haze. Before them, the misty river
stretched out like a sheet of lead, melting into a golden-
orange dusk. Beyond that, the English Channel. And 225
kilometers beyond that, Antwerp. The light was going fast.
Stone swallowed hard and nodded.

The Mallard grudgingly accelerated, sheets of spray
thrown out, the airspeed creeping up. A rowboat with a
man and a dog in it slipped by their starboard side, not
more than twenty meters away, nearly invisible in the
dusk.

Alarmed, Stone stared at the airspeed indicator. Thirty
knots – too damned slow. He glanced at Scott-Hughes who
shook his head.

'Downwind take-off,' Scott-Hughes mumbled in the
mike, distracted. 'Had to – bend in the river back the other
way. We'll be all right . . .' He hesitated, his cheek muscles
tightening. '. . . if we can clear that bloody thing.'

Stone lifted his eyes from the instrument panel. Over

the nose, emerging from the murk ahead, spots of red and green, haloed in the mist – the oncoming navigational lights of a ship. He could just make out the superstructure: some kind of a coastal freighter.

Airspeed indicator. The needle was kicking against the forty-knot marker, then forty-five. The Mallard was on the plane, bumping off wavetops, struggling to fly.

The ship was a distinct shape now, getting larger, spreading across the windshield.

'Not in the book but . . .' Scott-Hughes reached down and stabbed a switch, at the same time yanking back on the wheel. The Mallard groaned as it lifted off, staggering into the air. Scott-Hughes instantly racked the wheel over in a steep bank, the port wingtip lifting to clear the cargo mast as they skimmed past the ship, white faces on the bridge staring up at them. Then he slammed the controls forward and rolled to the left until his wings were level. The Mallard was shuddering on the edge of an incipient stall, the nose dropping, the river coming up fast. The Mallard skip-banged off the freighter's wake with a thud, then was airborne again, slowly gaining altitude.

Scott-Hughes was breathing heavily, the sound amplified in the intercom. He milked up the flaps, slowly easing back on the power and adjusting the pitch setting. 'Only tried that once before. Not good on the old girl.'

'You dumped the flaps?'

Scott-Hughes nodded as he cranked in trim. 'Instant lift. Instant drag as well. Not exactly how they teach you to fly, but whoever said that the world's a perfect place?'

Stone was sweating, his pulse loud in his ears. He concentrated on slowing his breathing. The Mallard had leveled off, only a few hundred meters above the river.

Ahead, the black waters spread out as they opened to the sea, hazy smudges of ships' running-lights scattered across the horizon. Scott-Hughes carefully eased into a shallow bank, adjusting his course to the east-north-east.

He lowered the instrument lighting to a faint red and settled into his seat.

'We'll stay low, approach Antwerp from the south-west, then pop up to traffic-pattern altitude.' He handed Stone a WAC chart. 'Look just a bit south of the city proper – Deurne Aerodrome. When we're within ten minutes' flying distance of the place, I'll call approach control and declare an emergency. They'll have to clear me in, even though I haven't filed a flight plan – probably catch hell in the process – but I'll talk my way out of it.'

'Customs, immigration?' Stone's passport was undoubtedly flagged by Interpol and they'd nail him on the spot.

'Not to worry. I'll land short, brake to a crawl before I turn off the active onto the taxiway. You'll jump out while I'm still rolling. Off to the weeds, wait a bit, then over the fence. It's probably no more than six kilometers to the docks and you shouldn't have a problem picking up a taxi.'

'What about you?'

'I'll muddle through – claim that I was by myself in the ship, fuel-transfer pump acted up. They'll let me off with a rap on the knuckles.'

Stone checked his watch – 21.21. Say an hour and ten minutes to Deurne, another half-hour into town if he could find a cab. He'd be at the hotel by 23.00. Stone prayed to whatever god was listening that Mac would be all right until then.

'How are you set for money, Stone?'

Not good but he could impose on Scott-Hughes only so much. 'I've got enough.'

'Behind you, in the back seat. Leather briefcase, inside left-hand compartment. There's a thousand pounds; always carry a bit of cash in case the plastic's not wanted. Take it.'

'Nigel – I can't . . .'

'*Take it!* Last thing you need is to run out of money.' Scott-Hughes dug down in the map compartment and pulled out the handi-talkie. 'Take this as well and stuff it in your case. It might take a bit of time to sort things out, but when you and your Scottish friend want to get out of Belgium, I can come and pick you up. Plenty of inland waters, lakes and such. You'll need to contact me to coordinate the pickup. Starting tomorrow morning, from ten in the morning onward until sundown, call on Channel 83. We'll use Mallard and *Snow Goose* as call-signs.'

'This thing can't possibly have the range to reach England.'

'Its range is limited to line-of-sight, but if I'm at 10,000 feet, I should be able to receive you from anywhere in the Lowland countries, provided you're in the clear.'

Stone slid the handi-talkie into Joss's attaché case, along with the cash, and pulled the zipper closed. Scott-Hughes might be a geriatric but he obviously had his act together. *My act, as well*, Stone realized.

'Where will you stay tonight, Nigel?'

'At the aerodrome. Holiday Inn. Call me there on the telephone if you're all sorted out by morning and we'll work out when and where to pick up the two of you. As I best recall, the Gat van Ossenisse estuary would be a suitable place.'

Scott-Hughes reached up and adjusted the elevator trim, then turned to Stone and grinned. 'Had a thought. If we can sort this business out by tomorrow, what say you and your lady join me for dinner. We'll make it a bit of a celebration. There's an old girl I fancy who might make it a foursome. Been courting her for three years now and have yet to get into her knickers. Calls me "Hot Screws" − very naughty, understand? − but she's a good sort.'

Tomorrow night. Best not to forget the champagne and roses, then let the old hormones take their course. 'Could we make it the night after, Nigel? Melissa and I had, uh . . . plans.'

Scott-Hughes was staring straight ahead, smiling. 'She's

quite lovely, Stone. I shouldn't wonder that you have *plans*. Shouldn't wonder at all.'

At 22.16, Scott-Hughes declared an emergency but declined the offer of an ambulance and crash vehicles. They touched down at 22.27, the amphibian's wheels squeaking lightly on the concrete.

It had all worked like a charm, with the exception of Stone's shoulder getting lanced by nettles and his hands being skinned on the fence. He crouched in tall grass for a few minutes, watching the Mallard waddle up the taxiway and disappear behind a row of hangars, then headed through a grove of trees toward a roadway where car headlights flickered.

Wary of being dumped in front of the hotel and possibly tipping the opposition, Stone paid off the taxi in the Grote Markt, and armed with a sketch-map supplied by the cabby, headed for Mac's hotel on Kloosterstraat. The area was wall-to-wall Renaissance, the peaks of the buildings crowded with statues. There were bronze horses rearing, stone saints imploring and gilded nymphs smirking, a mix and match of statuary which seemed it had been sculpted for the benefit of the local pigeons and the Kodak Corporation.

Stone mixed with the crowd, occasionally checking back for a tail, a little paranoid. The place was crowded, mainly tourists milling about, tramping on each other's toes, snapping pictures of the statuary, and probably getting their pockets picked.

He reached the western perimeter of the square and crossed over into Kloosterstraat. It was a narrow lane lined on both sides with low stone buildings, mom-and-pop stores on the street level with apartments over them. Different crowd entirely — mainly university students who were bar-hopping, hustling each other, kidding around, and arguing politics in three languages.

Stone ducked into a second-hand shop and bought a knapsack, black wire-rimmed sunglasses and a beret, on the theory that it would disguise his identity, make him look more European, not so obviously *American*. Outside the shop, he stuffed Joss's attaché case into the knapsack and slung it on his back, then checked out his disguise in the plate-glass window of a darkened chocolate shop.

The effect was that of an aging hippy who had probably slept through the upward-mobility lectures at the Harvard Business School. Still, the glasses hid his eyes, the beret covered his hair, and the knapsack gave him a vague student status. Not bad, he thought, adjusting the beret over his forehead, but he could faintly hear the inner man snickering.

The hotel was a four-story walk-up affair; neat but getting shabby around the edges. The desk clerk who checked him in was an old, stick-like creature who spoke passable English and chain-smoked Gitanes filters. Undoubtedly the night-shift clerk, and by his slightly Germanic accent, obviously not either of the two desk clerks with whom Stone had spoken over the phone. Stone scanned the pigeon-holes for number 303, Mac's room. The key was missing and there was no message slip in the box. Bad karma.

He checked in under the name of 'Talisker'. The master plan was to shift Mac immediately to his own room, then call Scott-Hughes at the Holiday Inn and set up an early-morning pickup.

Once out of sight of the desk, Stone double-timed it up the stairs to the third floor. The corridor was empty, just the sound of a television from behind one of the closed doors. He knocked lightly on the panel of 303. 'Mac . . . ? It's me, Stone.'

Silence, then a muffled voice, a woman's, speaking to someone else. Then a male voice, the creak of bedsprings.

A balding man with a dense mat of body hair and a sheet wrapped around his waist cracked open the door and squinted out, obviously puzzled, then even more obviously pissed off.

'Sorry to bother you,' Stone whispered. 'I was, ah, looking for a Mr Macleod. About this tall, a Scotsman. Thought this was his room.'

The man made a rude gesture with his finger, swore at Stone in French and slammed the door in his face.

Something was very wrong and Stone's guts were churning. He tried the desk clerk again. 'You have a Mr Macleod registered here?'

Suspicious. 'You are asking why?' He methodically ground out his cigarette in a dirty ashtray.

Stone pushed a five-pound note across the desk. 'Just that I'm a friend of his. We were going to meet here. He was in room 303.'

The man took the banknote, expertly snapped it, folded it neatly and slid it into his shirt pocket behind the pack of Gitanes.

'He is with us, but in a different room. We moved him because he did not like the noise his neighbors were making. But now, he is out. He was looking for a drink . . .' The man grinned mechanically, revealing hideous teeth. '. . . And perhaps a woman, I think.'

'Any idea where he went?'

The desk clerk stood motionless, his face blank, looking through Stone. Then his eyes briefly dipped to his shirt pocket.

Stone sighed and peeled off another five-pound note.

'I recommended a place near the docks that the English sailors favor – a place on Oude Leeuwenrui that's known as the Comic Strip. Three hundred brands of beer and the women are *very* clean.' He made it sound as if the ladies of the establishment had all been awarded the Belgian State Seal of Purity.

'How long ago?'

Without moving his head, the man rolled his eyes up at the wall clock. 'A short time before you came, one half of an hour, I think. You would want me to call a taxi?'

But Stone was already out the door, running.

*

The clerk slumped down at his desk and pulled a slip of paper from the drawer, laid it out next to the telephone, fitted his glasses over his nose and dialed.

A man answered, repeating the telephone number.

'There was a man asking for Herr Macleod,' the clerk said in Flemish-accented German. 'He appears to be the same one that called twice before, asking for Macleod. I sent him to the place that you specified.'

A voice on the other end of the line asked a question.

The desk clerk said, 'I am sure he is the same one. He gave his name as "Talisker".'

The voice asked another question.

'No, he has just left the hotel. As we agreed, the information is worth 2000 marks, correct?'

The voice replied with one syllable and the connection was severed.

The clerk managed a thin smile. In the New World Order, information was the most valuable commodity.

The Comic Strip was a cave-like dump – long, narrow, dark and smelling of stale beer. The floors were laid with cracked tile, incredibly filthy. The walls were plastered over with fading comic strips, most of the characters sexually enhanced with giant genitalia which, presumably, the clientele had added over the years. On the left, a battered bar ran the length of the room. A postage-stamp-sized stage was jammed in the back as an afterthought where, under a red spotlight, a frizzled-haired hag with sagging breasts was gyrating through a badly coordinated bump and grind to the recorded strains of 'Stormy Weather'. The cigarette smoke in the room was thick enough to blow the bejesus out of a smoke detector. The rest of the floor space was littered with rickety chairs and kiddy-scale tables, each illuminated with a fat candle burning within a red glass globe, casting the entire room in a sickly rose hue.

Stone paused in the doorway. Not Mac's kind of pub at

all, he reckoned. Yet, there was a chance that Mac had set up a meeting here with someone who had information to peddle.

He scowled, trying to make out the features of the few customers sitting around, but there was so little light it was impossible. And although, according to the desk clerk, Mac had a half-hour lead on him, it might be that he hadn't even arrived yet, assuming he had walked or taken the tram. Given Mac's pinch-penny mentality, that was a distinct possibility.

Stone decided to establish his base camp near the door, then casually explore the length of the room. If Mac wasn't here, which seemed more than likely, he'd wait for an hour, and if he didn't show up he'd grab a taxi back to the hotel and wait outside in the street.

He took the third table in from the door, a good perch from which to check out who came in and/or left. A waiter appeared out of the gloom and Stone asked for mineral water. Not answering, the waiter sucked his teeth, pencil poised, waiting. Stone settled for a beer.

His eyes were slowly adjusting to the darkness and he looked around. Standing within earshot at the bar and jawing with each other were two sailors in filthy watch-coats, probably Aussies by their accent. The bar in front of them was littered with empty beer bottles and a smoldering ashtray. An emaciated girl in a dirty lemon jumpsuit with the zipper down to *here* ghosted by them, drawing her arm along one of the sailor's shoulders as she passed. The taller Aussie casually slapped her on the buns and told her to fuck off. The girl laughed in a tired way and took the Aussie's lighted cigarette from the ashtray before moving on, as if both she and the sailor had been through this routine before.

The waiter eventually arrived with a beer and took a five-pound note in exchange. From the blank look on his face, Stone had a premonition that he wouldn't see any change.

He had been sitting at his table for ten minutes when the door at the front entrance scraped open, then rasped shut. There was a subdued exchange in French, the scrape of chairs, a shifting of clothing, the clearing of a throat.

Stone glanced around, trying to keep it casual.

They stopped talking and glanced at him, then looked harder. The older guy remained expressionless but the younger one slowly smiled through barely opened lips, eyes dead, his right hand starting rhythmically to close and open, as if he were squeezing an invisible rubber ball.

Stone felt his throat constrict.

The older guy was heavy-set, had a deeply lined face and a beaked nose. He wore a rumpled sports jacket, a brown shirt and black tie. A chunky gold watch flashed from his wrist.

The younger one, a brush-cut blond with watery eyes, wore jeans and a fringed leather jacket over a rayon shirt that was buttoned to his throat. As Stone watched, mesmerized, the blond lazed back in his chair and slid his legs out, heels scraping along the floor. His feet were encased in alligator-skin boots with shiny steel toe-caps. The impression was a sure-enough, shit-kickin' urban cowboy. Cowboy smiled again, lips curled, teeth set hard together and so white they had to be mail-order.

On Stone's back was the knapsack. Within the knapsack was a canvas attaché case. And within that, the Beretta. Stone pondered the wisdom of getting the weapon and decided to make a go for it. He casually started to shrug off the straps, then froze when the Beak shook his head in a no-no while casually lifting the lapel of his sports jacket. Beneath the lapel was a shoulder holster which encased a monster Magnum revolver of the type favored by gun nuts who get off on pulverizing slabs of marble as a weekend hobby. Stone briefly reflected that imported American TV violence had corrupted the civility of Europeans to a degree greater than was generally recognized by contemporary sociologists.

His palms were sweaty, his knees gelatin. The Beretta was inaccessible for now. *Yell for the cops?* He couldn't, at least not just yet. If they got their hands on him, he'd end up in the clink for the rest of his natural-born, but it was still an option if things got out of hand, infinitely preferable to dying.

Run? The goons weren't going to kill him in here, but once he was out that door Cowboy would make dog meat out of him with those shiny steel-capped boots. 'A mugging,' the cops would call it.

The Aussies? They were his only ticket out of here – just amble over to the bar, buy a round, chum it up with them. Then suggest that they call a cab and hit a fancy club with their rich American mate volunteering to pick up the tab. The theory – simplicity itself – was based on safety in numbers.

His cogent analysis of the safety-in-numbers theory was blown as Cowboy began to circulate through the bar, apparently well known to the clientele. In less than five minutes – save for the Aussies who were now deep into a drunken shoving-match about who was going to pay for the next round – the remaining patrons hurriedly finished off their drinks, paid up and left.

The dancer packed it in as well. With the screech of a phonograph needle slewing across a record, the music abruptly died, the spotlight flickered out, and the hag evaporated behind the curtain with a hasty grind of her pelvis as the act's finale.

Cowboy was good, undoubtedly did contract jobs as his primary occupation. Stone watched as Cowboy gave a short stack of francs to the bartender, then leaned over and whispered to one of the Aussies. The Aussie grinned broadly, then whispered to his mate in a stage whisper.

The mate was less discreet. He lifted his beer bottle to Cowboy, then turned to Stone.

'Randy bugger, aren't you, mate? Not fair dinkum to

screw the man's Sheila without his go-ahead. Likely to lose your teeth, you are, lad.'

Stone knew the Aussies would be gone in a few minutes, once they finished their beer. The bartender had already scooped the cash out of the till and had headed for the stage, in pursuit of the hag, safety or both. The waiter was long gone.

He had less than a minute now, Stone reckoned. They'd do it in here at their leisure, then toss him in the alley, maybe a Magnum-caliber bullet up his ear to be sure.

Not Brunner's people, Stone guessed. Local lads, undoubtedly goons for hire, but that probably meant that one of Brunner's people was still around, had watched the hotel or had been tipped off by the desk clerk, then had laid on the party.

He slowly edged his chair around so he was facing the Beak. The Beak was tipped back in his chair, one shoe up on the table, relaxed. He lifted his glass in an ironic salute and cordially leered at Stone.

The Aussies were over Stone's right shoulder, still at the bar, with Cowboy lighting a round of cigarettes, all three of them laughing.

It was time to think about getting out of here. Stone calculated that it was a good twelve strides to the door – say three seconds minimum, five max.

He kept his body movements calm, his face blank, and took inventory.

Glass ashtray with half a dozen stubbed-out cigarettes in it. The ashtray wasn't heavy enough.

The beer bottle was more promising as a weapon but he discounted it, not sure that he could throw it accurately enough to take out the Beak.

Use a chair? Slightly better, but he had to fight on two flanks, to slow down both the Beak and the Cowboy at the same time. Once on the street with a head start, he'd have a chance.

He looked down at the red globe which glowed on his

390

table – the kind you found in a zillion cheap bars. The candle was guttering and had probably been burning for a long time. A pool of molten wax filled the bottom of the globe.

He picked the longest butt from the ashtray, straightened it and stuffed it between his lips, then lifted the globe to light it.

Out of the corner of his eye, he could see that the Aussies were draining the last from their bottles. The Cowboy was slapping one of the Aussies on the back, encouraging him to finish up.

The Beak was still tipped back in his chair. His eyes clouded momentarily as Stone lit the cigarette. The Beak, maybe dim-witted but with street savvy enough to sense that something was about to happen, started to lift his foot off the table when Stone lunged, knocking his own table into the Beak's, setting up a chain reaction which toppled the Beak backwards. Stone was on his feet, accelerating.

The Cowboy shouted something in French. Stone ignored him, his eyes on the prize. The Beak had neatly broken his fall, rolling sideways on the tiles, coming up roses. His hand was inside his jacket, the gun starting to come out.

With a slashing movement, Stone threw the molten wax in the Beak's face, then hurled the globe to the floor, leaping over it as it shattered, his left hand dragging a chair into the path to his rear.

Behind him, the Beak howled.

Stone made it to the door, had it open wide enough when the upper panel exploded in a spray of splinters. Stone dove, ricocheting off the concrete sidewalk, rolling, the knapsack taking the shock. Another blast, the spang of a bullet, splatters of concrete shards in his face, then, behind him, boot leather grating on the glass fragments. The Cowboy must have slipped because his shout screeched upward by four octaves into a falsetto scream.

Ten strides, fifteen, thirty, the hollow in his back aching

from the impact of the bullet he knew was coming, fifty strides, pick 'em up, lay 'em down, half a block, the wind of his passage whistling in his ears, lungs gulping.

His vision was blurred, something in his eye, the sidewalk scrapes burning his hands, his knee throbbing. He zagged to the left across the street, dodging past a panel truck, headlights in his face, brakes squealing, horn blaring.

Other side now, past a mail box, hemmed in by a warehouse front, through a pool of light from an overhead mercury streetlamp, running, digging down deep for breath. Another shot, close enough to feel the snap of a sonic shockwave, a car horn blaring behind him, the echo of his footsteps bouncing back from the warehouse walls.

Not an echo, he realized. Other footsteps, not his. Cowboy's. Gaining.

Corner coming up. Another goddamned overhead streetlight, perfect target. No good heading straight, easy shot. Have to turn.

Pounding footsteps behind him, sprinting, close, *damned close*, could hear the guy huffing air, that close. No time to get the Beretta.

He clawed at the brick of the building when he hit the corner and used it as a pivot to swing to the left, jammed on the brakes, hung a 180 U-turn, cranked his head down and charged.

Cowboy, one side of his face smeared with blood, was off balance, banking for the turn when Stone hit him hard amidships. They both went down in a jumble of windmilling arms and legs, Cowboy's gun clattering to the pavement.

Cowboy rolling over, on his feet like a cat, switchblade out and coming on like gangbusters, the bastard *grinning*.

Stone backed off and pivoted, the glitter of the knife flashing past his shoulder, slicing into the knapsack.

Cowboy overshot, stopped, then came back toward him,

slowly, deliberately this time, the knife point describing bright circles.

Cowboy hesitated for a second, then pulled a circular gold object on a chain out of his jacket pocket and momentarily dangled it in front of Stone, then jammed it back in his jacket. 'Now, the turn is yours, *mon ami*,' the Cowboy whispered. His mouth was bleeding and he spit blood. He shuffled sideways on the balls of his feet, lowered the tip of the blade to gut level, then lunged.

Stone danced backwards in a two-step as the blade whispered past his belly, then rammed his body forward, his hands going for Cowboy's arm. Elbow in his face, hot breath on his neck, the stench of garlic, Cowboy's knee battering into his crotch, both of them going down again, rolling, locked together.

In the distance, feet pounding, one of the Aussies shouting to the other. Stone caught a glimpse of their bodies strobing through the streetlight forty meters away, the Beak just behind them.

Stone had never tried it, just seen it done once by a logger in a Maine bar-brawl. Cowboy's face was inches from his own, his teeth gritted, hand tearing at Stone's throat. Stone smashed his forehead against Cowboy's nose, the pain stunning, a thousand brightly spangled points of light bursting in his head.

Cowboy squealed, the switchblade clattering to the concrete, blood gushing from his nostrils, clapping both his hands over his face. He rolled away from Stone, pulling his knees up against his chest, sobbing from deep back in his throat as if he couldn't get enough air.

Stone rolled off him, staggered to his feet and leaned down. He grabbed the switchblade and dug into Cowboy's pocket, his fingers connecting with the watch. He pocketed it, then stumbled into the darkness, trying to run, his legs rubbery.

It was a long alley, hemmed in by the brick walls of two-story buildings, just wide enough for a small truck to transit. The place smelled of rotting garbage and rancid cooking-oil. He chanced it and looked back over his shoulder as he ran. The two Aussies had pulled up under the streetlight and were bending over the Cowboy, the Beak lumbering up seconds later.

Stone's head was still muzzy but clearing. He picked up the pace into a ragged shamble, his knee throbbing with pain. At the far end of the darkened alley in front of him, perhaps 300 meters away, he could see the occasional blur of a car sweeping under a corner streetlight. Make it to there and turn right on the main street. Run to the next intersection and turn again. Keep going in the maze of streets until he lost them. The laws of probability would eventually confound his pursuers. Clever, clever Stone, he thought. Then the thought of the gold watch in his pocket sobered him.

He glanced back again. A cluster of shapes backlit by the streetlight coming at him. But not running. Spread out, methodical, walking, as if they somehow knew they had trapped him.

He had sixty, maybe seventy meters' head start and was gaining. He slowed down, trading time for distance, shrugging off the knapsack, digging out the attaché case and retrieving the Beretta. Cool, hefty, solid metal in his hand. How many rounds left in the clip? – thirteen, he guessed, not able to remember exactly. He chambered a round.

They didn't know he was armed, showed it by their casual confidence. He thought of snapping off a shot over their heads but discounted it. He might need an edge later on.

He picked up his pace to a steady jog, conserving energy but covering ground. Now less than 200 meters to the intersection ahead of him. He twisted his head, checking over his shoulder for a second time. His lead had opened up even more, perhaps as much as a hundred meters.

Running blind, his body brushed a garbage can, knocking it aside, the sound overly loud in the restricted passage.

A muffled voice off to the right asked something in French. Stone froze, crouched, listening.

Another voice, arguing. Both voices coming from a recess in the brick walls that had been almost unnoticeable in the dim light. Stone kept his head down, the Beretta ready, and edged to the corner of the recess.

Not a recess – actually a T intersection in the alley which serviced a narrow walkway between the buildings. The walkway terminated about thirty meters away in a set of steps and a door, probably a service entrance of some sort. On the left side of the walkway were a couple of windows whose glass panes had been painted over but were opaque enough to allow a dim light from within the building to illuminate the walkway.

A lighter flared. Two men were standing together near the end of the walkway under one of the windows. One of them lit the other's cigarette, then his own. In the brief flare, Stone saw that both of them were shabbily dressed, one in a jogging suit and watch cap, the other in an ill-fitting army overcoat and baseball cap. Bums smoking dope, Stone guessed, not a problem.

He looked back. Four of them now. The Beak had recruited the Aussies and, somehow, the Cowboy was still functioning after a fashion. Not hard to understand why the Aussies, three sheets to the wind and out for a lark, had bought into a story about a maiden wronged and *machismo* sullied. Actually, astounding to learn first-hand that chivalry was not dead in Aussieland.

The four of them had paused, jabbering among themselves. Good, Stone thought. Their indecision increased his lead.

Stone kept low and silently eased past the walkway, then headed for the far end of the alley, now less than 100 meters ahead. He kept to the sides of the alley, picking up the pace. The streetlight at the end would silhouette him, and the boys behind him might chance a shot if he wasn't careful. Less than eighty meters now and he would be able to evaporate into the winding city streets, maybe find an all-night theater, disappear, vanish.

Seventy meters. Headlights turning into the alley. A van, either cream-colored or light gray. A Toyota? But all vans looked alike to him, couldn't be sure. The van braked and the headlights died but no one got out. Just sat there, like a toad waiting for the fly.

Stone stopped dead, trapped.

He looked back. The four of them were still coming but not rushing it, confident of the squeeze play.

No escape upwards. The alley was solid brick, the walls windowless, no bloody fire escapes – didn't Antwerp have any goddamned fire codes, for chrissake? – no doors – *except in the walkway!*

He sprinted back, careened off the same garbage can and swung into the walkway. He figured he had less than twenty seconds.

The two men were still there. They shrank back from him, the one in the oversized greatcoat raising his hands over his head in surrender. Then Stone suddenly realized that they weren't men, just kids in their teens; hollow faces, unshaven, unbelievably grubby, stinking of crack, puke and body sweat.

Stone shoved past them, grabbed the door and yanked. It didn't yield, locked tight.

Stone pivoted and waved the Beretta at them. 'Open the fucking door! *NOW!*'

The kids were immobilized, their eyes blank, the thousand-yard stare.

From the corner of his eye, Stone noticed a thin sliver of light spilling on the windowsill. The blackish-green painted window was open at the bottom, a protective metal grill swung back to expose it. He tried raising it. The sash edged up a hair. It figured. The kids hadn't come through the door but had used the window to get out of the building! Undoubtedly homeless, they probably lived in the building or used it as a crack-house.

A shout echoing down the alley, a whistled reply.

If he left the kids here, they'd blab, and he needed them to show him the way through the building to an exit on the far side. Stone rammed the Beretta into the smaller one's gut. 'Through the window, *NOW!*'

The kid in the tracksuit was shaking, the other edging backwards, his hands still clawing for air.

Stone thumbed back the hammer, the click satisfyingly ominous. '*Narcs,*' Stone said, spitting out the word. 'You understand me – those guys are fuckin' *NARCS!*'

It was a word that transcended all language barriers. The Runt in the overcoat dove for the window, whipped it open and disappeared through it like smoke, Tracksuit sucking in behind him, Stone tumbling over the sill after them.

It was a basement with a single overhead light. The Runt pulled the grill shut, dropped a rusted bolt in the latching slot and slammed the window closed, locking it. With a swipe of the Beretta, Stone smashed the bulb, the filament frying in a brief flare, then dying.

Frozen in time, no one moving, just the sound of their breathing. Pounding leather on the walkway pavement, muffled voices. Sound of the door latch being rattled, then someone outside the window, shaking the grill.

'Saw the bastard, at least saw some sodding bloke. Wearing a great fuckin' coat he was.'

The other Aussie's voice. 'Weren't him, mate. Let's go. Time we packed this shit in and got outta here. Ain't no silly-assed game these wankers are playin'.' Their footsteps receded.

'No one back here, try the other side,' one of the Aussies hollered. Cowboy's voice answered, indistinct, swearing.

Long silence, just the sounds of still-ragged breathing. Then a muttered exchange in French. The Runt flicked his Bic, checked around until he found a candle which was jammed into the top of a whiskey bottle and lit it. The Runt held it up to examine Stone.

They were both eyeing him, probably trying to figure out whether they were going to rip him off or vice versa. Stone backed off four paces, stuffed the Beretta in his belt and gave them the peace sign with his fingers. His clothes were splattered with blood and solidified wax. Have to fix that.

He dug into his pocket and pulled out a five-pound note and made swapping motions with his free hand. 'Your tracksuit for my pants and shirt, savvy?' He pointed to Tracksuit's watch cap. 'That too.' He added another five.

They went for it. Stone and kids kept their distance, tossing clothes to each other across a mutually agreed-upon no-man's-land.

The sweatsuit was a near-fit, good enough for his purposes. But it was probably infested with cooties and he'd have to wash it as soon as he got the chance or get busted as a lousy indigent. That assumed he lived to see daylight.

It was time to blow town, he figured, Stone positive that there was nothing left in Antwerp for him to discover other than pain and death. The pocket watch had proved that.

To get the point across, he went through an elaborate mime, walking upstairs, peeping out windows, tippy-toeing through a doorway, exiting onto the street. He enhanced his performance with another fiver. The vacuous smiles and nudging of elbows proved that he had gotten through to them.

The kids led him through the basement, up a stairwell and into a hallway which branched off into abandoned workshops filled with rusting machinery. The place was littered with runaway kids, old men, dopers and winos — sleeping, peeing in the corners, flaked out, wrestling under blankets, heating spoons over Sterno stoves, shooting up, all of them dying inch by inch.

The Runt pointed to a door. He waved the fiver at Stone as a parting gesture. 'See ya later, dude.' It sounded mechanical, as if the kid had memorized it from a TV cartoon.

Standing in the shadow of the factory doorway, Stone

studied the nocturnal habits of Antwerp nightlife. Very little traffic except for the occasional bus and a few taxis. Across the street was a park that stretched out in a strip through several blocks. He made it to a clump of bushes, paused for a minute to make sure he hadn't been seen, then moved deeper into the trees, still paralleling the street in what he hoped was a northerly direction. Some traffic but no vans.

The park ended in a little wheel with a rim and graveled spokes, its hub a fountain. Stone ducked his head under, washed his face, then took a long drink.

Five hours to daylight, he estimated. Public transportation was out of the question but he needed wheels.

Across from the park were a couple of apartment houses. He'd probably find what he needed there. He was about to cross when he saw headlights turn out of a side street and head toward him. He waited, hanging back in the shrubbery. A gray Toyota van cruised by less than five meters beyond him, its pace slow and deliberate. Two men. He caught the driver's profile in the brief splash of street-light, then the license plate.

He was struck dumb, yet somehow wasn't; the van from Austria and the driver from hell.

Stone settled in and waited, his mind numb. He was almost positive that the driver was Joss. Still, somebody once said that you can't keep a good man down, even if he was missing a fingertip. What did the politically correct call it now in this age of touchy-feely newspeak? – physically challenged digital impairment? Probably.

Minutes later, the van returned from the same direction it had originally come from. Stone figured that they were cruising in circles, working their way outward in an expanding search pattern. He waited until the van turned down a side street, then legged it across the street.

He found four of them in the second apartment's vesti-bule, all ten-speeds. Three of them were secured by plastic-covered chains led through their rear wheels, but the fourth – probably owned by a nose-thumbing individualist with no understanding of parts interchangeability – was secured through the front wheel. It took him less than three minutes to swap parts.

Wheeling the hybrid bike on foot, he headed down the side street. He crossed over two more streets, then saw headlights and threw the bike over a low, spiked fence and ducked into a basement doorway. But it was an old VW with the radio cranked up, a girl driving.

He hit a major street and chanced it, pedaling hard, hunched over, making fabulous time. Twenty minutes later, he rolled into a lorry stop. Inside, he bought a flashlight, a roll of electrician's tape, four sets of batteries, a plastic bottle of detergent, a map of the Lowlands, a half-kilo of sausage and a flask of coffee.

Back out in the parking lot, he loaded the batteries in the flashlight and played it over the map, working out a back-road route to the sea. It would be a long night and a longer day.

Before mounting up, he looked once again at Mac's watch. The glass was cracked and smeared with blood, the hands frozen at 23.09.

TWENTY

Stone pedaled through the night, heading north and west on a network of secondary roads. He had taped the flashlight to the handlebars, but there was enough moonlight and he was able to keep it turned off for most of the time, except in the villages where he suspected that a cyclist cruising without lights would tweak the curiosity of the local constabulary. He needn't have bothered — the windows dark and secret, the cops in their jammies, cuddled up to their wives, probably dreaming of busting the chops of itinerant gypsies and unlicensed fruit peddlers or whatever it was that good Belgian cops dreamed of.

His route took him through the outskirts of Antwerp, then north toward the Dutch border. The map showed an area near the Belgian town of Clinge where roads on both the Belgian and Dutch sides of the border paralleled each other, no more than a kilometer apart and without any trace of an interconnecting road — and consequently, no likely border-crossing checkpoint. Since 1993, all border formalities in the EC had been theoretically discontinued, but Stone wasn't about to bet his personal freedom on it.

Near Clinge, he dismounted, lifted the bike over a stone wall and walked it through a rough pasture splattered with cow pies, until he intersected another road. It didn't smell different and he couldn't sense any change, however subtle, but his map professed to the sacred gods of Michelin that he was now standing on Dutch territory.

As he pedaled west, his mind kept drifting to Mac. Not that the gold watch proved anything other than Cowboy

401

and the Beak had grabbed Mac and that noses got bloodied in the process. They would cart him off to someplace remote to interrogate him, of course, and that argued against them killing Mac until he had exhausted his reserves. The Scot was tough, Stone told himself – could hang in there for at least twenty-four hours of grilling. The bloody, hopeless trick was to find where Mac was before those twenty-four hours ran out.

Still, the memory of the Cowboy's brief taunt still haunted him – 'Now, the turn is yours, *mon ami.*' Turn for what? He didn't dwell on it, couldn't.

He passed through Sluiskil at 03.50. Lights were on in some of the cottages, farmers and tradesmen yawning and scratching as they groped their way to the lavatory, women making breakfast, packing lunches, looking forward to the blessed peace that descended when the old man left the house for the day.

On the outskirts of Sluiskil he found a darkened gasoline station which had an outside water faucet. He stripped off his jogging-suit and underwear, saturated them with detergent, then scrubbed them under the tap, bubbles flying. Next, he splashed water on his goose-pimpled body and squeegeed it off with his hands. He hung his underwear over the handlebar to dry, wrung out the jogging-suit and shrugged into it, then mounted up and pedaled furiously, hoping his body heat would dry the thing. Terrific plan, except that the soggy fleecewear chafed at his crotch. He stopped and padded his privates with the watch cap, the effect of the woolly material like dull sandpaper. At least, he reflected, it kept him awake – something that was becoming increasingly more difficult.

The jogging-suit was damp-dry when he rolled into the outskirts of Breskens, a small town that overlooked the Westerschelde Estuary. He checked his watch. It was 05.10. Stapled on the inside of the map was a timetable for ferries, the first one at 08.00. Stone found a footpath which wandered down to a little stream behind a row of lindens. He set the alarm on his watch for 07.30, then flopped down on the bank facing east where the rising sun would dry him. For a few minutes, his mind fogged with fatigue, he gnawed on the sausage, then passed out, the partially masticated mouthful of meat as yet unswallowed.

He woke to the watch alarm beeping, the sun hot in his eyes, bits of sausage greasy in his mouth. His legs were aching, his testicles raw, his face unshaven, his hair matted. He knew he looked like a bum, felt like a bum and, by most reasonable definitions, was one.

After coasting down through the cobbled lanes of the whitewashed village, he slowly pedaled toward the parking lot that fed the ferry, pausing at the top of a small knoll which overlooked it.

His map had shown that there were five choke-points between Antwerp and Holland: constrictions through which anyone attempting to move north into the Netherlands would have to pass. The obvious ones were the A18 and two other secondary roads that passed through Essen and Putte. The fourth and fifth choke-points were the two ferries that crossed the Westerschelde Estuary at Perkpolder and here at Breskens. Last night in Antwerp, Stone had chosen the Breskens ferry route because it was the furthest to the west, almost on the North Sea, and consequently the least likely for a sane man on foot to have chosen because of its roundabout route. Of course, what the opposition didn't know was that they were dealing with a man of questionable sanity – Stone's secret weapon.

The burning question was whether Brunner had enough resources to cover all five exits. Somehow, Stone had no doubts that he did. There seemed a pattern to the way Brunner operated. He undoubtedly had a sizable gang of full-timers working for him, but when the situation required, it appeared that he pulled in local talent. Made sense, Stone realized. Keep the corporate payroll lean by hiring temporary workers when the workload demanded it. At least he had to give Brunner high marks for his management style.

The parking lot was empty, the few vehicles bound for the Netherlands already queueing up in the ship-boarding lanes beyond the toll booth. They looked harmless: only two cars, both driven by women, a flower-delivery van and a bread truck. But no gray van.

Stone paid the sixteen-guilder fee with a twenty-pound note, got ripped off on the exchange rate, protested, was met with stony silence, then, nursing his outraged sense of justice, wheeled toward a kiosk that was selling snacks. Ganged around the kiosk were a couple of dozen young cyclists, all of them probably kids on an early summer holiday, the majority of them decked out in Spandex neon-hued cycling gear. Their bikes were crammed with stuff; sleeping-bags strapped on rear wheel-racks, saddlebags bulging, electronic performance gizmos studding their handlebars, blaze-orange flags whipping from fiberglass staffs. Neat, Stone supposed, if you took pedaling down a road all that seriously. By comparison, he felt as if he had just pedaled out of the Stone Age, his bike lacking even a minimal degree of sophistication.

A chubby, cherub-cheeked matron behind the counter wiped her dimpled hands on her apron and studied Stone, obviously displeased that the Dutch immigration authorities were actually allowing people like *this* into her country.

His mouth was salivating. He got coffee, then picked out a handful of pastries, two bananas and a Tetra-pak of orange juice. He had to flash a ten-guilder note before she would hand over his selections. The woman examined the bill minutely, wrinkled her nose, then finally handed him the change.

He retired to the far side of the kiosk, demolishing the sticky buns and gulping coffee while he watched the approach road from the village.

Two girls in tight-fitting Lycra cycling outfits with nylon rain jackets rolled up and tied around their waists sauntered past him, one chatting rapidly, the other giggling in response. They each bought a box of raisins. When they passed him again, the one closest to him threw him a glance, neither hostile nor inviting, more out of curiosity than anything else. Stone grinned at her, a real beamer. She hesitated for a split second, then smiled back, her face fresh and open. 'Good day to you,' she said, her Irish accent softening the consonants.

'And good day to you, miss,' Stone replied with all the gallantry he could muster, wishing he had something more than a watch cap to doff.

The girls — whoops, the politically correct terminology was now *women* — who were probably not more than twenty-five, rejoined two wiry young men and the four of them lazed around, sharing the raisins and a bottle of milk as they watched the ferry approach the slip. They were totally at ease with themselves, giddy with life, eternally young, and seemingly invulnerable to the process of corporal decay. Stone found it hard to believe he had ever been that young, that innocent, or that invulnerable.

The ferry had just docked, cars beginning to disgorge. Stone finished off the second banana, getting ready to join the line-up of cyclists marshaling near the boarding-ramp.

Out of habit, he checked over his shoulder toward the village.

Beyond the fence, in the long-term parking lot that fronted the ticket booth, an Opel sedan had just driven up. Two men got out. The heavier one wore a large collar-brace around his neck, the younger one — a crew-cut blond in jeans and a fringed leather jacket — wore binoculars around his. The lenses glinted in the low morning sun as they swept the boarding-area.

Stone froze, edging back, putting the kiosk between him and the Cowboy.

The cyclists were getting ready, checking the straps on their saddlebags, adjusting bedrolls, joking amongst themselves. The girl who had smiled at him came over to the kiosk, her eyes slightly averted, the empty bottle of milk in her hand. She slipped it into one of the empty milk crates and started back toward her bike.

'Could I bother you a moment, miss?'

She turned to him, hesitating a heartbeat, a little embarrassed. 'I'm afraid that I have no time, sir. I must go.'

So must I, Stone thought. But not on a one-way trip with Cowboy and the Beak.

'I would like to ask a favor of you. From where you're standing, can you see those two men in the upper parking lot?'

She glanced up, then nodded.

'They're looking for me, miss. They would dearly love to tear my leg off and beat me over the head with the bloody stump. I, on the other hand, have grown attached to my leg. Would it be possible to borrow your cycling jacket and cap, then have you walk with me to your group where all of us, like old chums, will pedal over to the ferry and board it?'

'They are the constabulary, the police?'

'No. They are wanted by the police. They will be wanted even more by the police if they have their way with me.'

She smiled at him – soft, lovely green eyes, teeth the color of milk, the glow of ripe Irish peaches in her complexion – not quite sure that she should take him seriously. She brushed her red hair out of her eyes. Her face clouded momentarily. 'You're being honest with me, are you?'

'Totally.' He made a big deal about crossing his heart. 'It was an affair willingly entered into by two consenting adults hopelessly in love. The younger man you see up there – the one dressed like the Sundance Kid – believed that it was his right, rather than his sister's, to give that consent. Unfortunately, he took the news of our affair badly.'

'And the other man?'

'. . . The dreaded uncle, a blackhearted and vindictive man if there ever was.'

406

She studied his eyes for a moment, then said, 'I don't believe a word you say except that you're in trouble not of your own doing.' She smiled again. 'Come on with you. We'll see you aboard the ship but nothing more, understood?'

Stone, a Dublin Cycling Union jacket on his back and a Guinness Stout cap crammed on his head, joined the Irish Gang of Four.

The girl, whose name it turned out was Trish, held a brief huddle with the other three. The men seemed less than enthusiastic, but the other girl, Erin, seemed caught up in the game and took to Stone, draping her arm around his waist, chatting him up.

Along with a dozen or so other cyclists, the five of them rolled their bikes aboard and parked them in cycling storage racks, then clambered to the upper deck.

Stone hung back, using the Irish as a shield, trying to spot the Cowboy.

The Opel was still in the parking lot, someone now behind the wheel. Stone squinted against the hard glare of the morning sun. It was the Beak. You couldn't miss the nose. A plume of exhaust trailed from the Opel, probably getting ready to pull out. Stone's heart soared.

Then plummeted as he scanned the path between the parking lot and the ship. The Cowboy was at the snack kiosk talking to the fat lady who apparently sang, because Cowboy wheeled and started legging it toward the boarding-ramp, the binoculars slung by a strap around his neck banging against his chest, a fierce grimace of triumph on his face. The boarding-barrier was already down, the ferry hooting three blasts, the propellers churning muddy water, lines starting to be cast off.

It was either going to be now or later, no way out of it. Stone opted for now.

He ran down the steps from the upper deck, taking them two at a time, swung past the parked vehicles, and headed for the boarding-ramp entranceway.

The Cowboy was already there, arguing with a young deckhand. The Cowboy flashed a bill.

The deckhand hesitated, only seconds to make a decision, the heavy blast of the ship's horn reverberating through the ship's structure. He looked around, probably checking to see whether his boss was looking, then gave a quick nod.

The Cowboy started up the ramp, a smile of triumph on his face. The deckhand pocketed the bill and, seconds later, vanished down a hatch.

Stone had hidden behind a steel pillar, the Beretta ready, its shape concealed beneath his jacket. The Cowboy would have to pass within a few feet of him on his way to the upper deck. Stone, knowing that he would have just this one chance, tried to slow his breathing. The plan was to bash the bastard over the head, chuck him in a convenient life-jacket locker, and let God sort out the Cowboy's vital signs.

Stone didn't hear them coming. Two young men brushed past the pillar as if they hadn't seen him, heading directly for the Cowboy.

'And what is it you want, sir?' It was the taller of the two Paddies, Kevin. His voice was reasonable, almost friendly. From Stone's hidden vantage point, he could see their backs and just part of the Cowboy's face.

The Cowboy's reply was in French, the tone contentious, touched with arrogance. He started to push past them.

Patrick, the younger Irishman, took the Cowboy firmly by the arm. 'You're mistaken, sir. There's no one of that description in our group.'

The Cowboy cursed, in two words impugning both Patrick's legitimacy and veracity. He whipped his arm from the Irishman's grasp, then backed away, putting space between him and the two men.

'Just who is it that you're really after, sir?' Kevin asked, a harder edge to his voice.

'The Ameri-*kan* . . . Stone. 'E was with you.'

So the Cowboy knew his real name. Had Brunner given them that, or had Mac? Stone thumbed back the hammer.

'And what did he do to wrong you?' Kevin said, his voice backing off to a reasonable tone, a seeker of truth. The kid would make a great diplomat, Stone thought.

'He fucked my woman.' The Cowboy's voice was aggravated, out of patience now.

Kevin's voice lifted slightly. 'Your darling wife, was it now?'

'No, not my fucking wife, you ignorant, priest-sucking *merde. Ma femme*, my woman, my whore. Move out of the way!'

Stone saw it all in slow motion, as if frames of a film were individually jerked past a lens by a defective shutter mechanism. The Cowboy's hand was moving to the inside of his jacket. Patrick moved a nanosecond later, then Kevin – plastic-covered bike chains snaking out of their sheaves, then slashing across the Cowboy's chest and arms. The Cowboy howled, stumbling backwards, a nickel-plated Derringer falling from his hand, clattering to the steel deck.

The Irish had momentum going for them, rousting the Cowboy backward toward the knee-high barrier gate. The Cowboy tried for a testicular field goal with the capped boot, but he was off balance and missed. One final push by Kevin and the Cowboy cartwheeled backward over the barrier, slithered down the edge of the boarding-ramp and into the wake.

The Irish stood leaning against the barrier, seemingly relaxed as if they were watching a sporting event, following the Cowboy's progress as he awkwardly splashed toward the shore, cheering him on. When the Cowboy finally crawled up on the beach, they nodded to each other. Patrick picked up the Derringer, tipped the barrel down, removed the shells and pocketed the weapon, then turned and headed for Stone. Kevin angled off to the right for some reason, out of Stone's sight.

'Relax. We mean you no harm,' Patrick said easily,

approaching, his hands held to his side. Too late, Stone heard the rustle of clothing behind him.

Kevin pulled the jacket down over Stone's shoulders, pinning his arms from behind. Patrick took the Beretta, expertly decocked it, and tucked it in his waistband, his jacket hiding its shape.

There was a lot of heavy breathing but Stone didn't resist and the Irish didn't push it. Kevin finally released Stone's jacket, rearranged it on his shoulders and took him gently by the elbow, guiding him toward the stairwell. 'It's time we had a serious chat, Mr Stone,' he said.

The five of them stood on the upper deck, looking past the bow toward the smudge of land in the distance. The wind was light, not more than a few white caps flecking the sea. It looked like the ferry would make the Flushing docks in less than a quarter-hour.

Stone had told them a highly edited and condensed version of the story, no more than he thought was necessary to keep them neutral and out of it. He didn't want to tangle with the Irish and, with both of the men armed, it would be damned simple for them to turn him over to the cops. He kept the emphasis on Mac's abduction and his own quest to rescue the Scot.

'. . . So I was heading up to Europort on the Hook of Holland. Small town near there called Oostvoorne, some sort of a shipyard just north of there. That's where this boat, the *Cormorant*, was hauled out and it's the most likely place for them to have taken Mac.'

Kevin looked toward the shore for a few minutes, thinking, then turned back. 'They may be waiting for you on this side,' he finally said.

'How could they?' Stone answered. 'They'd have to go the long way around; drive back to Perkpolder, wait for a ferry to Zeeland, then head west on the A58. I figure it would take them at least two hours, more likely three.'

'They could call ahead, now, couldn't they? If you're

right about this man Brunner, then he has the resources to do that.'

True. Flushing, by its profile on the horizon, looked as if it were a good-sized seaport, and Stone figured he could hole up there if he had to. The disadvantage was that Brunner had him in a box, only two roads leading out of the town. Brunner could call in as many hoods-for-hire as it took, and in the meanwhile have plenty of time to squeeze Mac to a pulp, then pull up stakes, erasing his tracks as he did.

Kevin was still studying Stone, waiting for an answer.

Stone shrugged. 'I've got to get to Oostvoorne by tonight, regardless. Otherwise, the possibility is strong that Brunner will be long gone and Mac with him. I'll try for a bus out of Flushing.' Even in his own mind, it sounded ridiculously futile.

Kevin shook his head. 'That's the first bloody place they'll check, man. That and the self-drive agencies. And you obviously can't go on the roads with your push bike – find you in less time than it takes to tell.' Kevin nudged Erin. 'My charming girl, does your foolish father still favor you with a Barclaycard?'

Erin looked at him with suspicion but nodded. 'For emergencies only. He'll cane me if I use it without good reason.'

Kevin jerked his head toward Stone. 'Do you have money with you? Say a hundred quid?'

Stone nodded. 'Enough.'

'Then Erin will rent a minivan or an estate wagon on her fantastic plastic and you'll pay her back in cash. You'll hide the push bikes in the boot, let Erin drive. Find a pharmacy and buy some shaving kit to get those whiskers off your face. Erin can loan you some clothes and a scarf, bit of lip rouge and face powder so you'll look like granny on an outing in case this Brunner chap has people on the lookout for you. You'll both motor up to Oostvoorne. Stuff Erin in a hotel room for safekeeping and then go on about your business.' He pointed to a coastal campground about three kilometers south of Oostvoorne. 'The rest of us should be able to make it most of the way up the coast today. We'll camp here at Rockanje. Erin – you meet us there tomorrow morning 'bout breakfast-time.'

Stone didn't like it. 'I don't know whether this is going to work, Kevin. Like you said, they'll check all the car rental outfits in Flushing.'

Kevin shook his head. 'No, boyo. I'm not talking about hiring a motor car in Flushing. I'm speaking of the two of you going *back* on the ferry to Breskens, then cycling to Temeuzen. There's a Eurocar self-drive firm there.'

'*Back to Breskens!*'

Kevin slowly smiled, his eyes intent on Stone's. 'Since you've just come from there, I wouldn't expect that they'd be looking for you to come back, now would they?'

'But what about the three of you? If Brunner's people are waiting, they might recognize you from the Cowboy's description.'

Kevin fetched a package of Sweet Caporals out of his jacket and lit one. He shook the match out in the wind and exhaled thoughtfully. 'Wouldn't think so. Two dozen cyclists, a good two-thirds of us lads, most of us in our twenties. They'd have a hard time sorting us out from the pack. Besides, they'll be looking for you, Stone, not for us.'

Stone had to admit that it was workable. 'Just one question: why get involved in this, Kevin?'

Kevin shrugged. 'Why not? The Irish have this bloody-minded tradition of flocking to lost causes. Yours seems to qualify quite nicely.' Kevin nodded and Patrick moved around behind Stone's back and opened the knapsack. Stone felt a heavy weight thump to the bottom – the Beretta.

'Don't think you'll need that, boyo,' Kevin said, 'but if you do, shoot straight. We'd like Erin back in one piece.'

*

The ferry returned to Breskens and docked at 09.40. Stone checked out the parking lot and boarding-area from behind the hazed glass in the passenger lounge. More cyclists, an assortment of local cars, a few people on foot, but no Beak and no Cowboy. He wheeled his bike off alone, Erin holding back and waiting for his all-clear sign. He gave the fat lady in the kiosk the finger as he cycled by, then waved his arm.

With Erin following at a discreet distance, Stone pedaled into the village, keeping to the back streets. Clean of Cowboys, as far as he could determine. Kevin had been spot on in his assessment.

He signaled her and, speeding up, she joined him. They pedaled east on a disused coastal road, tires humming, Erin teaching him the words to Irish pub songs as they went. Nice kid, he thought, the wind warm on his face. She was sexy, uncomplicated, full of fun, untroubled by the future, no hangups about the past, a true innocent. Stone could remember only one time in his life when he had felt the same – on graduation from eighth grade with a position at second base nailed down, a new Wilson glove hanging on a peg in the hallway, and the whole, glorious summer before him.

They reached Temeuzen by 10.20.

The Eurocar firm had three Fiat Pandas and a VW Passat wagon.

Stone chose the Passat on the theory that it could hide the cycles without having to disassemble them. Erin's Barclaycard and international driver's license passed muster.

They stopped at a sundry-store where Stone, feeling incredibly stupid, bought a Bic disposable shaver, shaving foam, face powder, and a white shawl with local tourist scenes silk-screened on it. To round out the effect, he tossed in a pair of yellow-tinted granny glasses.

He scraped off the whiskers while she drove, ignoring her snide remarks. His skin smooth, he then powdered his face, added the shawl, a scarf and glasses. Checking the effect in the rear-view mirror, he had to laugh. Anyone taking him for a granny had to be either blind or from outer space. Erin suggested that he plump up his 'bosom' with wads of facial tissue. Stone damn well drew the line at that one.

The traffic was light and they made good time, retracing Stone's route of the night before. Instead of going all the way into Antwerp, Erin found a bypass and angled north. They crossed the unattended border at Putte, picked up the A58 to Bergen op Zoon, then headed west on the A29. Twice, Stone thought they were being followed, but both times the cars had turned off.

Stone's watch beeped at 11.50. Nearly forgot. He motioned her to pull off the road.

'What's wrong?' she asked, downshifting.

'Nothing. Have a radio schedule.'

She batted her eyes when he pulled the handi-talkie from his knapsack. 'And who would it be you're calling on that thing?'

'A friend of mine by the name of Scott-Hughes, an Englishman.'

She pulled over on the grass near a hedgerow and got out. 'Off to spend a penny. Give the Englishman my love and remind him to get his SAS fuckers out of Northern Ireland.' She smiled wickedly. '. . . Else we shall do it for them.'

He called Scott-Hughes on the hour. No contact. He tried again at five after. Scott-Hughes came back, weak but readable. 'Snow Goose, Mallard here. Not the best . . . bit scratchy. Missed your wake-up call this morning. How's your friend and where are you?'

'Mallard, Snow Goose back. My friend got picked up by the competition. Not a good situation over here, a few people looking for me. The only thing I've got to go on is the shipyard I mentioned to you. I'm about thirty klicks south-east of the town where the yard's located. Plan to look it over by mid-afternoon. What's new on your end? Over.'

'Made a few calls from my hotel at the aerodrome last night. Contacted the brother of the chap we talked about. He proceeded to kick down some doors. Bit of a fuss going on, top people involved now, wheels in motion. They have some initial results. The fisher-bird has flown off to Norway. Over.'

Stone frowned, puzzled. 'Fisher-bird has flown . . .' The *Cormorant*, of course.

'Mallard, this is Snow Goose back. You sure of that?'

'Positive. Can't discuss it on the air. I want you to call me on the land-line as soon as possible. Over.'

'When?'

Ten, fifteen seconds drifted by, nothing from Scott-Hughes, then, 'Sorry 'bout that. Starboard engine's running a bit hot for some reason, have to look into that. When? – say two hours from now. Be back on the ground by then, so to speak, and I'll be able to make a few calls before I talk to you, get an update. Call me at my estate – hold on – better make it where I keep the plane. The oil temperature's getting a bit high and pressure's falling. Looks like my fitter will have to check it out so the seaplane base will be the best place to contact me. Do you need the number?'

'Negative – I can get it through directory enquiries. Incidentally, have you had any chance to talk to my lady?'

'Spoke to her early this morning and I'll be speaking with her before I talk to you again.' Longer pause. 'I've got to shut the starboard engine down, be a bit busy but that's all in the game. Not to worry, she's an old girl but she lumbers along just fine on one lung. I'll be talking to you soon. Cheers.'

Erin had come back and was leaning on the VW, smoking a cigarette. 'What's the drill, Yank?'

'We'll upgrade your accommodations. No youth hostel. I need a hotel room with a telephone.'

She pursed her lips, considering. 'Anything else?' She shifted her weight, thrusting her hip out, accentuating her body. An interesting crease formed in her biking shorts and Erin smiled suggestively. 'Patrick won't mind, you know, not that we'd tell him. He sports around himself.'

It had been a long time, too long, but Stone had another lady in mind. 'No, Erin,' he said, smiling, 'but don't think I wouldn't love to.'

By 13.40, Stone had checked them into a meticulously clean and overly fussy hotel called the Zeeburg. It seemed to cater to geriatrics. Wizened men and women in sun-faded linens sat on the sun porch, vacantly nodding to themselves and sipping tea. The place smelled of talcum powder, lilacs and frozen memories.

Their room was small but sunny, overlooking the hotel's lawn where some children were playing. It was furnished with an iron bedstead, a bureau and a few chairs. The adjoining bathroom had a long, deep tub with lion's-claw feet, something that must have seen the light of day long before the turn of the century. It fairly screamed to be used. Erin took one look at it and dumped her rucksack on the bed, turned on the taps, stripped down to minuscule panties and a bra, gave Stone a lovely smile, and disappeared behind the door.

Hot and achy, Stone stripped down to his jockey shorts and called Southampton directory enquiries for South Coast Aero's telephone number, then direct-dialed.

Scott-Hughes came on, his voice tired, out of sorts. 'Where are you, Stone?'

'Hotel near Oostvoorne. Sounds like you made it all right.'

'Tiresome, but I've lost engines before, more often than I can remember. Ruptured oil pipe this time around. Tommy's already digging into the engine, quite appalled that something he worked on packed it in.'

Stone had to admire a man who took the loss of an

engine so lightly. 'What's this about the *Cormorant* taking off for Norway?'

'I tried to contact Air Marshal Lindsey last night but he was off on some NATO thing, couldn't reach him, so instead I rang up his brother, Sir Alfred. Sir Alfred's a pompous, bureaucratic type with a flawed political future, but he still has bags of old-boy connections. He got on to the Foreign Office last night and they cabled their embassy in Norway – had the commercial attaché there do some checking. The attaché finally tracked your ship down in a small wrecker's yard up near Bergen. They said that the *Cormorant* came in about two days ago, right on schedule. She's being cut up for scrap as we speak.'

It couldn't be, didn't fit. Stone flopped down on the bed, cradling the phone hard against his ear, trying to shut out the sounds of children screaming on the grassy lawn below the window. 'Nigel – what about the alloy tank that was supposedly installed in the cargo hold?'

'Not on board, not part of the salvage contract. The ship's equipment list indicated that an alloy fuel tank previously installed in the cargo hold had been removed and sold to a scrapyard in Holland before the *Cormorant* sailed for Norway.'

'You have the name of that scrapyard?'

Scott-Hughes sighed, the edge of impatience in his voice. 'I can enquire but I think you're flogging a dead horse, Stone. The alloy tank's disposition is immaterial. It was the *Cormorant* we were after. And she's finished – just cut-up scrap by now.'

Dirty lyrics were wafting in from the bathroom. Stone prayed that the guests in the adjacent room were hard of hearing.

'Look, Nigel. Mac was snatched by a couple of thugs last night and they tried to grab me. Why would they still be trying to bash us up if the *Cormorant* was a blind alley?'

'They were Brunner's people?'

'Local talent is my opinion, but I'm almost positive that

417

I spotted Joss last night in Antwerp. My guess is that he was running the show.'

'*Joss!* You said he had been killed, then cremated. You're becoming paranoid.'

'But I saw him, Nigel, at least I'm pretty sure I did. He drove past me in a van, the same one he was using in Rouen.' It sounded weak, tentative, Stone realized. He had been exhausted, it had been dark, just a streetlight to see by. Yet, he was sure.

Long pause. 'I find it hard to believe, Stone. And there's one other aspect to this that's come to light, something that I couldn't discuss over the radio.' There was the tinny sound of hammering in the background, then an air-powered tool zapping off nuts. 'Are you familiar with SOSUS?'

'Just vaguely. Fill me in.'

'It's a form of acoustic-listening technology, Stone. Back in the seventies, the Americans planted hydrophones along the routes the Soviets would most likely use to run their subs into the Atlantic. Very sensitive things – could pick up the sounds of subs, identify them by characteristic noise signatures, could even determine what direction they were going and how fast they were moving. Obviously, the SOSUS sensors could pick up anything else – whales passing gas, shrimp chirping, the lot.'

'I've got the picture, but what's that got to do with the current situation?'

Scott-Hughes put his hand over the mouthpiece and shouted something, then came back. 'Sorry about that. Tommy had a question for me. Let's see – we were talking about SOSUS. Sir Alfred rang Scotland Yard, much against my wishes. Claimed there was no sense in half-measures. As a consequence, a very senior man from Special Branch by the name of Cartwright drove down from London this morning – arrived just minutes after I arrived back from Antwerp. They've got this thing in hand, Stone, and Cartwright took great pains to lay out what they're doing – to convince me so that I could convince you not to muck up their investigation.'

'Seems to me that, to date, they've done bugger all.'

'You're wrong. They've taken the potential threat to the Chunnel quite seriously. Cartwright told me that the Euro-tunnel people installed a string of hydrophones along the Chunnel route over four years ago. Every hundred meters, from one side of the Channel to the other. They obviously seem to have anticipated in their original security planning that there was the possibility of an attack on the Chunnel from the seabed. Cartwright told me that the Eurotunnel people would be able to pinpoint immediately any attempt by divers or a drilling rig to scour out the boreholes or drill new ones.'

'And let me guess. The hydrophones over the crossover cavern are out of action.'

'Quite the contrary. They're working perfectly, have been since the Chunnel construction was first started. Monitored round the clock by technicians on both the French and English sides of the Channel. And any attempt to cut their electrical connections would set off alarm bells. Foolproof, so says Cartwright.'

The problem was that *foolproof* implied that only fools would try. And Brunner was no fool.

'One other thing, Stone.'

He rolled over on his back and stared up at the ceiling. Brunner had sunk a lot of money into this project. Stone couldn't imagine that he would overlook this possibility, even if the information was closely held. Which implied Brunner had inside information.

'You still there?' Scott-Hughes snapped.

'Yes, I'm still here. Just thinking.'

'Special Branch is now doubly convinced that the *Cormorant* thing is – was – a red herring. Two days ago, they found the second ethylene oxide tank truck.'

Stone pricked up his ears. 'Where?'

'In a lorry-repair garage near East Harling, not more

419

than twenty kilometers from where they found the first tanker. The ethylene oxide had been transferred to another vehicle, most likely another tanker truck of some sort. But the Yard was able to identify the brand and lot number of the tires from their tracks – distinctive tread design, a discontinued Yugoslavian brand, very few of them imported into England. The Yard's already circulated a bulletin to garages, repair shops and inspection stations, and to every policeman in the British Isles as well as the Eurotunnel security people on both ends of the Chunnel. Cartwright is positive that they'll find the truck within days.'

Stone's back muscles were aching, his right leg throbbing along the old fracture lines. Maybe the English *were* right, that the threat to the Chunnel was from within. Still, he had an obligation to Mac, regardless of the outcome.

'Nigel – I hear what you're saying, but I've got to carry through with this thing. I'm going up to the shipyard this afternoon.'

'That's not on,' Scott-Hughes shot back. 'Cartwright says that your instructions are to return to England. Implied that the authorities will overlook your past indiscretions, assuming that you'll cooperate with them.'

That put Stone's hackles up. 'Since I'm not in England and not a British subject, I damned well don't see that they can do diddley-squat.'

'Not sure about that, Stone. Cartwright was quite adamant. Quoted chapter and verse about the public confidence being at risk if you start spreading tales, invoked the Official Secrets Act, that sort of tripe. Also implied that some of the high mucky-mucks in government would be badly embarrassed if it was made to look as if they didn't have a firm grip on the situation. Told me to make it clear to you that I'm to pick you up as soon as possible, no excuses.'

'What about Mac?'

'That's a moot point. You don't have any hard evidence

420

that he's actually missing, do you?' Scott-Hughes paused. 'Look, Stone. This thing is getting out of hand at my end. Sir Alfred promised to keep your and Melissa's name out of it, but somehow Cartwright pried the information out of him. Cartwright's a reasonable chap and he's confident that he can sort things out for you and Melissa as long as you cooperate fully with him. So before you make any hasty decisions about going on a fool's errand, you'd best first speak to Melissa. Hang on a second. Here comes Tommy with the bad news.'

There was a muffled conversation in the background, then Scott-Hughes came back on the line. 'Seems I have an oil leak on the starboard engine oil-cooler as well. Tommy's ordered the part from an outfit in Miami who're sending it by Federal Express. Should be here by mid-morning tomorrow. So the earliest I could pick you up would be tomorrow, probably late afternoon. Any possibility that you could get back to England on your own in the meanwhile?'

'I can't chance it, Nigel. Interpol's got my photo and description.'

'Then you'll have to wait it out. Tuck in at your hotel, keep your head low and get some rest. Once I get the Mallard fixed, I'll call you on the VHF as soon as I'm airborne and every hour on the hour thereafter. Start monitoring the radio for my call – say 15.00 tomorrow onward.'

'Where will you pick me up?'

'There's a protected bay to the west of you on the coast, place called Zwarte Hoek. I can land there. You'll swim out to the Mallard and we'll be back to the Hamble River in less than two hours. And mind you call Melissa. She'll knock some sense into your head.'

'How do I get in touch with her?'

'She apparently wrapped things up in London more quickly than expected. Ring her at my estate. She's waiting for your call – quite concerned about you, I'd venture.' He gave Stone the number and rang off.

Stone groaned. It had been sheer stupidity on his part to believe that Scott-Hughes could solicit help without running into bureaucratic entanglements.

The door to the bathroom opened. Erin was neatly gift-wrapped in a towel, her freshly washed hair piled high on her head.

'You through with your Englishman?'

'Yep, but now I have to call someone else. I'll be out of here in a few minutes if you don't mind putting up with me that long.'

'Doesn't bother me a bit; rather enjoy your company.' She gave him a lustrous smile, pulled a chair to the window and sat down, her legs stretched out, feet on the window-sill, then started combing her hair.

Stone tried to keep his eyes averted. The towel was slipping. He direct-dialed the estate's number.

The phone rang six times before she picked it up, breathless.

'Yes?'

'It's me.'

'Thank God! You sound like you're ringing up from next door. I've been worried to death. How soon will you be here?'

'Ah . . . there's a problem, Melissa. I'm in the Netherlands — a little hotel on the coast south of the Hook of Holland. Mac's gone missing. I've got to track him down before I can come back. I owe it to him, understand?'

There was a soft, strangled sound from her end. 'Stone, Nigel called me from the seaplane base less than twenty minutes ago and he told me you'd be calling. He stressed that you've got to come back as soon as possible, pleaded with me to convince you not to stir anything up at the shipyard in Holland.'

'Yeah, I sort of got that impression as well.'

'Did he mention this man Cartwright?'

'More or less. Cartwright doesn't exactly sound like a happy camper.'

She drew in her breath, then sighed, agitated. 'It goes deeper than that. Cartwright's from Special Branch. He arrived at Nigel's estate this morning just a few minutes after Nigel arrived back from Antwerp, read the riot act to him for interfering with an ongoing criminal investigation by Scotland Yard. I had just come up to the house from *Snow Goose*, expecting that you had come back with him, when I saw Cartwright's car pull in. I didn't want to interfere and stayed out on the patio. They went to the kitchen for tea but didn't know I was there and, later on, I didn't let on to Nigel that I had heard anything.'

'What was the conversation about?'

'I couldn't hear everything, could only get snatches of it, but enough to know that somebody by the name of Lindsey told the Foreign Office that we're involved. The Foreign Office got on to Special Branch and that's how Cartwright became involved. Somehow, Cartwright has the idea that you're possibly trying to divert Scotland Yard's attention to the Continent while the actual attempt on the Chunnel is being mounted in England. Very simply, he wants to get his hands on you.'

He gritted his teeth, wincing. So Nigel hadn't told him the full story, just hinted around the edges. 'Do they know about the *Snow Goose* yet?'

'I'm fairly sure Nigel didn't say anything. After Cartwright left, Nigel told me that he had told Cartwright I was with you in Belgium. Said he was trying to protect me for as long as he could. But with Scotland Yard involved now, it's only a matter of time. They'll start investigating, and one thing will lead to another. I've provisioned the *Snow Goose* and filled the fuel tanks. As soon as I'm finished talking to you, I'll sail her down to the Isle of Wight and anchor in Wootton Creek, an out-of-the-way spot Pieter's taken me to years ago. Meet me there. We'll get out of England as soon as possible, before we get any deeper in this thing.'

But there was still his obligation to Mac, wasn't there?

423

he realized. He still harbored some dim, irrational hope that Mac was alive, and the van Velsen shipyard connection was the only thing left he had to go on.

'Look, Mel. I'll be in contact with Scott-Hughes on VHF, Channel 83, tomorrow afternoon at 15.00. By then, I should have a much better idea of what's going on. Assuming that Mac's safe and everything's under control, I'll have Scott-Hughes pick me up and be back to the Solent no later than six in the evening. He's sailed all over the Solent and probably knows it like the back of his hand, so he'll surely know where Wootton Creek is. I'll have him drop me off there. We can be in international waters by sundown.'

'Just take care. You don't want to trust him too much, Stone.'

Stone frowned, puzzled. 'Why do you say that?'

'Just a feeling, nothing that Scott-Hughes said directly. But he's in trouble with the government. Cartwright is putting pressure on him, threatening him with all manner of things. Something about the Official Secrets Act and a violation of flight regulations. Said they could take his flying license away from him and charge him as an accessory unless he cooperated. Cartwright also told Nigel that he'd damn well play by the Queen's rules or suffer the consequences.'

Oh God, he thought, wearily. It seemed that he had this reverse Midas touch — where everything he messed with turned to shit. What had probably started off as a lark for Scott-Hughes had gone sour and Scott-Hughes, like everyone else in the universe, looked after number one first when it came to the crunch.

He sighed. 'Thanks for the advice but don't worry. I'll handle him, Mel.'

An odd sound distracted him and Stone looked up, puzzled. Erin was making a noise, deep in her throat, almost a soft growl. Her eyes were closed, her face turned up to the sun, and she was smiling as if thinking of something amusing. He had to admit it: she was enticing – a lithe, sleek, young animal basking in the early summer heat. The towel had slipped further, exposing the top of her lovely, freckled breasts. Stone swallowed, suddenly conscious that he had the beginnings of an erection that was slowly transforming his jockey shorts into a rumpled pyramid.

Melissa's voice had just the thin edge of alarm in it. 'Stone . . . are you still there?'

'I'm here.' He swallowed again, closing his eyes, mentally willing his organ to lie down and die, trying to blank out the image of Erin's body which was burned into his retinas.

Her voice softened. 'I want you back, Stone, in one piece. I've missed you terribly. I'll forgo the moonlight and roses. Just come back safe.'

Another noise. Stone opened his eyes – a mistake. Erin had stood up, the towel slithering from her body, leaving her splendidly naked. The nipples of her breasts were hard. Stone couldn't take his eyes away from her.

She slowly sauntered over to the bed and sat down beside him and began to massage his back. Her fingers then moved over his rib-cage, lightly tickling him. Stone couldn't help it, snorted a suppressed giggle. He reached around behind him, trying to move her away, but his hand touched her breast, the touch of her flesh incinerating his hand. He yanked it away as if it had been burned.

'Did I say something funny?' Melissa's voice was puzzled.

'Cold,' Stone said. 'Just sneezed.' Erin's hands were completely around his waist, moving relentlessly in a two-pronged pincer attack on his crotch. Involuntarily, he began to breathe heavily as her fingers slipped under his jockey shorts.

'Come on, now,' Erin whispered overly loud in his ear. 'Put that silly thing down and do your manly duties.'

'Stone! Is someone there with you?'

He was panicked, his mind wildly flip-flopping, half on Erin, half on Melissa. Erin proceeded to wrap her legs around his waist, pulling him backwards against her, rubbing her body against him. He frantically tried to push her away, connected with the wrong part of her anatomy, and she moaned in part-pleasure, part-pain.

'Stone! Answer me.'

He tried. 'No one's here with . . .'

'Ooooo, not so damned rough, Yank.'

'STONE!'

'Hey! Wait a minute. It's not what you think! I'm with a friend, nothing . . .'

She was shouting into the mouthpiece, her voice crashing against his eardrum. *'YOU CAN ROT IN HELL, STONE, FOR ALL I CARE!'* The connection was broken, replaced by a jarring dial tone.

He wrestled away from Erin and frantically redialed.

The telephone at Nigel Scott-Hughes' estate on the Hamble River, a galaxy away, rang for more than a minute but no one answered.

TWENTY-ONE

The Hook of Holland, 15.00, 14 April

The phone slipped from Stone's fingers, a devastating sense of loss and frustration overpowering him. He had dragged Melissa into this damned thing, endangered her life, her freedom, and in return she had given him support, strength and love. And now this. She would leave England without him, had to, and he couldn't blame her.

Erin had scrambled off the bed, snatched her towel from the floor and moved out of reach to the far side of the bed as if she sensed impending violence. Her voice was hesitant, contrite. 'Was she . . . was she someone . . . *special?*'

Stone nodded dumbly. 'Don't sweat it, Erin . . . just the only woman I ever loved.'

The room was almost silent, only sounds of children drifting up from below and the faint rustle of starched curtains stirring in the wind.

Her voice was hoarse. 'Oh Mary, Mother of God, I surely didn't know. I thought it was some old bag of a secretary that you were talking to, all that business chat. I was just having fun . . . didn't mean . . .'

The anger was growing in him like a malignant thing, out of control. He wanted to squash Erin, to tear her bloody head off, but also deep within him he knew damned well that he could have prevented it. Just a look, a shake of the head, a few simple words. He had set himself up to fail, never thinking of the consequences. *Story of my life*.

He stood up and dragged on his clothes. He pulled out sixty pounds and dropped the notes on the bed. 'That'll cover the room and the phone calls. I've got to get going.'

'Stone . . . *please!* I can explain it to her!'

'Then you better put your goddamned explanation in a bottle and throw it out in the sea because that's where she's headed.' He slammed the door behind him.

Trying to blank out his anger, he headed the Passat north. At a garage on the edge of town, he asked a kid who was sweating a tire onto a rim where the van Velsen brothers' shipyard was located.

Fifteen minutes later he pulled into a dead-end street fronted on one side by concrete-block warehouses and on the other by a scattering of two-story brick apartments, their postage-stamp lawns gone to weed, most of their windows boarded over.

At the far end of the street he could see the entrance to the van Velsen yard, its gate marked by a huge, faded sign, the paint peeling, the plywood delaminated. From this distance, he got the impression that it wasn't much of a shipyard. More like a junk-littered mud flat enclosed by a chain-link fence with a few galvanized sheds scattered around at random, the lot of them slowly rusting away in the salt air. A mobile crane stood like an awkward, one-legged bird, gawking over the mess.

He parked the Passat half a block up and got out, keeping it between him and the yard. Stone took the Beretta out, chambered a round, and stuck it under the band of his jogging-pants. He threw the knapsack in the trunk and locked the car, then moved cautiously down the street toward the gate.

It was ajar, the lock undone. He edged through it, then ducked into the shadows of a shack set off to the side, squatting behind a trash barrel and taking in the scene.

What he hadn't been able to see from the road was a separate building tacked onto the main workshop, the structure in slightly better repair than its peers, a half-dozen pots of wilting flowers speckling its window ledges.

428

Parked in front of the building was a green Fiat hatchback with Dutch plates, a faded peace sign plastered on its rear bumper.

He took his time, taking inventory before he committed himself.

Four sheds in all, some portable staging, stacks of paint-splattered lumber, jumbles of scrap metal, and an open shed where a motor-driven winch was connected by cables to the marine railway. Stone guessed the operation was teetering on the edge of bankruptcy.

About the only thing in good repair was the marine railway. He had seen plenty of them in Maine – had always been surprised how small they were in relation to the vessels they could haul. This rig was obviously old, but the tracks which led down to the water were shiny from recent use and the cradle that was used to haul ships looked as if it had adequate capacity.

At the edge of the yard where the mud flats oozed into weed-clogged tidewater, there were three large shipping containers, stacked side by side, all of them painted a dull green. It clicked – Mac had mentioned that the surveyor told him about three containers that had been trucked in from Germany while the *Cormorant* was hauled out. He made a mental note to check the interior of the containers for any trace of what they might have contained.

No one around, he was confident of that. Stone stood up, easing his leg muscles, the sweat clammy on his body. And no sign of the van, although the yard was crisscrossed with fairly recent tire tracks. Time to get on with it. He loped across the yard, heading for the building where the Fiat was parked.

The door was ajar. He pushed it open, one hand behind his back, gripping the Beretta. There was no secretary, no clerks, just an older man slouched over a scarred desk in the back office, spearing bills onto a spike.

The man looked up. *'Kom binnen!'*

Stone walked in. 'You speak English?'

The man scowled, distracted, then nodded.

'I'm looking for a man named Macleod: tall, balding with sandy hair, big nose, Scottish accent. I think he was here very recently – maybe last night – probably with two other men who were driving a gray Toyota van, Austrian plates.'

The man's face clouded. He looked at Stone, lips open and distorted, working his tongue around his teeth as if a piece of food were lodged in a crevice. He finally shook his head. 'I know nothing of these men you're looking for.' He gestured to the pile of slips in front of him. 'I'm busy. If you have work for the shipyard, state your business. Otherwise, get out.'

'The *Cormorant*?'

The man lifted his thick bifocals over his thinning hair and leaned back in his chair, the frame groaning under his weight. 'What about the *Cormorant*?'

'Where is she?'

'She has sailed. You can see for yourself.' He nodded toward a grimy window. 'To where, I don't know nor do I give a damn. Not my business or yours, is it?'

'My Scottish friend was interested in the work that your yard did to her. He must have contacted you.'

'No one by that name contacted me and we did no work except to haul the *Cormorant* up on the ways, do some lifting with the crane and arrange for the survey.'

'You did welding in the forward cargo hold.'

'We did not. Only two of us work this yard, my brother and me. I subcontract out all the other work. It's very bad times for small yards. The damned fish are gone from the North Sea and there's no trade for small coasters. My great-grandfather built this yard, and three generations of van Velsens before me ran it at a profit. But now it's all super-this and super-that; great piles of shit that bulldoze the seas, run by accountants and staffed by prissy old women who are afraid to get their hands dirty. There's no decent work for a yard like mine any more.'

'But you worked on the *Cormorant*.'

The man leaned forward and planted an elbow on the bills, his fingers cradling his fatty jowls. He stared intently at Stone. 'Just who the hell are you?'

'A man looking for his friend. He's missing. What you tell me decides whether I call in the police or not.'

Drawing a handkerchief from his pocket, van Velsen honked into it, examined the product and jammed it back into his pocket. He sniffed. 'All I need now is the *smerissen* – the cops – bothering me. Enough *godverdomd* laws as it is. I've got nothing to hide so leave the cops out of it.'

Stone made a point of considering it and finally nodded.

Van Velsen sniffed again. 'About three weeks ago, an old Dutchman from Utrecht came in and made arrangements to haul out a 500-ton coaster, the *Cormorant*, the maximum tonnage we can handle. He wanted an insurance survey. I suggested Hans Roders – surveys most of the coasters around Europort – but I told the *Utrechtenaar* to save his money. I've known the *Cormorant* for half a century. She's finished. Hull plating's like rotten cheese and her engines should be in a museum. Told him that, straight out, even though it might cost me business. But he still wanted her hauled. Was willing to pay all the costs up front, 9000 guilders, regardless of the survey results.'

'So you hauled her.'

'*Ja*. Even after she failed the survey, the crazy *Utrechtenaar* said the owners loved her and were determined to put her back in service. Said he'd rent the yard for two weeks if he could bring in his own people to do the work. Neither my brother nor I have had a holiday in four years. They paid our regular wages, the utilities and 10,000 guilder extra. You think I'd turn that down?'

'You didn't think that was odd?'

'Shit! I've got a load of bills and after expenses I'm lucky to have enough left over to pay the interest on them. One more bad year and I'll lose this place.' He banged the table with the flat of his hand. 'Hey! A ship comes in and a ship goes out. If I'm not here to know what goes on, then I'm not responsible. And I couldn't care less about what they're doing, as long as they pay in cash.'

'They did some modifications on the ship. What were they?'

The man settled deeper into his chair, then lit a fat cigar, studying Stone. 'Some sort of fuel tank, the *Utrechtenaar* said. Put it in the cargo hold. They were going to bring in their own welder from Finland to fillet the seams but he wrapped both his head and his Saab around a lamppost. They had to get a local man, fellow named Holwerda. A day later, just before I was scheduled to leave for Amsterdam, two flat-beds rolled in with stacks of prefabricated plate under canvas. I handled the off-loading with the crane, transferring the plates from the trucks to the deck of the ship. All high-quality alloy by the look of it. Damned thick, maybe twenty millimeters, the end cap sections shaped like they were cut from an orange. The rest of the plates were collars that fitted together into a tube. Once the plates were on deck, they wrestled them into place by hand. Holwerda, my local welder, had to align them first, then run a bead along the seams, both inside and out. Took him nine days to finish the job, he told me.'

To Stone, the tank sounded like a gigantic aluminum salami. 'How big was this thing?'

Van Velsen stuffed his upper lip between his teeth, chewing on it, eyes distant, then looked back at Stone. 'From what Holwerda told me, about eighteen meters long, six meters in diameter.'

'What do you think it was going to be used for?'

'There was an American working for the *Utrechtenaar* — "Turner" was his name — said it was experimental — some sort of bio-mass composter. Planned to shovel waste garbage and cow shit into it, then use the methane gas to run the engines. Ask me, they got that idea out of the comic books.'

'So you were away from the yard while they did most of the other work?'

'Like I said, Amsterdam. Spent a week and a half with my cousin. Came back three days ago. They had finished outfitting and welding, just wanted to be launched and take on some shipping containers that had come in from Germany. I used the crane to transfer everything to her deck. They unloaded the contents of the containers in the aft cargo hold and when they were finished I lifted the empty containers with the crane and stacked them down at the end of the yard. Turner, the American, told me that someone would come and pick them up in a couple of weeks.' He looked at another bill, scowled and jammed it on the spike. 'After that, they moved to a mooring in the outer harbor. Steamed out of here the next evening about sundown.'

'And that was when?'

Van Velsen looked at Stone as if he was deaf, dumb or had Alzheimer's. 'I already told you. She steamed out of this port in the evening, two days ago, the twelfth of April.'

It wasn't possible. Pigs didn't fly and neither did ships. 'You're *positive*?'

His lips compressed, van Velsen nodded mechanically. 'You see the port captain if you don't believe me. Just as I said, two days ago come this evening.'

'How many men did they have working in the yard?'

'Varied. Seven, eight at the most. Mostly Germans, other than the *Utrechtenaar*, the American and an Australian who spent most of his time in the engine room.'

Probably Allen, Stone thought. 'Does the name Brunner sound familiar? Older man, good-looking, silver hair?'

The Dutchman shrugged. 'There might have been but I wouldn't know.'

'What kind of ground transportation did they have?'

'Didn't, except for a rental truck.'

'But where did they stay – some hotel around here?'

'The men came in every morning on a couple of rubber boats with motors strapped on.'

'From another ship?'

The Dutchman flicked the cigar's ash on the floor, unconcerned. 'Probably. Didn't ask. Europort's big. Must be over sixty or seventy ships in the harbor at any one time. I told you before, it wasn't my business.'

Stone shifted, anxious to get going. 'Mind if I take a look around the yard?'

The Dutchman stood up, swept the bills into his desk drawer and switched off the desk lamp. 'I'm closing the shipyard now, going to a funeral. You come back tomorrow and you can snoop around all you want. But no cops, understood?'

Stone nodded. 'By the way, what was the local welder's name again – the man who worked on the *Cormorant*? And where can I get in touch with him?'

'Holwerda. Henk Holwerda. You want to see him, you come with me.'

'You said you were going to a . . .'

'. . . A funeral – right. Holwerda died the night he finished off the *Cormorant*. Worked on her fourteen hours a day, too much sweat for my taste, but he told me the money was good.'

'What did he die of ?'

Van Velsen upended an imaginary bottle. 'Bad heart, drank too damned much. I could see it coming for years. The man loved his *jenever*, put a bottle to bed every damned night of his life except his birthday and then it was two.'

One more door closed, one more corridor cut off. Brunner had swept the trail behind him free of tracks. There was an empty place in Stone's gut.

The Dutchman hung back, closing windows, locking his desk. Stone took his time walking to the gate, his eyes examining the ground. The tire tracks which led from the gate and down to the marine railway were indistinct, weathered by several days of wind and morning dew. But just inside the gate, there was one set that he hadn't noticed before. Fresher than the rest – not a truck, the wheelbase too narrow. The tracks led through the gate and turned left, paralleling the fence, straight toward the containers. Later, he thought.

The port officer's office was on the top floor of a concrete box which overlooked the massive maze of Europort. It resembled a control tower with outward-slanting tinted glass, the interior fitted out with consoles, radios, radar scopes and status boards. Stone was brusquely directed to a back office by a whiskered port captain who must have taken *Moby Dick*'s Captain Ahab as a role model, complete with *basso profundo* vocal cords.

A chubby older woman, her calm Indonesian face barely clearing the counter, met him at the enquiry desk. He asked whether she had records of all the ships that entered and left Europort.

'Of course. It is all in the computer.' She patted the machine as if it were a gifted child.

'The *Cormorant* – a coastal freighter, probably Dutch or German registry, about 500 tons. She sailed recently – the twelfth. Do you have a time when she left and her destination?'

The woman tapped the keys and watched the screen scroll through several frames, then freeze. 'She cleared port at 19.41 hours the day before yesterday, bound for Bergen, Norway. The owner is listed as Weshiem-Munden GmbH of Hamburg.'

Pay dirt. 'Do you have a listing of her cargo, her crew, anything like that?'

The woman cocked her head, birdlike, examining the screen. 'She carried no cargo, in ballast, you understand? A special sailing permit was required because she was not insured. A notation here shows that she was to be scrapped and her name removed from the Netherlands Ships Registry once the wreckers returned her papers.'

She frowned, turning back to the computer and stroking a few keys. 'The crew list would not normally be in the computer but the master's name always is: William G. Allen, Australian, first-mate's ticket, licensed all oceans, 1000 tons, oil and steam propulsion, papers current and in good order.'

'Allen?' So it had been the Australian. Which probably meant that the *Valkyr* had been in Europort as well.

She looked up, a pleased smile on her crinkled face. 'Is that of help?'

It wasn't, because neither pigs nor ships flew. Or traveled through time. It was as if a magician had shown the audience a coin in his right hand, closed it and opened his other to reveal the same coin. But it wasn't the same coin. It just *looked* the same.

Stone did mental gymnastics, working backwards. 'Did you have any other freighter of the same tonnage, the same owner, maybe even a sister ship, leave Europort — say between six and twelve days ago?'

The woman looked genuinely distressed. 'You must know the name of the ship before I can search. The computer is not instructed to answer such questions and, in the span of time you speak of, well over 300 ships left Europort.'

'Please, it's important,' Stone said. Then something occurred to him. De Ruiter had let slip about the *Cormorant* being only one of a series of ships built for some Dutch coastal line back in the forties, all of them bearing the names of seabirds. 'How 'bout letting me browse through your computer for a few minutes?'

She looked genuinely shocked. 'That would not be allowed.' But then her face folded into a smile. 'But I *could* print out all the ships' names for you to examine.' She actually winked.

Stone was scanning through a fanfold printout eight minutes later. He found, surprisingly, eleven ships named after seabirds. He underlined them and went back to the desk.

The woman found it on her fifth try – the *Pelican*, out of Rotterdam, bound for Iceland. Five hundred tons, in ballast, owned and operated by that fine old reputable firm in Hamburg, Germany – Weshiem-Munden GmbH. Brunner, the illusionist, had dazzled his audience with an elaborate shell game.

'Just one last question: do you have a listing in your computer for a yacht by the name of *Valkyr*? Probably in port about the same time.'

She smiled sadly and shook her head. 'Yachts we would not enter into the computer. Only commercial vessels. I'm so sorry.' She said it as if she meant it. Too bad, Stone reflected, that all the world's bureaucrats weren't this helpful. He thanked her profusely and left.

There was one last thing to do.

The shipyard was closed, the sun gone down, the last of twilight blurring the outlines of the buildings. A low deck of clouds had been driven in by a west wind, smothering the light.

Instead of trying to get through the gate which was now secured with an enormous padlock, Stone drove down to the end of the street until he was opposite the containers, then pulled in tight against the fence. He stripped the floor mat from the driver's side and slung the knapsack on his back. One last check. The street was deserted except for a scrawny brown dog who scuttled between the buildings, sniffing and occasionally marking his territory.

Stone climbed to the roof of the Passat, draped the floor mat across the razor wire and climbed over, dropping to the ground on the other side. He realized too late that getting back over the fence would be a bitch. A Stone, much like pigs, didn't fly.

All three of the containers had been stripped clean of their shipping labels. The inspection hatches of two of them were unlocked, the interiors empty except for unmarked packing waste and splintered lumber.

The third container was padlocked. It took Stone ten

anxious minutes rummaging around the yard until he found a steel bar. The padlock didn't yield but the container's hasp did.

He swung the inspection door open and the smell hit him – the fetid stench of vomit and human waste, overpowering.

He snapped on the flashlight, terrified of what he might find. He didn't see the shape at first, his view blocked by balled-up newspapers and a couple of crates. He took a deep breath and ducked through the low door, sweeping the beam in strokes along the cavernous aluminum container. Beyond one of the crates, burned-out cigarettes littered the floor and, next to it, the beam of his flashlight illuminated naked feet, bound together with duct tape, shoeless. Minus toenails.

Bending down beside the crumpled form, he swept the papers aside.

'Oh Jesus, Mac, oh God – what did those rotten fuckers do to you?'

Macleod was lying in a pool of congealing blood, stripped to his slacks, his mouth, ankles and wrists strapped with duct tape. Two ropes – one tied around his ankles, the other around his chest and under his arms – were knotted to cargo tie-rings welded to the walls of the container. Mac's chest was covered with cigarette burns. What was left of his dentures lay crushed on the floor, pulverized under someone's heel. Stone couldn't bear to look for more than a few seconds, the bile already rising in his throat.

His nerves raw, stomach churning, Stone touched Mac's throat, feeling for a pulse. The body was still warm. Barely. And there was a pulse but it was a feeble thing, just the slimmest suggestion of life.

Cushioning the flashlight between his neck and his shoulder, Stone hurriedly fished his knife out and carefully cut the tape binding Mac's mouth, then peeled it away as gently as he could. Mac winced, his eyelids fluttering, then opened his eyes, slitted against the hard glare of the flash-light. There was a spark of recognition. His lips moved, trying to speak, but it was a faint, hoarse whisper.

'*Dear God . . . don't!* Who are . . . ?' His eyes widened. 'Stone . . . ?'

Stone leaned down, close to Mac's face, touching it gently with his fingertips. 'Yeah, Mac — it's me, Stone. You'll be all right. Hang on, friend, hang on, dammit, hang on.' Stone slit the rest of the duct tape and the ropes, peeled off his jogging-jersey and laid it over Mac's chest, then piled the wadded newspapers around the Scot for what little insulation they would provide.

Had to get help; police — no, medics. Medics first. Ambulance. How? Call box. Call box back up the street near the main intersection, had seen it, used it as a landmark coming back from the port captain's office.

Mac moaned a little, trying to lift his hand.

'No, Mac. Take it easy.'

'It was . . .'

'Who?'

'Jaw . . . Joss. Other . . . called him that . . . outside after . . . left me. They were going . . . coast. Meet . . .' His eyelids clinched shut, a look of pain transformed his face to a mass of furrows, lips compressed, bloodless.

'To meet whom, Mac?' *Or what?* 'They were going to meet the *Cormorant*, was that what they were saying?'

Mac tried to nod, his features easing.

'Where, Mac? Where were they going to meet the *Cormorant*?'

'Freezing . . . just . . . freezing. Like chill . . . childer's . . . riddle something . . . don't . . . member title.'

'I don't understand, Mac. *Where?*'

'*Freezin'* . . . just . . . *Freezin'*.' Mac's neck was corded, the tendons jumping out as he tried to lift his head up. The effort was too much and it fell back, rolling to one side.

Stone bent down, massaging Mac's shoulders, his neck,

trying to get the circulation going. 'Mac – I've got to leave you. To get an ambulance. Ten minutes, not more than that. You can hang on.'

'Stone . . . !' His eyes had opened wide, his lips working but hardly any sound coming out, his gums black. 'Six . . . six . . .' He swallowed, tried again. 'Sixteen . . . uth . . . pairs.'

Stone bent down. 'What, Mac?'

'Pair . . . z. Pairs.'

He couldn't wait any longer. 'Mac – ten minutes. That's all. Just hang on.'

He was almost out the container's door when he heard Mac, his voice raw but stronger. 'Get them, Stone . . . get . . . them.'

I will, Mac. I surely will. God as my witness.

Stone sprinted to the gate and blasted the lock off with three shots from the Beretta. He swung it open wide, then legged it to the VW. The call box on the corner was busted, the coin mechanism jammed. He found another one two blocks up. The number for emergency medical services was flagged with a red cross on the glass partition. Stone dialed the number, was answered in Dutch by a cool, efficient voice who, unfazed, switched to perfect textbook English when Stone told him to pull his thick Dutch head out of his fat Dutch ass. He told the voice where to look, that a man was going to die unless they moved and fast. The voice started to ask Stone who he was as he slammed the handset into the cradle.

He drove back to the street that led to van Velsen's yard, checking his watch, and parked half a block short, slumping down in the seat below the line of vision. Three minutes, twenty-one seconds later, an emergency medical services vehicle, lights strobing, a horn warbling, wheeled past him, the words *Academisch Medisch Centrum* splashed across the side in red letters. It braked at the last second and veered into the street that led to the yard, followed seconds later by two cop cars screaming in from the opposite direction.

In less than six minutes, the ambulance came wailing back from the shipyard, one of the police cars in front of it running interference. Which meant that the second cop car was still on the scene, investigating.

Instinctively, Stone wanted to follow the ambulance but knew he couldn't. All that could be done for Mac now would be taken care of by people far more competent than a glorified coalminer from West Virginia.

He was about to start the VW when a green Fiat with a peace symbol on the bumper whipped past him and turned into the street which led to the shipyard. He was puzzled at first, then realized that it was likely the cops had called van Velsen in to find out just what the blazes was going on at his shipyard. Obviously, van Velsen would be less than thrilled when he found out the nature of the enquiry, and Stone had zero doubts that the Dutchman would finger him as the villain, rather than coming clean about his somewhat dubious dealings with the *Cormorant* crowd. As the Dutchman had said, 'None of my business, is it?' The likely result would be that the cops would soon start throwing up road blocks with a warrant out for Stone's arrest.

Time to go. Stone cranked up the Passat and headed south.

He timed the lights so he wouldn't have to stop and be exposed to the curious scrutiny of other motorists who pulled up alongside him. Out of necessity, he had given Mac his sweatshirt and now he needed to replace it with something – a jacket, a sweater, anything. There were a few stores still open but a hairy-chested American breezing in and paying in pounds sterling would raise more than eyebrows. It was the Irish he had in mind for one-stop jersey-shopping.

As an excuse to barge in on them, he'd tell them that he had forgotten to leave Erin's bicycle in the rack outside the hotel. He didn't look forward to meeting up with her again and, if he guessed correctly, Erin had probably told her Irish buddies about the Yank's lewd and lascivious behavior to cover her own guilt. And why not? He'd be tempted to do the same thing if he were in her position. It was just a matter of toughing it out, getting a shirt, then finding a place to sleep for the night. Tomorrow was . . . tomorrow, and he'd figure it out when tomorrow came.

In less than a quarter of an hour, he rolled into the town of Rockanje. The dubious merits of having to ask a local for directions to the camping-grounds were solved when he spotted four bicyclists with Swedish flags sewn on their jackets pedaling west out of town. He hung back, following them, and was rewarded for his patience when they turned off into a grove of trees marked with the 'VVV' marker that designated Dutch campgrounds and hostels.

He parked the VW on the far side of the trees that blocked the view from the road and wandered through the campsite, his nostrils filled with the smells of food cooking and marijuana burning. A pickup volleyball game was in progress off to the side, the back-and-forth chatter in Scandinavian. One team was made up of women, the other men. Watching the ladies play, Stone reckoned that purveyors of brassieres in Scandinavia were probably going bust.

The Irish had set up their tents on the far side of the campground and were grouped around a small fire, frying sausages and drinking beer.

Kevin was the first to notice Stone.

'Ah, the Yanks are coming – at least one of them. Looks like you gave someone the shirt off your back, boyo.'

There was no rancor in his voice, just easy banter. Stone caught Erin's eye and she shook her head slightly. So she hadn't said anything. Surprising.

Patrick lobbed him a can of Fosters beer. It was ice-cold.

Why not? he thought. What am I saving my liver for, anyway? He popped the top and sank down on his haunches next to them, taking a long pull. God, it tasted fabulous. Three more cans of this and he'd be in the Out Back . . . the far Out Back.

'Any luck in finding your Scottish chum?' Trish asked. She had been swimming, her hair still wet, a blanket wrapped around her. Stone hadn't noticed before but beyond the campgrounds was the sea, now bristling white in the rising wind.

'I found him,' he said. 'He was alive but not by much. They took him to a hospital.'

'Any idea of who did it?' Kevin was stirring the fire, adding a couple of twigs, his eyes averted.

'Pretty sure.' He took another pull on the beer. 'I brought back Erin's bike — completely forgot about it when I left her at the hotel — but I need to borrow a shirt or a jacket. Walking around half-dressed is likely to cause some problems for me.'

'The police?'

Stone nodded. 'Possibly.' He explained about van Velsen's semi-involvement. 'He'll say I did it to cover his ass or maybe even because he thought I did it.'

Kevin nodded, then glanced at Patrick who nodded his head almost imperceptibly. 'We already know. It was on the radio less than five minutes ago. Repeated the bulletin in three languages.' He sorted through his saddlebag and fished out a fake chamois shirt, L. L. Bean, no less. 'Lose this and I'll have your guts for garters. Trish gave it to me for my twenty-sixth. Cost her a packet but I'm worth every cent of it.'

Stone slid into the shirt, glad to have something on his back with the evening chill coming on.

'The *garda* know you're driving a Passat,' Patrick said casually. 'They found the floor mat you left on the fence and matched it up through a VW dealer who traced it back to the hire-car agent. Also said you were armed and

443

dangerous and had discharged a firearm; not happy about that at all. Whom did you shoot?'

'The lock off a fence, worse luck.' Stone sunk down between the two girls. He felt compelled to contact Scott-Hughes, tell him what he knew, but realized it was damn little. Macleod had tried to tell him something he thought was important, but Stone couldn't fit the pieces together. Had to think about it; maybe he could come up with something once he had had a little time alone to think. 'Are there any telephones around here?'

Kevin shook his head. 'Probably back in the village, but I don't think it would be a good idea for you to go wandering about. The police bulletin indicated that the man they were looking for is an American. There aren't that many around these parts this early in the tourist season and your accent would give you away. Erin said that you had a radio transmitter of some sort. Why not use that?'

'Can't right now, not until tomorrow.' Stone explained about Scott-Hughes and the Mallard. 'He's got to be airborne at a fairly high altitude to reach me.'

Kevin shrugged. 'Look, first thing, we'd best move your Passat. You have the keys?'

Stone handed them over and Kevin tossed them to Patrick. 'You and Erin drive the Passat back on the route we came this afternoon. Dump it on a side street in Haassluis, leave the keys in it so somebody will nick it, and use the bikes to come back here. Won't take you more than an hour.'

'What if we're stopped?'

'What if you are? The car's rented out in Erin's name so if anybody asks, she can show the papers. Get on with it – there's a good lad.'

He pulled two beers from an insulated vinyl cooler, handing Stone another, keeping one for himself.

'Suppose you tell me what is *really* going on.'

'I've told you as much as I should. It was originally just

a job. Now it's become a personal thing. I don't want to get you and your bunch involved.'

'Seems we already are.' Kevin arched his eyebrows.

Stone considered the idea. Ditching the car would probably be considered a felony in the Netherlands. The Irish were already sticking their necks out for him and he might as well warn them how easily they could get them lopped off if they went any further. 'About a month ago, I was called in as an engineering consultant to help access the vulnerability of the Chunnel to a terrorist attack that seemed in the making. Everything I've found out thus far indicates the terrorists will attack it by anchoring an old coastal freighter over the Chunnel. Using the ship as a diving-platform, they'd be able to use hydraulic dredges to clean out boreholes that were drilled along the Chunnel route some years ago by the French. The boreholes would then be packed with explosives. The problem is, the English cops have been conned by the terrorists into believing an attack will be from the inside of the Chunnel with a truck loaded with explosives. Scotland Yard is leading the charge and they seem hell-bent on ignoring the stuff that I've come up with.'

Kevin gave him a wary look. 'The English are stubborn sods. If they had any sense they would have got out of Northern Ireland thirty years ago. Doesn't surprise me at all.' He paused and lit a cigarette. 'Who are these people who are trying to bomb the Chunnel?'

'Rent-a-terrorists, not politicals. Led by a German by the name of Brunner. Obviously, someone is behind them, paying for the job. But I haven't a clue who that might be.'

Kevin took his beer and slugged down a mouthful. He leaned back, looking up at the cloud deck. 'Looks like our good weather's at an end. Rain tomorrow,' he said, then moved closer to the fire. 'You understand that there are radicals in Northern Ireland – such as the IRA – who would love to see the Chunnel blown. It would hurt Great

445

Britain's prestige, cut her trading revenues, which in turn would mean fewer pounds dedicated to the suppression of Irish nationalism.'

'People will die if the Chunnel blows.'

'That's a common enough condition of life in Northern Ireland, isn't it?'

'I'm talking about thousands.'

Kevin breathed out heavily. 'My older brother's a Provo. No education, but he's paid for mine, said they needed brains to help in the Struggle. I once believed that I could change the system with pure reason so I began my degree in philosophy. But I learned very early on that while logic has its beauty, it's also too far removed from the law, and the law is what must be on our side if we're to win. So now I'm reading law, you understand? If we're to do it, it must be peacefully, through the courts. Still, the Provos would love to see the Chunnel come crashing in.'

'Macleod, my Scottish buddy who now, hopefully, reposes between clean sheets, once told me that the IRA probably wouldn't get involved because blowing the Chunnel would be too indiscriminate. The Chunnel's destruction would kill not only Brits but American tourists, French businessmen, Danes, Japanese, Italians, Germans — a whole smorgasbord of nationalities. Not the best kind of publicity for the "Cause", is it? Particularly to the Boston-Irish who kick in most of the money for the IRA.'

Kevin studied the ash on his cigarette for a few minutes and flicked it into the fire's embers. 'You're probably right. Not that the Provos wouldn't love to see it happen if it could be proved to be the work of some other group, but I have a feeling that the Brits will try to blame it on the IRA anyway, regardless of who does the job. And that would escalate the cycle of violence.'

He rubbed his nose, thinking. '. . . But let's say that if Patrick and I, both of us known to have IRA family connections, were to help you prevent the Chunnel's destruction, it might sit very well with the British press. Possibly an opening. Give Irish moderates credibility, a public platform to explain that there's a sensible way to resolve the question of Northern Ireland – through the courts and public discourse and not with bullets.' He nodded to himself. 'And if it goes wrong, you'll be witness to the fact that we tried to prevent it and blunt any British accusation that the IRA was involved.' He smiled tentatively at Stone. 'What do you think?'

Stone was impressed. Here was a kid in his middle twenties who had the political acumen of a seasoned politician. An Irish one at that.

'What's your last name, Kevin?'

'Murphy. Kevin J. Murphy. Why?'

'I have a hunch that I'll be telling my grandchildren I knew you.'

Kevin snorted. 'That assumes you'll live to have grandchildren, doesn't it, Stone?'

05.50, 15 April

He woke in the first light of morning, a sleeping-bag thrown over him, a cycling jacket pillowed under his head. He got up and stretched, then ambled down to the sandy shoreline, unlimbering. Felt good, the old breaks in his bones protesting, but nothing serious.

The sea was a curious gray-green in the fragile lemon light of not-yet-dawn, whitecaps marching to the orders of the south-west wind, long plumes of foam breaking off the wavetops as the water shoaled. The cloud deck was rendered into a thousand tattered black banners, streaming overhead. And he could smell rain, pitied the seamen who had to make a living offshore in this kind of weather. And thought of her. He wasn't very conversant with God but he prayed that she'd be all right.

A footstep crunched on gravel behind him and he turned.

Erin.

'Good morning, Stone. I put some coffee on. It's near enough ready.'

He nodded, not answering.

'I can't say much more than I've already said.' She was staring at the sea, her hair flowing back in the wind. 'It was a stupid thing I did and I'll be eternally sorry for it. I'll make it up to you in some way, I promise you that.'

He nodded again. She meant it in a kind way, no sexual overtones. He wanted to reach out and touch her, to reassure her that it was all right. 'I'm okay,' he finally said. 'It was my fault as well because I let it happen.' He turned and gave her a weak smile, putting his hand out.

There were tears in her eyes but she was smiling. She took his hand and squeezed it very hard, then turned and ran back up the beach toward the campsite.

Vaguely depressed, he sat down on the sand, idly scooping up handfuls of the stuff, letting it run through his fingers. Like sand in an hourglass, he mused. Time running out.

The only thing open to him now was to get in touch with Scott-Hughes on the handi-talkie this afternoon. *Tell him what I know, not that it's much to go on.* The percentages were very high that Brunner had substituted the *Pelican* for the *Cormorant*, but how to prove that? The two ships had rendezvoused somewhere. Brunner would have painted out the old name and painted in the *Cormorant*'s. The papers would have been switched, a few traceable items moved from one ship to the other to complete the illusion. But even that evidence was gone now, the remains of the *Pelican* either on the scrap heap or, more likely, in the furnaces.

The only thing left for him to work with was what Mac had overheard. *Something he was trying to tell me, just couldn't get it out. About a riddle* . . . A riddle about what? A puzzle-book, a poem, a novel – something like that, because Mac had referred to a title. Still, it didn't make sense. He shook his head, defeated.

'Not exactly top of the morning, is it?' Kevin hunkered down beside him, two aluminum mugs of coffee in his hands. He passed one to Stone, took the other and blew across its rim, the steam whipping away. 'Sleep well?'

Trish had come down with him but she had walked on to the edge of the surf, skirting the waves as they rolled in, head down, examining the sand.

'Like a brick,' Stone answered.

'Shouldn't wonder.' Kevin took a sip, then set the cup down in the sand, fished out a pack of cigarettes and lit one. 'Sent Patrick into town for a newspaper and a sniff around for any police. Don't think we'll be moving today in this weather. What's your plan?'

'Don't have any. Macleod knew something, was trying to tell me. I'd like to get to a phone, call the hospital, but I doubt they'd let me talk to him. Probably on medication, drugged to the eyeballs, based on the shape he was in.'

'More than likely the police are monitoring enquiries. They'd try to trace the call. Forget that, mate.' Kevin paused, curious. 'Do you remember anything of what he told you?'

Stone bobbed his head. 'There wasn't much – just individual words and snatches of sentences, didn't make any sense. He was pretty groggy, tongue swollen, his dentures smashed up. He was trying to tell me where the *Cormorant* had gone to. Kept saying "Just freezing" . . . and "chill"-something. Maybe "children".'

He took a bite out of the coffee and swallowed, bitter freeze-dried stuff but loaded with a synapse-bursting blast of caffeine. 'Also, something about a riddle. And "sixteen pairs".'

Kevin studied the horizon, silent for a long time. 'If it wasn't exactly "chill" or "children", then would it be something very close to that?' He put his hand on Stone's

449

arm. 'Don't answer just yet. Think about it carefully.'

Stone did. 'Could be that he said "childers". Yeah, now that I think about it, he said "childers". It was just that he couldn't get the whole word out the first time.'

'And he also mentioned a riddle? Are you *sure* of that?'

'Positive.'

Kevin stood up, swirled the remains of his coffee in his mug and drank it. 'Macleod told you *exactly* where the boat had gone to. It's just that you probably never heard of the place. Let me talk to Trish to make sure. She's the one with half a degree in literature.'

Stone watched as Kevin caught up to Trish, slid his arm around her and continued on up the beach, their heads together, talking intently.

Stone didn't want to get his hopes up. He waited for a few minutes, then wandered back to the encampment to get a refill.

The next time he looked, the two of them had headed back, hand in hand. Trish was doing the talking, Kevin nodding. He passed by Stone without a comment and ducked into his tent, then backed out, a bicycle saddlebag in his hand. He pulled out a map and spread it on the ground. Trish stooped down beside Stone and pointed to the map.

'It's there,' she said softly. Her expression never changed. 'Did you ever hear now of a novel titled *The Riddle of the Sands*?' she asked.

Stone shook his head. 'Don't think so.'

'A wonderful sea story about a small boat sailing in the barrier islands fronting the Dutch coast, written early in the century by Erskine Childers. Born in London, but his sense of justice transformed him into an Irish patriot. He took up our cause, ran guns from the Continent to Ireland, spied on the British. And wrote that book. Every school-child in Ireland knows his name. Childers died for his troubles in front of an Irish Free State firing squad early in the twenties.' She turned and looked into his eyes,

450

unblinking. 'Kevin said Macleod used the words "just freezing"?'

Stone nodded dumbly.

'What he was trying to say was "Juist" – an island in the German Frisian archipelago. That's where your *Cormorant* has gone to.'

TWENTY-TWO

Stunned, Stone studied the map. Starting just north of the Hook of Holland and scattered along the Dutch and German coasts was a continuous chain of islands laid down in a shallow arc paralleling the coast. The chain continued along the northern coast of Germany, all the way to the Danish border.

Trish pointed to one. 'Juist Island.'

It was an elongated barrier island, not more than a couple of kilometers on its major axis, situated on the eastern side of the River Ems, a few kilometers from the mainland of the German coast.

'Looks to be a perfect place to anchor a small ship,' Kevin commented. 'A ship could tuck in behind the island and be protected from the North Sea. It's remote, not much of a place according to the guide; mainly sand dunes, summer cottages, a few small hotels, and no industry to speak of except fishing.'

It would indeed do nicely, Stone thought. A calm anchorage where two small coastal freighters could raft up and swap identities. Also, a perfect jumping-off point for a run down the English Channel. And conveniently, within German sovereign territory. Brunner would feel right at home there.

Stone turned to Trish. 'This book Childers wrote – any mention of "sixteen pairs"?'

Trish pursed her lips. 'It doesn't sound familiar and I've read *The Riddle of the Sands* twice, perhaps three times. It's basically a small-boat cruising story set around the turn of

452

the century — actually more than that — a true classic of sorts.'

'What else did Macleod tell you?' Kevin asked.

Stone thought about it. 'That's about it.'

Kevin shook his head. 'Then the "sixteen pairs" referred to something other than Juist Island and the *Cormorant* — something he thought you had to know.'

They were still kicking around the 'sixteen pairs' thing as they shared a tin of peaches when Patrick wheeled in, fresh melons, a quart of milk and a newspaper stuffed in his pannier. He tossed the paper to Stone.

'A police artist's likeness of you in the Rotterdam paper. Not particularly flattering.'

The face that leered out at the reader was unshaven, the eyes wild, the hair all wrong. Van Velsen had a vivid imagination, if not an accurate one. Stone scanned the article but couldn't decipher the Dutch.

'I didn't dare ask anyone to translate it,' Patrick apologized. 'Didn't seem wise. As to cops, there aren't any obvious road blocks but there were a couple of unmarked cars with whip antennas, manned by serious-looking types and parked off to the side of the road leading north from the village. I'll check again this afternoon.'

So they were looking for him, that much he could be sure of. There was nothing he could do until his radio schedule with Scott-Hughes, and it seemed that the best policy would be to stay put in one place and not show his face to the local gentry.

Just before nine, it began to rain, the wind now blowing close to gale force. The campground had a *kampwinkel*, a small recreation room equipped with a ping-pong table and coin-operated washers, dryers and soft-drink machines. Most of the cyclists migrated there, trading lies, drinking beer, tinkering with their bikes and playing table tennis. Stone, not wanting to draw attention to himself, squirreled away in Kevin and Trish's tent, alternating between dozing and reading a book of incomprehensible Irish poems about growing up in Dublin.

Kevin woke him up fifteen minutes before the radio schedule and handed him the VHF's battery pack which he had recharged at an outlet in the recreation room. 'Good luck on you, Stone.'

The rain had stopped but the cloud deck was still solid. The wind had shifted to the south-west and was blowing even harder, forty knots plus, Stone calculated. He couldn't bear to think of her trying to thrash her way south against this stuff.

Listening to Channel 83 at 15.00 hours, he heard Scott-Hughes call twice but was unable to make contact. Scott-Hughes had said he'd be airborne about then and probably wasn't up to a high enough altitude. Stone tried again at half-past the hour. No contact. He decided to conserve his battery and waited impatiently for Scott-Hughes' call at 16.00.

Exactly on the hour, Scott-Hughes blasted through on the frequency, his signal extremely strong.

Stone answered back. 'Mallard, Snow Goose here. How copy?'

'Five by five. I'm at 4000 meters on instruments, directly over the Dutch coast. Solid cloud all the way up. Don't think I can risk putting the old girl down in this weather but wanted to make sure you were all right. Bit of fuss according to this morning's broadcast on Radio Netherlands. Cartwright's less than pleased.'

Fuck Cartwright, Stone thought bitterly. 'Look, Nigel. I found Mac at the shipyard. He had been left for dead. He's in a hospital, *Academisch Medisch Centrum* somewhere around the Rotterdam area. Have Cartwright get someone over there to look after him. Mac will verify what I'm about to tell you.'

Burst of static, a voice in the background, Scott-Hughes mumbling something with his hand over the mike. 'Stand by, Snow Goose. Got to go over to the air traffic control frequency for a few seconds. They're a bit put off with my inability to maintain the assigned flight level. Can't help it, getting kicked all over the place in this turbulence.' He repeated that he'd be back in a few seconds and switched channels.

Drumming his fingers, impatient, Stone waited.

A burst of static, the voice broken up, a signal much weaker than Scott-Hughes'. 'Talisker . . . ight Watch — switch . . . quency to Channel 68, I rep . . . Chan . . . 68 . . . ten min . . . after your contac . . . ott-Hughes . . . copy?'

A white-hot rush flashed through his nervous system. Stone mashed down the transmit button. 'Ah . . . Night Watch, this is Talisker. Say again . . . ?'

Scott-Hughes crashed through on the frequency.

'Is that you calling, Snow Goose?'

He had been about to call her again, not even sure that it was her, then hesitated. She had warned Stone about trusting Scott-Hughes so he acted on his gut instincts, lying.

'Mallard, this is Snow Goose. Someone else was on frequency, broke up your transmission, but I think they switched to another frequency. Go ahead now.'

Hesitation, then 'What's your position, Snow Goose?'

Devious question, which deserved an equally devious answer. 'Same place as yesterday.'

Scott-Hughes didn't immediately come back, and when he did Stone briefly heard another voice in the background. 'Cartwright's been in touch with the Dutch authorities. According to them, you checked out of your hotel yesterday. He's quite concerned with your, ah, activities over there. He's made arrangements for you to give yourself up to the Dutch authorities. They'll waive any charges and see you safely over to England where we'll meet you. Just turn yourself in to them. You'll be far more useful to us on this side of the Channel.'

Useful in what way? — stamping out license plates, making small rocks out of big ones? Stone was infuriated.

Scott-Hughes had sold out to Cartwright. He thumbed the mike button. 'Negative, Mallard. Not until I finish some business over here. The ship that was trashed in Norway was the *Pelican*, a sister ship of the *Cormorant*. Brunner made a switch. The *Cormorant* is anchored behind Juist Island in the German East Frisian Islands. I don't know for sure, but I'm also willing to bet my ass that the *Valkyr*'s parked right next to her.'

There was a very long pause. Scott-Hughes was either digesting this or, more likely, someone in the aircraft with him – probably Cartwright – was prepping him for his response.

'Interesting, Snow Goose. I'll pass that information along to Cartwright. Should certainly be checked into thoroughly. However, Cartwright is even more convinced than ever that the attempt will be from the English side. A sighting of the truck with the, ah, special tires was made by a garage attendant just south of London when the truck stopped to refuel. Drove away before, ah, Cartwright's people could get there, but they've got the situation well in hand.'

The stupid bastards just didn't get it! 'Mallard, this is Snow Goose back. Tell Cartwright to pull his head out of his ass! The fuel truck is either a backup alternative to the main effort or, more likely, a staged diversion. I'm telling you, Brunner's going to use the *Cormorant*. Over.'

Again, a long silence, the empty frequency hissing with background noise, probably precipitation static, he guessed. She was out there, he thought, or had he just imagined it? The transmission had been faint and broken, easy to confuse it with . . . But he knew it was her. Only she and Mac were aware of the Talisker thing. He hadn't imagined that.

He was on the shore, sheltering behind a stunted pine. As he stood there shivering in the cold wind, he heard the distant rumble of aircraft engines.

'Snow Goose, this is Mallard. Didn't copy all of your last

transmission. Please give me a long count, see whether I can tune you in a bit better. Over.'

Stone depressed the mike button, not connecting. 'Roger, Mallard. One . . . two . . .' He released the mike button as if it had burned him. What in the hell was Scott-Hughes talking about? The VHF rig in the Mallard was crystal-controlled like all other modern VHFs. You couldn't 'tune' the damned things.

The sound of the aircraft engines was louder now. Suddenly, not more than half a kilometer out to sea, a twin-engine turboprop thundered past the shore, the thing no more than fifty meters above the wavetops, the fuselage bulging with black radomes and antennas, RAF roundels on its wings. It wasn't an aircraft type that Stone recognized but it resembled the Lockheed Orions that the US Coast Guard in Maine used on long-range search and rescue missions – the type of aircraft that would have radio direction-finding gear installed along with all the other black-box goodies.

Scott-Hughes was back on the frequency, his voice strained, overly loud. 'Can't hear you, Snow Goose. Give me a long count again, old boy. Over.'

'*Old Boy*', *my ass*, he swore. He listened for another minute. The sound of the engines died, then came back faintly from somewhere to the north. He waited even longer. The plane, like a persistent bird dog, was quartering the coastline, sniffing for the scent.

His voice angry, Scott-Hughes came back on the frequency. 'Stone – this is Mallard. Let's finish with this damn nonsense. The Dutch authorities have a good idea of where you are and it's only a matter of time. Cartwright's with me. Give up now and he pledges that he'll clear things up if you're innocent. And just to humor you, he's willing to send a Coastal Command aircraft to the Frisian Islands to see whether the *Cormorant*'s anchored there. I'm returning to Burnham-on-Crouch to refuel but will be off at first light in the morning in the event that the authorities haven't taken you into custody. I'll monitor this frequency at all times while airborne. Do you copy, Stone?'

He copied all right. He made the final transmission short so that the Orion wouldn't have time to get a bearing on him.

'Tell Cartwright he can shove it where the sun doesn't shine.'

He flicked to Channel 68 and waited ten minutes, his nerves jangling, pumped full of adrenalin, not really believing she had called or would meet the schedule.

Nine minutes and fifty-three seconds later he heard her, positive that it was her, her transmission weak but not as broken as before.

'If you're receive ... press ... mike button three times.'

He did.

'Received that ... Listen ... me in exactly two hours on Chan ... 6. I say again, Channel 6. Acknowledge, with three clicks, please.'

She was trying to sound either officious or impersonal for the casual listener, a very smart move considering the circumstances.

He mashed the button three distinct times.

'Received that ... okay. Now off and clear.'

He checked his watch: 16.09. Sitting down on the sand, he switched off the handi-talkie and stared out to sea. There were a thousand questions rushing through his mind, none of them answerable. But there was one thing that he did know – that she was coming for him.

17.55, 15 April

The wind was still blowing hard but the cloud deck was breaking up, slanting shafts of late afternoon sunlight sweeping the green, foam-flecked sea. Stone checked his watch for the fifth time in as many minutes: 17.58 – eleven minutes to go.

'She'll call,' Kevin reassured him. 'The question is, boyo,

458

whether the Englishman caught on or whether the RAF are still listening in. That's the rub, isn't it?'

Quaint way of putting it, Stone thought. If Scott-Hughes or the boys from Coastal Command were listening, there was the potential for an unmitigated disaster. Not only would they be able to get a fix on him, but she'd be trapped as well.

The VHF radio on board the *Snow Goose* was a good one and, more importantly, its antenna was at the top of the mainmast, extending the range. Given those parameters, the radius of her signal would be between fifty and sixty nautical miles. She would be closing on the Dutch coast, anywhere between the Belgian–French border and Texel in the Dutch Frisian Islands; over a hundred miles of convoluted coastline. And within that span of distance, there had to be twenty or thirty harbors she could put into. The question was, which one? And how to communicate it to her without tipping off a third party to its location. He thought he had the answer.

'Did you find it?'

Kevin pulled out his wallet and slipped a plastic-laminated card from one of the pockets. Stone examined it. There was a calendar printed on one side and an advertisement for a Stockholm office-supply firm on the other. Along one edge was a ruler laid out in millimeters. 'One of the Swedes loaned it to me. All I could find,' Kevin said. 'Will it do?'

'It'll have to,' Stone answered.

He went to the shoreline and sat down, then removed the map from his shirt pocket. He unfolded it carefully, keeping it pinned with his legs to prevent it from whipping away in the wind, then did some measuring. Once he had double-checked the numbers, he switched on the handi-talkie, punched in Channel 6 and turned up the volume to its maximum setting. And waited.

Her transmission was on schedule, much louder than either of the previous two.

'You there, over?'

'Roger. Keep your transmissions short, okay?'

'Good idea. Can you give me an idea of where you are?'

'Yes, but not directly. There's a book I was given as a gift by a terrific lady. It's about vacationing in the Lowland on a budget and there's a fold-out map inside the book. I have a copy right here in my hot little hands. Question is, do you have a copy as well?' She damn well better have it, he thought. After all, she published *Holland on the Cheap* and took the credit as the editor.

Fifteen, twenty seconds dragged by.

'Yes.'

'Measure up from the bottom edge 34.3 centimeters and in from the left-hand edge 9.8 centimeters.'

'34.3 up, 9.8 in, correct?'

'You've got it.'

A longer wait.

'I have it. But I can't get in there – far too shallow.'

'Then you pick the place and give me its location in centimeters from the top and right-hand edges of the map.'

'Stand by, this will take a bit of time.'

He had to smile. If Scott-Hughes or the RAF were monitoring the channel, they'd be tearing their hair out because without the exact same map, they'd have no way of knowing.

'You ready?'

'Shoot.'

'Exactly 35 down and 49.8 from the right-hand edge.'

'Stand by.' He plotted it twice to be sure. It was south of him, about a two-hour hike, on the far side of a causeway that linked Goeree and Schouwen. His plotting mark fell directly on a magenta circle with a sailboat inside it which was labeled *Binnenhaven* – undoubtedly some kind of a small-boat marina. He keyed the mike. 'I've got it. Eleven letters in the word, right?'

'You can count! It will take me five – no, make that six hours to get there.'

'I'll be there.'

'There's a condition you should know of.'

Her voice was dry, firm, no warmth to it. Stone's happy heart lurched, arrested in mid-beat.

'What's that?'

'I'm repaying a debt. Don't read anything into it more than that.'

Stone took a deep breath, then slowly released it.

'I understand,' he said. But he doubted she ever would.

The Irish had cooked up tinned bangers and instant mash.

'Did you get through to her?' Trish asked. She handed him a paper plate heaped with food.

He folded his legs under him and sat down. 'She's six hours out. Be in just after midnight. On your trip up from Vlissingen, you took the coastal road. Do you remember a yacht marina on the Goeree side of the causeway – a place called "Binnenhaven"?'

Wiping his mouth with his cuff, Kevin nodded, still chewing. 'Hole in the wall. We stopped for a breather and got water. Is that likely to be the place?'

Stone nodded. 'Think so.' He wolfed down the rest of the food and tossed the plate in the fire. 'I've got to get going.'

Kevin shook his head. 'No, we've got to get going. Patrick cycled into the village this afternoon while you were sleeping – talked to a local teenage punk rocker who wasn't overly fond of the police. The Dutch found the Passat, keys still in it. They're putting out the word that you're on foot. Moving south overland won't be a problem until you get to the causeway that spans the Haringvliet, but the kid says they've set up a road block there, and on all the other causeways leading south as well. We've discussed the thing and agreed. We're going with you, that much we can do.'

He had been prepared to do it alone but he was going to be eternally grateful for any bloody help he could get. 'How do we handle the causeway?'

Kevin looked up at Stone with a lecherous grin. 'And am I to believe that you never heard the expression "beauty blinds"?'

Stone and Kevin took off on foot half an hour before sunset. Hardly the word for it, because the cloud deck had folded back in on itself, swallowing the last of the fading light, the hard south-westerly wind rising again. They kept on the edge of the shoreline, letting the surf erase their prints.

'What about Trish and Erin?' Stone asked. The shoreline's surface was like quicksand, loose and soupy, making the going difficult. Random gusts of wind kicked up spatters of sand grains from the low dunes which stung their skin, and the bugs were out with a vengeance.

'They'll be along presently,' Kevin grunted, his breathing labored. 'Should see them at this end of the causeway if all goes well.'

Stone swatted a mosquito which had worked its way under his collar. 'How 'bout Patrick?'

'He'll be about half a kilometer behind the ladies. Bringing up the arse-end of the pack to make sure the trail is clean, you might say.'

The spongy sand sucked at their feet, their socks saturated, the grit trapped in their shoes chafing at their skin. It was enough, Stone thought, to make you swear off beaches for a lifetime.

'What about your bike?'

'What about it?' Kevin paused and lit a cigarette. 'None of the lot back at the camp will nick it. I'll pick it up tomorrow when I get back there after helping save a worthless hide. Not to worry.'

By twenty after, the causeway was in sight. Stone had half expected a bridge on pilings but, instead, it was a dike, the roadway on its crown, the slopes on either side of the dike tapering down to the sea over jumbled rip-rap, then flattening to sand and pebbles along the shoreline. Waves, a good meter high, thundered in, bashing spray.

Stone squinted in the failing light. A white car with red stripes was parked halfway across the causeway, the parking lights on. Cops.

'What now?'

'We wait,' said Kevin.

About ten minutes dragged by, the light failing, the dusk deepening into a muzzled gray as a bank of mist rolled in from the sea. While they waited, a handful of motor cars trundled over the causeway, each one of them flagged down by the cops. The procedure seemed to be for the vehicle's occupants to get out while the trunk and interior of the vehicle were searched. The *politzi* were being thorough in a way that only the Dutch could be.

'There they are,' Kevin said, nudging Stone. Two pinpoints of feeble light jittered onto the causeway. Stone could just make out the indistinct forms of two cyclists, slowly pedaling south, their battery-powered headlights jiggling on the bumps. Indistinctly, Stone could hear their voices and an occasional giggle carried on the wind.

'Let's go,' Kevin said.

They skirted along the shoreline, keeping their heads down, running in spurts, then dropping down where the sand edged the rocks. The spray saturated them, the wind chilling their bodies.

Without warning, a spotlight on the cop car lanced through the dusk, sweeping along the seaward shoreline. They were both running, had only a split second to pancake into the graveled sand. The spotlight swept over them, lingered for a few seconds on a rocky patch a few meters behind them, then continued up the shoreline.

'Might have seen our tracks,' Stone panted, his lungs like old leather – the payback for those twenty years of smoking.

A guttural male voice hailed in Dutch from the direction of the cop car and Stone could just make out the profile of a man walking north toward them on the roadway above, the beam of his flashlight sweeping from side to side, probing the slopes of the dike and the shoreline beyond. At the most, they had thirty seconds before the cop pinned them in his beam like butterflies to a specimen board. Stone assumed that the cops in the Netherlands carried side arms and were willing to use them.

He pulled his knapsack off and began to dig into it.

'*No fucking guns!*' Kevin whispered.

'Wasn't planning to, for Christ's sake. Going to throw the goddamned thing away – don't want to be caught carrying it.'

Erin and Trish pedaled past where Stone and Kevin lay, less than ten meters away, the two of them singing bad harmony off key, not a care in the world.

As if he hadn't heard them coming until now, the cop suddenly swung the beam of his light at them and yelled something, his voice hard.

One of the girls swerved out of his way but the other's bike suddenly wobbled, the front wheel skidding, the machine tumbling, crashing into the cop. There was a thin squeal of pain, the cop swearing, and the tinny rattle of metal as the upset bicycle skittered across the concrete.

'*Now!*' Kevin said in Stone's ear.

They headed into the surf, waded to neck high and started to swim.

Stone was in trouble from the beginning, the knapsack on his back slowing him down, filling with water.

About twenty meters out from the shoreline, they turned south, paralleling the causeway, Kevin leading by default. The seas were rough, the going lumpy. Stone was taking on water, his breathing out of sync with the curling waves, his throat and eyes burning with salt.

Endless, it seemed, not making headway, couldn't believe that the cops hadn't heard them thrashing around. He turned his head, side-stroking for a minute, and realized that there was a full-blown squabble going on in front of the cop car, its headlights on now, two figures in blue bent over, Trish's red hair haloed in the beams, Erin stretched out on the pavement, wailing like a banshee.

Fantastic. Command-performance quality, he figured, then reached out, grabbing another handful of water, and collided with Kevin.

The Irishman spat out a mouthful of water, dog-paddling. 'Float on your back for a while, mate. Think the current's with us.'

So it was. Like soggy corks, they wallowed in the waves, getting colder by the minute but regaining their breath, then started doggedly to stroke south again, the home stretch.

Ten minutes dragged by. He was getting colder, his legs cramping, Kevin somewhere off to the left. When he was lifted by a wave larger than the rest, he caught a glimpse of flashing red and green buoys, the glimmer of a lighted building set back on pilings, the outlines of masts swaying in the chop.

Less of a sea now, in the lee of a rocky breakwater off to his right, past a bobbing buoy, his arms aching, right leg knotted by a muscle spasm, his lungs burning with cold fire.

One hundred meters to the shoreline, fifty, then ten. Exhausted, he stroked and, as he pulled through, his hand brushed pebbles. He kneeled, then stood up awkwardly in the shallow water, stumbled up the beach and collapsed next to a row of beached sailing dinghies, the halyards of their masts slatting in the gusting wind.

Kevin staggered up from the beach and dropped down beside him.

'Not exactly a slice of cake, was it?' The Irishman blew his nose between his fingers. 'Rough as granny's chin, wasn't it, now?'

'Whose idea was that performance on the causeway?' Stone asked. God, he had to get in better shape. Had almost lost it out there.

'Don't have a clue but it was bloody marvelous, wasn't it? The girls were just going to flash their knockers and chat the boys up a bit. Must have improvised.' He peeled off his sweater and wrung it out. 'Bloody fucking cold. Catch our bloody death. How you doing, Stone? Old age got to your bones yet?' He seemed to be on a high, enjoying it, the bugger.

Damned if he was going to admit it. 'I'm okay.' Stone checked his watch: 21:52, two hours before she was due.

Together, they pulled some vinyl cockpit covers from the dinghies and wrapped themselves in the material, then jogged in place, trying to get their circulation going.

It wasn't more than ten minutes later when Erin and Trish rolled into the parking lot, their voices low but excited.

'Hey, down here,' Kevin stage-whispered.

The girls parked their bikes and pushed their way through a hedge. Trish wrapped her arms around Kevin and kissed him soundly.

'How was that for high drama?' Erin asked. She was nursing a brush-burn on her arm, overdoing it a bit.

'What happened to the cops?' Stone asked. From where he was, he couldn't see the causeway because of fencing that fronted the marina.

'They're undoubtedly where we left them,' Erin answered. 'Nice old lumps, really. Very polite once things were sorted out. Offered to call an ambulance, they did. We told them we were on the way to the marina to meet our fellows, would swab my arm with alcohol and put a sticking plaster on it once we got here.'

'Do you think they saw us?'

'Shouldn't think so. I did, only because I was looking for you, but the surf is so noisy that it would be sheer accident if they did.'

'What about Patrick?' Stone had the vinyl cover up tight around his neck, blood starting to warm up, his whole body tingling. God, what he wouldn't give for a hot shower.

'Should be along shortly,' Trish answered. 'He was going to chat up the police, tell them he was planning to take a degree in law enforcement, how much he admired policemen with *real* experience. And, of course, try to casually find out exactly what they knew about you.' She paused. 'Look, there's half a dozen motor cars in the marina's parking lot so the bar must be open. Patrick's to meet us there and in case the police check, it's best we put in an appearance.' She kissed Kevin once again and the two girls headed for the building whose lights flickered through the swaying trees.

They were back in less than five minutes carrying two paper cups filled with some sort of a sweet liquor. Stone tried the stuff – enough to take your head off, but it sure as hell set fire to what they called the cockles of your heart.

Trish bore reasonably good news. 'Patrick's just arrived, said the police were still on the causeway but were scheduled to be pulled off at midnight.'

Erin was the conveyor of the bad news. 'Oh, they're after you, they are,' she told Stone. 'European-wide manhunt. Connected you with the fire-bombing of a building in France and two deaths. A man in Antwerp identified you, said you were in a bar there, nearly killed a couple of Australian sailors. And they know your name, have a proper photograph of you in the papers. A reward of 10,000 ecus for information leading to your capture.'

He groaned inwardly. He trusted them, had to, but he couldn't involve them any longer. 'Look – you guys have done a lot for me but it's better that you get out of here. Just forget you ever met me.'

Kevin made dissenting noises in his throat. 'Can't. I'm without a push bike and it would seem queer to the police if I came straggling over the causeway in wet clothes. Trish and Erin brought their sleeping-bags and tents. Should be an open place away from the clubhouse to set our gear up. We'll overnight and try it in the morning.' He turned to Trish. 'You and Erin should hop back to the bar. Ask the owner whether you can camp on his grounds, then hang around until most of the patrons are gone. Come down and get me when you've got the tents pitched, that's a girl.'

When they had left for the bar, Kevin settled down beside Stone on the gunwale of a dinghy. 'What's your plan now?'

'I don't have a clue. I'm what you'd call "supercargo". Melissa's picking me up but I have a strong feeling that she may want to drop me off once we clear Europe. I can't see her having me on board all the way to the West Indies.'

'You mean she'd sail the Atlantic by herself?' Obviously, this concept of a woman's capability didn't fit in with Kevin's less-than-liberated Irish perspective.

'There's the autopilot. And she'll be able to pick up crew in Gibraltar or the Canaries. Like I said, I'm supercargo.' Stone hadn't explained the relationship or its recent deterioration and Kevin was gentleman enough not to ask, except for a curious sideways glance.

They sat in silence for a while, both of them sipping their firewater. Kevin eventually stood up, stretched and looked out at the horizon. 'What time did you think she'd be in?'

'By midnight, maybe a little sooner.'

'Try "a lot sooner", Stone.' He pointed.

Against the night sky was a darker shape, ghosting past the breakwater. No running-lights, the sails down, the engine just ticking over. She swung the *Snow Goose* hard over, the hull shape foreshortening as it turned, the ketch pivoting through a half-circle. He heard the change in pitch of the engine, the prop thrashing water as it reversed.

Stone cast off the vinyl cover and ran for the dock, stumbling in the darkness. She had the ketch bow into the dock, lines ready.

He secured the bow line, then warped in the stern. Kevin was suddenly beside him, helping to heave on the line.

The dark shape of the dog was forward, padding slowly aft, a low rumble in his throat.

'No, Sailor,' she said softly. *'Down.'*

She had been bent down in the cockpit, flaking lines, then slowly stood up, her hands kneading her lower back. In the subdued glow of the engine instrument lights, she was unrecognizable – encased in bulky foul-weather gear, the fabric stiffened with salt. She eased the hood back. Her hair was matted, face stained with streaks of grime, eyebrows whitened with crystals.

'Hello, Stone,' she said wearily. 'You look like something the cat dragged in but I'm hardly the one to talk.'

He found it impossible to speak, had nothing adequate to say, stood there like a ten-year-old kid in the presence of a stern adult.

'Who's your friend?' she said. She eased down onto the cockpit seat, her head slumping.

God, she had to be exhausted, he thought. Thirty-six hours at sea in a gale through some of the heaviest shipping traffic in the world, probably without sleep.

Kevin leaned over the rail, his hand stretched out. 'Kevin Murphy. Very pleased to meet you. Heard a lot about you, Melissa.'

'I'm sure you did.' There was no warmth in her voice, more like a recording than anything.

Stone stood there, crazy to touch her, hold her, but his damned feet were planted to the ground, his tongue an invalid.

'Get aboard,' she said. 'Just let me sleep for a few hours and we'll get off before dawn. Don't want to have Dutch immigration poking around, do we?'

Stone pulled himself up over the rail and hunched down beside her in the cockpit. 'Thanks,' he said. God, it sounded inadequate. He touched her shoulder tentatively but she didn't react, as if she couldn't feel anything. Her head was nodding, then she jerked it upright.

'Sorry . . . so bloody tired. Can't keep my eyes open.

Will you straighten up, Stone – get a couple of spring lines on and some fenders out. I've got to get in my bunk before I pass out.'

'Yeah, of course. Go ahead. I'll take . . .'

There was a shout somewhere up near the marina building, then a flashlight's beam zagging through the trees.

He hadn't noticed the steps before, off to the far end of the dock, hidden by shrubbery. A string of Christmas-tree lights winked on, faintly illuminating the stairs, then the glare of overhead dock lights flooding the entire length of the marina seafront.

'Oh God, no, not now . . .' She stood up, teetering, and slumped down again. Stone caught a flash of Kevin ducking down behind the coachroof.

The flashlight was connected to a heavy man in a plaid shirt and bow tie, one end of it undone. He came lumbering down the dock, a clipboard under his arm, glasses pushed back on his forehead, the lenses glinting in the floodlights.

He lifted a hand in casual greeting and pulled up opposite the cockpit. '*Goede avond*. Welcome to Binnenhaven, as we like to say, the friendliest place on the coast. I don't have you down on my list. Did you make a reservation?'

Stone stood up and leaned over the lifelines. 'Sorry about that. No reservation. Didn't think you'd be full up.'

The man stuck out his hand. 'I'm Adriaens, filling in as dockmaster while he's away.' He scratched his chin. 'I can take you for tonight but I'm full up for tomorrow. Have to be out by noon. Sorry.'

'No problem,' Stone said. 'Actually, we just put in for a couple of hours, problem with the water pump. Be gone early morning.'

The man's face clouded. 'Still, have to charge you for the dock space. Sorry, but we all have our rules.' He handed Stone the clipboard. 'Fill it in, please.'

The form was quadrilingual – Dutch, French, German and English. Stone began to tell lies with the ballpoint pen, pulling phony names and places out of a mental hat, anxious to satisfy the old man, get him out of here. Forms were forms. Fill them in, nobody cared what they said as long as they got their money. He scribbled, illegible as he could make it.

As he wrote, he noticed the man walking along the dock, appraising the *Snow Goose*. He paused opposite Sailor and offered his hand. The dog tentatively sniffed, then dropped his head between his paws, eyes hooded. The man hunched his shoulders as if the interest was mutual and strolled back, picking at something on his neck.

'Been out in the shit, have you? Must be bad in the Channel. Used to fish on weekends before my back gave out.' He looked down, just now noticing Melissa who was stretched out on the cockpit cushions, her head cradled in her arms, oblivious. 'Looks like we lost one. She all right?'

'Fine. Just a little tired.' Stone signed the bottom of the form with an indecipherable scrawl and handed it back. 'What do we owe you?'

The man was studying the form. 'Can't read your writing. What was your last port?'

Stone started to answer, figured that 'Europort' would sound reasonable, but she woke up with a start, disoriented.

'Wha . . . ?' She slowly wiped the flat of her hand across her face, groggy.

'Last port, I asked. Your last port?' Adriaens cocked the pen, ready to write.

'Southampton,' she said, then slowly shook her head, trying to wake up. 'No . . . Hamble. Hamble River.'

The Dutchman's hand froze. He looked up slowly, squinting at Stone. 'She said you came from a foreign port, from England?'

Hunching his shoulders, Stone nodded. 'Doesn't matter, does it? No immigration procedures on the Continent now, right?'

'Doesn't apply,' Adriaens said, stiffening his back. 'Ships must still clear in if they're coming from a foreign port,

471

even yachts. It's the rule and you must promptly inform the authorities.'

Stone tried to put on his most honest face. 'Look, Adriaens. We're tired and they'd charge a packet for overtime. What say if we let that go till morning? We're bushed.'

Adriaens frowned. 'I don't know . . . I could be fined for not . . .'

Stone reached down to his knapsack and fumbled out his wallet, then peeled off a twenty-pound note.

'Does that take care of things? We'll call immigration first thing in the morning. Just want to clean up and get some sleep first. You understand?'

The Dutchman took the money, feeling the limp bill, still soggy. He slowly nodded, the fat under his chin collapsing into accordion folds. 'I suppose it will be all right.' But his voice wasn't convincing. He backed away, lifted the clipboard in a shallow salute and headed back down the dock. He turned once and looked over his shoulder, then slowly climbed the stairs.

Kevin waited until the dock lights had gone out, then stood up and walked aft. 'You think he believed you?'

'No, but my guess is he likes the money more than he cares about the regulations.'

Kevin nodded. 'Probably right. Need any help? If not, I'll get along.'

Stone shook his hand. 'You and the rest of your bunch have done a lot, Kevin. More than enough and my thanks for it. I'll write when I can, let you know how it works out.'

She was snoring softly, her foot twitching. He looked down on her, his heart breaking. Somehow, he would get through to her, had to.

'Take care of yourself and the lady, Stone.' Kevin nodded toward Melissa. 'My guess is that it will work out.'

They shook again and Kevin jumped down to the dock, waved, and headed for the stairs.

He propped her up on her feet, worked his way down

the companionway backwards hanging on to her, Melissa slumped against him. The dog was right behind them, protective but not making unfriendly noises.

He eased her out of her foul-weather gear and sea boots, laid her out on her bunk, pulled the covers over her. *Sleep well, my lady*.

Softly pulling her cabin door closed, he next switched on the light over the nav table. Her course was laid out on the chart, a stair-step of pencil lines zig-zagging up the Channel, neatly labeled with the time, course and distance. He leafed through the log. She had kept a complete record, except for the last forty-odd miles on her approach in from the sea. The log recorded winds between force six and nine, gale winds most of the way. And all alone, he thought.

It was more of a vibration than a noise. He couldn't work it out at first, then realized it was the sound of feet pounding down the dock.

Oh shit! he swore.

He popped his head out of the hatch. Kevin and the two girls were running toward him, Patrick another twenty meters back.

'Get the engine going, Stone! He called the cops.'

Stone scrambled into the cockpit, twisted the key, heard the engine fire on the first turn.

Kevin was casting off the dock lines, the girls scrambling over the rail, Patrick pushing the bow away from the dock.

Vaulting over the rail, Kevin landed on deck, twisting his foot, collapsing into the cockpit. *'Bloody hell!'*

'You okay?' He didn't throw it in gear, didn't want to commit yet. Had to get them off the boat. This wasn't something that the Irish should get involved in.

'Just twisted it, nothing . . .' He looked up at Stone. 'For God's sake, man, get going.'

'I can't let you get involved any more than you are. You and the bunch — get off the boat. They'll never know. Come on, Kevin — move it!'

'You're not listening, Stone. We're already involved.

473

The rest of the patrons had gone, just Trish, Erin and Patrick left. The Dutchman came back, muttering about smuggling, said he was heading up to the office to call the customs authorities. Patrick followed him, knocked him over the head with a piece of firewood and tied him up with his belt. Now, you bloody fool, will you get this thing moving?'

It seemed like a damned fine idea to Stone.

TWENTY-THREE

Snow Goose, 03.07, 16 April

He put his back into it, forcing the helm down another spoke. The next sea, like a blundering drunken giant, lurched from out of the darkness and smashed into the topsides. In the dim wash of the running-lights, his eyes burning from the lash of the wind and salt, he caught a flash of the spume, torn from the crest of the wave and shattered by the impact into fractured green glass, whipping aft toward him.

He ducked, trying to avoid the fusillade of spray, then was hammered by the solid stuff, its impact driving the breath from his lungs. The water flowed away as *Snow Goose* wallowed in the cross-sea, the spent sea sucking at his body, trying to tear him loose.

Stone coughed and shook his head, trying to clear his blurred vision, felt for the thousandth time icy trickles infiltrating the gaps in his foul-weather gear, eating the heat from his body.

The *Snow Goose* now tore free, slowly accelerating. Spent seawater cascaded down the deck in a wave, smashing against the coachroof, bursting upward, then washing aft, flooding the cockpit.

As her bow rose to the next wave, she slowed to a stagger, teetered on the crest, then stumbled and fell. Her bowsprit speared the slick, black trough, then slowly rose again, white water streaming from her forefoot in a shaggy beard.

He had let her come up into the wind too far and the storm trysail luffed, canvas drumming, the bronze sail slides clattering. He spun the helm over, heading off again, the sail filling with a thunderous *whump*, the mast groaning in its step, the shrouds twanging, the whole hull shuddering.

Jesus, he thought. *How much longer can she stand up to this sort of punishment?*

He had her on the port tack, holding a rough heading of 285 degrees mag, had been since they cleared the shallows west of Binnenhaven four hours ago. No real navigation, no log, no bearings, just the erratic readout of a soggy loran which slurred through a stream of numbers, pausing occasionally to spit out a dubious fix. How accurate it was he couldn't guess, but he was damned sure he wasn't making progress to the south, instead being driven slowly west-north-west, into the North Sea. Fine by him for now – get sea room in a blow, said the old fishermen of the Maine coast. And sea room he would need aplenty before he tried to turn south.

His skin crawled thinking of the risks she had taken. She had been through these same seas as well, by herself. But the wind had been behind her, the waves toppling in on themselves in the ketch's streaming wake. The autopilot had freed her hands, given her breathing room, but Stone had found the autopilot couldn't handle the erratic, clashing seas when it tried to steer a windward course – instead just mindlessly bulldozed through them and, in so doing, subjected the hull to the hammers of hell. Once, in the few minutes during which he had tried using it, the autopilot had been overwhelmed, the bow falling off dangerously, a sea the size of a barn breaking over the entire length of the ketch, the classic broach and knockdown.

He had kicked out the autopilot clutch and wrestled back control, but it had been too close a thing, the smell of the sea's corruption the same as it was in the mines when you hit a methane pocket – that rotten-sweet, cloying scent of near-death.

But there had been no choice. They would hunt for him,

476

he knew. How long the marina manager would take to get his act together was an unknown, but he would, and then it would hit the fan in a glorious splatter. They would scratch their collective asses as they looked at the charts and conclude that he had to head north-east toward the Denmark Straits, running before the wind as any sane man would. And that's where they would look first – for a sane man heading north-east.

Not west-north-west where he was headed, nor south-west, where he would steer once he had sufficient sea room and could tack, because he *knew*, was *positive* that the wind would shift, was willing to bet everything he had on it.

The barometer had bumped along near the bottom of the scale for the last three hours, but it was now climbing, three millibars in the last half-hour. He guessed that an intense low-pressure cell was somewhere down south, probably in the Bay of Biscay, racing eastward, driven on the breath of the jetstream. As the low plowed into the coast of France, soaked the plains of Guianne and finally broke its back on the Pyrenees, the wind would start to clock around from south-west to south, then to the south-east. And as it backed, it would ease, please, dear God, it would ease.

Twenty minutes ago, Erin, tough as a brick, had passed up a mug slopping over with cocoa and brandy. By the time he got it to his mouth it was half seawater, but he drank it and was thankful for its bite. He shouted his thanks but she couldn't hear him, had just given him a clenched-fist salute and a grin, then ducked below, slamming the hatch behind her as a sea broke over it.

His eyes burning with salt, his hands raw, his ears hammered senseless by the wind, his body shivering, Stone steered. He could make it to the dawn and by then Melissa could spell him with five hours of sleep under her belt. That is, if the damn boat held together that long.

A wedge of light at the top of the hatch widened as the

hatch slid back. Patrick's head cautiously popped out. 'Got the weather forecast,' he yelled. Stone checked ahead for a smooth patch and waved his arm.

Patrick scrambled aft and snapped his safety harness around the binnacle support. He had tried to spell Stone off during the second hour outbound, but a full gale was a lousy classroom in which to learn the skills of an offshore sailor. Stone had finally told him to go below, keep an eye on things, check the bilges. And listen up on BBC Radio 4 for the shipping forecast.

'They're still calling it a south-westerly gale, force nine: Forties, Dogger, Humber, Thames, Dover and Wight.'

'How about the banana belt; Finisterre and Biscay?'

'Still gale force down south but backing to the east by dawn and decreasing to force five.'

The sea, not to be ignored, cuffed the topsides with a breaking wave which slopped into the cockpit, drenching them. But it was not a malicious thing, just a reminder. Stone eased the helm, water running down his nose, and paid attention to his course.

He had been steering by the feel of the wind on his face and the luff of the trysail. He glanced down to check the compass. It was oscillating around 260 degrees. Backing already, he thought, pleased as a kid with an all-day sucker.

'Trish doing any better?' Stone asked.

'Still sick,' Patrick yelled back. 'Like a dog.'

'Kevin?'

'Ankle's ballooned up, has some ice on it — Erin's fussing over him like Mother Teresa.'

'Melissa?'

'She woke up half an hour ago, groggy, splitting head-ache. Wanted to come on deck but I pushed her back to her bunk, told her you were on watch. She made a face and asked me to pass a message to you.'

'Like what?'

'She said to watch out for the potholes.'

Stone had to smile. 'Were you able to figure out when the tide turns?' Up until now, the tide had been running down-Channel, bucking the south-west gale, lumping up the seas into something Mr Maytag would have fancied.

'According to the tables, it's slack water now, starting to run up-Channel,' Patrick shouted. 'Is that bad or good?'

'Both. The seas should smooth out but the current will be against us.'

'Any idea where we're headed?'

Stone shrugged. 'The hell out of Dutch waters and eventually to the south. Beyond that, it's up to the lady. It's her boat and I'm just driving.'

The Valkyr, 03.28

Billy Allen, Master under God, duly licensed by the Australian Department of Transport, empowered to command motor vessels not exceeding 1000 tons on all oceans, sat rooted in the upholstered helmsman's chair, his feet braced against the stirrups, his hands gripping the arm-rests. The autopilot was holding the *Valkyr* reasonably steady but she tended to wallow badly in the cross-seas, inducing a sickening roll. He checked over the instrument panel. Course 290 degrees more or less, speed averaging 6.7 knots, the rpm gauges of the three IMU diesels barely ticking over. Annoying as hell, because the *Valkyr* was built to rip through this crap at thirty knots plus. Pound your guts out it did at that speed, but better than this bloody rolling. He turned and checked with the American.

'How's the scope look, Turner?'

Turner was braced in the seat behind the radar repeater scope. 'More or less the same heading, same speed, wiggles around a little like he doesn't know how to steer straight. Half the time, the boat's down in the troughs between the waves and I lose her. How long you think they'll keep this heading?'

'If I knew where they were headed, you'd be the first

to know.' Allen fetched a cigarette from a pack and lit it. Turner, he reckoned, was bloody wizard on fitting out the pneumatic and electrical stuff which Brunner had installed in the Tank, but his sloppy work on the radar grated on Allen's nerves. That and the fact he incessantly picked his teeth with his fingernails.

Turner, leaning back, scratched his neck. 'Hey, buddy. Staring at this radar for three hours straight sucks. It's frying my eyeballs out and that bozo's not going anywhere. What say I knock off early and head down for chow?'

Allen glanced at his Rolex. Still half an hour till Turner's watch was over. 'Who relieves you?'

'La Cucaracha.' The Bolivian's name was actually Carlos Mendez, but the nickname had stuck – as long as you didn't use it in Mendez's presence. To do that was to invite a knife blade shoved in your guts – overly sensitive to ethnic slurs was Carlos.

Allen shook his head. 'Cookie's off watch, Turner. The bitch kept him up half the night making stuff for her while she was on the radio with Brunner. He won't be back on till six.'

Turner wasn't about to be deflected from bugging out of the last half-hour of his watch, but he added some bait to make the deal sweeter. 'So no big deal. I'll make the chow myself. I'll go down and hustle up some eggs. Also saw some ham in the chill-room – cut off a couple of slabs, throw it in the skillet along with some sliced spuds. Make enough for both of us, be ready to chow down by the time you get off watch.'

Allen considered it. Hadn't eaten much since yesterday evening when they left Juist Island, with only a dry sandwich this afternoon.

'The yacht still in the same position relative to us?'

Turner nodded. 'Yeah. Twelve miles dead in front, same speed, just where it's been since we picked it up two hours ago.'

Ham and eggs sounded good. 'Right,' Allen grunted. 'Get

on with it. Make mine over easy, lots of ham, forget the potatoes. And Turner . . .'

'Yeah?'

'Wash your fuckin' hands first, right, mate?'

Snow Goose, 03.49

Stone swore under his breath. The wind, which he thought had been slowly backing, had clocked around again, pushing him onto the same old west-north-westerly course of 290. And he was uneasy. The *Snow Goose* would soon be penetrating the northbound shipping lanes. Visibility was nil and he didn't want suddenly to be staring down the bow wave of a tanker doing twenty knots as it plowed north for the Denmark Straits. Two hours ago, he thought he had caught the truncated profile of an unlighted ship's superstructure on his port quarter. He had stared into the stinging wind and driving spray, trying to make her out, but even if she *had* been there, she vanished: maybe nothing more than an apparition concocted by his own stir-fried brain.

He worked at visualizing the North Sea in his mind. If he tacked, say around dawn, they'd be able to lay a course of roughly south which would push them in toward the coast of Belgium. Not good, but if the wind shifted eastwards, as he thought it eventually would, they would have a clean, one-shot run, right out the Straits of Dover and into the Atlantic. He decided to hang on to this heading until dawn when Melissa came on watch and see what she wanted to do. Her boat, therefore her decision.

The hatch slid open and Patrick popped his head out. Stone waved him aft.

Patrick scrambled over the deck and dropped into the cockpit. He fished around in his jacket pocket and came up with a candy bar. 'Tried to heat some beans but the pot flew off the stove and they spilled on the floor. Thought this might do you for now.'

Stone took it, used his teeth to tear the wrapper off and bit into it. It tasted like desiccated grub worms.

'Granola,' Patrick said. 'Found a whole box.'

At least it cut the taste of salt in his mouth. Stone mumbled his thanks and chewed on.

'Anything on the news?'

'In about ten minutes, BBC World Report.' Patrick was wedged down in the forward part of the cockpit, looking aft. 'Say . . . I didn't know there were buoys out here.'

'A few, but they're mostly north of us. You see one?'

'Thought I did. Red.' He pointed over Stone's left shoulder. 'Saw it as we came off the top of the last wave.'

'See whether you can time the flashes, give us an idea which one it is.'

Patrick stood up, bracing himself against the cockpit coaming, one hand on the mizzen shrouds. 'Must have been mistaken, don't . . .' He craned his neck, pointing. *'Hang on, there it is!'*

Red didn't sound right. Stone had expected to pick up one of the lighted buoys that marked the southern side of the northbound shipping lane, probably buoy MW3. Except, according to the chart, it was a green flasher, once every six seconds. 'Time it,' he said, a little aggravated.

'Ah – can't actually time it,' Patrick said. 'It's on for a while, then off, as if it were sometimes down in the trough between the waves where I can't see it. Actually, I think it's solid red all the time.'

Stone turned, fear clogging his throat. He didn't see it at first, then did as a wave lifted the ketch. Red. The light moved, some green showing to the left of it. *Oh hell, not like this!*

He threw the helm over, hard aport, the *Snow Goose* responding sluggishly. He knew almost immediately that she didn't have enough speed on her to get through the tack. She came up into the wind, hung there, the trysail flogging, her speed dying as the bow pounded into the seas, damn near dead in the water. He reached down, frantically tried to start the engine but it was stone cold. It grunted over a couple of revs before the relay chattered.

Batteries damn near flat, had to switch over to the other bank, no time, looked up again, Patrick just standing there like a twit, frozen, staring at eternity and yet not knowing its name.

The thing was blacker than the night, blotting up a good chunk of the horizon. Stone could now see both of the running-lights, the red a dazzling ruby, the green now just a splinter of emerald, as if it were refracted through the edge of the lens.

The thing slid past the bow of the *Snow Goose* like a dream of death, its bow wave breaking against the topsides of the *Snow Goose*, the stink of diesel exhaust sucked behind it, the wind actually blocked for a second by its passage.

The ketch's trysail shook, then filled with a clap, *Snow Goose* finally falling off on the port tack, heading south. Stone, his heart thudding, eased in the helm, letting her gather speed, then brought her back carefully, hard on the wind. He glanced down at the compass. New course, 180. He thought about trying to tack back to the old course but decided not to. He had enough sea room and might as well start to make some distance down-Channel.

As the trawler's stern light drifted to starboard, he watched it grow dimmer, dissolving into the spray and darkness of the storm. The overtaking trawler had come down on him from behind, both of the vessels heading in roughly the same direction, the trawler's course only slightly divergent from his. A very near thing. Ships that passed in the night were a damn-sight better proposition than those that collided and sank. At their closest point of passing, Stone doubted that more than fifteen meters had separated the two vessels. He also doubted that the trawler's helmsman had even seen the *Goose*'s puny stern light or had kept a watch on radar, probably mesmerized by the flicking wiper blades or brain-dead from boredom.

Patrick was slumped down in the well of the cockpit, shaking.

Stone touched him on the shoulder. 'Don't say anything about this to the rest of them, right?' There was no point in crying over milk that hadn't been spilled.

Patrick nodded dumbly, then gagged and vomited.

The Valkyr, 04.11

'Where is Turner?' Carlos the Cucaracha asked, obviously irritated. He had turned up three minutes early for his watch, typical of the Cucaracha.

'Galley.' Allen couldn't stand the bleedin'-heart bastard, always on somebody's case about that Shining Path political crap. They were pushing it in Europe now, trying to Mao-tize European radicals who had never come in from the cold. Joss knew Carlos vaguely, had done the recruitment with Brunner's blessing, but Allen didn't much care for whacko political types.

Carlos leaned down and studied the scope. 'I cannot see the vessel.'

'Look dead ahead, twelve miles, bearing 290 magnetic, making about seven knots. Sometimes the return isn't too good. She's built out of wood and that makes for a rotten return. On top of that, she's end on to us and the seas reflect back a lot of clutter on the scope. Take your time and you'll eventually pick her up.'

Impatient, Carlos selected a greater range setting and turned up the gain. 'I see the ship now. She has altered to the right by at least fifteen degrees and she is moving faster than seven knots. Perhaps nine, possibly ten.'

Allen was too tired to argue, and he had learned from a couple of other verbal run-ins with Carlos not to tangle with him.

'Set the cursor on the return like I showed you before and give me a heading,' Allen said. His stomach growled in anticipation. Turner would scarf up all the tucker unless he got down to the galley pretty damned quick.

Carlos fussed around with the radar's controls. 'With the bearing cursor on top of the return, 307 appears in the upper right window.'

So the ketch had altered course slightly, Allen thought, mildly surprised. He didn't know much about sail-boats, actually, didn't give a fuck about them. Bloody stupid to go to sea with canvas as a means of moving the boat when all you really needed was a couple of good diesels.

Switching the autopilot to standby, Allen turned the helm a few degrees and watched as the repeater compass drifted to starboard. He steadied out on 305 and reengaged the pilot. Then he added a bit of power, slowly edging up the *Valkyr*'s speed to fourteen knots.

Dieter, yet another one of Brunner's ex-Stasi gonzo types, finally arrived, his coffee mug slopping over. Allen gritted his teeth, knowing the stains would be hell to get out of the carpet.

'You're late, *Mein Führer*,' Allen said, trying to get a rise out of the Kraut.

Dieter gave him a look of loathing and slid into the helmsman's seat without comment. He silently thumbed through the log, tapped one of the transfer pump gauges with his fingernail and, seemingly satisfied, sipped his coffee.

It pissed Allen. Bastard might have had a lot of sea-time, as Brunner claimed he had, but Dieter was an insolent sod. Allen grabbed an overhead rail and swung into the companionway leading belowdecks, then turned back to Dieter. 'If the yacht alters course again, give Brunner's bitch a call on the intercom. She's scheduled to give Brunner an update at 05.40 before he pulls the plug. And keep the radio scanner volume turned up. The yacht hasn't made any transmissions as yet, but if they do, Brunner will want the details.'

Dieter did not turn to acknowledge Allen's instructions, just nodded vaguely.

Uneasy for no particular reason that he could put his finger on, Allen clumped down the stairs to the galley. He figured it was just the lack of food after a rough night. Be bloody glad when this job is over, mate.

The Cormorant, 05.19

Karl Brunner slouched against the rail of the wing bridge watching the *Cormorant*'s crew on the foredeck roll out massive spools of wire cable in preparation for anchoring. A sea, larger than the rest, broke against the bow, throwing heavy spray, but the five men, most of their working lifetime spent at sea, ignored it.

Brunner was more than satisfied with them – solid professional types composed of former men and officers of the now-dismantled GDR *Kriegsmarine*. All of them had been members of an underwater strike team, seconded to Brunner's command back in 1987, when the KGB had been directed by the Stasi to tap into a NATO underseas teleprinter communications cable which led from northern Denmark, across the Skagerrak Sea, to the southern coast of Norway. On that job, Brunner had lost three of the team of eleven, but the job had been a success. By comparison, this job would be a stroll in the park. And at 50,000 deutschmarks each for the job, far more appealing. It was too bad, he thought, that they would never live to spend it.

Over the last two hours, the wind had gradually shifted from south-west to southerly, then south-easterly, and its velocity had moderated to under thirty knots. The *Cormorant* was headed directly into the leftover swells, making only six knots – very slow going because he had standing orders for the helmsman to favor the weak bow sections and thin hull plating. But the *Cormorant* had stood up well enough on the trip down from Juist, and there were less than five nautical miles to run before she was in position.

He returned to the protection of the glassed-in bridge, nodded to the helmsman, and poured a cup of coffee from the thermos. In less than twenty-four hours, he would be finished with the project and headed south to the Med on the *Valkyr*, if events proceeded as he had planned. He smiled ironically to himself, uneasy with his choice of words. *If* was a tenuous word, not normally part of his vocabulary. Perhaps a sign of advancing age, he thought, when caution began to erode confidence and the mind became averse to risk.

A hand appeared over the edge of the bridge deck. Maas, his lungs wheezing, climbed the last few rungs that led to the wing bridge and swung on the hand grip into the seat behind Brunner. He wiped his hands on a rag, gradually recovering his breath.

'What was the problem, Hans?' There had been a slow leak in one of the modified high-pressure steam pipes, and Brunner was now concerned that some of the ninety-two others might be defective as well. Maas had calculated that they would only need sixty-two for the job but, like all engineers, he worshiped redundancy.

Maas slowly lifted his shoulders, then let them sag. 'It wasn't a problem caused by Turner's welding after all. Both the pipe and the end-caps were leak-free. I traced the problem to a defective shut-off valve so I switched it out of the manifold system. No point in trying to repair the valve and refill the pipe with the compressor. There's not enough time.'

'But the rest of them?'

'Perfect — all over 210 bars, the specified pressure.'

Maas had devised the setup. He had originally calculated that a compressed-air supply, equivalent in volume to 1100 scuba bottles, would be required both to supply air to the divers and to power the hydraulic dredge that would be used to scour out the boreholes. Using that many scuba bottles was obviously out of the question, but the

Dutchman had come up with a neat alternative. By using ninety-three sections of high-pressure steam pipe, each thirty centimeters in diameter and twelve meters in length, then welding the ends shut and installing valves so that each of the pipes could be filled with compressed air to a pressure of 210 bars, he had achieved roughly the same pressure and volume of air as could be contained by 1100 standard scuba tanks.

While the *Cormorant* had been anchored in the lee of Juist Island alongside the *Pelican*, the steam pipes, caps welded to their ends, had been clamped to the floor of the *Cormorant*'s aft cargo hold and their valves manifolded together with a network of pipes. From the manifold led two high-pressure hoses – one to the outlet on the chamber and the other fixed to the hydraulic dredges that would be used to scour out the boreholes.

'What about the Semtex. Unpacked from the barrels yet?'

'All done. It's stored in the nets on the outside of the Tank.' He fished a key from his jacket and handed it to Brunner. 'The firing mechanism is in the compartment next to the hatch.'

Far ahead of the *Cormorant*, Brunner saw the wink of a red light: two longs, two shorts. He put his hand on the helmsman's arm. 'Reduce your speed to steerage way until the men are back on board, then resume speed.'

He swung to the bridge and clambered down the ladder. There was a hint of light to the east, and as he walked to the boarding ladder he could just make out the inflatable assault boat as it banked through a turn and swept in alongside the *Cormorant*'s hull.

A bow line whispered over the rail, was grabbed by one of the deckhands and secured. Joss was the first one up the boarding ladder, water dripping from his neoprene wetsuit, a transparent plastic camera housing dangling by a strap from his left hand. He saw Brunner, gave him a thumbs-up and padded over.

'How did it go?' Brunner asked.

Peeling off his hood, Joss nodded. 'Tough. The current on the bottom wasn't slack like the tide tables predicted. Bitch of a time moving around — started to run short of air.'

Not really interested in whether it had been difficult or not, Brunner only wanted to know whether it had been done. 'Let's get out of the wind,' he said. He led Joss through a side door and into the wardroom.

Brunner nodded casually at Joss' finger. It was encased in a protective rubber sheath, bound with some kind of waterproof tape. 'Does it still bother you?'

'Has anyone ever told you that you're a filthy, sadistic bastard, Brunner? I understand the reason why you wanted my fingertip but, for Christ's sake, why didn't you get Horst to lay on some morphine? Fucker took it off with a bolt-cutter and the only anesthetic he gave me was a shot of brandy. Swear to God, that cocksucker enjoyed doing it. Damn near passed out.'

'My apologies . . .' Brunner found himself loathing this tiresome, whining incompetent — the only one he would truly be glad to be rid of. '. . . But it was an operational necessity and, as you can see, the deception succeeded admirably. I would add that, in all likelihood, your Interpol file has now been relegated to the archives of those vicious criminals who have passed on to their just rewards.' He held out his hand. 'We're wasting time. The camera, please.'

While Joss slumped down on the settee, Brunner unscrewed the wing nuts of the camera's waterproof housing, lifted out the first Polaroid print and examined it carefully under the desk lamp. Captured in the glare of the camera's strobe light was a slender stalk which rose out of the seabed, terminating in a spherical bulb.

'Any identifying model numbers on it?' Brunner asked.

Slumping down opposite him, Joss nodded. 'It's a 58–01 Mark 4. English job, built by Marconi, five kilohertz broadband. Identical to the American 409 Mark 3 that you briefed me on.'

Based on the information that his 'client' had modemed in by satellite, Brunner had known that there would be acoustic sensors strung across the English Channel along the route of the Chunnel, providing Eurotunnel security personnel with a means of listening for any man-made activity on the seabed. That had cost them a fortune, he thought. But if Joss had done his job properly, Eurotunnel's investment was wasted.

Joss lit a cigarette, then reached across and picked up the second Polaroid, examining it, then skidding it back across the table to Brunner's side. The camera had captured a gloved hand sliding a perforated cylinder over the SOSUS transducer. 'Neat gadget you had whipped up. Whoever gave you the details of the SOSUS sensors knew what the hell he was talking about.'

Commander Gregori Michaelovich Petrof, a Russian naval intelligence officer, now living in a St Petersburg cold-water flat on a 300-rouble pension – but soon to take up residence in a fashionable bungalow in Barbados – had sold Brunner's ex-Stasi contact an intelligence file garnered from a career spanning two decades in anti-submarine warfare. More important, Petrof had also provided the rough designs necessary to defeat any one of four different models of SOSUS sensors used by NATO, for it was obvious that Eurotunnel would have leaned on NATO for a solution to the Chunnel's seabed security.

Technically, the problem was that you couldn't just clap the marine equivalent of earmuffs on a SOSUS sensor because the technicians who monitored the unit would immediately notice that the sensor had suddenly gone deaf, triggering an investigation of the sensor's health and well-being. Nor, for the same reason, could you cut the underwater cables that carried the sensor's signals to the monitoring processors.

The Soviet solution – low-tech, relatively cheap and virtually foolproof – had been to encase each targeted NATO SOSUS sensor in a foam-lined canister which was equipped with sixteen miniature transducers – each transducer nothing more than a waterproof high-fidelity loudspeaker. The transducers were connected by an undersea cable to an acoustic pickup positioned a kilometer away on the seabed. Thus, what the SOSUS signal processors heard were underwater sounds generated 1000 meters distant from the actual SOSUS sensor's location. In the same way, the Soviets had opened acoustic windows in the SOSUS line, allowing their subs to slip through without detection.

Brunner had contracted with an Italian firm to build the units, their intended use being 'underseas marine mammal tracking'. The Italian firm, not one to ask questions, didn't raise a corporate eyebrow. The fee they were paid by the Hamburg firm of Weshiem-Munden GmbH had been sufficient evidence of the order's legitimacy.

The *ears*, as Brunner referred to them in his private diary, had been extravagantly expensive. Now, he would soon find out whether they had been worth it.

'Were you able to install all of them?' Brunner asked.

Joss held up his right hand, fingers spread, only the thumb tucked under. 'I had trouble with one of them on the checkout. It's installed at the far end of the line but I wouldn't trust it.'

It's good enough, thought Brunner. With four SOSUS sensors neutralized, 600 meters of the seabed over the Chunnel was now deaf. In time, the Eurotunnel technicians who analyzed the output of the sensors would detect the anomaly, but that time-frame, Brunner guessed, would be measured in days, not hours.

The Valkyr, 05.36

She lit another cigarette from the butt of one still burning and stared out the porthole at the gray wash of sea. The wind seemed to have gone down but there were low banks of fog on the sea. She was tired and a low-level headache ground at her temples.

The destination of the sailing yacht concerned her. The alert for it had been broadcast from a Dutch coastal station, Radio Goes, shortly after midnight. The name of the yacht was not known, only that a marina dockmaster suspected smuggling and, for his trouble, had been brutalized. He had described the vessel as an English ketch, manned by a man and his wife. A dog had been on board as well – a large, vicious terrier of sorts.

Yet, incredibly, the Dutch marine authorities had apparently made no connection between the smugglers and the terrorist that the police were seeking. It was a typical case, she guessed, of one bureaucratic hand not knowing what the other one was doing.

Immediately after the Radio Goes broadcast, Brunner, well to the south of the *Valkyr*, had called her on the scrambled single sideband radio, sure that it was Stone.

The time the ketch had left Binnenhaven was a known. The authorities believed that the ketch would head northeast, driven by the gale. Brunner believed differently. He was sure that Stone would head west into international waters, *then* south.

The *Cormorant* had left the anchorage at Juist Island first, the *Valkyr* remaining at anchor for another twelve hours, then leisurely steaming south for the rendezvous at 17.00 when Brunner would be finished with the job and ready for the pickup.

But based on the Radio Goes transmission, Brunner had radically changed the plan, telling her to find the ketch and shadow it. With the *Valkyr* blacked out and running at thirty-one knots, it had taken them slightly more than two hours to intersect the ketch, make an identification and start to trail her. The question that gnawed at her now was what Brunner intended to do. He had a phobia about revealing his plans and never informed her in advance of his intentions, but she had an idea of what he would tell her to do and she was anxious to get it over with before the cloud deck broke up. She was sure that by mid-morning, the Dutch authorities would have aircraft over the North Sea, searching for the ketch, and she had no desire for the *Valkyr* to be spotted anywhere near the wreckage.

The Icom 3000 single sideband transceiver was warmed up. She checked her watch. Karl was one minute late – unusual for him.

She picked up the microphone, about to call when his voice broke through the crackling static.

'Bravo, this is Alpha. Do you read me?'

'I read you. Switch.' She flicked the scrambler on and waited until the green confidence light blinked. She thumbed the mike button switch again. 'How do you hear me, Karl?'

'As if you were at the bottom of a barrel but, still, good enough. What's your location and weather?'

'Approximately halfway across the North Sea on a line drawn between the Hook of Holland and Great Yarmouth, England. The ketch altered course slightly to the north about two hours ago and picked up a couple of knots, possibly running under both sail and engine. I checked with the bridge ten minutes ago. She's still in position, still on a 305-degree heading. The winds have moderated and gone easterly, some fog about and getting worse.'

'Strange – I would have thought Stone would have tacked to the south by now. Where do you think he's headed?'

She had the chart of the North Sea and the English Channel laid out on the desk. 'Great Yarmouth seems the obvious destination. It has a good harbor. My guess is that he'll turn himself in to the police, try to cut some kind of a deal. I don't know what he's learned, Karl, but it isn't worth our while to take any chances. We do it now or never.'

'He still hasn't used his radio?'

'No. We've had the scanner on all night. Nothing.'

There was silence on his end, as if he was considering his options. Then, 'I had hoped that he'd run for it, create a diversion that would tie up the English, but you're right. We can't afford to let him get back to England. Is there any shipping in your area?'

'Very little. We're already past the Noord Hinder light-ship that marks the northern limit of the deep-water shipping lanes. Dieter reported to me less than ten minutes ago that there's no vessel except the ketch within a thirty-mile radius.'

He sounded satisfied. 'Very well. Take care of it. Make sure that you get the masthead antenna first so he can't transmit, then use the RPG-7 to blow out the hull at the waterline. There may be some debris. Pick up anything that's identifiable. If the Dutch and the English authorities think he's still afloat, they'll center their efforts on an aerial search up in your area which will keep them away from mine.'

She jotted down his instructions and underlined them. 'The time of the rendezvous remains the same?'

'The same, 17.00 hours.' There was a delay, someone talking to him in the background. 'We're almost into position and there's work to do. I'll sign off now.'

'Good luck, Karl, and take care of yourself.'

He laughed, his tone sarcastic. 'I appreciate your deep concern, Francine. If I, by some great misfortune, were to die, there wouldn't be any way for you to get into the Luxembourg account, now would there?'

'I didn't mean that, Karl!' she shot back, but the frequency was now silent.

The Cormorant, 05.50

The wind was down to twenty knots but the fog, light until an hour ago, had thickened. A heavy swell was still running, but Brunner was pleased. In some ways, the conditions couldn't be better; not that he had a choice.

The *Cormorant*'s engines were slow ahead. Brunner leaned over the Raytheon GPS satellite navigational receiver, his instructions to the helmsman precise.

'Now slow ahead on your starboard engine, slow astern on the port and shift your helm . . . all right, bring her up to the wind, easy . . . good, now steady on . . . no, port, port . . . steady, now engines to neutral.'

The liquid crystal display crept to latitude 51° 04' 58.23" north, longitude 01° 23' 02.22" east. Brunner abruptly chopped his arm downwards and the helmsman shouted to the deck foreman, 'Let go!'

The anchor cable screamed out through the hawse pipe, then slowed as the *Cormorant* drifted slowly to leeward, finally fetching up in a depth of thirty-five meters with 240 meters of cable played out.

He waited until the *Cormorant* stabilized dead downwind, then nodded to the helmsman. 'Drop the aft one.'

The helmsman picked up the tannoy loudhailer. 'Now let go the stern anchor.'

A squeal of cable, a hollow splash.

'Now come ahead on both engines, dead slow,' Brunner said.

The *Cormorant* crept ahead, the forward anchor cable slowly reeling in, the after cable slowly paying out.

'Both engines neutral.' Brunner inspected the GPS. The readout hunted for a few seconds, then stabilized.

Maas leaned over Brunner's shoulder and checked the readout. 'Considering the size of the swells, Karl, quite acceptable.'

'Within twelve meters, Hans. Not exact, but good enough.' Brunner nodded to the helmsman. 'Secure engines, but leave the generator running. I'll need electrical power for a bit longer.' He checked the bulkhead chronometer and compared it to his diving watch. 'Sixteen minutes until slack water. Have both Franz and Joss set the detonators and double-check for anything that might

495

float free. We'll muster on the forward cargo hatch in twelve minutes.'

The helmsman, perhaps forgetting that he was no longer a bosun's mate in the GDR Baltic Fleet, snapped his heels together, saluted, then headed for the lower deck on the double.

Brunner leaned back on the stool and lit a cigar. 'We've come far in these few months, Hans.'

'You know you should not smoke, Karl. Not before this.'

'Indulge me, my friend.' Brunner smiled, exhaled a stream of smoke, then tapped a blip on the radar scope. 'This one worries me. He might see us.'

'You're an old woman, Karl. Fifteen miles off, heading away from us. Another ten minutes and we'll be out of range of his radar.' Maas checked the S-band radar detector and shook his head. 'Besides, his signal is feeble. Probably an old set in need of adjustment. He won't notice us.'

'You're probably right, Hans. Better that we get on with the job. You check the crew and make sure that they're ready to go. I'll be down in a few minutes.'

Maas stood up, zipping his jacket, then smiled. 'I've looked forward to this, Karl – never had the chance to see my work first-hand. I think you'll find it satisfactory.'

'I have no doubts about your calculations, Hans. None whatsoever,' Brunner said. The old man smiled, then worked his way down to the deck.

He took his time, enjoying the cigar. Maas, unlike the rest of them, was a man he would miss. So few dedicated technicians left in these days of instant gratification and shoddy workmanship. Refreshing to have known him.

He finished off the cigar and stubbed it out, then carefully switched off the radio and radar. He clambered down the ladder to the steel deck, then headed forward to the cargo hold.

Joss was waiting for him, his tanks, mask and regulator laid out on the deck.

Brunner checked his watch, then glanced over the side. Bits of sea grass and debris floated sluggishly past the *Cormorant*, the current almost slack. He nodded to Joss. 'Get on with it. We'll see you on the bottom.' Brunner swung a leg over the cargo hatch, then looked back at the seven men assembled on the deck. 'Let's go.'

Joss waited until they had filed past him and followed Brunner into the cargo hold. A flare of light from within the Tank flicked on, followed by the sound of a metal hatch slamming shut. There was the hiss of pressurization, then the clang of a hammer against metal – Brunner's signal that they were ready.

Using a flashlight, Joss scanned the checklist one last time.

1. Engine room: firefighting seacocks, port and starboard diesel engine seawater intakes, generator seawater intake
2. After cargo hold: refrigeration heat-exchanger intake
3. Foredeck: firefighting seawater intakes 1–4

He worked his way through the *Cormorant*, keeping his movements careful, not taking any chances. To trip and fall, to sprain an ankle or cut into his wetsuit because of a careless movement, would screw up the whole operation. Slow and easy, he thought.

As he opened each seacock, he checked the inflow, then moved on to the next one. All in sequence, precisely timed. A marine architect, a *Kraut* marine architect, because Brunner didn't trust any other nationality, had made the calculations. The Kraut had guaranteed the results to within thirty seconds.

Joss finished his rounds, sloshing his way back to the main deck. The *Cormorant* had already settled perceptibly, her movements sluggish. She was down on her marks by perhaps a meter and sinking on a fairly even keel, just a bit down by the stern. Right on. He checked his watch. Thirteen minutes, twenty-three seconds.

He moved to the foredeck and strapped on his tanks, checked his regulator, adjusted his weight belt, then sat down on the edge of the cargo hatch and waited.

Five minutes ticked by, and he realized that the *Cormorant* was settling more slowly than he expected – maybe barnacles in the intakes which were slowing the inflow.

Best to get on with it, he thought. He padded aft and opened the door to a waterproofed electrical panel. His flashlight picked out four newly installed switches. He mentally reviewed the sequence, then fingered the first two. There was a dull, hollow thud, followed closely by a second one.

In the engine room and well below the waterline, two loops of primacord – three meters in diameter, plastered to the hull with duct tape and tamped with clay – detonated, blowing ragged disks of steel plating away from the hull. What had been a controlled inflow of seawater now became a gushing flood.

Joss hesitated, then fingered the last two switches simultaneously. Two muffled thuds rumbled out of the forward cargo hold, disks of steel plating on either side of the hold blowing outward.

The old bucket started to settle at a much faster rate. Joss carefully pulled on his flippers, spat in his diving mask and pulled it over his head, checked his regulator, then jumped feet first over the side. He stroked clear of the *Cormorant*, then turned back and watched her settle. Two underwater floodlights were switched on and he followed her down as she sank through the murky water.

In the slack water of the English Channel, the *Cormorant* finally settled upright, restrained in position by her anchors fore and aft, the hole blown in her hull on the port side of the forward cargo hold eighteen meters away from the silted boreholes at Station CH.27,088.23 of the Chunnel Crossover Cavern.

Behind his diving mask, Joss grinned. The Kraut naval architect had been right on the money.

The Gwendolyn III, 06.20

The vessel, an old wooden trawler, thirty-one meters in length, wallowed in the swells, her engine dead. The skipper, Charlie Miller, was down on his hands and knees, bent over an open hatch, peering into the engine space. The man below him was wrapped around the engine, working with a set of wrenches. He gave the spanner a final tug, snugging down a fitting, then looked up. 'Try her again, Charlie. The effing filter was packed up solid with sludge. The fuel you got in Oudeschild at such a good price was contaminated. Told you that old bastard mixes crude heating oil with his diesel to shave his costs. Heard that twenty times over.'

Charlie gritted his teeth and hit the starter again. The Perkins diesel ground over, caught, coughed, then slowly picked up rpms, the exhaust billowing black soot. He eased the clutch in and slowly advanced the throttle until the old tub was making an honest nine knots.

The man from the engine room fiddled with the engine for a few more minutes, wiped oil off the block with cotton waste, then clambered up on deck, closing the hatch behind him. He paused in the lee of the pilot house and lit his pipe, then swung in the door and slammed it behind him, chafing his hands.

'The old girl's running a bit rough, Charlie. Needs new bearings.'

'You think I'm deaf, Billy? You can hear the bloody things knocking half a mile away. That thing eats more oil than fuel. How much on the last trawl?'

'Three hundred kilos, maybe four. Hake, some sole but mostly trash fish.'

Charlie shook his head. 'Not enough by half.' He scratched a few numbers in his ledger and totaled them up. 'That lot will pay the fuel and wages but not a damned bit left over for maintenance.' He looked to the west where the fog seemed to be thinning. 'We'll put in for the night and try again tomorrow. Otherwise, in these seas, we'll tear up the nets.'

Always tomorrow, Billy thought, but after four days in the North Sea he looked forward to dry land, a hot meal, a bed that didn't roll, and a tumble with the old woman.

Charlie smeared the condensation on the windscreen, trying to see into the thickening fog. He turned back to his first mate. 'She won't push much faster, Billy, and she's rolling in this beam sea like a pig wallowing in swill. Set the steadying sail. And make damn sure you vang it down hard. I can't afford to pay to repair a ripped sail on this trip.'

Billy sighed, knocked the ashes out of his pipe and swung out the door of the pilot house. He looked aloft. The mast was visibly creaking in its tabernacle, the shrouds alternately taut, then slack. The *Gwendolyn* was buggered out, he figured, not many trips left in her, and he'd been on her too long. Didn't trust her any more, hadn't for the last two years since he had found rot in the garboard strakes. Miller had told him to patch it with cement because he couldn't afford a proper job.

Billy let go the sail gaskets and heaved up on the halyard. With a *crack*, the sail flogged, then filled. He sweated up harder on the halyard, cleated it, eased the sheets and set the vang. He took one last look astern. A gull, hanging on the edge of visibility, squawked and wheeled down the wind. *You'll be back on dry land before I will*, he thought, a little jealous.

The Valkyr, 06.27

'Not my ass,' Turner muttered, squinting into the radar scope. '*Yours*, Herr Kaptain Katzenjammer.'

Dieter, a half-eaten ham sandwich still in his hand,

500

shoved him aside and checked the scope. The return was very weak and far to the west. It had been stationary but now it was beginning to move.

'All right, all right. There is no problem,' Dieter grumbled. 'I will come up on her very quickly.'

The companionway door slammed against its stop, Allen out of breath. He ran over to the radar scope and checked it.

'What the fuck's going on?'

Turner was ready with an excuse, like a little kid, trying to shift the blame. 'Stone's boat stopped dead in its tracks about thirty minutes ago. Dieter decided to slow down, left it on autopilot and headed for the galley to get a pig's knuckle popsicle or some such shit. That's why we're so far behind.'

'But you can see it now, right?'

Turner nodded. 'She's out at nineteen miles. Bad return but she's there all right, headed 305 degrees, nine knots like before.'

Allen turned to Dieter. 'I just finished talking to the bitch. Brunner's given her his marching orders to destroy the sailboat. Go get the Cucaracha out of the sack. He'll be on the RPG-7. Tell him to put at least two shells through the waterline so she sinks quick. You and Herman will be equipped with Uzis. I'm taking over on the helm and Turner will stay on the scope.'

'Do you desire me to set up the 20-mm?' Dieter loved the damned thing, could field-strip it in five minutes, change barrels in eight and didn't waste ammunition. Something of an artiste on the cannon, old Dieter was.

'Won't need it, mate,' Allen said over his shoulder. He rocked the throttles forward, the IMU engines picking up the beat, the speed slowly rising to thirty-five knots. Allen did a quick mental calculation. He had an overtake of roughly twenty-five knots, had to close an eighteen-mile gap. Figure three-quarters of an hour before they'd be within range. Goddamned fog. Still, he'd be right on top of the ketch before they could see him. Which meant Stone wouldn't have time to get off a radio transmission.

Dieter was halfway out the door. 'Hold it, Dieter,' Allen called after him. 'On second thought, set up the 20-mm. As soon as you can see the boat, shoot out the antenna, then work over whoever's steering.'

Dieter grinned, then actually licked his lips.

The Gwendolyn III, 07.14

Charlie Miller leaned back in the seat, packing tobacco into his briar. Good lad, Billy – should be in his bunk by now. Not that bright, but a willing hand. He'd call Freddie out about nine to take over the watch and get a kip hisself. Long night, rotten catch, and it would be good to be back in port for a night.

He checked the loran, plotted the fix and readjusted the autopilot to a heading of 301 degrees magnetic.

Barometer coming up good, wind down, the seas stretching out. He hoped the fog would thin out as he closed the coast; usually did and, if it didn't, he'd feel his way in with the depthsounder. Couldn't afford radar, even the cheap sets the Nips were flogging – just one more piece of trash you had to maintain. Had to laugh at the younger lads who worked their trawlers out of Great Yarmouth. They wouldn't think of going to sea without radar, any more than they'd walk through town with their fly buttons undone. Yet Charlie had been trawling the North Sea for forty-seven years now without getting a scratch on the *Gwendolyn*'s topsides. Just took a touch of common sense, it did.

He lit his pipe, sucked on it and leaned back, reflecting on his dubious future. The *Gwendolyn* had been steadily losing money for the last three years. Nothing left out there except tin cans and bottom trash, the fish gone, small bleedin' wonder, what with drift-netting, pollution and such.

She was fully insured, and sometimes Miller wished the old girl would just quietly sink at the dock. Take the insurance money and start walking inland with a pair of oars over his shoulder until some damned fool asked him what *those* things were.

He smiled. Yes, he would pack it in for good, far from the sea. Find a little cottage with a plot of ground inland, dear old Brenda to take care of him, potter around in the garden, drink a few pints with the lads in the evening. And, above all, dreamless sleep, even when the autumn gales howled in the eaves – an old seaman's hard-won rest.

He sensed, rather than heard, the vibrations, then looked out the pilot-house window. It was a bloody great thing, shark bow throwing spray, pulling up beside him, no more than twenty meters off. Dumb bloody dingbat – just what the hell did they think they were doing, too damned close by half. He looked more closely at the yacht, saw a man on the foredeck with something on his shoulder.

Miller flung open the pilot-house door and angrily swung his arm, motioning the thing off. Bloody idiot. One slip of the helm and there'd be a collision. No reaction. Some shouting between the man on the foredeck and another man coming out on the wing bridge, some kind of machine in his hands.

Charlie Miller ducked back into the pilot house and grabbed the handset of the VHF, the channel selector already set to 16, the emergency frequency. 'Yacht on my quarter. Head off, you damned fool!'

He heard a flat, low-pitched *crump*, then an explosion, racking the old girl somewhere aft, felt her buck under the impact, starting to roll sluggishly to starboard. He hit the fire gong to wake Billy and Fred, a cry of anguish rising in his throat, no bloody damn sense to it . . .

The glass of the pilot house exploded inward, shards shredding his body, the life snuffed out of him as cannon shells scythed through the structure, reducing it to fragmented kindling.

The *Gwendolyn III* dived as she turned turtle, the seas washing over her port bulwarks, cascading down her deck and into the gaping hole where her pilot house had been, then flooding her belly. She didn't pause as she corkscrewed under, gone in less than a minute. Only shattered planking, a few balks of timber and a slick of oil marked her passing.

The Valkyr, 07.18

'Blast his bloody balls!' Allen screamed, wheeling the *Valkyr* into a looping turn. Before he had been able to veer off, Carlos had fired the RPG-7, which was followed by the harsh stutter of Dieter's 20-mm. It had been over in seconds.

The bitch was perched behind him, hanging on to the back of the helmsman's seat. He could feel her breath on the back of his head, smell its tobacco-tinted staleness. Brunner might think she was the best lay this side of Singapore, but Allen detested her holier-than-thou phoniness and flop-wristed posturing.

'You're responsible for this fiasco, Allen,' she snapped at him. 'Of all the stupid blunders. Karl will be . . .'

'Shut your mouth, lady. I'm sick and tired of you and your bleedin' opinions. It was Stone's sailboat I saw last night, saw it plain in the night glasses. And that's what we followed, until Turner or the cockroach kid screwed up on the scope. Forget this mess. It's over. We've got to get south.'

'No! Not yet. Karl said to pick up any debris that would identify the boat.'

'He was talkin' about the sailboat, you stupid bitch!' Allen rolled out on a south-westerly heading. Brunner was expecting the *Valkyr* to show up by 17.00 prompt, and Allen knew which side his bread was buttered on. He eased

504

in power settings until he had slightly over sixteen knots showing on the speedo. Brunner had been adamant: get the *Valkyr* to the rendezvous at 17.00 — not before, and not after.

'What about Stone?' she demanded.

'What about him? If you order me to start looking all over the North Sea, write it in the log and sign it proper, because if we're not there on time, Brunner will be in trouble and I'm not going to be the one that's responsible.'

There wasn't any response. The companionway door leading to the lower decks slammed behind her.

TWENTY-FOUR

Snow Goose, 07.50, 16 April

The wind, apparently loath to make the forecaster out a liar, had slowly backed into the east and moderated to a manageable sixteen knots. There was fog, but it had lifted into a low overcast, occasionally patchy with a weak sun trying to crowbar its way through the ragged scud.

At daybreak, what there was of it, he had considered waking Melissa, but decided to stay on watch and make her the gift of a few more hours' sleep. He had already scaled that barrier of fatigue so familiar to long-haul truckers, players of all-night card games and tenacious drunks: where the mind was spaced out and the body's coordination shot but the nerve-endings sparkled with improbable electricity.

Sometime after seven, Stone had switched to the alternate bank of batteries and started the engine. With a flood of juicy electrons now pouring into the batteries, power to spare, he had kicked in the autopilot and watched to see how she'd handle it. She did, although the wake resembled a child's crayola scrawl. He fiddled with various settings on the autopilot and, gradually, the wake straightened. He was pleased with his instant mastery over microchips, but the thing he loved about the autopilot was that it didn't talk back or bitch that it had to go to the head or ask you to bring up a cold beer.

He checked the compass. The *Goose* was averaging 215 degrees magnetic, a clear shot out of the Channel with the sheets eased. Time to get moving. He dropped the trysail, hoisted a single-reefed main, hanked on the staysail and rolled out the high-cut Yankee. She surged ahead, bow wave foaming, the knotmeter kicking up over ten knots as she heeled to the wind. Lovely.

For a few minutes, he hung on to the mizzen rigging, face to the wind, reveling in the glory of it. The swells had stretched out and the *Snow Goose* loped through them, throwing a little spray but her motion easy. Compared to the violence of the gale, she loved it, tossing her bowsprit in abandon, her rigging humming a discordant A below middle C, the hull vibrating with energy. As his mother had once told him, you'll never appreciate the apple pie until you've choked down the asparagus.

He took a slow look-around, scanning the horizon. It was barren, only tired waves breaking occasionally with skeins of matted seaweed and the ubiquitous plastic trash of a careless civilization scarring the surface.

Leaving the autopilot to tend the helm, Stone went below. The main cabin was a mess, baked beans splattered on the counter and cabin sole, the upholstery soggy from a leak around the skylight, the smell of stale puke and sweaty bodies assaulting the senses.

Erin was asleep, balled up under the salon table, a sail-bag pulled over her legs for warmth. Kevin was flaked out on the pilot berth, snoring, Trish wedged in beside him asleep, one arm shielding her eyes, the other one flung over Kevin's chest. A distant snore confirmed that Patrick had taken over the forward stateroom.

He padded softly to Melissa's cabin door and eased it open a crack. She was stretched out, still clad in her foul-weather gear, knees braced against the bulkhead, shoulder hunched against the lee board, a pillow clutched in her arms. The dog was flopped across the bottom of the berth, his head hanging over the edge of the berth, pink tongue lolling. He looked up and wagged. Stone closed the door gently, then lit a burner on the stove, filled the kettle and set it on to boil.

Erin stirred, groaned and lifted her head, banging it on the underside of the table.

'*Fooking* thing,' she said to no one, then crawled out, massaging her scalp. 'Oh – it's you. Still floating, are we?'

He leaned back against the galley bulkhead, spooning mouthfuls of jam, munching on Graham crackers, ravenous. 'Better weather now except for the fog. Probably burn off by noon.'

The door to Melissa's cabin opened and she poked her head out, now in jeans and a woolly pullover. 'What time is it? My watch died last night.'

'Morning. Just shy of eight,' he answered. 'Sleep okay?'

'Like a stone.' She wrinkled her nose as if the word was distasteful. 'Like a log. Who's on watch?'

'Otto.' He made jerky, mechanical steering motions.

'The autopilot?'

He nodded. 'We're on the English side of the Channel, out of the shipping lanes. Visibility about a quarter of a mile and I don't figure that there's much in the way of fishing traffic out there after last night.'

She slumped down on the settee, still groggy, and looked around the salon with the bewildered disbelief of a child who has just learned that even Mickey Mouse farts occasionally. She scowled at the couple interlaced on the pilot berth and settled her gaze on Erin. 'Who are *these* people, Stone, and what in hell are they doing *here*?'

He wanted to charm her, give her a bit of the old Stone, the carefree, feckless lad of happier days; drag her back into his net, which of late had badly frayed. 'Either visitors from outer space or Ireland – take your choice. They were advised a sea voyage might rid them of noxious Continental vapors. Melissa – meet Erin.' He made an attempt at flinging out his arm in a grand gesture, but succeeded only in banging his knuckles on the salon table.

Erin smoothed her hair with a stroke of her hand. 'Nice to make your acquaintance. You're Stone's ladyfriend he told me about, are you now?'

'E pluribus unum.'

Erin cocked her head slightly, not understanding.

Melissa gave a dismissive shrug. 'It means "one of many".' She paused, the moment pregnant, the connection suddenly made, her eyes slowly narrowing, a dangerous vertical crease furrowing her brow. 'Were you – just by some odd chance – the one who was with Stone when he called me from Oostvoorne?'

Erin didn't answer but, not one to hide her light under a basket, grinned.

Melissa went ballistic. 'Stone – you rotter! You mean to tell me you brought your . . . your . . . floozie on *my* ship? *Get out of my sight!'*

He suddenly found the need to get topside and scan the horizon for the bow wave of an errant quarter-million-ton crude-carrier which would, hopefully, sweep him from the deck and into peaceful oblivion. If he had any idea of eavesdropping, he was disabused of it, the companionway hatch slamming shut behind him. He fervently hoped that the rumble of the engine would drown out the bloodletting that would now ensue.

That's it! he thought. Erin, under fire and undoubtedly reluctant to confess, would clam up, leaving only one obvious conclusion.

Twenty minutes oozed by. Melissa finally came up on deck, her eyes puffy from crying. She shoved a mug of coffee in his face, her silence deathly brittle.

He experimentally tasted the coffee, expecting the bitter, sludge-like texture of instant freeze-dried – the crud that slicked-down account executives in trendy advertising firms touted as the New Age Nectar of the caffeine-addicted masses.

Instead, it zinged his tastebuds, filled his mouth with glory, spoke eloquently of shimmering mountains and tropical uplands, of macaws squawking and Monarch butterflies golden in the sun.

'Blue Mountain,' she said. 'I thought you might like a

cup before going off watch.' She hesitated. 'My way of saying thank you for keeping things together through the night.'

His tongue was atrophied, brain traumatized. She had done it once again – actually thanked him for something, her intent sincere, yet turning him into an awkward, zit-faced teenager with shit for brains and his tongue locked.

Before he could recover, she stood up and wandered forward, her steps in sync with the softly heaving deck, first checking the set of the main, then fussing with the tension on the topping lift, making it clear that she was capable of a generous gesture but that it was not to be misinterpreted as friendship or compassion.

Kevin clambered out of the companionway hatch, a bit off kilter, favoring his still swollen ankle. 'I'll take over the watch, Stone,' he said, his smile lopsided. 'Turn in and get a kip. Melissa said she'd coach me for a while, make sure I don't run any stop signs.' Perhaps, out of compassion, he made no reference to the debacle that must have gone on below.

Stone considered the mechanics of the confrontation between Melissa and Erin, although he knew that it was Christopher L. Stone who had been on trial. Had testi-monials of his character been given, extenuating circum-stances considered? Had there been both vigorous prosecution and defense, a filing of depositions, due delib-eration then reduced sentence as he had hoped, or had there been just a summary judgement condemning him to eternal banishment?

Stone glanced forward. Melissa was still fussing, snug-ging down on the drawstrings of the canvas anchor-winch cover.

'Did she say where we're headed?'

Kevin eased down on the cockpit cushions and lit a ciga-rette. He puffed, exhaled, then compressed his lips, think-ing. 'She made mention of La Coruña on the northern coast of Spain – thought it would be safe to put in there for water, fresh veggies and to drop off excess baggage. Then on to some place in the Caribbean – Aruba was the name of the place, I think.'

Reassuring to know, Stone thought, that she ranked his worth in the same category as a duffel bag. Wordless, he nodded and went below.

Down below, he paused at the foot of the companionway. The salon table gleamed with a fresh coat of wax, the cabin sole freshly sponged, berths made up, the smell of lemon oil on the paneling, the stainless steel in the galley shimmering with cleanliness.

Trish was just finishing up, cleaning the portholes with paper towels, Patrick and Erin forward in the guest cabin, packing their gear away in overhead lockers.

He had figured on commandeering the pilot berth but the Airedale had already reclaimed territorial rights, now snoozing peacefully.

Trish must have heard him and glanced over her shoulder. 'You're probably looking for a place to bed down?'

'I'd considered it.' Christ – he was dead on his feet, didn't care where he bunked down as long as it was roughly horizontal and reasonably dry.

She sprayed some more cleaner on the glass and polished it with a paper towel, her face turned away. 'Melissa said it was all right to use her cabin,' she said over her shoulder.

It wasn't what she said, but how she said it. With the suggestion of a smirk in her voice.

Stone opened the door to Melissa's cabin. The berth was freshly made up, clean sheets, everything stowed. A piece of cardboard lay on the berth, the words 'TAKE SHOWER FIRST' scrawled on it with a felt-tipped pen.

Almost in a stupor, he mechanically peeled off his foul-weather gear, stacking the salt-encrusted pile on the cabin sole. His skin was raw, itching, hair matted, eyes gritty, he was incredibly weary, impossibly depressed.

Opening the shower compartment's frosted-glass door,

he reached in and twisted on the hot-water tap, waiting for the water to heat up, then slid in, eyes closed, his face turned up to the sweet, hot spray. It washed over his face and body, carrying away the gritty salt crystals, dissolving the gummy deposits in the corners of his eyes, caressing his body. He soaped down quickly, then rinsed. About to shut off the water, he opened his eyes.

Beneath the taps was another cardboard sign done with a felt tip, the words blurred and spotted with dribbles of water: 'SAVE WATER! SHOWER WITH A FRIEND'.

The compartment door clicked open behind him and she slid in, the space so tight that their bodies were jammed against each other. He froze, immobilized.

'Let me do your back,' she said softly. She soaped his shoulders first, working down his spine, then followed the crease of his buttocks with one hand, easing his legs apart, her fingers cradling his testicles. With the other hand, she reached around and took his cock gently in her hand as if it were a wounded bird and soaped it, moving her closed hand with agonizing tenderness along its swelling shaft. Star-spangled bombshells burst in Stone's head, his knees weakening, flesh quivering.

She turned him toward her. She placed his hands on her breasts, cupping them. 'Very gently,' she whispered. 'As if you wanted me — as much as I want you.' He did and he did.

And as he did, she closed her eyes, head back, her lips parted, melting against him, her groin pressing tight against his, then capturing his distended appendage between her legs, slowly rubbing it between the insides of her thighs, an agonizingly slow march to madness.

He thought he was going to explode when she put her arms around his neck, her head on his shoulder. 'Lift me up into you.'

He did, his hands cradling her buttocks, kissing her hardened nipples, amazed at their salty sweetness.

She locked her long, lovely legs around his waist, squeezing tight. Her voice was hoarse, water streaming over her face. 'I love you, Stone, God how I love you. Now – *please.*'

He did, my God, how he did.

He woke sometime after noon, thin slivers of sunlight streaking the sheets, climbing in jagged steps up the molded paneling. She was fitted to him, her front to his back, a set of not-quite-matching spoons. He could feel all of her – the twin pressures of her breasts, her heart beating, the fine down of her belly, the tickle of her lips on his shoulder-blade, the breath from her nostrils on his neck, soft and even, stirring strands of his hair.

'You awake?' she whispered.

He hesitated for a few seconds, so much at peace, not wanting to break the melody that played in his head. 'Halfway. I dreamed I made love to a woman who said she loved me. Was that real or just part of the dream?'

She put her arm around him, played her fingers down his chest. 'I love you, Stone.' She said it simply, a matter of fact.

'When you came on deck with the coffee, you'd been crying. I was sure that was the end of it.'

She pressed her lips against his neck, gently kissing him. Her touch electrified him.

'I had been crying,' she said, '. . . but it was from sheer, dumb happiness, and because it was so damned funny. Erin's description was . . . well – you wouldn't want to know.' She laughed, not exactly a sound, just a vibration deep in her throat. 'I should loathe her, I suppose, but that's impossible. She's so – I don't know how to say it – perhaps "blithesomely innocent". A cuddly wood nymph, every man her Pan, juices flowing, libido bubbling over, never a thought for the consequences because in her mind there aren't any.' She readjusted her head, her hair spilling over his shoulder, tickling him.

'You understand, don't you? I'm never going to let you go,' he said, '. . . not for any woman, ever. You have to

513

know that.' His unspoken question was whether she had let go.

He felt her head move slightly, nodding. 'That's why I came north for you, just that I didn't understand exactly why at the time, didn't want to think about the real reason because it might have frightened me.' She paused. 'I know what you're asking, Stone. I loved Pieter once and the two of you would have been great friends. He was a man so very much like you it scares me: loving, oddly shy as if he wasn't quite sure of himself when he should have been, yet charming if you could read between the lines. And, like you, like me, he had his faults. But Pieter's part of the past, an old friend I'll miss. But he's gone. Now, it's you and me . . . us.'

It was the only answer he needed.

He rolled over so he could see her. She smiled, a little embarrassed. 'My boobs are too small, aren't they?'

He wondered how breasts so perfect could be described as small or large or anything else. Perfect was perfect. 'Hummm . . . let's do a reality check.' He lifted the sheet and set his lips down on her breast, touching the nipple with his tongue, his lips just brushing the aureole.

She closed her eyes and folded her arms around his neck, gently drawing him down to her. He felt her body move upwards, ever so slightly, then a bit more urgently but still restrained. Then she shifted slightly, arching her back, opening her legs, and he moved in response to fit his body to hers.

When he could wait no longer, she took him into her, a feeling of completeness sweeping through his body, home at last.

She whispered to him not to move, to lie perfectly still, as if to imprint the memory for both of them. Then, finally, they did.

Under the waterproof floodlights, Brunner watched as three of his divers wrestled another section of pipe into the borehole and opened the air-feed valve. There was a delay of ten, fifteen seconds. Then, from the end of the flexible steel pipe, there was a black eruption of silt, pebbles and great gouts of air, immediately caught up by the tidal current and swept away.

Maas had adapted a South African commercial marine dredge for the project. It consisted of a high-pressure air hose which pierced the wall of a flexible steel pipe – the pipe slightly less in diameter than that of the borehole. The air hose ran down the interior length of the pipe to its mouth, then curved upwards in a U-shaped fitting. As the air from the hose jetted upwards into the pipe, it mixed with the seawater and, as it rose, created a suction which siphoned silt and pebbles from the bottom of the borehole. It worked like the proverbial charm.

The dredge was eating the compressed air from the tanks housed within the hull of the *Cormorant* at a rate roughly a third faster than Maas had calculated, but that still left a twenty-two per cent margin in reserve.

The flexible dredging pipe was marked with yellow bands, giving an indication of how deep it had penetrated the borehole. This one was down twenty-seven meters, six meters to go, the adjacent borehole already scoured out to its complete depth. Brunner was more than satisfied. His timetable was running fifteen minutes ahead of schedule.

He gave a thumbs-up to one of the men and flippered his way toward the *Cormorant*, breasting the weak tidal current.

As he swam, he checked his diving watch. Nearly slack water, the current due to reverse and run north-east in another fifteen minutes. Maas had told him from the very beginning that the seabed of the Straits of Dover was racked by furious currents, their velocities sometimes running as much as four knots. Maas's conclusion was that working on the bottom would be difficult if not impossible during maximum tidal flood or ebb. But Brunner had anticipated the problem, intentionally sinking the *Cormorant* in a position that was perpendicular to the current's direction, pinning her hull in that position by locking her between the fore and aft anchors.

Like a magician conjuring up an elephant, the *Cormorant* suddenly loomed above him in the murk. He swam over the sill of the jagged hole in the *Cormorant*'s hull which the primacord had blown open, into the Tank's 'vestibule', then climbed the short metal ladder.

His diving mask broke the surface and he shucked it off, then shut off the valve on the air-supply line that trailed behind him.

Maas was sitting on a camp stool next to the electrical distribution board, hunched over, checking the ampmeters and making notations on a clipboard. He turned and blotted sweat from his face. 'How does it go, Karl? Are they on schedule?'

Kicking out of his swim fins, Brunner crawled up into the Tank. An airtight hatch door had been built into the outer part of the 'vestibule', but with the interior of the Tank now pressurized to 7.5 bars, the pressure of the seawater on the outside of the Tank was counteracted by the interior air pressure, allowing the hatch to be left in the open position for easy access.

'Borehole number one is completely cleaned out, all the way to thirty-two meters. Number two is twenty-seven meters down, approximately six meters to go. We'll be able to start enlarging the bottoms of the boreholes as soon as Joss and Gunther have the equipment set up. How are the batteries holding up?'

Electrical power had been the one aspect of the project that Brunner had been concerned with. Maas's original specifications had been to use nickel-cadmium batteries encased in a waterproof container within the hull of the

516

Cormorant, with power cables from the batteries led to the Tank's electrical distribution board. The electrical demands had been predictable: six underwater floodlights, interior Tank lighting, and power for the VHF radio; the total electrical demand requiring twenty heavy-duty nickel-cadmium batteries wired in parallel.

But the American supplier had faxed Maas six days before the *Cormorant* sailed from the van Velsen yard, informing him that the delivery of the ni-cads would be delayed — a problem with the Environmental Protection Agency which had mandated that production cease until more effective cadmium dust filtration units could be installed at the firm's Ohio plant.

So Maas had been forced to use the lead-acid batteries as substitutes. They were substantially larger than the ni-cads and the waterproof container originally fabricated could not be adapted in time to house them. The only solution had been to fit them on the floor of the Tank. Dieter in particular hadn't liked it. He had been the quartermaster in one of the GDR's submarines, an old *Echo* class sub the Soviets had sold the GDR at a ridiculously inflated price. Experienced in the hazards of lead-acid batteries for subsurface propulsion, he had warned that when the batteries were charged, explosive hydrogen gas would be given off. Maas had calmed Dieter's concerns by arranging to have the last charging cycle carried out in the ventilated machinery spaces of the *Cormorant*, then installing them in the Tank, all prior to sinking the ship. Dieter had shrugged and grudgingly given his blessing.

Still, Brunner didn't like it. The lead-acid batteries had been laid out in a row on the floor of the Tank and wired together. One had to be damned careful moving around so as not to get entangled in their cables. It wasn't a tidy arrangement and Brunner was a tidy man.

Maas checked the wattmeter. 'We're ahead of the consumption curve, Karl. I had expected to use three kilowatts of power by this time but I've only used 2.2. We're in good shape – enough power for another six hours of operation.'

But it would only take three and a half more hours before they were finished, giving Brunner a margin of an extra hour to tidy up before the *Valkyr*'s pickup time. It was more than enough.

Once the dredges had penetrated to the bottom of the boreholes, the air pressure would be increased so that they could scour out a crude bulb-like cavern at the base of the borehole, enlarging it from eighty-five millimeters in diameter to roughly half a meter. Next, the cavities would be inspected by a fiber-optic cable and, if satisfactory, the bulb-like caverns and then the entire length of the boreholes above them would be packed with Semtex plastic explosive – in all, 1356 kilos of the stuff, according to Maas's calculations – over three times as much as the computer projections had specified in order to collapse the roof of the Chunnel for the entire length of the Crossover Chamber.

Brunner wiped his hands on a towel, withdrew a roll of plans from a plastic tube and studied them.

Once a breach had been blown in the side of the Crossover Chamber, the inrush of sea would rapidly erode the Chunnel's walls, ever widening the breach. Dr Herman Fiche, formerly a fellow of the Danzig Institute of Marine Hydrology, had made these computer predictions for the modest fee of 200,000 marks. Fiche had projected that the inflow of seawater would initially be 3280 cubic meters of water a second, rising to over 8000 cubic meters of water a second once the 'borehole access is fully developed by detonation coupled with subsequent inrush erosion'.

How precise calculations were, Brunner thought – a dumb computer, first eating numbers, manipulating them, then spitting out the results. Yet it had no way of knowing or caring what those numbers really signified.

Obviously, the Crossover Chamber would flood. The Chunnel's sump pumps, designed to deal with an inflow a tenth the volume, would be overwhelmed. Fiche had projected that the Chunnel would be completely flooded within forty-eight minutes. What Fiche had not projected was that between six and eight trains, roaring through the Chunnel at speeds in excess of 150 kph, would collide with those walls of water. The trains and their carriages would derail, accordioning into scrap, then flood with water under enormous pressure. The Chunnel would become a thirty-two-kilometer-long tomb, filled with twisted metal and pulped flesh.

How many would die? he wondered. Perhaps not as many as had died in the Dresden firestorm that February night half a century ago, but sheer numbers didn't concern him, as long as the old lady and her spawn were among them. For after all, he concluded, it was the symbolism that mattered. Your mother for mine.

The Snow Goose, 13.42

Trying not to wake her, Stone eased out of the bunk and pulled on jeans and a T-shirt. She mumbled something, then turned over and buried her head in the pillow.

He grabbed a sandwich from a plate in the galley, picked up a can of soda from the fridge and climbed the companionway ladder.

The air was warm, the wind down to ten or so knots. The sea had smoothed out to slick rollers, no whitecaps breaching the swells, a hazy and ill-defined sun occasionally breaking through. Visibility had picked up to a mile or so, and seagulls followed in their wake. He felt fabulous, alive, wonderful, in love and loved, the best of all things possible.

Patrick was on the helm, Erin lying on the deck forward, reading, the Walkman plugged into her brain.

'How's it going, Patrick?' Stone wrapped a fist around a mizzen shroud, then swung into the cockpit.

Patrick stretched his arms and yawned. 'Good. A lot better than last night, I'd venture.'

Indeed, Stone thought. 'Where's Kevin and Trish?'

'Guest cabin. They came off watch at noon. I'm on till 16.00.' He cocked his head a little. 'And how are things . . . below?' He had paused before speaking the last word, as if discretion had caused him to choose it carefully.

'*Things* below are fine, Patrick, me lad.' His mind stretched out to weeks on a sunlit sea, flying fish skimming the waves, awesome sunsets, crisp tropical dawns, and the company of the woman he loved.

Patrick smirked a little, thought better of it, and shifted his expression into neutral. 'Incidentally, I've been monitoring your walkie-talkie thing. Heard the Englishman on the radio calling you. Twice now in the last hour. I thought it was a good idea not to answer and I didn't want to, ah, wake you up.'

'Good man.'

'But it was bloody odd, Stone. He identified himself with something like "Mallard, flight of one". Does that make sense to you?'

Stone wondered whether it did. 'Flight of one' implied that the Coastal Command's Orion wasn't airborne and trying to sniff him out with a radio directional finder. What Stone really wanted to know was whether they had found either the *Cormorant* or the *Valkyr* parked in the lee of Juist Island.

He decided it was worth the risk as long as he kept his transmissions short enough so they couldn't get a directional-finder fix on him.

'Back in a minute, Patrick.' Stone headed for the companionway, dropped below and turned on the *Goose*'s VHF, flipping the channel selector to 83. Better than the handi-talkie, a full twenty-five watts with a good antenna on top of the mast. If Scott-Hughes was at altitude within a 200-mile radius, he'd hear the call.

'Mallard, this is Snow Goose. You copy, Nigel, old fruit?'

No answer. He tried again. This time Scott-Hughes came back, weak but readable.

'Mallard back to Snow Goose. Where are you, Stone? I've been concerned.'

I'll bet my ass you've been worried, Stone thought. He thumbed the mike switch. 'Same old place, Nigel. I've been tilting at windmills, eating Gouda cheese, snapping pictures of pink-cheeked ladies in lace hats – the usual stuff. Heard a rumor that you're flying solo today.'

'Cartwright's not with me, Stone. And Coastal Command's packed in the operation. It's all over. I wanted to get the word to you before you did anything else stupid.'

'Whaddya mean, they packed it in? What about Juist?'

'Nothing there, old boy. Coastal Command overflew the anchorage yesterday evening and then checked it again first light this morning. Macleod's information was wrong.'

'You mean that somebody's actually checked on Macleod?'

'Cartwright was able to persuade the Foreign Office to make some enquiries. Macleod's condition is stable but he's under heavy sedation. The medicos seem to think he can be medivac-ed back to Scotland in a week. Very close thing – shock, loss of blood and concussion.'

There was a pause as if he were trying to get the words right in his mind. 'Stone – I give you my word. Cartwright and his people have no further interest in you.'

'Charming. Just exactly why is that, Nigel?'

'A tanker truck supposedly loaded with a non-flammable pesticide showed up at a Chunnel shuttle loading-dock in Folkestone at 06.20 this morning. The Eurotunnel security chaps spotted the same tread design on it as the Yugoslavian brand Cartwright's people had identified. Instead of pesticide, there were 25,000 liters of ethylene oxide on board and some sort of a detonator linked to a black box on the belly of the tank.'

'Who was driving the truck?' He was willing to bet that it was a Kraut.

'A Welsh lad – had a proper transport license, worked the odd job on contract. Seems he was wounded in the

Falklands War, had a history of mental instability – seems he lost quite a few of his chums in a blundered frontal attack on Port Stanley. He blamed Maggie, the press, Parliament, the Army, the arms manufacturers, almost anyone you could think of. Seems in the past he had sent several anonymous letters to the London papers, threatening to kill those responsible, and the handwriting matches up. But he swears he knew nothing about the contents of the tanker or the people who hired him.'

'Did anyone bother to check whether a certain ship or ships are anchored within sight of the White Cliffs of you-know-where?'

'Coastal Command did so twice yesterday and once again this morning. I made a pass over the area myself less than an hour ago. Nothing . . . absolutely nothing there. Cartwright took you seriously, Stone, and so did I. We had to. But the area you speak of is clean. Nothing unusual on the sensors either, according to Cartwright.'

Stone rested his head against the paneling, feeling its coolness hard on his cheek. What did he really know? he asked himself. Odds and ends, scraps of information. But nothing specifically to tie the *Cormorant* or Brunner to an attempt on the Chunnel from the seabed, other than the drilling logs, and even that was a tenuous theory – an enlightened assumption at best. Maybe Scott-Hughes was right – that it was finished.

He glanced down at the chart. Patrick had plotted a fix at 13.00; roughly an hour ago. Stone spanned the distance off with his fingers. Another hour and a half and they'd be abeam of Dover, not that far from the Crossover Cavern. With a change of heading – he guessed about eight degrees – they'd sail right over the damned thing. Yet, he had no desire to go anywhere near it – a dead issue. He picked up the mike again.

'Mallard, Snow Goose. You still there, Nigel?'

There was a subdued grunt on the frequency. 'Thought for a moment that one of those windmill blades had bashed you, Stone. Seems you and Quixote have more than a little in common. Yes, I'm still here but I'm getting a bit low on fuel. Think I'll head back to Southampton unless you'd like a ride. Might consider the offer. The Dutch authorities are still perturbed with your activities and they're looking for you. Tenacious people, the Dutch.'

'Thanks for the offer, Nigel, but I think I can make my own way home.'

'Will we see your face again on our foggy shores?'

'Not likely, Nigel. Not bloody likely.'

A long pause. 'Perhaps that's best.' A pause, then, 'I'll say cheerio, then. Send me a postcard when you get to wherever it is you're going. And Stone . . . understand that I did what I had to do, just as you did. I give you full marks for persistence, regardless of how misguided.'

He knew that Scott-Hughes had tried to help him. He could also appreciate the pressure that Cartwright had put on him. It was just a matter of priorities, and he couldn't blame Scott-Hughes for having to choose the priority that favored his own self-interest. Still, Stone owed him a lot. He thumbed the mike.

'Adios, Nigel. Might write a book someday about this fiasco and, if I do, I'll make sure you're wearing a white hat. And, Nigel . . . my sincere thanks. I truly mean that.' And, strangely, he did.

'God speed, Stone.' There were two clicks and then the frequency was silent. Stone flicked the VHF off, a little unsettled. He turned on the AM radio and hunted through the broadcast bands. A dance band was playing something old, actually recognizable. Nice. A change from the screech of fusion, rap, and heavy metal — always wondered why the environmental freaks didn't lobby against pollution of the eardrums.

He pulled a Coke from the fridge and popped the tab, still trying to work it out in his mind. The whole thing vaguely depressed him, much like an argument with a friend that was unresolved. He tried once again to put all the pieces together. Everything had hinted at a sophisticated attack on the Chunnel from the seabed. Yet, it was obvious that he had got it wrong – that Brunner, or whoever he represented, had actually planned to destroy the Chunnel from within. And if that were the case, the *Cormorant* had been the deception and he, Stone, had been the agent selected to perpetuate that deception. Still, it didn't *quite* fit. The fuel-air bomb attempt by the Welshman smelled of the obvious, almost as it were meant to be discovered.

Still, he couldn't make the argument that the seabed was vulnerable to attack. The SOSUS sensors would detect any attempt to scour out the boreholes and, certainly, anchoring a vessel in the vicinity of the Crossover Chamber or anywhere else along the Chunnel's route was a potential threat that Eurotunnel security had devised countermeasures for.

Yet, he was still convinced that the Crossover Chamber was the weakest link and, consequently, the most vulnerable part of the Chunnel.

He examined the chart and plotted the location of the chamber. It was only five nautical miles from the cliffs of Dover, and any vessel anchored there would be visible to the naked eye. Which argued for a submarine or a submersible research vessel, but that concept was ludicrous. The purchase of a sub or a submersible by a private party would be impossible without twitching all manner of official eyebrows. And without a doubt, the SOSUS sensors had been installed with just that improbable possibility in mind. Eurotunnel had covered their bases, as had Cartwright and his people.

He finished off the Coke and crumpled the can, then chucked it into the gash bin. He had beat the whole thing to death and come up empty-handed, as usual. It was time to let it go.

He climbed back on deck and sat down on the coachroof,

more at peace with himself than he had been in a very long time.

The visibility had improved slightly, maybe to three miles, the wind down to eight knots — a lazy, hazy day. Off to port, a heavily laden tanker headed down-Channel. Big mother. He hoped that visibility would remain reasonable through the night, give them a chance to get out of the Channel approaches and into the open Atlantic where traffic would thin out. Then south. Melissa had estimated between twenty-five and thirty days to Barbados, then another three to Aruba. *Aruba.* It had an exotic ring to it.

Erin was still forward on the deck, lying on her back, paperback spread open on her stomach, eyes closed, the Walkman earphones plastered to her ears. Her toe was twitching to an unheard tune, her lips moved, soundlessly singing the lyrics.

He stood up, stretched and ambled forward, then plunked down on his elbows beside her. She opened her eyes, smiled, and pulled off the earphones.

'I guess I owe you,' he said.

'You don't owe me anything, Stone, except a good fooking, but it looks like you already got that.' She said it with a sly smile, a raunchy joke shared between old friends and not for public consumption.

'She's nice, Stone,' Erin added, her voice softer. 'Lot of guts for a lady to come bashing all that way to Holland for you in bad weather. I just hope you're worth it.'

He hoped so as well.

She patted him lightly on the back as if he were a good kid who had done his homework. 'I'll light a candle for you both if they ever let me back into the Church which is bloody doubtful. Last time I gave confession, I thought the old boy on the other side of the wicker was going to have an orgasm.'

Stone smiled, imagining.

She lay back down, pulling the headphones on again, then sat up again, propped on her elbows. 'BBC world news just coming on. The forecast should be directly after that if you're interested.'

He was. He went below and flopped down at the nav desk, checked his watch when the time-tick beeped, then grabbed a pad of paper and ballpoint to catch the forecast.

The announcer had a smooth, unctuous accent which oozed upper-class overtones. In a bored voice that implied he'd much rather be off at his club drinking with the chaps, he laid down the travails of a weary planet before his listeners. It was as if he were an indifferent sales clerk who offered shoddy goods for sale and didn't really give a damn whether the customer was interested or not.

There were the usual food riots in Albania, an expanding hole in the ozone layer which scientists were futilely attempting to plug with yet another over-funded study, an organ transplant scam in Poland involving the cadavers of mental patients, and a grisly bit about UN peace-keepers being 'necklaced' by insurgents in the Transvaal.

Stone heard the snick of a door opening. Melissa, barefoot and dressed in jeans and one of Stone's shirts, the tail of it knotted around her waist, padded out of her cabin and sat down beside him, sleepy. She leaned her head against his shoulder.

'What's up?' she asked.

'Nothing much. Just waiting for the shipping forecast.'

'Want some tea?'

'No thanks, just finished a Coke.'

She nodded and got up, pecked Stone on the head with a kiss, lit the gas burner and set the kettle on.

The announcer blathered on, now into the news of regional interest. The Scottish nationalists were calling for yet another referendum. A woman in some village that sounded like Tiddley-Bottoms-Ups-and-Downs had hit the lottery and was going to spend the proceeds on a home for quadriplegic pigs. And Princess Margaret, having fallen ill with an unspecified malady, would be unable to accompany the rest of the Royal Party on their state visit to the Elysée Palace.

Melissa was munching a cookie. 'Not likely.'

'What's not likely?' he asked, distracted.

She pushed a strand of hair away from her forehead. 'That thing about Princess Maggie falling ill. Bollocks. She's as healthy as a horse. Just that she can't stand playing the role that she's condemned to by birth. The only one of the Royals that I've ever had much respect for.'

'Wasn't really listening. Something about the Elysée Palace.'

The kettle whistled. She poured steaming water into the cup and added a tea bag, then proceeded to dunk it. 'Saw something in the paper three or four days ago. A contingent of the Royals is heading off to France sometime this week including Queenie, the Queen Mum, a slew of ministers from the Department of Transport, plus various other puffed-up toadies from British Rail. Dedicating the new high-speed rail line from London to Folkestone, making the trip from London to Paris by Eurotunnel in under three hours. The Royals are going over there to kiss the Frogs and turn them into Euro-princes.'

A chord reverberated within him, too low to hear, the vibrations rapidly fading away, something he couldn't quite hear.

The announcer had been rattling on in the background and the forecast was now on. Stone scratched down the specifics: winds in the North Sea backing, force five, showers before dawn – Humber south to Portland, winds going light and variable, patchy fog, tomorrow fair – Biscay, Sole and Finisterre westerly, force four, clearing.

He tossed the pen back in the cuddy and folded the page of the notebook. 'Reasonable forecast,' he said.

'After the stuff we've been through, idyllic.' She rattled her spoon against the wall of the cup, stirring. 'Let's bunk down on deck tonight and watch the lights of Kent slide by. I'll miss England, Stone. I don't think I told you but my mother was born in Bermuda. She married my father when he was posted there, but I grew up in Cornwall, did most of my schooling there, then worked in London for a publishing house until I met Pieter. Regardless of anything else, once you've lived in England, you are forever British. And for all their quirks, Stone, they're a noble breed.'

Somehow, deep down in his bones, he believed that as well. They were good people who gave much better than they got. And, yes, it would be nice on deck under a waning moon with the lady of his choice, watching the coast slide by – that and other things. 'I think I could handle that,' he said.

She pulled a stern face, the smile not quite suppressed. 'No hanky-panky under the blankets.'

He went over and kissed her, almost afraid that if he showed how much he loved her, the dream would evaporate.

'No promises,' he promised.

The Cormorant, 14.22

The most difficult task was finished. The boreholes had been cleaned out and the bulb-like cavities at the base of the boreholes enlarged to more than a half-meter in diameter. Working in coordination with Brunner by sound-powered phones, Franz had uncoiled the fiber-optic cable and snaked it into the mouth of the borehole, then lowered the viewing head until it bottomed.

Crouched over the viewing monitor that was set up in the Tank, Brunner inspected each of the cavities in turn. The chalk marl composition had eroded irregularly but the general dimensions of the cavities were satisfactory. In the flat, white light of the lamp that was attached to the optical cable viewing head, Brunner noted with satisfaction that in a few places rough concrete – the outer shell of the Chunnel's liner – had been exposed by the high-pressure jets. The boreholes, as it turned out, were even closer to the axis of the Chunnel than the drilling log had indicated.

Only Franz was still outside of the chamber, tending to the fiber-optic cable's placement. The men who would actually load the Semtex sat on the crude benches of the chamber, resting, waiting for the command.

Maas leaned over Brunner's shoulder and pointed to a metal protrusion in the borehole cavity.

'What's that, Karl?'

Brunner zoomed up the magnification with the tap of a key, then spoke into the handset. 'Franz – rotate the viewing head clockwise, just the slightest bit.'

The image on the screen jiggled, then slewed to the right in small, jerky movements.

'Good enough, Franz – hold it there.' Brunner adjusted the contrast. 'A rock bolt, I think, not a sensor.' He turned to a desk that was bolted to the chamber's wall and picked up a catalog. He thumbed through it, then stopped at a page and showed it to Maas. 'It's a rock bolt all right, Hans. Simmons-Rand split set, type SS-46.'

'Good. Just that they'll have to be careful when they lower the detonators so the wiring doesn't foul on the rock bolt.'

Brunner nodded, then spoke into the headset. 'Franz – pull the fiber-optic cable all the way out. We'll start loading the Semtex as soon as Joss places the detonators.'

He turned to Joss. 'Get on with it. I've already attached the electrical cables. Three detonators per cavity with the wires led back here to the Tank. Then line the men up in a chain so you can pass the blocks of Semtex from one man to the next. And don't bother tamping the Semtex down unless one of the blocks gets hung up in a borehole.'

Joss nodded, puffed out his cheeks and blew, obviously tired. 'Okay, let's *raus*, you cocksuckers.' The men got to their feet, pulled on their masks, then attached individual compressed-air hoses to their regulators. The air hoses were each thirty meters long and were fitted into a manifold on the outside of the chamber, that manifold in turn fed by a larger-diameter high-pressure hose that led from the drilling pipe compressed-air tanks located in the hull of the *Cormorant*.

Only Brunner was outfitted with scuba tanks, the obvious reason being that he had to be highly mobile, constantly moving between the boreholes and the chamber to supervise the process. At least, that's what he had told the men.

He checked his watch: 14.32 hours. Francine would be listening out for him continuously now, right up until the pickup.

'Hans – switch on the VHF circuit breaker and switch off breaker number fourteen.'

The dial light of the Icom VHF blinked on. Brunner switched the set to Channel 6, turned up the volume and waited. The set was quiet except for a very low-level background hiss.

On the outside of the chamber, an electromagnet, deprived of the current that kept its jaw clamped together, relaxed. The fifty-meter coil of coaxial cable which had been held in position by the jaws drifted free, a foam plastic float at the end of the cable rising toward the surface, the coaxial cable reeling out after it.

The plastic float had been designed by Maas to resemble a fisherman's fish-pot float. The only difference was that the brightly painted stick that stuck up out of the float was not wood but rather a thin tube of fiberglass. And housed within the fiberglass tube was a VHF whip antenna.

The Valkyr, 14.36

She sat at the navigational desk, nervously picking at her nail polish, slightly uneasy. Again, Karl was late for his schedule – this time by six minutes.

'Where are we, Allen?' she called across the expanse of the bridge.

Billy Allen glanced at the GPS satellite positioning receiver. 'Exactly 46.8 miles from the pickup point. We're dead on schedule – be there in two hours and twenty-four minutes.'

She scratched the information down on the margin of the chart.

'Bravo, this is Alpha. Do you read me?'

His voice was distorted due to the scrambler and the high-pressure air that he was working under, raising the pitch of his voice.

'Alpha, this is Bravo,' she answered. 'You're weak but readable. We're forty-six miles out and making eighteen knots. On schedule. Over.'

'Good. Any problems?'

'None.'

There was no point in telling him about the failed attempt to sink the *Snow Goose*. The trawler had never had a chance to put out a distress call and no search and rescue advisories had yet been issued by the English coastal radios. That would come later, perhaps much later, she hoped.

As for Stone, she had monitored his long exchange with the *Mallard*. She had no idea where Stone was but it didn't matter – the deception played out by the tanker had worked perfectly and, from the conversation, it was obvious that the English authorities believed that the threat to the Chunnel was at an end.

Brunner sounded pleased with her report. 'Excellent. Things are going well here. I should be finished in less than an hour. Are our guests on schedule?'

She glanced toward the small television set flushed into the bulkhead which she had been monitoring. The camera panned from the Queen, who had just lifted her hand in a majestic benediction, to the crowd of loyal Royal-watchers – mainly older women with a scattering of rapt teenagers and tourists thrown in. The nobility was separated from the masses by a stalwart wedge of bobbies.

At the last minute, one of the women held up a hand-printed sign that read 'GOD BLESS YOU' and the crowd cheered. The Queen, decked out in a tasteful linen suit, sensible low-heeled shoes and a floppy-brimmed hat, smiled pleasantly, waved again, then carefully boarded the steps of the Royal Train, followed by a contingent of nobility, in turn trailed by the official party – a mixture of DoT bureaucrats and British Rail managerial wallahs.

There were only four railway carriages in the Royal Train. The route would take it from London to Folkestone for a round of ribbon-cutting, then undersea through the Chunnel and on to Paris, arriving at the Gare St Lazare by 18.22. That is, it was scheduled to arrive at 18.22.

She keyed the microphone. 'Our guests are just leaving – perhaps three minutes behind schedule, but I'm sure that adjustments will be made so that they will be there on time.'

The Royal Train, based on Karl's calculations, would pass through the English Crossover Chamber at 17.55, plus or minus three minutes. By then, Karl would be back aboard the *Valkyr* and they would be forty-one nautical miles south of the Chunnel, headed for the Mediterranean at thirty-five knots, just one more vessel mixing in with hundreds of other ships outbound from the English Channel, no connections to tie them to the tragic event.

'Very well. Please reconfirm that you will pick me up at exactly 17.00.'

She glanced over at Allen.

'Piece of cake,' he said.

'I reconfirm 17.00. Billy has double-checked your accommodations. The air conditioning is fine and he thinks you'll be quite comfortable. I have nothing further on this end, over.'

'Very well. Wish me well. Alpha is off and clear.'

She hung the microphone on its fitting and eased back into her chair, then held the glass of wine against her cheek, the bite of the cool glass chilling her skin.

She didn't care for Brunner, his heavy-handed manner or his overpowering ego, but she had to admire his courage and determination. If it went wrong, if their arrival at the pickup point was late by more than a few minutes, he would die an agonizing death. And if he did, she would never be paid the two million.

He had read her well. His continued good health was ensured by her own enlightened self-interest. But that was what business relationships were all about, wasn't it?

TWENTY-FIVE

Snow Goose, 15.02, 16 April

The late afternoon sun, muted by haze, had turned the sea to a dull, hammered copper. The wind, warmed by the land, was abaft the beam, down to less than nine knots, the oily seas now no more than sluggish swells.

Stone was stretched out on top of the coachroof, his face to the sun, eyes closed, half dreaming. The *Goose*, sheets eased, rolled slightly in the swell, her sails softly slatting, making a lazy seven knots.

He could occasionally hear raised voices as Kevin and Patrick, both of them with their shirts stripped off, drank beer and argued politics in the cockpit. Politics seemed to be a disease of the Irish, totally incurable and occasionally terminal. But never boring.

The heat of the frail sun soaked into his skin, warming him, making him drowsy, the soft wash of the quarter wave lulling his senses.

Voices drifted up from belowdecks. Trish and Erin were in the galley, starting to put the evening meal together, both of them singing in soft harmony about a boy from Bantry Bay who had gone away, far over the foaming sea. Nice. Stone sighed, contented.

There was the sound of someone on the companionway stairs behind him. He grunted and slowly rolled over. Melissa had come partially up the companionway, pausing, her head just level with the coachroof planking, inches from his.

She touched his nose with the tip of her finger. 'You're getting a sunburn, Yank. Keep that up and you'll be able to pass as an Appalachian redneck . . . not that you really aren't one.'

He touched his hand to her face. 'I'll let that pass. What's up?'

She held up the newspaper that Patrick had bought in Holland. 'I was cleaning the nav station and noticed it on the shelf. Is this really you?'

It was the Interpol photo. 'Good likeness, I thought. Note the mad eyes, the bulging brow and the squashed brain-cage.'

She looked back at the article, reading on, occasionally pursing her lips, half smiling.

'You actually sprecken zee Dutch?' he asked.

'Dribs and drabs. Pieter taught me a little and I picked up some on my own.'

'What's it say about me?'

'Nothing particularly complimentary.' She finished the short blurb on the front page and turned to the interior of the paper for the balance of the article. She snorted. 'Says you're wanted by the US authorities as well – something about tax evasion. Really, Stone – you seem to take delight in thumbing your nose at the authorities.' She read on, laughing occasionally.

'Inherited that from my old man,' he said, yawning. 'He figured that you could never win in court against unjust taxation so you had to fight them with . . .'

'Stone! What was it that Macleod said to you that you couldn't make sense of . . . something about sixteen pairs?'

He swallowed, suddenly alert. 'Yeah . . . sixteen pairs. Something like that. Why?'

'Look at this!'

He shuffled his body parts, peering over her shoulder at the article. On the page opposite the article about him were two file photographs: one of the Queen, the other of the French President. And beneath that, an old photo of the Chunnel breakthrough taken when the French and British tunnel workers first linked up mid-Channel in 1990. The article was several paragraphs in length and a side-bar gave a schedule of events.

She translated as rapidly as she could. 'The Queen and her party are going to *Paris* on the *sixteenth* of May. That's what Macleod was trying to say. You told me his bridge-work was broken. Think about it, Stone – how he'd have trouble enunciating the "s" in Paris. So when he said it, "Paris" came out sounding like "pairs".'

'When's the sixteenth?' He had left his watch on the cabin dresser. He grabbed the paper from her hands, saw that it was published on the fourteenth, did some mental pushups. Patrick had picked it up yesterday, therefore today was the fifteenth, tomorrow the sixteenth. '*Jesus* – we've got to get hold of Scott-Hughes. They'd never believe me, but maybe they'll listen to him.'

The conversation in the cockpit had stopped, both of them listening. Patrick wrinkled his forehead. 'Didn't hear you – something about the sixteenth?'

'It's tomorrow, right? You got this paper yesterday. It's dated the fourteenth.'

Patrick shook his head. 'You've got it wrong, Stone. *Today's* the sixteenth. The paper I bought in Rockanje yesterday morning was an evening edition from the night before. The morning papers from Rotterdam hadn't arrived yet.'

Stone scrambled past her, down to the navigational table. He checked the output of the loran and plotted their current position. The *Goose* was already four miles south of the Chunnel route. He scaled off the distance between the Crossover Chamber's position and the *Snow Goose*'s present position with the dividers – 7.2 nautical miles, bearing 305 degrees magnetic.

He poked his head up through the hatch and yelled aft to the cockpit. 'Hey, Kevin – you've been on watch. Remember seeing any ship to the west of us – roughly three-quarters of an hour ago?'

'Just a hovercraft out of Dover that crossed behind us

heading for France. That and some kind of an excursion boat well inshore and headed south.' He shielded his eyes against the glare and pointed. 'It's still there, off to the west, probably headed back to Dover.'

'Nothing else? How 'bout you, Patrick?'

'Truth to tell, I didn't notice. What's the row about?'

Stone dropped down the hatch. 'Check the newspaper, Melissa. Is there a timetable saying when the Queen and her party pass through the Chunnel?'

'It says here that her train was to leave from London this afternoon after due pomp and exhausting circumstance, stopping at the Folkestone terminal around 17.32 where surplus government red tape is to be cut. In the process, Eurotoady executives are to trundle aboard for a glass of free champers and fish eggs. Then on to the French side for a repeat performance, and finally, up to Paris in time for much more pomp and truly exhausting circumstance, culminating in a reception at the Elysée tonight.'

He wasn't listening to her now, distracted, pecking at the pocket calculator. Seven point two miles back from the *Snow Goose*'s current position to the Crossover Chamber. Say they made eight and a half knots motorsailing with the engine cranked up to max, it would take about fifty-one minutes. He turned to her. 'We have to go back.'

She slowly shook her head. 'Stone – don't you see, it's over. Just as Scott-Hughes said. They found the truck with the fuel-air bomb stuff – *today*, the *sixteenth*. The *Cormorant*'s gone, God knows where, but it's gone and the *Valkyr* with it. Brunner used your borehole theory as a diversion to throw the investigation off track. It's obvious now.' She gripped his arm. 'Please – let it go, Stone.'

He bit down hard on the inside of his cheek. She was buying into it, just as he had bought into it, and just as Cartwright, the Yard, Scott-Hughes and everyone else worth mentioning bought into it. But he was convinced that Brunner had planned a two-pronged attack. Redundancy was the hallmark of the man and Stone just couldn't shake the feeling.

'Look, Mel, it's your vessel. I can't force you to go back but it's important to me. Mac tried to tell me two things – where the *Cormorant* had gone and when the Chunnel was going to be blown. They had already left him for dead meat, so I'm damned sure there was no deception intended in what he overheard.' Frustrated, he shook his head. 'Look, Mel – Mac went through hell to get that information and give it to me. I owe him, that simple.'

She stared out the porthole. 'What if there's no ship anchored there?'

'I'll dive anyway. You've got tanks in the fo'c'sle. I want to check the seabed for myself, see whether there's any signs of recent activity. The loran's accurate enough to locate the Crossover Chamber within twenty yards or so. If nothing's there, we're finished with it – you have my word.'

She finally nodded, sighing. 'You're a very stubborn man, Stone.' She gestured toward the horizon. 'Fog bank's starting to roll in from the west. Visibility isn't going to be all that good, but let's get on with it.'

They gybed over, sheeted in and hardened up on the wind, then started the diesel. By twenty after, the *Snow Goose* was heeled over on the port tack, close-hauled and making over nine knots.

The Cormorant, 15.27

Joss was the last man back to the Tank. He pulled himself up the ladder and broke surface under the harsh glare of the fluorescent lights, slick as a seal, water streaming from his wetsuit. Brunner, Maas and the six others were sitting on the benches, slumped over, limp with exhaustion.

Brunner looked up. 'You finished?'

Joss ran his hand through his hair, then toweled his

face. 'Both boreholes loaded. Ran a continuity check on each of the six detonating circuits, all okay.'

'What was the final Semtex load in the boreholes?'

Joss checked his plastic knee-pad where he had scrawled the final tally with a grease pencil. 'Six hundred and nine kilos in number one borehole, 713 in number two. The Crossover Chamber roof will crack like an eggshell when that stuff goes up.' He picked up a plastic bottle of water and swallowed. 'When do we start decompression?'

'16.00 – twenty-nine minutes from now. Do all of you have your decompression tables?'

There were tired nods all around because these men knew the routine, had done it hundreds of times before. Diving at this depth and for such a prolonged period of time had saturated their blood with nitrogen. Ascent to the surface would be a long, arduous process. Polypropylene lines that were marked at three-meter intervals would be tied to the superstructure of the *Cormorant*, then uncoiled. Each diver, still connected by his high-pressure air hose to the tanks within the hull of the ship, would start to ascend, pausing at each marker for the prescribed interval, allowing the nitrogen gas to work its way out of his bloodstream. Failure to follow the decompression schedule would allow the dissolved nitrogen gas to boil in the bloodstream – a hideous death with every joint screaming in agony, the body doubling up into a fetal ball, then death by embolism. It was called the 'bends' for good reason.

Brunner stood up. 'All of you stay put for a few more minutes and rest. I'll connect the firing timer.'

Franz made motions to get up. 'You're getting old for this sort of exercise, Karl. I'll do the hookup.'

Brunner smiled. Franz was the best of the lot. A professional, to be sure, but also a man he would have liked to have known better. And a superb chess player. 'Stay where you are, Franz. Do you think that after all I've been through I'd be denied this pleasure?'

Brunner reached up and took the last set of charged

scuba tanks from the rack, connected the hose from his regulator to the fitting, checked the pressure gauge, then slung the apparatus on his back. 'I'll be back in a few minutes,' he said, then slipped the diving mask over his face and eased down the ladder past the open hatch, the water closing over him.

The floodlights were still on, giving the seawater an opalescent translucency, sediment slowly drifting on the current like motes of dust in sunlight, a grouper working against the tide, its mouth jawing as if it were an old woman muttering to herself.

Brunner paused outside of the hatch. Because of its location at the far end of the Tank, no one sitting on the benches had a direct view of the hatch unless they turned their head. To be sure, Brunner checked through the quartz glass viewing port installed adjacent to the hatch. All of the divers were hunched over, their eyes closed, resting, only Maas still alert, scratching on his notepad.

Brunner waited for a few more seconds, then slowly and carefully pulled closed the hatch, trying not to make any sound. Next, he rotated the two locking levers into position.

He rested his head against the skin of the Tank, listening. No sounds of movement, only the tinny murmur of muted conversation.

From a flap stitched onto his wetsuit, he withdrew a clevis pin and inserted it into the latching lever so that it could not be moved from the inside of the Tank. He repeated the sequence on the second lever, then tested both of them for movement. With the insertion of two clevis pins, he had converted the Tank into a crypt.

He listened again. The voices were badly distorted but someone raised his voice in a question. Seconds later, the upper locking lever rattled, then the lower one. A face then appeared at the viewing port – Maas's – then moved away as if he had been shoved, replaced by Franz's. His expression was first of puzzlement, then anger. Brunner backed away into darkness, not wanting Franz to see him, even more so, not wanting to see Franz's face. Again.

Shouting inside now, the voices high-pitched and distorted. He recognized his name being called, then a blitz of curses. Someone banged on the hull of the Tank, at first regularly, then louder and more frenetically.

Brunner flippered to the top of the Tank where the high-pressure air hose led in from the hull of the *Cormorant* and terminated at a Y-fitting. One branch of the Y led along the top of the Tank through steel supply lines to the outside manifold where the divers' high-pressure air hoses were attached. The other branch of the Y led to an external valve, then through a fitting on the skin of the Tank to a regulator within, providing emergency air to the Tank's occupants. On that outside fitting, a separate standard industrial gas cylinder had been strapped down in a bracket and attached by a hose to the fitting. No one except Franz had asked Brunner its purpose.

'It's a thirty-minute emergency back-up air supply, Franz. Pure oxygen,' Brunner had casually explained. 'In the event that the hose from the main air tanks fails, we can switch over. Give us time to isolate the leak and repair it.'

'How's it activated?' Franz had asked.

'With this valve.' Brunner touched the bronze lever. 'For emergency only, of course. I like to ensure that all the contingencies are covered.' Franz, a professional to the core, had nodded his approval.

Now, Brunner slowly threw the lever, closing off the main air supply to the Tank, transferring it to the industrial gas cylinder. The contents of the cylinder on top of the Tank now flowed into it. It was nitrogen, not oxygen, despite the green color-coding and stenciled letters on the cylinder which marked it as oxygen.

This was not an act that he took pleasure in. He had worked with each one of these men, gotten to know them as individuals, not ciphers. Except for Joss and Maas, all fine Germans and dedicated professionals. Franz in particular. In a lifetime, Brunner had only met one or two men he felt totally at ease with — like-minded in outlook, a companion to share unguarded moments with, a sounding board for ideas, and a sympathetic friend to share a bottle with in either victory or defeat.

Nor was it the money. He had already paid them. Numbered bank accounts from Switzerland to the Grand Caymans would now go unclaimed.

No, it had been a decision based solely on security. Inside the Tank were eight men who knew his name, his identity, and had lived aboard the *Valkyr* while the *Cormorant* was hauled out at van Velsen's yard. When the Chunnel was destroyed, there would be an investigation of a magnitude never before seen. Brunner had known from the beginning that he couldn't risk their sworn silence because, inevitably, one of them would talk, either for money, because he was drunk or to save his own skin.

Brunner inhaled deeply, exhaled slowly, then moved hand over hand along handholds to a cabinet welded to the outer skin of the Tank. From within a second pocket sewn to his wetsuit, he withdrew a key and unlocked the cabinet, opening the lid and exposing the firing timer.

Joss had coiled the electrical lines that led to the boreholes at the base of the cabinet, and Brunner picked them up, one bundle at a time, checking their color-coding and making sure that their contacts were clean.

He wrapped the naked copper ends of the insulated wires around the terminals and screwed the self-locking wing nuts tight, then set the timer. Backlit liquid crystal numbers glowed on the readout and the battery confidence light winked on. It was a unit that had been built in the German Democratic Republic, precision-engineered and tested to fifty atmospheres of pressure, capable of taking a 100-G shockload, virtually guaranteed against failure by the precision engineering and quality materials that had gone into it. One would not expect less of a German instrument.

He did a final circuit continuity check, his heart thudding, the realization quite clear to him that over a thousand kilos of plastic explosive were being set on a hair trigger.

The light glowed green and steady. He squinted at his watch, set the timer to 17.46, then tripped the switch. The steady green glowing light began to blink at one-second intervals, counting down. Any number of unknown events could delay the schedule of the royal party, but his final check with the *Valkyr* by VHF radio would provide an updated timetable.

Brunner slowly flippered up the *Cormorant*'s deck and sheltered down in the lee of the cargo hatch. He would wait out the time for the nitrogen to act, conserving his air and body heat, not thinking about the men inside the Tank. But he found that difficult to do.

At least their deaths would be quick and painless, he rationalized. As the nitrogen gas built up in concentration, each man would first feel relaxed, then slightly giddy, as if he had had a few quick glasses of wine, then nothing. In less than fifteen minutes, they would all be dead. Technically, the manual called it nitrogen narcosis. But a French diver had coined the phrase 'rapture of the deep'. It was a term that was appropriate.

It was cold at this depth – much colder than the surface water. He wanted sunlight, the smell of the sea wind, texture and perspective rather than featureless black, but he knew that would come – soon.

He squinted at his watch again, the tritium-coated numbers dim. Thirteen more minutes before he would switch the valve back to compressed air, making the Tank's atmosphere breathable again, for he still had one last task to undertake in there.

When Allen was ten minutes from the rendezvous point, he would make one last call, giving Brunner an update on the train's schedule, allowing him to readjust the firing timer before he started his ascent.

And that was the dangerous part. The prescribed decompression procedure was to ascend slowly to the surface, stopping every few meters for a specified number of minutes to allow the nitrogen gas in the bloodstream to be absorbed into the body tissues. The only problem was that the total time necessary for decompression from this depth after being down so long would be close to eight hours, time that Brunner didn't have, had never planned on, despite what he had told his men.

Of necessity, he had chosen the only alternative method, in theory without risk, in practice potentially deadly. It all depended on timing.

After dropping his weight belt, Brunner would slowly rise from the depths, not pausing to decompress. By the time he broke the surface, the *Valkyr* would be alongside the fishing float, ready to pick him up. There was a maximum of eight minutes for him to get into the one-man decompression chamber that was bolted to the afterdeck of the *Valkyr* before the bends began to affect him. Once he was in the decompression chamber, it would be immediately pressurized to 7.5 bars – the same ambient pressure as he was presently being subjected to. Then slowly, over the next eight hours, the pressure would be decreased in timed stages to normal atmospheric pressure – a full decompression cycle based on the US Navy diving tables. And by then, the *Valkyr* would be off the coast of Portugal, heading south. He would assume command and set course, not for the Mediterranean as he had told Allen and Francine, but to the Cape Verde Islands to refuel, and then on to Brazil. Brunner had made the arrangements well in advance but had kept them to himself. Pulling off the destruction of the Chunnel had been one thing. To survive and be able to spend the rest of his life in both peace and obscurity was another, and he had put an enormous effort into both endeavors.

There was just one thing that made him uneasy —
reentering the Tank, now inhabited by eight dead men
who had trusted him with their lives.

The Snow Goose, 15.55

Stone stood on the foredeck, his back braced against the
mainmast to steady his body, sweeping the north-west
quadrant with the binoculars. He estimated they were less
than two miles from the Crossover Chamber, only another
nine minutes to run. The sun was gone and the haze ahead
was consolidating into streamers of condensed moisture
as the temperature dropped. Further inshore, the blocky
outlines of the cliffs of Dover had been erased by patches
of fog.

He refocused the binoculars, trying to sharpen the
image. As yet, he couldn't see anything except a blank sea,
patches of weed and the occasional herring gull. Somehow,
he wasn't surprised. Melissa had implied it and she was
probably right: a bloody fool on a bloody fool's errand.

He padded aft in bare feet to the cockpit and rechecked
his equipment. Of the six scuba bottles, only two had
retained their full charge, the others in various stages of
depletion. It didn't matter. One tank would do him. He
figured he'd have enough air for a descent to the seabed,
ten or fifteen minutes down there for a look around, then
the ascent back to the surface with a one-stage decompression stop at fifteen feet that would last a quarter of an
hour; a rough guess but close enough.

The wetsuit — apparently Pieter's — was a tight fit on
him. It was made out of neoprene foam but the stuff had
deteriorated — a little on the stiff side with a couple of small
rips along the shoulder seam where the glue had given
out. On the left shoulder was a canvas pocket which contained a couple of grease pencils and a marlin spike —
apparently a modification that Pieter had patched onto the
wetsuit for his own purposes. It would have to do.

The face mask was in bad shape, the rubber seal crazed with surface cracks; probably from ultraviolet deterioration. He had greased the lip of the seal with petroleum jelly in the hope that it would stay relatively watertight, but at depth he knew that he would have problems with the damned thing leaking.

The *Goose* was on autopilot, Patrick on watch. He had ducked below a minute ago, but had just come back on deck. 'Just checked. Loran reads 1.3 miles out. See anything yet?'

Stone swept the horizon once again. 'Nothing.'

More and more, he was growing convinced that what he was doing was just plain damned stupid. God only knew what dangerous junk littered the seabed. He had examined the chart in the area of the Crossover Chamber and found it densely speckled with the symbols of shipwrecks, most of them probably from the Second World War. And then there was the tide to consider – a real bitch when it came to working on the bottom. Still, he kept telling himself, he had come too far not to carry through.

Kevin followed Patrick up the companionway, a tidal-current manual in his hand. 'Checked the tables. Quarter-knot of current moving down-Channel but it will be increasing. Flood tide in two and a half hours.'

'Anything on the VHF?'

Kevin hunched his shoulders. 'Normal traffic. Erin's scanning the most used frequencies. Doesn't sound like there's any ship traffic in the vicinity except a couple of coastal fishermen.'

God, the desire for a good, stiff drink almost overwhelmed him. What in hell was he doing, going down to a depth of thirty-five meters in water loaded with silt and strewn with jagged iron, and for what? To bolster his ego, to make good on a promise, or to prove something? None of the above, because it was more than that, wasn't it? He had been in a tunnel once when it blew in. No one deserved to die like that.

He sat down on the cockpit thwart and strapped on his flippers, trying to get his nerves together.

She came on deck, lugging a canvas sack. She spilled the contents onto the deck – a separate set of diving gear, along with the underwater torch and some other stuff. 'I'm going with you.'

'*Bullshit*. It's my deal, not yours.'

'Stone, I didn't come all this distance to help you kill yourself. I rather had in mind a long relationship. What if you get in trouble or get snagged on something down there? You know the rules of diving – you work with a partner. I'm going with you.'

'. . . And leave the Irish to fend for themselves? That's just plain nuts. Wind's getting up, and the fog's thickening. What if the engine quits; what if a ship comes steaming out of the fog headed for the *Goose*? That doesn't cut it, Melissa. I'll be down no more than fifty minutes, probably less.'

Patrick had gone below to check the loran again. He popped his head up out of the companionway. '. . . Less than half a mile to go!'

He took her by the hands, pulled her to him. 'Hey, there – calm down. I've got to go down and you've got to stay here and tend the store. It's called "division of labor".'

She nodded, grudgingly. 'All right. You're right for once.' She bent down and picked up a diving knife which was encased in a plastic sheath. 'Strap this on. It was Pieter's. He'd want you to have it.'

He couldn't argue with her.

'And this,' she said. She lifted a blaze-orange life vest from the pile and placed it over his neck and chest, then buckled the strap. 'Carbon dioxide cartridge inflates it from this pull cord or you can blow it up manually. Just in case, right?'

He smiled at her, sheepish, feeling a little like a kid being sent off to school by his mother who had to make sure that her little, darling boy had a clean hanky and enough lunch money.

Four and a half minutes later, with the *Snow Goose* head to wind and the sails luffing, she let go the anchor. The chain rattled through the gypsy, then slackened as the anchor bottomed. The *Snow Goose* fell back under the influence of the tide and wind, then fetched up hard in seventeen fathoms as the anchor dug in and held.

She set the chain snubber and came back to him, pulling off her rust-streaked gloves.

'I dropped on Patrick's signal. The anchor should be within ten meters of the position you gave him, give or take a little. Follow the chain down and don't get too far from it when you're on the bottom.'

She glanced at her watch. '16.08. I want you back in fifty minutes or I'm coming for you, understood? And don't take any short cuts on the decompression.'

He nodded, then kissed her awkwardly and went over the side.

16.09

The temperature of the water hit him like an electric shock, flashing his nerves and knotting his stomach. He kicked downwards, his torch out ahead of him, its beam illuminating small flecks of sediment, the occasional fish, and a vagrant tendril of weed torn loose from the bottom of a ship or a far shore.

Pressure on his ears, hard and piercing. He swallowed, then valsalvoed, clearing them, stroking down into blackness with his right hand, his left trailing over the links of anchor chain.

Stupid. Swore at himself for his tunnel-vision obstinacy. It was a black streak in his personality which had landed him in trouble more than once – just didn't know when to quit when he was ahead. Just down and back for a quick look-around, he promised himself. If Brunner had been dorking around down there, he would see evidence. If not, home free.

He checked the depth gauge on his wrist. Forty-eight feet. Should have taken more lead weights, felt a little buoyant, maybe the neoprene fabric still taking on water and not saturated yet.

Down through sixty-eight feet. Anchor chain starting to curve out in its catenary, arcing in a gentle curve toward the north-west, the metal of the links still warm from the sun but now rapidly cooling.

He thought he saw a glow ahead, not definite, more of a suggestion. *BUFF*. What John Lawrence, an ex-Navy SEAL who had often done commercial diving with Stone, had called them: 'Big, ugly, fuckin' fish'. Saw them down deep, all lit up like billboards. Bioluminescence was the term. Something BUFFs used to attract the opposite sex or maybe their prey. *Come and get it! Two for the price of one, everything must go* – the big come-on.

Flicking off the underwater torch, Stone tried to localize the source of the glow. He loathed deep-dwelling fish: bony bastards with weird shapes and gaping jaws. Made your skin creep. He kept his mask aimed in the direction of where he thought the glow was, willing his night vision to accommodate. He slowed his descent, holding back a little, just a thin flutter of irrational fear nagging at his nerves.

Then paused in his descent. No sound except for the rattle of his own breathing and the jerky exhalations of exhaust air, breaking into snapping bubbles, then ballooning as they rose toward the surface.

He could see better now. He strained, damning the cold trickles of water invading his mask. He arched his head back and cleared the mask, then looked again harder.

A glow. Almost sure of it now. But, curiously, steady, not moving or pulsing as a BUFF would.

He headed down again, this time more slowly, link by link. He found that he was holding his breath, had to work at keeping his breathing steady, his heart rate starting to pick up the beat.

The glow was stronger. As he drew closer, it broke apart into two separate blobs of illumination, still no more than bilious yellow glimmers, but there, for damned sure, *there*.

He checked his depth gauge. Ninety-eight feet. Ten more feet and he'd be on the bottom. Some trick of current swallowed him in a cloud of silt – black, greasy stuff. It felt slimy, and he wanted to push it away, couldn't. He used both hands, frantic, heading down the chain hand over hand, trying to get free of it.

He broke into clearer water, the lights still roughly ahead but slightly off to one side, now brighter. Not two lights as he had thought, but two separate concentrations of lights, clusters of three in each blob.

Definitely not a BUFF. Steady, unwinking, unmoving. *Man-made. Powered by electricity.*

A shudder ran through him, not from the cold. His left hand hurt, then he realized he was gripping the chain in a vice-like grip.

The chain, its arc flattening to a shallow slope, led him on. He took it slowly, a few links at a time, keeping his scan going, the pressure of his blood pounding in his ears, deafening.

The lights were hard, distinct points now, still below him and off to the left. And behind the lights, he could now make out a slabbed metal wall, dull black with streaks of rusty brown. He pulled himself down the chain another few meters. Closer now, he could begin to pick out rows of rivets, a crudely painted waterline, a Plimsoll mark, portholes, the ghostly loom of superstructure. Forward, about where the cargo hold would be, the hull plating was blown open below the waterline in a circular hole about three meters in diameter, the metal bright, not yet even showing the haze of rust. A welding torch or explosives had obviously done that work. *Recently.*

Beyond the loom of the lights, the ship's shape slowly

melded into the blackness, but, even though invisible, its hulking presence was overpowering, palpable. Although he could see no other markings or nameplate or hailing port to identify her, Stone knew he was looking at the sunken hulk of the *Cormorant*.

Oh, the tricky bastard. The alloy 'fuel' tank in the forward cargo hold, the rust-riddled hull unfit for sea duty coupled with the substitution of the *Pelican*, the drilling logs, the now-you-see-it-now-you-don't diversion of the fuel-air bomb threat – all of it now made perfect sense, no longer an academic supposition but solidified into a neat package with all the bows tied on. How Brunner had defeated the SOSUS sensors he didn't know, but not surprisingly, Brunner had pulled it off.

His chest felt tight, a grinding in the back of his head, screwing down into his cortex. Then he realized he was hyperventilating, light-headed, nerves wired.

Got to get out of here! his synapses shrilled. Overwhelming desire to flee – back to the surface where it was safe, to get away from this cesspool of murky shapes and black unknowns. But deeper down inside him, something was starting to boil, the anger seething up, the realization that he had been had – manipulated like a dime-store puppet, laughed at and patronized, used and abused. And left for dead.

The adrenalin was starting to pump, anger overcoming fear, his emotions metamorphosing into something rock-hard, a determination to survive, outlast, outwit, win.

Get it together, his mind screamed. He consciously slowed his respiration rate. Three seconds in, hold it, three seconds out. His tunnel vision cleared, heart rate slowing, mind starting to come back into focus.

How long had he been down here? Not that long; he checked his watch. Twenty-four after the hour. He had been sucking on the air tank for sixteen minutes, about thirty-four minutes left, less twenty or so on the way up for decompression. So he had fourteen to get the job done.

Assuming that he could figure out what the job was.

Odd. Still no movement, no guys in black hats flitting around in wetsuits, as if it were a stage setting but with no actors. How long had Brunner's people been down here and where were they? Just starting, taking a break or finished and vamoosed?

He scanned the floodlit area more carefully to see whether he could pick up on how far they had progressed. The two light-stands were set up about four meters apart. Logical that they would be positioned to illuminate the working area. He looked harder, saw the slightly mounded areas in the glare of the light, a bundle of insulated wires, half covered with sediment and sand, snaking out of the bottom, then merging together into a bundle, leading off toward the hull of the *Cormorant*.

The firing circuit wires — had to be.

Which meant that the boreholes were already loaded with explosives and the detonators set in place. But where were Brunner's troops? Gone? Possible, but it didn't seem likely because the floodlights had been left on. Last one out shuts off the lights, right? Inside the alloy tank? Brunner might have planned to use the tank as a decompression chamber, assuming it was strong enough; slowly cycle it down to ambient sea-level pressure over a number of hours, allowing for decompression, then he and his buddies doing a free ascent to the surface for pickup by a mother ship — undoubtedly the *Valkyr*.

He had to get word back to Melissa to get on the VHF and call for help; wondered whether that would result in the Brits doing bugger-all, whether they'd believe her? Unlikely, but he knew she'd die trying.

Back to the surface to tell her? — no, didn't have the time or the air reserves. Had to cut the wires that led to the boreholes. Possible?

Only one way to find out — had to see whether he could cut the wires, knock out the lights so that Brunner's divers couldn't find him in the darkness, then get back to the surface and get the hell out. They might try to splice the wires, but if he hacked off a long enough section it would buy additional time. Simple in theory, perhaps more difficult to execute. Paused. Not a good choice of words — *execute.*

Something to write on ... He fingered the life vest, yanked at the buckle and pulled it off, regulator and air hose in the way, sucked in a deep breath, ducked out of his mask, cleared the life vest strap over his regulator and crammed the mask back on, bloody thing full of water, two hard exhalations to clear it, still leaking like a sieve.

Had to chance it; couldn't write without some light. He rotated his body away from the two clusters of floodlamps, masking his flashlight with the palm of one hand, letting only a thin sliver of light leak out between his fingers, printing with the grease pencil on the broad back of the life vest with the other.

> BOREHOLES LOADED, TRYING TO DISARM
> GET OUT NOW & MAYDAY DOVER
> WATCH OUT FOR VALKYR!!!!!!

He looped the life jacket's waist strap around the anchor chain, buckled it, tested it for ease of movement, then yanked the CO bulb's inflation cord.

The life jacket's air chambers puffed out in a fizz of gas. He let the fabric slip through his fingers, up and away like a beautiful balloon, prayed that it didn't hang up on the chain.

Then he studied the area around the floodlamps again. The bottom was dead ground, no movement, just the occasional swirl of sand where a bottom-dweller burrowed. An eel eased through the light of the floodlamps, unperturbed, stemming the current.

Going to be a one-shot operation, in and out, because there wasn't any elegant alternative to the direct approach: skirt around behind the floodlamps so he wouldn't be spotlighted, cut the firing circuit wires off where they entered the boreholes, then break the floodlamp bulbs. If – hell of a gigantic word, *if* – Brunner's people were still in the Tank, it would take them time to realize something was wrong, to organize, to get new floodlamp bulbs and an extra length of cable and then to splice the wires.

Maybe he'd buy half an hour's delay, perhaps more. Worth it, his only possible shot. He unsheathed the knife, then flippered toward the bottom, his nerves screaming.

16.28

Still conserving air, Brunner hunched in the lee of the *Cormorant*'s cargo hatch, inhaling and exhaling slowly, massaging his legs and arms to keep his circulation going, just waiting until the time had run out.

Now that it was done, it bothered him less, the memory of their faces, the sound of their voices, their individual mannerisms already fading from memory.

It had been necessary, of course, an operational requirement. He had been taught that when you sent men into battle, some were bound to die. But it was the objective that mattered, and if that was won, the equation of gain versus loss was more than balanced. Yes, he admitted to himself – they had died by his hand, but not in agony. And not in vain. They had been in it, partly for the money, but they too remembered Dresden, had relatives and friends there, and that agony still festered in the national soul of Germany. No, it had not just been for the money. Not for any of them, except Joss.

He checked his diving watch again. Thirty-three past the hour – time to go. From his position behind the cargo hatch bulkhead, he swam through the opening and flippered down toward the top of the Tank. Once on top of the Tank, he ran his hands along the smooth metal, feeling for the Y connection. His hand closed over it, then gripped the valve and rotated it back to its original position. A surge of compressed air whooshed through the line, flooding the Tank. Now the atmosphere inside would be breathable again, enough so for him to remove his mask and regulator, then make final contact with the *Valkyr* on the VHF before starting his ascent. It was almost over.

He slowly flippered down to the level of the hatch, brushing past a pair of curious codfish. Using his flashlight to illuminate the latching mechanism, he removed the two clevis pins and tried rotating the locking levers. The bottom one opened easily as he expected, but the upper one moved only a few millimeters before jamming. He heaved harder, putting his whole weight on it. It gave slightly, then opened.

As he pulled the hatch door open, the positive pressure within the Tank sent a gush of air boiling past him, the effect momentarily startling him. He forced his heart to slow and worked his way up the ladder, his face mask finally breaking through the surface. He eased the mask back on his forehead, wary.

All eight men were sprawled on the floor of the Tank, their mouths open, jaws slack, limbs akimbo at grotesque angles. What they had thought, what words they had uttered in those last few seconds of semi-consciousness, were an unknown. He tried to avoid looking at them but he found it difficult not to. Franz in particular. He lay on his side, his arms and legs at awkward angles, fingers splayed out, eyes rolled back so that only a small crescent of his irises showed. Beside him was one of the heavy-duty marine batteries, the cables disconnected from its terminals. What Franz had attempted in those last few minutes was obvious – to use one of the thirty-kilo storage batteries as a battering ram, to break the quartz glass of the viewing port in what would have been a vain attempt to reach the outside locking levers. Even Franz must have realized it would be futile because of the thickness of the glass, but he was a man to attempt the impossible, even if the odds were non-existent. Brunner turned his head away, his stomach roiling, a bile taste in the back of his throat. He swallowed and tried to clear his mind, to concentrate on what he had yet to do.

He stood up, kicked out of his flippers and padded to the far end of the Tank where the VHF was located, then snapped on the power supply. Nothing. Fringe of panic tickling his guts. He checked the power cable – intact as far as he could see, then traced it back to the circuit breaker. The switch was off, probably Maas's doing, his obsession with conserving power. Relieved, Brunner switched it on and heard the rush of background noise from the VHF.

He triggered the mike button.

'Beta, this is Alpha. Do you read me?'

Allen's voice came back instantly, very loud, even though they were both using minimal transmit power. 'I copy you, Alpha. Switch.'

Brunner flipped over to the scrambler. 'Allen – what's your position?'

'Less than six miles out, but we've got a bloody great bag of shit on our hands, mate. Distress call went out over Channel 16 seven minutes ago. Woman's voice. Didn't hear all of it, just Dover Harbor Radio coming back to the call. Something about an attempt to blow up the Chunnel. Dover didn't sound like they were buying it but told whoever it was to stand by while they called to someone higher in authority. On top of that, I got a radar return on my scope and the vessel's in your vicinity. Patchy fog up here so I can't make out what kind of vessel it is yet but I should be able to in four or five minutes.'

Brunner's stomach lurched, his throat suddenly constricted. Had to think, no time to, just the obvious.

'Beta, this is Alpha back. Listen up, Allen. How soon can you be over my position?'

'I'm right on schedule, maybe a hair early. Figure 17.00 hours at the very latest. I've got her up to forty-one knots, and Dieter's rigging the boarding ladder. The decompression chamber's been checked out and it's all set.'

It would take him seven minutes to rise to the surface, which meant that he had to be clear of the Tank no later than 16.53.

'What's the latest on the train's progress?'

'Francine's been watching it on the telly. They're running about three minutes late but no more delays expected.'

'All right, got that. Now listen carefully. Pick me up as per schedule but get off this frequency and back on to Channel 16. If either the vessel which called the Mayday or Dover Harbor Radio tries transmitting, I want Francine to hold down the mike button and start whistling in it.'

'What in bloody hell for?'

'Use your head, Allen. The *Valkyr's* transmitter is 125 watts. The hash from your signal will jam communications between the vessel and Dover Harbor Radio.'

'What about this vessel I got on my scope?'

'If it represents a threat, sink it and make sure everyone on board is finished off unless you want eyewitnesses left to identify the *Valkyr*. Now get off this frequency and back on to 16. I'm shutting down now.'

'Rog . . .'

But Brunner had already flipped off the power switch. He walked across the floor, slippery with body waste and seawater, sat down at the top of the ladder to pull on his fins, then shrugged into his scuba tank harness.

He checked his watch: 16.49. Which gave him four minutes before he should start his ascent. Just one last thing to take care of – to adjust the timer so it fired three minutes later. To come this close to success and not to optimize the results would be both stupid and unforgivable.

Stone was in darkness, the floodlamps facing away from him, using his hands to propel himself along the bottom. Insanely, he wished he had worn gloves, worried about brushing a toadfish, had done that once, nearly blew his circuits, then he smiled, realizing that a fish was the least of his worries.

The borehole mounds were only meters away beyond the light-stands. Once he got to the wiring bundle, he would be spotlighted under the floodlamps. The space between his shoulder-blades burned hot.

He cautiously moved forward along the bottom, the bright circles of lights spilling over him, little swirls of sediment spiraling up from the bottom in reaction to his movements. He grasped the bundle of wires, examining them. Three pairs per borehole, twelve in all. Six detonators! But it made perfect sense – Brunner's passion for redundancy. He hesitated, the knife in his hand. There was a slim possibility that cutting through them would trigger the firing signal, but there was no choice. He began to hack at the wires, trying to keep his mind blank.

Tough insulation, some kind of braided wire sheath, not just plain stranded stuff, hadn't seen this crap used before in demolition wiring, maybe something new . . .

A movement flickered on the periphery of his vision, the image blurred by the condensation in his mask. He turned his face upwards, trying to see what . . .

A flash of slick brightness, a momentary glint of metal in the floodlights, a shock of pain along his left arm, then another body in black hammering into him, tearing at his mask, fingernails raking across the skin of his face.

Instinctively, he reached out with his left hand, grabbing the man's wrist, wrestling him in tight so he couldn't get leverage, trying to get his own knife into the guy's guts. Left arm howling with pain, burning in a searing streak from shoulder to elbow, must have cut deep, losing blood, tendrils of black already staining the water.

The man was clawing with his free hand at Stone's mask. Stone brought his own knife up, slashing, point catching flesh, ripping into wrist muscle and tendons. The man closed in, death grip, locking Stone's head in the crook of his arm, knees pumping, trying for the groin.

Desperate, Stone kicked off the bottom, clouds of silt blossoming up, the guy's knife only a whisper from his throat, their regulators so close they banged off each other, bursts of air boiling out of their masks; he could hear the guy screaming at him from behind his mask.

Up, like acrobats, whirling, pivoting, swirling, head over heels, tumbling, colliding with one of the light-stands, the thing overturning, silt boiling up, visibility shot to hell now, Stone fought for his life.

The man wrenched his arm loose, then, slashing down, missed as Stone back-pedaled, pushing off the man's lower body with his flippers, back-flipping in a loop, kicking hard and coming back in, arm extended, knife straight out going for the man's chest, missed, point snagging on something, yanked upwards, air boiling out in a great gout of bubbles from the man's air supply hose.

Lost him, silt clouding the water, visibility zero, flippered backwards into darkness, then began to twist around, knife extended. Where there was one guy, there would be more.

Leaking blood. Stone quickly ran his knife-point along the left arm, cutting away the neoprene, then twisted it around his biceps in a tourniquet, tying it off with an overhand knot.

Took inventory. Arm hurting like hell, maybe a good sign, no nerves cut, but he was leaking blood, dizzy. Air supply low, starting to feel the restriction in his mask, flipped to the reserve, give him ten more minutes, not enough for decompression. Screw it! Get to the firing circuits and cut them, priority one.

He flippered back toward the floodlights. One of the light-stands was face down in the silt, the other still standing. He memorized the position of the firing cables, then, using the grip of the knife, bashed in the bulbs, fizz-pop as the filaments burned dazzling bright, then short-circuited and died.

Blackness, feeling for the cables, found them in a bundle, hacked at them, protective cover tough, had to saw, not making it, would take too long to cut through the suckers. Follow them – had to terminate at some kind of timer, might be able to disable it.

He drew himself, hand over hand, along the cables. Thunked into something hard – groped at it with his hand, slimy metal, rivets, then the edge of sharp metal. Explored the jagged steel with his hand, realized it was the opening that had been blown in the hull of the *Cormorant*. He followed the cables through the opening, felt the blackness intensify, claustrophobic, sensed space squeezing in on him. He gripped the cables, his fingers brushing greasy deck plating.

The cables canted upwards and his fingers followed them, felt the edge of sheet metal, a cabinet or housing of some kind, the cables leading into it. He floated up to the cabinet's height, saw green luminous numbers flickering – the bloody firing timer!

Cautiously, he felt the cables, running his fingers along them until he touched the terminal posts. He yanked, but the cables wouldn't budge, screwed down tight. He tried working the terminal wing nuts loose, couldn't, damned things self-locking. Had to break them off, hammered at one of the terminal posts with the handle of his knife, felt it begin to yield, pounded it the other way, felt it snap. He snatched the bundled wires away from the timer, his skin crawling, knowing that the jarring of the mechanism could have set it off. But didn't.

He stood upright, felt the wall of metal in front of him which supported the firing cabinet – smooth machined sections, curving as they rose – the Tank. And off to the right – a dim shaft of green light. He realized it was coming from some kind of entrance. He swam toward the opening, his knife ready.

16.54

Brunner was on his hands and knees on the floor of the Tank, his head down, retching up seawater and bile. His lungs were burning, throat raw. But he was alive.

Cursed himself. When his air hose had been cut, he had panicked, flailing backwards, mask filling with water, blind. He had lashed out with his hands trying to protect himself, then blundered into the hull of the *Cormorant*, felt for the hole in the hull, through that opening, then the glimmer of light, went for it and broke surface into the fetid atmosphere of the Tank, lungs starving.

He knew he would never have made it to the surface, had taken too much water in his lungs. He vomited again, knotted pains contracting his stomach muscles, hand bloody and burning but workable.

Watch still working, fifty-five past the hour, *Valkyr* nearly in position over him, had to start the ascent – *now*.

He yanked the mask and regulator from one of the dead men. His scuba tanks were empty, the air exhausted through the cut hose. But there were still high-pressure hoses on the outside of the Tank. Hook into one of those and start the ascent, then only minutes to the surface and safety.

How many out there? Just the one man he had seen, but there were bound to be others. Had to concentrate, found it difficult but an idea worked its way through the fog. Without light he would be invisible, just part of the blackness.

He stumbled across the floor of the Tank, had to push one of the dead men who blocked his path to the switchboard aside, fingers feeling down the row of switches, yanking numbers six and seven, killing power to the floodlamps.

He turned, heading for the hatch, fitting the diving mask on, pulling the straps tight.

Sound — the clank of metal on metal. He saw exhaust bubbles breaking the surface of the hatch opening, someone coming in. He froze. Needed a weapon, anything. Fumbled for his knife, then realized he had dropped it, frantically searched for something, anything.

On the deck in front of him was the lead-acid battery that Franz had disconnected from the bank. He bent down, prying his fingers under the bottom edges, and hefted its twenty kilos of dead weight over his head. He was ready, knew he had to get the timing just right, wait until the man's head was fully exposed.

Hair and scalp streaming water, mask and regulator breaking through the surface, the top of the man's tank, his left hand reaching up for another rung, a knife in his right.

The man pushed the mask up on his forehead, eyes squinting, his vision blinded by the glare of the Tank's interior lights. Obviously disoriented. The man tried to scramble up the remaining rungs of the ladder but his tank snagged on the rim of the hatch.

It couldn't be him but it was. 'Stone!' Brunner screamed, then heaved, the battery slipping in his bloody hands, tumbling end over end.

Brunner had a strobe flash of Stone's face in the frame of the hatch, then Stone flinging his arm upward, trying to fend off the black shape tumbling toward him, deflecting it, not quite, the battery smashing into his faceplate, its trajectory now altered, finally impacting against the ladder, the walls of the cells fracturing, the electrolyte spilling across the floor.

Brunner sank to his knees, gasping. In the lights of the capsule's hatch, below him in the black water, he saw Stone, faceplate cracked, water filling the mask. Stone was exhaling great globs of air, his movements spastic, black blood flowing from his forehead.

Exhausted, heart jackhammering, Brunner slumped to the deck, sucked in, filling his lungs, trying to squeeze air into his bloodstream.

Something wrong! His throat burned, acrid smell, taste of metal in his mouth. He gulped air again but his lungs seared with fiery pain. He hacked explosively, felt as if his body was tearing itself apart, chest heaving in convulsions, couldn't stop himself, sucked in again, molten glass eating out his throat, tissues blistering like hot fat, streaming tears, looked down, blurry yellow-green-brown gas swirling as the battery acid mixed with seawater.

He was screaming, but no sound came out. He needed to tear his chest open so he could get air, his fingers clawing at his wetsuit, nails clawing and breaking.

Incredible agony, a firestorm consuming him, flames eating his flesh, couldn't take . . .

With all the strength he had, he reared up, then smashed his head against the rim of the hatch. There was a brilliant explosion of light, then dimness, pain dissolving magically, sight fading to gray to black, to nothing.

His lips formed the word *Mutti* as he died.

16.57

Stone rose slowly, spiraling upwards, his body limp. His mask was flooded but he had no energy left to clear it. Mostly breathing out, exhaling, the compressed air in his lungs expanding as he rose, dimly remembering not to hold it in – he would explode like a cartoon character. He smiled faintly at the image.

Heart still kicking, but the left arm was shot, useless, no feeling. Always wanted to learn to play the piano, maybe get a synthesizer, program in the chords, do it one-handed. *God*, for just one look at the sun, ah shit. So close, so far away.

Didn't want to think about decompression because there wouldn't be any — painful way to go, the bends were. Had seen one guy — no, didn't want to remember what it was like but couldn't push the image away — poor bastard howling at the stars, flopping around the deck of the diving barge like a fish out of water, eyes bulging out of their sockets.

Air intake back-pressure increasing, sucking the last of it. Only chance now would be to stroke for the surface, but he couldn't seem to get it together; anyway, nice now, little fuzzy around the edges, calm, just drifting like a leaf on the summer wind.

Only ten minutes' more air would do it. Not a full, by-the-book decompression but enough, maybe, just enough.

Had always heard that drowning was not a bad way to go. Just gulp in like a guppy. Remembered a guy once they fished out of a pond. Peaceful face, like the going was easy.

Lighter above. Could see the distortion of the surface, seas running, as if he were looking through a distorted lens.

He sucked once more but no air came. El finito, buddy. Thought about pulling the mask off so he could see properly but couldn't, no energy. He fumbled with the catch on his weight belt, hadn't thought about that before, el stupido. God — tough to undo, like the thing was welded together. Ah, hang on — catch moving, then the belt falling, up, up, up and away, sunlight stronger, dumb fish cruising by, givin' me the eye, curious, maybe I'm breakfast, not-so-special-of-the-day.

He broke through the surface. Eyes bleary with salt water, like wearing dirty contacts; he shook his head, seawater slopping over his face.

Light mist, fog bank further out in the Channel, smooth, oily swells running.

In the distance, something sticking up, maybe quarter of a mile. Mast of some sort, he thought. Weird — the thing was folded in half like a straw bent by the wind. Further offshore, greasy smoke rising but couldn't see what it was coming from. Then heard whacking in the distance. Choppers?

He raised his arm to attract attention and sank beneath the surface. Dumb, should have brought a dye marker. He resurfaced, took a deep breath, sank again, stabilizing, popping up again. How long before the pain came? — major joints first, pain you couldn't believe, said the manuals. Didn't matter anyway. Too weak to keep this up for long. Empty tanks added a little buoyancy but it was awkward, likely to roll him over on his face. *God, I'm cold. Freezing.*

He heard three short *blaps* of a foghorn rolling over the water and echoing back from the fogbanks.

Another deep breath, relax, going down, women's things, fall sale of earmuffs, next floor toys for boys, stabilizing, coming up, breaking the surface, deep breath, starting down again . . .

High-speed whine, like a buzz saw, louder. Another deep breath, going down, wished he had the willpower just to open his damn mouth and take in a lungful of water. Read about a guy in Aussieland could breathe the stuff, stay under for hours. *Guinness Book of Records*; nope, remember now — phony, had a scuba tank stashed on the seabed.

Up again, breaking the surface. First twinges of pain in his knees like little needles. Now it starts.

Shouts, the buzz saw rasping in his ears. Splash. Opened his eyes, going down again, catching the shape of a gray whale, fat and saucy, like a Macy Thanksgiving parade thing hovering over him. Almost laughed.

Something rough tearing at his tank harness, pushing him down, down, mask torn away, cramming something in his mouth. He sucked instinctively like a newborn child. *Air!*

Stone opened his eyes. She was holding him, trying to fit his lips over the regulator, her face magnified by the water, nodding, squeezing his good arm.

Down again. Pain hard in his joints, then magically diminishing.

Down deeper. The light fading but the compressed air sweet as a June morning's. Sucking in hard, the fuzzy edges firming up.

He rested his head against her shoulder, thought he could feel the heat of her body, molded himself to her, not just for warmth.

Scene dissolve, fade out, fade in. No sense of seconds, minutes ticking away, just drifting. She pressed her mask against his, staring at him. *I love you*, he thought. More than love. Indescribably more than love. Whatever that is called.

Up. She was kicking her fins, languidly, not too fast, rising upward slowly in stages toward the light. Hovering again – minutes, hours, an eternity. Sunlight and shadows above. The shape of a boat outlined against the brightness. The *Zodiac*, gray whale, Moby Dicky boat. Cute.

Fascinated with the bubbles. Suck in, exhale . . . equals bubbles. Smiled, but couldn't with the regulator in his mouth. Tried to count the bubbles. Back yard, still just a kid, running in the evening shadows, first fireflies of June blinking in the trees, a hoop dipped in soap streaming bubbles, the old man laughing softly, his arm around his mother's waist.

I'm forever blowing . . .

Now up again. Breaking the surface, another shout. Hands pulling him in over the inflated rubber gunwale, his eyes open now, Patrick grinning, Mel heaving herself up beside him.

She took the regulator from his mouth and he breathed air. Real air. Clean air, heavy with the tang of salt and the smell of damp English countryside blown offshore on the evening wind. And felt her sweet breath on his face, just as she slid in the needle.

She leaned over him . . . smiling.

Alle alle in free, he thought, sliding into unconsciousness.

EPILOGUE

Kent, England, 03.20, 17 April

He drifted upward from the bottom, the sightless depths beneath him gradually transmuting to iridescent pearl. Shafts of defused light filtered down around him, illuminating quicksilver flecks which drifted past on a sluggish current.

As he gently exhaled, the bubbles from his mask gurgled upward toward the interface of sun and sea above him, expanding as they rose. There was a movement at the limits of his vision and he slowly turned his head to watch, curious. A spangled shoal of fish swept by him, rainbow-hued, fins of intricate filigree. He tentatively tried to touch them but, as one, they swooped away.

The sea, enfolding him in its warmth, felt safe. Safe? He decided, for some unknown reason, that it was – *safe*.

Dazzling bright above him, he broke the surface, inhaled, then exhaled, listening to his breath rattle through watery lungs. His head hurt in a vague, indefinite way, his face numb, as if it wasn't there. He tried to wiggle his nose, felt a dull twinge of pain.

It was another place and time but he wasn't sure where or when. Something missing in between that was faintly remembered but not recallable. Bothered him in a vague way, but not to worry.

He smelled something vaguely tropical. Oranges? Not quite; its tangy scent mingled with a harsh pungency.

Sounds: footsteps on tile, the light chime of a bell, muted voices, and the sound of his own raspy breathing.

Stone willed one eye to open, then the other. Dark. He

tried to move his left arm but couldn't, the thing entombed in concrete. Then moved his fingers under the cast. Creaky things, as if they couldn't quite remember the commands.

He struggled against gravity and inertia, his scalp prickling with sweat from the exertion, then was able to roll onto his other side. He groped with his right hand, fingers testing shapes. Bedstand, glass of water, buttons on a pad. Chain. He pulled it. Let there be forty watts of light and there was.

She was asleep in a chair, a blanket thrown over her body. Hair drifting over her shoulders, lashes dark and impossibly long. Her face was sunburned, her nose peeling. She breathed slowly, her lips slightly pursed as if her dreams were sweet.

Stone relaxed and settled his head back onto the pillow, drifting down into the sunlit sea.

Sometime, 21 April

He woke again later, disoriented. No idea of the time of day, the drapes drawn, just a smear of dull light leaking through the heavy fabric. Above him, three plastic bags of fluid hung from a metal rack, tubes leading down and disappearing beneath the sheets. He found it difficult to concentrate, his limbs aching in every joint, his body burning with heat. He focused past the molded nose guard that was taped to his face, watching the fluid in the bag drip, counted twelve drops, his lips frozen forming *thirteen*, and slid back into unconsciousness.

10.41, 3 May

Drapes parted, Venetian blinds partially open, bright slats of sunlight laddering the wall. He could smell food and his stomach rumbled tentatively. He had to pee, badly. Some kind of bathroom on the far side of the room. He tried to ease himself into a sitting position but was defeated by weakness and pain. He groped for the button on the night-stand and pushed it.

Heels tapping on tile, a pause, voices, then the door opening. A starched white origami sculpture floating on black hair above a brown face appeared. She pushed the door open, then closed it softly behind her. She gave him a professional smile.

'How are we feeling today?' Her accent was West Indian, Bajan probably, warm and golden as butterscotch pudding.

'*We* feel like hell. Look, can you get some guy to give me a hand. I have to take a . . .'

She held a finger to her lips. 'In polite society, Mr Stone, we refer to it as "spending a penny".' She picked up a white enameled object from beneath the bedstand, folded back the sheets and fitted him to it.

He froze, mortified.

'Think of a babbling brook, Mr Stone. It *does* help relax the muscles.'

It burned and he had to grit his teeth but was rewarded with a distant tinkle, then a rush.

'*Very good,*' she said, as if he were a small child who had accomplished a difficult task worthy of praise. 'We certainly must feel better now.' She removed the urinal and set it on the floor, then dabbed him with a towel and replaced the sheets. She adjusted the blinds to let in more light and turned back to him. 'Perhaps we would like something to eat to celebrate our first day back on planet Earth?'

He looked at her carefully for the first time. Her skin was without the slightest blemish, the shading of Bailey's Irish Cream. Lovely high cheekbones, eyes widely set, the suggestion of dimples and calm, confident lips.

'Where is she?' he asked.

The nurse cocked her head marginally.

'Melissa . . . ?'

She shook her head slowly. 'I'm not familiar with the name.'

'She was here last night. Sitting *right* there.'

She frowned. 'No visitor was here last night, Mr Stone. Or for that matter, during the last fortnight.'

'How long . . . ?' He made a vague circling gesture with his finger.

'. . . Have you been with us? This is your seventeenth day with us, Mr Stone. You had lost quite a bit of blood when they brought you in and there was the later complication of an infection. But Doctor thinks you'll be fine now.'

He touched the plaster cast on his left arm and the bandage on his chest. 'When does this come off?'

'Doctor will see you shortly and answer your questions, I'm sure.' She checked a clipboard which hung from the foot of the bed and looked up. 'It seems that we may begin to take some solid food.' She inclined her head slightly. 'Perhaps we would like something special?'

His stomach rumbled in anticipation, the dormant juices now starting to flow in anticipation. '*We* could handle a couple of eggs over easy, bacon and coffee. With an order of fries on the side.'

She favored him with a suppressed smile. 'I meant marmalade or jam. With our toast and tea, Mr Stone.'

5 May

Scott-Hughes trundled in two days later, a rainy Thursday afternoon. Stone had been dozing when he appeared in the doorway with a spray of fresh-cut flowers and a briefcase. He put his finger to his lips, closed the door behind him and twisted the lock, then eased into the chair facing the bed.

'Cartwright finally allowed me to see you. Been trying to for over a fortnight. You're looking rather peaked, I must say.'

Stone propped himself up on his elbows. 'Didn't think I'd be seeing you again, Nigel. Where's Melissa?'

'Thought you might ask. She's fine and sends her love

570

– told me that you were not to start mucking around with the nurses, particularly the Irish ones.'

'I want to see her.'

'That's not on, Stone. Cartwright won't allow anyone in to see you and I'm told you're scheduled for another ten days of rest and physical therapy prior to being released.'

'But she was here, wasn't she? I remember . . .'

Scott-Hughes nodded. 'A Royal Navy Sea King helicopter brought the two of you to this facility the evening of the, ah, the incident. Mrs van der Groot insisted on staying the night with you. Cartwright debriefed her the following morning, then released her on her own recognizance, pending further enquiries. Quite frankly, old boy, the powers that be would just as soon she leave the country, providing that she pledged not to leak word of the disaster.'

'*Disaster! I ripped the firing wires off the timer. It couldn't have blown!*'

Scott-Hughes lifted his hand in supplication. 'Please keep your voice down. But you're quite right. No real harm done. The disaster I speak of is a call for an investigation by certain members of Parliament into a rumored underwater terrorist attack on Eurotunnel, the effort supposedly funded by highly placed British nationals – the chairman of the board of a cross-Channel shipping firm by the name of Coosworth who is now conveniently dead, as are four of his board members – all of them distinguished notables. The tabloids don't have any hard evidence as yet but they're playing it up. Still, nothing definite, mind you – just rumors at this point.'

'That hardly qualifies as a disaster.'

'Public trust and confidence, Stone. Eurotunnel shares are off sharply since the rumor first leaked out and, consequently, the 300-odd banks holding mortgages on the Chunnel are skittish, not to mention thousands of Eurotunnel shareholders.'

Stone scratched at his beard, now in its third week of growth. 'The same thing always happens when some raghead blows up an airliner. Nobody wants to get anywhere near a plane for a while, then, three weeks later, everybody forgets about it.'

'Goes deeper than that, old boy. Calls into question the competence of our government intelligence, law enforcement and security agencies to protect our citizenry from terrorism. Goes even deeper — Special Branch with their noses bloodied, Lloyd's running their own operation against all the rules, MI5 and 6 fumbling around, trying to cover their arses. And imagine the reaction of the EC high mucky-mucks on the Continent. Absolutely apoplectic!'

Scott-Hughes examined his eyeglasses and buffed the lenses with his handkerchief, wiping away an imaginary smear. 'No, Stone. This has to be swept under the rug. It's a dead issue, isn't it? Pure *Alice in Wonderland* stuff.'

'What's likely to come out in the enquiry?'

'Nothing, of course. There wasn't an attack on the Chunnel, never happened. All the protective devices worked, security intact, business as usual.'

Stone looked at him in disbelief. 'Someone will dive on the *Cormorant* someday, Nigel. Hard to explain that away.'

'Gone.'

'*Gone?*'

'Dismantled, I should say. Piece by piece with underwater cutting torches. Carted off into deep water at night and sunk. Boreholes cleaned out and grouted. Brunner and his compatriots buried at sea — with proper ceremony, I might add. It goes to show that when someone at the very top end of government decides to do something, it gets done properly.'

'The *Valkyr* . . . ?'

Scott-Hughes raised his eyebrows. 'Officially, I wouldn't have the slightest idea. Unofficially, I heard a rumor from a chum of mine in Coastal Command that a vessel by that name was approached by a Royal Navy Sea King helicopter which demanded the right to land on board the vessel and interview the crew members. Unfortunately, the Sea King was fired upon by the vessel in question. As a consequence, a flight of RAF Tornadoes was dispatched to protect the helicopter. All keen chaps, veterans of the Iraq or Bosnian thing, hot-blooded the lot of them. Seems more shots were fired by the vessel in question resulting in the Tornadoes overreacting with Harpoon missiles. All of that just a rumor, of course.'

Scott-Hughes paused for a second and inspected a spot on his tie. '*They* expect your cooperation, of course. Wouldn't do to have you telling tales out of school, now would it?' Withdrawing a document from his briefcase, Scott-Hughes tossed it onto the sheets. 'Official Secrets Act. Your signature, I believe.'

'I never signed . . .'

'But you did, Stone, when you were questioned by people from Special Branch shortly after admission. Perhaps you don't remember but it's your signature I'm told, and properly witnessed by two doctors in this facility, both men of unquestioned honesty. Then there's the matter of some gentlemen from the Justice Department of your country. They have been making enquiries out of your London embassy. Seems they would like our government to hand you over to them once you're released from here. Questions of tax evasion and damage to government property.'

It had 'squeeze play' written all over it. 'What's the deal, Nigel?'

Scott-Hughes lowered his head slightly, rubbing his forehead with his fingers. 'The *deal*, as you put it, is that you give your word to remain silent. In return, Macleod – who, by the way, is on the mend – will be paid for his work with a matching sum paid to you as well – £60,000 each, as I recall. Certain arrangements that I'm not at liberty to discuss will be made to ensure that your exit from England will be unimpeded by either American or British authorities, provided that you don't dally around too long.'

There didn't seem to be any point in spitting against the wind. There were more important things on his agenda. Stone shrugged, then nodded. 'You *did* say £200,000 each, didn't you, Nigel?'

Scott-Hughes hesitated, his lips compressed, then sighed. 'I think that could be arranged, Stone.' He got up, adjusted his jacket and neatly shot his cuffs so that just the right amount of impeccably white sea-island cotton showed. 'I'll be back in a few days to check up on you. Keep well until then, and, by the way, there's a chap waiting outside in the corridor to see you. Third cousin to the Queen, twice removed, Duke of something or other, generally spends his time in New Zealand pottering around in Maori digs. Dreadful man, all elbows and knees, German side of the family, harelip. Still, best they could dredge up without alerting the Fleet Street *paparazzi*, I'm afraid.'

'What in blazes is . . .'

Scott-Hughes raised his hand. 'High honors, old son. Your name inscribed in the hallowed hall of heroes. Norman Schwartzkopf, Jack Ryan, Ike, Patton, the Australian chap who invented the muttonburger. But in your case, 'fraid that public knowledge is circumscribed by the Official Secrets Act. Still, you can wear your gong in the bath. Heavy thing. Clanks very nicely.'

'You're shitting me.'

'Stone – *please* humor the man. Embarrassing for him as well.'

'How do I address him?'

'"Freddie" will do nicely.'

'What's the nature of the honor?'

'Don't know exactly. Knave of the Garter, I should think.'

15 May

Stone sat on a bench under the shade trees, the grounds of the hospital parched by the early summer sun, locusts buzzing.

He still had not heard from Melissa, nearly a month now. Couldn't even dig an address out of Scott-Hughes who remained very vague. According to Scott-Hughes' brief account, the *Snow Goose* had lost her mast and had been holed just above the waterline by an RPG-7 fired from the *Valkyr*. Apparently Kevin had prevented the *Valkyr* from getting off any additional rounds by picking off two men on the *Valkyr*'s foredeck with the Beretta — at a range of over fifty meters, which Scott-Hughes had thought quite impressive, even for an Irishman. Immediately thereafter, two Sea Kings arrived and the *Valkyr* had broken off the attack, heading south at high speed.

While Patrick and Melissa had searched for him in the dinghy, Kevin, Trish and Erin had pulled off the impossible by stuffing cushions into the hole and working the bilge pumps to keep her afloat, but it had been a near thing. *Snow Goose* had been towed into Dover with her decks awash, temporarily patched by an underwater diver, then towed to a shipyard on the south coast of England for an insurance survey and repairs. Lloyd's of London apparently seemed quite willing to cover the repairs.

He wondered about the Irish gang of four. Missed them, actually. Gone back to Dublin, he guessed. Like him, political lepers, despite their having given all for Queen and Country.

As for Melissa, he had heard nothing from her. Scott-Hughes had made vague noises about her being up in London with her father, then on a trip over to France to clean up her affairs. She hadn't even taken the time to drop him a postcard.

Stone felt alone. Very much alone. But at least alive.

He looked up and saw the Morgan wheel into the parking lot, Scott-Hughes unfolding himself from the cockpit, then striding across the burned lawn toward him in his comical bouncing gait. He was wearing a white linen suit and a raw silk shirt with a Panama hat turned up at the brim.

Scott-Hughes settled down on the bench beside him,

removing his hat, and dabbed at his brow with an immaculate white handkerchief, then withdrew a bulky envelope.

'You're leaving today, Stone. The Home Office has released your passport and your requisite £200,000 fee, in unmarked bills, I might add. Macleod's fee will be hand-delivered to him tomorrow. I would add that all of this took more than a few people in high places to apply pressure. As I thought, your visa was canceled, *persona non grata*. They'd like you to leave as quickly and as quietly as possible. Arrangements have been made to drive you to Heathrow.'

'What about Melissa?'

'What about her? Still not back in England, I'm told. The authorities, those unfeeling brutes, are unwilling to let you hang about until she returns. You'll just have to catch up with her later.'

If this was the way it had to be, so be it. He'd fly into New York, then grab the first plane out for the Canary Islands where she'd planned to stop and wait for her there.

He reached for the envelope but Scott-Hughes delicately pulled it away. 'There's one small snag, Stone. A gentleman from your embassy who doesn't seem to trust our people insists that he drive you to Heathrow, just to ensure that you actually board the plane.' He nodded toward the circular driveway in front of the Admissions Building. 'Chap there in the black Buick. And it would seem that people from your Justice Department will be waiting at the other end in New York.'

'You *rotten bastards*! You gave your word . . .'

Scott-Hughes nodded. 'Quite right, Stone. That your exit from England would be unimpeded. But there was nothing that could be done to dissuade your embassy people. And if they wished to get stroppy, they *could* force extradition which would undoubtedly raise quite a ruckus in the press. Consequently, our people in the Foreign Office thought it would be better to handle it quietly.'

'They'll throw the damned book at me, Nigel. I'll probably pull three years in the clink at a minimum.'

Scott-Hughes handed over the envelope and stood up. 'I think not, Stone. Given time, these things work themselves out. Just trust me.'

He looked up. A porter was headed down the path toward the Buick with a small overnight bag packed with the few clothes Scott-Hughes had bought for Stone's release from the hospital.

Scott-Hughes helped Stone to his feet and together they headed for the Buick. Stone eased himself into the back seat and settled against the cushions, his body still stiff. Scott-Hughes leaned over and offered his hand through the window. 'I've done my best for you, Stone. It wasn't enough, but then again, it never could be in comparison with what you've done for my country.'

The Buick pulled away from the curb, Scott-Hughes still standing there, his hand now lifted in a formal salute.

Suburbs flowed by, then scattered fields, the countryside of Kent, narrow lanes, a village with a dirt-smeared child waving from a doorway. The wind was westerly, fields of grain rippling, cumulus clouds building in the afternoon sun.

'So you're Stone,' the driver said. 'Heard a lot about you.' He glanced back over the seat. 'Name's Folley.' He didn't offer his hand.

He was short and balding, sunglasses, a gray suit that hadn't come off plain pipe-racks.

'Who you with, Folley?'

'State. I glanced through the reports on you, Stone. IRS has a bug up their ass but it's really some bozo called Kagg that's pushing it. You mess with the Agency?'

Stone could see Folley smiling in the rear-view mirror. 'No more than they messed with me,' he answered. *Kagg*, he thought. Given the resources of the CIA, the evidence would be overwhelmingly against him. Three years in prison now seemed trivial in comparison with what they were going to give him.

'Might as well relax,' Folley said. 'Should take a couple of hours to get up to Heathrow. But I'll have to take your passport and the money you're carrying before I put you on the plane.'

'What for?'

Folley hunched his shoulders. 'Evidence, but don't sweat it. You'll get a receipt.'

Folley slowed for another town, downshifting.

'Billingshurst,' he said. 'Another six miles and we'll be on the A24, get off these back roads and make some time. We get to Heathrow early, I got meal chits for both of us, courtesy of Uncle.' He grinned.

On the far side of Billingshurst, Folley started to accelerate, then jammed on the brakes as a delivery van ran a stop sign on a crossroad and stalled in front of them, blocking the intersection. A man got out of the van, ignoring the Buick, and ambled around to the front of the van, opening the hood.

Cursing, Folley mashed his horn. He lowered his window and stuck his head out. 'Hey, asshole! How 'bout moving that thing!'

Stone caught the flash of a movement through the side window. Two men in dirty boiler suits, both with ski masks over their faces, moved in next to the Buick, Colt snub-nosed .38s in their hands. Two more on the other side, the back door opening, hands reaching in, Folley screaming bloody hell as the two men on the driver's side hustled him out of the Buick and into the back of the delivery van.

They dragged Stone into the street, shoved him down a side alley and into the back of an old Rover saloon, one of them pushing in alongside him, the other clambering into the driver's seat. The door slammed as the driver accelerated, wheeling out of the alley and turning right, then a quick left, along a dirt lane, across a small bridge, then onto asphalt again, heading south. More than half an hour passed but neither man spoke, the driver concentrating on the road, the man beside him continually checking behind them.

Stone started to ask a question but the man shook his head.

The Rover sailed over the top of a rise, the flash of the sea before them, silver in the sun, stretching out to the south, ranks of white caps marching before the wind.

The man beside him had been staring back through the rear window, then, apparently satisfied, he peeled off the mask and threw it out the window. He turned to Stone. 'Relax, mate. We'll be there in a few minutes.' It was Kevin, grinning.

'Kevin – what the blazes are you . . . ?'

The driver had his mask off, stuffed it under the seat and glanced back over his shoulder, laughing. Patrick.

A sign flashed by, *Littlehampton*.

'Hey! Where . . .'

'You're not the only one who's *persona non grata*, boyo,' Kevin said, lighting a cigarette.

'What . . . ?'

'Didn't your mother tell you that patience is a virtue? Scott-Hughes said we'd have no more than an hour's head start so hang on and enjoy the ride.'

The Rover whipped past a row of houses, through a shopping district, past a marine store, a grocery, then down an alley. The alley opened on to a dock where a yacht with gleaming new spars lay alongside with lines singled up to the dock, exhaust water kicking in spurts from her transom.

Her arms and legs were deeply tanned, and she was dressed in shorts and one of his button-down shirts. Her hair stirred in the wind like wheat before a summer storm. For a second, she seemed frozen in time, unable to move, her expression between puzzlement and shock. Then her lips parted and she smiled, yet tears were streaming down her cheeks. She broke and ran to him, her arms out, both laughing and crying and calling his name. *Stone*.

Star Shot
Douglas Terman

The electrifying thriller from the
bestselling author of *First Strike* and *Shell Game*

Shot down over Vietnam, US pilot John Bracken is interrogated, tortured and broken by Lu, a cold-hearted Eurasian KGB agent. Finally he returns home, only to find himself forced out of the service in disgrace. Twenty years later, on a charter trip to Florida, Bracken's peaceful new life as a yacht skipper is shattered when he is dragged into the world of international terrorism.

With the US space shuttle and its payload of top-secret Star Wars technology standing sabotaged on the launchpad, Bracken comes face to face once more with his hated former tormentor in a heart-pounding battle of wits on the high seas . . . racing to prevent the most devastating act of terrorism ever conceived.

'This is a *must* read . . . spies, Star Wars technology, revenge, hate and heart-stopping suspense, all carefully crafted into a taut zinger of a tale.'   Stephen Coonts

'A page-turner . . . pulls you headfirst into a world of danger and intrigue.'   Larry Bond

'A stimulating, totally captivating thriller.'   Ernest K. Gann

ISBN 0 00 617809 X

HarperCollins Paperbacks – Fiction

HarperCollins is a leading publisher of paperback fiction. Below are some recent titles.

You can buy HarperCollins Paperbacks at your local bookshops or newsagents. Or you can order them from HarperCollins Paperbacks, Cash Sales Department, Box 29, Douglas, Isle of Man. Please send a cheque, postal or money order (not currency) worth the price plus 24p per book for postage (maximum postage required is £3.00 for orders within the UK).

NAME (Block letters)_____

ADDRESS_____

_____